BELVEDOR AND THE GOLDEN RULE

BOOKS IN THE
OLLEB-YELFRA UNIVERSE
BY ASHLEIGH BELLO

A Myrmaid's Kiss

The Belvedor Saga

Belvedor and the Four Corners

Belvedor and the King's Curse

Belvedor and the Desert of Secrets

Belvedor and the Trail of Fire

Belvedor and the Golden Rule

BELVEDOR AND THE GOLDEN

RULE

ASHLEIGH BELLO

Light is light and dark is dark,
but never shall they live apart.

BELVEDOR AND THE GOLDEN RULE
Copyright © 2022 by Ashleigh Bello

Second Edition: February 2022

Originally published as:
Belvedor and the Golden Rule (parts three and four) February 2020

Cover design by Mirella Santana.
www.mirellasantana.com.br
Cover photography by Jessica Truscott (Faestock).

Map and chapter illustration copyright © 2021 by Jessica Khoury.
All rights reserved.

No part of this book was written using the help of ChatGPT or any generative artificial technologies.

Other publications by Ashleigh Bello in the Olleb-Yelfra Universe:
Belvedor and the Four Corners
Belvedor and the King's Curse
Belvedor and the Desert of Secrets
Belvedor and the Trail of Fire
A Myrmaid's Kiss

For more information, visit: www.ashleighbello.com

ISBN-13: 978-0-9987974-8-9
ISBN-10: 0-9987974-8-0

10 9 8 7 6 5 4 3 2 1

*To all the Belvedor Bookworms who
have stuck with me since the Four Corners.
Thanks for giving me the opportunity to share
my stories, my truest magic, with you.*

*For all my friends turned family.
From every chapter of my life to every corner of the world,
you've shown me what 'home' truly looks like
and what 'adventure' really means.*

CONTENTS

ACCEPTANCE — 1 —

THE IN-BETWEEN — 16 —

FIRE MEETS WATER — 31 —

LOST TIME — 46 —

STARR CAVERNS — 69 —

MASTER OF EARTH — 87 —

ONE HEART — 109 —

THE WAY FORWARD — 124 —

GUARDIAN RELICS — 129 —

FLAME IN THE NIGHT — 152 —

MASTER OF SWORDS — 175 —

CITY OF GUANAMARA — 193 —

GHOSTS IN THE NIGHT — 211 —

SLIVER OF LIGHT — 226 —

REINCARNATION — 263 —

SAILING SOUTH — 287 —

SEA OF SAINDORA — - 313 -

READY OR NOT — - 343 -

INTO THE SHADOWS — - 376 -

ALLIES — - 397 -

MARCH TO FREEDOM — - 434 -

BEAUTIFUL CHAOS — - 465 -

THE CHOSEN ONE — - 493 -

CURSES AND VOWS — - 513 -

THE FINAL FREE FALLS — - 545 -

THE ECLIPSE — - 578 -

ALL THAT REMAINS — - 595 -

AS FATE WOULD HAVE IT — - 625 -

EMBERS RISE — - 640 -

CITY OF THE FOUR CORNERS
THE JAR OF STONE
UNDOR
Agrarian's District
Healer's District
Vanishing Tunnels
Creator's District
Warrior's District
Tombs
Draminet
NICORA FOREST
BLACK SAND DESERT
BELGRADIA
Fate's Pool
KAMPAULO
MORIAMO
HIGH CITY OF SAINDORA
SEA OF SAINDORA
Empress Isle
N
NW
NE
W
E
SW
SE
S
OLLEB YELFRA

BLANCOREN MOUNTAINS
NORTH LUOSE
SOUTH LUOSE
ZAMBIENTH
The Greenhouse
LANZATARÉ
Island of Idris
IMPENETRABLE FOREST
The Treehouse
Starr Caverns
GUANAMARA

"The only rule that has any true merit is the
golden one, a rule of balance. The Golden Rule
stems from the beating heart of the world,
And for all its wonders and all its evils,
that's the heart of us all."

- King Damas, High City of Saindora
Volume IV, Belvedor and the Trail of Fire

PART ONE

I

ACCEPTANCE

JEOM WOKE TO A POUNDING HEADACHE. When he opened his eyes, he found his brother's.

"Demetrius!" he said in a gasp, sitting up so quickly that he felt dizzy. "What's happened?"

As the daze of sleep dissipated, everything hit him all at once—he looked Demetrius up and down and immediately sank to his knees, beside his chair.

"Brother, I'm so sorry for what I've done," he said, laying his head across Demetrius' lap. "I never meant... I never meant..."

He couldn't even pass the words from his lips as shudders took over his body. He began to sob, waiting for his brother to inevitably push him away again.

"I forgive you, Jeom." It had been Demetrius' voice, but Jeom could hardly believe that he'd uttered those words; he looked up to find Demetrius staring down at him with an expression that, oddly, seemed to resemble love.

He was sure he hadn't heard him correctly. "What—"

"I *forgive* you," he repeated, firmly. "I know what happened wasn't your fault. I know it wasn't. Please, be calm. Everything is all right now."

All right? Nothing is all right!

"You may forgive me, but I shall never forgive myself," he replied, stomach tangled in knots. "I failed you, brother."

"No," said Demetrius, patting him on the back, "you saved me. You and Gabriel got us all to safety after that horrid night. I have my life and *you* to thank for it."

Jeom sat back on his heels, looking away.

"Never thank me," he said, bitterly. "I don't deserve that. Not after what I did to you… and Tobias."

He could barely stand to draw breath, so much guilt and sadness bearing down on him. *I killed Tobias. I mutilated my own brother.*

"I'm fine, Jeom, really," said Demetrius, gently. He laid a hand on his shoulder.

Jeom wouldn't meet his gaze.

"Come on, just look. It's not all bad." Demetrius sat back, wiggling his foot. "*See*, I still have one good leg to hobble around on." He nodded to a wooden staff leaning against the doorframe; Jeom had crafted it for him long ago. "I use my staff for support when I want to walk."

At this, Jeom perked up, slightly. He hadn't thought Demetrius would ever be able to do anything like walk again…

Demetrius patted his silver-capped knee with a grin.

"That's right," he said. "I can still get around fine. Just need time to get my leg a little stronger, to make up the difference when I stand. Diveena gifted me this nifty traveling throne, though, for when I want to give my leg a break and work out my arms instead."

He flexed his biceps.

"I mean, please, the necromancer did me a favor. Now I have *no* trouble getting attention." He tossed his hair back. "I'm both funny and have a great war story to tell."

When Jeom looked again at his brother, he did *seem* well enough, in a new sort of way; Demetrius returned a warm smile, one that he had thought he'd never see again.

"Strength can be found in many forms, brother, and overcoming challenges builds it more than anything." He spoke with astute awareness. "I was weaker with two legs. And as soon as you accept what has already come to pass, you will be stronger, too."

Jeom gulped. It was all so unnerving.

This is not the broken man I dragged to shore.

But it wasn't just Demetrius. It was everything. Jeom's present was completely unfamiliar—this place, this person.

Where are we?

"We'll be all right," said Demetrius. "Now, you must come. There's someone you need to meet. I've been waiting for so long to introduce you."

Demetrius spun in his chair toward the door for Jeom to follow; he wore gloves on his hands, expertly manipulating the large, wooden wheels on each side of his seat to control his direction.

"How *long?*" he stuttered, feeling his expression twist in concern.

Everything felt... off, as if he had awoken in another dimension, one where he wasn't expected to worry over the burdens of the past. Alas, they remained with him, weighing heavy on his heart—he knew this was *his* Olleb.

He scratched at his chin, eyes growing wide as he felt the full, prickly beard beneath his hand.

"A month and some days," said Demetrius. "You're always such a late sleeper." He chuckled.

A month and what now?

Demetrius flew out of the door, and Jeom shook off his stupor.

"Wait! Really?" he called, racing after him; suddenly he understood just exactly why Arianna had been so sour upon waking from her injuries in the South Luose Well Center… and she'd only had a few days to catch up on.

All questions blew out of his mind as soon as he stepped outside; he was so stunned by the view that he had to cling to the railings in front of him.

He stood on some sort of bridge and felt as if he might float up, up, and away, into the sky, if he were to let go; it was like the Palace of South Luose had somehow found its way into the treetops, a treasure trove of woodsy nooks and alcoves expanding out all around him, leaf-laden caves begging to be explored.

"This is impossible," he whispered, daring to lean a little forward to try to scope the height. *What is this place?*

"Impossible?" said Demetrius. He laughed again—a joyful sound that Jeom had been sure he'd cut out of him for good. "Come on. I just know you're hungry! I'll explain everything on the way to where we're going. Promise."

He flashed him a quick thumbs up, showing off one half of their six-pointed-star scar—a secret little signal they'd developed to let each other know all would be well, as long as they had each other. *Is Demetrius really still my… brother?*

Jeom felt more tears wet his eyes, but he wiped them away.

He followed Demetrius over bridge after bridge, never releasing the railings; his legs still felt a bit numb and wobbly, and he was somewhat weaker than when he'd fled the Greenhouse—although not as much as he would've expected after being unconscious for a month.

Why am I not thinner, after being bedridden for so long?

Every question that flitted into his mind made his heart pound even harder. He looked after Demetrius with disbelieving eyes, the vines magically manipulating around him to help him across the more challenging pathways, twisting with a mind all their own it seemed; he didn't even bother to ask, but his mind screamed in protest.

Where in the Olleb are we?

Once they were on a steadier walkway and Jeom caught his bearings, Demetrius slowed. He began to relay unfathomable stories someone called Diveena had shared with him about their location, her acquaintance with Talis and the guardians, and even her Golden Age heritage.

Did he say… elf? Jeom's mouth fell open.

Demetrius slowly nodded; a smirk stretched across his face.

"That's right," he said. "She's the one who's kept you so well taken care of."

Jeom blinked a couple of times as he tried to keep up. "With… magic."

"Yup," said Demetrius, lifting his finger. "*Elf* magic."

Jeom's tongue had gone dry, his jaw still wide open.

Demetrius sniggered at him.

"Close your mouth! You're going to catch flies this high up."

Jeom's heart warmed, happy to listen to Demetrius' bad jokes for the rest of his life. *Are we really all right?*

"She said you'd wake today, so I came to fetch you," he added. "It's like having Lessa around. She's *always* right." Jeom felt the warm feeling vanish, something sharp returning in its place. "She and Gabe are both waiting for us in the dining nook."

After a while longer, they ducked into a large alcove with several long, narrow tables that looked as if they'd been chiseled straight from the tree they were in; one was topped with baskets of fruit and bread for the taking, and Diveena—the last remaining Nicora elf of Olleb-Yelfra—was seated at it.

"Jeom Kane, why *hello*," she said in a strong yet soothing voice. "I've heard so much about you." She opened her arms in a welcoming gesture. "Please, sit. I've been dying to meet you, to have a little chat."

He pointed to himself, his feet stuck in place. "*Me?*"

His voice came out with a noise that sounded a lot more like Sano squealing than a man talking.

Diveena nodded, a smile warming the stern features in her face.

Demetrius gave him a reassuring nudge forward, so Jeom forced his feet to move. He awkwardly plopped down across from her—looking at Diveena was like staring straight into the sun. She exuded power, beauty, and serenity all at once.

He averted his eyes, scratching again at his bushy beard and wondering how long he'd have to live with it; the more he settled into this strange present, the hotter he realized it was.

Demetrius wheeled over to the table and plucked at the food absentmindedly; there was silence, just the uncomfortable sound of his brother chewing loudly.

Jeom cleared his throat, meeting Diveena's probing eyes. "So... you're an elf?"

"And you're a dwarf," she replied, matter-of-factly, her smile growing wider—Jeom felt his face redden, and Demetrius practically choked on the sip of water he'd been taking, trying to hold back his laughter.

"*Half*-dwarf, apparently," Jeom mumbled, shrugging his shoulders.

A look passed between Demetrius and Diveena, but Jeom couldn't quite place it...

"Wonderful. Then, we're all caught up. I'm glad to see I don't have too *much* to explain," she said, gently. "Demetrius forewarned me that you'd bombard me with questions. Where would you like to begin?"

He had barely formed a thought before they were

interrupted.

"Jeom!" The sound of Gabriel's voice was *such* a relief. Jeom felt his whole body loosen. "It's good to see you, mate."

He turned to find Gabriel standing in the entrance, beaming so widely that his chubby cheeks squished toward his eyes.

"Can you believe all of this?" he said, scanning the dining nook.

"Absolutely… *and* also not even a little," said Jeom with a contented sigh—he was just glad that they'd all arrived somewhere whole.

Gabriel gave him a quick hug around the shoulders and then sat down at the table; he passed out mugs filled to the brim with something cold and bubbly. "It's not like the stuff we used to brew back at my tavern in South Luose, but it'll do."

They clinked their cups together.

"How long have you been back at it, then?" asked Jeom, sipping the drink; his stomach rumbled, so he reached for the bread, suddenly ravenous.

"Just about a week," he said. "Demetrius was the first to wake, though."

Demetrius' smile faltered. "You guys were in pretty bad shape. More so than I."

"I found both you and Gabriel passed out on the beach from exhaustion," interjected Diveena. "Demetrius tells me you rowed the entire way, three men and a horse!" She tasted her drink, every movement so poised.

Jeom noticed a silver marking on the back of her hand, wrapping around her wrist. *An elf,* he thought with the shake of his head.

She set down her cup. "If that's not true strength and determination, I don't know what is."

"Tobias' compass led us to the nearest guardian across the sea," explained Demetrius. "If not for him, I'm not sure where we would've ended up."

Jeom felt the room still around him, the guilt crashing back down; Gabriel cleared his throat.

"To Tobias," he said, raising his glass once more; the others returned the gesture, but Jeom could barely lift his without crying.

AFTER A LONG WHILE of filling their bellies and catching up on all that he'd missed—including things about his own dwarf-given gifts and the ancient Golden Age pact that supposedly linked him and his brother—Jeom began to feel extremely uncomfortable.

He tugged at his clothes, fanning himself. "Is it getting warmer in here? Is it just me?"

He chugged his cup of water, wiping his brow with the back of his hand.

"Why don't we get some fresh air?" said Demetrius.

Jeom nodded, and they excused themselves from the table.

"How are you feeling?" asked Demetrius after they'd gone outside to the bridge; Jeom was gulping down air as if he'd never breathed before in his life. "I know it's a lot to take in. You've been awake for barely two seconds, so just take it slow."

"I'm scared, Demetrius," he replied after finding his bearings. "The girls…" He brought his hand to his temple. "And you have powers now? And… we're in the *middle* of nowhere. And—"

He let out a moan of frustration, his thoughts completely jumbled.

"And it's a lot," he replied, gently. "I know, but it's nothing we can't handle together. We'll just take it one day at a time."

Jeom looked off toward the treescape. "I'm very glad you're..." He cleared his throat. "You seem good."

"I am good," said Demetrius, a sureness in his voice.

He knew that he meant it. In fact, he actually thought that his brother seemed more secure in who he was now than he ever had before.

Jeom plucked at a vine leaf hanging near his head; he couldn't be certain, but he felt as if it tugged back in defiance. He let it be, and sighed.

"Are you worried about them?" he asked in a low voice.

"I worry about them every moment," said Demetrius in a serious tone; his newfound glow seemed to dim. "About all of the guardians."

Jeom put a hand on his shoulder. Then he sat down, letting his legs dangle off the bridge—side by side, they both looked toward the city that lay far off, hidden somewhere in what felt like a never-ending jungle.

"*So*, what now, then?" Jeom asked, overwhelmed by the choices.

"We have to do our part," said Demetrius, "and hope that the others try to make the best of whatever hand they've been dealt." He ran his fingers through his long, wavy hair. "We all know the goal. It hasn't changed. We just need to tackle it differently now."

"How?" said Jeom, looking to him, so many doubts in his mind. "We're separated from everyone but each other... what are we supposed to do alone?"

"I think it's been made quite clear," said Demetrius. "In some grand game of chance, you and I were marked by this... this agreement made between dwarves, elves, and humans centuries ago—"

Jeom shook his shoulders in silent laughter, still trying to wrap his head around that one.

Demetrius smiled.

"I *know*," he said with a little laugh of his own, rolling his eyes. "It's insane, but then again…" He lifted his hand to show off his birthmark again, reaching for Jeom's as well. "You know what I mean?"

Jeom returned his smile, internally so grateful that he did know; they could always practically read each other's minds, and he was so glad that the horrors that had passed between them hadn't broken their link.

I didn't break us. He's still my brother.

They grew quiet, and Jeom could sense the shift in energy. *We have to actually speak of it sometime. I owe him to listen.*

He braced himself.

"The day you…" Demetrius sucked in a deep breath. "The day this happened—"

He gestured to his missing leg.

Jeom's jaw tightened as he tried to hold in his emotions, to allow his brother the space he more than deserved to express his.

"Do you remember the moment at the end?" he continued. "You would have killed me," Jeom couldn't help his whimper, so Demetrius hurried on, "but after the first blow from the axe, when I lifted my hand to shield my face, I felt this *power* explode out of me." He gazed at his hands with a look of disbelief. "I know that's what stopped you, and what released you from Sir Vladamor's hold." He looked up, finding Jeom's gaze. "Do you?"

"I remember," whispered Jeom, wanting so badly not to.

He glanced to his hand, to his own star mark.

"I could feel that I was possessed. I sensed everything that happened, but I just *couldn't* make my thoughts connect to my body… I couldn't stop." He clenched a fist, the mark made even more prominent now. "It was like I was trapped inside of myself, with someone else making the decisions."

"It *wasn't* your fault," implored Demetrius—this time Jeom didn't object. He glanced to Demetrius with sudden understanding.

"You're saying that you used magic, aren't you? *That's* what you're trying to relay?"

Demetrius shrugged, a sheepish grin playing on his face.

"I think it may have been the elf in me," he said with a wink. "Or, *maybe*, it was the foolproof protection of this pact?" He shook his head. "I've honestly no idea. Diveena wouldn't go into too much detail about it without you to hear."

Jeom huffed. "If I didn't know any better, I'd say we found ourselves a new master," he said. "Sounds like she has another important magical lesson waiting to impart on us."

"Don't they *all*."

They shared in a laugh, and suddenly the air felt lighter, the future brighter.

"We're meant to symbolize dwarves and elves in harmony with the human race," said Demetrius, shifting his hands up and down like a balancing scale, "so it wouldn't be farfetched to assume that whatever enchanted pact we're part of comes with magic that prevents us from fatally harming one another?"

"Sounds like the elf in you just needed a little nudging to come out, then," said Jeom, prodding him in the ribs. "Welcome to my world."

He kicked his feet in the air, unable to deny just how beautiful that world was.

"Too many theories," said Demetrius, chewing on his lip. "I don't think Diveena even really knows what to make of it, if I'm being honest."

"Really?" Jeom cocked his head to look up at him.

Demetrius grinned, lifting an eyebrow. "Well, she shared with me all her most precious elven secrets but was tight-lipped about that?"

"Ah, I see your point," said Jeom, nodding. "She's probably just as much in the dark as we all are." He pouted. "I bet Lessa could figure it out though…"

"Surely, she could," said Gabriel, surprising them; he seemed giddy from the brew, swaying a bit as he walked toward them.

"Do *you* think they're safe, Gabe?" asked Jeom, peering up at him with worry—he was their elder guardian, and he'd risked his life for him and his brother. An optimistic word from him would make Jeom feel a whole lot better about things.

"Honestly," he mused, "*I* think they are, but thoughts don't mean much in a war." He seemed to suddenly grow sober. "We need to find out what happened to everyone."

Demetrius inhaled deeply, gripping the wheels of his chair; Jeom knew he was anxious, just holding it back for his sake.

Why would he do anything for my sake? I need to pull it together… I'm not the one who suffered here.

"They're strong," stuttered Demetrius. "Stronger than us combined."

"We should go and look for them," said Jeom, jumping to his feet. *I will be strong for you, Demetrius! I can bring our family back.*

Demetrius shook his head, laying his hand on Jeom's arm to settle him.

"No," he said with a firmness unlike his usual self, and yet with a gentleness that was even greater than usual. "Now that we know who we are, Diveena can teach us, train us in *our* type of magic. This is how we do our part, Jeom. We're here for a reason. And wherever Lessa and Arianna are, they're there for a reason, too."

"But… we're not supposed to split up," mumbled Jeom, looking to Gabriel for guidance.

"And yet, here we are," said Gabriel, obviously in agreement with Demetrius. "Destiny has no direction, yet people are always searching for the right path. Fight her not and maybe she'll lead you somewhere worth going."

"Tobias?" said Demetrius.

Gabriel chuckled, fanning himself, mockingly. "What, you think I came up with that on my own? Why, I'm flattered."

Oh, Tobias, thought Jeom, sadly.

He wasn't sure whether his heart would be fully mended or fully broken by the time these conversations were done.

"We've come so far as a family," said Demetrius after consideration, "and distance won't change that. In fact, I'm sure it will only make us stronger." *If we ever see them again.* "I just know the girls would see it the same. We have to continue to build our strength and position before this battle draws to a close, *if* we want to play an influential part to help end it on our terms."

Gabriel laid a hand on Jeom's back.

"With Demetrius coming into magic, well, he's going to need to try and get a handle on all that before we jump into battle again," he said. "We could lose more than we already have if we rush into anything. You understand?"

Jeom felt that punch again to his gut—he would never let any harm come to his brother again. He would die before that happened.

"Completely," he said, finally feeling sure about something.

"Good," said Gabriel. "Then I'll leave you both to whatever it is that brothers do."

He waved as he left, seeming drunk again, and cheerful.

Demetrius opened his arms out wide, taking in the beautiful sunset that was upon them; he sat so confidently, as if he knew everything would turn out all right in the end.

"I like this new you," said Jeom. "Where has this been hiding all these years?"

Demetrius shrugged.

"I guess sometimes you have to lose things, in order to make room for something better."

Jeom returned a solemn smile. "Let's take Diveena up on her offer," he said. "She can train you, teach you more about your power over nature—"

"But not just me, Jeom! More about your powers in creation, too." Demetrius grew ecstatic with his brother's acceptance. "You could understand better how to wield the Axe of Crissy, and properly control whatever magic it holds that the King has been so eager to get his hands on."

Jeom winced; he didn't ever want to think of that axe again.

He fingered the tube at his side, concealing the priceless artifact he'd found in the Vanishing Tunnels so long ago—it held special powers and secrets he still had yet to uncover.

He considered Demetrius with a startling spark of hope, an idea surfacing.

Maybe the axe holds a magic strong enough that it could help me build my brother something new to stand on.

His creator mind churned, already mapping out a plan to fashion him something more comfortable for support, just as he'd fashioned him the staff for protection.

"Your confidence will return, brother," said Demetrius, knowingly.

"Yes, yes, but then what?" he asked, wanting to move on. "How do we know when it's the right time to make a move? We just wait for something to happen?"

Demetrius smirked, fingers tapping the arms of his chair. "If the last few years are any indication of how this is going to play out, then *yes*, that's exactly what we do."

Jeom reached for his brother's hand and squeezed it tight.

"I love you," he said.

"Always have, always will," replied Demetrius, squeezing back.

They stayed like that for a moment—a half-dwarf and half-elf, feeling more whole than they ever had before—staring toward the horizon.

THE IN-BETWEEN

IT HAD ALREADY BEEN SEVERAL MOONS of searching for their friends.

Arianna's hands and legs ached from clenching so tight to Solza's back for hours on end. But after a while, she began to crave it, the deafening silence. She could live in the sky, she thought—just the calming sound of the wind beating in her ears, and the stars twinkling forevermore in her sight.

Arianna and Solza had never been so connected, and the skies were starting to feel like they belonged to her now too, just as much as they belonged to her avatar.

Solza made a grand avatar dragon of Olleb-Yelfra, clearly born to fly. After completing her final phase of transformation, she was now able to manipulate all of the elements. She confidently wielded her power over the air to create speed on the winds beneath her expansive wings, putting as much distance as possible between them and the City of Saindora.

They rested and replenished during the long, hot days, and flew only with the cover of the dark.

At the end of the seventh night, the sun finally started to rise again in the sky, hovering like a plump orange over the sea; Solza gradually began to drop lower; they emerged from a large, puffy cloud in a burst, as if a dandelion's seeds had been blown apart with a *whoosh*.

Moments later, they were hovering so close to the water that Arianna could feel the soft sprays of the ocean tickle her skin.

A twinge of excitement ran through her every time a new sunrise came—it meant that they were nearing their destination, that they could possibly reunite with Lessa and Eli.

But what if Solza loses Sano's scent? Or what if he's been separated from Lessa and Eli? What if they're all...

Arianna could feel Solza's mind press into hers, urging her not to worry. She shook her head, pushing away the anxious thoughts, focusing instead on the lull of the water...

It was mesmerizing, this endless bright, rippling turquoise.

The reflection of Solza's white belly shimmered atop the waves in line with the glistening sun; it appeared as if a silver beast lurked just beneath the surface of the sea, following them always and about to emerge at any moment.

With a giant, arching splash, something *did* break through the waves from below.

Arianna gasped as a true dweller of the underwater world surfaced to greet them—it was a fraction of the size of Solza's shadow.

"A whale!" said Arianna, pointing ahead.

A jolt of happiness made all the hair rise up on her arms, the sea gifting them with such a rare sight today—she'd only ever witnessed this creature in her studies. She stretched out her fingers to try to graze the gentle beast, but it sank beneath the waters before she could.

She was sad for only a moment—Solza veered to the left just as a pod of dolphins gracefully jumped up to welcome them into their domain.

"*Hmm… they're like me?*" Solza mused, slowing a bit to observe them.

She was equally as enthralled with all the peculiar life that flourished with the water's blessing.

"*Nothing like you,*" said Arianna, knowing that she referred to her dolphin form. "*You are so much more.*"

"*Beautiful, though,*" said Solza in delight—she made strings of delicate water dance around her kin, zigzagging between the pod as if she swam alongside them.

"*As are you,*" replied Arianna in awe.

The dolphins raced after Solza for a while, but they were no match for an avatar dragon. They soon fell behind.

Arianna turned around to try to glimpse them one last time.

She stiffened, eyes wide open, trying to decide whether or not what she saw was real or just a distorted image from the waves; the dolphins were gone, but something had appeared in their place.

Someone was watching them.

"Syrifina?" Arianna's voice was carried off into the salty breeze.

Solza took a sharp turn, forcing her to look ahead and focus on her grip.

"*She's here?*" said Solza.

Arianna didn't miss the anxiety in her voice.

When they were steady, she turned back around, staring at the same spot—nothing was there.

"*I think I was just imagining it.*"

"*Hmm…*" said Solza, clearly unconvinced.

It *could* have easily been a trick of the mind, her thoughts merely wandering over the witches of the water.

And yet, it rarely ever is just my imagination… not these magic-filled days.

Had the mother of mermaids been spying on them all this time? After all, the Sea of Saindora *was* her domain, and they had been following it a very long way from the High City.

"*Do you think that we're close?*" asked Arianna, growing impatient with the journey.

The last thing she or Solza desired was a reunion with Syr-ifina Myr, or any of her water-bred minions, not before they located their friends. And never again would also be fine.

"*I think so, Master,*" said Solza, sensing her unease. "*You have to trust me.*"

"*I do. I'm just…*" Arianna couldn't bring herself to finish her thought.

"*I'm scared, too,*" murmured Solza, "*but I left them in good hands, so I pray that 'good' is what we find.*"

They glided at an even slower pace now, keeping their eyes peeled for the next daytime campsite.

"*I see land!*" roared Solza. "*I thought they'd be sailing still, but they must be around here somewhere. I think we've made it.*"

"*Are you saying what I think you are?*" said Arianna in a steady tone. She felt Solza smile.

"*Yes, Master. I can sense that Sano is very close.*"

Arianna felt so much nervous energy rush through her then. "*Are you sure?*" she said in a shaky voice. "*I don't see anything…*"

She tried with everything to squash her exhilaration down, not wanting to be disappointed; she'd had enough experience with the ocean to know that it could certainly play games on wary wanderers—all she could see was an infinite stretch of water.

"*Quite,*" said Solza. "*Use your magic. Your eyes unaided aren't nearly as strong as mine.*"

She flapped her wings harder, aiming for whatever land she claimed lay ahead.

"*You wouldn't mind?*" asked Arianna, chewing on the idea.

Her anticipation grew, but she remained hesitant. She just couldn't bring herself to be hopeful until she saw the proof for herself.

"*My sight is your sight,*" said Solza, matter-of-factly.

Arianna closed her eyes. Then, she emptied her mind, just like Mother Adunni had taught her to do in Moriamo.

The avatar state of being was easier to call now. In fact, after spending so much time under the blanket of suppressive magic during her imprisonment with the King, Arianna found that it had become second nature to summon; it was as accessible to her now as conjuring her regular magic, if she concentrated and Solza concentrated too.

They had come a long way since their bonding in the Nicora Forest, and so much time apart had only reaffirmed that they were much stronger together.

Arianna gave a long exhale, letting Solza's magic flood through her. When she opened her eyes, she could *really* see—a new world expanded out in front of her, washing the old, dull version of the Olleb away in a blink.

She glanced to the waters; the varieties of blue and green hues she found there were so striking that she lost her breath momentarily. And when she gazed forward, her sight stretched much farther than her human eyes could have ever hoped to attain.

Arianna let out a little scream of joy.

"I see it!" she said as a distant terrain came into view.

Trees shot up around a hilly base for miles; it was possibly the most enchanting green she'd ever seen, like a lake of emeralds glittering against the shore underneath the sun.

She beamed. "It looks like a jungle."

"*Told you so*," said Solza.

Arianna rolled her eyes.

"And look! There's a city there, too, beyond the trees," she said, drinking it all in. "Do you think that's where they are?"

"*I don't know, but we're going to find out*," said Solza, flying faster toward the trees. "*Sano* is *here*."

Arianna held on tight, praying to every god and goddess she could think of that she might find her friends soon, hiding somewhere in these mysterious hills—the air grew thick with a sweet, sticky taste as they drew nearer, and the fresh scent of nature hit them in a burst when they came upon the shore.

A white stretch of beach with rosy pink accents swathed a long, narrow coastline. The water here looked as if it shimmered with jewels, the rowdy waves taking on the sparkling sand in masses.

Black boulders dotted the beach sporadically, jutting up to the sky from both the sand and the sea. And the deep blues of the water were made even richer against the dark walls of stone.

Farther up the shore, the sands became overrun with vines that made it look as if dark green snakes slithered out from the trees and across the beach in droves, but pink flowers bloomed from the vines every few inches.

As the beach receded, the nature grew extremely dense.

The sand-slithering vines met giant bushes and twisted up boulders on the edge of the jungle. There, thick trees sprouted to the sky in a great tangle, weaving in and out of each other like a giant bird's nest; tall, lanky flowers with budding yellow petals grew up alongside them, trying to find pockets of sun, and prickly, bright green plants decorated the ground at their base.

All the nature entwined in such a way that Arianna wasn't sure that she'd be able to locate a footpath through…

"*We could fly straight over, into the city*," she thought—

but she knew it was a bad idea.

"*People will see us,*" said Solza with a nervous start. "*What if I scare them?*"

"*There's no 'if' about it,*" said Arianna with a sardonic laugh. "*They would be wise to be frightened of you; however, that's not our goal.*" She remembered King Damas' warning. "*We need the people to join us… not run from us.*"

"*I agree,*" said Solza. "*Let's find a way through the trees.*"

They circled the beach, trying to locate a good entry point.

"*Wait, I see something over there!*" Arianna had spotted a small cove, tucked away between the sand and sea.

She steered Solza toward it.

Boulders peppered the shallows on this side of the beach, tightly enclosing the area and blocking any waves—pockets of deep water grew so still that, even from such a height, Arianna could spot rainbow-colored fish swimming back and forth beneath the crystal-clear surface.

Solza perched atop one of the taller boulders so that they could scan the vast area.

"By gods, I don't believe it!" said Arianna, her voice bouncing between the rocks.

She nearly toppled off Solza's back from disbelief.

Three remarkable ships were docked before the cove, gently rocking atop the azure waters.

"How can this be?" she said in a daze—Arianna recognized the ships. She had helped form the inspiration to build them in the first place. "*But I thought they'd only built one…*"

She would never forget the moment when she'd watched the hopeful start to a fleet of such ships burn down during the battle of Zambienth—and yet, here it was, resurrected from its ashes and multiplied by three.

The wooden wings of dragons stretched out wide to form the sides of the ships, gold paint shimmering like scales. And giant, gilt heads were positioned at their fronts. Each ship was so big that Arianna thought they could fit a hundred people on board, easily.

Large white sails flapped in the wind, painted with the familiar emblem of the guardians. However, as she looked closer, she realized that emblem had been decorated with new life. "*Solza, are you seeing this?*" she said, staring toward the sails in utter shock.

The symbol of the Four Corners had been merged with a fierce, golden dragon, its wings outspread and teeth bared in the center—a black snake hung limp in its mouth.

She hugged Solza, heart pounding in eagerness. "*What aren't you telling me, girl?*"

"*There's much we haven't spoken of yet, Master,*" she said, a smile in her voice. "*Your friends should be the ones to explain.*"

Arianna could barely contain herself. "*Then, come on. Let's find them! We can land over there.*"

"*At once, Master,*" said Solza, mirroring her excitement.

Solza set down on the beach with a heavy thud, sand spraying out all around them as her thick claws dug into the earth; Arianna slid down her back in the same second, a puff of magic cushioning her landing.

As Solza began to shift into her more agile snow leopard form, Arianna's connection to her sight was suddenly severed.

It took her a moment to find her bearings, but when she did, the ships had completely vanished.

"What... where did they go?" she asked, panic rising up in her throat. "*They were just here. I... what's going on?*"

"*They're cloaked with magic,*" said Solza, eyes locked on the waters where the ships had just been. "*Such enchantments don't work on avatars. We see all.*"

Arianna waved her hand in the general direction, fearful that everything she'd just witnessed had been some sort of mirage.

"*But the guardian ship in Zambienth had been cloaked with magic, and I could still see it…*" she said, "*because I'm a guardian.*" She took a step toward the area, still searching. "*Why would this be any different?*"

"*Maybe they took extra precautions this time around?*" said Solza, uncertainly. "*Last time the Shadow Resistance could see it, too. Maybe now they can't.*"

Arianna gave a curt nod, trying to remain calm.

"*You're probably right,*" she said after a moment, releasing her tension. "*Any guardian would be smart to hide such vessels from wandering eyes.*"

She couldn't wait to find out more about their origins, let alone who had traveled here upon them.

"*Just as long as they're actually there and I'm not going crazy.*"

"*Oh, they are,*" said Solza, reassuringly, still staring ahead. "*And so magnificent.*"

Arianna couldn't fight away her twinge of jealousy. She just had to see them again, too, so she said the first revealing spell that popped into her mind. "*Vertodiso!*"

As the magical word left her lips, the grandiose guardian ships reappeared in a ripple, as if they had been hovering in the astral plane just waiting to be called.

Arianna staggered backward, craning her neck to take them in fully—they were even bigger than she had first thought.

She shook her head of the wonder, letting out a slight whistle.

"*I don't understand how these could have possibly been built,*" she said, gawking. "*By who? And… so quickly. It took months to build just the one.*" She could barely form a proper sentence. "*How—*"

"*It's possible they had more help this time,*" said Solza, sounding much too coy.

"And when did you become so knowledgeable?"

Solza was clearly hiding something from her, and it was rather annoying… since now they shared thoughts.

"I've always been so, Master," she replied. *"That's why we can communicate in your language now, yet we cannot communicate in mine."*

She hummed a lovely laugh that made Arianna's heart swell with warmth.

"Knowledgeable and sly, I see."

Arianna tickled Solza under the chin; she purred.

As the magic waned and the shimmering ships vanished again, she spotted something vastly smaller yet even more astounding bouncing on the waves—it was the boat she'd built with the boys.

Jeom… Demetrius!

"Please, let this be real," she yelled, running over to it.

It was anchored to a large rock in the sand, and it was badly battered; it looked as if it had barely survived another trip across the sea.

"It's theirs!" she called back to Solza; her avatar was already inspecting the edges of the jungle, pawing at the ground. *"They must have landed here, too. But… are you sure it was Sano's scent that you caught?"*

"Oh, I'm positive," said Solza, sounding just as surprised. *"Destiny probably has something to do with this, but I'm certain that—"*

Solza sniffed at the air, suddenly padding back and forth.

"Quickly, follow me." Her tone grew serious, anxious. *"Sano is very, very close. I can sense him just as surely as I can you."*

Solza started off at a run, headed straight into the thick of the trees; Arianna didn't hesitate to follow, stumbling down a thin, sandy path behind her.

She ducked beneath long, swaying vines and dodged

bristly bushes as they zigzagged through the tangled green terrain—there was no rhyme nor reason to their trail, so they'd
never have a hope of finding their way back to the beach if
they got lost.

But Arianna knew Solza wouldn't lead her astray.

The trees and plants were sticky with life, and the air was
so muggy that Arianna felt water condense on her skin. It was
like they traveled through a never-ending cloud, which proved
much more difficult to do on foot rather than in flight.

The sound of waves was quickly replaced with the voices
of stealthy insects the farther they navigated away from the
beach, and the haunting melody of unknown wildlife filled
their ears.

The sand eventually morphed into long grasses and
muddy ground; Arianna wasn't sure if Solza's fur would still
be white by the end of the trek, and she hoped that the beautiful cloak Jillian had gifted her wouldn't be ruined either.

Soon, it began to grow dark.

The light fell in sporadic rays to the jungle floor, the
bunchy treetops becoming too dense to let much through.
However, Arianna took comfort in that the sun was still out
there, shining.

"*Something doesn't feel right,*" said Solza, abruptly stopping in the middle of a small clearing.

"*What is it?*" said Arianna—her heart wasn't just beating
now, it was banging in her chest like a bass drum.

They had been walking for hours.

We're so close to finding someone, I know it.

All her instincts were shouting at her to keep going. But
she also knew that at any moment something terrible could
snatch the possibility and hope straight from her grasp.

Nothing is ever certain.

"Tell me, girl," said Arianna. "What is it?"

"*I could sense Sano so strongly before,*" she said, her voice trembling, "*but now I can't sense anything at all. It's like our connection was suddenly broken. He's just… gone.*"

Arianna's excitement began to wear off in the face of this obstacle—she started to think a bit more clearly, working through the problem.

"*That city we saw in the hills was also a long way off, Solza. And, honestly, it seems like we've been going deeper into this jungle instead of up and out… Do you think you maybe got turned around somewhere?*" She scratched her head, looking back the way they'd come. "*Maybe we can retrace our steps to pick the scent back up.*"

Solza peered at Arianna with helpless eyes.

"*No, I felt him,*" she said. "*In my heart. I know this is the right direction. It's just… everything has gone all fuzzy now. I can't see where to go next.*"

Arianna suddenly had an epiphany as the word 'direction' bounced around in her mind.

"*It's magic, strong magic. Has got to be!*" she exclaimed.

"*What do you mean?*" said Solza.

"*It's just like you said with the ships,*" said Arianna, hands on her hips. "*Maybe someone doesn't want to be found.*"

She recalled how Demetrius' enchanted compass, their one last hope to try to find a way off Idris, had stopped working on that island; Jeom had tossed it to the waters out of anger, only for them to realize later that the compass had never been broken at all—the island was the problem. It had been concealed by Syrifina, interfering with the guardian relic's directional magic.

"We must be close to something important," said Arianna.

She turned about in circles to try to find a way to overcome what was, surely, another magical barrier; Solza sniffed at the ground again, searching for any clues as she followed her master's train of thought.

Arianna stopped, staring to the treetops—the sun

spotlighted her through the jungle canopy, birds soaring high overhead.

"*We need to get an aerial view,*" she said with determination. "*We have to clear the trees. Whatever this enchantment is, it probably won't touch the skies.*"

"*Brilliant!*" said Solza, her avatar magic already surging.

Without wasting another second, she morphed back into the black and white dragon of Golden Age dreams; Arianna stepped into the bubble so that she too was engulfed in the transformation—once again, a dragon and dragon rider were merged.

Arianna looked up and then closed her eyes.

With one forceful flap of her wings, Solza launched them into the sky, smashing through the treetops with ease.

As soon as they were free of the jungle, Arianna could feel the weight of foreign magic roll off her back.

I knew it, she thought.

"*You were right!*" said Solza, feeling it too.

They circled the area they'd just left, careful not to fly too far from where Sano's scent had been, and careful not to soar too high for curious city eyes to potentially spot them…

With their new view, they noticed that long, skinny rivers wormed their way through the jungle, sprawling out in every direction. It looked as if a spider with a hundred legs was carefully weaving an intricate web of green.

Arianna couldn't help but think, *Trap or haven?*

The rivers were so crisp and clear that she saw the reflection of the clouds and of Solza in the mirror-like waters.

"Are those—"

She shook her head of the silly thought, but she had *almost* considered that she'd seen a stretch of bridges built straight into the treetops, heavily obscured by nature.

They circled a moment longer, and then Arianna shrieked a mixture of nerves and delight. "Down there!"

She steered Solza toward an enormous open field.

As they drew closer, they were both astounded at what they saw—scores of people dotted the field, battling one another in sync as what looked to be trainers shouted commands.

It was unlike any group training Arianna had ever been a part of in her younger years; she swore she heard the sound of laughter traveling through the air, and cheers of triumph.

Warriors aren't taught to laugh in the King's land.

"What is this?" she muttered, spying on the scene below— her excitement began to falter, replaced quickly with caution. "*Do you know this village?*"

Large tents and tables had been placed all around the vicinity, and there were small fires going on as some people cooked. She even saw an area dedicated to healing—people's battle wounds were being patched up with care, not nearly in the same manner she had grown accustomed to seeing in the Jar.

Oh, Cyn…

She shook her head, forcing herself to focus on their surprising discovery.

"*No, I don't,*" said Solza, soaring a little closer. "*But it looks like soldiers… training for something.*"

"*Let's be careful, then,*" said Arianna, not wanting to be noticed—she tried to urge Solza higher. "*We don't know who commands this army.*"

"*Don't we?*"

Solza made a sharp dive toward the ground before Arianna could respond.

Everyone in the field froze, eyes to the sky with their weapons now limp in their hands. Then, the shouts came—cries of fear and shock as a dragon seemingly dropped from the heavens.

The ones directly beneath Solza quickly scattered like ants; her giant wings expanded, slowly rising up and down until her claws sank into the earth.

She reared her mighty head to the sky and let out a deafening roar that quieted the area, fully clearing the vicinity around them. Then she lowered herself to the ground so that Arianna was now in full view of the onlookers, sitting atop a dragon.

"By gods, it's her. It's Arianna Belvedor," someone said. "And a… a—"

"A dragon!" exclaimed someone else.

A wave of excitement, babbles of disbelief, seemed to blow over the field, whistling like the wind through the grass.

Arianna wasn't sure who was in more shock, these strangers or her, but she knew that she wasn't in any immediate danger.

Solza could level this field in a minute, she thought.

Cautiously, she slid down from the dragon's great height, with all her nerves gathered in her chest.

At least, I have my swords. And my dagger… just in case.

Before her feet had even touched the ground, someone pushed through the crowd, running straight toward her; she would have recognized those blue eyes anywhere.

In the next second, Lessa's arms were wrapped around her, so tightly that she was sure that no one could ever rip them apart again.

FIRE MEETS WATER

"ARIANNA, BY GODS!" CRIED LESSA, tears in her eyes. She was a beautiful, blubbering mess. "Is it really you? I just can't believe this."

Arianna laughed, feeling so much joy in her heart that she could hardly stand it.

"Me either," she stammered. "I'm… surprised to see you, Les." She thought of the Four Corners, of their devastating separation. "I'm so glad you're all right."

She meant that more than she could possibly show with words. In fact, she wasn't even sure if her words had passed her lips for how stunned she was in this moment.

"*Me?*" said Lessa. "We've been worried sick about you since Solomon stole you off!" She hugged her tighter. "I was beginning to lose hope."

Her voice was muffled, lost to Arianna's cloak.

"You? Lose hope?" She gently pushed Lessa to arm's

length. "I don't believe that for a second."

Lessa tried to smile back, her lips quivering with emotion; and Arianna could do nothing but smile.

"We tried to get your whereabouts," said Lessa, concern lacing every word, "but we heard nothing of you since that day, Ara. I thought—" She bowed her head, wiping her eyes with the back of her hand. "I thought that Solomon killed you."

"Solomon gave it his best shot," said Arianna, bitterly— her thoughts shifted toward him, toward their seemingly never-ending journey across the Olleb.

Toward Moriamo. Toward the King.

He really did…

She wondered what he'd been doing every day since the night she'd left him glaring up at the sky, watching her escape on a fire-breathing dragon.

"He delivered me straight to King Devlindor… as promised," mumbled Arianna.

She swallowed back her emotions, every memory as painful as sucking down the revealing potion that had ripped away her Aridyn identity—sometimes she could still feel the King in her head, the ghost of him digging around for her secrets. And sometimes she could sense the swathing loneliness he had left in his trail, tempting her to give up the fight.

She shuddered.

"It was only with luck that I got away before he was done toying with me."

Lessa whimpered, shaking her head.

"No… the *King?*" She began to sob harder, burying her face in her hands. "I'm so, *so* sorry. I just don't—"

Arianna cocked her head to the side.

"Sorry for what?" she said, softly, pulling Lessa's hands away from her face. "Les, you haven't anything to apologize for. There's truly nothing you could've done. It was inevitable that Solomon would catch up to me one day."

Lessa gazed at her with such sorrow in her expression, taking the time to really consider her now.

Arianna felt her cheeks grow warm under the scrutiny. She tucked her hair behind her ears and brushed off her cloak.

Pointless.

She hadn't thought much about her appearance since the day she was handed over to the King, but she was certain she must look like the living dead after such a trying journey; she also hated giving Princess Elisa *any* consideration, but if not for her occasional kindnesses to try to soften her brother's blows, Arianna would have probably been unrecognizable.

Lessa's tears came harder then; Arianna was still in such a daze that she hadn't even shed one.

"Eli, he wanted to go after you right away," she said, "but I… we… *couldn't.*" She let out another strained sob. "*Oh*, I'm so sorry that we couldn't."

"I completely understand." Arianna squeezed her shoulder. "I *really* do."

It was clear that Lessa had been holding on to a heavy load of guilt after they were forced apart, and it made her heart twist; she knew exactly how her friend felt, for she had been feeling the same way all this time.

"Nothing that happened to us was in your control," she added. "I made the decision to go with Solomon quietly, so that the rest of you would be safe."

She pointed to herself, trying to force Lessa to *really* hear her—they had both suffered enough.

"I made that decision, Les. *Me.* There was nothing you could've done to stop me, and, frankly, nothing you could've done to stop Solomon from taking me. Not in that moment."

Lessa tilted her head, biting down hard on her lip.

"But look at you…" she whispered—yet more tears fell, though she tried to suck them back. "I can't even begin to imagine what you've been through, Ara. I just…" She peered up at her, face pained. "King Devlindor, *truly?*"

Arianna returned a solemn nod, averting her eyes.

"It wasn't all bad," she said with an unconvincing shrug—she focused on her time with Odessa, on the one good thing that she had experienced there. "I made a friend… in the end."

Though, one I'll never see again.

Lessa swallowed, still trying and still failing to restrain her emotions…

Arianna had never seen her face such a bright pink before. And seeing her friend's reaction made all that she'd suffered hurt even worse—there hadn't been nearly enough peaceful nights soaring through the skies with Solza to erase the damage the King and Solomon had inflicted on her soul.

"Eli was right," said Lessa, hardening. "We should have gone after you."

Arianna tried to concentrate. Her thoughts were so jumbled, racing with questions. *Where's Eli?*

Her attention shifted to him, of their last, dreadful moments together, and of some of the best—a dance beneath the stars, a sandstorm kiss, a horseback ride alongside the sea.

"*No,*" she said after a moment, running her hands through her tangled hair. "Eli's feelings were… noble." Of course he would've insisted to go after her. He as much said that he'd follow her anywhere, and Arianna doubted that the threat of another dungeon would have stopped him. "But yours were brave. You did the right thing."

She put both her hands on Lessa's shoulders, giving her a gentle shake.

"Listen to me," she urged. "I don't blame you, nor any of my friends, for a thing that happened to us back there. We're on a dangerous path, and that's none of our faults." She lowered her voice, thinking of Talis. "And I hope you wouldn't hold anything against me either. Can we just start afresh?"

"There is *nothing* I hold against you," said Lessa—so firmly that Arianna knew she had guessed her train of thought.

She let out a relieved sigh, unburdening herself from the hard decision to help Master Tayshin wipe Lessa's memories back in Zambienth; in the face of all that had been lost, they were both lucky to even still have each other.

"The *only* person to blame for any of this sleeps in a palace with a crown by his bedside," said Arianna, staring at her intently. "And, Les, I've seen it."

Lessa gaped back at her, glassy-eyed still. Then, she returned a firm, accepting nod and they embraced once more.

"How did you escape?" she asked, collecting herself. "If you were in the King's hands? I can't even begin to—"

"Narrowly, just a few nights ago," said Arianna, tersely.

She couldn't stomach thinking about the torture she'd suffered in such a blissful moment…

So easily had she blocked it out with only crisp, starry skies and boundless waters in her vision over the last several days. But it was all flooding back now that she'd found the comforting arms of a friend.

"It's a long story. Not for now," she added when Lessa looked at her funny. "But I've been going crazy with worry over you and Eli for months just the same. I thought you'd be fated to the Tunnel of Tombs. How did *you* escape? And for the second time around…"

Every nerve in Arianna's body was burning with curiosity.

"Not without a lot of help," said Lessa, mustering up a smirk. "*Speaking* of, how were you even able to find us out here, in the middle of nowhere?" She scratched her head, brow furrowing. "This jungle is a long way off from Saindora and heavily protected to avoid this very situation. Although, I'm very glad our safety measures have been proven imperfect."

"Solza," said Arianna, glancing up at the dragon hovering protectively over them both. "It was all her. If she hadn't come to my rescue when she did, I'd be at the bottom of the sea right now. We reunited a few nights ago, and she reassured me that she'd left you in good hands."

Solza gave a little grumble of support.

"*Told you so*," she sang.

Arianna ignored her, trying to suppress a giggle.

"It's the only relief I've felt about your fates since we separated. She followed Sano's trail and led us here. Whatever magic you're using to protect these trees doesn't reach the clouds." She shook her head of the lingering disbelief. "Now that I see you with my own eyes, I can finally believe that you're safe."

Lessa put her hands on Arianna's cheeks.

"You better believe it!" she said, her eyes finally dry. "We're not finished here yet."

Arianna laughed. "Hmm… still have a few more lives left in us, I suppose."

"But wait…" said Lessa, eyebrow raised, "what do you mean that Solza *reassured* you that we were alive?" She looked at her with an incredulous stare. "How so?"

Arianna teetered on her heels, grinning up at her avatar dragon.

"It's *such* a long story," she said.

She placed her hands on her hips, still staring at Solza.

"*How do I explain that we can speak to each other now? I'll sound ludicrous!*"

"*You're on your own for that one,*" said Solza.

"I see," said Lessa—she returned a warm smile, then Arianna wondered if she would even have to explain anything at all.

Arianna looked her over again; it was hard not to notice that Lessa appeared to have gone through a lot of changes since they'd last been together.

Her hair was cropped short, reminiscent of the first time

she had met her, and her cheeks were flushed a healthy pink.

In fact, she appeared to be *glowing* with health, all over.

Whatever time had passed for her must've been for the better. Good, she thought.

There was something strangely different about her now, in the best of ways.

Solza nudged Lessa from behind with her snout, vying for her attention. A rumbling sound originated from deep in her throat, and it was full of affection.

Lessa placed her hand on her scaly cheek.

"Solza, girl, by gods…" she breathed, utterly beguiled by her presence. "Just look at you." She slid her hand over the smooth, black scales, and Arianna saw that it was shaking— probably with both fear and delight. "Sneaking away like that! We've been worried sick over you, too, you know?" She smiled. "But mischief does you quite good, I see. You do take after your master."

She glanced back to Arianna, a happily dazed expression on her face.

"A dragon, Ara. A *dragon*." She shook her head, looking into Solza's electric blue eye. "In all that we've learned about avatars, this still always seemed so unimaginable. Yet, here you are… living, magical proof that the Golden Age can exist again."

"I know," said Arianna, stepping back to get a good look at Solza too. "Beautiful, isn't she?"

Her avatar was a giant on this field—her body stretched out so long that it appeared as if a small hill had suddenly pro- truded up from the flat grassland, clearing some of the sur- rounding trees.

"Stunning," replied Lessa with a nod. "I wonder if Sano has it in him?"

Arianna crossed her arms at her chest, looking around. "Where is that little—"

Sano plopped onto her shoulders at that very moment, as if waiting for his turn to be in the spotlight; Arianna squealed, making a cradle for him with her hands.

He slid into her open arms, excitedly, a tiny, warm ball of fur. It felt so familiar, so comfortable.

"Oh, Sano!" She snuggled him into her chest. "I'm happy to see you good and well. You're one lucky little monkey."

She peered lovingly into his bright orange eyes, tickling his stomach.

"I'm sure he does have the fire in him," said Arianna after a moment, considering Sano with new appreciation. "All avatars do. Although, I think it's less about him and more about the both of you, together."

"And what makes you say that?" asked Lessa as Solza and Sano became entranced with one another; they shared a connection that even the girls would never quite understand.

However, Arianna could sense Solza's elation at the reunion just the same.

"Well, quite similar to the first connection we made with our avatars, the last transformation is also made as… one," explained Arianna, interlacing her fingers. "Like some kind of magical union."

"Are you giving *me* the lessons now?" said Lessa, gawking at her. "Sano, are you hearing this?"

Sano bounded onto Lessa's shoulders, wrapping his tail around her neck.

"That's right," said Arianna, smirking back at her. "I've actually learned a fair bit more about avatars since our lessons with Kassime." She couldn't wait to tell her about the secrets hidden in the swamp village. "I think I may *actually* know some things you don't for once."

She placed her hands on her hips, beaming with pride.

"My, my," said Lessa with an astonished chuckle, "I see we have much to catch up on, then."

"If you have any stories quite like my own, I'm afraid we may need weeks to get through it all," she replied. "If only we could return to simpler days."

"Well, I might not be able to solve the world's problems in a night, but I have *just* the thing to get us through storytelling," she said with a wink.

Arianna realized only now how much they truly did have to discuss—months' worth of separation, adventures, and horrors, and countless new mysteries.

And thank the gods that we can unravel them together.

"Follow me," said Lessa. "Too many eyes and ears here. Let's get somewhere private so we can speak more freely." She looked her up and down again, worry etching her features once more. "There'll be plenty of time for proper introductions later. You need to rest."

Arianna had been so absorbed and ecstatic about finding Lessa that she'd all but forgotten the crowd around them; there were hundreds, she thought, listening intently to their conversation and still humming with excitement.

She had absolutely no idea who they could be, and hardly had the capacity to guess for all the things swimming in her mind. However—seeing as they were smack in the middle of a jungle that went on for miles before any civilization was known—she was sure the answer would surprise her.

"Where did all these people come from?" she said, staggered by the audience. "And where even are we?"

They watched her with gaping mouths, seemingly waiting for something.

"What are you all standing there for? Carry on! Nothing to see here," shouted Lessa, shooing them away with confidence.

They were immediately obedient, though they took their time clearing a path for them.

"Come on," said Lessa, pulling her along. "Let's get you

settled now, shall we? We need to have a serious talk."

"All right," said Arianna, feeling a bit uneasy. "Solza, mind showing off a side of you that's a little… less imposing?"

"*Fine*," hummed Solza. "*Though I quite like the way they're looking at me now.*"

Arianna scoffed. "*You're so modest.*"

Solza gave a tinkling laugh—one that only Arianna could hear—then began to shrink down from the dragon of legends into a sure snow leopard of present day; there was a collective gasp, even from Lessa, as an enchanting web of magic spun around her.

"Gorgeous!" Lessa clapped her hands. "Her transformation has grown to be absolutely extraordinary."

They'd both witnessed countless avatar transformations by now—and the beautiful magic which accompanied them—but Solza's shifts through the elements had become even more spectacular.

The people watching could hardly contain themselves, pointing and shouting with fervor.

"Let's get out of here while we still have the chance!" said Lessa, hurrying her away from the crowd.

They pushed through throngs of people, Sano just along for the ride and Solza prancing close by Arianna's side.

Arianna kept her head down, following closely behind Lessa.

It was impossible not to overhear her name being threaded throughout the gathering.

"Don't be daft," someone screeched. "*Of course* that's her. She looks exactly like the wanted portraits."

"I knew she was alive," said a young woman. "No one can hold down Belvedor!"

"See, I *told* you it was all true," whispered a boy as they passed. "All of it. She's the one!"

Arianna frowned. *The one for what?*

"Lessa, who *are* all these people?" she asked.

She thought her face must be the color of the sun for how hot she was feeling—arms reached out to touch her, everyone trying to lay even a finger on her robes.

"The city isn't for miles," she prattled on. "Where are we going? What's going on here?"

"I'll tell you everything soon," said Lessa with a little whine. She stopped, turning to look at her. "But frankly, you already know."

They quickened their pace, until finally they broke through the crowd, out of earshot of everyone.

Lessa looked like she was bursting to talk, as if the answer lay right behind her teeth, just dying to break free; she led Arianna up the side of a tall hill and paused at the top.

"Look," she said, pointing down at the field they'd just left. "Just *look* and tell me you don't understand what you see?"

Arianna peered out over all the people, trying to wrap her head around it. "I don't understand what—"

Before she could even finish her sentence, her mind had already caught up.

The commotion of Arianna's arrival began to slowly die down now that she was out of their line of sight, and those below went back to what they'd been doing before she had landed...

Training for something.

With a closer look, Arianna could make out groups of young men and women practicing in archery, swords, axe-throwing, and hand-to-hand combat. Instructors yelled directions, and peers gave feedback round after round. And she could hardly believe her eyes when she noticed other groups using magic... spells from her enchanted beginnings: levitation, summoning fire, healing, and more.

"It's an army," she uttered, mouth ajar—the words had

just spilled out.

Lessa squeezed her hand.

"*Your* army," she said, slowly. "Ara, don't you see? We did it! We really did it."

She was practically jumping with joy.

"How?" stuttered Arianna, unable to blink.

In all her time held captive, she hadn't even *thought* of this as a possibility. She had only ever found room to hope—with great effort—that her friends were still alive somewhere out in the world, hanging on by a thread, surely, but alive.

This, that they had somehow gathered an army and had begun to train them as such, was an *exceptional* outcome.

Had Odessa seen such a lovely vision before her untimely end?

"When Solomon took you," said Lessa, "Eli, Noah, and I made a plan to rally the Warrior's District." She took a deep, satisfied breath. "We told our story. We told them everything, and, because of your spell to lift the memory magic from that night we first escaped, they believed us!"

"You mean to say that these are freed district slaves?"

Arianna felt her mind tumble through a glorious golden tunnel, filled with new possibilities. *Can it really be true?*

"But how did you escape the mountains and travel so far with so many?"

She couldn't tear her gaze away from the field; everywhere she looked was like a new piece of a puzzle coming together to form the picture of her dreams.

She saw herself, Jeom, Demetrius, and Lessa multiplied by the hundreds—learning to fight and spell magic, just like a flashback to their own introductions to the charmed world.

Arianna understood plainly now just how far they'd truly come and the impact their adventures had made on the Olleb. Her imagination and hopes had finally caught up with her reality—this was a moment to mark in history.

"Through the Vanishing Tunnels, of course," replied Lessa. "With a little help from some friends." She nudged her, playfully. "Damon and Jacob give their regards."

Arianna thought she could melt into a puddle from happiness. The grin on her face actually began to hurt her cheeks, but she just couldn't stop smiling.

"Welcome to my world," she murmured, thinking of her first friendly ghost encounters.

"Unfortunately but fortunately," said Lessa, knowingly. "Ghosts are quite frightening, if you ask me."

"Well, I'm glad they were able to help guide you safely out of the Warrior's District," she said after a moment, staggered by all Lessa had accomplished in such a short time. "Jacob and Damon are kind souls."

Lessa paused, smiling at her strangely.

Arianna raised an eyebrow. "*What—*"

Lessa took Arianna's hand and pulled her to the very edge of the hill.

"Ara, look again," she urged. "It's not *just* the Warrior's District."

At first, Arianna didn't know what to make of her statement as the freed slaves below swirled back and forth under the bright sun. It was hot, so those dueling were in lighter garments.

However, those watching, in waiting, or performing other tasks were draped in familiar robes, district cloaks—and red wasn't the only color. *Purple. Blue. Green....*

Arianna's hands flew over her mouth. She looked to Lessa, eyes wide. "All the districts? All of the *districts*, Les? No..."

"Very much, *yes*." Lessa nodded, chin held high. "Creators, healers, agrarians, *and* warriors are all accounted for down there. We freed *everyone*."

"The Four Corners no longer exists?" whispered Arianna.

She finally felt her eyes water, and there would be no

holding the tears back once they started to fall.

"The slave city no longer exists," said Lessa.

Arianna couldn't make a sound, but she managed to mouth, "How?"

"After the warrior-slaves were won over, it's not like anyone could really stop us from taking the others," explained Lessa. "The regulators in the Four Corners know nothing of magic, and with an entire district on our side, the rest were easily persuaded." She looked down to the field. "Really, the tricky part wasn't even escaping into the tunnels. It was after we were out of the mountains and in the King's land of law-abiding citizens." She smiled. "More than *just* freed slaves are down there preparing to fight now."

She patted Sano on the head, peering down at everyone with pride.

Arianna gaped. " *What—*!"

"More on that later," said Lessa with pride. "So much more. But since we landed here, the other guardians and I have been training everyone in magic."

"Others?" Arianna felt the warmth of a tear roll down her cheek. "It's really happening, isn't it?" she said.

We have an army!

But she was sure there was a bigger explanation to be had—the number of people in this field certainly didn't even come close to the number which had occupied the Four Corners. *Had?*

"It is," said Lessa in a serious tone. "And none of this would have been possible without you, Arianna." She shrugged. "In fact, I had to channel my inner warrior for your district to even *consider* listening to me." She waved her hand, looking back over the hill. "This is your army, Ara. They're here for you, for your dream of freedom."

"We all share the same dream," said Arianna.

She hugged Lessa around the waist, and they gazed out

over the field together.

"Yes, we do," she replied. "Now, come on. I promise not to spare a detail if you don't, but first let's get you somewhere more comfortable."

Arianna was hesitant to leave this view behind.

Her hopes had finally formed into something tangible, something that she could see with her own eyes. It was as if one of her greatest wishes had been plucked from her mind and drawn in ink on a page of history—the City of the Four Corners had fallen, the Jar finally opened. And the people that had been locked away there had at last come together.

The balance is shifting. The Golden Rule is skewing in our favor.

She followed Lessa into the jungle, suddenly very eager to return to Saindora.

4

LOST TIME

LESSA LED ARIANNA AND SOLZA DOWN the other side of the hill and away from the clearing. They traveled deep into the trees. After a while, the sounds of an army-in-training faded into the soft hum of the jungle.

They walked for a long time in silence.

So many thoughts ran through Arianna's mind that she couldn't possibly yet translate them to words. For now, she put her focus on this new, wild world that was the jungle.

They passed thick, moss-covered trees that dominated the terrain, giant roots bulging from the earth so that they could climb across them like bridges. Bright green, circular leaves created arches over their path like a continuous umbrella, and their trunks and limbs intertwined with each other like long-lost lovers.

Thin, yellow plants covered with bulbs also dangled over their heads, and flowers of every kind cropped up from the soft soil or peppered the trees, insects creeping around them greedily; Arianna wished she could just soak everything in, but she was forced to keep her focus on her footing to keep from falling face-first into the mud.

Lessa abruptly stopped and Arianna nearly toppled into her.

They stood before a grand tree. It towered over them; there was no way to even see the top.

Lessa was just staring toward the canopy, seemingly searching for something among the leaves. She whispered a phrase that sounded foreign to the ears.

Arianna's instincts told her it was some sort of spell, the way it slid off her tongue. However, she didn't immediately recognize the words from any of their lessons in magic.

"All right, up we go," said Lessa.

After making sure their avatars were close, she took Arianna's hand—a waterfall of vines dropped down from the treetops, like ropes spilling from the sky.

Arianna shouted, "Lessa—!"

The nature seemed to spring to life all around them. And she realized that there was some sort of wooden platform beneath their feet, hidden expertly among the leaves and dirt. With a jolt, it began to slowly travel up.

"Just relax," said Lessa, giving her hand a squeeze. "You're safe with me."

She remained so at ease, her eyes never leaving the sky, clearly enjoying the climb to the top.

Arianna let a long exhale escape her lips, trying to calm her skittering heart.

What in the gods' names is up here?

They were already so high into the trees that she could barely see the forest floor anymore. She kept her focus on Lessa.

Not soon enough, the platform came to a gentle stop, her

ears popping with the height.

Arianna sucked a breath in through her teeth, following Lessa off the platform and onto a sturdy, wooden bridge; she held tight to the banister with sweaty palms. There was no river to catch her if she fell this time.

"By gods, Ara, didn't you just fly a dragon across the Sea of Saindora?" Lessa howled in laughter. "One would think you'd be over your fear of heights by now."

"I *trust* Solza," she grumbled back.

She moved as if she walked through molasses, her avatar gently nudging her along.

"*She has a point, though,*" said Solza with a little chuckle.

"*Hush! You're making me dizzy,*" whined Arianna, praying that the contents of her stomach would stay put.

Lessa shook her head, a bemused smile on her face. "What, and you don't trust the trees?"

Arianna tossed her a frown. *Can everyone just please be quiet?*

Every time she glanced over the rail, she thought the ground was going to rush up and meet her; she held on tighter.

"Well, you had better learn," said Lessa, urging her forward. She threw her arms out wide. "Welcome to the Treehouse. At least, that's what we've started calling it."

Arianna took another deep breath, full of all her height-fighting courage. She lifted her eyes from her feet and suddenly wasn't scared anymore—the Treehouse expanded out in front of her like a spectacular painting.

It pulsated with life and magic, so much so that Arianna mused that if she *had* fallen, something probably would've reached out and caught her.

Vines and tree limbs acted like levers to lift several wooden platforms across the canopy up and down, people coming and going. And with just one glimpse around, she could tell that this network of huts in the sky went on and on; structures had been somehow built in and around the treetops farther than the eyes could see.

"How did you find this place?" she said, her intrigue eclipsing her fright.

"I was guided across the waters," Lessa said in a shaky voice. "Like you, I suppose."

Arianna didn't miss her change in tone. "By who?" she asked.

"Who do you think?" she replied, staring at her with an expression that suggested she should *know* the answer.

The name left Arianna's lips without a second thought.

"Syrifina…"

"*So that was her in the waters!*" Solza said. "*She was watching us.*"

"*I'm both shocked and unsurprised,*" said Arianna. She looked to Lessa. "You've really encountered her again?"

She nodded. "Wherever the water touches, she has eyes. You know this."

"That I do," she said through her teeth. "But I *don't* know why she would've helped you…"

She tapped her fingers on the banister, waiting for worse news.

"She's been more helpful than you could imagine," said Lessa, steadily. "Kind, even."

"Anything she does out of kindness is questionable," said Arianna, curtly. She narrowed her eyes. "Did you offer her something? Oh, *please* tell me you didn't make another deal with that sea witch."

Lessa scoffed.

"I've offered Syrifina enough," she said, a sharpness forming in her expression. "I owe her nothing more, and she has asked nothing of me."

Arianna returned a nod, chewing on the inside of her cheek.

If anything, she owes you.

She would never forget how Lessa had aided greatly in solving the mystery of the Myr sisters and their untimely deaths; she had discovered Sir Vladamor sucking the souls and magic straight from the entranced mermaids' bodies, only to capture and store their remains on his belt. For what, they had yet to discover...

"All right, fair enough," she said, releasing her tension in a whistle of air. She spoke more calmly now. "But how would Syrifina know where to find such a place as *this*? A treehouse, as you call it?"

"Well," said Lessa in a lighter tone, "I guess you can say that she has a lot in common with the one who built it..."

"Who built—"

Lessa smiled, twisting Sano's tail around her finger.

"*Just* follow me. You'll see soon," she said. "Every answer just begs another question, so I'd rather do this somewhere we can sit. Been on my feet all day."

Arianna chuckled. "I suppose you're right."

"*You have no patience, Master,*" said Solza.

She patted her head. "*I suppose you're right, too.*"

"Good," said Lessa. "There's an empty nook near my sleeping quarters where we can put you and Solza. Just a short walk away." She waved them forward, skipping across one bridge to the next until Arianna wasn't sure which direction they'd come from. "This place is unlike anything, Ara. She's really given us a haven up here, a new utopia. It's more than we could have ever hoped for... after everything."

Arianna couldn't hold back yet another question. "She?"

Lessa grinned at her over her shoulder. "You're incessant, you know?"

Arianna shrugged. "*So?*"

"Her name is Diveena," she replied with a laugh. "I'll make a proper introduction for you in the morning."

Arianna froze. "Did you say… Diveena?"

"*Master, could it be?*" Solza sounded just as shocked.

"*Fate is fate,*" said Arianna, shaking out of her stupor—Lessa hadn't even noticed the pause as she walked. "*I suppose that we'll find out soon enough.*"

Arianna and Solza caught back up with her; she led them across several more bridges until they found themselves in an area that was elevated above all the rest.

From up here, Arianna had a bird's-eye view of not only the lush green jungle but of the sea from which she'd come and of the city she hoped to one day discover; she became immersed in the gorgeous backdrop, starting to feel even more of herself return so far from the King's grasp—free and full of the eagerness to explore.

She was also starting to understand more where Lessa's obsession with heights came from…

How much safer could one get from the dangers of the world than up in the sky away from it all?

She could reach out and touch the clouds if she wanted.

The perfect place for hiding.

"What city is that, beyond the trees?" she asked, her eyes drawn to the twinkling lights of fire and soft trails of smoke far off in the distance. "Do you know?"

"It's called the City of Guanamara," said Lessa, allowing her a moment to stop and stare. She came to her side. "Apparently, it's home to many creators and agrarians."

"Jeom and Demetrius would love it, then," mused Arianna. Her stomach knotted. "Have you… heard anything of them? And Eli and Noah, shouldn't they be here with you?"

She had been so overjoyed at finding Lessa that she had all but forgotten the others.

As her excitement ebbed, making room for the worries hovering above her just like the clouds, she couldn't help but think of everyone else who was absent from this reunion.

"Oh, there's so much you've missed," said Lessa with a solemn sigh—Arianna wondered if the solemness came from the fact that she'd missed so much *or* that the answer was unpleasant.

Sano decided to take leave at that moment. Clearly tempted by the heights, he leaped off Lessa's shoulders and disappeared into the trees.

They watched him for a minute, silence lingering in his place. Then, Lessa turned to Arianna, eyes glittering.

"There's just so much to share with you," she said. Her solemness appeared to shift into an overwhelming contentment. "Ara, Jeom and Demetrius were the main reasons why Syrifina led me to this shore…" Arianna felt herself hanging on to every word. "She was leading me *to* them. Knew where they had landed after escaping Zambienth on the water."

"They're really here somewhere?" A surge of relief rushed over her. Their boat on the beach had tipped her off, but she wouldn't believe it until she saw their faces for herself. "They're alive!"

She was staggered by their luck. But it was a fleeting cheerfulness—she thought of the last thing she remembered of the Kane brothers.

"And what of Demetrius, his leg—" It all came rushing back to her now, all of the horrible things. "Is he…"

She didn't even know how to finish her sentence. *All right?* Who could be all right after such a traumatic experience?

"They were… with us for a while," said Lessa, looking away; her energy shifted to something darker. "But they've gone now."

Arianna's excitement vanished, replaced with a lump of dread in her throat.

"What do you mean 'they've gone'?" she said, cautiously. "Where did they go, Les?"

She couldn't believe that the boys would leave Lessa here

after only just reuniting. Something was wrong.

Lessa ran her fingers through her hair.

"It's fine, really," she said. "At least, I *think* it is. We have to sit down and discuss everything."

"*Oh, I hope they're safe...*" said Solza.

Before Arianna could protest, Lessa opened the door to the nearest cottage and led them inside.

When the door shut, Arianna had no more patience. She didn't even care to look around.

"Tell me what happened," she demanded, readying herself for the worst.

She sat down, and Solza lay on the floor by her feet; Lessa plopped into a chair and began.

"The boys were already here when we arrived, healthy as I've ever seen them," she said. "Demetrius... *oh*, you wouldn't even believe it if I told you. He's more whole than ever before."

"Demetrius?" said Arianna, cocking her head. "But how?"

She had trouble picturing him as such. He had been merely a shell of himself when they'd left him, as had Jeom.

"I guess all this nature really did him good," said Lessa, squirming in her seat—Arianna knew she was leaving something important out, but she let it slide for now. "Jeom and Eli have really taken to each other, too, always dueling. I'm not sure who's better these days, but Jeom is *finally* learning to better control the powers of the Crissy Axe."

All Arianna had heard was 'Eli.'

Lessa scooted her chair closer to her.

"Gabriel is to thank for everything, you know. He watched over Jeom and Demetrius on the journey here, found Diveena, and has been helping to further train us all." She lowered her voice, as if to tell a secret. "I *think*... with all of us back together again, we could have a real chance at winning this."

Arianna felt as if a jolt of electricity had sizzled straight through her bones.

"Are we really all back together?" she mumbled, unbidden tears welling again in her eyes.

She blinked them away, and Lessa nodded.

"We really are, Ara."

"I hope so," she replied, staring at her hands. Her thoughts moved in a darker direction. "I'm afraid the time for the truest test is nearing. We have no choice but to be ready for it now."

A heavy silence floated in the air, but Arianna refused to let it linger.

"How is Eli?" she asked, changing the subject. *Where is Eli?*

"Oh, the people love him!" Lessa gave a tiny clap. "He's really stepped up as a leader in your absence. He's come a long way since South Luose."

"As have we all," Arianna replied.

She felt a tightness in her chest; there was no bad news delivered as of yet, but she could tell Lessa was hiding something from her, skimming around the details.

"Why are they not here, Les?" said Arianna, trying to keep calm. "Please, just, out with it. Spare me the niceties. Where are our boys?"

Lessa leaned back in her chair.

"I can get nothing past you," she said with a tight smile.

Arianna did not return it.

"Just, *please*, don't do anything rash," added Lessa, holding up her hands. "Promise me." She dug her nails into her leg. "I know how you can get."

Arianna gave a weak nod, sealing her lips together and crossing her arms at her chest.

Depends on what it is, she thought.

"*I agree,*" said Solza, sitting up on her haunches.

Lessa rolled her eyes, surely knowing that Arianna would never keep such a promise.

"Oh, all right then," she said, huffing. "Jeom, Demetrius,

Eli, and Gabriel... they all left a fortnight ago. Trekked back into the Impenetrable Forest."

She pointed toward the outside.

"You mean, a trip to the City of Guanamara?" said Arianna.

She clenched the sides of the chair, for she knew there was more; Lessa shook her head.

"No... not to the city. They went the other direction. Diveena, she sent them west. They're searching for a place called the Starr Caverns."

Arianna had never heard of this place. She squeezed her eyes closed for a second.

"For *what* reason?" she asked, her voice pitching. "What happened to staying together?" She began to spiral, her hopes of assuring that the rest of her family was alive and well suddenly obliterated. "You *just* found each other! Why couldn't she have sent anyone else? Why them?"

"Because, Ara, only those truly connected to the Golden Age and all the magic that comes with it will be able to locate who Diveena believes still exists."

Lessa stared at her intently, watching every flicker in her expression as her words sank in.

Arianna reined in her frustration.

"You mean... only guardians?" she said after a moment.

"*Not* exactly," replied Lessa—another tight smile.

Arianna wasn't sure if the low growl that sounded had come from her or Solza.

"We've run out of time," said Lessa, throwing her hands up. "You just said so yourself. Wars have already broken out all over the Olleb, and we're going to need all the help we can get to come out as the victors." She pulled in a big breath. "So, we all agreed that this was one more chance worth taking. Myself included."

Arianna brought her hand to her head, feeling a bit

dizzied; she glared in Solza's direction.

"*Wars?*"

"*I'm sorry, Master. Just breathe,*" she purred, her voice ringing through her mind with a much-needed calming effect. "*Let her explain. Much has happened since you were taken…*"

"*But you kept things from me.*"

"*I had to,*" she said, gently. "*For your own good.*"

Arianna gritted her teeth.

"Go on," she said, turning back to Lessa.

"I take it that you hadn't heard… about the wars, then?"

Arianna focused on the floor.

"I've been either in hiding or imprisoned for the last six months," she snapped—Lessa flinched.

Arianna closed her eyes, reminding herself that her anger was misplaced. *Never forget.*

"No… I hadn't," she added.

"Well," said Lessa with a nervous expression, "that does complicate my story a bit. Let's just start with the good." She sat up straighter. "You'll be pleased to know that we're racing toward our end goal now. The King's regime is unraveling right underneath his nose, and it all started with you!" Her eyes drifted toward the window. "*However,* we do need more support to secure our army. That's why the boys left… to find help."

Arianna stood. "This is too much."

She was barely able to process her surroundings, let alone that her beloved friends had ventured back out into the dangerous world to try to recruit more non-believers to join those already gathered. That somewhere out there, true battles for freedom had already begun.

How had I not known any of this?

She felt for the hilt of her dagger, thinking of Solomon, thinking of the King.

They hid everything from me. Would've let me die in that

dungeon never knowing the truth!

"*But they couldn't hold you,*" said Solza, firmly. Arianna caught her fire-filled gaze. "*And now you know. The Guardians of Gold have risen.*"

"I knew it would be," said Lessa, getting to her feet.

Arianna heard the tinkling of glass as she retrieved something from a cabinet.

"Here, take this. You look exhausted."

She handed Arianna a cup filled to the brim with something red.

"Prillyberry juice or wine?" asked Arianna with a smirk; she was instantly disarmed by the promise of either.

Lessa wasn't to blame for her world news blackout. She was just the messenger.

Down with the King! And Solomon, too.

"Drink up," she said with a grin.

Arianna sipped what was surely a fine red wine, though there *was* also a hint of the familiar bitter taste of prillyberry juice, somewhere in there.

It had been ages since she'd even thought of the old luxuries they'd enjoyed before things had turned so serious—prillyberry juice had saved them more times than she could count in the early years after their escape, and wine had never failed them before.

She felt herself relax as soon as the drink touched her tongue.

"You're getting good at this," said Arianna, smacking her lips. "I barely tasted it that time."

"There's nothing that prillyberry juice *or* wine can't fix," said Lessa. "I figured a combination was worth a try."

They both laughed, and instantly any tension between them fell away.

"It's brilliant," said Arianna, taking another sip. "You're brilliant." She stared down at the dark red contents of her cup.

"I'm sorry, I'm just so overwhelmed by everything…"

Lessa placed her hands on her shoulders, eyes glowing silver. She didn't need to speak; Arianna could feel the powerful healing magic that she called—*Helthra saludis emencia*.

It rushed through her body, a tingling sensation spreading across her limbs.

When Lessa pulled away, Arianna examined herself; all her visible scratches, cuts, and bruises were beginning to fade. And she hadn't even realized how much she'd been hurting until the pain was taken away.

"By gods, so you're *really* getting good," said Arianna, watching as she tended to Solza next. "Shall I call you master yet?"

Lessa snorted, settling back down in her chair with a cup of what looked to be water.

"Not quite yet. But my avatar magic has grown, too," she explained. "I can channel Sano's healing powers a lot easier now. His unique ability is much more effective than mere prillyberry juice. That combined with the knowledge Talis bestowed on me…"

"I see," said Arianna, bowing her had.

She raised her glass and Lessa joined her; they needn't speak of that dreadful moment just yet.

With Arianna a little caught up and a little calmer, Lessa launched into the full story of their time apart. She started with her tales from the Four Corners, of how she bewitched the districts with the truth. And from there, an even bigger adventure unwound…

She and Eli had literally retraced the steps of journeys Lessa and Arianna had first experienced together—this time taking over the cities as they went.

They started at the beginning, with the dreadful Village of Draminet.

"EACH TOWN AND CITY we've passed through, we've taken, establishing a foothold," said Lessa. "Some have been more difficult to hold than others… but people have been persuaded to listen to our side given just the indisputable reality that the district slaves walked free beside us."

She gazed toward the open window again, the sun still high in the sky.

"But magic, unfortunately, *can* prove difficult to use as persuasion at times," she added. "Especially with the older generations. Some people are absolutely terrified of it, and feel safer turning toward the King."

Arianna let out a sarcastic laugh. "If only they knew."

"*Right?*" said Lessa. "But it doesn't matter." She waved off the non-believers just as easily as swatting a fly. "Everyone has a choice. A good many have followed us and are in training as we speak."

"What else?" said Arianna, hungry for every word; she leaned forward.

She felt almost as if she walked alongside Lessa in her memories as she spoke of the last six months—by the thousands, they marched through South Luose and stole back the palace from the Shadow Resistance, loosening their grip on the city.

They passed through several new municipalities that bordered the sands and the Nicora Forest, each now with a wavering loyalty to King Devlindor. And they followed Eli safely across the Black Sand Desert.

"We took back Zambienth too—" said Lessa, searching through her past; a shadow haunted her expression.

Arianna saw the shine in her eyes; she reached out a hand.

"I'm sorry about Talis," she whispered, knowing where her thoughts had turned. "Trust me when I say this, he lies in your heart… and you still in his."

Lessa sniffled. "I know." Her voice was barely audible.

As if he'd sensed her sadness, Sano bounded in through the window on a cushion of air. He settled into Lessa's lap protectively.

She cleared her throat and started up again, holding Sano close.

"When we reached Zambienth, we discovered Rowina there in hiding, with some of the other elder guardians who had escaped." She looked to Arianna, a determination in her eyes. "Shadow Resistance may have captured the city that awful night, but they couldn't hold the Greenhouse. *Especially* not after we showed back up to stake our claim. It remains intact."

Arianna felt more of her fear deflate, leaving her stunned. *The Greenhouse survived…*

"*It's as strong as ever*," said Solza, proudly.

"After we unseated the regulators and interim city keeper," Arianna's jaw dropped, "we organized in Zambienth with the Greenhouse as our base. And with so many young creators on hand, we were able to continue where we had left off… building guardian ships."

Arianna absentmindedly stroked Solza, hardly able to comprehend such a story.

"Yes, I… I saw them when Solza and I landed on the beach here," she said. "They're truly grand."

Lessa beamed bright.

"That's just the start of it, Ara," she said, growing excited. "There's a fleet of them in the making back in the pyramid city." She pointed to the door. "All the people you saw today down at the camp makes up just a *fraction* of who we liberated from the Jar, as well as the cities between there and Zambienth."

She smiled, seeming to rather enjoy Arianna's surely

astonished expression.

"We've had to split up to be able to hold down the territories."

She was talking eagerly now, hands flying all around as she tried to help Arianna picture all these wonderful victories.

"Eli has really taken charge of all that. He's a natural." She softened her voice with a somber shake of her head. "Alas, we *have* lost people in the process… many in fact. The battles with the King's followers have been bloody at best."

Arianna felt her stomach twist again, but Lessa didn't allow her even a second to inquire.

Who? And would their lives be worth this?

"But still, we have seen many successes," she continued. "King Devlindor has been pulling back his main army and the Shadow Resistance closer to Saindora. Things are looking quite optimistic… as of yet."

Arianna let out a long whistle, Lessa finally pausing to take a breath.

"Funny, the King was never so forthcoming about any of these failures with me," said Arianna. She let out a derisive snort. "Though, now I realize why he tortured me so."

"Your turn," said Lessa, turning serious.

Arianna gazed to the floor.

"Cyn and Iris are dead," she said, breaking the news quickly. "He killed them and made me watch."

Lessa's hand flew over her mouth.

"No, please," she said between her fingers. She balled her other hand into a fist, pounding her thigh. "That monster! I can't even fathom…" She reached out to Arianna. "I can't even fathom it. I'm so sorry."

Arianna glanced at Solza, not wanting to meet her eyes… not wanting it to be real.

"All that you've accomplished in these last months, it doesn't matter to him," she said, gravely. "King Devlindor will *never* back down. Not even with the Guardians of Gold creating such mayhem in his realm. He's too confident in his powers, his position. Maybe even more so than before, now that we've challenged him." She finally looked up. "He enjoys it, I think."

Lessa nuzzled Sano, looking unsurprised.

"I fear that it's part of his plan to thin us out before we reach the High City," she muttered. "And… it's working." She crossed her legs. "Even still, I think we actually stand a chance against him."

"Is that why this Diveena has sent our boys out to look for more help?" Her thoughts drifted back to the Kane brothers. To Eli and Gabriel. "Because you think the King's strategy is to thin us out?"

Lessa hesitated. "Yes, but…"

"But, *what?*" snapped Arianna, unnerved by her own sharp memories of the King's power.

"Well, I… I don't want to alarm you more than you already are," said Lessa, "but the group has been gone a little longer than we'd planned."

Arianna felt her throat tighten. "How *much* longer?"

"A few days… give or take," she said, staring too hard at Sano.

Arianna pursed her lips.

"If they're not back by this time tomorrow, we're going to go find them," she said, leaving no room for debate. "I'm not losing anyone else."

"I've already packed a bag," agreed Lessa. She looked up, playing with a stray thread from her clothes. "I know they're fine… I just want to be sure."

Arianna relaxed in the face of her friend's worry—and at seeing that after even six months apart, they were still on the same page.

"Do you think they could be just slowed down a bit?" she

asked. "You know, with Demetrius' leg and all?"

Lessa let out a barking laugh, startling both the avatars and Arianna.

"Trust me," she said, "if anything, they'll be trying to keep up with him now."

Arianna frowned, having trouble imagining that he could somehow be more agile with only one leg. But she decided to save that query for Demetrius.

She gazed around the room, finally taking it in—it was striking in its simplicity, its rawness, blending right into the nature that surrounded it on the outside.

"So what is this place, *really?*" she asked. "And who is Diveena?"

"She's a miracle," breathed Lessa.

Arianna sipped her wine, trying to hide her skepticism.

"We've been fortifying ourselves here under her protection and guidance," continued Lessa. "We plan to take Guanamara next, and she's been helping us strategize a way."

"And then what?" said Arianna, unable to picture what it meant to 'take' a city.

"Then you can see for yourself what it looks like when the Guardians of Gold come into power," she replied.

Arianna looked to the ceiling.

"It all seems to be happening so fast, when before it felt like the days were just dragging on and on to even get to the start of all you've described," she said. "I feel like I've been sleeping and have woken up to a brand-new world."

"Oh, we wouldn't enter the new world without you, Ara," said Lessa in all seriousness. "Not *ever.* We were making plans to rescue you from Solomon, but we knew you had probably already been taken to Saindora. We couldn't risk not being *completely* prepared before marching there."

Arianna felt a twinge of jealousy. *Making plans… when I've been doing nothing.*

"At least you got to see some action," she said, gazing through the window. "It seems I've missed out on everything." She waved her hand, hating Solomon more and more. "I've just been chased to the end of the world and back and missed it all."

"You haven't missed a thing!" said Lessa with a chuckle. "We're just warming up. The King and his Shadow Resistance won't be taken easily. You know that. We may have started the battles, but we need your help to guide us to the end."

Arianna closed her eyes.

"I don't know if I'm ready to meet him again," she said, softly. "I know that when I do, it will be for the last time—whether or not we win."

Lessa went over to the cabinet to grab the canister of wine; she filled her cup back up to the brim.

"When you do, I'll be right by your side," she said. "Now tell me… what happened to you there? How did you escape from Solomon and the King?"

They both slid to the floor atop a plush rug, Solza and Sano snuggling close.

"I didn't…" said Arianna after a moment. "Not alone anyways. And by the time I did, they'd already inflicted enough damage for me to remember forever. They'll be coming for us and soon." She grasped Solza. "I almost didn't survive—"

She took another long sip of her drink, the liquid warming her from the inside out.

"The King is pure evil," she added. "If it wasn't for Odessa, I would've lost my mind for certain."

"Odessa?" asked Lessa. "Who—"

"She was the daughter of Ophelia…" explained Arianna. "A seer."

Lessa's mouth formed a big 'O', and Arianna held out her glass for a refill. Then she dived into the many details of her own wondrous and terrifying adventures; she told Lessa everything.

TOGETHER, SHE AND LESSA TRADED months' worth of stories between them. When they came up for air, the sun had
fallen beneath the trees to be replaced by the moon; Solza and
Sano were fast asleep on the floor.

Lessa gave a big yawn, stretching her arms above her head
so that her shirt lifted up—Arianna's eyes widened as she
caught a glimpse of her stomach.

"Lessa, you've grown so… big," she said; she hadn't noticed before, for she was wearing loose-fitting garments.

Lessa immediately put her arms down, twisting a piece of
hair around her finger—she gazed anywhere but directly at
Arianna.

Arianna gave a little start, nearly dropping her cup.

There was something *very* familiar about her appearance
now that she cared to look closely; she recognized it from her
time spent in the cities and in Moriamo.

"Lessa, you're not—" She scooted closer, laying a hand on
her belly. Her skin was plump and hard beneath her palm.

"A baby?" she gasped; the avatars stirred but didn't wake.
"By gods, are you going to have a *baby?*"

Arianna sat back, gawking at her; Lessa had clearly gone
through a major transformation all her own.

Her hand drifted protectively to her stomach, just a small
bump there now.

"Yes, I'm having a baby," she said, trying to hold her voice
steady; her bright blue eyes were rimmed red with tears. "I'm
having a baby—"

Her voice cracked, and Arianna was certain of where her

thoughts had gone…

The only children she had ever known to be free flashed through her memories, hidden in a magical swamp from the King's far-reaching rule. Then, she remembered vividly the moment she was handed her cloth as a child—number twenty-two—before she was escorted into the Four Corners alongside all the other child-slaves who were old enough to leave the Opalls.

Arianna grasped Lessa's hands tightly, peering into her eyes.

One of the strongest women she knew would not be undone by fear of the King. She would *not* allow it.

"I promise, by all the gods and goddesses watching over us now, no harm will come to your child. That baby will be born free. Do you understand me?" she implored. "This world is not the same one that we entered. We have cut it open and bared its truths, and there will be no burying them again. The King cannot have us back."

Lessa nodded, wiping her tears away.

"I can't have a child just to hand it over to death, Ara. I can't."

"You won't," she said. "You won't." She leaned back, forcing a smile onto her lips. "But, Les, just wow… I can't believe that you're pregnant! This is quite unexpected. I have to hear more."

"There's not much more to tell," she said with a shy shrug. "I'm not *exactly* sure how much time I have until it comes, but Diveena thinks several months still. It definitely happened sometime after we landed here." She blushed, the brightest pink yet. "There was a lot of… rejoicing at the reunion with the boys. At least, for me and Jeom anyways."

Arianna threw her head back in laughter, and suddenly warmth blew back into the room.

"Well, Jeom certainly isn't one for patience, is he?" she said with a chuckle. "What a way to celebrate, indeed! I don't think there's anything more precious than a child."

She remembered them fondly from Moriamo; and she hoped with all her heart that there were more survivors than losses from that dreadful night.

"She's just a little nugget now," said Lessa, glowing with delight. "I'm so happy to be able to share with you."

"*She?*" Arianna raised an eyebrow.

"I just have… a feeling," said Lessa, biting her lip. "I think, it's a girl."

"If it is a girl, she'll be lucky to be even a little like you," said Arianna. "What will we call her, then?"

"Well, *if* it's a boy, Talis Jr.," said Lessa, eagerly.

Arianna beamed.

"Of course," she said. "But if your instincts are right?"

"Snow," she replied with a sureness.

Arianna gave her a quizzical look. "I thought you hated the snow?"

Lessa shook her head with a solemn expression; Arianna understood.

For, really, how could anyone hate the snow? It was the only thing that could paint over the Olleb's wounds with something pure and clean. And now that there was no snow in sight, she could definitely appreciate it more.

"No matter where I was in the Four Corners," said Lessa, wistfully, "the snow always made it beautiful, always brought the hope and happiness to a dismal situation. I *thought* that I hated it back then, but when we returned to the Jar, I realized how much I actually missed it sometimes." She smiled. "Snow is but water, and water fills the most beautiful oceans where the *most* enchanting creatures reside… so it seems, in fact, that I love the snow dearly."

Lessa moved her hand back and forth, the wine in Arianna's cup beginning to swirl as she manipulated its water-like elements.

"Snow," mused Arianna. "A fine name, indeed." She thought of her conversation with Talis in the afterlife, of the wonderful setting he'd created for them. "Your very own snowflower, born in the coldest of places yet still needs sun to shine—a rarity."

"I can't lose her," said Lessa, a dark look crossing her eyes again. "If we fail, I will lose her."

"We won't," Arianna assured her. "That child will never see anything like the Jar, no matter what happens. I promise you this."

The two talked well into the night until the wine was nearly empty, musing over a world like the Swamp of Mori-amo where children roamed free under their mothers' care and where the King was nothing but a bad dream. Both giddy with happiness, they fell into a fit of giggles over the magic of their imaginations.

"You should sleep now," said Lessa after a while. "The sun will rise soon enough, and I know Diveena will want to ask you even more questions. You'll need your energy for tomor-row."

She got to her feet and went toward the door, tiptoeing over Solza and Sano; they'd curled themselves together across the soft carpet between them.

"Stay," said Arianna, dragging herself into the large bed in the middle of the room. "I've been alone a long time."

Lessa didn't protest, crawling in next to her. She pulled the covers to her chin. "It's just like before."

"Nothing is like before," mumbled Arianna. "But I'm so glad you're here now."

Her eyes drifted closed, and for the first time in months, she slept soundly.

STARR CAVERNS

JEOM CLUTCHED THE AXE OF CRISSY, cutting away the branches and tree limbs as he walked; everything seemed to grow denser with each step, the nature a tangled, incomprehensible heap in this part of the jungle.

He led the way for Demetrius, Gabriel, and Eli who followed on horseback.

Each time Jeom swung the axe to do away with the Impenetrable Forest's incessant obstacles—Diveena had done her job *too* well—Demetrius would respond with a sigh of annoyance. Then, he'd wield his newfound magic to shift the trees and bushes before they could come to any harm.

Gabriel and Eli tried and failed to hold their amusement behind their teeth.

"*Yeesh*, you're no fun," said Jeom, his palms sweaty around the staff of his weapon; he glanced over his shoulder, rolling his eyes at Demetrius.

He'd come a *long* way with his powers over these short

months.

Demetrius shrugged, smirking back at him.

They had been doing this same dance for days; they were so comfortable together again, returned to such high spirits as brothers, despite all the horrors, that sometimes Jeom had trouble believing it was all real—yet here they were, on an adventure meant solely for them.

"And you're a menace!" called Demetrius, his laughter bouncing between the mammoth leaves hanging over their heads.

When Jeom heard his brother's laughter, he thanked all the gods—or, as Diveena would correct him, goddesses—that he had come back to him whole. There had been a moment when he was sure that he wouldn't…

Diveena was to thank for everything, a godsend herself. Not only had the elf coaxed them all back to perfect health but she'd helped both him and his brother discover a new realm of powers—ones gifted to them as the chosen ones in the incredible shared history between elves and dwarves.

"Do you think there's even anything out here to find?" he heard Gabriel ask. "I know Diveena has faith about this place, if it still even exists, but I'm starting to think that this journey was a fool's errand. It's taking much longer than we planned. We need to return to camp soon."

They had all agreed before the start of their trek that Gabriel—the only elder guardian among them—would have the final say as to when this adventure would be over.

Jeom knew that if he remained uncertain of their progress much longer, he would overrule them with a decision to return.

"It's not a waste of time!" implored Demetrius, using the compass to guide them; he wanted to reach the Starr Caverns just as badly as Jeom. "We'll have our answers soon, whether we find anything or not."

"That's true," said Eli, "but if there is anything out here

worth knowing about... anyone, we had better find them soon. Sorry, boys, but I'm with Gabe. If we don't turn back in about a day or so, we'll run out of supplies *and* surely be missed."

"We can't go back empty-handed," said Jeom, thinking of Lessa and the child she was growing.

She's probably trying to send the entire army after us by now, he thought.

And knowing her, she could succeed with little effort; she'd truly grown comfortable as one of the guardian leaders. But, with any hope, Diveena could offer her enough reassurance to keep her from sneaking off in the night to search for them.

"If there's something out here that could help us, we have to know."

They just needed a little more time.

They marched onward, through the seemingly never-ending tunnel of trees, taking turn after turn with the guardian relic as their only source of direction. As Jeom twisted the double-sided axe in hand, leading the way, he could almost imagine that he was navigating again through the Vanishing Tunnels.

His mind traveled back to that distant yet life-changing moment—sneaking through a maze of tunnels and doors, searching for freedom, with new friends and a rediscovered brother by his side. Beneath the Blancoren Mountains they had learned a great many things, including the story of King Undoriamus and the Axe of Crissy...

He had now studied the dwarf king's weapon and its special properties at great length, having pried from Diveena every bit of knowledge she had about its masterful creation.

I still can't imagine that such a treasure belongs to me...

The scales of wings had been etched across both silver-edged blades so that when Jeom wielded the axe, calling to its magic, it always appeared as if a royally armored dragon took off in flight. And he had even come across the surprising discovery that the stones of aura and ora held a significant place in its foundation, just like his friends' guardian relics—if one looked closely, the pitch-black frame of the axe glittered like tiny crystals in dark liquid, while the stones that created the eyes of the dragon skull swirled with vibrant hues, eternally glaring at its challengers.

The Axe of Crissy and its powers were unfathomable at best, but Jeom understood it much better now, as well as his Golden Age ancestry…

Just as the element of earth was attributed to elven heritage, water to that of mermaids, and fire to dragons—all some of the most esteemed magical beings known to the Olleb since its beginnings—dwarves were celebrated masters of air.

Wind was the *first* known natural creator ever to have existed; its powerful gusts had been slowly carving and shaping the earth each and every day, for always.

And just as surely as the gods created Olleb-Yelfra, they had created dwarves and wind as one—their magic was naturally in tune with it, tied to it, for no creator's tool could offer as much precision as that of mastering the element of air.

The Axe of Crissy was a profound instrument in channeling such magic; because of its unique and exceptional properties, King Undoriamus' people had sealed it away using a *blood* magic enchantment, during the King's ambush on their city.

Once it was under protection bound by kinship, not even the King's armies could break through the axe's barrier.

Until me…

Jeom thought back to when he *first* laid hands on the weapon. A chill came over him, even on this muggy day.

The axe's impenetrable chamber, one which the High King of the Olleb had been unable to open with all the magic to his name, had simply fallen away at Jeom's touch; all the dwarves of Undor had died during the siege on their kind, trying to protect the sacred weapon he now held in his hands.

I am, somehow, their kin.

He no longer questioned it, just wanted to deserve it.

He thought of King Devlindor's attempts to retrieve the grand weapon, of Demetrius, of all the sacrifices that had been made in its name.

I will never let him have it! Down with the King.

Jeom squeezed the axe tighter and could practically feel its magic pulsing in his veins, awaking every nerve in his body— as if to say, '*You're one of us, Jeom. Protect this with your life.*'

He closed his eyes a moment, silently reciting the words of the plaque he'd deciphered and memorized in the abandoned city, located near a statue of King Undoriamus himself. It had taken him many moons, but he finally comprehended what the last part of the inscription had meant.

To truly tap into the axe's powers, '*…the beholder must have unbendable loyalty and strength…*'

In oneself, he thought.

Jeom accepted who he was now—half-dwarf, brother to a half-elf, and a leader in a quest that could ultimately change the world.

As his fingers wrapped around the staff, he could feel the wind whistling within the weapon, affirming his decisions. And with the strength of a swing, he knew he could blow his enemies off their feet, its elemental magic now his to control.

Jeom had finally been made into a true believer, and he would do everything in his power to do the right thing by his chosen family, both blood and not.

We must win this war, or die trying.

He swung the axe, its blade effortlessly slicing through the thick arm of a low-hanging tree in his path. He carried forward, ignoring Demetrius' curses in the background.

"OVER THERE," SAID GABRIEL, yanking Jeom out of his thoughts; he felt as if he'd been sleep-walking, dreaming of the dwarf city and its exquisite architecture, its unparalleled treasures.

"Look alive, man!" said Gabriel, an excited pitch in his voice. He leaped off his horse and rushed ahead of Jeom.

"This must be it," said Demetrius in awe. He guided his horse forward into the shallow stream ahead. "This has to be Starr Caverns, just like Diveena promised."

Eli followed right behind on Phantom—the two had become inseparable again, ever since their grand reunion.

Jeom followed everyone's gaze and let out a little laugh.

"I'm *not* going in there," he said, shaking his head.

He was staring straight into the wide, open mouth of a rocky cavern; Jeom thought if they took one step inside it would clamp down on them.

It's a deathtrap—suddenly, his memories traversing the Vanishing Tunnels turned a lot more bitter.

Moss and vines grew up the sides of the dark stone so that it seemed to melt right into the trees, like a portal to another world.

A dark world?

It had been carved out in the middle of the jungle at the end of a long river they'd been following; if Demetrius was right, that river would lead them straight back to the campsite.

"What, *you*… afraid?" chided Eli with a grin.

He unmounted Phantom and tied him to a nearby tree.

"Do the Vanishing Tunnels ring a bell? Literally, the dwarves had those tunnels *changing* directions," he shot back. "I'm not eager to reexperience that."

Eli patted him on the back.

"Don't worry, Jeom. I'm sure there's a couple of friendly

ghosts in there ready to lead the way."

Jeom shoved him off, his whole body shuddering.

I hope there aren't really ghosts in there...

Eli skipped away.

"Will you two behave?" said Gabriel, walking closer to the cave. "Let's just check it out. We didn't come all this way to turn around now."

"He's not wrong, though," said Demetrius, "about the tunnels..."

The boys were all silent for a moment, standing side by side in front of the cavern, all lost momentarily in their district pasts.

Jeom let out a loud moan, tossing his head back as he realized something. "Are you thinking what I'm thinking, Demetrius?"

"Probably." Demetrius nodded. "It does have a certain familiar... *quality* to it, doesn't it?" he replied.

"How do you mean?" said Gabriel, hands on his hips. "Familiar to what?"

"Well," said Demetrius, "if there *are* any more dwarves left in the Olleb, even in another tribe, this would be a perfect hiding spot for them. The City of Undor was built miles beneath the ground, and the entrance was a foreboding cavern tunnel, quite like this."

"Oh, I see," said Gabriel with wide eyes, considering their findings with new understanding. "I wonder... could Diveena's inkling have been right, then? Did dwarves survive—"

"Diveena sent us here for a reason," said Jeom, commanding his axe to conceal itself once more. "Let's go and find out."

His fear fled in the face of hope.

Maybe there's something in here that could tell me more about who I am. Why Demetrius and I were chosen...

He watched with pride as Demetrius slid down from his

horse; the prosthetic leg he'd crafted for him had held up nicely on the journey so far, though he was already thinking of new ways to enhance it when they returned to the Treehouse.

"Gabe, you mind?" said Eli, nodding to the broken branches scattered on the ground. "We'll need some light down there."

"Good idea," said Gabriel, picking them up and handing them around to the group.

Closing his eyes, he called to his magic—the branches crackled with rosy flames in the next second.

One by one, they entered the cavern.

Once they stepped through the mouth, almost instantly, they felt relief from the hot, sticky day—cool, wet stones shielded them from the outside heat.

It was a massive cave, their firelight doing little to showcase the true width of the area.

Mammoth, jagged columns lined their path, so they held on to them for balance. And they followed a sharp, downward slope, taking care with their footing.

The sound of trickling water from the outside stream echoed eerily around them, creating a soothing ambience. It had, evidently, snuck its way into the cavern, flowing somewhere deep down that they had yet to see.

They maneuvered through waxy formations that shot up from the ground, like trees made of stone; some reached so high that they connected with their brethren hanging from the ceiling, and they shone nearly translucent with the aid of fire.

There were clusters of crystalized chandeliers, dangling low enough that they had to duck around them as they continued their exploration. And sharp spikes, dripping with dew, hung from white, cloudlike ceilings—the texture was so ribbed that it seemed as if ripples of sparkling snow had frozen overhead.

Vines and flowers of the jungle had also crept their way into this cave, petals glowing with florescent pinks and whites; they crawled up the walls and drooped from the chandelier-like structures.

"This place is magnificent," said Demetrius, gently caressing one of the flowers.

When he brought his torch too close, the petals instantly sucked back into a tight bulb—as if to hide or protect itself from the disturbance.

"They must not like the light," said Gabriel, leaning over his shoulder to look.

"*See*, Jeom," said Demetrius, moving the flame to a safe distance; the flower slowly opened back up. "They can sense pain."

"I suppose…" he said, feeling guilty for all the flowers he'd slovenly crushed in his life. "I'll try to be more careful."

For once, he actually meant it.

"It's strange, this place," added Demetrius. "There wasn't a single plant in the City of Undor. Remember?" Jeom nodded, recalling the enchanted painted forest they'd discovered there. "It's as if both of our kinds are welcomed here."

Jeom considered this as he gazed around, the light of his torch making monstrous shadows across the glistening cave walls; it could have been the perfect home for dwarves, another marvelous setting for mining and creation.

But Demetrius was onto something—the jungle had found its way in here, too.

Jeom thought it all the more beautiful, beholding the two natural elements joined together in the dark.

They turned the corner, and his thoughts turned with it—he became lost in deep, still waters that surrounded their path.

So this is where the outside stream went.

Tranquil, crystal blue pools sat on either side of this particular stretch of cave floor. And a sapphire reflection sparkled along the walls, creating a sanctuary of calming blue around them; anything that Jeom had considered 'dark' before was abruptly washed away in azure brilliance.

Thick columns of rock jutted up from the floor of the pools, glinting like gemstones in the light of their flames. And the entire cavern ceiling was reflected in the mirror-like waters, making it seem as if they could see to the very bottom.

Jeom leaned farther over the edge to prove his theory; it *really* looked as if he could simply swim to the bottom and back in one breath.

He scoffed.

"There's no way…" he muttered to himself.

It's just a mirage. There's no telling how deep that water goes. Eyes never lie… but mirrors do.

The more he stared, the deeper the waters seemed to grow.

"Careful, or you'll fall in," said Eli, pulling him back by his shirt. "Don't want to be something's dinner down here."

A giant eel had slithered out from an underwater passage-way, its electricity circling it in a protective shell as it hunted.

"Thanks," he stuttered, not wanting anything to do with such a creature.

"No problem," said Eli with a shrug. "Same rules apply in caves as with deserts… mind your surroundings so they don't mind you."

"Amazing advice." Gabriel laughed, hurrying onward with the others in tow.

Jeom kept one eye on the waters as they continued.

The deeper they traveled, the denser the vines and flowers seemed to grow, feeding off the small pools that now kept them company throughout their journey—one poured into the next, like a waterfall, going down, down, down.

After a while, Demetrius took over as guide. He was determined to follow the nature once again; and as his magic enchanted the plants to lead the way, no one was in a place to argue with him about it.

"Look!" he said, pointing up.

"I've never seen anything like this," said Gabriel, holding out his arm for the others to halt, too.

They stood on the ledge of a high cliff.

"It reminds me of the desert nights," said Eli, a dazed smile stretched across his face. "Ara would love this."

Jeom's breath caught in his throat at the vision before him. "Lessa, too."

He missed them both—feared for them the same way he feared for Demetrius when they'd been separated in the districts—every time they found themselves apart.

Ara, please be all right...

His family was still incomplete.

Rays of light poured in through minuscule cracks on a dome-like ceiling in this part of the cavern—it seemed as if stars danced all around the shadowy chamber, spotlighting a large lake of dark blue waters where the stream of pools had finally gathered.

Lanky trees, with bright red flowers dotting their canopies, grew up from its depths, and all around the sides of the cave to complete this underground oasis.

The cliffs they stood on now rose high around the water, closing it in like a bowl with a lid—the only way out would be to turn back the way they had come, *or* to jump in and see what they could find in the underwater tunnels that surely continued beyond this mysterious lake; the gaping hole of crisp, clear blue had no clear end in sight.

Option number one, please, Jeom thought.

He glanced over to Demetrius and knew they had reached the end of their journey.

The sounds of the jungle slipped back into this part of the cave, calling them to return to the Treehouse... though, a quiet echo surrounded them still, begging them to stay.

"Over there!" said Eli, pointing across the waters. "It's a boat."

Jeom followed his line of sight.

Sure enough, a light blue boat, worn with time, had been tied to one of the leaning trees. He also noticed a narrow passageway where the pool may have once been open to the outside—it was now closed off with rocks.

"Maybe an avalanche?" mused Demetrius, craning his neck to see.

Jeom wiped the sweat from his brow.

"That or someone didn't want their tracks to be followed," he said—he thought of Undor, of the lengths his brethren had taken to hide it from people like King Devlindor.

"Either way, someone was here before," said Gabriel, nodding.

He was excited, eyes darting around everywhere, searching for more hints of life.

"Yes, but they're gone now," said Demetrius, growing frustrated. He turned to Jeom, brow furrowed. "Why would Diveena send us all the way here if there was no one to find?"

Jeom shrugged.

"Beats me," he said. "Why do these ancient, all-powerful women do anything?"

He pouted and crossed his arms, begrudgingly remembering Syrifina Myr. *Probably because they can.*

"Well, from the looks of it, they've been gone a *long* time," added Eli. "A boat with such craftsmanship doesn't rot like that overnight."

Jeom scrutinized it closer and had to agree.

He could tell a master creator's hand when he saw it, and this boat had been touched with skill. From the way it looked now, he thought it a permanent fixture of this lake, and one that had been there for decades—maybe even centuries.

He lifted his gaze back to the starry ceiling. Then, he tilted his head, squinting his eyes to make out a picture forming there.

"By gods, that can't be." He gasped, nearly losing his balance—Eli grabbed the back of his cloak to steady him.

"Careful, mate," said Eli. "Lessa will have our heads if we don't bring you back in one piece."

Jeom grunted in response, still focused on the ceiling.

"Demetrius, take my hand," he said, desperation in his voice.

He was still staring up, unblinking.

"Why?" said Demetrius.

"*Just* do it," he urged, holding it out wide for him.

Gabriel and Eli were engulfed in conversation, sizing up the scenery and making mental notes of what to bring back for Diveena, information that might be of value in her search.

Jeom felt Demetrius' palm lock together with his, his gaze now lifted too.

"I don't see—"

"Look closely," he said, pointing to the spot he was fixated on; Demetrius' grip tightened.

There, among the cracks in the cavernous ceiling, was the clear outline of a six-pointed star.

"I don't think Diveena sent us here to find *anyone*," said Jeom, squeezing back. "She sent us here… to find ourselves."

With their palms still clasped, their marks began to glow bright.

Jeom felt as if their hands had been fused together. He knew they wouldn't be able to let go, even if they'd tried.

"Your eyes," stuttered Eli—Jeom barely noticed, feeling his hand grow warmer. "They're glowing!"

There was a blinding flash of light, erasing everything around them. When it died away, all Jeom saw was Demetrius by his side.

"What happened?" he asked, looking around—nothing

could make him let go of his brother's hand now. "Where are Eli and Gabriel?"

Demetrius glanced around too, seeming just as confused.

Before they had time to figure it out, their attention was drawn to the lake—several boats had swiftly gathered in what appeared to be a wisp of smoky magic.

Jeom could hear his own heartbeat pounding in his ears, growing faster and faster; the air was silent, heavier than before, as if all his senses had been dulled.

"I think, I recognize this charm," whispered Demetrius, leaning forward for a better look. "It's memory magic. Just like with the giants' enchantment we witnessed back on Idris."

Jeom let some of his tension go, realizing he must be right.

"I hope so…" he said, concerned for Gabriel and Eli.

But magic never seems to react the same way twice.

"How are we even seeing this, though?" asked Jeom. "And why not the others? The giants' magic we experienced didn't exclude anyone."

"I have an inkling that this has something to do with us, and us alone," said Demetrius, gesturing to their clasped hands.

"It's not like we haven't held hands before," said Jeom, shaking his arm.

Demetrius twisted his lips, thinking hard.

"I'm not the spell master here," he said after a moment, "but maybe this place somehow triggered a particular memory?" He shrugged. "I don't know, but our bond obviously goes deeper than a birthmark."

"Well, I could've told you that, brother," said Jeom with a wink.

They turned their focus back to the lake, watching together in awe as a sure memory played out before them.

It wasn't hard to deduce that the historical gathering was made up of elves, dwarves, and humans…

Everyone present began to lock hands, linking the boats on the water. All eyes then lifted toward the starry ceiling, each person chanting the same, rhythmic verse.

It was a clear declaration to the higher beings of the Olleb—the congregation had taken an eternal oath of alliance before the known gods and goddesses of their world.

"Are you hearing what I'm hearing?" stammered Demetrius, his palm growing sweaty. "It's the blood magic pact Diveena described to us! She was telling the truth. By gods, it's all true."

"Then… this is where our story began," said Jeom, trying to memorize every second. "No wonder she sent us here."

He huffed, tossing his head back.

"But seriously, *why* is everyone so clandestine about everything that has to do with the Golden Age? It's maddening! She couldn't have just said… 'I'm sending you two to a questionable cavern in the jungle, to see if some old mind magic trick ignites when you hold hands with your brother. By the way, it's about the blood magic pact that made you who you are'?"

There was a second of silence, and then Demetrius burst out laughing, tears in his eyes.

"To keep things interesting, I suppose," he said after a moment. He turned serious. "What should we do?"

"Wait, watch, and remember," said Jeom, mouth agape as the memory unfolded to reveal even more.

In the next moment, King Damas, Master Lethander, and King Undoriamus appeared at the center of the lake, their boats regally dressed for the occasion, highlighting the best of their people.

They passed around a dagger with a glittering black blade.

Demetrius looked at Jeom, eyes wide. "That can't be what I think it is—"

"Let's just keep watching," answered Jeom in a shaky

voice. But he was thinking the same thing.

King Undoriamus and Master Lethander made a large cut on the palms of their hands and then joined them together, adding their voices to the magical song. Then, King Damas sliced open his palm as well, calling forth his powers within.

When the true king of Saindora placed his hand over that of the noble elf and dwarf leaders, a vibrant magic began to whirl around them, intertwining them as one. The magic rose to the top of the cave, settling in a twinkling pattern on the ceiling overhead—it was the enchanted outline of a six-pointed star.

Jeom felt a chill run across his spine.

The magic fell away, the cave darkening once more.

"It is done," said King Damas, his voice resonating throughout the cavern. "Peace be with us, brothers, for generations to come."

"Peace be with us," replied King Undoriamus and Master Lethander.

The witnesses gathered began to clap and cheer, shooting celebratory magic into the air.

The noble beings released their hands.

The memory magic faded away like a rolling fog across the lake, leaving Jeom and Demetrius stunned.

"We have to uphold this pact," said Jeom with fervor—he'd come to the realization that each point of his half of the star mark *must* represent the binding cut from each one of them; he felt as if their noble blood ran through his veins. "We must carry on our legacies with honor."

Jeom blinked the tears out of his eyes, finding his brother's—they were also shimmering.

As if of one mind, they let go of each other's hands and lifted their fists to their chests.

"Hail to the World! Hail to Olleb-Yelfra," they shouted out, their voices echoing off the cavern walls.

Jeom felt a renewed devotion to their cause, and he was sure Demetrius did too; they'd been given all the reassurance they needed as to what their purpose was, and it was enough to carry them through to the end of this war without giving up.

Eli's voice broke their focus. "Care to explain that little outburst, fellas?"

Jeom and Demetrius turned around to find that Eli and Gabriel had, thankfully, joined them again now that the memory magic had worn off.

They looked utterly confused.

"Yeah, you went silent there for a while," said Gabriel, giving them a worried look. "Then you just started yelling out of nowhere, *so…*"

Demetrius and Jeom looked at each other, speechless.

"You both really are brothers, aren't you?" said Eli, hands on his hips. "You're a strange bunch."

"More than you know," said Demetrius with a nervous grin.

"Well, what happened then? What kind of magic was that?" asked Gabriel. "We didn't see anything, *but* I'm guessing you did. Out with it now."

"It's a dwarf and elf thing," said Jeom with a sly grin. "Not sure you humans could understand."

Gabriel and Eli scoffed; Jeom had never felt prouder in his life.

"Oh, please, *now* he wants to be called a dwarf?" howled Eli, jokingly. "Well, that's that, then! Something's wrong with his head. Let's get out of here. Cavern air isn't doing you much good, boys, and seems there's nobody home."

Jeom glanced back at the lake.

"It is time to return," he said, growing serious. "We have a war to prepare for. If there are any dwarves or elves still out there, they're counting on us to make their homes safe again for them to come out of hiding."

He frowned.

"But I don't think there's anyone else in a position to help us now," he added, "even if they are still alive… somewhere." He hoped they were. "We'll just have to be enough as we are."

He looked to Demetrius. *We are enough.*

"You've grown so wise, brother," said Demetrius, squeezing his hand again—there was no glow this time, no warm feeling, but Jeom was certain that if they *did* call to their magic, something would come.

I wonder what else we can do, together?

Demetrius let go.

"Let's get going," he said. "There's a lot counting on our success. More than we could have really understood before."

Gabriel and Eli flashed each other concerned looks.

Jeom smiled.

"We'll explain on the way," he said.

He turned on his heels, ready to get back to reality.

"Come on, now!" he said in high spirits, waving them forward. "I can't keep my lady waiting on me. She's got a mean streak, that one."

"Not worse than Ara…" said Eli in mock fear.

"Definitely not," said Demetrius with a whistle.

Laughter trailed them all the way back through the tunnels and out into the fresh jungle air. Making haste to return back to camp, they left the Starr Caverns behind, seemingly empty-handed.

Though, just like Arianna, Jeom and Demetrius now held the peculiar power of a star all their own—they only needed to join hands to feel its magic.

6

MASTER OF EARTH

WARM RAYS OF SUN roused Arianna from sleep as they snuck in through the large window. She sat up, taking a proper look around; in the morning light, the Treehouse truly was beguiling.

Plants were stitched to the walls, and the bark of an enormous tree spun the room around her like a cocoon, as if she sat in a nest of thick branches. Glass fixtures fused into the ceiling bathed her in dancing lights, channeling the sun from the outside, and beautifully bizarre insects had made a home here too, exploring the space as if they also needed somewhere to hide.

Her heart quickened—Lessa was no longer beside her, Sano nowhere to be found.

Before she could panic, the buzz of people from somewhere beyond the door reached her ears.

"*Don't worry, Master,*" said Solza with a yawn that

sounded more like a snarl. "*You didn't imagine anything. They're just outside. They didn't want to wake you.*"

Arianna relaxed.

"*You know me so well,*" she replied.

"*Better than anyone, I think,*" said Solza, haughtily. "*We share the same mind.*"

Arianna laughed, enjoying how light it made her feel. *I can breathe easy for once.*

It was a delicious, comforting moment to realize that the dreamlike events from the night before had been real.

She placed her feet on the floor and padded across to the window. She pushed back the sheer curtains to peer out. Waving branches with bouquets of pink flowers were set against the breathtaking backdrop of a deep blue and lavender sky.

She spotted Lessa on a bridge just below the level of her nook; Sano teased her from the trees, hopping about from limb to limb.

"You're getting so fast," said Lessa, showering her avatar with praise. "I'll still catch you, though!"

Arianna watched in admiration as she manipulated a large ball of water into the air, playfully trying to target him with it.

There was a sudden splash and a squeal from the trees—Lessa burst out in giggles as Sano plopped into her arms soaking wet.

"Better luck next time, buddy," she cooed as he shook dry.

Arianna smiled, shaking her head.

"*Let's join them, Solza!*" She was about ready to dart outside. For the first time in a long time, the promise of a new day filled her with motivation, joy.

"*Might you consider a bath first?*" said Solza, pressing her cool nose into her foot—she retreated quickly. "*You could use it...*"

Arianna shooed her off, tickling her with a bit of magic. "*Like you're any better!*"

Solza retorted with a soft bout of air magic; Arianna got a whiff of herself and recoiled.

"A bath it is," she said, glancing over to the fresh basin of water ready and waiting—Lessa must've prepared it for her. "But you're coming with me."

The next hour was filled with scrubbing the jungle and seven days of dragon flight off her and her avatar; Solza was not at all cooperative, and most of the water ended up on the floor.

After they'd both dried off, Arianna pulled on the clean clothes Lessa had left out for her and readied to leave. And, *just* in case, she strapped her swords in the sheath across her back.

"*Ready?*" said Solza, her fur coat back to its normal shimmering standards.

"*More than ever!*" She threw the door open, and they both stepped out onto the walkway.

Arianna whistled—the sunlight glistened over everything.

"I can't believe this place is real."

"*It's quite something,*" agreed Solza, her warm voice awakening Arianna's mind in the most delightful fashion. "*I shall fly with Sano, Master?*"

There was no hiding her eagerness to join her friend in the treetops.

"*Of course,*" said Arianna, albeit a bit reluctantly—she tried to shake off her reservations.

We're safe here.

"*Just… stay close,*" she added.

"*I won't go far,*" said Solza, clearly also revitalized by this new, hope-filled chapter in their lives—she shifted into a beautiful owl, perching on the rail of the bridge.

Arianna hadn't had the opportunity to really stop and appreciate her avatar's air form yet; Solomon had made sure of that…

Solza's black and white feathers glittered under the sun, and large, electric blue eyes seemed to see everything in the vicinity. Arianna also thought her unusually large, bigger than any of the other owl species that she'd learned about.

Solza unfurled her massive wings, soaring gracefully into the trees; Sano pounced off the air and tree limbs to chase after her.

Arianna cupped her hands around her mouth. "Be careful!" she called after them both.

"Oh, there you are," said Lessa, waving up to her from the bridge below. "You're finally awake. Come down and join me for breakfast, won't you? Diveena is waiting to greet us, and I'm sure you could eat something."

Arianna suddenly realized her hunger, her stomach growling so loudly that she almost thought Solza had transformed back into a snow leopard.

"Gladly!" she said, beaming down at her. "I'm famished."

She glanced from side to side—there were several bridges and nooks built above, below and all around her, an open-air maze of sophisticated architecture throughout the trees.

"It's as if the Swamp of Moriamo has been lifted to the skies," she mumbled to herself.

Jeom probably lost his mind upon arrival here.

Arianna wondered how its existence was even possible; the Treehouse was surely doused in even more magic than the Greenhouse had been, to be supported so high up… what's more, it seemed to comfortably support a plethora of visitors.

Lessa clearly left something out of her story last night. There's more here than meets the eye.

The people in this enchanted sky village started to wake, drawn out of their nooks by the early daylight. They scuttled about the bridges with a mission on their minds.

Arianna spied on them for as far as her sight could reach, curious as to what each of the freed slaves had been tasked to do—many young people descended on the enchanted platforms, presumably to trek back to the larger campsite and training grounds.

A night was not enough to go over everything, she thought. *There's still so much to understand.*

She felt so behind everyone, eager to catch up and prove herself useful again.

"Which way do I go?" she called back to Lessa. "It's like the Vanishing Tunnels up here!"

Lessa scoffed.

"Miss, could I be of any assistance?" Someone had snuck up behind her.

"I know that voice," said Arianna with a start—a jolt of excitement ran through her. She whipped around, her hand flying over her heart in relief. "Oh, Noah!"

He ran to her, nearly toppling them both over the side of the bridge as they collided.

"Noah, just look at you." She laughed, ruffling up his forever-unruly hair.

They embraced.

"Ara, you've been such a stranger," he said, taking her hand in his. He smiled down at her.

Has he grown taller since we last met?

"Been hiding from us all this time, have you?"

Arianna pressed her hands against her cheeks to steady her mind—another wonderful reunion had left her staggered.

"Well, your company is just *so* dreadful," she teased after a moment. "I was hard-pressed to leave Solomon's captivity and drag myself here."

She wiped her eyes of the happy tears.

It wasn't until now that she comprehended just how much she had missed this familiar face from her district days—Noah was proof of a life before Lessa, Jeom, Demetrius, Eli, *and* the enemy they'd made of King Devlindor.

Just like her dear, sweet caretaker, Noah had always remained a steady beacon of light amid the dark, since her beginnings.

As the silence between them lingered, the darker memories they'd suffered together in the Jar began to seep through the magic of this moment; she was sure they did for him as well.

Noah's smile faltered into something more serious—such an unnatural look for him.

He drew her into another hug.

"I'm so glad you did find your way to us," he said. "The thought of never seeing you again, on top of Liam…" His voice cracked. "I couldn't bear it."

Her insides twisted. "You've heard, then?"

He nodded into her shoulder, squeezing her tighter.

"I'm sorry that I couldn't save him," she said, swallowing the growing lump in her throat—her mind wandered to that dreadful night, but she shook out of the downward spiral. "Oh, just *look* at you, Noah."

She pushed him to arm's length so they could look at each other.

"He'd be so proud of how far you've come. Liam would be beside himself if he could see us now." She gently slapped him on the chest. "I heard you even helped Lessa and Eli free the districts!"

"Someone had to step up," he said with a shy shrug. "I was just following your lead."

Arianna looked him over with pride.

She could hardly believe the sight of Noah before her eyes, of how strong and courageous he'd become after facing a life-altering change—plucked from the Jar and dropped straight into her fantasy world filled with magic.

"Come on, then," he said, tugging at her hand. "There's loads of people waiting to meet you. But first things first. You must be fed!"

"Always your number one rule," said Arianna with a laugh.

They signaled to Lessa that they'd meet her in the dining nook and started down the walkway.

Noah chatted ceaselessly about all the adventures he'd experienced with Lessa and Eli since their escape from the Four Corners. Overcome with excitement at discovering this new world of potential, he gushed over their battles to take down the King's regulators and all the wonders he'd witnessed thus far.

Arianna saw in her young friend a bright and magical future to be had—the same future she wanted for everyone else.

This is why we fight. Never forget.

They took turn after turn, traveling across the plethora of bridges and footpaths; she couldn't make sense of up from down.

They ducked beneath low-hanging leaves and branches as they maneuvered the winding walkways, and she was careful not to let her eyes travel too far toward the ground for fear her body might follow. It was a busy morning, people running this way and that, so she tried her best to blend in next to Noah.

However, her arrival had stirred up quite the commotion...

Anytime they passed someone on their path, they would shamelessly gawk at her.

"Why do they keep staring at me like that?" said Arianna, attempting to hide her face behind her mane of wild curls.

"Haven't you heard, Ara? You're somewhat of a legend now," he replied, pausing on the bridge.

Noah threw his hands into the air, theatrically.

"*The* Arianna Belvedor, escaped slave of Warrior's District. A defender of the oppressed in Olleb-Yelfra. A symbol of hope for all district slaves to come together as allies in the joint quest for freedom! Uncovered a world of magic, and defied the tyrant king in one fell swoop that's shaken the land awake—"

Arianna slapped him on the arm, then buried her face in her hands.

"Noah! You're such a… *hush*," she demanded, her cheeks running hot as everyone stopped to listen.

They smiled and waved at her from both above and below.

"And *then*, the great Belvedor warrior, famed Guardian of Gold, landed on our shores on the back of a dragon, no less! She is no martyr yet, folks," he continued, addressing all the curious bystanders—Arianna almost died when they started applauding. "Neither snake nor wolf can hold her back from her destiny."

"Noah, I swear by all the gods," she hissed, "I will have your head if you don't shut up *right* now."

Arianna feigned reaching for her swords; the gathering crowd responded with such enthusiasm that she couldn't help but laugh along with them.

"All right, all right." He chuckled, raising his hands in surrender. "Show's over, people. Move along. I'd like to keep my head right where it is, *thank* you."

He turned to Arianna, grabbing her by the shoulders as the crowd scattered, excited chatter trailing behind them.

"Sorry 'bout that, but don't you get it?" He cocked his head to the side, a quizzical expression on his face. "Everything we've done here… you're the face of it all! These people have only followed us so far because of *your* story and courage." He poked her over her heart, in the same spot where her double-digit identity used to be. "You've risked everything to open our eyes, and now we see."

Noah winked at her before disappearing into a large structure that spanned two levels of the Treehouse.

Arianna followed him inside, climbing up a small flight of rickety stairs that wrapped around the bark of a thick tree—a huge room opened up before them at the top, the tree trunk at its center.

People were seated on the floor, hovering around slabs of unfinished wood, tables low to the ground.

They plucked from baskets of fruit, pulled at loaves of bread, and piled up their plates with meat and eggs—all seemingly cooked with the splendors of magic. The smell of food wafted deliciously about the area; Arianna's stomach roared.

"Welcome," said a tall woman, rising from her seat.

The bustling room went silent.

She carried herself with a visible confidence that made Arianna innately take caution—delicate yet commanding, in a startling way.

A long sheet of silvery-blue hair draped across her shoulders, and she wore a garland of gentle yellow flowers atop her head, like a crown.

"We've all been waiting for you for a long time," she said. "Come now. Don't be shy."

She sat back down, seated cross-legged; the room began to stir again, coming back to life with the sound of voices.

Lessa was already sitting at the table with a plate of food to her name.

"Don't worry," Noah whispered into her ear. "Diveena's harmless."

Just one look at her told her otherwise. *I know a warrior when I see one...*

She was clever to have brought her swords.

Noah took Arianna by the arm, leading her across the room; every person they passed on their way nearly broke their neck to try to get a good look at her.

"This is Diveena," said Lessa in a high-pitched voice. She cleared her throat. "She's the one I mentioned to you, yesterday."

Diveena offered a slight nod, and Arianna returned it.

Such a highlife mannerism, she thought.

They observed each other in what felt like an

excruciatingly long moment.

Lessa didn't know this yet, but Arianna had been thinking of this woman in the back of her mind for months. She hadn't known what to expect then, or if she'd ever even find her…

And now that she had, she wasn't sure what to do.

"Arianna Belvedor," said Diveena in an inquisitive tone, gesturing for her to sit down on the other side of the table, next to where Noah had settled in. "I was hoping you'd find your way to us, as all your family has. Join us, won't you?"

The statement sparked something of irritation for her.

She returned a tight smile.

"Speaking of my family…" she said, trying to be cordial. "You sent them, *alone*, on a wild hunt into the jungle for new recruits?" She stayed standing as she questioned her. "It's not safe out there for us. I would like to understand why, before I agree to dine with you."

She heard Noah's intake of breath but ignored it.

Lessa and Noah were accounted for, but what of Jeom, Demetrius, Gabriel, and Eli? Arianna hadn't forgotten them yet, and she wouldn't rest easy until she saw them again.

Lessa was trying to get her attention from beside Diveena, clearly uncomfortable at this exchange, too, but Arianna kept her eyes forward.

She wanted to skip the small talk and get right to the meat of it—she hadn't come all this way just to find out that her boys still needed saving. And, if they did, she wasn't going to waste another second on breakfast.

Diveena didn't seem perturbed in the slightest by the confrontation, considering her with even more interest.

"They're still not back yet," added Lessa, turning to Diveena with pleading eyes. "What if… something's happened to them? They *should* have returned by now, like we discussed."

"You wish to go after them," said Diveena, matter-of-factly.

"If they're in trouble, then yes. Of course," said Lessa, a bit taken aback.

"I see," she replied, taking a sip from her cup. "I couldn't very well stop you from following their tracks. Though, I don't find it necessary."

Lessa looked back to Arianna, shaking her head in confusion; Arianna slowly sat down across from them, trying to quiet her growing reservations about this mysterious woman.

She didn't want to come off as completely ungrateful, for she knew that, somehow, this person was to thank for the existence of the Treehouse at all.

But who was *she* to send her friends back into the wilderness in search of something, or someone, that may not even exist, amid all the dangers that they knew surely did?

Now is not the time for careless risks.

"You don't find it necessary for us to see if our friends are alive?" said Arianna through gritted teeth.

Diveena turned her gaze on her, and she became nearly spellbound by the gleaming emerald eyes—she looked to her hands, not letting herself become intimidated… or trapped.

Something strange about Diveena reminded her of Syrifina's hypnotizing powers.

If I can withstand an evil king, I can hold my head high for this.

She lifted her chin, gazing back at her, determined to get answers.

"Go, if you must," Diveena replied, evenly. "You have free will here, and I won't waste energy to try and stop you." She smirked. "I've heard what happens to those who get in your way, young dragon."

Noah snickered; Arianna shot him daggers, and he suddenly became very interested in a piece of bread.

"However, an inkling does tell me they're more than fine.

They're right where they're supposed to be," she said. "Besides, the Impenetrable Forest is my territory, and the trees tell me all. I think I'd know if your friends were in any kind of danger. They've spent months under my care, and I would certainly go to their aid if I got wind of trouble."

Arianna gaped at Lessa for help, but she seemed so reassured by Diveena's response that she'd already gone back to eating.

"I don't understand…" said Arianna as Noah passed her a full plate and a cup of water. "What did you expect them to even bring back from the middle of nowhere? Solza and I flew over this terrain. It's just jungle for miles, save for the City of Guanamara."

"Does one need to bring back something tangible for the journey to have been worth the time?" Diveena wagged her finger at her before she could reply. "You're just having trouble accepting this, because it wasn't *your* journey to take."

Arianna balled her hands into fists under the table.

"Don't play coy with me," she snapped. "I've had enough of that to last me a lifetime from elders that I actually trust. I've no idea who you are to make demands of my friends. If anything should happen to them—"

"Ara, now just calm down a minute," said Noah, standing up. "You don't—"

"Stop," she said, holding up her hand. "I want *real* answers, now. I've been shuttered in the dark long enough."

He sat down, clamping his lips tight.

"What exactly was the grand plan here, and who is *she* to make such decisions after all the risks we've already taken with our lives?" She glanced at Lessa. "You said so last night… what if they don't come back?"

Lessa stood up from the table, garnering everyone's attention.

"Arianna," she said, firmly, "Diveena… well, she's not just

any elder. I didn't want to overwhelm you last night with so much, but she is," Lessa gestured to Diveena, "the last remaining elf of the Nicora Tribe."

Arianna felt her entire body tingle with nerves, eyes flicking to Diveena and Lessa, then back.

"She created this labyrinth in the skies in hopes of offering sanctuary to other surviving elves," she added. "Sadly, centuries have passed by with no sign of anyone else like her…"

Diveena humbly smiled at Lessa.

"But she's welcomed *us* here now, and we owe her a great many thanks. She's been guiding us since we arrived, sharing her knowledge in magic and of the Golden Age with our entire camp. She deserves your respect, Ara, whether you trust her yet or not."

"Yeah, she's on our side," said Noah, nodding along.

Arianna took a sip of water and nearly choked on it as Diveena brushed her hair back, revealing the slightly pointed ears she recalled elves to be known for.

Thin, silver tattoos swirled up the backs of her hands and around her wrists like bracelets, and she wore long chains around her neck—now, as she really looked at her, Arianna could not *unsee* the resemblance to Master Lethander and the other ghosts of the Nicora Tribe.

"An elf?" she gasped, finding her voice; Lessa sat back down. "Talis… he told me to find someone named Diveena. I never thought that you'd be—"

"Talis?" stuttered Lessa, eyes widening. "What do you mean that Talis *told* you? Before he died?"

Diveena looked confused too.

Arianna felt a pang of guilt for having even mentioned his name.

"No, Les, I'm sorry," she said, looking at her hands. "I… I saw him and Keeper Kassime in the astral plane. I was searching for you when Solomon first took me from the Four

Corners, to try and get you a message. Talis and Kassime found me instead. They told me to find someone named Diveena," she nodded to the elf, "to trust in her."

"I see," mumbled Lessa, eyes watering.

"I'm *really* sorry," she said again.

Diveena placed her hand on top of Lessa's.

"It's all right to mourn him still," she said with a knowing expression. "I was quite upset, too, to hear of his passing. Talis was a good man. Mourn him, but do not let his memory cloud your future."

Lessa gave a curt nod, looking away; Arianna could tell that she and Diveena must've had a similar talk before.

"You knew him?" asked Arianna, quietly.

"I surely did," she replied. "He had traveled through the Impenetrable Forest during a time when he'd lived in Guanamara. Quite like your Gabriel, he had been searching for something." Diveena sighed. "We both were, I suppose. It was hard times back then."

She tore apart some bread and passed it down the table.

"We were drawn to each other by the magic. And unlike most humans I had encountered since the ruin of my tribe, he knew about my kind. Talis introduced me to the Guardians of Gold to show me there was still a fight to be had, and in exchange, I helped him to master his craft. Elves are excellent agrarians, you see. Therefore, we know all the best ingredients that healers call for." She looked to Lessa. "Wouldn't you agree?"

Lessa perked up.

"Wait… you actually *taught* him healing magic?" she said, sniffling. "I thought that Master Tayshin—"

"Oh, Master Tayshin taught him a great wealth of knowledge, I'm sure," said Diveena with a tinkling laugh. "Though, I certainly hope he didn't take *all* the credit for Talis' master status." She tutted as Arianna and Lessa smirked at each other. "There is no one craft that can truly be mastered without first understanding the others. Indeed, I taught him the agrarian fundamentals, with an elf's touch to aid his practice."

"How's that now?" asked Noah, so clearly enraptured by this new realm of possibility.

"Well," said Diveena, "a creator must understand the need of the warrior to master weaponry fit for a battle, right?" Noah nodded. "So, just as the creator needs the warrior, the warrior must become the expert in handling the creations from the creator."

She plucked a grape from the bowl at the center of the table.

"A healer mixes their remedies with the fruits labored over by the agrarian, and an agrarian is only as good as the health of his land and animals." She plopped the grape into her mouth. "An old tome from my childhood. It's the Golden Rule—one of balance—one I think you all know well by now, *hmm?*"

Arianna smiled to herself as she connected that picture of the Four Corners to the Golden Rule. *It's up to the interpreter to decide what the prophecy truly means.*

Diveena smiled back. "The Golden Rule stretches across many themes in life."

"So… Talis taught you of the Guardians of Gold, and in return, you helped him master his craft?" said Arianna, scratching her head.

It was hard to imagine Master Churry as anything other than an older, wiser healer—she hadn't spent much time thinking of his upbringing.

She considered her own past. *I suppose no one is born knowing their greatest gifts.*

"Among other things," she replied. "The Greenhouse might very well be one of my favorite creations, with Talis' help, of course. A little sorcery and elf magic can go a *long* way, I daresay."

"That was you?" Arianna's mind was quickly shifting from skeptical to thrilled.

Noah and Lessa were nodding along to her story, obviously already well in the know about a lot of things.

Arianna shoved a big piece of bread into her mouth, finally comfortable enough with her company to eat.

"When he said a friend helped to build the Greenhouse, we never imagined elves still existed." She spoke through a mouthful.

"I requested my existence was kept secret," said Diveena, her expression softer. "Even among the guardians. I couldn't risk being found by those less than noble, but recently, I've felt things beginning to… *change*. I knew it was time to come out of hiding, that fate was calling me out from the shadows of the trees. Then, to my surprise, I found Gabriel."

Arianna bowed her head, embarrassed by her premature outburst from earlier.

"I'm sorry I was so quick to throw accusations," she said.

Lessa was more than right—Diveena deserved her upmost respect, whether or not she agreed with the decision to send her friends away. She couldn't wait to tell Solza about their host.

A true elf, by gods!

"I'm just worried over the boys," she added. "I haven't seen them in so long, and when I discovered that they were here, I…"

"I understand your worries," said Diveena, gently. "I just do not share them."

Arianna looked up; Diveena was, in fact, perfectly calm.

"But how do you expect them to sway anybody with only Gabriel wielding magic?" she asked, less accusatory now. "Who do you anticipate they'll find in these… Starr Caverns?"

"Their collective magic is exactly why I sent them on such a quest in the first place," answered Diveena. "Jeom, as you know, is of the dwarf bloodline." She placed her hands in her lap, her green eyes boring into hers. "And Demetrius is of mine."

"*What?*" Arianna was sure she'd heard wrong.

"It's true," said Lessa, her expression bright.

"How is that even possible?" she said, pressing her hands into the table to steady her pounding heart.

"Just like everything else, I'd wager," said Noah with a smirk.

Arianna gawked at him.

"Drink your water," he said. "Your throat must be dry with your mouth hanging open like that."

Arianna gave him a playful pinch. Then, Diveena launched into the tale of a pact between elves, dwarves, and humans.

She explained that, with a sprinkle of fate and magic, the Kane brothers had become the embodiment of all three to ensure their species could always coexist with each other, in harmony.

"I sent the boys on a journey not to sway others to our side but to fully understand their beginnings. You, of all people, should understand just how important that is… to understand who you really are."

Arianna was still trying to figure that out.

"If, along the way, they stumble across any remaining dwarf or elf tribes that might still be in hiding, I'd call that a bonus," added Diveena. "Jeom's dwarf bloodline has been completely wiped out, and I am all that remains of the Nicora Clan…" She paused, a shadow crossing her expression. "But there's nothing to suggest that the same fates befell other tribes of the Olleb." She took a deep breath. "There were many of us once upon a time. And, like me, they could very well still exist."

Arianna found this an incredible thought to feast on, but it still sounded like a fairytale.

"In all honesty, it sounds like you sent them off chasing ghosts…"

"Ghosts have a lot of stories to tell," said Diveena with a wink—Arianna couldn't disagree with that.

She laughed.

Diveena continued, "The Impenetrable Forest is as large as a sea, and over the years, I've felt… *things.*"

"Things? What *kind* of things?" asked Lessa, leaning forward.

"Sensations that suggest there are others like me out there," said Diveena. "Whiffs of familiar magic here and there, a tingle on my skin or in my mind. I never thought anything of it, but when you all landed here on such a wave of change for the Olleb, it gave me hope that *maybe* there were others out there like me, and like you all, who had not yet bent under the King's weight completely."

She shrugged.

"And the Axe of Crissy has such power that if any creation has felt the magic of a dwarf, it will know. Demetrius and Jeom both have the innate ability to track their own kind. They just have to tap into it." She tilted her head to the side. "Why do you think Demetrius' compass led them to me in the first place?"

"I thought it was because you're an honorary guardian…" said Lessa, raising an eyebrow.

She smiled, shaking her head.

"What I am is an elf," she replied, resolutely.

Arianna could find no words; her imagination unwound even further to let these ideas sink in.

If such strong, magical species still existed somewhere in the Olleb, there could be an even greater opportunity to roll this dark age back into a golden one…

"Yet, *if* I'm wrong," said Diveena, "what's a couple of weeks spent looking? Time where Jeom and Demetrius can explore their new powers freely? Eli and Gabriel are more than capable guardians to help guide them safely home, when it's time."

"All right," said Arianna, resigned to Diveena's explanation. "Well, I do sincerely apologize for jumping to conclusions. I feel a bit crazy, after the King…"

She couldn't go there.

"No need to apologize," she said; Arianna thanked her for not letting that silence linger.

She wasn't ready to talk about her time in captivity again, not with so many listeners around.

"You've been through a lot," she added. "It's not unusual to jump to conclusions based on experience, but you should learn to remain open that your conclusions may be wrong." Diveena touched eyes with Lessa and Noah as well. "You're all still *so* young, so many lessons ahead. You may feel you've grown since years past, and you surely have, but do not forget how many years could be ahead for you. Just think of all there is still yet to know."

There was a moment of silence as her words settled around them.

"Well, Arianna's *always* wrong," murmured Noah into his cup—he flashed her a sly grin.

Unable to resist her reflexes, Arianna shoved him from his seat; Noah toppled over sideways in a fit of laughter, and the seriousness in the air shifted into something lighter.

"I really missed you," he said, getting to his feet.

"Missed you too," said Arianna, rolling her eyes.

"Now that introductions are over," said Diveena with the clap of her hands, "it's time for you to formally address your followers. They've been eager for your arrival. Let's not keep them waiting. We have plenty of time to grow familiar."

"Followers—" Arianna looked uneasily between Lessa and Noah.

"That's my cue! By gods, *finally.*"

A small girl with short, spiky hair plopped down onto the floor next to Arianna, stealing Noah's place.

"You're Arianna Belvedor?" she said, her voice strained.

"That I am," said Arianna, leaning back. "And… you are?"

"I'm Kiki," she said with confidence. "A *good* friend of Noah's."

"The best," he said, dryly. He moved around the table to gather more food.

She glared over at him. Then, she turned her attention back to Arianna, sitting as tall as she could.

"It's my *complete* honor to finally meet you," said Kiki.

She gave a slight bow, and Arianna balked; Noah threw his hand over his mouth, laughing through his fingers.

Lessa was beaming.

"In the King's name, really? Can you *please* calm down, Kiki?" whined Noah as he squeezed in next to her.

He took a big bite of chicken, mouth full as he spoke.

"I told you that I'd make an introduction." He looked to Arianna. "Her impatience rivals your own, Ara. But she's all right."

He nudged her in the arm, and Kiki swatted his hand away.

Arianna chuckled.

"I see. Well, any friend of Noah's is a friend of mine," she said, warmly. "Are you from Warrior's District, then?"

Kiki nodded, lifting her chest proudly—she had a stern face, yet a frame that made her seem so much younger than she probably was.

"I was there when Solomon pitted you against Lessa," she said, brow furrowing. "That monster." She huffed, and

Arianna looked away. "I was one of the first to join your cause once Lessa offered us the opportunity. At your service, miss!"

"Is that so?" said Arianna, glancing to Lessa.

Lessa nodded, still smiling.

"Not everyone in the campsite or who has joined is a former slave, though," added Noah. "We picked people up from the cities along the way, too." He patted her on the head. "You made *quite* a lasting impression in South Luose and Zambienth, by the way. Rumors have spread, traveled farther than I think maybe even you have."

"Yes, but *not* every place in the world has been swayed by our story and our fight," said Lessa, giving Noah a stern look—as if to say 'don't sugarcoat it.'

Arianna was so relieved by that. She'd spent enough time being lied to in this world.

"Quite right," said Diveena. "There's still much change to be had. Although, this is the first dent I've seen in the King's rule since the Golden Wars... your efforts are surely something to be proud of, and I'm honored to support you as your host. I look forward to seeing what will happen next in the saga of Arianna Belvedor—"

She suddenly got to her feet; everyone else stood, too, out of respect, leaving Arianna the only one sitting, with all eyes on her.

She gazed up at Diveena, finding herself still stunned by everything. *An elf... in real life.*

"Let us wait no longer." Diveena held out her hand for Arianna to take.

She grasped hands with the last remaining elf of Nicora and stood. Then, she followed her out of the dining nook and onto one of the many platforms.

Noah, Kiki, and Lessa were trailing behind.

This time, instead of Lessa, Diveena called to her magic to ignite the nature-fueled lift—it was, by no means, the same.

"I'll teach you a similar spell," said Lessa. "It's not quite an elf's touch, but you'll at least be able to get up and down from here on your own."

Arianna barely noticed her as the nature around them began to twist and wriggle to life once more, slowly lowering them from the Treehouse to the ground.

7

ONE HEART

THEY TOOK THE SAME BEATEN PATH Arianna had followed Lessa down the day before, retracing their steps to the campsite—the sounds of metal on metal, and crackling blasts of magic, filled the air as they neared.

"Are you sure that no one will be able to hear all this noise?" asked Arianna.

"For miles, this part of the Impenetrable Forest has been veiled by my magic, and it hasn't faltered yet," said Diveena, not even trying to conceal her pride. "You're safe here, as long as you don't go *too* far past the campsite." She pointed ahead. "My magic doesn't extend much farther than this."

Arianna recalled that Solza had held on to Sano's scent for miles past the beach; she'd only hit Diveena's blockade when they were too deep in the tree-laden terrain to ever find their way back out again, no hints of a trail nor path in sight.

"It doesn't extend to the skies either," she said, watching

as an explosive spell fizzled away, just before it cleared the treetops.

Diveena nodded.

"I have nothing to do with the skies," she replied. "They can do as they please."

They reached the base of the large hill and began to climb.

Every step upward made her nerves ignite—she already knew what magnificent view she'd find at the top.

How will I ever get used to this? she thought, as the training campsite unfurled before her eyes.

Arianna beamed down at the fantastic events expanding from the base of the hill to the outskirts of the trees…

A real army in the making.

The people trained hard, maybe even with more ferocity than her peers had during her Warrior's District days. It made her ponder over what might be the bigger motivation—fighting to win freedom from a terrible place or fighting to win freedom from the terrible person who had created it.

We fight for a new type of freedom now. A permanent one.

But mere weapons could not defeat the King's armies, nor his Shadow Resistance—this Arianna knew. They would need to exercise strong, skilled magic to turn the tide in their favor.

Observing the apprentice guardians now, she suddenly grasped what Lessa had tried to explain to her the night before… as excited as she was at the thought of marching an army to the doors of the Saindora palace, these new recruits proved the equivalent of newborns compared to their enemies, especially in magic.

We'll need all the help we can get in the final battle to come.

So, if there *was* anyone left to find, with experienced magic and willing to fight, Arianna understood that it was worth taking the time to look. She just hoped that Demetrius and

Jeom's trek proved a risk worth taking.

"Please keep them safe," she whispered, so softly that only the wind might hear.

People began to spot her and the others. Slowly, the dueling and training drills came to a stop, the magic ceased, and a crowd gathered at the base of the hill.

One by one, Noah, Kiki, Lessa, and Diveena moved out of the way to reveal Arianna.

Like smoke rising to the air, a steady stream of excitement began to stir through the crowd.

Now, Arianna was the one being observed.

She wanted to make her way back down the hill, to hide in her little nook until she was sure what she was meant to do next. *How do I fit into all this?*

The last six months of her life had been stolen from her, and now she wasn't sure where to start in moving forward.

Diveena placed her hand on the small of her back. "They just want to hear the words you carry in your heart, to know surely that they're the same ones they carry now, too."

"Trust me," said Lessa, nudging her in the ribs. "If I could do it, then so can you."

"Do *what?*" she asked, looking at her sidelong.

Kiki laughed. "Why, they want to hear you speak! We all do."

Noah smirked, nodding along with his friend; and Kiki was looking at her just as adoringly as everyone else was from down below.

Arianna dug her heels into the ground, nerves squeezing at her lungs and heart.

"No way am I giving a speech right now!" she said.

Diveena kept her hand on her back; she was, unsurprisingly, strong. She forced Arianna to the edge of the hill.

"You must," she said, a command in her tone. "*Your* army needs to believe in *you*, Arianna. Or they will not win."

Hundreds of curious faces peered up at her, waiting for her to find her words. *I don't want to let them down...*

She returned a feeble nod.

"But where am I even supposed to start?" she murmured.

Diveena released her grip.

"Why don't you just start at your beginnings?"

She stepped back, leaving Arianna alone, on a nature-made pedestal of the Olleb, to ponder who she was and where she'd really begun...

The Warrior's District? When I escaped the Jar? Dying and then living again?

She'd started over at so many major chapters in her life that she wasn't even sure which version of herself remained at present—she'd experienced so many beginnings.

So many chances. So many do-overs.

Life after Aridyn? Life after Solza? Becoming a dragon rider, a Guardian of Gold? Surviving Saindora and the King?

Who was Arianna Belvedor, truly, and why should these people follow her?

She chewed on her lip, twisting her necklace around her finger, absentmindedly. She pinched the soul of the star between her fingers, willing any words to come. When she glanced back to her friends, Noah just shrugged, shooing her forward, and Lessa flashed her an awkward and unhelpful smile.

Arianna let out a huff of frustration and turned her gaze back to the crowd.

For a fleeting, painful moment, with so many hungry eyes feasting on her, she was reminded of the punishment platform in Saindora. Of Cyn and Iris...

Of Solomon's betrayal. The Princess's questionable support, and of the King.

Her insides burned with rage, her eyes with tears; she wondered how on earth she could ever describe who the enemy really was and why she fought. *Never forget!*

After a painfully long time, someone from the crowd spoke up, piercing the silence that had settled around the field.

"Is it true what they say? Is it true you've faced King Devlindor in the flesh?"

She couldn't pinpoint the face of who had spoken, but the voice made something in her stir to life.

"Who said that?" she called back, shielding her eyes from the sun.

The crowd parted, revealing a chiseled young man with golden skin and a confident stride.

He glittered with sweat, hair swooping to his shoulders, and he clasped a sword. Black tattoos poked out of his shirt. And a radiant smile was stretched across his beautiful face—it was one that Arianna surely recognized.

"Eli," she breathed, unable to even blink.

She felt so warm with happiness that her knees went a little weak. She shook her head, trying to shake off the daze.

She knew what love was—she loved her friends dearly.

And she also knew heartbreak; Liam and Solomon had taught her that hard lesson.

With Eli, though, something had always felt different…

The truth was that she had feelings for him, even if she had yet to admit them to anyone out loud, even if she had yet to define them for herself.

But she knew for certain that it *was* love—the kind that could surely lead to a worse type of heartbreak, and one that terrified her more than all the rest.

She used to think that she didn't have time to be scared in such ways, not until this nightmare they lived in was over and the war was won. But with Eli in her sights again, it scared her even more to keep trying to lock those feelings away.

I can't miss my chance again. Nobody lives forever. There will never be a perfect time.

King Devlindor had impressed this upon her so well that Arianna was still surprised she'd made it out of there alive, to see any of her loved ones again.

With this in her mind, she recalled Eli's haunting words from one of their last nights together in Zambienth…

'One can't prove their love by setting it aside. And if a war is coming, then love is the one thing you should be holding on to tight, not pushing it away. That's the only way you'll win. That's why you're fighting in the first place.'

Arianna had been too defensive to really hear him then, but she could hear him now.

In their time apart, she'd learned through difficult trials that love was one of the *only* things that made this fight worth it in the end… something he'd known all along.

Her passion to fight and to risk her life in the ways that she did boiled down to love every time—love for her family, friends, and for the beautiful world they'd been granted.

She was ready now to give in to her heart, and to let Eli have a piece of it.

She opened her mouth to respond with any of these revelations, but nothing came out. She might've thought someone had cast a spell to steal her voice, if she wasn't still so shaky and scared at the thought of addressing such a large audience.

Is this really happening?

Eli smirked—his beautiful, persuasive, heart-melting smirk—as if to say, '*Yes, Arianna, this is really happening.*'

He stepped aside, gesturing to none other than Demetrius, Jeom, and Gabriel.

Arianna brought her hands to her chest, nearly going faint from relief at seeing the boys safe and sound again.

Jeom showed off the dazzling Axe of Crissy with zero modesty, and Demetrius was actually standing on *two* legs—one made of flesh and one made of metal. He held his staff firmly in hand.

She shook her head, disbelieving. *Do my eyes deceive me? Is that really them?*

"Jeom!" she heard Lessa shout from behind.

"They're back," cheered Noah, pumping his fist in the air.

There was a wave of clapping, people shaking their hands and welcoming them home.

It was in this miraculous moment that Arianna found her voice. Seeing her friends again, together as one, she was reminded of the promise that they'd all made to each other long ago…

That's what these people need to hear from me today. That's where this all began.

She hardened herself and peeled her eyes away from the ones she loved.

"It's true—" she started, her voice carrying down to the curious crowd.

All was silent again as everyone turned their attention back to her. There were hundreds of people gathered, maybe even a thousand, if she dared to count.

But this was nothing like the King's punishment platform…

This platform is all mine.

"After our escape from the districts and uncovering the many mysteries of the Olleb, my friends and I made an oath," said Arianna. "We vowed to share all the magic we had discovered and, consequently, bring King Devlindor to his knees," her words grew louder, "make him pay for the *lies* he's fed to us all, and the hurt he's caused to our land."

Arianna considered the people then, finding so many emotions among their expressions—haunted, impassioned, excited, angered, and scared.

In all of their faces, she recognized her own.

"I know your pain," she continued, softer now. "I know your anger and sadness, for I've lost… many friends." She bowed her head; others did too. "And by the end of this, I fear we will say goodbye to many more."

She looked back up, unblinking—her voice felt like fire in her throat now for how badly all she wanted to do was speak, to share her story.

"But I look at you as you are and rejoice that you're here at all, free from your shackles!"

She locked stares with Jeom and Demetrius.

"So far, my family and I have stayed true to our promise. We've tried to shed the light of truth on the darkness that's swept the Olleb. Sharing the truth is the *only* way to have a chance at defeating the King, and now our magic has started to spread—"

Electric bursts of colorful spells suddenly shattered in the sky, shaking the vicinity.

Scattered cheers sounded, the people clearly becoming em-powered by her words; their enthusiasm fed her own.

"And yes, I *have* faced the King," added Arianna, her words landing as sharp as her swords. "I was brought to him in chains, betrayed by a friend, but I would not bow. I would not bend."

She frowned, remembering each lash of the King's power just as surely as she remembered the number he'd forced her to become for so many years.

My name is Arianna Belvedor! We are slaves no longer!

"With his magic, he brought me to my knees, against my will," her voice grew louder, "as he has all of Olleb-Yelfra!"

There were shouts of agreement, sporadic curses to his name.

Her gaze drifted to the sky; she felt her purpose settle around her as more magic burst in the air.

She lifted her hand to calm the riled crowd.

"Soon, the rising sun will mark three hundred years that Kyrone Devlindor has ruled us," she continued. "We *cannot* let another century begin where this selfish monster may call himself King."

They responded as if in chant—"We will not! Down with the King and his kingdom!"

It came like music to her ears. *But do they really understand what's at stake?*

"Look around," she said after their chants had ebbed, "at the faces who surround you. This is your family now, the Guardians of Gold. These are the people who will live, or *die*, at your side in the battles to come. This is why you train." Nervous eyes flicked around, considering one another with new understanding.

Arianna glanced back to Lessa; she returned a firm nod of encouragement.

"Keep going," she mouthed.

"The King's wrath is true," said Arianna, demanding back everyone's attention, "so train hard and protect each other as sisters and brothers. Your life and the life of your Olleb depends on each other... every *single* one of us." She swept her eyes over the crowd.

They stood silent and still.

She stood up straighter. "What say you?"

There was not even a second of hesitation—they roared their approval, sending even more magic toward the clouds in explosive, vibrant bursts.

Arianna lifted her hands out in front of her to join them; she felt her powers ignite, swirling deep in her belly. She looked to the sky, the sun as her witness, and called to her deepest magic as a Guardian of Gold.

Unite us, she thought, focusing her mind.

She felt an enormous tug on her energy, and the people down below began to buzz in delight, gawking at their hands—the guardian symbol had been magically etched into everyone's palms.

"We're all dragons now," she said with confidence, thankful that her intended spell had worked on such a grand scale; everyone here deserved their new status, and the magic agreed.

Arianna raised her golden-marked palm toward the sun; Lessa, Diveena, and the boys were the first to join her.

Then, one by one, the newest guardians all lifted their hands—a shimmering wave of gold danced across the field.

Arianna could barely even smile for how happy she was, tears blurring her vision. But the magic didn't stop there…

The *biggest* image of a dragon she had ever seen was suddenly conjured up from the communal gesture.

The more guardians, the bigger the dragon, she thought, proudly, thinking of the first time she'd seen such a thing conjured in the Greenhouse. *And now we've multiplied by the hundreds.*

The dragon hovered between the treetops like a guardian ghost protector; there were gasps of awe from below, everyone staring and pointing up.

Arianna was impressed too, though it was nothing compared to the real thing.

"*Solza, come now*," she commanded.

"*I'm already here, Master*," she replied.

In the next moment, Arianna felt her energy surge, in the delicious way it did when her avatar was near.

There was another collective shriek from the crowd—Solza appeared from over the trees in a *whoosh*, sending a much-needed breeze across the field with the flap of her wings.

She circled the meadow before making a ground-shaking landing directly behind Arianna upon the hill; Diveena, Lessa, Noah, and Kiki were already gone, making their way toward the others down below.

Arianna could feel Solza's breath, heavy on the back of her neck, warm and welcome as the mighty beast showed everyone who she answered to.

"All of us, we are *free*, Guardians of Gold," said Arianna, walking forward. "No matter what happens next, Kyrone Devlindor is no longer our king, and that is something to rejoice in. Let us make this known and see that the balance is brought back to our land. Down with the King!" She drew her sword into the air and everyone followed. "That is our oath!"

The crowd roared again with new fervor, throwing their weapons and fists to the air.

"*Show them what you're made of*," said Arianna, courage overwhelming her. "*What we all have within.*" She pressed her hand upon Solza's leg with support and authority.

Solza reared her mighty head to the sky; her jaw erupted with a stream of fire.

There were screams of joy and fright. The sound that had left her throat alone was terrifying enough, but the fire was *truly* magnificent.

Solza clamped her jaw shut and the flames were instantly extinguished, singeing nothing but the clouds. And with the swoop of Solza's tail and a bit of magic, Arianna lithely climbed atop her back, positioning herself right at the base of her neck.

Solza crouched down for leverage and then propelled high into the sky, circling the trees. Slowly, she began to lower back toward the ground until they were almost skimming the tall grasses.

The people raced after them, forming a wide circle in the center of the field. They shouted their support, jumping and hooting as Arianna and Solza drifted above them.

Arianna could feel her magic stirring within her. Their combined force made her hair raise and clothes float around her, as if she and Solza defied gravity in this moment.

Faintly, she wondered what they might look like in the eyes of their new followers—*Terrifying? Glorious?*

She'd learned by now that magic could be either. And no

matter what she did with it, her irises would glow silver just the same.

Arianna's voice rained down on them.

"We may have been bred in the Four Corners, but we beat with one heart—"

She felt the fire that ran through Solza surely burning within her chest. She clung tightly to the horns on her back, leaning forward as she spoke.

"No matter what district color you may wear on your shoulders, we are *all* warriors now. Hail to the World!" she yelled, spit flying from her mouth.

"Hail to Olleb-Yelfra!" they all bellowed back, fists pressed firmly against their hearts.

With one giant flap of her wings, Solza settled gently in the center of the meadow.

The crowd came running.

Arianna slid down Solza's tail and landed on her feet, but before she knew it, she was being thrust again into the air; the people lifted her up, bouncing her back and forth on their arms, sounding their praises and their passions.

It was such a joyous moment, and it seemed to last forever.

Alas, Arianna's glory was quickly outshone by her dragon. The crowd set her back on her feet at the edge of the circle and turned their sights on Solza.

"*Be gentle with them,*" said Arianna as they swarmed her to get a better look, Sano joining in on the fun.

"*I will try not to eat them, Master,*" said Solza in a sardonic tone.

Arianna laughed as she outstretched her wings, clearly showing off and loving every second of it; everyone paid her compliments, itching to lay a hand on a glittering scale or a horn.

"*How about, just try not to let all that attention go to your head,*" said Arianna—Solza let out a roar of a chuckle.

Arianna put her hands on her hip, shaking her head as she relinquished the spotlight. Then, she turned around to find Lessa, Jeom, Demetrius, Gabriel, and Eli all waiting to greet her.

Arianna ran to Jeom and Demetrius before she even had time to think straight.

"Oh, look at you!" she said, pinching their cheeks to make sure they were real. "I can't *believe* you're really here. We were about to send out a search party."

"We didn't want to miss the show," said Demetrius, scratching the back of his neck as he gaped up at Solza.

Arianna beamed, planting a big kiss on his cheek.

"But, Ara, *how* did you find us?" said Jeom, his usual baffled expression plastered across his face.

I missed this so much.

"With a lot of luck and a little bit of magic," she said, hugging them both together. "It's a long story."

"I can't wait to hear it," said Gabriel, a huge grin on his face.

Arianna reached out her hand to him.

"I'm certain you have a tale of your own," she said, her face still buried in Jeom's cloak. "*Thank* you, Gabe."

She knew the Kane brothers would've never made it here alive without Gabriel to guide them.

He returned a humble nod. "It's my honor to serve the guardians."

There were so many words to be spoken and so many questions to be asked; Demetrius and Jeom hugged her back, so snugly that Arianna thought they might break one of her ribs.

She could tell by just one glance that Jeom and Demetrius had changed, even more than she could've imagined after the details she'd learned of their growth.

She saw now that Demetrius' leg, or lack thereof, seemed

to have only made him stronger—his smile bigger, his confidence greater. And, sure enough, she recognized his elven powers almost as quickly as she'd noticed his new metal limb.

He's truly found his magic!

Jeom, on the other hand, was just much more *man* than she'd ever noticed him to be, no longer a lost creator boy stumbling through an enchanted world. He appeared so poised now, his grip on the Axe of Crissy surer than it had ever been. And he stood taller, ripped with more muscle than she thought even necessary.

I can't imagine what his ego's like now... She snorted a little as he squeezed tighter. *Oh, he's really just showing off! Must be the dwarf in him.*

Nevertheless, there seemed to be a sureness about the Kane brothers that definitely hadn't been there before... as if they now walked as one and knew exactly where they were going.

After a perfect moment, the boys relinquished their embrace; Jeom returned to fawn over Lessa, and Demetrius and Gabriel were gawking up at Solza.

Someone else took her hand, pulling her to the side and away from the others.

It was as if a swarm of firebugs had gone into an uproar in her stomach. She turned.

"Eli, I..." She lost her words the second she found his face.

The last time Arianna had laid eyes on him, he'd been risking his life to save hers; in her time spent in the Saindora Dungeon, she'd reflected on that moment a lot, among many others...

She felt utterly guilty for how hard she'd made him work for her trust, always blocking him out, fearing he might betray her again—even after he'd proven himself so worthy of forgiveness.

Eli gazed down at her now with a solemn expression, as if reading her mind.

"The past doesn't matter in this life," he said, the sound of his voice so soothing. "We only have now." He tucked her hair behind her ears, gazing down at her with such devotion, such love.

The fluttering firebugs turned into a swirl of fire in the pit of her belly. It moved slowly across every inch of her body until landing in her heart, burning there—just as warm and comforting as her magic.

"Ara, my feelings for you are unchanged," he whispered, his lips close to hers. "And I pray to every goddess and god that has placed us back on the same path now that you grant me permission this time..." He took a deep breath. "May I, please—"

Arianna didn't even wait for him to ask. She pulled him into her chest and kissed him with a passion like never before. Eli wrapped his arms around her, lifting her off her feet, and the rest of the world vanished.

THE WAY FORWARD

AS THE DAYS DREW ON, Arianna finally learned the answer to a question that had been gnawing at her mind ever since the ambush in the pyramid city—*what were the fates of the other elder guardians? Had they been luckier than Cyn and Iris? And Vance, who was captured at the beach and never seen again?*

Rowina, the old Greenhouse caretaker, had never even left Zambienth. She, along with Margery and Sergios, had kept hidden away in the Burrows for months. When the freed district slaves—Lessa and Eli in the lead—showed up in a storm at the sandy city gates, the elder guardians joined their ranks.

Together, they unseated the interim city keeper and took back the Greenhouse. And just as they'd accomplished in the other provinces bordering the Black Sand Desert, they wiped out any regulators or Shadow Resistance who tried to stand in their way.

Quickly and peacefully, they began to convert the

innocent citizens of Zambienth to their side, until soon the great pyramid city no longer bowed to a king.

Rowina, Margery, and Sergios assumed the responsibility to protect their base there, beginning to train new followers for the battle to come; Lessa, Eli, and Noah took to the seas, continuing to spread the story of the Guardians of Gold and praying for a way to locate Arianna and the Kane brothers.

City after city, they left their golden mark.

Finally—with the help of Syrifina—they reached the shores of the Impenetrable Forest. They reunited with Jeom and Demetrius, and discovered Diveena as a new master and friend to help guide them throughout the rest of their journey.

Margery had since arrived at the Treehouse, after a short mission to take several seaside villages; she'd brought with her much-needed supplies to support their jungle branch of the army as well as news of yet more success for the guardians—Nico and Master Tayshin had made it safely to the Greenhouse.

Arianna couldn't have been more thrilled and stunned to also learn that many families and friends from Moriamo had been welcomed through the city gates at their heels, safe and sound.

The arrival of children and the other magical people of the swamp village were proof enough to persuade any citizen who still held doubt in their hearts about the King's treacherous lies…

Thus, the City of Zambienth was pronounced the guardians' greatest victory in the ongoing battles to date—everyone there believed in their cause, and believed in Arianna as the chosen one to see it through…

From then on, with such a strong hold on one of the most populous and influential cities in all of Olleb-Yelfra, a new age had truly begun to unfold.

The King's regime is crumbling within his hands. We can

win this! We're so close.

The youth liberated from the Jar, along with people who had shed their shackles from the King even after earning citizenship, flew into training for the next great battle to come, invigorated by all that had already been achieved.

And now, with Arianna leading as the prime example of what a warrior *should* be, the jungle unit trained with even more dedication.

It was strange, to say the least, for her to find herself at the head of such a gathering. But she settled into her position with both humility and strength, focusing all her energy on readying those who had vowed to join her in the final fight for freedom.

Just survive!

They were risking everything for her dreams of a better future, so she would give all that she had in the hope that they succeeded, their lives intact at the end.

Each day, from dawn to dusk, the newest apprentices practiced with weapon and magic, Arianna by their side; when night fell and the camp rested, the original Guardians of Gold tried to form a foolproof plan for the march to Saindora.

Between Arianna, Diveena, Lessa, Demetrius, Jeom, Gabriel, Eli, and Margery, and even Noah and Kiki—they'd earned their place as leaders during the downfall of the districts—everyone had agreed to take the City of Guanamara as the next logical step before infiltrating the High City. Once this major province was secured, a smaller party of guardians would be sent back across the land to persuade as many inland villages as possible to join them.

If all went according to plan, the Guardians of Gold would thus control a good majority of the Olleb—the King would have no choice but to surrender the throne.

Arianna had recited their tactics over and over, for weeks on end, until everything started to feel real; they were nearly ready to notify the Greenhouse of the last piece in their battle strategy.

The guardians were preparing for an attack of their own to finally bring this war to a conclusion. They were no longer willing to play defense, once the majority of the territories were acquired…

Unless Master Tayshin or the other elders in Zambienth took issue with anything they'd outlined—and Margery was sure they would not—it was *almost* time to launch their fleet.

Ahead of Margery's arrival, Rowina had sent word to the Treehouse that the last ships would be complete in just a matter of months. They'd be able to carry everyone from Zambienth willing to fight; the two guardian strongholds would rejoin on the water and, together, make one last journey across the Sea of Saindora to the High City.

Once they reached the King's shores, they intended to unite with their land-based allies.

Then, they would storm Saindora and the palace, claiming it back for Olleb-Yelfra, wielding all the magic and weaponry in their arsenal—they would not stop fighting until King Devlindor *and* his Shadow Resistance were no longer a threat.

Arianna was integral in helping to strategize around the King's final moments, having spent so much time on the inside of the palace *and* sharing his mind; her freshest memories combined with that of the elder guardians' knowledge gave them the upper hand.

Days turned into weeks, weeks into months, but finally they had worked out almost every possible angle of attack to end in their favor… all but one.

Before they even reached Saindora, there was a single, *very* important task to accomplish, and everything else depended on its success—regardless of how many cities they claimed, how many people they recruited, the only way to face King Devlindor, evenly matched and in his own territory, was to destroy the King's Shadow.

If they could remove Sir Vladamor from the picture, the lead guardians were confident that their battle strategy could prevail, with few casualties on their end. And only when Sir Vladamor was dead, Saindora secured, and King Devlindor unseated would the Guardians of Gold declare victory.

There was just one problem—they had *no* idea how to kill a necromancer...

For how does one kill something that has mastered death?

GUARDIAN RELICS

THEY PORED OVER OLD AND NEW MAPS, old and new battle sequences, trying to determine the best ways not to die;
Arianna's mind began to wander, drifting back to the long
hours trapped in the Saindora Dungeon with Odessa.

She retraced her steps during her ghostly walk through the
Hall of Maps and counted the lines on the King's pallid face
as he slept. She remembered King Damas and Prince Neas,
fondly, their glittering forms the only thing of comfort in the
snake's sleeping pit. However, mostly, she kept returning to
the memory of the towering black door.

Its barrier magic had been so strong that it was able to defend itself against her touch, *even* though she had been in an
astral state; the royal ghosts had guided her there for a reason,
so she added it to the top of her stack of the many magical
mysteries yet to be solved.

I have to find out what's behind that door.

At the next break in conversation, she described its location to the others, pointing to the general area on the map of the palace—Lessa and Eli had teamed up to create a spectacular rendition of the King's domain.

"Does anyone know what's down here?" she asked. "It's important… I think."

Margery recognized it almost instantly.

"Why, that's how Talis was able to escape the palace the first time we tried this," she said, tracing her finger around the exact spot where the door was tucked away. "With the aid of Solomon and Princess Elisa."

Arianna pursed her lips; she couldn't help but question their motives, even then.

"It leads to a vast underground level," added Margery. "A storage cellar or something. He told us so upon his return."

Fleetingly, Arianna pondered what might be kept down there, then her thoughts became consumed by the Princess…

When she'd revealed to the other guardians that the King's very own sister had been her savior in the end, they just couldn't believe it had happened again.

What does she have to gain by protecting guardians, betraying her brother and sovereign right under his nose?

It was the question of the century.

Some mused that Princess Elisa had developed a soft spot for the guardians, fueled by her obvious love for Solomon. Others spread rumors that Solomon had been swayed permanently to the dark side once she'd sunk her claws into him, her selfish motives never to be trusted…

If the King were to die, Princess Elisa Devlindor would hold the *only* blood claim to the throne, though Arianna could hardly imagine this as a possibility; King Devlindor selfishly believed in a future where he would always exist to control it, and the last remaining royals had never named children who might solidify the claim to the throne for their bloodline.

Will he forever refuse to die?

Arianna fumed at just the thought of his suffocating grip continuing to squeeze the Olleb's life away.

Out with tradition! Nothing is immortal. Once the King is gone, all the rules will change for the better.

Her head was spinning with all the possibilities that could mark the end of this journey—the Guardians of Gold taking power. The King keeping power. His sister stealing the throne with Solomon by her side…

Nothing is certain. Odessa had taught her that.

There were so many ways that she saw this going, and they were inching closer to finding out what conclusion their choices might bring.

She could practically hear Solomon's past lectures reverberating in her mind as her imagination ran off. *'Focus! Don't be so impatient. Time will unfold all.'*

Arianna heeded his old warnings now more than ever.

They had to be patient and plan slowly, meticulous with all the details. There was no room for error this time, for if they failed, King Devlindor would ensure that the Guardians of Gold would never get another chance again—this he'd promised.

The only thing she knew with confidence about this journey was that she'd left a trail of blood behind her on the way to wherever she was headed; she prayed to every god and goddess she knew the name of that she wasn't leading her faithful, young army straight to their deaths.

Just breathe.

She and Lessa began to recite the plan again.

"Is that all, then?" said Jeom, wryly, his eyes glazing over as he listened to the girls painstakingly comb through every detail for the hundredth time.

"I *think* that's all…" said Arianna, pacing back and forth—she was trying to memorize every footfall she'd soon take between here and the King. "Except for Sir Vladamor."

At this, Jeom grew more serious, his brow furrowing as he stared at the map; Lessa hugged him around the neck.

"It's all right," she murmured into his ear. "We'll think of something."

Jeom disappeared into his thoughts for a moment as he tickled Solza behind the ears, happy to have her company again—he had been *very* vocal about his preference for her snow leopard form, rather than the dragon form that could easily take his head off in one bite.

"Does anyone have anything else to add?" he called across the room, his voice filling the large space.

He was met with silence, his words fizzling away into the chirps and creaks of the jungle; it beckoned them to come back outside.

Arianna stopped pacing and glanced up—everyone was looking anywhere but at Jeom.

On the other side of the room, Gabriel and Margery were poring over her map of the Golden Age, trying to solidify the best route for their ships to take to Saindora. Noah and Kiki assisted them by pushing pins back and forth across the blue-painted waters; it was a miracle that Lessa had even been able to hold on to this prized possession for so long, keeping it safe while Arianna was away.

Solomon had gifted her this treasure long ago, marking the beginning of their voyage across Olleb-Yelfra…

Arianna thought it fitting that it would now also help mark the end.

Demetrius and Eli were huddled in the center of the room near Jeom, concentrating hard on the map of the palace and surrounding city—it was spread out on a grand wooden table that had been carved straight into the heart of this nook, crafted from the tree it was built around.

Eli was giving instructions to Demetrius, who moved

small pebbles back and forth across the top, trying to predict the places they'd most likely encounter the King's right hand and to smooth out the new battle sequences Eli had most recently dreamed up. He'd discovered a knack for battle strategy, his talents as a warrior and experience in city regulator units proving very valuable now.

They were crouched over an intricate layout of the palace hallways, one which Lessa had expertly drawn up from the guardians' combined memories.

Arianna walked over to observe, trying to visualize the future along with them. It was imperative that everyone hold the same image in their minds, in order to execute their plans seamlessly.

She watched intently as Demetrius slid the tokens across the wood, Eli whispering the critical components behind each move—black represented the King's armies and gold represented the guardians.

They were nearing the throne room, black pebbles thinning out the closer they got, the gold surrounding all the major corners of the palace, from the outside in…

Arianna didn't even realize she was holding her breath until Sano jumped up onto the table. He scared the life out of her, scattering the gold pebbles everywhere as he tried to steal them away.

Those hovered around the map had been so sucked in, too, that it took them a moment to realize what had happened—Arianna knew that, like her, they had been envisioning themselves nearing those great glass doors, wondering what type of monster they might find inside.

Tamed? Defeated? Or agitated, claws out, willing to fight to the death, no matter the cost to his so-called people?

Would he even be there at all?

Everything was a presumption—some things they just couldn't plan for.

"Sano!" scolded Lessa, scooping the little monkey into her arms. "You're so mischievous. Give me that."

She pulled a black pebble from his paws before he could swallow it. She placed it back down on the table among the scattered gold.

"Sorry everyone," she said, wagging her finger at Sano.

"Isn't he supposed to be… more intelligent than most animals?" said Noah, scratching his head.

Lessa scoffed.

"Oh, he *is*. But he likes attention just as much as the rest of us, and I've been really busy lately." She nuzzled her cheek into his. "Sorry, buddy," she whispered to him.

Arianna looked down to Solza and frowned. *We all have.*

"*Don't worry about me, Master,*" said Solza, nudging her shins affectionately. "*The male species just lacks patience. Especially the ones in our family.*"

Arianna laughed, glancing to Sano… she *swore* he had just stuck his tongue out at Solza.

Eli wasn't paying any attention to the exchange, his gaze still pinned on the map; he suddenly looked up, standing tall, a determined expression chiseling out his features.

"We have to try and eliminate the necromancer *soon*, immediately after we take Guanamara," he said, addressing the room—everyone present gathered back around the table. "We have to try something. If he's anywhere near the palace when we send our people in, we're doomed. They're nowhere skilled enough to handle that… *thing*. I can't see any way out of this with him still lurking around to thwart our plans."

He gestured to the mess Sano had made of his pebble army.

Arianna scanned the map, quickly rehashing the path they'd outlined through the palace to corner the King—if they were intercepted in any major way, lost too many warriors, before reaching King Devlindor, they might not survive him.

"We could lure him here?" mused Demetrius, gesturing to the room. "Into our territory and ambush him, like he did us."

"Vladamor would annihilate anyone you send after him, or anyone you draw him near," said Gabriel, shaking his head. "We can't let him near this sanctuary."

"Yeah..." said Jeom, "and just imagine what a necromancer might do to your precious nature." He shook his head in warning.

Demetrius shuddered.

"All right, scratch that," he said, focusing on a wilted flower on the wall—he used his magic to bring it back to its full potential.

Arianna had to agree, recalling Sir Vladamor's abhorrent strengths.

"Honestly, I don't know how the strongest of us would even fare against him, regardless of the location we're in." She touched eyes with Jeom, Demetrius, and Lessa. "He raised an entire army from the dead *just* to battle the four of us."

She pouted, grinding her teeth as she thought.

"Besides, he'll be more prepared than we are if we don't know how to kill him... and he's already hunting us, per the King's wishes. Let's not make it easier for him to figure out where we are."

"Pray he doesn't find us before we find him," said Margery, placing her hand over her heart.

"Well, if Ara can't handle him, then who can?" asked Noah, throwing his hands up.

"We've only ever escaped him by luck," said Lessa, chewing on her lip.

"I wouldn't call any encounter with him lucky," said Jeom, head bowed. "Not to mention, he has the power of possession. He can get inside your mind... just like *that*."

He snapped his fingers.

"We won't let him this time," promised Lessa, hugging

him around the waist.

He gazed down at her with such adoration, then he kissed the top of her head, and Sano's, too.

Eli moaned in frustration, pulling at his hair. "If we could *just* figure out his weakness."

He swept the pebbles to the side and started at it again.

Arianna contemplated him from across the table, still unable to help being slightly distracted when he was around; the more he demonstrated his confidence and courage as a warrior on this dangerous quest, the more she wanted to be near him.

He looked up, catching her eye with a wink.

The firebugs started buzzing again in her belly, and she was sure their heat was displayed all over her cheeks.

This is exactly why I was hesitant to get close to him in the first place. Now, focus! Think of the necromancer's ugly face and figure out how to pummel it.

She put her head back to the unsolvable problem at hand—they'd all been over this a thousand times, digging for an answer that didn't seem to exist.

"I don't know much about necromancers," said Kiki, her voice small yet sharp, just like her, "but, maybe, there's a way to just... wound him? While we carry out the rest of the plan, you know? Couldn't we just lock him up somewhere, possibly?"

Eli cocked his head to the side as he looked at her, thinking, and there were murmurs of interest from across the table.

"He'd be less of a threat that way," said Lessa, glancing up to Jeom, "if we could injure him... slow him down somehow."

"But still a threat, nonetheless," replied Jeom, firmly.

He nodded to Demetrius.

Arianna considered the boys with the necromancer in mind and immediately felt just as angry as she had on the night when the unspeakable had happened—without ever even being seen, Sir Vladamor had used his dark magic to force a ghost to possess Jeom's body and do his terrible bidding, almost tearing him and his brother apart for good in the process.

Down with the King, and his pet!

She couldn't wait until they unlocked the secret to the necromancer's end.

"At least we still have the Axe of Crissy," said Demetrius, flashing his brother a grin. "And now you really know how to use it."

Jeom squared his shoulders, surely thinking of all the ways he'd like to get Shadow Resistance blood on those blades.

"Here, here," said Arianna with a knowing smirk.

"*Hmm,*" said Margery, her gaze flicking to Gabriel. "I hadn't really considered this yet, just been thinking of how to fully get rid of him. But Kiki's idea… that *was* what we tried to do last time."

Kiki perked up, silently shimmying her shoulders.

"Show off," Noah mumbled with an eye roll; Kiki stuck her tongue out at him.

Arianna smiled—their friendly banter always made these difficult planning sessions a little less daunting.

"How did you do it before?" asked Eli.

"Let's see…" Margery tapped her chin, looking into her past. "Vance and I did a big bout of magic out in the open, near the borders of Saindora," she replied. "The Shadow Resistance has eyes everywhere, so we knew the King would send Sir Vladamor to investigate and put a quick stop to it. The plan was to lure him to us while another group of guardians infiltrated the palace. Vance had a brilliant idea on how to trap him using a strong barrier spell, but it wouldn't have lasted long."

She sighed, surely saddened for his loss. The guardians had performed a small farewell ceremony not too long ago to honor his sacrifice, as well the losses of Cyn, Tobias, Iris, Keeper Kassime, and Talis. They had also given a heartfelt send-off to Liam, Odessa, and Mother Adunni.

"I'm honestly not even sure if it would've worked," she added, "but, regardless, it *would* have given enough time to the other guardians to get their job done. We knew what we'd signed up for… the only reason we survived our part was because the necromancer never showed up."

She was met with silence—they all knew where Sir Vladamor had gone instead.

Arianna felt a twinge of sadness in her chest. *At least the King has no more seers to control,* she thought. *They won't see us coming this time.*

Margery let her head fall back, closing her eyes, surely seeing the faces of more friends she'd been forced to say goodbye to, much too early.

"And yet the question remains the same, either way," said Arianna, tapping her fingers on the table. "Trap, wound, or kill… *what* is the weakness of a necromancer?"

Everyone at the table seemed a bit unsettled—nobody offered up any more thoughts. They'd truly hit a wall.

Not even the guardians back in Zambienth had shared any useful information to help solve this conundrum.

To make matters more complicated, Arianna had also started to get the sense that many in this room feared the necromancer even more than the King; she wondered if this was holding people back from discerning how to handle him.

Sir Vladamor was a familiar nightmare for them all.

He did most of the dirty work on the King's behalf, and almost everyone gathered here now had felt the might of his power at one point in time or another.

Arianna, though, would not be fooled by his shadowy tricks—the master of something as monstrous as a necromancer was to be feared above all else. She had faced King Devlindor, looked him dead in the eyes, and knew that he was the truest form of monster that walked the land.

"His weakness is the same as his strength," said Diveena, her delicate voice drawing everyone's attention.

She had been sitting quietly in the sill of a window, observing.

Although she was always welcome to these elder guardian gatherings, Diveena didn't usually attend nor contribute to their strategy sessions. She was more comfortable sharing her magic and knowledge down at camp rather than planning warfare; in fact, she'd already gained such strong support among the people that Arianna thought she could lead their army single-handedly, if she so chose.

But a role in leadership wasn't what she desired.

As the elf instinct was not to meddle in such human affairs, Diveena preferred to keep somewhat in the shadows, staying true to her Nicora traditions. But when the guardians *really* needed her, she was always there to nudge them in the right direction.

She'd become another revered master to them all, and Arianna thanked Talis every day for his hand in bringing her into their lives.

Demetrius cleared his throat.

"Umm… what was that now? Do you happen to know something, Diveena?" He looked just as flabbergasted as everyone else. "Do *you* know what his strength is?"

All eyes turned on her.

"You know just as I," she replied, so matter-of-factly that Arianna wanted to shout back at her—*uh, clearly we don't!*

She refrained.

Diveena tilted her head to the side, squinting her eyes, considering each one of them. After too long of a moment, she answered.

"A necromancer's greatest strength is control over death."

Jeom rolled his eyes, and Lessa threw him a 'reel-your-attitude-in' glare in the same second.

"Am I not right?" snapped Diveena, not missing his reaction.

"Well, you speak an obvious truth," said Jeom with a shrug, "but I don't see how that helps us solve anything…"

Diveena smiled, daring him to challenge her further; he opened his mouth to respond but thought better of it.

She hopped down from the windowsill and padded across the room to the table. She plucked a black pebble from the map, before holding it up for everyone to see.

"Death is just another way of viewing life," she finally responded, placing her hand on Jeom's shoulder. "Death may try to overcome life, but life is its equal."

She brought the pebble to her lips—a gentle kiss—and when they looked again it had been transformed into the color of gold.

She locked eyes with Arianna. "One cannot exist without the other."

"One cannot exist without the other," repeated Arianna in a whisper, clinging to her thoughts as they led her somewhere new.

"That's it!" she exclaimed; Jeom's last encounter with Sir Vladamor had suddenly popped into her head. "Perhaps… just *perhaps*, there's a way we can seek the help of a different form of life, one that has a little more experience with death."

Arianna caught Lessa's attention and her eyes grew wide—she knew they were thinking the same thing.

"Ghosts!" they both yelled in unison.

Diveena gave a slight nod, returning to her corner to let them draw their own conclusions.

Arianna felt all her hair rise on her arms, the thought stirring something up inside her, motivating her—finally they at least had an idea to explore.

"*Something is certainly more than nothing, Master*," said Solza, sharing in her excitement.

"Jeom, when the terrible thing happened back in Zambi-enth," said Arianna in a rush, "you were possessed by the ghost of a woman. But whatever magic sparked between you and Demetrius broke the ghost's control over you and, subsequently, Vladamor's control over the ghost."

"Yeah?" he stuttered. "So?"

"Well, that poor soul had been *forced* to do the necromancer's wishes. She told me she hadn't wanted to… that she was sorry."

"Sir Vladamor made her do it," added Lessa, gently.

"*All right…*" said Jeom, his voice cracking. He spoke through his teeth. "And your point?"

He grabbed for Lessa's hand as Demetrius shifted uncomfortably on his feet—these were the last details in their history that any of them wanted to recap.

"When we were in the desert, the ghosts he was controlling turned on him, too," continued Arianna. "Somehow, I helped them gain back their free will. They came back to *life*, in a sense… I think." She waved her arms in the air to try to make sense of her own words. "Anyways, they drove him away. That's my point! He was scared, the necromancer… they frightened him off!"

"But wasn't he scared of who the ghosts represented?" asked Demetrius, crossing his arms. "Not of the ghosts themselves."

"That, I don't really know," said Arianna with a shrug. "Though, if death is his greatest power, then life, as Diveena says," she gestured to her, "*must* be his greatest weakness. Life he cannot control."

She glanced around the room, arms wide with enthusiasm—nobody looked as sure as she felt.

"Look," she said, "what I mean is that maybe there's a way we can call to that life to help us. Or we could try and figure out how those connections were broken in the first place, so that he can't manipulate death against us again."

As crazy as it all sounded, Arianna knew that her incoherent thoughts made, at least, more sense than anything else suggested so far; there were murmurs of consideration around the table.

"And who were these ghosts, exactly, that you saw in the desert?" inquired Gabriel. "Do you have any idea?"

"They were… uh…" Arianna flashed a nervous look at Diveena.

Lessa, Demetrius, and Jeom mirrored her anxiety.

She lowered her voice out of respect. "They were the ghosts of the fallen Nicora Elven Clan…"

Diveena instantly became alert.

"You saw my clan?" she said—a silver sheen slid around her irises, her magic flaring up.

Arianna returned a soft nod.

"Master Lethander, your father… he spoke to me," she said, cautiously. "He's the one who told me to gather my friends and followers, that a war was again coming, and for us to be ready. He said their souls would remain on this plane until the Olleb was put right again." Arianna met her eyes. "They are waiting."

A tear, shimmering silver, slid down Diveena's cheek. She didn't respond, withdrawing into her own thoughts.

Arianna muttered an apology.

She had hoped, for a long time, that this topic might never come up—how could one simply tell the last remaining daughter of a ruined tribe that they'd met her ghost of a father in a desert?

"I'm sorry, but I *still* don't get it," barked Jeom; for once, Arianna was happy for his interruption. "How would this help us weaken the necromancer?"

"Sounds like a dose of his own medicine might send him running," said Lessa as she mindlessly twisted a ring about her finger—it was a priceless piece of jewelry, one that Keeper Kassime had given to her before his untimely death.

The stunning guardian relic was made of the same aura and ora stones as Arianna's dagger, Demetrius' compass, and Jeom's axe; the band had been forged from the familiar starry black stone, and it was topped with a jewel that looked as if it had been plucked from a vibrant sky, a blend of indigos, blues, and greens swirling together like dyes in water.

As Lessa continued to twist it back and forth, Arianna noticed a shimmer beginning to radiate from the jewel and around the band.

"Les," she said, though her voice barely came out.

Everyone else had homed in on the ring now, too.

"What… what is it?" she asked Jeom as he gawked down at her. "Is there something on my—"

He brought her hand to her face so that she could see.

Her mouth fell open as she examined her ring. "What in the gods' names?"

Gradually, as if the sparkling properties of the ring had lost all sense of gravity, tiny lights began to rise into the air like minute stars or twinkling specks of dust. They expanded so quickly that there wasn't even time for anyone to voice their thoughts.

The lights merged together as one, floating over the table like an electrified cloud; night had already fallen, so the mysterious mist illuminated the room with a soft glow that rivaled the torches on the walls.

Everyone squeezed in closer around the table, settling into the surrounding chairs—they stared, silently, in awe, as they watched the cloud fill with wisps of people from their pasts.

Diveena stood back.

"Jeom, look, it's more mind magic," said Demetrius, pointing up.

"I think this is in the palace attic back in Luose!" said

Jeom, on the edge of his seat. "What I'd give to go back."

"Talis," said Lessa with a yelp, her hands flying over her mouth. "It's really Talis… do you see him there?"

She reached for Arianna's hand.

"I see him," she said.

Like Lessa's, Arianna's eyes had filled with tears at just the sight of Master Churry, seemingly alive and well in this ethereal moment. What's more, Cyn was there, too, chatting his ear off—only innocent smiles warmed their faces, nothing to suggest that such bleak futures awaited them.

"Dammit, Cyn…" She wanted more than anything to pull her from this fleeting past and into her present. She could barely choke out her name. "I'm sorry."

Eli's hand curled around her own beneath the table, just a soft squeeze to let her know he was there.

"Just breathe," he whispered so that only she could hear.

She squeezed back. He let go, placing his palm gently on her thigh.

"Thank you," she mouthed.

"By gods, I remember this night!" said Margery, clutching at the table as she watched the memory hungrily. "It was just after we had all agreed to plan an attack on the King… much like today." She jumped up. "Oh, look! There I am."

Arianna followed her gaze and, indeed, found a much younger version of Margery gliding around the room, so tall and statuesque. She had the same bookish air about her back then as she did now, but Arianna knew Margery to be quite tough on the battlefield—she was a skilled sorceress with much to offer.

Arianna had learned some of her sneakiest tricks from her.

"I always wondered what it had been like before I found the guardians," mused Gabriel, eagerly observing every moment. "It's beautiful… to see them all there, so at peace."

"We were naïve," said Margery, growing grim.

She looked to her hands.

"But *how* are we seeing this?" said Eli, mouth agape—Arianna remembered what it was like the first time an old memory magic spell had engulfed her.

"It's Kassime's ring," she said, knowingly. She looked to Lessa with pride. "You must've tapped into the unique power it possesses somehow."

She glanced back to Diveena, and she returned a single nod.

"I *knew* you'd figure it out sooner or later," said Demetrius with a clap. "Tobias said all guardian relics have something else to offer, in addition to aiding in astral projection. Just like my compass!" He swiveled in his chair. "Ara, your dagger must have other gifts as well. Have you found out anything more?"

She just shook her head, unable to peel her attention away from Cyn and Talis; guardian relic magic was one mystery Diveena was determined to let them figure out on their own.

"Is there any rhyme or reason to this?" asked Lessa, gaping down at her ring.

"The mind magic I spelled your trinket with is… unique to other forms," said Diveena, finally speaking up. She circled the table. "It stores every memory of the one who wears it. Only a true guardian can tap into its powers to view those memories." Her eyes followed Talis. "So, this would be displaying the memories from the viewpoint of—"

"Kassime!" said Jeom, jumping up. "I knew I recognized that voice. He's there too. These *have* to be his memories."

Everyone around the table started to wiggle in even more delight as they spied on many of their fallen friends and heroes from the history books.

"Is *that* Nico?" said Lessa in disbelief as a young, chubby boy bounced around the room. "Tell me it's not…"

"He's put on a few pounds since I last saw him," said Arianna, beaming. "Hasn't aged a day."

Margery giggled, nodding her agreement.

A door opened in the past, and Arianna spotted Solomon padding across the room toward Cyn; a lump swelled in her throat almost instantly.

The energy darkened as all eyes turned to him, on the wolf entering Keeper Kassime's line of sight.

"I wonder… why this particular memory?" asked Arianna.

Solomon passed around drinks to Cyn, Talis, Nico, and, presumably, Keeper Kassime. Then, the young guardians put all their focus on what appeared to be the Golden Age map.

Solomon took care to explain to Cyn what they were working on, both laughing all the while as she tried to keep up. And, as Keeper Kassime paced around the table, Arianna even observed Master Tayshin showing Talis the lay of Saindora.

There was long-gone Iris, too, frowning down at Sergios—he was babbling on and on in his thick, alluring accent while she cleaned her sword.

Vance was busying about mixing potions, Margery alongside him. And Rowina also made an appearance, naturally gathered near the wine, along with many others that Arianna had never gotten a chance to know much about.

It was a time when the Guardians of Gold had flourished under Master Tayshin's leadership… and Solomon's loyalty.

"They all look so happy," said Lessa, placing a hand atop her rounded belly—Arianna was astounded at how much the baby had already grown since her arrival.

"We were happy," said Margery, wiping the tears from her eyes. "Because we didn't know what we were getting ourselves into. We were *too* confident. There was so much potential… but we failed."

Gabriel laid a hand on her shoulder.

"You didn't fail," he said. "Our time is now."

"But *why* are we seeing this?" asked Jeom, repeating

Arianna's question.

"Ah," said Diveena, lifting a finger. "That's where this magic is truly interesting."

"How so?" asked Lessa, eyeing her ring with wonder.

"Well, we all know that magic has a mind of its own, yes?" said Diveena; there were nods of acknowledgment around the room. "This mind magic, in particular, is selective with which memories to release." She shrugged. "Based on what, who can say? All I know is that with this type of magic, though the memory may *seem* quite random at first, the purpose is usually revealed in time."

"Just like with the compass," said Demetrius, excitedly. "It guides you to where you need to go, to other guardians. But until you get to where you're going, the destination is always unknown."

"And what grand fun that's been," whispered Jeom.

"Exactly," said Diveena, throwing him a wink.

"*Hmm*, as cryptic and confusing as Talis Churry himself," said Lessa with a solemn smile.

"As well as Keeper Kassime *and* Master Tayshin," said Arianna. "Of course, they'd be the focus."

"That's odd… you find it cryptic?" said Diveena, narrowing her eyes as she observed the ghosts of the guardians at their finest. "This glance into the past seems quite timely to me. Surviving failure is the only way to succeed."

They all considered her statement, observing a moment of silence as they witnessed a time when the Guardians of Gold had only really just begun.

Arianna realized she knew exactly why they were being shown this memory now—it was a reminder of their beginnings, of the purpose of this all, family and faith working together toward a brighter future.

"This was the day the portrait was painted, wasn't it?" she said, glancing to Margery. "The one that hangs in the

Greenhouse and in the Luose attic?"

"Why… yes," she replied with a smile, not taking her eyes away from the magical mist. "It sure was."

She pointed to the other side of the clouded memory where the figures from their past all started to gather and pose in front of an artist aided by magic; Keeper Kassime appeared to be walking toward them until all they could see was this gathering of young, hopeful guardians, their smiles and laughter filling the air.

"Kassime, get over here!" called Cyn, waving at him to hurry.

"We're not doing this without you, brother," said Solomon, laying his arm snug across Talis' shoulders.

"There's space next to me!" sang Nico, standing on his tiptoes. "Looking good, Kassime. Like a slice of—"

"Oh, dear, was he going to say apple pie?" said Cyn with concern, glancing around at everyone. She rolled her big, brown eyes. "*Ugh*, you were… weren't you?"

Nico beamed back at her.

"You have a problem," she said with a giggle.

There were friendly snickers all around.

"All right, all right," Kassime said, huffing. "Move over, then. Make room."

He moved closer to the smiling group, and the clouded memory began to slowly fade away.

The bright, smoky mist broke apart by its seams, separating again into minuscule specks. Then the magic sank back into the black band of Lessa's ring.

Arianna couldn't shake the fresh images of the young guardians whirling in her mind, and she knew they would stay with her for a long time to come. She was again inspired to honor their memory.

She had gazed upon that portrait many times—the original Guardians of Gold forever memorialized in one of their happiest moments, youthful and glowing with pride. And looking around the room she stood in now, at those left standing and those new to the fold, she sensed the same hopefulness for their future.

"*Wow*," said Kiki, breaking the silent awe that had settled around the table; she and Noah had been watching quietly the entire time. "Just… wow."

"It's truly an honor to be a part of this," said Noah, giving her a gentle hug around the shoulders.

There were strong responses of agreement from everyone.

Eli stood, picking up one of the pebbles on the map; Diveena plucked it from his hand, placing it back down.

"What—"

"Come, children," she said, a glow in her eyes and a command on her tongue. "There's time yet to discuss the looming dangers of this life. You fight so that the world can continue forward in happiness. This does not mean you should ignore happiness now, when it's presented, as the past has just so kindly reminded us."

"How do you mean?" asked Demetrius with a smirk. "What do you have up your sleeve, Diveena?"

"You guardians *deserve* something to celebrate for once," she said, shooing everyone toward the door. "You've come far in your teachings and trainings, so let us take a moment to honor your successes and clear our heads of the future for one night."

"A party?" squealed Noah; this time he was the one shimmying. "Am I hearing this right?"

Diveena grinned.

"Go, freshen up," she said, not leaving room for indecision. "Everyone has been making preparations all day. I daresay the festivities have already begun."

"But what are we celebrating, exactly?" asked Arianna. She bit down on her lip, looking to the map. "We're still not ready…"

"We bear witness to a time when the Guardians of Gold have once again enriched their vow from being passive by-standers, protectors of knowledge, to becoming active warriors who not only protect it but fight for it," she said. "That, in and of itself, is something worth celebrating."

"You don't have to ask me twice," said Jeom, sniffing at his dirtied clothes—they trained so much these days that Arianna hardly remembered what any of them looked like clean.

Demetrius mimicked his brother, his nose scrunching up at the smell; they both fell into a fit of laughter.

"All right, I'm off! Must look dapper," said Noah. "I think I might have a chance with Kiki."

He winked at her, then flew out of the room, leaving everyone to try to stifle their amusement as Kiki blushed red.

"He's in for a *world* of pain," she mumbled, a wobbly smile on her face.

She stomped out after him.

"We'll meet you all there," said Lessa, tugging at Arianna's hand. "Come with me to get ready."

Arianna glanced at Eli for help, a smirk sitting on his lips.

"We deserve to relax a little," he said. "Don't fight it."

"Fine, I won't," said Arianna, giving in to Lessa. "But we *still* have to solidify this plan about Sir Vladamor. We've barely just grasped an idea about how to get him out of the picture." She addressed everyone still there. "Let's all recon-vene in the morning."

Margery laughed.

"My, *my*, you really are the spitting image of Bell, you know? When he was the one barking orders about battle plans." She put her hands on her hips, considering her. "It's nice… familiar."

Arianna was momentarily stunned at the statement.

She knew that Margery referenced the trustworthy and

strong Master Bell who had just graced their presence, the ghost of the Solomon who existed now. And no matter how much she tried to suffocate the feeling, she just couldn't help but get a pinch of proudness in her heart at such a declaration… that she might be anything like the masterful teacher from her past.

Lessa pulled her out the door before she could push the thought from her mind.

IO

FLAME IN THE NIGHT

IT WAS DUSK NOW, the sun beginning to fall back behind the trees and a waning crescent moon already in the distance, eager to take the spotlight this night.

Arianna and Lessa had been happily surprised to find spectacular outfits waiting for them in their quarters for the evening's events; Diveena always seemed to have a way of conjuring anything they needed, and with their newly found connections to major hubs around the Olleb, there had been no shortage of quality goods at the Treehouse.

The girls were putting on their final touches, both adding a little splash of magic here and there for some extra *oomph*—they truly sparkled tonight, like two firebugs lost among the treetops. Arianna admired herself in the mirror for a moment as Lessa placed the last pin in her hair.

"I think that about does it," said Lessa, twirling in front of the mirror.

"Job well done, I have to say," said Arianna, grinning at their reflections. "Reminds me of our highlife days."

She boasted elegant wrappings of a deep red, Lessa's of flowing baby blues; both garments were dotted in subtle gold patterns, the fabrics fluttering out behind them like soft butterfly wings every time they moved.

Lessa gave a mock curtsy, and Arianna returned it.

She felt like her best, proper self in these clothes but also felt a bit more exposed than usual—they offered nothing of function for a warrior constantly under attack, so she took care to secure her dagger in the sheath at her thigh.

Just in case…

She thought of the last occasion when she'd taken the time to get properly dressed up, and it actually wasn't in South Luose—the Village of Moriamo flashed through her mind, the vibrant welcoming festival they'd thrown in her honor. The dancing, the food… the beautiful people. *Gone.*

Scattered to the winds, in search of a new home, just like her.

Arianna took a deep breath, trying not to let those darker memories dampen the celebrations tonight.

At least there are survivors… We're all survivors.

"Solza, aren't you coming?" she asked, shifting her focus to her snoozing avatar.

Solza let out a big yawn in response. She was stretched out across the carpet, her tail swishing about lazily.

"I think that's a *no*," said Lessa, tickling Solza under the chin. "Maybe if she had a little encouragement?"

She threw open the door and cupped her hands around her mouth, calling for Sano.

A flash of bright white fur against the nighttime jungle backdrop burst into the room, bringing a gust of wind with it; Sano landed in Lessa's arms in the next second.

"He's ridiculously fast now!" Arianna called, her hair

settling back down around her shoulders. "I barely saw him that time."

"He's really perfected air and water," said Lessa. She shimmered with pride as she peered down at him. "We're still working on earth, but he's come a *long* way since he first found me in the trees."

She planted a kiss on his head.

"Well, go on then, Sano," urged Arianna. "Show Solza what you're made of."

Sano batted his moon-like eyes at her and then leaped from Lessa's arms to the floor. Upon landing, he transformed into the stately white wolf—with a fiery stare—that they'd all first met in the Four Corners. He padded across the room toward Solza, nudging her impatiently with his nose.

A low rumble started in Solza's throat.

"*Oh, all right… I'm coming,*" she snapped.

Arianna chuckled. "*It will be fun! Let's get going. You can sleep soon enough, you lazy cat.*"

Reluctantly, Solza got to her feet, and Arianna slipped on her shoes.

"Ready, Les?"

Arianna caught a glimpse of Lessa in the mirror; her eyes were suddenly rimmed red with unfallen tears.

"What's the matter?" said Arianna, spinning around to look at her properly. "Do you want to sit down a moment?"

"No, everything's fine," she said, bowing her head. "It's just… this *baby*, Ara." She plopped down on the bed, looking at her belly. "She won't stop moving, yet there's nowhere to go."

She let out an exasperated sigh, but at least she was smiling.

"Here, come feel."

She gently grabbed Arianna's wrist and maneuvered her hand around her stomach; Arianna felt a little nudge from whatever new life lay inside and froze.

"That was definitely a warrior's kick!" she said, hoping to feel it again. "Incredible."

Lessa snorted. "Well, if she's not careful, she's going to kick her way right out of me before we're both ready."

She grew flustered again, her moods everchanging from one second to the next as of late.

"What is it?" said Arianna, letting her hand fall away. "Does it hurt when she moves?"

"Sometimes it can be unpleasant, but… it's not really that," she said, shaking her head. "She's just making my mind crazy!" She threw her hands up, waving them in the air like a madwoman—indeed, Arianna thought she was a bit crazy. "I feel like I can't think straight sometimes. I'm all over the place. And now's really *not* the time for my mind to be going."

She huffed in frustration.

"I know Snow will be worth all this trouble," she added, rubbing her stomach, "but tell me something, Ara, *why* can't the men be the ones who carry the child, *hmm*? Jeom is already a bit nuts anyways."

Arianna howled in laughter, relishing how unhindered she felt at the moment, free.

"I would hate to see him become any more foolish than he already is," she replied after a moment. "Diveena says babies can do that to you, though, before they're born. I guess, we must have missed that training when we skipped out on being citizens…"

Arianna smirked down at her, hands on her hips, thinking quite the contrary—since the first day they met, she and Lessa hadn't missed out on anything.

"But don't worry, you're not acting any stranger than normal."

Lessa wiped away her tears, letting out a contented sigh.

"Thanks," she said with a sniffle.

A knock came at the door.

Arianna peeked outside and was pleased to find Jeom and Eli standing on the walkway, sheepish grins on both their faces. They looked as handsome as ever, donning stylish vests that showed off their chiseled chests, perfect attire for such a warm night.

"Hope we're not interrupting, ladies," said Eli, leaning in the doorway. "Someone told us you were both in need of escorts."

"*Wow*, you both clean up good," said Arianna, a little shocked to see Eli in anything other than a warrior's ensemble.

Diveena had selected outfits for them that also paid homage to their district beginnings—Jeom stood proudly in purple and Eli confidently in red, their garments both decorated in thin, gold embellishments that matched the girls'.

But she couldn't take her eyes off Eli... reminded of the first time she'd ever opened a door to his beautiful face.

So much had transpired between them in the last few months at the Treehouse that it made her dizzy still. And the more time they spent together, the deeper their connection grew—there was no going back, and she would never want to.

Jeom cleared his throat, blocking Eli from view.

"*Yes*, Arianna, I know I look good," he declared, tugging at his vest with a smug expression.

"Good gods," said Arianna, rolling her eyes.

He winked.

"Not too shabby yourself," he said with a look of approval.

The ruby red pins in her hair caught his attention; he began poking at them without a lick of finesse.

"Why thank you," she replied, slapping his hands away with a laugh. "Lessa's inside. Go on now."

She stepped aside, opening up her arm wide to welcome him as if he were a highlife entering a palace.

Jeom flashed a bright smile, puffed out his chest, then

walked into the room. He bowed low in front of Lessa.

"Miss," he said, planting a kiss on her hand.

His smile fell to concern.

"Wait… why do you look like you've been crying? Is something wrong?" He looked her up and down, frowning. "I plan on dancing with you tonight, you know, so tell me what to do so I can ensure that happens."

He looked nothing if not sincere.

"Oh, I'm fine, really," she said, eyes averted, looking slightly embarrassed. He hugged her close. "I just feel so… uncomfortable in my own skin, lately."

She shifted awkwardly on the bed.

"I'm sorry," he said, squeezing her hand. "But Diveena said you're more than halfway there. You'll be back to normal soon." He tilted her chin up, lowering his voice. "If it's any consolation, you look more beautiful now than yesterday, *and* every day before that. And tomorrow, I daresay you'll grow that much more lovely to my eyes."

"Same to you, Miss Belvedor," said Eli, coming to stand beside her.

He grasped her hand, twirling her into his arms with as much grace and grit as he did when wielding his swords in a duel he was sure to win.

They locked eyes for a moment, and Arianna felt as if they looked upon each other for the very first time again.

"Laying it on a little thick, aren't we, boys?" said Lessa.

Her voice drew them out of their bubble.

Arianna glanced her way just as she gently kissed Jeom— she still couldn't get over how wonderful it was that two of her best friends had found such a bond with one another.

"They've clearly already found the wine," she said, smirking up at Eli; she could smell the sweetness of it on his breath.

"Damn, caught red-handed!" said Eli to Jeom, his gaze still pinned on Arianna.

He flashed his signature grin that always made her fluttering firebugs return.

"My, you really *do* look stunning tonight, though," he
said, shaking his head. He ran his hand through his hair. "You
don't need magic to charm me."

Jeom stole the moment with a barking laugh. "Oh, and
I'm the one laying it on thick? *Please!* Meet the master."

He began clapping at Eli, who bowed to his applause.
Then he helped Lessa to her feet.

"You're a buffoon," she said, smoothing out Jeom's vest.
She tossed Eli a smile. "*Both* of you."

Arianna broke out in a fit of laughter that couldn't be
quelled.

She pushed Eli away.

"Yeah, real smooth…" she said, every word making her
laugh even more.

He shrugged, smiling still.

"Can't let Jeom show me up all the time," he said. He held
out his arm. "Shall we, then?"

Arianna composed herself. She looped her arm through his
and relaxed into the moment.

They all made their way to one of the enchanted platforms, Solza and Sano trotting closely at their heels.

Just as they were preparing to descend, a voice sliced
through the silence of the night.

"Wait for us!" Demetrius called to them from somewhere
behind.

He was rushing toward them, vines twisting about like
some kind of nature-made octopus had swallowed him whole;
he wore an emerald vest dipped in gold, and sun-kissed flower
patterns bloomed all around the fabric to match.

Gabriel was racing alongside him, trying his best to keep
up.

They reached the platform within seconds.

"Not *again*," said Gabriel with a moan, gasping for air; Demetrius gloated. "I'll never win. Next time… no… magic!"

He pulled in breath after breath, clenching his ribs with one hand.

"Deal," said Demetrius, shaking his other hand, firmly.

"Maybe a little more training and a little less dining nook," chided Jeom, poking him in the belly—Diveena *had* spoiled them rotten at every mealtime since their arrival.

Gabriel playfully shoved him off.

"When you're my age, you'll understand, kid," he said, wiping the sweat from his brow.

"All right, enough jabbering. I'm ready to dance. Hang on tight!" said Demetrius.

His eyes streaked with silver and the platform jolted to life beneath them.

EVERYONE WAS ALREADY down at the campsite—the night around the Treehouse was as quiet as ever, save for the sound of what Diveena deemed whistling frogs, drowning out the silence with their nighttime lullabies.

Arianna had spent countless nights listening to them. They'd become somewhat of a comfort to her, coaxing her into peaceful sleeps or encouraging her to focus. Sometimes their song rang so loud that it actually turned into a calming hum that chased away the worrisome thoughts in her head, like a voice telling her to remain optimistic and keep going.

On this night, though, as they traveled the familiar path through the jungle to the meadow, the song accompanied them like an inspirational melody, lifting their spirits even higher in preparation for the festivities.

Along the way, the trees took on strange, shadowy shapes in the night that reminded Arianna to take caution, even when all seemed safe; she focused on the comforting pressure of the dagger against her thigh with every footfall.

It wasn't long before they heard the rumble of music and laughter rise up to their ears, the wafting smell of delicious food coming with it. When they reached the top of the hill, Arianna saw roaring pink fires in the middle of the field, people dancing around them like nothing else in the world mattered—it appeared as if she spied on the ghost of the Village of Moriamo in full swing, like she'd stumbled into another memory enchantment.

Everyone was dressed in glittering garments, making it seem as if a flock of wild nocturnal birds had taken over their training grounds. And colorful bulbs of bright magic twinkled in strings above the party; Arianna imagined it like a swarm of fairies, observing the humans in dance from a distance.

Diveena's doing, certainly.

Some groups of guardians were lounging about in the grass, staring at the decorative magic in awe. Others were picking over a long table stacked high with food and drinks.

She spied Noah at the table, one arm wrapped tight around Kiki and one reaching for food; Arianna smiled to herself, realizing that others were also starting to make room for love in the new world they were shaping...

As if possessed by the spirit of celebration, Sano raised his head to the sky and started howling, his voice carrying across the meadow—the moon had spotlighted them on the hill.

Everyone down below stilled, looking their way. Then, they began to cheer, lifting their cups to the air.

"Now that's my kind of entrance," said Jeom, waving back with gusto.

"All this attention is really starting to go to your head," said Arianna, giving Sano a gentle pat.

Jeom snorted.

"*Me?*" he said, hugging her around the waist. He opened his arm out wide, forcing her to look again—they still had an audience. "You know this is all for you, Ara."

"*He's not wrong, Master,*" said Solza.

She felt her cheeks redden as she took it all in; she waved nervously alongside him and then hurried down the hill with the others in tow.

Arianna made a beeline for Noah—when they reached the table, they were all quickly swept up into the fun.

She couldn't remember a time when she'd danced more than on this night, taking turns about the camp with new and old friends. Some hours later, she went to rest by one of the fires, trading adventure stories with Margery, Diveena, and other well-traveled souls.

Jeom and Lessa stole much of the attention as they slowly drifted along to the melodic tunes of an instrument spelled to never let the music stop. And Gabriel and Eli chased Demetrius around the field, magic sparking through the air in trails behind them.

At one point, Diveena had even taken it upon herself to decorate Lessa's baby bump in silver paint, as she explained how revered mothers used to be in elven culture; Arianna couldn't believe that she had let her do it, but Lessa showed off the artwork proudly, her stomach glowing through the sheer and flowy fabrics.

Even Solza and Sano were enjoying themselves tonight as they bounced between the fires, displaying their unique talents any chance they got; the trainees fawned over the avatars like the animal kingdom royals they were, giving them the extra attention they deserved for sharing their masters so much.

When the night grew thicker, Eli graced the party with a song of his own, one anyone from Warrior's District would recall. He strummed the strings of a guitar loudly and proudly, his voice booming over the chords as the fires roared along with him in the background; he stared at Arianna the entire time:

With a warrior's might,
We arrive to the fight.
If the enemy is real,
Then their blood will taste steel.
Hoorah! Hoorah!

No, we don't lay down our swords
With only mere words.
Raise them high to the sky
And protect what is ours.
Hoorah! Hoorah!

With a warrior's might,
We will fight.
We will fight.

And with a warrior's soul,
We will win,
Or we'll die.
Hoorah! Hoorah!

Arianna was the first compelled to join him in song. She jumped to her feet, fist pounding the air, and shouted, "Hoorah, Hoorah!"

Soon all the Warrior's District survivors had stood to dance, waving their weapons in the air and bellowing the verses over and over until the night was drowned out with their voices.

When the crowd took over singing, a mind of their own, joining arms and swaying back and forth, drunkenly, Eli abandoned his guitar and grabbed for Arianna's hand to make a run for it.

He led her a safe distance away from the rambunctious group.

"Walk with me?" he asked.

"Gladly," she said, overwhelmed by all the merriment.

"*Solza, will you be fine on your own?*" she said—she hadn't seen her for hours, and was sure some trainee had swept her off somewhere; their minds connected. "*I'm headed back with Eli now.*"

"*Of course!*" she replied, not worrying over Arianna in the slightest. "*These people are just the best. Good night, Master.*"

"*Good night, Solza! Don't have too much fun.*"

Solza laughed warmly.

Arianna and Eli snuck back into the jungle while they still had the chance. They remained in silence for a good while, and she appreciated it after all the commotion. It felt good to just walk off all the food and wine, the cool nighttime breeze refreshing after dancing so much.

The trees swallowed them whole, and it was suddenly very dark.

"Do you mind?" said Eli, picking up a fallen branch.

Solza ven immito, she thought—a fire grew at its tip.

Using the makeshift torch to light their way, Eli walked a little ahead; he never let go of her hand and always remained on the lookout, even though they were in the safest space they had maybe ever been together.

She understood him well.

Their minds worked alike; they were warriors who had seen true bloodshed—she never fully let her guard down anymore either.

And while she didn't need anyone to protect her, it was, at least, nice to know that someone *felt* like they needed to protect her...

Arianna considered him now, the light of the fire casting a warm glow around them both. She truly thought Eli a beautiful man—he had a lean, muscular build and hair that had grown so long that it brushed his shoulders. And skin much like her own, darkened each day they were under the sun.

As they walked this jungle path together, hand in hand, she wondered how many more moments like this, peaceful and still, would be left to them; she thought of their cold desert kiss, the first time they had been truly alone…

I should've never let go of his hand.

Arianna could feel the nights ticking away, faster than she cared to realize; life had changed so drastically, from one day to the next, since the first step she'd taken on this journey that it was hard to even keep track of who she was anymore.

However, her roots remained the same.

She knew that somewhere inside of her Twenty-Two still existed—a small seed that had sprouted into so many bigger things.

Never forget.

The red cloak with the silver number embroidered at the chest and the tattered blanket that had been her safety net for so long… they were still there, forcing her to hold on to the *why.*

Why she had found Lessa Thur in the first place, and Jeom and Demetrius, too. *Why* she had killed Grinda Risso, God-frey, Ophelia, and taken countless more lives with her swords. *Why* Solomon had chosen the dark path that he traveled. And *why* Kassime, Talis, Cyn, and so many others had had to die for her to live.

Down with the King!

She closed her eyes a moment, homing in on the sound of the whistling frogs; tonight, she didn't want to drown in her past, didn't want to think about the meaning behind so many things that had happened the way that they had, nor what that meant for the future…

She only wanted to focus on the now, being here with Eli, in the safety of the trees—for the present was fleeting, and she knew that more truly than anything.

A while later, they reached the hidden platform.

Eli dropped the torch to the ground and stomped on it, the fire instantly extinguishing. They both stepped on, and Eli pulled Arianna close to his side.

She whispered the words to a spell she'd learned to coax the platform awake, then they rose up, slowly, toward the starry sky.

The higher they went, the quieter the night grew—everyone was still down at the celebration.

When they arrived and exited onto the empty walkway near Arianna's nook, they were compelled to stop and take it all in. They leaned across the rail, peering down toward the blackness of the treetops.

If Arianna squinted, she could *just* make out the tiny firelights and enchanted strings still blazing from the ongoing festivities.

She raised her eyes to the sky, becoming absorbed there. A blanket of milky stars created a backdrop that started from the base of the jungle hills, rising tall to the clouds—it appeared as if diamonds had been stitched to midnight-colored silk and stretched out across the world.

"It's *so* black, isn't it?" she said.

Eli moved closer to her, following her gaze.

She knew he was likely connecting the patterns of the stars in his head, lost there, too… as he often was.

"It reminds me of the desert," he said with a wonder-filled whistle. "Of that night."

Arianna placed her chin in her hands.

"You just wouldn't give up," she said with a mock sigh.

"What's the fun in that?" said Eli, wrapping his arm

around her waist. "Besides, you were well worth the wait."

She laughed, pulling away from him gently.

"Well, I'm very glad you didn't," she said in a soft voice.

Things had certainly changed since Zambienth.

The time she had spent imprisoned in the Saindora Dungeon, alone and away from her friends, had made her grow faster than any other challenge she'd faced thus far; each day she had thanked the gods that she still lived, and each day she had wished for just one more.

During that time of self-reflection, she also came to realize that grudges and anger were worth letting go of in the end. She didn't want those to be the last things people remembered of her... or the last things she remembered of herself.

Take nothing for granted, no one.

But the biggest lesson she'd received from that terrible experience was that there was no way of knowing *when* the final moment with someone she cared for would be.

Cyn...

Arianna would never get to say goodbye, or tell her how much she had meant to her. She was just gone, forever, like a smothered flame—only the memory of its brightness remained.

She had promised herself after that day to *never* leave behind such a difficult realization. If she had the chance to see her loved ones again, she vowed to make sure that they knew just how loved they were.

Thus far, she'd lived up to that promise with Lessa, Demetrius, Jeom, Noah... and now Eli; she put her trust in the stars to carry her message on to those already gone.

"You know what the sky *actually* reminds me of tonight?" said Arianna, tilting her head, her eyes dancing between the specks of fiery light.

"What's that?" asked Eli, inching closer still.

"Aurora," she whispered, drinking it in.

She'd never noticed it before, but now…

She slipped the blade out from its sheath at her thigh and held it in her palms, remembering how she'd named it for the aura and ora stones long ago in the Vanishing Tunnels. She admired its shimmering black blade now, sparkling just like the sky above.

"Yeah, I can see that." Eli nodded. "Your dagger also reminds me a lot of Solza, though, if you ask me." He leaned over her shoulder to get a better look. "Her eyes… that flaming streak. Know what I mean?"

Arianna had also drawn such conclusions before about Solza and the dagger, wondering if they could be connected, somehow. But it had been just a farfetched thought, and she'd never leaned into those musings.

However, as she considered the weapon, Eli's statement made something else click.

She fixated on the yellow streaking through the black jewel in the pommel, recalling a memory—a falling star, chasing away the dark, leaving behind a bright trail of…

Fire!

"Eli, that's it," she said as she gazed upon the dagger with new and eager eyes. "You're just brilliant!"

She had a very strong feeling growing in her gut that urged her to do something out of the ordinary. *Fate hasn't steered me wrong yet.*

Her blue-eyed, fiery-hearted avatar had successfully mastered all four stages of the avatar cycle *and* had single-handedly brought the dragon race back from extinction overnight; together, they had finally found their fire.

Eli was staring at her with a quizzical expression. "What do you—"

Without a second thought, Arianna spoke the phrase burning in her mind.

"*Solza ven immito!*" A small flame ignited in her palm.

Compelled like a magnet—the blaze bouncing in her hand, brilliant and warm—Arianna grasped the pommel of Aurora.

The jewel instantly reacted, the streak of yellow inside igniting with her touch. It began to sizzle and writhe with a life she'd never known it had.

Eli jumped, letting go of her waist, but he didn't say anything to break her concentration—she knew that he realized the importance of the moment.

Something big is coming. I can feel it.

They both focused on the dagger.

It was as if the dragon etched into the blue, green, and violet metals of the guard began to breathe a fire all its own, straight into the sparkling black of the blade; its peculiar properties shifted, swirling like a tiny, powerful portal that opened up to another part of the universe.

She held on tight, feeling the energy of the blade slide into her veins; her hair began to float all around her, her magic racing.

She didn't know what to make of it, couldn't stop it.

Unless I let go, she thought.

Arianna squeezed the pommel tighter, burning her flame brighter—the most magnificent magic she had maybe ever witnessed exploded into the night.

"By gods!" cried Eli, shielding his eyes. "What's happening? What did you do, Ara?"

The night lit up like a lantern all around them, engulfing them.

"I don't know," she stammered—whatever this was, the magic was draining. She could barely hang on now. "I just had an inkling that I was supposed to call my fire. I'm not sure *what* kind of magic this is, but I'm sure it has to do with Aurora's special guardian gifts." Her flame continued to feed the dagger, her hand shaking. "Finally, I've tapped into the relic's true powers."

They both gaped in astonishment at the sky—the same deep colors that made up the weapon's rare craftsmanship poured out in a torrent, settling above them in a stormy wave the size of Solza in her dragon form.

The magic twisted and expanded overhead, showing off beautiful, smoky shades, like a colorful, electric cloud had been added to the night. It danced there, ominously, thick ribbons of dark, dazzling hues painting the air, Arianna's fire snaking throughout it.

"That's two in one day! Incredible," said Eli. "But the magic feels strange somehow, doesn't it?" He gawked at the enchanted veil, unblinking. "Do you feel that, Ara?" He shrank back a little, as if afraid the cloud might absorb them. "It seems… *dangerous*. I wonder what it does."

Arianna returned a subtle nod, knowing what Eli meant but not sure how to articulate it into words of her own.

She was drawn to the magic yet frightened of it all the same. Something told her that if the blade had been buried in flesh, Aurora's gift would take on a very different shape…

It was powerful, alive, like an animal with a hunger all its own—a dragon watching over its territory, ready to open its fire-filled jaws and strike should a threat come too near.

Not too long ago, Solomon had shamed her for her failure in discovering what the dagger could *really* do, but now she was so close. *What are you trying to tell me, Aurora?*

She was staring the answer in the face but wasn't ready to see.

But she knew in her heart that it—whatever *it* was— would reveal its true self in due time.

Arianna tore her eyes from the sky and looked to Eli.

"It's going to happen soon," she said, gravely. "I can feel it. The Olleb is ready now."

"I can feel it too," he replied, stiffening.

He placed his hand on Arianna's wrist, on the hand which held the dagger, her fire still burning there; she instantly relinquished her magic, knowing that it might treat him differently.

As she let go of her flame, it was as if the animal soaring in the sky had been called back into its bottle and swiftly locked away—like an avatar obedient to their master.

The night grew dark again in a flash, the twinkling of stars and an even thicker silence left in its place.

"Well… I suppose that's our cue," said Eli, a staggered smile on his lips. He rubbed the back of his neck, still staring toward the sky. "Strange world we live in."

"Indeed," said Arianna, gawking at Aurora.

When the lightning in the pommel stopped stirring, she sheathed the dagger back at her thigh.

Eli cleared his throat.

"Good night, then, Arianna." He gazed at her with wide, curious eyes, like he'd just experienced magic for the first time. "You… you really are an amazing woman, you know?" He shook his head, seemingly lost for words. "You make me believe in this enchanted life over and over again."

He reached out and gently stroked her cheek, as if he needed to ensure that she wasn't a figment of his imagination. He sighed, appearing so content as his fingers slid against her skin.

"However long we have," he said, stepping closer, "no matter what happens, I'm with you in it." He leaned in, kissing her goodnight, lightly, warmly, on the lips.

He pulled away to leave, but Arianna didn't let him go.

With a warrior's reflex, she grabbed his vest and kissed him back like there was no tomorrow.

PART TWO

MASTER OF SWORDS

THE DAYS CAME AND WENT until Arianna had counted another month gone by in the hills of the Olleb, away from the eyes of civilization and under the watchful spirits of the trees. She and the other guardians had fully developed their powers and skills through the training of those newer to magic. And soon, their guardian army began to show true promise.

While Arianna was eager to put their training to the test, she was grateful for the extra time they'd been granted to hone their strengths. They would need every ounce of power in their arsenal to secure Saindora.

Alas, they had received word that the King was on the move, his armies trying to regain control across the Olleb—they had to act soon before he succeeded in loosening their grip.

Eli continued to orchestrate and lead battle sequences akin to the plans they'd all agreed on, Noah and Kiki offering their support. Likewise, Margery and Gabriel headed up trainings in battle magic, teaching the new swarm of freed slaves just what it meant to be a Guardian of Gold.

Lessa and Demetrius leaned into their core skills—she led workshops on the basics of healing, in the hope that everyone present could have the potential to keep each other alive; and he shared the key to being a good agrarian so that no one would go hungry along the way.

"Sustenance and strength go hand in hand," he would say, repeating the motto from his district days.

"It is the Golden Rule," Diveena would agree, impressing its importance upon all those who would listen; she assisted in any way that she could, mainly through the upkeep of the Treehouse and restocking of supplies.

Jeom and Arianna were at the center of it all, leading one-on-one combat training drills, crucial to the success of their plan. They tested the strength of the most practiced warriors in both magic and metal, instructing them in all the ways they'd learned how not to die—these would be the young men and women tasked with leading small units across Saindora when they were ready to split up.

Jeom also made sure the entire camp knew how to make a basic weapon on the go, and Lessa ensured that anyone within reach of a bow and arrow could aim and shoot.

For once, everything seemed to be in their control. It was only a matter of time now before they would be ready to reunite with the Greenhouse guardians and march together against the King's armies.

However, there was still just *one* last nagging question to be answered before they could—how to stop the necromancer?

In her heart, Arianna knew that ghosts were the answer…
Somehow.

She had no idea where to even begin in recreating the moment in the desert; there had just happened to be an army of ghosts gathered at the time. Nor did she know how they had been able to break Sir Vladamor's magic and turn on him at the *exact* moment when she needed help most.

We need help now.

She had a strong feeling that Diveena held the key, that something in her old mind could guide her in the right direction. And the closer they got to being ready to march, the stronger that feeling grew. Though, if she did have the clear answer, she wasn't giving it up easily.

Diveena was a strict believer in self-discovery, true to form of anyone she'd ever considered a master or respected elder.

Arianna wanted to roll her eyes just thinking of how frustrating she could be. *Just like Talis. Just like Master Tayshin… Mother Adunni, Odessa, Kassime, and even Solomon, too.*

Diveena had deemed Demetrius her official apprentice in the elven ways, but her teachings were not exclusive to him. She offered Jeom insight into his axe-wielding and royal dwarf heritage, and she gave Lessa and Arianna lessons on their elemental powers when they trained with their avatars.

Solza, especially, took to Diveena in kind. They shared a special connection—they were both blessed with the power to revitalize the earth in a way that Arianna couldn't quite comprehend.

It still amazed her when she thought back to first discovering Solza's unique ability to literally breathe life back into the earth; it had been just a small piece of land that she had healed on the outskirts of the desert. And yet, considering this enchanted jungle for what it was now—knowing that Diveena had created this all herself using the *same* type of magic— proved just how far that power could potentially grow.

Diveena was master of many things, as was true for most enchanted beings with such capacity for knowledge, but Arianna revered her most for her skills as a master warrior.

The ancient elf had tested her to new levels, with so many

centuries of practice under her belt.

Arianna had learned more about defending against surprise attacks in real, rugged terrain than ever before. They used the trees as their battlefield, darting back and forth from behind the massive trunks, tripping over the tangled, soft grounds, and clambering up and around the uneven hilly areas.

After a particularly difficult duel one afternoon—Arianna could never even *dream* of beating Diveena—she sat to rest on a thick, aboveground tree root. She needed a moment to herself before she returned to the campsite, to the swarm of guardian apprentices counting on her.

She took out a cloth to wipe the muck from her swords, savoring the calm setting of the jungle—it had been a long time since she had really stopped to appreciate her cherished weapons, for they reminded her of broken memories she'd rather not dwell on now.

She pulled the cloth over the shining, curved steel, wiping it back and forth until they again shone bright and silver, like Solza's claws. And she cleansed the rainbow jewel collection decorating the handles, ones surely mined from the City of Undor; she'd never seen anything like them elsewhere.

There, sparkling clean. Like new.

She put the dirty cloth back in her pocket, then ran her finger across the inscription that appeared on each blade.

"I never could translate it," she mused aloud. "It's been so long since I really looked… I almost forgot there was still a puzzle here, traveling on my back all this time."

"May I see?" asked Diveena.

She had been focused on a large patch of dried grass, steadily turning it from its colorless state to something lush and green; Solza was concentrating with her, following Diveena's every magical move.

Her magic flowed through her body as an extension of her,

just as the earth seemed to be an extension of her; with this observance, Arianna began to understand her own avatar powers a little better.

Solza had given her the gift of elemental magic—magic as old, wise, and strong as the mermaids, elves, dwarves, *and* dragons combined. And when she opened up her mind to let them all pour in, she found that they were all now an extension of her, too, just as she considered the swords in her hands.

"Of course," said Arianna, gently presenting her priceless weapons to the elf.

Diveena hopped up from her position, leaving Solza to practice conjuring her earthly magic on her own.

The way she walked was like a dainty dance, so lithe and subtle with every step, like a loose leaf following the unpredictable path of the wind. It was the same way she had destroyed Arianna in every duel they'd ever had.

She wished for that kind of agility during swordplay, studying Diveena's movements even now to try to better understand the mind behind them. She tried not to be too hard on herself, for who could beat a Nicora elf with all the magic of her tribe embodied in her?

But still… *I absolutely hate to yield.*

Diveena sat down next to Arianna, turning a sword over in her hands.

"May I ask how you received these?" she said, drawing Arianna away from her thoughts of another lost battle.

She could forget sometimes that she was in the presence of an ancient being. Then there were moments where she would catch Diveena in a sort of concentration and could almost see her magical mind bubbling, with powers and knowledge that she couldn't even begin to understand—quite like now.

She looked so serene, lost in her tangled, enchanted thoughts. Her eyes streaked with silver, the earth around her reacting to her very breath.

"Master Bell gifted them to me on the day of my escape from the Four Corners," said Arianna in a low voice, watching closely as Diveena continued to examine her swords.

A faint smile crossed her lips. "*Litra et litra, é deurct et deurct*," she spoke, softly.

She brought two fingers to her lips and then pressed them against one of the blades—a golden spark shimmered through the inscription, as if returning her gesture.

A chill ran up Arianna's spine, and she twisted around to look at Diveena in full view.

"Don't tell me you understand this?"

"Of course I can," said Diveena, casually. "How can you not?"

Arianna pulled her hair from her eyes.

"I've *never* seen this language before, Diveena." She chewed on her lip, eager for more details. "Solomon never told me what it meant…"

Diveena chuckled, her voice blending into the melodic jungle background.

"You may not have seen it written elsewhere," she replied, "but you have certainly heard it enough." She beamed, brightly. "Why, this is my language, child." She happily repeated the phrase.

Arianna was stunned that she could suddenly put a tangible voice behind the inscription. *Litra et litra, é deurct et deurct*, she thought, trying to memorize the intonation of every word.

"These are elven-made, you know?" added Diveena. She sat crossed-legged now, twisting the swords around and around, wind whistling through the blades. "*Not* dwarf."

She balanced one sword on her finger, seemingly testing its weight; Arianna already knew it was light as a feather.

"Most humans thought that only dwarves could make fine weaponry like this," she said, "but it was a false belief we planted many moons ago so that we wouldn't be taken advantage of…" She shrugged. "By your kind."

Arianna gawked at her, thoughts reeling. "I didn't think that—"

"It wasn't often that elves spent time crafting weapons. And even less often would we craft them for a human or being outside of our tribe. Those were rare occasions," she explained. "But when we did, they were always for good reason."

She gazed at the swords with fondness; silver tears began to well in her eyes.

"I would recognize the skill of this craftsman anywhere." She swallowed, her voice dropping to a whisper. "My father made these."

"Your *father?*" stuttered Arianna; she could sense Solza snap to attention. "Are you saying… you mean that Master Lethander, the leader of the Nicora Elven Clan, crafted *my* swords?"

Diveena nodded, lips pressed into a firm line.

"Yes, I am." She traced the words on the steel with her fingertip.

Arianna's mouth formed an 'O' but no sound came out.

Diveena let out a heavy sigh, blinking away her tears.

"I haven't seen a weapon made by his hands since…" She smiled sadly, her body wilting a bit. "Well, it's been quite some time. These were made just before my tribe fell, actually." Arianna clung to every word. "As part of our birthright, elves are gifted a single elven-made weapon, all embedded with our tribe's most protected jewels."

She fingered the colorful gems welded into the hilts, then she narrowed her gaze at Arianna.

"I know I don't have to remind *you* about the kind of power the most precious stones of the earth can contain. And when they're carefully crafted into magic-blessed weapons like these," she shook her head, "you just never know what they're truly made of then…"

Arianna nodded, thinking of Aurora; she'd since shown the other guardian elders its bizarre fire-aided trick.

"Solomon told me, a long time ago, that these swords could teach me many things… if I let them."

She allowed her mind to slip back into the comfort of a world where Solomon had been a friend.

"And have they?" asked Diveena, cocking her head to the side.

Arianna thought about this question for a moment, contemplating his gleaming weapons in the elf's hands.

"I suppose… they have," she replied with sudden realization. "Their lessons have been endless, honestly."

She had killed with those swords, saved lives with them. And she'd learned *all* about her power to control someone's fate with just one swing of a blade—it was a coveted power, indeed, but above all else, it was to be respected.

Arianna had trained for countless hours now with those metal arms, and had put them into real-life practice more times than she'd like to remember; it was in those moments, those tangible seconds, when she'd come to understand that her weapons—and her choices with those weapons—could be the end or the beginning of something… *someone.*

When a life had been taken, blood on her blade with no putting it back, that was when she learned the most.

"Good," said Diveena. "These weren't gifted to your master lightly, and I'm sure he did not give them away lightly either. He must really believe in you."

"Maybe at one time he did," she said, the real truth of him hitting her like a slap in the face.

"You must have trust," said Diveena, firmly, enunciating every word. "Sometimes, even in those who seem least deserving."

Arianna looked at her, questioning; Diveena held her gaze.

"So I've been told…" she replied, raising an eyebrow.

Diveena wasn't going to elaborate.

She glanced back to the swords, frowning.

"These, at least, have earned my trust," said Arianna, thinking of all the ways Solomon had destroyed it. She looked up. "But why didn't you mention this sooner? We've battled many times… you must've known."

Diveena smirked. "Because the time is now," she said, evenly.

Odessa flashed across Arianna's mind. *'Everyone has a choice. No use always harping over the why.'*

Arianna sighed, letting that one go. She had more important questions on her mind.

"Where do you think Solomon found them, then?" she asked. "They couldn't have been given to him by your father. He wasn't even born before Master Lethander was…" Diveena's expression hardened; Arianna cleared her throat. "Could he have stolen them, maybe?"

Just the thought of more treacheries under his belt immediately disgusted her, enraged her.

Diveena suddenly let out a chiming laugh.

"Elven weapons cannot be *stolen*," she said in a gasp, as if it were the most ridiculous statement to have ever been made. She wagged her finger at Arianna. "That's part of their magic, silly girl. Haven't you noticed? Are you not surprised that such priceless treasures are still in your grasp? *You*, who get lost at every turn."

"*She does have a point, Master*," mused Solza, lightly. "*You even lost me, and it's, frankly, very difficult to lose an avatar. We're quite literally connected by the soul.*"

Arianna bristled.

"*Oh, hush up*," she said, shooing Solza away.

Her avatar giggled, entertaining herself with a treasure trove of jungle grub to investigate.

"You mean to say… they're charmed?" asked Arianna—even as she spoke the question, she felt her own magic react with the answer.

Diveena pressed the tips of her fingers together, thinking.

"You could say that, I suppose," she said after a moment. "But it's more like they have a soul all their own." She patted her heart. "They will always find their way back to their rightful master."

She leaned forward with a curious gaze, as if inspecting Arianna for something, her eyes probing.

Arianna pulled back, uncomfortable with her closeness.

"If Solomon had them for any such time," added Diveena, "they were surely gifted to him, willingly. And they chose to stay at his side for a reason." She poked Arianna in the chest. "That goes the same for you, child."

Diveena gestured to the swords still in her lap.

"If *you*, Arianna Belvedor, have been able to hold on to these through all your trials and troubles, then they were surely a gift. And they've agreed to name you their master now."

Arianna gulped, peering down at the weapons, trying to see any hint of life within them.

"*What aren't you the master of… Master?*" said Solza, unconcerned.

Arianna pressed her back against the trunk of the tree. She had never thought about this before, never considered that the swords were still in her possession by more luck than should be possible. But she couldn't deny Diveena's words.

Solomon's swords have always found their way back to me. Aurora, too…

Through countless battles and near-death experiences, even journeys across the desert and sea. And enslavement by the King!

Arianna ran her hand through her hair, trying to wrap her head around all this.

"Who do you think gave them to Master Bell?" she asked, suddenly. "You know, don't you?"

A sly grin grew across Diveena's lips.

"Well, now that you ask... it was I who gave them to young Solomon," she said, holding her head high. "I had gifted Talis Churry a bow—"

"You mean, *Lessa's* bow?" Arianna was glad she was sitting down. "By gods."

Diveena nodded.

Arianna chewed on her lip; she couldn't wait to tell her.

"And these," she handed the swords back to Arianna with care, "were my gift to Solomon. For his loyalty to my friend, to me, and for his faith in the magic that once was. As Talis would agree, I never saw his faith falter."

"I'm sorry to be the bearer of bad news, then," said Arianna, feeling her heart constrict, "but Solomon is not who you remember."

Diveena was already in the know about his betrayals, but Arianna hadn't realized they'd had any kind of relationship before... not like with Talis.

"Do not be sorry," said Diveena with the wave of her hand. "I'm certainly not. How happy I am to know what a wonderful journey these creations have experienced under the guidance of guardians such as yourself and Solomon Bell—"

Arianna opened her mouth to protest, but Diveena held up her palm.

"No matter if he became lost along the way," she said, her voice growing louder, "his story *still* starts as a noble one."

Diveena's gaze flicked to Solza—she was digging, mindlessly, in the earth.

"We all have darkness within us, don't we, Arianna?" she said, softly, still looking at her avatar; Arianna looked, too, wondering what she saw there. "Can we truly blame those who eventually can no longer fight it? Especially with as dark a world and life as the one Solomon was living in, a double one?" Diveena shook her head. "No, I don't blame him at all. I fell beneath the weight of darkness once too."

Arianna was speechless.

She didn't want to acknowledge it, but she suddenly realized that Solomon's predicament must have been quite like Keeper Kassime's to some degree.

Even though his face had remained the same throughout the years, he had been playing the part of the King's wolf *and* a Guardian of Gold since he was even younger than she was now. That he was finally compelled to choose a side—after more than a century of playing both—wasn't that shocking, now that she really cared to think about it.

"It's funny, isn't it…" said Arianna, after a moment. She stared at her swords, admiring their history and their connection to this place around her, to this spectacular being sitting next to her. "How things come full circle like that in the end?"

"They always do," said Diveena with a knowing smile. "That's the Golden Rule."

Again, she spoke the elven phrase inscribed on her swords. The words rolled gently off her tongue, like a familiar song.

"*Litra et litra, é deurct et deurct.*"

Arianna perked up. *Diveena was right!*

She did know what the phrase meant.

"Light is light, and dark is dark…" she breathed. "The Golden Rule."

Diveena returned a nod, looking quite pleased with Arianna for once.

"It's been with you all along," she said.

Solomon's voice filled her head then. *'I chose you because you are worth choosing.'*

Arianna gazed up, fighting away the sadness creeping back into the empty spaces he'd left within her.

But, why, Master Bell…

There she found the sun, bursting through the thick canopy of trees. Its fiery ring burned bright and full overhead.

"The Golden Rule seems to be the answer for a good number of things these days," mumbled Arianna. "But it seems to mean nothing *and* everything all at once."

"*Hmm,*" said Diveena, also looking up. "I suppose it does. Everything has an opposite and an equal. Nothing is created alone, and nothing is meant to exist alone. That's why the King has evoked such chaos here… he's continuously fighting the natural balance of things with his choices. Each one worse than the last." She tilted her head back and forth. "For instance, a necromancer can't exist very long in the world without an animancer cropping up now and then."

Arianna thought her heart had actually skipped a beat. "What did you just say?"

Diveena tucked her long hair behind her ears. "I take it that this isn't the first time you've heard this term?"

Arianna shook her head.

Diveena seemed to consider something a moment, then got to her feet.

"Animancers are rare, in fact," she said, pacing the area. "I haven't seen one since the time of the dragons. The darkness is normally much more persuasive. But, like my father used to say, in the darkest hour, all you need is a touch of fire."

Arianna felt a prickle crawl up her spine as Diveena circled her with her eyes. This was the fourth time in her life that she'd heard the word 'animancer' spoken. Deep down, she knew it was a mystery that could help define something more inside of her.

Odessa had mentioned the word after she had awoken from a dream that was, in fact, no dream at all, and the ghost of Prince Neas had uttered it on another night her astral body had explored the palace. However, the *first* time she had heard this word was from the mouth of Sir Vladamor himself—in the Black Sand Desert—before he had fled for his life.

Life… she thought.

"What does an animancer do, exactly?" asked Arianna, determined to stay rooted to this spot until she knew.

"As before, this you already know," said Diveena, pressing her hand to the trunk of a tree—Arianna wondered if she could feel its heartbeat, its soul speaking back. "If a necromancer controls death, then an animancer—"

"Controls life," answered Arianna, flatly. She stared at her, unblinking. "*That* is the weakness you speak of to destroy Sir Vladamor… an animancer?" She sheathed her swords, standing. "*Me?*"

Diveena nodded, another faint smile on her lips.

"That is your answer," she said, her voice so casual that it made Arianna want to scream. *Me?* "Just as Sir Vladamor has the power over the dead in more ways than one, an animancer's powers are known to manipulate life."

"But in what way?" she said, opening her arms out wide. "How?"

Solza curled around her legs, trying to calm her. "*You're spiraling, Master. Just breathe.*"

Arianna pulled a deep breath in through her nose.

"*How many more surprises are left, Solza? It's maddening!*"

"*They are surely endless, if we've learned anything at all,*" she replied, the deep echo of her voice soothing.

Diveena laughed.

"Settle down," she said. "Things are not always as complicated as they seem, Arianna. Sometimes, all you need is to take a step back to see the bigger picture."

A wall of flowers began to spring up from the ground, growing tall all around Arianna and Solza in a circle; Diveena's eyes were again shining bright as she influenced the earth.

"Remember," she added over the sound of petals peeling

open, "magic has never discriminated. It may have a mind all its own, but it's only as good as the beholder. It can easily be swayed between light and dark."

The nature bloomed in a beautiful crown around her. Then, it began to shrivel up, slowly turning black before her eyes... all by Diveena's hand.

"I don't understand," groaned Arianna, distraught as the flourishing flowers fell to muck at her feet.

She scooped up the dead remnants in her palm, and Solza sniffed at them, warily.

"The power of an animancer and a necromancer are one and the same," said Diveena, finally. "It just depends on how the magic is being used." She patted Solza on the head. "Just think of what your avatar can do. She could just as easily grow a tree as she could destroy it."

"*We use our powers only for good!*" retorted Solza.

Her voice shook, and Arianna felt just as confused and defensive.

"But I'm not—"

"There is only one way for a necromancer's hold to be broken over the souls it has claimed," said Diveena with a serious tone. "And that is by an equal opposite force of powerful magic. When you told me that you were somehow able to break Vladamor's spell that was trapping the ghosts of my family, I knew right away what you were."

Arianna recalled the elven ghosts in the desert who had helped her. They had been so expressive in their gratitude, yet, to this day, she still hadn't a clue of how she'd managed to free them in the first place... all she remembered was that a strange sensation had built up from within at a time when the necromancer held her life in his hands.

"Tell me," said Arianna, focusing her thoughts, "how does one become such a thing as an animancer?"

Maybe if she could understand that, she could better

understand why this was a power belonging to her in the first place.

Diveena sighed, shaking her head.

"You really need everything spelled out for you, don't you? You beguile me constantly, sorceress, truly." She tutted her tongue at her. "Alas, I *do* see why Solomon chose you."

Arianna's eyes widened, but Diveena continued on before she could question her on something new.

"If the powers of a necromancer and animancer are one and the same, just wielded differently, *then*…"

She looked to Arianna, waiting for her to finish, but Arianna needed to hear her say it.

Diveena threw her hands up in frustration.

"Then the transformation *must* be the same as well."

"The *Onasyuda* spell," gasped Arianna, feeling as if all the wind had been knocked out of her.

"Exactly," said Diveena, growing excited. "It is a very dangerous, difficult type of magic. One only ever conducted in a crisis or with malintent. Vladamor's transformation was done with insidious intentions, this we know. He chose the darkness and thus was overcome with something completely dark." She gestured to Arianna. "Now you—"

"Were in a crisis," stammered Arianna.

She thought back to the moment everything had been put into motion.

"It was the first day I met Talis," she said. "Solomon brought him to me after I was wounded in a duel." She let out a frustrated howl. "A *foolish* Warrior's Challenge I could not win. I would've died if not for his help." She perked up, tearing through her memories to try to find the prize. "And again, in the desert! Sir Vladamor forced me to undergo the spell once more… tried to turn me to the dark."

"Well, it seems you did die, both times, in fact," said Diveena, nodding. "And both times, you *chose* the light."

Arianna didn't need her to recap the experiences for her—she remembered Death's clutch well.

"But how do you know any of this?" she asked, her voice pitching. "You weren't there!"

Diveena let out a barking laugh.

"If it's taken you this long to just figure out who *you* are, then you have no hope at ever understanding me, child. Just accept the words I'm offering you."

Arianna couldn't help but crack a smile. "Fair enough," she muttered, crossing her arms at her chest.

Diveena laid a hand on her shoulder, smiling.

"Your powers will manifest in time," she said, gently. "You're young yet. Vladamor has had centuries to practice, knowing what he is. And now that you know, maybe you will grow, too. In any case, the light is there for you, if and when you need it. Astral projection, possession, manifestation—you need cast no spells nor use props for support. The light within will guide you always. It's chosen you just as much as you've chosen it."

"Just like Solomon's swords?" replied Arianna, her words shaky.

"Just like *your* swords," said Diveena.

Arianna straightened her back, returning a firm nod.

Diveena looked toward the falling sun.

"I must return now," she said, spinning on her heels. "Lovely dueling you today. You're getting better. Just think less. Let your heart guide your hand, not your frazzled mind." She chuckled.

Arianna's voice caught in her throat as she watched her go.

Diveena began to walk toward the open field of the campsite, leaving Arianna feeling completely confused. Just before she reached the break of the trees, she turned back around.

"It's interesting, though," she said. "Animancers are yet

rarities, but I'm inclined to say that there has never been, at least in my time nor the time of my ancestors, an animancer *and* avatar master as one and the same." She laughed again, the sun spotlighting her. "You just never know what surprises the world has waiting after each sun that sets."

"I suppose there's a first time for everything," Arianna called back. She knelt down to stroke Solza.

"That there is, young sorceress," said Diveena with a softness. "I hope such… exciting possibilities do not end with you."

Arianna felt her throat run dry.

Diveena disappeared into the meadow, leaving her alone with her thoughts.

"*It's all right,*" said Solza. "*We will not fail.*"

"*I pray so…*" said Arianna.

"*At least, now you know who you are,*" said Solza.

Arianna scoffed.

"*Hardly,*" she said. Their minds shifted to Sir Vladamor. "*But I'll figure it out.*" She and Solza locked eyes. "*I think we're ready for the first phase in our plan.*"

12

CITY OF GUANAMARA

"IT'S NOW OR NEVER," SAID ELI, addressing the table of lead guardians. His words landed like a heavy hammer, decisive. "Once we take the City of Guanamara, everything we have planned will fall into place."

There were murmurs of acknowledgment from around the table.

"Are we ready?" said Eli with confidence, palms pressed hard against the wood—his gaze was steady, touching all the eyes present. "Everyone must agree before we march."

They had rehearsed their action steps innumerable times. Every member of the guardian army, from the elders to the newly appointed, could recite the plan by heart. And each person had just as an important part to play as the next for it to be successful.

When the sun rose, a select group of warriors—led by Eli, Gabriel, Lessa, and Arianna (Noah and Kiki joining the group)—would march through the Impenetrable Forest to the borders of Guanamara, a city scattered among the hilly jungle, though miles away yet. And just as Lessa and Eli had done so many times before, they would convince the citizens there to join their pursuit against the King, bolstering their numbers even more ahead of the looming battle for the throne.

It was fitting that Guanamara would be the catalyst to the face-off with King Devlindor, for it was the largest province in close proximity to the City of Saindora. They had all come to an agreement not to delay the inevitable further by attempting to take any other regions after that—from the North to the South, all the major cities were accounted for.

And once they hit Guanamara, the King would be able to sniff them out, quickly.

It will have to be enough, thought Arianna, listening intently as the elders confirmed their consent, one by one.

Diveena planned to accompany them only to the border of the jungle; she had agreed to keep watch from the trees and report back to the campsite on the outcome of the siege.

While her powers would prove a valuable asset to any fight, it was too risky to expose her before this war had barely begun. They didn't want her to become a target after she'd been so careful to stay hidden and alive—she was, after all, the last of her kind.

What's more, if any trouble stirred, she had made it *very* clear that her first priority was to protect the Treehouse and reinforce the defenses around her lands; Time would decide whether or not she would interfere when it came to actual battle.

Jeom, Demetrius, and Margery would also remain a safe distance from Guanamara. Despite the boys' insistence that they should join the girls, the guardians needed their strength at their home base for an equally important responsibility— they were tasked with holding down the campsite and fortifying the handful of ships docked on the shores for the voyage they'd been built for. Once Diveena confirmed that Guanamara was in the control of the guardians, they would need to swiftly prepare the rest of the army for the next phase of their plan… the true beginning of the war.

With Guanamara secured, the Treehouse guardians would send word to the City of Zambienth to organize the rest of their warriors and fleet; they'd finally be ready to set sail and meet on the waters.

On this journey, before they reached Saindora, Arianna was determined to master her gifts as an animancer. And once *all* the guardians were reunited on the waters at the point they had mapped out, she would lead her newfound army across the Sea of Saindora to again set foot in the High City—this time with the intention of taking over.

"Arianna," said Eli, drawing her attention; everyone else had already stated their agreement. "What say you?"

All eyes turned to her.

"Down with the King," she said, resolutely, her sword raised high.

ARIANNA'S SMALL GROUP WAITED in the safety of the trees, hidden among the lime green bushes and tangled vines. It had been hours of watching and waiting for the sun to set to allow them proper cover.

Thanks to Diveena, the element of surprise was truly on their side; no one but guardians knew the whereabouts of the Treehouse group.

They'll never see us coming, she reminded herself, trying to quell her nerves.

Eli and Lessa had also noted that this city was somewhat smaller than others they'd conquered before…

"It should be fairly easy to gain with magic on our side," Lessa whispered, her sureness palpable. She tickled Sano under the chin; he was perched on her shoulder in his monkey form.

Arianna nodded, hoping that Lessa was proved right and wishing she felt just as confident.

"*Try not to worry so much,*" said Solza—she sat on her haunches, patiently waiting by Arianna's side. "*Lessa and Eli have done this before. I've seen them in action. Everything will go smoothly.*"

Guanamara was a place overrun with nature, claimed by the trees. The charms of the Impenetrable Forest seeped in through the cracks in the cobblestone and decorated the sides of sophisticated structures sprinkled far throughout the hills.

The city center had been built upon flat ground and was what they spied on now—they observed citizens going about their business, like any normal day.

Like there weren't wars breaking out all across the Olleb.

From this point of view, it seemed that Guanamara stretched out thinner and thinner, until the jungle took it back over, somewhere in the hilltops where their eyes couldn't reach.

Arianna noted that there weren't as many city regulators roaming around as they'd anticipated…

"Likely spread out across this vast territory, just like the city," said Eli. He smiled.

Arianna relaxed a little.

"I'm sure you're right," she replied, feeling her confidence grow.

The less regulators united, the less resistance we'll meet.

"*This will be over quickly,*" said Solza, affirming her thoughts.

They had calculated a much bigger defense than

Guanamara actually appeared to have. And even if there *were* others distributed among the hills, the guardians would be able to pick them off more easily in small numbers—their first attack would be on the city center and the palace.

"After that, everything should be a breeze," said Noah.

He and Kiki bumped fists.

"If the wretched sun would just set," she whined.

Gabriel glanced back at the nervous young warriors gathered with them. He brought a finger to his lips.

"*Shhh.* And don't let your guard down."

Arianna took his words to heart as they all settled back into silence, waiting for the dark to come.

Never forget.

Another hour passed, and with it, her excitement and impatience doubled—Arianna didn't spot a single Shadow Resistance member hidden among the city regulators here. They appeared to be mere men and women, with no knowledge of the sorcery that was bubbling up across the land.

Word of Arianna and her armies, apparently, hadn't snaked its way through the jungle just yet.

We'll have the magical upper hand, just as Lessa and Eli experienced in their first journeys outside of the Jar!

She glanced down to Solza, thinking of how strong they were together, especially in the face of magicless citizens.

All of her optimism pooled at the surface.

Everything we prepared for is really about to happen.

Eli lifted his finger to point out someone roaming through the bustling crowds, citizens cowering in his presence.

"City Keeper," he mouthed.

They all watched him, their number one mark.

Arianna had to stifle a laugh—this frail, blond-haired man with sharp, bird-like features hardly seemed a threat.

But if he had been put in a position of power, he was, certainly, just as cruel as his master. She steadied her eyes on him, reciting the first step in the strategy to take over Guanamara.

"*Remove the fear-inducing leader who kisses the heels of the King,*" she said in her head.

"*Then his followers will be more open to exploring another path,*" added Solza.

Arianna nodded. "*We have to show them that they have another choice.*"

The sky darkened, and her heart drummed faster in her chest. She wanted to leap through the trees and reveal the new and golden path awaiting these people, if only they knew the truth.

She felt as if she'd waited *so* long for this moment—years, months, days, hours—yet now it seemed as if everything was racing toward the end, no chance of keeping up with the tick of the clock. Now that the time for action was here, it felt as if the days had flown by with not even a moment for her to catch her breath.

Another hour passed, the city keeper gone, presumably back in his palace.

The sun fell, suddenly all at once, behind the hills, the golden embers waylaid by giant clouds that casted shadows across the entire town.

Arianna felt Eli's hand wrap around her wrist.

"Almost time," he said, keeping his voice low.

She was itching to make herself known, to remove the hood from her face and show the people here that there was freedom beyond the King's rule; if Eli's hand hadn't been steadying her now, she might've already blown their cover.

Her skin prickled with magic, and she felt resilient with Solza lending her powers.

But were those standing with her now just as ready?

She looked around the group, everyone swathed in cloaks of the deepest black to blend in with the real regulators—except, instead of golden snakes threaded at their backs, they boasted dragons.

People could die on this very night, Arianna thought. *My people…*

This was the only consideration that made her not want to rush the future.

It was an inevitable consequence every new guardian had acknowledged as worth the risk in the name of freedom from the King. And in trainings at the campsite, the variances of skill proved the same as in the Jar—some people were just more naturally skilled than others.

Arianna and her friends, the first of the Four Corners to steal back their freedom, had been lucky in that their respective district placements couldn't have been more accurate from day one. Fate had spoken, and it had been true and kind to their hearts' greatest aptitudes.

Alas, the same couldn't be said for everyone…

Arianna had witnessed some deemed as agrarians, creators, or healers display stronger skills in dueling than some who had been named warriors in the Jar; while each person boasted unique strength, it quickly became apparent that King Devlindor's selection process in the Opalls had been imperfect.

Most who had found themselves in the guardian army had displayed a desire to be part of the fight to come. However, eventually, the elder guardians had had to draw the line—not long after Arianna's arrival, they came to an agreement that each person should be evaluated for their skill as a warrior.

Those who could not hold their own against the more experienced fighters with a weapon had to prove their skill in battle magic, or that they could conjure any magic at all. If their control sufficed, they would be permitted to join the frontlines.

If not, they were strongly advised to help out the cause in other important ways—creating weapons, farming the land for food, and developing their skills as healers.

Many had been dissuaded from the ultimate battle for their own good, but there were a number of young people who had refused to take their advice, too proud to stand by and watch from the sidelines. They had made their choice.

Arianna looked around and saw them now, the ones who she knew might not make it back to the Treehouse if anything went wrong—they had all been raised in the Warrior's District.

She fully understood and respected their want to sacrifice. She would have never stayed behind either.

She brought her fist to her heart. *May we all survive.*

As dusk finally settled over the City of Guanamara and the streets began to clear, Gabriel formed a huddle with the group.

"Night has fallen," he said, uttering the words that would launch them into action. "Are we all set?"

"Definitely," said Noah, his expression eager. He twisted his fingers around the staff of an axe.

"More than ready," said Lessa.

She patted the silver and blue bow at her back, then she patted her belly.

"Are you sure you can do this?" asked Arianna to Lessa. "It's not too late to turn back, you know?"

Her stomach had grown so big now that her arm could easily rest on it when she had her bow and arrow strung.

"Don't you start on again!" she barked.

Lessa could hardly see her feet, but she was determined to keep up every step of the way.

"All right, all right," said Arianna, jumping back in mock caution. "Sorry I said anything."

Gabriel let out a low laugh. "I'll keep an eye on her."

"No, I'll keep an eye on *you*," retorted Lessa, pointing at him. Her irises flared silver.

"Whoa…" said Noah, holding up his hands for calm. "We'll *all* keep an eye on each other." He grinned.

Lessa rolled her eyes at him.

The little life growing inside of her certainly hadn't slowed her down yet, and it was her choice to make—as much as this was Arianna's fight, it was Lessa's too.

Still, she couldn't help but worry for her friend who now had the most innocent of lives to protect...

Wherever Lessa went, so did baby Snow. And right now, they were marching straight into danger.

Her expression must've revealed her doubts, for Eli gave Arianna a gentle hug around the waist, whispering in her ear.

"Just breathe," he said. "We're all going to be fine."

He didn't even know how much those words meant to her. It was the resounding hum of her subconscious sparking to life with lyrics of calm every time she felt scared. *Just breathe.*

She pressed her forehead to his. Then she pulled away, drawing her swords.

Eli slid his blade from the sheath at his hip and turned to address the group of fifty volunteers huddled around them.

"This is it," he said, rolling up his sleeves so that the tattoos on his arms were made visible. "Our future begins here. You know your roles now. Just stay safe and remember the goal at hand. Once this city is secured, we'll all meet at the base of the palace."

No one needed to speak—they held up their palms, the golden dragons a show of solidarity beneath the cover of the trees.

They readied their weapons.

"Let's go!" said Gabriel, guiding a large group straight into the city center; he would lead the charge to wrangle the bulk of the regulators patrolling the streets.

Kiki was part of Gabriel's entourage, too, so Noah gave her a strong hug goodbye.

"Give 'em your worst," he said.

She flexed her muscles. "Don't I always?" He returned a

dazed smile. "See you on the other side!"

She blew him a kiss, and he pretended to catch it in his palm. Then she skipped off behind Gabriel, swinging her flail alongside her.

"Is this what love is?" Noah asked, floating back toward Eli.

"Hmm… it just might be," he replied, his gaze flicking toward Arianna.

She turned away, pretending to fiddle with her swords so he couldn't see her face turn bright red. *I'm certainly in love,* she thought, *but, by gods, I would never say it out loud!*

"*Focus!*" growled Solza.

Arianna jumped at the intrusion.

"*I know. I am…*" She gripped the handles of her swords tight, thinking of the future—with Eli, with Lessa, with baby Snow. "*I'm focused.*"

Down with the King!

Arianna and the remaining guardians watched Gabriel and the others pour out of the jungle, moving stealthily as one through the city center. They disappeared up the main path, as planned.

"Our turn now," said Lessa, taking a deep breath; Sano was still on her shoulders, his orange eyes like bulbs of fire in the night. She looked to Arianna. "Be safe, all right?"

"*You* be safe," she said, sternly, reaching for her hand; her gaze settled on her stomach.

"Don't worry about us," said Lessa with a wink. "We'll be just fine. Besides, Sano has my back. Don't you, boy?"

Sano nuzzled her neck, affectionately.

"I know you will," said Arianna with a firm nod; she and Sano together were a force to be reckoned with. "See you soon."

Lessa smiled. Then she made her way out of the trees, another group of eager guardians following at her heels.

Lessa's role was to head through the central part of the city to warn citizens that a strike against the King was coming. Just as she had first done with Noah and Eli in the Warrior's District, she would visit homes, one by one, revealing proof of magic and trying to persuade the vast majority to their side.

As evidenced in the takeover of the Four Corners and other major cities, many times people stood down out of sheer fear in the face of the unknown—an enchanted demonstration proved a much more powerful statement than metal force.

Those who refused to believe were left behind, alive—as long as they did not stand in their way.

After almost everyone had gone from the hideout, the dark streets of Guanamara swallowing their friends whole, only Eli, Arianna, and Noah remained—their duty was to quietly take care of the city keeper and secure the palace.

Arianna imagined every step of the way.

In a few hours, their small army would assemble outside of the palace gates, along with any new additions from Guanamara. By the time the palace regulators realized something was amiss, the battle would be won.

"Let's not waste time," said Noah, marching ahead.

Eli grabbed him by the hood, yanking him back.

"Stay behind me," he commanded.

Begrudgingly, Noah let him pass—originally, incapacitating the city keeper was supposed to be a two-person job, but Noah had insisted on sticking with her during this mission.

She didn't have the heart to refuse him.

They stepped out of the jungle into the quiet streets, the thick night enveloping them like a blanket. They kept to the outskirts of the city, following a long, windy path down to the palace, just as Diveena had mapped out for them.

"Can we pick up the pace, at least, *Sir* Eli?" said Noah after a while. Arianna snorted. "I can't let Kiki have all the fun. We have a bet going."

"What bet?" asked Arianna, slowing in step with him.

Eli walked ahead, Solza by his side, eyes darting over every angle of the sleeping city; they had yet to see a soul.

"Who can take out the most regulators," he replied, swinging his axe back and forth. "I have to win. Kiki *always* beats me. This time, though, I have the upper hand since we're on palace duty. Lots of regulators for the taking!"

"*Noah…*" chided Arianna. "We agreed to try and not leave a trail of bodies behind us this time."

Eli laughed from up ahead.

"Gods, I forgot about that silly bet," he said. "Yeah, please don't get axe-happy on us again." He slowed to their pace, a smirk on his lips. "But what's on the table?"

Arianna punched him on the shoulder, and the boys both snickered, trying not to make too much noise.

"How did I get stuck with you two?" she said with a scoff. "Can we please just—"

The palace loomed ahead of them, a mammoth fortress sprawled out between the trees; they all grew silent, the weight of their responsibility settling back with them, heavy and real.

"Let's go," said Arianna, turning serious.

She led the way forward.

The Palace of Guanamara was a grandiose structure. It reminded her so much of the Luose palace charms, trees crawling up all around it like an impenetrable barrier. But unlike her former highlife home, this was nestled right at the base of a steep hill.

It appeared to be just one story, stretching out flat across the earth from one side of the hill to the next. Ponds and gardens surrounded it at every angle.

When they reached the bottom of the hill, they were forced to make themselves visible in the streets—there appeared to be only one way into this palace.

A wide river cut it off from the rest of the city, no gate

needed. A sturdy stone bridge waited to greet them.

It stood empty, welcoming, the passageway to the future.

With Arianna in the lead, they crossed the bridge, stopping right before the palace. Like a hillside inching along the river, layers of warm, earthy tones, red and brown, stretched out before them. And dark windows glared down from every angle, daring them to get closer.

"Let's get out of the open," said Arianna, hurriedly. "Come on, Solza."

They surveyed the palace, pinning themselves against the walls.

"I don't see any regulators at the front," said Eli, glancing back, "but I don't think we should go in that way. We'll lose the element of surprise."

Arianna agreed.

"There's a door over here," said Noah, jiggling a lock some way down. "Locked."

Arianna rushed to his side. "Here, let me."

She sheathed one of her swords so that she could free up a hand. She rested her palm on the door handle.

It had been a long time since she'd needed to use this particular spell, the first she and Lessa had ever learned together. But as the words left her lips, Arianna couldn't help but feel even more empowered—it was a strong reminder of just how far she'd come.

"*Operium undrio!*"

There was no hesitation. The lock clicked open.

They slipped inside, finding their presence joined by a palace regulator; he looked very shocked to see them.

Arianna could tell that he was trying to figure out whether or not they were also regulators; she credited Margery for thinking of such a distracting disguise.

He reached for his sword in the next second.

Eli was faster.

He pinned him to the wall, pressing his hand over his mouth before he could scream and wake up the entire palace.

"Let him go," said Arianna. "He won't be saying anything."

Eli shoved him to the floor, and Noah kicked his weapon a safe distance away.

Arianna stood over the regulator, pointing the tip of her sword at his neck; Solza was snarling above him.

He drew in a breath. "Wait—"

Cementas cuerpal, she thought.

He went rigid, everything but his eyes freezing.

"That should hold until we're gone from here," she said, savoring the magic buzzing through her veins.

She sheathed her other sword, hoping she wouldn't need to use it tonight; it felt strange to be on the other side of things, to be the one in control, after what she'd experienced in Saindora...

"Ara, *please,*" said Noah, glancing down at the regulator. "Kiki will never let me live it down if I don't get any blood on my blade. Did you have to—"

"You should never wish for blood!" said Arianna, glaring back at him. "In this world, some wishes can be granted."

Noah bowed his head.

"No, you're right," he mumbled. "Sorry... I'll take this more seriously."

She returned a curt nod, stepping over the regulator.

"So far, so good," said Eli from down the hall. "There was just one guard here. Let's get to the keeper now. Can't risk him sneaking away if we're discovered too early."

They followed in his footsteps, headed toward the keeper's wing of the palace as stealthily as possible.

It proved easy; they quickly and quietly immobilized one regulator after the next.

In fact, it was *so* easy that Arianna felt like she could have time to explore the halls of this robust palace.

She wouldn't stray from their plan, though she did let her eyes wander…

The palace was airy and dark, the same earthy tones from the outside making their way in. Grand windows gave birth to a breathtaking view of the jungle, and from here, it didn't appear that they stood within a major city at all.

Crackling fires burned in large pits in every room they peeked into, and lush rugs with deep colors lined the cold stone floors. Vast portraits, chockful of the wild creatures that lurked just outside, decorated the walls so that one could never forget they were in the heart of a jungle; they were colorful, vibrant, reminding Arianna of Solomon.

Noah stopped to gawk at the stuffed heads and clean skulls of large beasts pinned to the walls. A fur rug was also sprawled out in front of a hearth, fashioned from what had once been a bear.

Arianna thought of the dragon rider tapestry in Moriamo, of the first avatar that had taken shape as such an animal; she glanced to Solza, disgusted by this garish display of some of Olleb-Yelfra's most beautiful creatures.

She was certain this entire chamber was a nod to the King's rule that animals were permitted as anything other than pets, one she now understood to be a scheme to stop the creation of new avatar masters—thankfully, much like his efforts in trying to suffocate magic, that plan hadn't worked either.

"*I don't like this, Master,*" stuttered Solza, pausing in front of the rug. "*Why would someone do this?*"

"*Don't look at it,*" said Arianna, urging her along. "*It's just a reflection of this cruel world the King built, but tonight that changes.*"

They continued to roam the palace, and Arianna began to feel too comfortable in the lonely halls, too safe.

"Has it normally been this quiet when you've done this

before?" she asked—they opened door after door, finding all the rooms empty. "We only passed a handful of regulators so far." She thought of her time in South Luose. "It seems odd…"

"It *is* odd," agreed Noah. "In the other cities we've taken, there have definitely been more people holed up in the palaces."

The edge in his voice made Arianna grow nervous; Eli didn't respond, and she grew more nervous still.

"Maybe they're just sleeping, in a different wing somewhere," she said, not sounding too certain. "This place is massive."

"From what I can gather, we're nearing the keeper's chambers," said Eli. He looked around. "And speaking from experience, there *should* be more security, especially down here."

Noah pushed open another door, slowly, then threw it wide. He whispered the word for fire so that a little flame grew in his palm, casting a soft glow in the chamber.

Arianna smiled with approval. *He's been practicing.*

"If they're sleeping," said Noah, "then why are all the beds empty?"

Arianna peeked in behind him, determining in just one glance that this was a highlife's quarters.

"Something's not right here." Eli had stopped in his tracks, his words echoing her own thoughts.

Arianna turned toward him, her skin prickling in fear. "What do you—"

Without warning, he raced ahead to the end of the hall, throwing all caution to the wind.

"I was right. This is the city keeper's quarters!" he called back.

He kicked the door open, brandishing his weapon. Then he looked at her and Noah over his shoulder, a shadow crossing his face; he lowered his sword.

Noah paused. "Empty?"

"Empty," replied Eli, his voice stifled by the stillness in the air.

"No…" said Arianna—this wasn't how she'd imagined this going. This wasn't part of the plan. "But it doesn't make sense. How can all the highlife quarters be empty? We saw them in the streets only a few hours ago. They *must* be here somewhere. Could there be some kind of gathering tonight?"

"A formal gathering with the attendants *and* the cooks? All the people of the palace?" said Noah, scratching his head. "I don't think so, and I haven't seen nor heard any palace staff since we stepped foot here, come to think of it… aside from the few guards we took care of."

"Attendants and such are normally up long past sundown," said Eli, walking back toward them and seeming just as confused. "They've proven the easiest to sway to our side in the other cities. But I don't—"

Arianna turned to face them both, hands shaking, stomach in knots.

"It's an ambush," she uttered. "They know."

"What?" said Eli. "What do you mean?"

"They know! They must've been tipped off somehow," she shouted, pacing back and forth. Months of preparation unraveled before her eyes, too quickly for her scattered thoughts to catch up. "If I'm right, then—"

Lessa and Gabriel flashed in her mind.

"Gods, we have to go, now!"

She spun on her heels and ran back through the halls, no time to explain her conclusion, no time to think.

"*I'm right behind you*," said Solza, mirroring her dread; Noah and Eli kept pace behind her.

One of the most useful things Solomon had impressed upon Arianna in the districts was to go with her gut on the battlefield. *'If something feels off, run.'*

Her intuition had never steered her wrong before, and right now, it was urging her to go faster. She barreled down the main hall toward the front doors, not caring about the noise she made—there was nobody to wake.

The closer they got to the entryway of the palace, the heavier her worries weighed in her chest. And when they arrived at the doors, she felt nothing but terror.

"I'm sure there's some kind of explanation that doesn't mean…" Noah cleared his throat, hope thick in his voice as they all stared ahead. "I'm sure it will all be all right," he said.

"No," said Arianna, growing cold, "it won't be."

"Prepare for a fight," said Eli. He readied his weapon, sharing in her concern. "Someone's, unfortunately, caught up to us this time."

Arianna laid her hands atop the door handles and pulled.

GHOSTS IN THE NIGHT

THE DOORS SWUNG OPEN, fresh air pouring into the hall. Like a veil being lifted, the palace revealed them to the outside world.

Arianna wanted nothing more than to slam the doors shut and pretend this future didn't exist.

She had been wrong before, to think that she'd known who would or wouldn't be able to hold up in a fight—for, as she looked out into the night, staring from the foot of the doorway out toward the bridge, she found them all dead.

A silent scream rose up from her chest. She reached out her hand to steady herself against the doorframe; Solza had stilled in place, and Noah and Eli were petrified alongside them.

It appeared as if almost every single one of the fifty volunteers for this mission were scattered across the palace grounds. *All dead…*

She squeezed her eyes shut, trying to erase this reality, wishing to go back in time and figure out where they'd gone wrong. What choice had they made in the past that would've led to such a future as this? In all their planning, how had they not foreseen whatever plagued them now?

This cannot be.

She called out for Odessa, for her to turn back the clock and lead them down a different path. She called out to the gods and goddesses of the Olleb, the ones who were supposed to be watching over them from above, protecting them.

This cannot be, please!

When she found the strength to open her eyes, her heart shriveled in the face of the glaring truth—they were gone.

"Maybe… maybe some are still alive?" said Noah, his voice barely a whisper, his body trembling.

Their friends stared back at them with wide eyes, cold and empty.

"Maybe," said Eli, his words quivering. "We should check, just in case."

He took a step past the doorway, but Arianna put her hand out to stop him.

"Don't," she said, gravely. "They're gone."

"But how do you know?" stammered Noah. "Some might still—"

She shook her head, decisively, her gaze set beyond the steps where the line of bodies started—the souls of those who had fallen *were* still among them, though now in ghostly forms, lingering near their bodies.

What's more, Arianna was sure this spill of life went on and on, farther than they could see from this vantage point.

"How do you know?" said Noah again. He slammed the butt of his axe to the ground, demanding an answer.

She turned to him, a solemn sigh loosening from her lips. She squeezed his shoulder, forcing him to focus on her instead of the sprawling massacre.

"They remain here with us… but only in spirit, Noah." She spoke in clipped breaths, trying to keep from crying out herself. "They're not coming back to us in this lifetime."

She turned back around, observing the ghosts of her warriors, her followers. Their shimmering forms were the only light shining against the swathing darkness of this night.

"You can see them?" he asked, bewildered, face stricken with tears.

She nodded. "I can."

His mouth dropped open. He looked around, expectantly. "But I—"

Eli reached for his hand, gently tugging him to his side.

"Let her do her thing," he said. He gave Arianna a reassuring nod.

Arianna stepped forward, all ghostly eyes on her.

"My friends, what's happened to you here?" She spoke in an unsteady voice, feeling as if her knees might give way beneath her. "And why do you linger?"

They needed answers quickly if they had any chance of surviving this sinister evening.

"We can't move on," replied the frightened ghost of a young former creator-slave; she had been so capable with both weapon and magic… and yet, she had still died. "We're stuck, Arianna."

Moans and howls of sadness echoed through the night, confirming her statement.

"Something's keeping them tethered here," Arianna told Noah and Eli. "Their souls… cannot move on."

An ice-cold prickle skittered up her spine as the words passed her lips.

"This doesn't make any sense," said Eli, squeezing his eyes shut a moment. A tear slid down his cheek; he still held tight to Noah's hand. "Can you find out what happened, at least?"

His voice pitched with desperation.

These were his warriors, too.

Arianna knew he must feel just as responsible for their fates as she did—the guilt weighed heavy.

"Who could've done this, and *so* quickly?" he said. "We couldn't have been separated for more than an hour."

Arianna looked to the yawning moon, shoulders sagging.

"Not who… *what*," she replied in a defeated tone. "I don't have to ask." She unsheathed both of her swords—they'd see blood tonight after all. "There's only one who can violate the rules of death in such a way."

She glanced back to Noah and Eli; fear had knitted them together.

"Sir Vladamor has found us." She tightened her grip on her blades. "Keep your eyes peeled and stay behind me."

Solza nudged her gently from behind. "*Oh, Master, I'm so sorry*—"

"*Stay behind me*," she repeated, sternly.

No one had the energy to object, moving close together.

Arianna began to walk forward, her swords hunting for a necromancer.

THEY RETRACED THEIR STEPS toward the city center, following the trail of bodies like a map. More ethereal eyes met Arianna's every step of the way—the palace grew smaller behind them, and the line of bodies grew denser.

The ghosts of their friends watched them silently… in sorrow, with knowing. Riddled with confusion, anger, and pain; she felt all of the same emotions. But she felt them in her physical body… in her heart that was still *beating*.

Never forget.

This moment would haunt her forever.

"I'm sorry I couldn't help you," she said, meeting the gleaming stares of everyone she passed. "I'm so sorry."

Her words melted into an echo, like the haunting whisper of the wind—but she could do nothing for them now, and they asked nothing from her.

The city seemed utterly quiet, as if it were holding vigil in the face of so many suddenly departed beneath its watch.

Lessa. Where's Lessa?

Her heart slowed in her chest as she stepped over body after body, searching for her face and praying not to find it. So far, she counted a death toll in the high thirties, young men and women from every district. Many of whom she had trained with, broke bread with, shared hope with…

"Everyone's dead," whimpered Noah, checking all the bodies they passed; his hope was diminishing by the minute. "All of them, gone—"

His words were replaced by a heart-wrenching cry, his voice bellowing out into the night.

Arianna and Eli whipped around, swords raised.

"Oh, no…" said Eli, lowering his weapon. "Not Kiki."

They both stiffened, both trying to remain strong.

They couldn't crumble like poor Noah. They couldn't let their guards down yet.

Just survive.

Arianna gave Eli a single nod, and he understood her unspoken words; he knelt down, forcibly setting Noah back on his feet.

"We have to keep going," he said, taking him by both shoulders. "There will be time for this later. I'm sorry, but pull it together."

Noah sucked back his tears, flashing one last glance at his lost love.

"I'm coming back for you," he said with courage, leaning all his weight on his axe; Eli patted him on the back.

Arianna swallowed, staring straight into Kiki's shimmering face; the ghost of this young, fearless warrior offered her a faint smile of encouragement, a gesture that said keep going.

Arianna returned it, focusing on her breath. On the silent prayers in her head. *Lessa... please, please, please.*

"*Everything will be all right, Master,*" said Solza. They walked side by side. "*We'll get to the bottom of this.*"

Arianna couldn't bring herself to respond; however, she knew that Solza would sense her hopelessness.

When they came to the top of the hill, the city and jungle unraveled before them to unveil the flat city center. They stopped dead in their tracks, as if they'd hit a wall.

Instead of a faction of their army waiting to greet them, as they'd planned for so long, it was the King's—and at the head of his army was Sir Vladamor himself, cloaked in the full costume of the King's Guard.

Arianna saw him sitting there, atop his horse, and recoiled. It felt like experiencing a horrible déjà vu, though she knew this was no such thing...

For the second time in her life, she prepared to face the necromancer and his army, and with only a handful of friends by her side. Fortunately, there were no skeletons flanking him now, no broken bones and fallen swords spellbound from their graves to add to the impending fight.

But Arianna wasn't sure if she should be relieved just yet, for, instead of the dead, he had surrounded himself with warriors of the flesh—Guanamara city regulators, the keeper included, were fanned out behind him like a shield.

Sir Vladamor snapped his fingers.

Torches lit up throughout his army, illuminating their numbers and casting an eerie glow about the streets.

Noah gasped from behind. "There's too many..."

The necromancer locked eyes with the city keeper; the flaxen-haired man stepped forth from the crowd, dragging someone by the neck.

The earth gently rumbled beneath their feet, Solza seething.

"Lessa…" Arianna's voice barely came out. Her entire body seemed to have gone numb.

She watched in horror as the scrawny man handed Lessa over to Sir Vladamor.

He slithered down from his decorated horse and grabbed her by the wrist with a golden-gloved hand, his bony fingers burrowing deep into her skin.

"Ara!" Lessa cried, struggling against his grasp—her bow and arrows were scattered amid the bodies of those closest to his army. "Get out of here." She looked around in a panic, as if registering the staggering death toll for the first time. "He killed them… He killed them all."

Arianna followed Lessa's horrified gaze as her eyes settled upon the body closest to her. Another dear friend, gone.

There, at the necromancer's feet, lay Guardian Gabriel, frozen in time as he reached for his sword. His ghost was just as still, stunned by his own death…

Lessa screamed out again, and Arianna finally felt the true weight of their losses—she couldn't move a muscle.

Time stilled around her. She was frozen, too.

She felt someone move behind her, a steady hand at her back.

"Breathe," Eli said, forcibly, his voice nearly lost to the thoughts drowning her mind; she was sifting through memories, trying to determine how… *Why?*

He inhaled through the nose, and exhaled through the nose, urging her to do the same.

Arianna let her eyes float closed, then she pulled in a deep, centering breath, unclenching her muscles.

He cannot have her, too.

Her eyes flew open, and she squeezed the hilts of her swords so forcibly that she thought they might snap right off. Her magic tingled beneath her skin as she prepared to give the necromancer a *true* fight this time around.

We will not surrender!

"*Ahhh*, and there you truly are," said Vladamor, surely seeing the silver flood Arianna's glare. "What a delightful surprise, indeed." He tightened his grip around Lessa until she stopped wriggling. "I traveled here to find the ones they call the Kane brothers, and instead I'm greeted with the King's most wanted prize… *and* the second runner-up. Two avatar masters for the price of one."

He laughed, then he pressed the golden nose of his mask against Lessa's neck and sniffed, drinking her all in.

Arianna could see the tug on her soul as he did—if he wanted to, he could suck it right out of her until her best friend was no more, fated to death like the rest of the guardians here.

Lessa whimpered, shriveling away from him; she grew paler by the second.

"*Yes*," he said with a hiss, "quite the treat."

"Let her go," growled Arianna, inching forward.

Her strongest battle magic sparked from her hands all the way down to the tips of her blades; they vibrated within her palms, itching to strike.

"No, I don't think I will," said Vladamor with a derisive snort. "You're not really in a position to bargain with me this time."

"How did you even find us?" said Eli, finding his voice.

He walked forward, too, not letting Arianna leave him behind.

Sir Vladamor cocked his head to the side, considering him a moment, probably trying to figure out who this brave new addition was to Arianna's team.

"I've been hunting the slave brothers ever since you all escaped the Shadow Resistance in Zambienth," he replied. "The King desires the Axe of Crissy, among *other* things."

Arianna shuddered, knowing he meant her.

"Since I wasn't able to obtain it in the takeover of the Greenhouse, I followed its scent across the sea, only to lose it some months ago." He appeared cross at the memory. "I couldn't very well go back empty-handed, you see."

He tutted his tongue against his teeth, shaking his head.

"No, the King would *not* be happy with me then." He opened up his arms, seeming to gaze around in pride. "However, to my great surprise, the scent found me again… somewhere in the Impenetrable Forest the axe's magic was being used."

His voice grew sharper, darker. He squeezed Lessa tighter.

"So it seems, in fact, that Fate is on *our* side, Twenty-Two."

Arianna gritted her teeth.

Eli leaned in to whisper something in her ear.

"It had to be when we journeyed outside of Diveena's protective barriers," he explained in a rush. "He must've been able to track our use of magic when we went searching for help." He looked to his feet. "I never thought—"

Arianna turned away from him.

"Not your fault," she said, curtly. "There's no changing the past, and now isn't the time to dwell on it."

He nodded, moving back.

Her gaze lingered on the departed warriors scattered around them—she couldn't help but contemplate how much that little excursion to the Starr Caverns had cost them tonight… and maybe even the entire war on freedom.

I hope it was worth it, she thought.

Sir Vladamor continued gloating.

"Since your friends were able to disappear so successfully,

I assumed they were being aided by strong magic…"

He paused, seemingly hoping for elaboration.

Arianna didn't offer it.

"*Well*—" his voice slurred, and she could just make out the smooth accents of the Nicora Elven Clan, similar to Diveena's "—there was no good way to ensure the upper hand in such a vastly dense jungle, nothing around for miles." He tossed a dismissive glance to the trees. "So I waited in the nearest city for them to come."

He gestured to the shadowed streets of Guanamara.

"I reasoned that they must've been lost and would eventually find their way here, *if* they had any luck at all." He kicked at Gabriel's body; Gabriel's ghost winced. "Turns out the luck was all mine! This is a much better outcome than I could have ever anticipated, and I'm sure that the King will agree… the Kane brothers can wait." Arianna could practically hear the wicked smile in his voice. "You guardians, like rats to a trap."

"We spotted you lot coming from a mile away," added the city keeper with a sneer—his voice sounded just as feeble as he looked.

"Stop it!" cried Lessa. Her eyes streaked with silver, and she ripped out of the necromancer's grasp. She threw herself over Gabriel's body, trying to protect him. "Stop it. Just leave him alone."

Sir Vladamor mocked her, his horse pawing the ground near her head.

"Silly little dragons," he spat down at her. "You think the King isn't aware of what the guardians are doing? You impudent children!" His golden mask glared sharply underneath the light of the torches. Black eyes—like the Pit in the Warrior's District—dark and deadly, stared out at them. "How do you think King Devlindor won the Golden Wars to begin with?"

He scoffed, his cloak fluttering out behind him in the

building wind; Arianna couldn't be sure if it was natural or enchanted.

"Your ploys have not got past him, and he has a plan all his own," he continued. "You think just because a few cities now know the secrets we've been hiding, just because some have chosen a new side… that you can win this? Take the crown… from *us?*"

His voice grew louder, filled with disdain.

"Quite the contrary. You're only solidifying your own demise." He sliced his hand through the air, and a nearby pillar was obliterated by his magic. "And you're wasting our time."

"Enough!" said Arianna, standing her ground. She couldn't take another word of this victory speech. "I said, let her go. *Now!*"

Lessa looked up, her face blanching as she locked eyes with Arianna—they both knew there was no way she could make it the short distance between Sir Vladamor and them, *alive*, if she tried to run.

Lessa shook her head, another whimper escaping her lips. After so much preparation, this was the worst possible outcome… an ambush by the necromancer, *again.*

And there was nowhere to run this time, no more star magic to wipe away this nightmare with a flash of light.

Sir Vladamor cocked his head to the side, his cutting gaze drawing Arianna in from beneath his gleaming mask; she just *knew* he was smiling.

"I know you want to, so come and get her," he said. He opened up his arms, as if to present Lessa for the taking. "I dare you to try."

Arianna made a move forward, propelled by her rage, Solza in tow.

Eli caught her by the elbow. "Don't give him what he wants, Arianna!" Noah looked like he was going to be sick, keeping behind him. "And we all know what he wants… what the King *really* wants, is you."

Solza let out a snarl, feeling just as conflicted as her master in this moment. "*But we have to help her!*"

"If you let him get his hands on you again," he added, "Lessa is done for, regardless." He tried to get her to look at him. "Ara, then we've lost this thing for good. You hear me?"

Arianna ripped out of his grip. She stayed her ground, tearing her gaze from Lessa to look upon Eli. She searched for any answers in his eyes but found nothing there.

"He can't have you," he implored, his own brooding stare filling with emotion. He swiped his sword at his side. "I'll die before I let them have you again."

"And I will die if Lessa dies!" she choked out, tears swelling in her eyes—she could hardly believe her friend's life was on the line like this. *Snow's too…*

"We won't let that happen, Ara," said Noah, mustering his courage; he wiped his eyes and came to stand bravely by their side.

Sir Vladamor gave a roar of annoyance.

"If you come to me, willingly, girl, I *promise* to return your friend in one piece," he said, coaxing.

Arianna remembered the last promise he'd made her.

"You don't have a noble bone in your body," she called back.

He shrugged.

"You wouldn't want her to get harmed, now would you?" His hand flew over his mouth. "Oh, I must beg your pardon! I mean, *they*…" Arianna felt her heartbeat quicken. "She's expecting soon, I see."

Sir Vladamor tapped his finger on his chin, mocking—the metal echo from his mask grated against the insides of her mind.

"*Hmm*, now I wonder what the King would have me do with a baby guardian?"

Lessa's hand flew to her stomach, her other hand still clinging to Gabriel's robes; the night seemed to grow heavier, sucking them in deeper.

"What should we do?" asked Noah, drawing Arianna's attention back to him and Eli.

"I... don't know yet. Let me think." She racked her brain for the answer.

They were profoundly outnumbered. And Sir Vladamor was holding his dark powers, a looming threat, over one of their own...

Arianna wouldn't take a chance with Lessa's life.

She looked around at the dead covering the ground and suddenly knew exactly how they'd died—their souls had been sucked dry, stripped from their bodies, now just empty shells with barely the remnants of the light they had once held.

He must've done the same thing to them as he did to me in the desert.

And she was certain that it had happened quickly and quietly, a small piece of comfort in such morbid times.

The only reason she had survived Sir Vladamor's magic was because he had been toying with her, trying to turn her to his side with the *Onasyuda* enchantment.

"*We can't let him take Lessa's soul,*" said Arianna, honing all her focus. "*Any ideas, Solza?*"

"*I could transform,*" she said with a low rumble, staring ahead at Sir Vladamor, a fierceness in her eyes.

"*No,*" said Arianna, firmly. "*He would immediately respond to the threat. Lessa wouldn't make it.*"

Solza huffed in understanding. "*I'm out of ideas, then. But Eli's right. You cannot surrender.*"

Arianna chewed on her lip, thinking hard.

Yet, if I don't... if we attack at all, he'll kill her with the snap of his fingers.

Her eyes flicked to Noah and Eli, knowing he'd add them

to the pile of dead as well.

Not a single soul was safe around this monster…

Her enlightening conversation with Diveena about Sir Vladamor's weakness slipped into her mind—the necromancer's control over death truly was the *same* as controlling life. Arianna could see that plainly now.

As long as there was any form of life nearby, he could take it into his hands and do what he pleased. And what pleased him were evil, terrible things.

Yet, somewhere inside of Arianna was the key to the *Onasyuda* powers, too.

"*If I could just do what I did before, back in the desert…*"

She tried to call forth the elusive powers of an animancer—nothing. She howled in frustration.

"*I just don't know if I can, not in time.*"

"Ara, what do we do?" said Eli.

She ignored him, still concentrating on whatever it was that was inside of her—the key to killing the necromancer.

"*Keep trying,*" said Solza, reassuring her as best she could. "*It may be the only way to save her now… All of us.*"

Arianna gave a firm nod, trying with every ounce of energy she had to pull her animancer powers into her grasp.

This had always been the plan; however, she was supposed to have more time to master the magic on the journey to Saindora, *before* coming face-to-face with him. She hadn't even begun to understand such magic, and now all she felt was fear.

A comforting hand suddenly rested upon her shoulder, drawing her away from her suffocating doubts.

It didn't belong to Eli nor Noah.

Sir Vladamor staggered backward. "Impossible!"

The last time Arianna had seen him so shocked was when the ghosts of his brethren had chased him off. She looked up to see who had joined them.

Diveena was there by her side, glowing like a silver beacon

of hope on this bleak night.

"Let me take it from here," she said with a solemn smile. "After all, he *is* family." She glowered in his direction, then looked back to Arianna. "You have acted bravely, child. The powers you seek will surface when they're ready. For now, let us work to avenge these young lives lost… together."

Arianna felt her entire body nearly collapse with relief.

"*Thank the gods!*" said Solza, putting words to how she felt.

Arianna just wasn't ready to battle him alone yet, for she didn't understand the part of her that could…

She gazed at Diveena with pure reverence.

The hand that had rescued some of her closest friends, and that had always watched out for the guardians, was now reaching out to save her from drowning, too. This rare being, the last noble elf of the Nicora Clan, had finally stepped out from the shadows of the trees—and to help humans, no less.

It was a moment to be recorded in history. *If we survive.*

Times were nothing like that of the Golden Age, but Arianna again saw proof of hope that the Olleb could return back to her glory days. Or, maybe, even come to realize something far better than before.

She thought of Talis now—his faith had lifted Diveena out from the darkness long ago, and now she was returning the favor.

Arianna and Lessa locked eyes; she saw the hope shining there as well.

"Hang on," she mouthed.

Lessa returned a firm nod, composing herself.

If everyone let go of their fear of the unknown to help one another, as Diveena did now, they *might* just stand a chance… and live to see a more unified future.

The elf moved in front of Arianna to address her fallen brother.

14

SLIVER OF LIGHT

"DELIRA?" MUTTERED VLADAMOR, finding his balance. He lifted his mask for a better look at her; his bony, skeletal face almost seemed remorseful in its expression, delighted even, at seeing a ghost from his own past. "It cannot be…"

"Try again, you foul creature," said Diveena, her voice cracking like a whip.

Her fingers grasped the hilt of a slender sword. Gold traced the metal in delicate designs until it formed the jewel-studded hilt; it was the very same one she'd used to best Arianna in countless duels.

She paced forward, her stance as strong and as sure as ever.

"How cowardly must you be," she said—it was not a question. "Centuries pass and yet you continue to hide behind spiteful tricks to gain the upper hand. In all this time, all your power… you *still* cannot find the bravery to fight fair?"

Sir Vladamor started, as if he'd not been expecting such a

response. He shook out of his daze.

"*Why*, if it isn't Diveena," he replied, straightening up. His lips twitched downward, though he tried to hide his clear disappointment. "My old eyes deceived me for a moment." He narrowed his gaze. "And yet a ghost you prove to be. Hello, *sister*. It's been a long time."

Diveena's magic swelled, like an aggravated beast ready to pounce at the slightest provocation. "You're no brother of mine."

Her words rolled through the night, like a powerful punch, landing straight in Sir Vladamor's face.

He grunted.

"I never wanted to be…"

He seemed to experience an epiphany then, growing incensed. He balled his hand into a fist, taking a step in her direction.

"I just *knew* someone had slipped past me that night." He pointed an accusatory finger at her. "You're the reason why I never obtained the rest of the magic from our tribe!" He sneered, pursing his lips. "And you call *me* the trickster. How did you escape us?"

"Our magic is not yours to have," she replied, her jaw set. "The trees whispered for me to hide—" she twisted the sharp blade round and round in her hand, a snake ready to bite "—not long after word reached the Nicora Forest about my father's *death*." She exhaled through her nose, and the trees breathed with her. "Or don't you remember him?"

Something like a smile formed on his lips. "I remember spitting on his body," he said with pleasure.

Diveena's magic pulsated again, causing such an intense friction between her and Sir Vladamor that Arianna had the good sense to stand back; she pulled Eli and Noah with her.

And with all attention now on the two ancient elves, Lessa took the opportunity to crawl as far away as she could get.

Although, not before slipping what looked to be a weapon of some sort from Gabriel's robes and into her own; the ghost of Gabriel smiled.

"Master Lethander did you a mercy by letting you live after what you did," shouted Diveena. "If not for you, Delira would still be alive!" Arianna thought Sir Vladamor actually winced. "This time, you won't be so lucky."

Diveena bared her teeth, a snarl rising up from her throat as if she'd morphed into a wild animal. Suddenly, she reminded Arianna much more of Syrifina Myr than she would've liked to admit.

She had never seen her in such a state before, though she imagined this must be quite like the version of Diveena that Talis had first discovered in his younger years… unhinged with remorse, driven by revenge, a thriving jungle decaying at her touch.

Diveena's recent wisdom about magic echoed in her mind.
'It can easily be swayed between light and dark.'
Arianna saw proof of this lesson now; Diveena rippled with a dark and dangerous energy… and it was absolutely terrifying.

"This is the Nicora Clan's new home," she declared, "and you are *not* welcome here, Vladamor." His name curled off her tongue like acid.

"We'll just have to see about that." He returned the slightest bow of his head—the universal signal for a duel to begin.

Then, he gestured to the city keeper.

"Stop the girl!" the keeper ordered, pointing in Lessa's direction; she had almost reached the safety of the trees.

City regulators were on her in the next second, yanking her back into danger.

"Let me go!" she wailed, kicking and struggling with everything she had.

But just as suddenly as her eyes filled with silver, her magic fizzled away, leaving her defenseless.

"There's Shadow Resistance here," Arianna said to the boys. She recognized Lessa's frustration as she tried to conjure magic— dark sorcerers must be hidden among the regulators. "Be on the lookout."

She tried to pick them out of the crowd, but she couldn't be certain who the culprits were in such a large gathering.

She glanced down to Solza.

"*There can't be that many here,*" Arianna noted; she still felt the strong pulse of her magic in her grasp. "*Otherwise, only our avatar gifts would work.*"

"*Best keep your defenses up anyways, just in case,*" warned Solza. "*Don't let them in.*"

She nodded in agreement.

Arianna had had enough experience with those wretched enchantments back in Saindora that she was confident she'd developed a significant resistance to them. She now had the strength and know-how to ward them off once they'd been spelled, before they could sink in to incapacitate her.

However, at least she and Solza were reunited now, just in case they wore her down. "*Of course, but I wonder how—*"

That's when it hit her…

Lessa had the same insuppressible magic to her name, avatar magic. So why wasn't she using her elemental powers against the regulators?

Arianna looked around, frantically. *Where in the gods' names is Sano? How did they even get their hands on Lessa with him protecting her?*

The answer was surely dreadful, for he wasn't anywhere in sight. And if Lessa was separated from Sano by any measurable distance—or if he was badly hurt—her avatar magic would certainly feel the effects.

She glanced to Lessa, not a flicker of magic coming to her aid. *Sano, please be all right.*

Neither Lessa nor Arianna had mastered their elemental gifts to a high enough degree to succeed without support—they both required the direct aid of their avatars in order to wield them.

She drew closer to Solza. "*Stay close, girl.*"

Mother Adunni would be displeased, but Arianna couldn't help but wish for a little bit of that shadowleaf potion right now...

Before she even had the chance to survey the rest of the area for a clue about Sano's whereabouts, Sir Vladamor's dark magic exploded out from him, aiming straight toward Diveena.

Arianna, Solza, Eli, and Noah were thrown off their feet from the blast; Diveena conjured a pillow of earth to cushion their landings.

They jumped back up, brandishing their weapons—Solza her teeth—to help in any way they could.

"Go!" Diveena cried out as Arianna and her friends rushed again to her side—her magic sent them flying backward once more. "Rescue Lessa, and persuade who you can to our side. I can handle this. There's still a chance here."

She seemed strained already, using all her effort to block Sir Vladamor's forces; dark spools of shadow rippled from his hands and chest, searching for more souls to take.

"Be careful," said Arianna, wishing she could help somehow.

"Go!" she yelled again, this time not to be disobeyed.

Everyone, shadow and not, gave a wide berth to the necromancer and elf as they locked into a deadly battle.

"*Master,*" said Solza, vying for Arianna's attention—their minds had homed in on the same thing, panicked. "*Sano is wounded. I can feel him somewhere, but his energy is very weak.*"

"*Go and find him, Solza,*" she commanded, even if a little

reluctantly. "*I can cope without you here. Just... don't go too far.*"

Solza turned to leave.

"*Come right back to me if you hit trouble!*" A rock seemed to solidify in her stomach—she wouldn't be able to survive it this time if they got separated again. "*Promise me.*"

"*I will, Master,*" she replied, already shifting into her owl form. "*I promise.*" She flapped her wings and was off, rising high above the battle and the city to begin her search. "*Call should you need me.*"

Arianna watched her leave, feeling their connection already ebb; she clung to it, unwilling to let it fully go.

"Come on. It's now or never!" She tore her eyes from the sky. She signaled for Noah and Eli to prepare for battle. "Lessa needs our help."

"Forty to one?" said Noah, lifting his axe with two hands. He snorted, glaring ahead at the enemy. "That's *nothing.*"

"I think I'll join you in that bet now," said Eli, giving him a nod of approval.

Noah laughed something wild, surely keeping Kiki in his mind's eye—it morphed into a warrior's cry, tears flying from his eyes as he ran ahead.

Arianna and Eli caught up to him quickly.

Together, the three warriors—three Guardians of Gold—raced toward the gathering of what looked to be maybe a hundred regulators, all itching for a fight.

"*Luzcora!*" Arianna's swords sparked into life.

"*Solza ven immito,*" she heard Noah say from behind her, following her lead—the head of his axe burst into flames.

Eli struck his sword at a regulator who had strayed too far from the pack, blood already drenching his blade before the battle had even begun; he swept up her discarded shield and slid back into formation with Arianna and Noah.

"*Umm,* a little help here?" he said with a tight smile—

between Arianna's electrified blades and Noah's flaming axe, he did appear the opposite of threatening.

They stood, back to back, and the regulators closed in.

Arianna concentrated on Eli's sword until his blade licked with fire. He jumped and shook his head with an astonished expression.

"I just love it when you do that," he mumbled with a smirk.

Arianna couldn't help but smile a little, too, rejuvenated by the opportunity to fight back. They deserved a dose of revenge after such incredible loss tonight, but if not for Diveena's intervention, they would've most certainly have had to yield…

We can still win this, she dared to think, holding tight to Diveena's optimism.

The regulators slammed into them like a crashing, ruthless wave—and, side by side, they persisted, months of training not yet wasted.

"Noah, *now's* the time for blood!" screamed Arianna, forcing her charged blade straight through her first attacker, armor and all; she ripped it back to her side with no remorse, enemy blood spilling to her feet.

"Ay, ay, Captain!" he called back, twirling his axe with a skill he'd gained not from the Warrior's District but from countless drills between Gabriel and Jeom.

Eli was not to be left behind, already leaving a trail of broken regulators in his wake, his sword spitting fiery sparks every time it struck down. And as a former regulator himself, there weren't many tactics his opponents could use to surprise him.

Soon, the four remaining guardians in Guanamara were fully immersed in outright war—every strike of their weapons and release of their magic was an act of retribution for those that had already died on this night.

Down with the King!

Arianna remained at the front of their guardian triangle, wielding her deadliest magic just as decisively as she wielded her swords; she didn't have eyes on Lessa anymore, but she would soon.

She used her avatar powers sparingly, already feeling the tug on her energy levels without Solza near. However, when she felt like the numbers were too much for her and the boys to handle, she didn't blink an eye at using her elemental control to even things out.

She felt the wind whistling in her chest, filling her whole.

Solza is still in her air form, she thought. Still flying high, safely, over the battle.

With a boost of confidence, she stepped in front of Noah and Eli, lowering her weapons. Then she cupped her lips and blew—the group of regulators surrounding them collapsed in seconds, the air pressed out from their lungs.

They stepped over their bodies, preparing to fight the next layer of regulators barring them from Lessa.

Numbers don't mean a thing, Arianna thought.

Magic was quickly equalizing the battlefield.

As the night continued to light up around the city center, some of the opposing warriors began to flee the scene; they'd take one look at the regulators scorched from magic and run the other way as Arianna and her friends advanced, weapons singing with spells that no ordinary armor nor shield could withstand.

"These people clearly have no idea what they've gotten themselves into," she called to the boys. "They don't know the truth yet." *They don't know who their King really is…*

Some, but not all.

There was still a great many left, fighting on behalf of Sir Vladamor and the King, maintaining the chaos.

Arianna felt a heavy sword land hard against her own before she saw the face of who held it—she shoved it off, readying to release her magic at her newest opponent.

The city keeper stood to face her.

"Ah, and finally we meet," she said, crouching low as he circled her; she was buzzing with adrenaline, magic, and the confidence to win. "Sure you want to do this?"

She sent another surge of electric magic through her swords—they glowed like lanterns in the night.

The keeper spat at her feet.

"You thought you could just come into my home and take my city from me in my sleep?" he retorted, swinging his broadsword back and forth with two hands—it seemed too big for him to handle. "How well did that work out for you now, *hmm?*"

His blade suddenly sparked to life, just like hers, sizzling with a dangerous energy.

"Shadow Resistance," she breathed, grinding her teeth. She gripped her swords tighter and looked around, searching for more silver glinting eyes. "How many of you are there here, hiding?"

She hadn't felt the sting of anyone's magic yet; if there were more, they were clearly biding their time, waiting for a command.

That, or focusing all their energy on holding Lessa. *Baiting me...*

They knew she would come.

The keeper started laughing, not missing the concern wrinkling her expression. "More than you clearly think."

A jolt of fear raced through her, stabbing at her courage—how much had they underestimated the King? In all their planning, all their assumptions about this move or that, how much had they missed?

Clearly... she bitterly thought in response.

She stepped over the body of one of her own to face him.

He flashed her a jagged-toothed smile.

"And thanks to you, we no longer have to live in the shadows, little girl. Do you even understand the favor you've done us?"

He mirrored her every step… the way that Solomon had taught her to move.

She focused, putting her guard back up to the fullest.

Do not underestimate him, she reminded herself. *The King selected him as keeper of one of his most formidable cities for a reason.*

"You forced us out into the light, and now the entire world will know of King Devlindor's greatest powers! You have done nothing but *help* our cause, pushed us into the next phase in our rule." He let out a long sigh of what sounded like relief. "Now, we no longer have to hide."

She tripped over uneven ground as she tried to take a step back.

He lunged, blasting her with spell after spell.

His strength and agility took her aback; she struggled under the continuous force of his magic, furiously trying to regain her balance and control—the moment she had hesitated, she'd lost the upper hand.

Arianna howled in fury with the effort it took to block him, sweat dripping into her eyes. She was drowning under his skill, taking hit after hit. Tasting blood, metal, and magic.

Too late did she come to understand how this poor excuse for a man had gained such a powerful position under the King's regime in the first place—he was an undisputable *master* in battle magic, in war.

Arianna barely had time to think of her counterattacks, and she was growing tired. She gripped her elemental magic, preparing to release whatever might come.

The city keeper struck first.

He slammed his sword into the ground so hard that the cobblestone exploded out from the tip of his blade; the blast knocked the wind out of her, as well as any thoughts of conjuring magic, avatar or otherwise.

She flew backward with a yelp, shielding her eyes.

Eli was there to break her fall—their weapons landed right behind them.

"Are you hurt?" he asked, rolling out from under her.

Her ankle was definitely twisted, but she hobbled to her feet.

"No," she said, pinching the stitch in her side; the city keeper was advancing, and her bravery was slipping.

She looked up into his dirtied face—he'd clearly had a go of it as well.

"We have to save her," she said. She placed a hand against his chest. "Eli, we *have* to."

"We will," he said, resolutely, placing his hand over hers. "But they're showing their cards now. They have magic."

She peered over his shoulder, keeping one eye on the keeper. "I know," she said, quickly. "But so do I."

She simmered as the keeper neared, a smug look on his face; she wanted to rip it right off him.

She made a move toward her swords, but Eli stopped her.

He gripped her by the shoulders, shaking her gently, forcing her to breathe.

"You can't take them all by yourself, Ara. You're zapped, and they're just getting started." His gaze bore into hers. "This was part of their strategy… tire us out. Hit us hard when we least expected it." He shook head his head. "Don't get cocky here. We never had the upper hand tonight, and we still don't. We won't be enough. Not like this, so *think*."

His words were sharp yet gentle, soft yet pointed—and they were just what she needed to hear.

Don't get cocky! Don't fight with your ego, fight smart.

Eli gestured to Noah—he was struggling to hold his ground against a pair of sure shadows.

"You're right, you're right," she said. "Just give me a second." She pressed her hand to her forehead to think—they literally only had seconds.

The keeper was almost upon them.

She guessed that his use of magic had been the permission for the other Shadow Resistance supporters to expose their true nature; she counted about fifteen men and women with silver-streaked eyes in black cloaks.

She looked up, the night riddled with gray, smoky clouds.

"When Solza returns, I can take them all out," she said, hoping her avatar had felt her distress.

She took a deep breath, silently reassuring herself of that statement... *I can. I will.*

She looked back to Eli; his expression was full of concern.

"We just need to buy some more time," she pleaded—the only other option was to run, and she was not leaving this gods-forsaken city without Lessa. "As long as Diveena keeps Vladamor's attention, Solza and I, together, can level the rest of them."

She inhaled, deeply, tugging again at her connection with Solza. "*I need you!*"

"All right, then let's buy you some more time," said Eli—he clearly wasn't ready to call it quits yet either.

He dropped his arms back to his side, flinching from the movement; he was bleeding.

Arianna nodded back at him, relaxing a little to know he was still in this with her...

She again looked over his shoulder; the city keeper had lifted his sword to strike, and Eli's back was his blade's closest target.

She outstretched her hand and shouted at the top of her lungs, "*Ni passe!*"

A protective barrier exploded around them, taking all of her energy with it; it wouldn't last for long, but it would give them a couple of minutes to regroup.

"We can do this," she said, clinging to her last bits of energy. She locked eyes with Eli. "Just have a little faith, all right?"

"In you?" He chuckled, as if it were the silliest of statements. "Always."

She forced a smile, then pressed her palm over his wound. He winced.

Helthra saludis emencia, she thought. His skin slowly began to stitch back together.

He gawked all the while.

Arianna pouted at the result. "I'm no Lessa, but I suppose that'll have to do for now."

"Good enough for me," said Eli, flexing his somewhat-healed arm. "Thanks."

He gave her a quick kiss on the cheek, then he lifted a handful of nuts from his pocket.

"How much time does this buy us?" he asked with a sheepish grin—the barrier reverberated around them as the city keeper tried to tear it to pieces.

Arianna beamed. "What made you think of—"

"After all our practice duels, I've learned to always carry a little something with me now…" He shrugged. "Just in case you get that look on your face again, when you almost killed me during training that one time." Arianna smirked, thinking, *Which time?* He pointed a knowing finger at her. "This look."

"You *never* cease to surprise me," she said in delight, scarfing them down—her energy levels boosted, her magic surged.

Just enough for now… "*Solza, are you there?*"

The barrier faltered, the city keeper still throwing everything he had at it.

Arianna used their remaining time to mend her ankle the best that she could, then they scooped up their weapons and readied to fight.

The city keeper blasted through their protections in the next second, with one big swing of his sword. But this time, Arianna was ready for him.

Levantis bora! she thought.

He flew off his feet, hurtling through the sky toward the trees.

"That should keep him busy for a while," she said to Eli. "Stay close to me."

Noah was running toward them.

"Need help!" he called out in a panic, waving his axe in the air; it was no longer on fire.

The more seasoned sorcerers were chasing after him, their shadowy magic on the hunt.

Arianna jumped in front of Noah, reflecting their dark enchantments back at them—they were forced to run in the opposite direction, forced to reckon with their own wicked choices.

"We stick together now," she instructed Eli and Noah.

They quickly reformed their triangle with Arianna at the front.

She was the strongest in magic out of the three of them, but she didn't have enough energy to magically aid herself *plus* the two of them anymore.

Instead, she blocked any charmed attacks from fatally harming the boys. And they focused on battling the traditional way, weapon against weapon.

Just like they had trained their guardian apprentices to do back at the Treehouse, Arianna, Noah, and Eli combined the best of their strengths on the battlefield, leaving no friend behind. And like this, they were able to carve, slowly, through the opposition, slowly toward Lessa—Sir Vladamor would have graves of his own to dig, too, after all was said and done.

He and Diveena were still deeply concentrating on their own feud. The skies shook from their magic, the ground rumbling beneath their feet with every blast; it looked, sounded, and felt as if a wild thunderstorm and powerful earthquake were happening all at once.

And with Arianna and the King's Guanamara shadows throwing their deadliest magic tricks to the air alongside them, those who had never had an encounter with the enchanted world were quickly weeded out…

It was a miracle they'd even lasted this long.

Arianna recognized the fear in the faces of many regulators who knew nothing of magic, too scared to even stand their ground anymore in a fight. It was a harsh reminder that not all those battling in the name of the King were in the know.

Their remaining opponents started to thin out quickly—dead or deserters.

It didn't take long before Arianna was up against a number she could handle on her own, even without Solza.

"*Where are you, girl?*" She could hold them off for now, but she *would* need her avatar to finish this.

"Eli, it's time for the next phase in our plan," called Arianna after a while. She released another heavy blast of magic, her opponent spinning off their feet. "You're up! Take Noah and do what we came here to do. I've got this." She readied her next defensive spell. "Trust me."

Eli and Noah had battled with honor, but it was her against *only* Shadow Resistance now—weapons were no good here.

And it was taking more energy to protect the boys than she had to give at the moment.

Eli hesitated, his expression conflicted.

"*Go,*" she mouthed, looking at him sidelong.

He loosed a long breath and sheathed his sword.

"Be careful, and *think* first," he reminded her, tapping his finger to his temple.

"I've got this," she said again, flashing a shaky smile; she couldn't lose focus.

Noah opened his mouth to protest. "What—"

"That's enough blood for now, Noah," she said.

He pursed his lips and nodded.

She turned away from them, concentrating hard on the enemy.

"Good luck."

Eli grabbed Noah by the arm, and they slipped away before the next explosion.

ARIANNA DANCED ACROSS THE CITY CENTER, spells and enchantments chasing her with every footfall. But she kept eyes and ears on the boys all the while—they hadn't gone too far from her line of sight, keeping to the outskirts of the battle area.

It was the guardians' only opportunity tonight to try to persuade the unknowing regulators, and other citizens, to their side. They had to take it.

Our friends can't have died in vain.

A shadow's spell nicked her in the shoulder; she pulled in a hiss through her teeth as her skin broke open.

Eli had certainly mastered persuasion after so much practice across the Olleb. He could talk anyone into anything, but he could, especially, talk someone into becoming a Guardian of Gold—his words *were* gold, spinning the most beautiful dream, a gleaming picture of a life that everyone wanted.

"The King has lied to you!"

Arianna heard him address a gathering huddled along the outskirts of the trees; they hid behind the vast trunks, using them as shields against any residual magic.

"Why do you think we're out here fighting?" he said, pacing before them. "For *your* freedom!"

He pressed a hand over his heart.

"My friends and I are already free. We escaped from the King's oppression, but we were forced to battle tonight in the hope of staying that way, and in an effort to show *you* the light." He opened his arm out wide. "See what's plain in front of your eyes!"

Noah pointed to Diveena and Sir Vladamor with his axe, their tangled magic enough to turn a non-believer into a believer, instantly.

"The one you serve has not been truthful to you, nor any of us," Noah said in a gentle tone, his face a trustworthy one. "We mean nothing to the King. He only craves power, control over everyone… *everything*. Even if that means keeping us from magic—"

He found the strength to conjure a small, pink flame in his palm. He offered it to a fearless young woman to hold, trying to prove it wasn't only destructive.

"The fact that you can grasp this flame in your palm proves that you have magic," said Eli, standing beside him. "It belongs to you, yet the King has tried to take it."

The young woman's eyes glowed in awe as she stared at the fire in her hands; her peers seemed to lean in a little closer to listen.

Eli's voice grew louder.

"I don't even have the ability to create magic," he said. "Not everyone does, but it *is* a part of my world that I've come to accept. An incredible part that deserves to be free." His eyes flicked to Arianna—she was beginning to struggle. "We've come here to offer you the chance to take part in that freedom. To earn your life back, outside of a tyrant's rule, and to see what the Olleb is really made of… and I assure you, she's beautiful. *Nothing* like this dark, decrepit land the King has thrust upon us."

The City of Guanamara was fully awake now, citizens fleeing down different paths, hidden within the jungle or behind the buildings that sat a safe distance away—but they still kept a close eye on the battle, trying to understand what was going on.

More and more crept their way toward Eli and Noah, toward the group of potential guardians, curious to hear the coaxing words of this invader.

"You do not deserve your magic!" shouted Arianna as the city keeper again stepped into her path, sword blazing.

It was just him and her now, the last man standing between her and Lessa; the rest of his shadows were dead or wounded, or taking time to recoup their magic out of harm's way.

Arianna was about tapped for magic, too, but she wouldn't let him know it—she silently thanked Iris for the countless lessons in preserving energy when it came to using battle magic; Iris could've outlasted them all.

"Who are you to decide who deserves anything?" he said, a nasty scowl on his face. "You're nothing but a number, Twenty-Two."

Arianna opened her mouth to scream, but a guttural roar came out instead—she glanced back and Solza was running toward her, silver claws outstretched and teeth bared.

"Solza!" she cried out in relief.

A revitalizing energy began to pour into her body… Solza's energy.

She considered that this must be what the earth felt like whenever her avatar gifted it back its health—from dry and brittle to brimming with unconquerable life.

Arianna whipped back around just in time to lift her swords and block the city keeper's magic.

"You'll regret that," she retorted, sensing her fire burning again at its brightest—she prepared to let all the elements in her grasp do with him what they pleased, until he was nothing.

The city keeper suddenly let out a cry, falling to his knees.

Arianna blinked, feeling her magic drift away; she looked to her hands, confused.

I don't think I did anything…

He dropped his sword, twisting his arm around behind him to try to reach something.

That's when she saw the dagger lodged in his back, smoking with what could only be magic.

"That's for Gabriel!" yelled Lessa, her blue eyes lined in icy silver—without anyone left to hold the oppressive spells over her, her magic was again in her reach.

She stood, wiping herself off.

The city keeper barely seemed to notice her, still trying to reach for the dagger; his magic flared up as he finally grasped the hilt.

Both Lessa and Arianna prepared to intervene, but Solza got to him first.

She leaped to the air and landed on him with a mighty crash, her powers over the earth landing too, in full force—the impact alone had surely killed him.

Arianna cringed at the gruesome sight, Solza leaving bloody pawprints in her wake as she trotted back to her side.

"*Are you all right, Master?*" she asked, her voice full of worry.

"*I am now,*" stammered Arianna, sheathing her swords. She knelt down to hug her. "*I can forget how strong you are, sometimes… thanks for the save.*" She stood back up, looking around. "*But what took you so long? Did you find Sano?*"

"*I did,*" she replied—her tone suggested bad news.

Arianna braced herself.

"*I stayed with him for as long as I could, to protect him from…*" She peered, warily, in the direction of Sir Vladamor and Diveena; the earth rippled beneath their feet as another explosive blast struck the air between them. "*He's very weak, Master. I couldn't move him by myself. My guess is that he was trying to protect Lessa when the necromancer ambushed the other guardians. He must've gotten badly wounded in the process.*"

They both looked to Lessa.

Arianna didn't even have to say anything—Sano, clearly, was the only thing on her mind.

Lessa began to call out for him, screaming his name, not even bothering to acknowledge her or Solza.

"Les… *Lessa*!" said Arianna, running after her. She caught her by the elbow. "Are you hurt? Wait a second. Look at me."

Lessa seemed a bit taken aback as she took in Arianna, like waking up from a sleep

"You must be in shock," she said, examining her. "Try and calm down." She breathed with her, deep and slow, until Lessa's breathing became steadier.

"I… I…" Lessa shook her head, lips quivering. She gazed around, eyes glassy with unfallen tears, seeming to see everything all at once. "I can't believe that everyone's gone—" She hugged Arianna tight, breaking down into a sob. "I couldn't stop him, Ara! I tried, but he…" She whimpered. "I couldn't do *anything* to stop him."

"I know," said Arianna, hugging her back. "I know."

Eli and Noah were there in the next heartbeat, arms around them too.

"It's no one's fault," said Noah—he was also crying; Arianna wasn't sure if he'd ever even stopped since discovering Kiki's body. "We'll avenge our friends."

Arianna sucked back her tears. *Not yet. Just survive.*

The battle wasn't over.

Lessa pulled away from the embrace, unable to meet her eyes.

"There's nothing you could've done," said Arianna, setting her gaze on her. "Diveena's here, though. She came to help us." She tried to sound hopeful. "We're going to make it out of here and find a way to... to fix this."

Deep down, she knew there was no way to bring anyone back from the dead. There was no *fix* for a life lost.

Lessa nodded, seeming calmer.

"Les," said Arianna, cautiously. "I don't want to alarm you, but Sano—"

"Where is he?" she said, snapping alert; her eyes were still burning silver. "He's hurt, I can feel it."

Her gaze darted every which way, searching.

"Whatever Vladamor did to our friends," she ran a hand through her hair, "Sano took the full blast of it for me. That's the only reason I survived the ambush. That's when he remembered I had an avatar, too, and thought me better as a hostage."

Arianna raised her hands, not wanting to send her friend into a downward spiral—Lessa seemed fragile, to say the least.

"I'm sure he's fine," she said, averting her eyes to Solza. "We'll find him. Don't worry." She meant it.

She turned to assess Eli and Noah—they were both covered in blood.

"How did it go?" she asked, warily.

This was not quite the state she'd left them in; they appeared shaken.

"Some of them were coming around to hear our side," mumbled Eli. "But then most of them ran off." He used his cloak to wipe his blade clean; his sword hand was trembling. "Some dead."

"Lots dead..." said Noah, rocking back and forth on his feet.

"What? *Why?*" asked Arianna, cocking her head to the side. "It seemed like they were hearing you out before..."

"You don't want to look," said Noah, his face pallid, brushing off his clothes.

"Come on," said Eli in a troubled tone. "We can't remain out in the open like this. It's too dangerous."

He took Arianna's hand and guided them all to crouch down behind the cover of a large, fallen tree—the residue of magic glistened off its bark like steam.

From this vantage point, they had an unobstructed view of Diveena and Sir Vladamor; they remained at the core of the city center where they'd left them not long ago.

Since the battle had begun, Arianna hadn't really any opportunity to *see* what their duel looked like. Just felt, heard…

But as she watched them now, swathed in chains of mighty magic, she had the urge to run herself. *Should we?*

It was a terrifying display of power.

Diveena had summoned her greatest power over nature, the earth churning at her fingertips and magic rippling in the air around her.

Sir Vladamor had called on his most frightening magic, too—control over the dead.

Just as easily as he had rained death upon all their friends, he had used his despicable powers to raise them up again from the ground…

Arianna couldn't stifle her shock.

"Gods have mercy," breathed Lessa, her hand flying over her mouth.

For a moment, it appeared as if the fallen guardians had risen from their haphazard graves. No wounds to account for, bodies perfectly intact. *Alive.*

And yet, their eyes told a different story—eerie, empty stares looked back at her.

Dead.

"As soon as the people saw *this*," Eli gestured to the sickening scene, "they fled in a panic. It undid everything." He shook his head, sounding so defeated. "If *this* is magic, who would want any part of it?"

"This isn't magic," responded Arianna—she thought she might be sick. "This is monstrous."

"Some of them got killed as soon as they tried to run… from *us*," muttered Noah, head bowed. "They got scared and fled right out into the open. Blasted apart like that." He snapped his fingers, their tips stained in blood.

"Not your fault," whispered Arianna, trying to tell herself the same.

Her subconscious shouted a different message. *We should've never come here. This is all our fault, all this death. The King keeps winning!*

She, Lessa, Noah, and Eli all watched on in horror.

The dead hadn't moved a muscle yet, standing stone still—Arianna had an awful image of the skeleton army floating in her head. *Not again…*

She realized what Sir Vladamor meant to do next.

"No, don't!" she said, jumping to her feet. "Leave them in peace."

Solza whined in support.

Eli pulled her back down to safety; she let him, for she could not move.

The ghosts of her friends disappeared from her sight, their souls drawn back into their bodies; Sir Vladamor was manipulating them to do his dark bidding…

Just like with Jeom. Just like with the Nicora Elves.

Mindlessly, with one goal in sight, their friends all began to march against Diveena, weapons in hand.

Arianna could see the light snap back into the eyes of those she had called friends—alive yet not.

She knew their minds were being trapped by his, and there was nothing they could do to stop him. *Only one of equal opposite strength has a chance*, she thought.

Diveena's lecture echoed in her mind.

Arianna felt Lessa's hand on hers.

"This is truly horrendous," she said in a shaky voice. "Do you think Diveena needs our help?"

Eli chimed in.

"It looks like… like she's handling him still," he said, taking a knee. "We had better just stand back and let this play out. Don't want to do anything to distract her from putting this monster down for good."

Arianna didn't respond.

She didn't want to drain any more hope from this hopeless situation, but… *Diveena doesn't have the power to put Sir Vladamor down for good.*

"That's right. Take him down, sister!" said Noah. "She's got this. *Right*, Ara?"

They gazed at her with fearful expressions.

Still, she didn't respond.

Sir Vladamor's magic was undeniably strong; however, Diveena did *appear* his equal in nearly every way—she used her gifts to call forth mammoth vines and roots to pin the bodies back down to the earth where they belonged.

Powerful magic throbbed all around them, the necromancer and the elf sending blast after deadly blast toward one another, the jungle shrieking in response.

Lessa suddenly jumped up from her perch.

"Sano!" she called out. She peered all around the vicinity, distraught. "I can't feel him! I can't feel him at all anymore…" She screamed again, cupping her hands around her mouth. "Oh, no… no, no, no. Sano! *Where* are you?"

"He's not far," said Arianna, trying to reassure her, *trying* to pull her back down behind their cover; she resisted. "You would know, if he…"

She couldn't bring herself to finish her sentence, Lessa's eyes shimmering down at her in terror.

Arianna understood all too well the enveloping emptiness that came hand in hand with separating from an avatar—if they didn't find Sano soon, Lessa would break.

Arianna connected with Solza.

"*Where did you last feel him?*" she asked, hurriedly. "*I fear we don't have much time left.*"

"*On the other side of Diveena and the necromancer,*" said Solza, solemnly. "*He's in the midst of… everything.*"

Arianna felt herself deflate, looking up at Lessa. "Solza says she felt him near Vladamor. He's alive, but he's basically in the center of their war zone."

"*Solza* says?" asked Noah, raising an eyebrow at her.

Eli gave her a strange look just the same—but she *knew* that Lessa understood.

"Not now," said Arianna, peering over the tree trunk with care. "We have to locate Sano."

Lessa was standing on her tiptoes to try to survey the ground near the thick of the battle.

"Over there! I see him," she said, pointing, frantically.

They all looked in that direction and found a bright white mound of fur; Sano was lying directly behind where Sir Vladamor had positioned himself. He was again in his white wolf form, so his body proved easy to spot in the dark.

"Oh, gods, Sano!" Lessa's call was lost to another explosion.

She slid back down behind the tree, and Arianna covered her eyes to shield them from the debris flying all around.

"Get down!" said Eli, pinning Arianna to the ground just as Diveena landed another big blow to Sir Vladamor—the aftershock headed straight their way, leveling the standing trees in the vicinity.

They all cautiously moved back to their crouched positions when the dust had settled.

"He looks really hurt," said Noah, chewing on his lip.

"What do we do?"

"I have to go to him," said Lessa, standing.

She tried to slip away from the cover of the tree, but Eli stopped her.

"I can't let you do that. It's *too* dangerous."

Jeom had made them each promise to look out for her on this mission, and she knew Eli would not take such a duty lightly.

"I'm not asking," she countered. Her eyes gave a dangerous glow, but he kept his grip tight, determined.

Arianna gently tried to talk her down.

"Les, Eli's right. You can't," she said, prying his hand away from her before Lessa accidentally singed it off. "We just got our hands on you, and you… I know you're strong enough, but you just *can't*, all right?" She glanced to her belly.

Lessa's hand settled on her stomach, and she looked longingly to Sano, tears streaming down her cheeks.

"But I have—"

Arianna sighed, resigned to her next life-endangering choice. "No, I'll bring him back." She stood. "I'm going to try."

Lessa squeezed her eyes shut a moment and nodded. "Thank you," she said, softly.

"He's family," said Arianna with a shrug. "We do crazy things for family."

"No!" Eli tried to pull her back down, hand wrapped around her wrist in desperation. "You think I'd let you go out there alone—"

"I'm not asking." Arianna hoped he saw the apology in her eyes.

She sent a gentle but sharp shock to his hand; he let go.

There wasn't time to explain. She knew how strong the bond was between avatar and avatar master—if she didn't go herself, Lessa certainly would, and her friend had already lived through enough necromancer-induced turmoil for one night.

And I promised her we'd protect Snow…

She ducked out from behind the tree and braved the open.

Careful not to let Sir Vladamor see her, Arianna kept to the shadows of the battle area. She dodged blast after blast, flying trees, and stray enchantments, until she finally she reached Sano; she felt the eyes of her friends on her the entire time, Lessa even using her magic to cover her when she could.

She laid a hand on Sano's large belly—he was still breathing, albeit faintly.

"You're going to be fine," she said in a whisper. She signaled to the others that he was still alive.

Lessa's hand flew over her heart in relief; Eli waved frantically for her to return, fear *and* anger plain in his expression; and Noah cheered her on.

Arianna had no hope of moving Sano without support—he was massive as a wolf, much too heavy for one person to lift.

"*Seriously*, Sano… why aren't you in your air form?" *Nothing is ever easy.*

She wished in this moment that he was the little monkey she'd happily held in her arms so many times before…

"Darkness has done nothing but make you weak!" she heard Diveena shout, drawing her attention.

She sent another detonation of magic toward the necromancer, all while struggling to keep the walking dead on the ground.

"Who has been the one in hiding for centuries?" retorted Vladamor. "Darkness has given me all the freedom I desire. But *you*, you're bound to slavery by your own morals! That will be the death of you."

Levantis bora, thought Arianna, lifting Sano's body into the air.

She kept him as low as she could to the ground, careful

not to draw the necromancer's eye. Slowly, she began to make her way back toward the others, still keeping low and out of sight. She made it halfway.

As if tasting the magic she'd conjured with her mind, Sir Vladamor spun around and looked her dead in the eyes.

She stopped in her tracks.

Before she could even think her next thought, he had aimed an attack toward her. And at the same time, he redirected Diveena's spell toward her friends.

Eli and Noah dived out of the way, and Lessa shielded herself and Solza with barrier magic; the tree they'd been hiding behind was annihilated.

Arianna, on the other hand, had been so taken off guard that she had no time to defend herself.

"No! I won't let you kill another one of us," cried Diveena, summoning the earth to protect her.

Both she and Sano slammed to the ground, hard, caught in the middle of the resulting blast.

Arianna tried to regain her bearings, ears ringing from the explosion—Solza was suddenly by her side, nudging her to get up.

"It's a trick," she said to Solza, head spinning. She pushed on to her hands and her knees, glaring at the necromancer. "Diveena, watch out. It's a trick!"

He'd been waiting for an opportunity like this, for her focus to be swayed...

Sir Vladamor flashed a wicked smile back at Arianna, then he directed his next attack at Diveena, leaving her no time to defend herself.

She flew off her feet. She was coughing as she met the ground, blood staining her porcelain skin and pink lips; it appeared as if darkness poisoned her insides, his magic seeping into her body like tiny black worms burrowing into white sand.

Arianna didn't even know a name for this spell, but it was evident that it was of the worst kind…

She was too weak now to defend herself from the onslaught of Sir Vladamor's ghostly army; the bodies of their fallen friends began to land attacks on Diveena, one after the other.

"She needs our help!" said Arianna, levitating Sano a safe distance away.

Lessa ran to Sano.

"Thank you, Ara," she called back. "*Go!* I'll join you as soon as I know he's all right."

Arianna, Noah, and Eli ran to Diveena's aid without a second thought.

Arianna tried to block Sir Vladamor's attacks, but she quickly confirmed that—even with all her magic and knowledge gained—there was just no way she could possibly wound him, a necromancer. Not without accessing her animancer magic, at least. Solza remained by her side, lending her powers over the earth since Diveena was too weak to carry on.

Noah and Eli took up arms against the walking dead, though it was a terrible thing to raise a weapon against a fallen friend.

Just when they thought they would become buried beneath the onslaught from every direction, blazing arrows lit up the night sky and pinned the dead to the ground.

Arianna looked up to find Lessa, her bow steady in hand; with her next exhale, she let another enchanted arrow fly.

But even with all of them working together to fight him off, Sir Vladamor was still too strong…

"*I should shift now,*" urged Solza as she and Arianna focused on the flaming arrows. "*Fire may put them all down for good.*"

Eli caught her eye then, shaking his head. He recognized the thought crossing their minds—they'd been over this many times before.

"*Fire won't have a stronger effect on the necromancer than any other element,*" Arianna replied, repeating what they'd decided after countless strategy sessions. "*You'll be too easy to target. Just stay close to me. We cannot risk you now, especially not after what happened to Sano.*" Her gaze flicked to him; he still hadn't stirred. "*You're our greatest weapon in this war, and there's a much bigger battle to be fought once this one is over.*"

Solza accepted this, but Arianna didn't miss her comment. "*Will it ever be over?*" she thought.

Arianna prayed for the ending to come soon.

It was a difficult decision not to call on Solza in her dragon form during such a time of need, for her powers were great, indeed. But Sir Vladamor's weakness was still yet to be revealed. And she wouldn't risk Solza's life to try to test a new theory, no matter the cost—on this, the elder guardians had all agreed.

'*A dragon is too important to the war to gamble in the smaller battles.*' A message sent from the Greenhouse guardians to the Treehouse—signed by Master Tayshin, Sergios, Nico, and Rowina—had been enough to solidify the decision.

Arianna and Solza, instead, called on all the elements together, winding them into one in order to defend against his dark magic, to protect Diveena, until a way to escape presented itself; with Sano still unconscious, Lessa was forced to lean on her defensive spells and her bow.

Arianna's avatar powers had grown to be quite impressive, yet nothing seemed to weaken the necromancer long enough for them to gain the upper hand. In fact, he appeared to be enjoying the ensuing chaos.

A cry ripped through the night—Eli.

Arianna glanced over just as he fell to one knee, his hip bleeding. He covered the wound with his hand, crying out again as he tried to stand.

Little Kiki, raised back from the dead, had caught him in the side with her tried and true flail; his shield had long since been discarded.

Arianna felt his pain, the memory of one of Grinda Risso's favored weapons always fresh and bitter every time it flitted in her mind.

"Eli," she breathed, stricken with dread—she wasn't close enough to help, and she and Lessa couldn't lose focus on holding off Sir Vladamor.

Noah was frozen in horror by his side, staring at Kiki in shock.

"Kiki, *please*," he sputtered, tears streaming.

He raised his hands, pleading for her to stop, his axe falling to the ground.

"Noah, that's not her," screamed Arianna as the walking dead surrounded the boys from all sides. "Eli, you have to get up!"

He tried again, but he couldn't.

He looked up at her, shaking his head, eyes welling. "With you till the end," he mouthed.

Kiki lifted her weapon once more.

"*Eli, no...*" Her heart boomed in her chest, like one of Diveena's magical bombs had gone off.

The elf's voice burst through her mind.

'Death may try to overcome life, but life is its equal. One cannot exist without the other.'

Arianna knew she had the power to defeat the necromancer, to help her friends—if *only* she could tap into it!

She bellowed out into the night with the effort it took to hold Sir Vladamor off, yet not be able to stop him. She closed her eyes, connecting with Solza.

"*I need to make room for the animancer in me,*" she said in a panic, clinging to a faint idea. "*I can't reach it otherwise.*

You have to let go."

"*Are you sure, Master?*" said Solza, hesitant. "*Our defenses will fall…*"

"*Yes,*" she replied, mustering all of her courage. She looked to Eli; Kiki was about to strike. "*Now!*"

Her connection with Solza ebbed, subsequently ending her connection to her avatar powers. It felt wrong… dark.

"What are you doing?" Lessa yelled—she took on all the weight of Sir Vladamor's attacks, barely able to withstand him. "I need you!"

Without Arianna, he could end her in seconds.

"I'm here," she promised, eyes still closed, still searching for the light.

It was a terrible feeling, to let go in such a dire moment, a terrible risk, but Arianna saw it was the only way—they would all die here otherwise, regardless.

The strongest sensation suddenly pressed upon the walls of her mind, begging to be let in.

Onasyuda… It was the dimmest of thoughts, growing into something more. Then the thought came strong, taking her over completely. *Onasyuda!*

A new yet familiar energy filled Arianna, and she grasped it for dear life. She pushed it out in front of her, like a shield of light.

When she opened her eyes, she saw that it actually *was…* a shield of sorts.

As if the moon had fallen from the sky to hover just above the city center, a stark, white, blinding light had washed over the entire area, wiping it clean.

All the bodies Sir Vladamor had had in his control fell back to the ground.

"Ara, you did it!" said Eli, collapsing where he stood.

Noah was trying to hold him up.

"I'm sorry, mate," he said through the tears. He looked

down at Kiki, her body now crumpled and lifeless at their feet. "I just couldn't…"

"I know, Noah. I understand," said Eli, clenching his teeth and taking deep breaths through the pain. "No harm done here. Lessa can heal this right up."

He tried to smile, but he grew paler by the second. He was bleeding too much.

They wobbled over to stand behind Arianna, but she couldn't focus on them now.

She turned around in circles as the resounding cries of ghostly gratitude filled her ears.

Eli and Noah couldn't see, but the darkness around her had been lit up with the sparkling presence of every guardian taken from the world on this terrible night—and floating out among them, a leader for certain, was Gabriel, a brilliant smile upon his face.

Arianna couldn't help it. Her tears finally fell.

The blazing light within her kept shining through, still washing everything in a white sheen, like a safety net.

"You *did* do it, Arianna," said Gabriel, such pride in his voice. "I'm sorry that this didn't go as planned, but here you are, saving the day again." He gazed around the vicinity, at the guardians who still lived. "I hope to see you in the future, but not too soon, you hear? Do right by us… the guardians, I mean. We really needed you in this fight." He waved at her—a goodbye she wasn't ready for. "I pray that you're able to heal this land *and* live a long and healthy life to enjoy it."

"Gabe," she choked out. "I'm so sorry this happened to you." She bowed her head. "I'm sorry for you all… it isn't fair." She looked around at all the ghosts, all now free from Sir Vladamor's chains. "I *will* see us through this. I promise you that."

Their voices spoke out encouragement, praise, and warm-hearted farewells.

"I know you will," said Gabriel. "Of this, I have never had a doubt." He leaned in to whisper with a wink, "None of us have."

The guardian ghosts gazed to the sky, like someone had called them each by name.

"That's our cue," he said. "Send our farewells to the others, won't you?" A solemn smile played on his lips. "And tell Demetrius and Jeom to behave. I won't be around anymore to keep them in line…"

"I'm sorry," Arianna said again, her voice barely audible.

Gabriel turned serious, looking more like a wise elder guardian than she'd ever thought of him before.

"Don't let this be a setback, Arianna," he demanded, his voice strong and steady. "Let it fuel our fire to take back the Olleb."

"Of course," she replied with fervor, unblinking. "We *will* continue to burn bright."

He nodded, so much hope in his expression.

Kiki glided over, stealing the focus from Gabriel—she was looking longingly at Noah, knowing that he could not see her.

"Can you please tell him for me, Ara…" She swayed back and forth, nervously. "Well, *you* know." She gave a little shrug, gaze averted. "I loved him, I suppose."

If ghosts could blush, she thought that Kiki was surely doing it now—everything about her sparkled.

"I will," she replied with a reassuring nod. She forced a smile, trying not to cry anymore. "But he already knows."

Kiki let out a satisfied sigh, giving Noah a longing glance.

"Thanks," she said. She turned back to face Arianna, as feisty as ever. "And you've got this, all right? Don't give up for *anything*. You're our warrior. Our dragon!" She placed her fist over her chest. "Win or die!"

Arianna returned the gesture, standing up tall. "Win or die," she responded, enunciating every word.

Kiki began to glide away.

"Oh… and *sorry* about that," she added, her eyes flicking to Eli; she had a guilty look across her face. "I didn't mean—"

"He's got thick skin," said Arianna, waving it off. "And that'll be the perfect scar to remember you by."

Kiki's shrill laughter rang in her ears—she'd miss it.

Arianna met the eyes of each and every one of the guardian ghosts then, those who had trained so well for their moment to contribute to the fight for freedom. For this…

She tried to memorize their faces.

"Be free now," she said. "Your sacrifice is not a waste, and it will not be forgotten."

Arianna watched as their sparkling souls drifted off into the night sky as one, a group of fallen guardians rising to the heavens, sprinkling the stars above.

"You're learning well," said Diveena in a hoarse voice. She was still on the ground behind her, shivering where she lay. "He fears you now, and for good reason."

"Will you be all right?" said Arianna, glancing down to her. "What should I do—"

Diveena's eyes floated closed. She didn't respond, could barely breathe—the necromancer's darkness was spreading.

With the ghosts now gone, Arianna finally turned to him.

He had stopped attacking, giving Lessa a chance to scurry out of the way; she moved off to the side, standing in front of Sano.

Sir Vladamor was seemingly in a state of shock, trying to regain control over the bodies at their feet.

"That won't work now," she called to him, stepping forward. "Their souls are not yours to take!"

He growled, pacing where he stood. His ruby necklace swung back and forth like the pendulum of a clock.

"An animancer you are," he said with a hiss. "I *knew* it."

"Yes, and all thanks to you," said Arianna.

She stood protectively in front of Noah, Eli, and Solza. And they all stood protectively in front of Diveena.

"I am what you fear because you made me this way. *You* gave me this magic a second time around, but the darkness wasn't the only choice presented to me. I didn't have to forfeit my humanity to gain power." Arianna stood taller. "And now, I realize that I have the light enough to destroy you."

She called to that light now, knowing it would come.

With the wave of her hand, she sent a blast of white magic toward him; it felt so different than the spells she'd cast before.

She didn't need enchantments nor words to ignite this power—it had been lying dormant a long time inside of her, ready to be drawn on should she need it, just like Diveena had promised.

Sir Vladamor tried blocking the magic, but he was so taken aback that he faltered. He caught the blast with his arm and cried out.

She had never heard him scream…

It gave her even more confidence. *This is it! Once I take out Sir Vladamor, it's a straight shot to the King.*

If she could end the necromancer for the guardians, then, maybe, this trip to Guanamara wouldn't have been such a total disaster.

"Looks like you're bleeding," said Arianna, feeling this wonderful, new energy humming at her fingertips, ready to be explored.

Sir Vladamor covered his wounded arm with his golden-gloved hand—dark blood stained the gleaming cloth.

A dazed look crossed his monstrous features. He considered Arianna and the boys, all hovering over Diveena. Then his focus found Lessa.

He pulled his mask down over his face, gold and glaring.

Arianna's eyes grew wide. "Don't even think about it!" She

spun on her heels. "Les, watch out!"

Sir Vladamor released everything he had toward Arianna so that she had to stop and block it, to protect Diveena and the others; his necromancer powers were much more honed than whatever animancer gifts she'd tapped into.

In a smoky blink, he had Lessa by the wrist, Sano too weak to help her.

Sir Vladamor kicked Sano where he lay, and Lessa cried out, fighting against his hold.

"I have your light now," he hissed, speaking directly to Arianna. "My offer still stands… if you want her, come and get her. I'll be waiting." He smirked. "You know where to find us." *Us*—him *and* the King. "I can't promise that you'll receive her alive, but I suppose you'll try either way, now won't you?"

He bowed, mockingly, inviting her to war.

"Ara…" breathed Lessa, eyes wide in terror, one hand on her stomach.

Arianna blinked and they were gone, nothing but dark smoke rising into the air in their wake.

15

REINCARNATION

IT WAS A LONG JOURNEY BACK to the Treehouse, made even longer in silence. Arianna kept her eyes to the ground; every footstep felt like it weighed a thousand pounds more than the last, so heavy with sadness and worry. They'd lost some of their bravest guardians, including two of their leaders—Gabriel and Lessa—and they hadn't even marched to the true battlefield yet.

Not Lessa…

"*No, not Lessa, Master,*" Solza said, trying to fill both their minds with optimism—they'd since reconnected, and Arianna would *never* be asking her to break that connection again. "*Not Lessa. Not yet.*"

She couldn't think like that.

Lessa wasn't *dead…* just gone, separated from them.

Sir Vladamor's repulsive voice echoed through her thoughts, consuming all of her focus.

'You know where to find us.'

Of course, she knew. Sir Vladamor would have returned straight to the City of Saindora, straight to the King with his prize. And, just as he'd surmised, Arianna would absolutely follow him there to get Lessa back.

Just survive, Les. I'm coming.

They marched through the Impenetrable Forest at an uneven pace, away from the City of Guanamara and back toward the Treehouse. And the closer they got, the more dread they felt…

How could they show their faces there ever again? *We failed.*

How could they look their friends in the eyes and tell them everyone was dead? *Slaughtered in seconds.*

How can I tell Jeom that Lessa is—

"*No, Master! Not dead.*" Solza was desperate to believe that.

"Are you all right?" said Eli. He laid a hand on Arianna's shoulder. "You're shaking."

She jumped, shrugging away from his touch.

"I'm fine," she replied. "Just drained."

Diveena floated eerily out in front of their small procession, Arianna using all of her remaining energy to hold her up with the levitation spell.

Noah's voice croaked out for the first time in hours.

"You're overexerting your magic," he said. "If you want, we could switch for—"

"No," snapped Arianna. "I *said* that I'm fine." Noah lowered his head and fell back in step behind her. "Solza, just give me another boost, please."

Solza's eyes lit up, and Arianna felt her power rejuvenated.

But Noah was right—she was reaching her limits, even with an avatar boost .

She lifted her gaze from her feet to the treetops, trying to focus on anything else other than what the future might bring, yet this view was no better…

Every time they passed beneath an opening in the jungle canopy, Diveena's ghostly body would be spotlighted under sporadic rays of early morning sun. And each time, Arianna would cringe at the sight—she could plainly see Sir Vladamor's dark magic spreading beneath her skin, eating away at her light. It looked as if she'd been force-fed the contents of an ink bottle.

She was barely breathing, each breath a rasped gasp for air that sounded as if it might be the last.

"If we don't reach the campsite soon, I'm afraid she won't make it," said Arianna, watching as the necromancer's shadow crawled, hungrily, from limb to limb. "She's getting worse."

They'd tried, of course, but not even Sano could help her now. He was much too weak.

In fact, he'd barely been able to heal Eli's wound when he'd come around. Thanks to Sano, Eli now boasted a silver scar at his hip that would always remind them of Kiki's bold personality. But Arianna thought that even if Sano had been in perfect health, it wouldn't have made a difference to Diveena's situation…

She frowned, still looking up at her. *This isn't just any wound.*

What's more, Sano *wasn't* in the perfect health.

He may have been physically healed, from whatever magical remedy Lessa had used, but his spirit had been irreparably injured from being separated from his master. Too late had he awakened from his battle wounds in Guanamara to do anything but mourn Lessa's loss.

He had since returned to his monkey form; Noah held him safely in his arms.

He barely moved, as if he were sedated.

"*He's in shock,*" explained Solza. "*It's… not a pleasant*

feeling for us, you see… this kind of separation. He needs his master."

Arianna returned a nod of understanding.

"*I know,*" she said, not even wanting to remember the days she'd spent without Solza near. "I'm sure Lessa feels exactly the same."

She gritted her teeth and picked up the pace. *Never forget.*

"We're almost there," said Eli after a while. He was leading the way with a torch in hand.

Arianna focused on his flame. It flickered back and forth in the subtle wind that snuck between the trees.

Everything came rushing back to her then, the end of their Guanamara mission a sharp, stinging memory…

She had frantically tried to call to her animancer magic, anything to stop Sir Vladamor from leaving with Lessa in his grasp, but it had been too late. Her magic had blown straight through the space where they had been.

Sano had awoken in that moment, barely able to stand. He had let out a long, wailing howl into the night, and the sound had nearly broken her.

He had collapsed just as soon as he'd risen, and so did Arianna.

"Not again…" she had whispered.

And just as swiftly as it had come, her newfound magic had faded away, leaving her with nothing but an empty hollow in her chest.

Eli had tried to comfort her, tried to pull her to her feet, but she'd been in a sort of trance, unable to see anything other than that final moment before Sir Vladamor and Lessa had vanished; all she really remembered of the minutes after were the sounds of Noah's sobs and Eli yelling at her to snap out of it.

But Diveena's suffering had brought her back.

One whimper from their stricken friend was the only

reason Arianna had been able to pull herself together—they had to get Diveena back to the Treehouse right away, into a healer's hands, if they wanted even a chance at saving her.

No time to even bury their dead.

And since there was no one left of their group to stay behind and help fortify Guanamara, as was originally planned, Eli and Noah left a message, instead, for the citizens who had witnessed the battles and who had listened to them speak. Maybe they could still sway some people to see the truth.

Eli had crafted the words, and Noah had scrawled them over the city center's punishment platform, using enchanted fire to ensure they'd be seen.

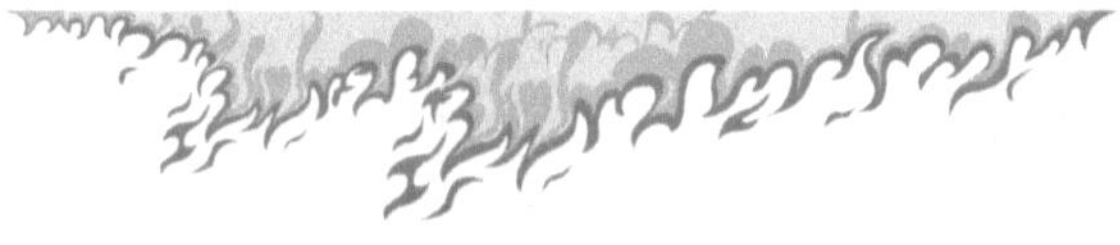

Not everyone bows to the King. Join us if you truly
desire freedom. The time is now. We'll converge in the
High City of Saindora to take back what is ours.
Hail to the Olleb!

- Guardians of Gold -

Their message had lit up the night with bright pink flames. And anyone who dared to read it would have a choice to make. Arianna had also left a message of her own…

She'd conjured a spell that she'd learned from Keeper Kassime, ensuring that, even in death, the Guardians of Gold could shine on—the dragons etched into the palms of all those lost to Sir Vladamor were ignited, the silhouette of a mighty golden dragon lured into the sky for all of Guanamara to behold.

Down with the King, and fire to his kingdom!

She wanted to burn everything to the ground, seeing nothing but that flaming rage flickering in her eyes. And if they didn't get Lessa back soon, she was sure that she would.

She ran through every moment of that horrific night in her head until they finally broke through the trees and into the meadow. The early morning enveloped them in garish light; Arianna wanted to retreat back into the darkness of the jungle.

Everyone was down at the campsite, huddled around dying fires and sprawled out in the grass—clearly, nobody had slept a wink, all waiting for the safe return of their peers.

As soon as Eli and his torch were spotted on the outskirts of the trees, a buzz of excitement blew through the field. The guardians began to cheer and clap, racing to greet them.

The sounds of celebration abruptly ceased once it was apparent that nobody else was coming, and once Diveena floated into view.

Jeom broke into a run; Demetrius was right at his heels, skating across the grass on a cushion of magic.

They all met in the center.

"Where's Lessa?" said Jeom, his voice an octave lower than normal.

He stopped in front of Arianna, his eyes boring down on her, daring her to speak anything other than 'she's right behind me.'

Arianna's lips quivered with just the thought of responding to him. She knew she couldn't utter a single word without tears falling. Unable to withstand the weight of his penetrating gaze, she looked to the sky. Then, she nodded to Noah.

With a sigh, he swung Lessa's bow and quiver of arrows off his back, and tossed them to Jeom's feet.

Jeom froze, staring at the bow. It was sleek, silver, and blue… and blood-splattered.

His lips pressed into a thin line, muscles twitching as he clenched his fists. He looked back to Arianna.

"Where is she?" His voice started as a murmur, then it boomed over the deafening silence that seemed to stifle the air, making it hard to breathe. *I can't breathe. Diveena can't breathe.* "Tell me!"

Jeom grabbed her by the shoulders, trying to shake the answers from her.

She opened her mouth to speak, but no sound came out. Just a desperate gasp for air as she began to weep.

"*No*… oh, no, Ara." He paced back and forth, pressing his hands to his face. "Please, don't tell me this. Don't tell me this. Is she—" He let out a moan of grief and sank to his knees; Arianna still couldn't speak, feeling as if a wave of water had slammed into her, suffocating her. "Is she?"

"She's *not* dead," interjected Eli, trying to comfort him and control the situation. He stepped in front of Arianna. "Lessa was… taken."

There were whispers from the gathering crowd; Arianna thought their expressions must mirror her own—horror-stricken, tear-stricken—to see their leaders in such shambles.

"Vladamor ambushed us," he said to Jeom. "We didn't stand a chance." He cleared his throat, addressing those in earshot. "Nobody else survived."

The Treehouse guardians began to panic. There were shrieks of anger and sorrow over the loss of their friends, demands for more information, battle cries to march into war right then and there. *'Down with the King! Down with the King!'*

"No…" said Jeom, standing—he towered over Eli, over everyone. "How could you let that *monster* put his hands on her?"

Eli shook his head, raising his hands. He took a step back. "We did everything we could to try and stop—"

Jeom lunged. "You promised me you'd protect her!"

He threw a punch that cracked into Eli's jaw and then he tackled him to the ground.

Eli shouted for him to get off, though he didn't fight back.

"Jeom!" yelled Demetrius—he called the earth to Eli's defense, trying to lessen the blows he was taking, but Jeom was as strong as a boulder.

"Enough!" said Arianna, finding her voice as the boys rolled around at her feet; the ground rumbled in response, Solza lending a little support—Eli had already taken enough hits in Guanamara. "Jeom, *please*, stop this. Don't take it out on him. If anything… it was my fault."

She bowed her head.

"*What?*" Jeom paused in his mindless attacks and glanced up at her with glassy eyes. His arm was looped around Eli's neck, Eli fruitlessly trying to pull him off.

She shook her head, tasting salty tears every time she opened her mouth.

"I… I couldn't stop him, Jeom. I'm sorry."

"You couldn't stop the necromancer?" he asked, enunciating every word, as if trying to understand the meaning behind each one.

She shook her head. "I *tried*, but I couldn't stop him," she spluttered.

Jeom released his hold on Eli and crumpled into a ball, crying out into the echoing quiet; Eli wiped the blood from his lip, laying a caring hand on his back without so much as a complaint.

"It's not your fault," Jeom choked out to Arianna, letting

Eli help him up to his feet. "We weren't ready for that... that..."

"Monster," spat Eli. "Vile, despicable creature from the bowels of the Olleb." Jeom shuddered with sadness, and Eli gave him a strong hug; his gaze found Arianna's from over his shoulder. "We are going to get Lessa back."

Jeom sighed. "I'm sorry for hitting you, mate," he said, averting his gaze. "I just... can't lose her again."

"We won't," said Demetrius, his expression dazed. He sounded as if losing Lessa wasn't even possible, clearly still processing all this awful information.

Arianna wished that were true, but she knew the chances of Lessa making it out alive got slimmer each second she was in the King's clutches. *Just survive, Les.*

Jeom collected himself with one clearing of his throat and one roar to the skies; then he extended a hand to Eli.

He accepted, shaking it firmly. "She's going to be fine. We will rescue her. We just... need a new plan."

Jeom returned a firm nod, and Arianna could already see his mind racing with dangerous ideas.

"Oh gods, but *how* did this happen?" stuttered Demetrius, snapping out of his stupor.

Arianna and Eli shared a glance; Eli gave a slight shake of his head and she silently agreed—now was not the time to tell the Kane brothers the part they had played in the situation.

Demetrius went over to Arianna, searching for any sign of hope in her expression; she stayed silent.

His gaze traveled toward the treetops, toward Diveena— she was still being carried by the levitation spell.

Everyone seemed to notice her all at once, creating only more panic.

"Healers... we need a healer!" called someone from the crowd—people were running back and forth, spreading the word. "Diveena is hurt!"

"Put her down, Ara," said Demetrius, his eyes widening in horror as he took her in completely.

Her skin had begun to gray, as if she were slowly rotting.

With as much finesse as she could muster, Arianna lowered Diveena to the ground and relinquished her spell. As soon as she let go of her magic, her knees gave way.

Eli was there to catch her. He lowered her gently to the grass.

"*Master, are you all right?*" asked Solza.

She didn't have the strength to respond. Didn't have the strength to tell her, nor anyone, that she *wasn't* fine anymore.

She leaned all her weight into Eli, for once, letting him cradle her; Solza nuzzled up against her.

A few volunteer healers came running to their aid, the crowd clearing a path for them—among them was Margery.

"What happened to everyone?" she demanded, looking between Arianna and Diveena.

Arianna blinked up at her, her tears dry. "Vladamor."

Margery sucked a breath in through her teeth.

"Necromancy," said Noah, hovering a few feet back; he still rocked poor Sano in his arms, trying to keep him calm. "A lot went down. It was—" His voice cracked, and he focused on Sano. "Basically, Diveena got hit pretty badly when she was trying to protect us from him."

Margery gulped, looking to Arianna. "And you?"

"I'm fine," she mumbled; Eli held her tight. "I just need rest. Help Diveena."

"But what of the others?" she asked. "What of Gabriel?" There was a remnant of hope left in her voice.

Arianna swallowed the lump in her throat, knowing they were about to squash it.

Margery glanced back toward the trees, expectantly.

"They didn't make it," said Eli, before Arianna found the courage to respond. "Me, Noah, Ara… we're all that's left."

"Please, help Diveena," said Arianna. "We can't lose her too."

Margery's mouth fell open, eyes watering, but she held back her breakdown for later—Arianna thanked her for that.

They needed an elder to lead them right now.

"Is there anything you can do?" asked Demetrius, his nails digging into his palms; he was Diveena's apprentice, and she was his pride and joy of a mentor. "There must be a way to help her."

Arianna prayed so, but hadn't figured it out yet; all eyes settled on Margery.

She appeared frazzled, clearly trying to focus her thoughts as her gaze darted back and forth.

"I learned a fair bit under Talis," she replied. Her words wavered. "But necromancy is… deadly. I don't honestly know that there's anything that can counteract such dark magic once it sinks in. It's utterly toxic to anything that it touches."

"Just like Vladamor," said Arianna through her teeth, her heart pounding as she thought of his claws around Lessa.

"You have to try!" cried Demetrius, kneeling down in the grass next to her. "She trusted us, and look what's happened to her."

Arianna flinched. *I'm sorry, Diveena*, she thought.

They should've never allowed her to reveal herself like that.

"I'll do my very best," said Margery, her voice of little confidence.

She began to enlist other healers for help, and they made Diveena as comfortable as they could while everyone stood back to watch; Demetrius held her hand all the while.

Eli and Noah offered more details to their peers about the lost night and the lost guardians, and Arianna and Jeom were huddled in deep conversation, already ironing out a rescue plan.

AN HOUR CAME AND WENT, the sun rising high in the sky. The healers had tried everything in their power to help Diveena, but nothing proved effective in combating the necromancer's magic.

Margery glanced to Arianna with such defeat in her eyes. She gave the slightest shake of her head.

Arianna wobbled to her feet, some of her strength returned; Eli lent her his arm to lean on.

They walked over to them.

"Demetrius," she spoke as gently as possible, "Sano's magic didn't even…" She cleared her throat. "It might be time to—"

"Something will work," he snapped. He didn't even look at her. He squeezed Diveena's hand tighter. "It has to."

Diveena suddenly fluttered her eyes open, for the first time since leaving Guanamara.

Arianna clutched at Eli's arm to steady herself. *Oh, please be all right!*

Margery and the other healers stood back to give them room, but their expressions weren't as optimistic.

"Demetrius," said Diveena, her breath clipped. "I'm glad… that you're here."

"Tell us how we can help you," he replied—Arianna thought, morbidly, that if this had happened to anyone else, Diveena probably *could* have saved them.

She coughed, dark blood dripping down her chin.

Demetrius carefully lifted her head into his lap, wiping the blood away with a handkerchief.

"This shouldn't have happened to you," he said, his voice wavering. "How can we—"

"Everything happens for a reason," she said. "There's

nothing—" Another frightening cough. "I can't be saved." Her lips were cracked, blood staining her perfect teeth. "His darkness sank too deep. I… I don't have the strength to fight it anymore."

"But there must be something—"

She shook her head, slow movements.

"It's… *too* late." Some of her normal sternness filtered through her pain. "You must promise me, Demetrius. You *must* remember us." This time, she squeezed his hand. "Never forget where you came from… my brother."

He bowed his head, a single tear rolling down his cheek.

"Of course, I won't forget you, Diveena," he said, trying to hold back his emotions. "I could never forget any of this." He looked around, desperate for help—nobody moved. He let out a little sob, gazing back to Diveena with such sorrow in his eyes. "All this… you gave it to us. We will *never* forget."

The gathering spoke their unwavering agreement, all clinging to each other in support, all waiting for the inevitable.

Arianna watched, too, with the same aching heart.

Never forget! Kill the King. Kill the King!

"Good," whispered Diveena. She glanced around at each of the young guardians she'd helped to raise, smiling weakly at them… at Arianna. "*Good.*" She locked her gaze on Demetrius, placing her hand upon his cheek. "Then we will never forget you."

Her emerald eyes suddenly morphed into orbs of silver, blazing bright, as if stars had replaced them; the silver magic began to spread throughout her entire body until every inch of her skin radiated with a shimmering light.

"Remember us," she said.

Her eyes floated closed, the silver vanishing.

Demetrius still held her hand against his cheek, his tears trickling onto her face. "Diveena! No… *wait*—"

He let out a gasp, choking on his words—the light within

her had pooled in the palm of her hand.

He let go, her hand falling back to her side, but it had already begun; the magic poured into his body as it faded away from hers.

Demetrius cried out in what was surely agony, yanking at the fabric above his chest, above his heart.

Jeom, Eli, and Arianna all ran to his side, looking down at him in horror; there were cries of concern from the bystanders.

"Brother, what is it? What's happening?"

Jeom reached out to help, but Arianna stopped him.

"What if Vladamor's spell was contagious?" she said in haste, throwing herself in front of him.

They all shared a glance of sheer dread. Was Demetrius now infected by the necromancer's dark disease?

"No, something is—" Demetrius let out another howl of pain, his head thrusting back, eyes to the sky. He lay flat on his back besides Diveena, crying out for her… crying out for dear life. "I don't know what's happening to me!"

His eyes began to glow like Diveena's had just been, frozen open in what could only be fear. They had flooded with silver, then his entire body followed.

"Somebody, help him!" Jeom roared, lurching toward his brother.

This time, Eli was the one to tackle him to the ground.

"Wait," he said, pinning him to the grass; his eyes swam with tears. "We *have* to wait."

Jeom stilled. Everyone stilled, waiting for Death to take another leader away.

Then Demetrius stilled, too, his eyelids falling closed.

Arianna held her breath, staring, unblinking, at Demetrius and Diveena. An eternity seemed to pass before she was able to let it go…

As if the life had been pounded back into his lungs, Demetrius woke with a deep inhale. The silver shell that had encased his body burst away, glittering in the air around him.

An exhale of relief whistled through the meadow.

"Demetrius," she breathed, her entire body sagging as it released the weight of her worry.

He blinked up at her, his brow furrowed—she wasn't sure if he could actually *see* her. It was as if he was lost in his thoughts.

"Demetrius?" she said again, warily.

He didn't respond.

Eli and Jeom jumped to their feet and ran over.

"Are you… hurt?" asked Jeom, kneeling down next to him.

Demetrius shook his head, pushing onto his elbows.

"Help me up, please." His voice sounded different… steadier.

Eli held out his hand.

Demetrius got to his feet, and they all surrounded him, waiting for him to say something more.

Arianna glanced to Margery; she appeared just as concerned, ready to examine him. "Maybe we can let a healer look at you—"

"Move back," demanded Demetrius. His focus was set on Diveena, giving her a wide berth.

"What?" Jeom trailed him. "Demetrius, are you sure—"

With a sound like raindrops on pebbles, Diveena's body suddenly began to dissolve. It was frightening and beautiful all at once, until, soon, all that remained of her was a glittering pile of gold and green dust atop the grass.

Jeom shrieked, jumping a foot into the air when he noticed she'd vanished.

"Move back," Demetrius repeated, eyes steady on the spot where she'd been.

Arianna felt the ground groan beneath her feet.

She glanced to Solza, who had since retreated to stand near

Noah and Sano.

"*Not me, Master… and not Sano.*" She sounded anxious.

Arianna dragged Eli back toward Demetrius and Jeom, not waiting to find out what it was. And with their remaining leaders setting the example, the guardians all formed a large circle around where Diveena's body had been.

Everyone but Demetrius appeared to be in shock at this strange occurrence, unnerved.

Suddenly, the ground roared, the force of the earthquake nearly toppling people to their knees.

The meadow broke apart at its seams, a crack in the earth originating from the green and golden dust—with it, a massive tree unearthed itself, as if the remnants of Diveena's body had literally been the enchanted soil from which it could sprout.

The tree was reinforced by a mass of tangled roots that crawled their way out from the ground, and it was topped with a thick head of sprawling, sparkling green leaves that curled all the way down to its base on long, swaying limbs.

Veins of silver seemed to pulsate on the outside of its trunk.

Lifeblood, Arianna thought.

When the earth stopped churning and the tree stopped growing, everything stilled. The tree stood steady as a statue, as if it had lived a thousand years in that spot—the jungle's living, breathing heart.

Noah let out a loud whistle of astonishment.

"I will never question you again, Demetrius," said Jeom, jaw hanging open. "Nature *is* alive."

Arianna had to crane her neck to even see the top of the tree. *Such a vision…*

It made her rethink everything she'd ever assumed about the many tree-laden terrains she'd trekked through during her journeys across the Olleb.

How had the Nicora Forest really come to be?

Eli ran his hand through his hair. "Um… what just happened here?"

Along with everyone else, he was stunned.

"I know what it was…" said Arianna after a moment—she was struck with a thought. She tore her gaze away from the tree and considered Demetrius. "It was a shift in power."

Demetrius let out a deep breath, and every plant and tree in the vicinity breathed with him.

All eyes turned to stare his way in disbelief, the jungle rustling with a mind of its own.

"Diveena gave me all her power, I think," he whispered, closing his eyes. "All her knowledge, it's flowed into me, just like she said it could. But I *never* thought—" He pressed his fingers to his temples, furrowing his brow. "I can feel everything. And their memories, too. It's like… like I was there." He shook his head. "It's too much. I can't do this!"

"You can, Demetrius," said Arianna, laying a hand on his arm. "You can handle this. It's what Diveena was training you for all this time." His skin was hot, bubbling with this newly earned magic just underneath the surface. "Focus. Concentrate on the here and now."

She knew what too much power could feel like… how dangerous it could be if he lost control.

Demetrius took deep, long breaths, in and out, until she felt him relax.

"Better?" she asked.

He opened his eyes.

"Better," he mumbled with a curt nod.

He gazed at the tree, sinking back into his thoughts.

"Is Gabe really gone?" His question hung in the air.

Eli cleared his throat. "Yes… I'm afraid he is," he answered.

"I'm sorry," added Arianna, still touching his arm. "I know how much he meant to you too."

Demetrius bowed his head; she could feel him trembling.

"Everyone is gone," stammered Jeom.

Silent tears overcame him as he stared ahead—the Kane brothers were crumbling before her eyes.

"Just breathe," implored Arianna again. She reached for their hands. "Breathe with me."

As their fingers wrapped around her own, she immediately felt more grounded. And she hoped they did too.

"What do we do now?" asked Noah; Sano was curled around his neck, Solza at his feet, and Margery had one compassionate hand on his shoulder.

Arianna took in all the rattled young guardians, everyone unsure of what to say or do.

It was evident that they hadn't fully felt the risks they'd signed up for in positioning themselves against the King… but now they surely did. Everyone here had lost someone, a friend, to Guanamara. And every one of them could've just as easily been in their friend's place.

She addressed Eli, Jeom, and Demetrius. "Stay strong. They need to hear us now, as one."

They agreed, and she let go of the boys' hands.

Together, they all walked forward, ready to lead again.

"If you didn't grasp the dangers we face as guardians before," said Arianna, her boys flanking her, "then now you do. We thought we had the upper hand when we marched on Guanamara, but we're playing at the King's game here." She looked to the ground before forcing herself to meet everyone's eyes. "We *always* have been, and he's not making it easy. He's had centuries of practice to keep us down, and we're only beginning to rise."

She pressed a hand against the bark of Diveena's tree, sensing the warmth of her encouragement flood through her even now.

"We can't stop if we want to win, no matter the stakes, but

King Devlindor and his armies are a *real* threat. We've openly assembled against a viper of a man with infinite power to his name, and he's prepared for a nasty fight." She felt the scowl wrinkle her face. "And we already know that he doesn't fight fair…"

"The King's Shadow destroyed some of our strongest guardians, our friends," said Eli, standing tall by her side.

"He's killed *two* of our beloved leaders," added Demetrius, glaring at the tree.

"And he's taken Lessa as bait," said Jeom with a sneer, flexing his muscles.

Arianna felt her rage burn even hotter. She unsheathed one of her swords just to feel the weight of it in her hand. All the anger she'd been holding in burst out with her voice.

"Guardians are not bait," she yelled. "We are dragons!"

The people were buzzing with restless energy—nodding along, mumbling curses in the King's name, whispering prayers for their fallen friends.

Arianna began to pace the circle, sword swinging by her side.

"Not all of us will make it to the other side," she said, gravely, "but some of us have to. This is the *last* Free Falls Festival the King will ever make us enter!" Her grip tightened around the jeweled hilt. "There have only been, and only ever will be, two ways out of this… win or die." She lifted her sword, pointing it toward the crowd, her gaze sharp. "*Win*… or die."

Their murmurs of praise grew into a loud steady hum. Weapons were being drawn, feet stomping the ground; Solza's low growl joined them.

Arianna returned a nod of approval.

"Those of you still standing here today," she continued, "be strong, stay vigilant, and keep your courage in your grasp. Because the Guardians of Gold will *not* let our friends die in vain!" She looked to Noah, and he crossed his fist at his chest; she thrust her blade into the air, sunrays glaring off the metal. "We must beat the King at his own game. Whatever sacrifice that means, we make it together, and ensure that we take his last breath in repayment." She swiped her blade through the air; it sizzled with magic. "Dragons, what say you?"

Her voice boomed out across the field.

Everyone threw their weapons into the air in a passionate fury, tears falling to the ground and a flood of shouts and curses on their tongues.

"Down with the King!" they bellowed back. "Hoorah, hoorah!"

The echo of their combined voices shook the jungle awake, birds and butterflies swarming out from the canopies of the trees, filling the sky in a thunderous burst; Solza let out a ground-shaking roar to join them, and even Sano seemed to be roused from his terrible trance, the wind whistling through the field with such force that the grass was nearly flattened.

Arianna closed her eyes a moment, soaking everything in, letting the resilient sounds energize her for what came next.

"There's been a change of plans," she called over the rumble of voices. She glanced to Eli, Jeom, and Demetrius—they were all pounding their fists in the air with the crowd. "We're going to the City of Saindora, *now*. We wait no longer."

"Hoorah, hoorah!" the crowd agreed.

She raised her hand for quiet, repeating herself, just to be sure everyone understood the importance of what she'd said.

"The final phase in our strategy begins now." She spoke in a steady voice, touching eyes with them all. "This is the part that will decide our future, what we've been training for. If anyone wishes to speak a concern, you have the floor."

Margery stepped up, and a hush fell over the field.

Arianna more than welcomed her to speak as the last elder guardian among them.

"I don't disagree," she said with a solemn expression. "I don't think anyone does at this point, but the Treehouse guardians won't be enough to invade Saindora alone..." She looked around. "We'll be slaughtered on sight. We *need* those in Zambienth to join us in battle."

There were mutters of support—that had always been the plan.

"She's right," said Noah, stepping up alongside her. "We need numbers, now more than ever." He fingered the handle of a dagger at his belt—Kiki's dagger.

"Let's get a message there quickly, then," said Demetrius, seeming a bit more himself. "We don't have time to waste."

Arianna and Jeom shared a glance; he nodded.

Solza pranced over to them when Arianna beckoned her.

"Leave that to me," she said with confidence, one hand on her avatar—Jeom's idea. "I'll organize the fleet in Zambienth myself, and then we'll all meet on the deep waters, just like we always planned."

"Wait," said Eli, shaking his head, his focus on Arianna. "You shouldn't go alone." He glanced at Solza, warily. "We can just send word the normal way..."

"Sending a crew will take too long," interjected Jeom, firmly. "We need to move *now*."

He ignored him, still looking to Arianna. "Then let me come with you," he said, closing the distance between them.

She lowered her voice, finding his gaze.

"No, I need you to stay here, Eli," she replied, a command in her tone. "You're one of the main leaders of this army." She gestured to the younger guardians. "With Lessa gone, they need your guidance right now more than ever." The crowd responded with sounds of agreement—he was one of their first leaders since the freeing of the districts, an important motivational figurehead. "And someone needs to watch over Demetrius while he figures out how to control his powers. I can think of no better person to do that than you."

Demetrius grimaced. "Oh, I'll be *fine*," he grumbled.

Eli frowned down at her. "But—"

She sharpened her gaze, and his words faltered.

"Jeom." She turned away from Eli before he found the courage to protest. "This was all your idea. Care to join me for the ride?"

He puffed out his chest. "It would be my greatest pleasure."

"All right then," she said, meeting the eyes of her warriors; Margery and Noah nodded their blessings, melting back into the crowd. "Anyone else have anything to add?"

Nobody but Eli tried to speak up. "Ara, I—"

"Don't worry," said Jeom, meeting his troubled gaze. "I'll take care of her. I always do. And *you* take care of my brother." He squeezed his shoulder, a serious expression on his face. "Deal?"

Eli hesitated a moment, but sighed, surely knowing that her mind was made up. "Deal."

The last thing Arianna wanted to do was separate from him again, but she had to put the guardians first, they all did.

"We need to do what's best for… our people," she said, letting the commitment of her words sink in. She took his hand in hers for only a moment, noting the familiar lines of callouses formed where he always gripped his sword; she squeezed. "I promise, it won't be for long."

He returned a firm nod, and she, reluctantly, let go.

Arianna addressed the crowd with orders, no more waiting. No more planning. *Time for action!*

"The rest of you, ready the ships and take to the seas as soon as you can. Set anchor in the location that we agreed, but do not drift too close to Saindora until we're all together." She touched eyes with Noah, Margery, Eli, and Demetrius—they all lifted their fists. "Listen to your leaders. Demetrius has the compass to guide you there."

"How will you find us, though... without a compass?" asked a young girl she'd trained with many times before, her apprehension plain.

She offered her a warm smile.

"We'll follow the South Star, like Eli taught us," she replied. "It's as good as any compass."

"Better," he chimed in, his frown faltering.

"Much better," she agreed, feeling some of her faith return.

Guanamara's mission may have been ill-fated, but not all of their strategy sessions and trainings were to be discarded just yet—they still had plenty of tricks up their sleeves to try to get ahead of the King, and now Arianna at least had *access* to the key to killing the necromancer.

Diveena's conviction, along with that of the Treehouse guardians, filled her heart whole again.

There's still a chance here... Saindora, here we come!

In a colorful burst, Solza transformed into the colossal dragon that never failed to take one's breath away. And with a magical *whoosh,* Arianna was situated on her back.

"Be safe," said Eli, watching her go with a pained expression.

"You too," she replied, blowing him a kiss on the wind— enchanted and electric.

He jumped a little in surprise, then flashed her one last charming smile to send her off in higher spirits.

"Thank you," she mouthed, grateful he'd come around.

Jeom swept Sano into his arms before following Arianna.

"Don't worry, buddy," he whispered, giving him a gentle hug. "I'll find Lessa for you. I promise." He passed him off to Demetrius. "Take care of him until we meet again, all right? And take care of yourself."

They pressed the palms of their hands together, two halves

of a whole, never to be broken apart.

"I'll see you soon, brother," said Demetrius, determination in his silver-lined stare.

Jeom returned a firm nod, then used the Axe of Crissy to manipulate the air element for a boost up onto Solza's back. He settled in behind Arianna.

"The necromancer said that the King is waiting for us, ready for us," called Arianna, commanding all attention—the guardians gaped up at her in pride. "Let's not keep him waiting any longer!"

With a mighty roar, Solza stretched her wings out wide and lurched into the air. Cheers of support chased after them on the wind as they slowly circled the meadow.

Arianna glanced down one last time to witness their friends waving them off. As she did, she *swore* the tree Diveena had left behind was waving, too, scattering nature's beautiful magic into the air in solidarity with the Guardians of Gold.

She beamed, urging Solza to fly faster.

"Hang on tight," she said to Jeom. "We're going to get our girl back."

16

SAILING SOUTH

ARIANNA AND JEOM REACHED the City of Zambienth under the cover of night, just a handful of days later. White pyramids jutted toward the sky from waves of black sand, Solza soaring high above it all.

"It's amazing," said Jeom, sounding stunned. They slowed down a bit. "From this view, it's truly all just… amazing."

"I couldn't agree more," said Arianna, peering down on the twinkling city that had been their home not so long ago. "How strange to be back after all that's happened."

From this vantage point, she saw just how truly complex Zambienth was. Bridges intertwined with each other in never-ending patterns—creating the Burrows—connecting the entire city from the top of the tallest pyramid to the bottom of the smallest.

She and her friends had never even come close to exploring all this city had to offer.

Solza veered to the other side of the city where the sea came back into view, black sand shimmering along the shoreline and stopping at the base of marble gray cliffs. Everything was so familiar, except—

"Over there! Do you see that?"

Arianna pointed ahead as a breathtaking pyramid rose into sight. It was even more spectacular than the city keeper's pyramid palace—a pointed top made of crystal so clear that it glinted like a diamond as the moon glared down on it.

She recognized it immediately.

"It's the Greenhouse, Jeom," she said, excitedly. "Just look!"

"Oh, wow, you're right," he said, leaning a little forward to see. "That's odd, though… isn't it? Isn't it supposed to be cloaked by guardian magic?"

She beamed.

"Not anymore," she replied with pride. "The City of Zambienth is no longer controlled by King Devlindor, remember?" She steered Solza toward the Greenhouse. "The Guardians of Gold no longer have to hide."

They both fell silent a moment as this truth resonated with them—so much had happened since their beginnings.

"Sir Vladamor has cost us too much pain," said Jeom as the earth neared, the nighttime breeze enveloping them. "We're so close to our freedom. If we don't all make it—"

"We're going to get her back," said Arianna. "We'll defeat the King and his shadow." *Shadows. Solomon, too.* She gripped Solza's horn tightly, her hair whipping all around. "I know we can do it. Just look at all we've accomplished so far. This city is *ours.*"

They hovered over the beach where the secret entrance of the Greenhouse was located—where the guardians had been ambushed by the Shadow Resistance, subsequently scattering them, it had seemed, to every corner of the Olleb.

Yet, together we rise.

Instead of wreckage from that lost battle, as she half expected, countless guardian ships were docked on the waters, each one larger than the next.

Jeom let out a loud whistle, and Arianna beamed.

"By gods, someone's been *busy*," he said with a chuckle of surprise. "I'm staggered! It… it almost looks like nothing bad ever even happened here. Right, Ara?"

"Time is funny like that," she replied—the tide had refreshed it all. "I honestly don't know what I was expecting." She cocked her head to the side, quickly counting, smiling. "It's just surreal they could create this many ships in such a short amount of time, even with magic. I was certain it would be less."

Roughly two hundred gleaming vessels bounced back and forth on the waves, dragons waiting to take flight across the sea.

"They have the bulk of the Creator's District here," said Jeom, "and who knows who else has found their base in Zambienth. When you pull people together to create, that's when the real magic happens."

Arianna smirked at him over her shoulder. "How wise you've grown."

He flashed her a wink.

"I know they sent estimates, but how many people do you think those could truly carry, now that you see them?" she asked.

"Thousands," he said, matter-of-factly.

Arianna's palms grew sweaty with her grip, her heartbeat quickening.

"*Thousands…*" said Solza, mirroring Arianna's astonishment.

She'd always known that their army was big, but seeing its potential with her own eyes really put things into perspective.

I can't believe we finally made it to this point.

"Let's set down over there," she said after a moment, guiding Solza toward the sand; she was eager to see these ships set sail.

Jeom and Arianna slid down to the ground, and Solza changed back into her snow leopard form. Then, they located the Greenhouse's secret entrance.

Arianna pressed her palm against the wall of a plain-looking cliff. The tingle of guardian magic pulsed through her hand, and a door appeared before them, singeing into the rock.

"You know, I guess we don't really even have to sneak in," Jeom mused as they tiptoed through the secret passageway.

Arianna had thought the same, but it felt wrong to just knock on the front door and announce themselves—they'd been in hiding for so long.

"Better to be cautious," she said, still wary to be back here after the last time.

Jeom grunted in response; they walked along in silence.

The tunnel eventually receded. There was a small opening at the end, covered in hanging vines; Arianna knew that just beyond that nature-covered doorway lay the center of the Greenhouse.

Home.

Without any finesse, Jeom pushed through the vines.

"Is anyone here?" he bellowed out, turning in circles with his arms spread wide.

Arianna's hair stood on end, as if he'd sent a jolt of magic through her.

"*Cautious!*" she hissed, giving him a kick in the shin—his voice echoed on for ages, bouncing between the thick, glass walls.

Solza paced forward, wary.

Jeom flashed her a toothy grin, not sorry in the least; he

acted brave, but Arianna could tell he was on edge, too, probably reliving very unpleasant memories.

Alas, nobody answered his call…

They walked farther into the main garden, where they used to spend so much of their time; the entire Greenhouse uncoiled around them, like memory magic taking over their senses.

Arianna breathed in deeply, relishing the eternal fresh scent of flowers from every region of the world, and she felt comforted by the glittering black sand walls that had protected her for so many moons; the passageways that would take her elsewhere in the Greenhouse tempted her to explore, and the calm lake in the center coaxed her to relax by its edges.

She tilted her head up and found the top of the crystal ceiling they had just flown over, the golden stars and moon pouring in their light—the spiral steps called to her to climb.

As if time had changed nothing, they curled around the massive, glass cylinder filled with desert sand. Its dancing blue flame still drenched the area in enchanted, natural light… still burned bright, in defiance of the King.

Just like the guardians.

"I really missed this place," said Arianna; Solza purred in agreement.

"Me too," said Jeom.

Snap! A ripple of sound cracked through the still air.

In barely a blink Arianna had unsheathed both of her swords, heart racing.

And with a booming scream, Jeom had leaped behind her. "What the—"

As if a veil had been lifted away from the entire area, hundreds of people suddenly surrounded them, weapons drawn and defensive magic stirring in the air.

Arianna crouched low, preparing to fight; Solza snarled, baring her teeth; and Jeom was still collecting himself.

Yet, the more she took in this enemy, the more she realized…

This isn't the enemy at all.

She softened her stance.

"*Stand down, Solza,*" she commanded, a smile on her face.

She sheathed her swords and nudged Jeom to catch on.

"Oh…" His voice came out in a shaky croak. He straightened up. "*Oh,* I see what this is." He threw his hands into the air, a smirk crawling over his lips as he now, cockily, stepped in front of Arianna. "We surrender!"

Arianna scoffed, rolling her eyes. But, just in case, she put her hands up too.

The people who had cornered them looked between each other, perplexed, still holding their weapons high.

"Who are you?" someone demanded.

Arianna heard worried whispers snake among the crowd. "Could they be Shadow Resistance?" She gave a derisive snort.

No one advanced, no one the leader—for their leaders were the ones they had waylaid.

Arianna and Jeom had been cornered by an entirely new group of young guardians.

Arianna couldn't stop smiling, thinking of herself, Lessa, Jeom, and Demetrius, just trying to make it out of the mountains with hardly any magic to their names.

What started out as only a small rebellion has now combusted into a far-reaching movement…

She considered that each day only felt more surreal than the last, the closer she got to returning to Saindora.

"Stop, stop, *stop!*" came a high-pitched voice from behind. "Lower your weapons, you idiots. For the gods' sakes. Do you have any idea who that is?"

There were grumbles of confusion as some of the guardians started lowering their blades. Those who did not found their weapons magically flung from their hands, as if a magnet had drawn them down to the ground.

Arianna and Jeom dropped their hands to their sides, trying and failing to keep their laughter behind their teeth.

"And where's your defensive spells?" the woman barked. "I shouldn't be able to unarm you so easily. *Yeesh*, novices. You better have smarter senses than this on the battlefield. These two could've leveled you in a second with pathetic shielding like that."

Jeom covered his mouth with his hand, his laughter bursting through his fingers.

"Rowina!" said Arianna as the crowd parted to let her pass. She ran to her. "It's *so* good to see you. You have no idea…" She was giddy with happiness. "I can't believe we're back."

"Oh, Arianna," she said, wrapping her arms around her—they were skinny but strong. "We were all worried sick after you disappeared that night!"

She pressed her cheeks between her dirt-covered hands, squinting through her big glasses to look at her properly.

The young guardians in earshot all gaped as they realized who she was—the name '*Arianna Belvedor*' started twisting through the air in an excited hum.

"And when you didn't show with Lessa and Eli…" Rowina shook her head. "Gods, we were so relieved when word came that you eventually found Diveena's care." She narrowed her gaze at her, sharp and studious. "Although, I wasn't expecting to see you again so soon… not at least for another month. Why are you—"

"It's a long story," said Arianna, her insides knotting with the bad news to be delivered, "but I'll fill you in soon."

Rowina bent down to scratch Solza behind the ear. Then she gave her attention to Jeom.

"And, Jeom, you've gotten much… taller," she said with a nod of approval; he shimmied with smugness. "The news of *your* survival was even more shocking." She smirked, hands on her hips. Then she turned more serious. "I'm glad you and your brother made it safely out of that boat."

Jeom lifted Rowina into his arms with ease, giving her a big squeeze. "Amazing to see your face again, too, Rowina."

'*Jeom Kane*' replaced Arianna's name on the tongues of the guardians, their interest only piqued more.

"Oh, put me down," Rowina said with a cackle, slapping his chest. She straightened her glasses as he set her on her feet. "Seems like Diveena has been treating you lot well enough." She looked back and forth between him and Arianna. "But now… where's Lessa and Demetrius? You're such the inseparable bunch." She cocked her head. "Have they not come with you?"

When they didn't respond, the smile vanished from her eyes.

"There's trouble," replied Arianna, gravely. She lowered her voice, not wanting to alarm any of these fresh warriors. "It's time. We've come to gather you all. We can't stall any longer."

"Sir Vladamor killed fifty of our best, and… he captured Lessa," said Jeom, his voice cracking on her name.

Outrage heaved throughout the Greenhouse—Lessa was, clearly, someone that many of these guardians here had personally gotten to know.

"I see," said Rowina in a clipped tone, her brow furrowed. "And what of Diveena? What does she say of all this?"

Arianna and Jeom shared a furtive glance, full of dread.

"She's dead," uttered Arianna, bowing her head out of respect.

"Gabriel, too," said Jeom, rubbing the back of his neck.

Rowina's face went pale, her eyes growing large beneath her frames. "*Dead?*"

Arianna had never seen her look so despondent before. She normally hid her emotions well.

"As I said, we cannot wait any longer," said Arianna; her skin ran hot with all the attention. "The Shadow Resistance knows we're coming, and we can't give them more time to prepare or pick us off."

Rowina pursed her lips, lifting her chin high and puffing out her chest.

"All right," she said, turning away from Arianna and Jeom. Her voice boomed across the Greenhouse. "You heard her, folks! Spread the word. Get everyone up and out of bed. It's time to go. We'll meet at first light in the city center."

"The city center?" Jeom raised an eyebrow.

"That's right," snapped Rowina. "The city center, everyone, at the crack of dawn!" She peered back at Jeom and Arianna as the Greenhouse guardians burst into action. "When we wrote to say that the city was fully ours, we *meant* it." She grinned. "Just wait until you hear who sleeps in the palace."

Arianna and Jeom both gaped at each other, squirming in anticipation.

"Just one more to go," said Arianna, "then we can start putting this world back together."

"Right you are," said Rowina, pinching her cheek. "Saindora will be the guardians' next sanctuary soon."

Jeom visibly relaxed, all the hope of her words written in his expression; he let out a big yawn and Solza caught it.

"You all look tired," said Rowina with a knowing stare. "I'm sure you had a long journey, so you had better get some rest now. I'll take everything from here and see you kids in the morning. Your beds are right where you left them."

She shooed them away.

Jeom, Arianna, and Solza were happy to leave the chaotic scene behind, guardians running this way and that, Rowina shouting directions after them.

They walked the familiar path to their old quarters.

When they reached the room, they didn't even bother to

say goodnight to each other. Their heads hit the pillows and eyes shut tight in the same second; Solza curled up in a ball on the floor.

What felt like only moments later, Arianna awoke with a start—Jeom was shaking her.

"Get up," he moaned, sounding exhausted. "We've overslept."

She blinked back at him, sleep still in her eyes. It took her a minute to even remember where she was.

"What'd we miss?" she asked, sitting up.

Jeom shrugged. "Not exactly sure, but we're late." He pulled her from the bed and handed her her swords; they were still in their riding clothes. "You too, Solza. Time to wake up."

Solza stretched her limbs and flexed her paws. "*I'm up,*" she said with a snip reserved for Jeom.

They both followed him into the hallway.

"How did you sleep?" she asked.

"Terrible," he said. "You?"

"Same…" she replied, quite sure they had both experienced an identical, all-too-real nightmare.

They entered the main gardens, everything now underscored by a bright morning sunlight; Arianna took a moment to remember Diveena.

"It's awful what happened to her," she said, letting her fingers brush one of the many brilliant plants that combed the vicinity. "She was such an incredible soul."

During the countless hours they'd spent stuck in this spectacular guardian sanctuary, she and her friends had often wondered how it had come to be. They had since learned that Diveena Lethander, an elf of Nicora and honorary Guardian of Gold, was owed their thanks… for this and so much more.

Jeom sighed.

"I hope Demetrius will be all right," he said. "Diveena taught me so much about my axe and the powers I inherited from the dwarves, but I have a feeling she only tapped the surface with him." He frowned. "After all, she couldn't have known her life would end so abruptly." He stopped walking.

With a howl of anger, he punched his fist into the silver bark of the large tree in the center of the gardens.

"Jeom…" said Arianna, cautiously; his hand was bleeding as he pulled it back. "You have to remain in control."

"I just feel like this is all my fault," he huffed out. He leaned his back against the tree and gazed at the lake with a glassy stare, unblinking. "It's always all my fault."

"What are you talking about? How could *any* of this be your fault?" said Arianna, gently.

He sank to the ground, and she knelt down beside him.

She took his hand in hers—using her elemental magic, she called forth the water from the lake, wrapping it around his broken skin. *Helthra saludis emencia.*

Jeom's hand slowly began to heal.

"Vladamor was after us… *me*," he said, a shadow crossing his face.

Arianna was taken aback. "How do you even know—"

"I got it out of Noah before we left," he said, "while everyone was fussing over Diveena."

Arianna opened her mouth to respond, but no words came out.

He looked up, glowering. "No point in trying to deny it, Ara."

She didn't.

Jeom pulled his knees into his chest, bowing his head.

"I know that he was on our trail because the King still covets the Axe of Crissy." He was seething with every word. "Diveena's barrier spell in the jungle had kept us hidden. That's what Noah said." He let out a groan of frustration, grinding his teeth. "But we just *had* to go searching for more answers… more, more, more." He spat onto the grass.

"Bloody Starr Caverns!"

Arianna looked away with apprehension, intertwining her fingers—she didn't want to hear this. Didn't want to know that Jeom thought their trip had been a waste of time…

A waste of life.

She shook her head of these thoughts.

The choice is in the past, she reminded herself, firmly. *Nobody knew the future.*

If they had, Lessa would've never agreed to let their boys go in the first place.

Jeom balled his healed fist, the skin red and raw.

"The moment I stepped outside of the Treehouse boundaries, the necromancer caught back onto us," he said. "And look what happened! Gabriel and Diveena are dead, the new recruits slaughtered, and they *took* Lessa." His eyes were rimmed with tears. "Who knows what will happen to her…" He sniffled. "To her, and… and…"

Arianna knew the name he couldn't bring himself to say. *Snow.*

Jeom let his head fall back, staring up toward the maroon canopy of the tree. "I should have never let her go, Ara."

She reached out a consoling hand.

"Jeom, you know that you couldn't have stopped her, even if you'd wanted to," she replied. "And you *did* want to, I remember." She forced a smile, but he didn't reciprocate. "Lessa's been on this journey from the start, and she's going to see it through, just like the rest of us… baby or not." He grimaced. "But *none* of this is your fault. Not Guanamara and certainly not what happened to her. We all knew the risks when we signed up to go against the King. Nobody blames you for anything."

She moved so that they were side by side, her back against the tree; she leaned her head upon his shoulder.

"We can't give up, all right? I'm just as determined as you

to get her back, but we have to stay focused," she implored. "Lessa risked her life for a reason, and you've risked your life for a reason, too. We all have, every day that we fight this brutal fight. But we *can't* forget why we're fighting in the first place."

She felt her heartbeat thrumming faster.

"This is so much bigger than just us," she said. "Than you, me, Demetrius… or even Lessa." Her lips quivered with the thought of losing any of her dear friends, but she swallowed back her tears. "If we get too distracted, we'll make mistakes. And if we make mistakes, then…" She closed her eyes. "Just, stay with me."

Jeom took her hand, giving it a gentle squeeze.

"Yeah," he said. "I know that you're right. I'm sorry. It's *just…*" He squeezed her hand tighter as his voice trailed off.

Arianna wrapped an arm around him. "I know."

She sucked in a deep breath, forcing herself to be optimistic.

"But we've lost Lessa before, and we got her back," she said, trying to keep her tone light. "The second time around should be *easy*, especially with an army on our side."

"Pray you're right," Jeom muttered.

Dear gods… she thought, holding that prayer in her heart.

The eerie quietness of the Greenhouse seemed to press into their bubble of worry then—they were very much alone.

"Come on," said Arianna, getting to her feet and pulling Jeom with her. "We're late as it is."

THEY CLIMBED THE TALL STAIRCASE and passed through the threshold of vines, entering the tiny room filled with old plants—one of the main entrances to the Greenhouse.

From there, they followed the familiar yet tricky paths through the Burrows; Solza led most of the way with her keen sense of direction. After a while walking, and meeting not a soul along the way, they came upon a bridge that opened up to a clear view of the city center.

The first thing Arianna noticed was that all of their 'Wanted' posters had been torn down; the symbols of the guardians had been painted in their place.

"Well, would you look at that!" said Jeom, flashing his first genuine smile since they'd left the Treehouse.

The low rumble of voices rose up to their ears.

They both peered over the banister to get a view of the gathering down below.

Arianna thought she might topple over the side of the bridge from surprise; thousands upon *thousands* of people had come together in support of their cause.

The massive crowd had all the makings of a morning commendation to the King. Yet, the leader who stood upon the platform to address them now was no city keeper—he was a Guardian of Gold.

And not just any guardian but the one who had started it all…

"Master Tayshin," Arianna breathed.

Of course, he's the one staying in the palace. She smirked.

He had the city's undivided attention, passionately speaking about their mission.

"The time is now!" he called out to them. "The King has openly waged war on the Guardians of Gold and has taken the lives of our friends, our comrades. For centuries, he has held his sword over our heads, but no longer! Now it is our turn to raise our blades against the Crown and demand justice. Blood for blood. You have trained well, so remember your teachings and listen to the guardians named generals, for they have the experience to help guide you to the end of this as safely as possible."

He gave a nod of respect to those flanking him, faces Arianna surely recognized…

Rowina, Sergios, Nico, and even the protectors from Moriamo who had made it out safely—Kayode and Tayo among them—were all there by his side.

Arianna was overwhelmed with joy.

"Remember," he continued, "we're no longer segregated by the color of our cloaks, by district, by skill. We are one." He lifted his fist into the air. "We are fighting for *one* united Olleb-Yelfra."

The crowd roared their acceptance, everyone more than ready to be a part of this new chapter in their world; Arianna gawked down at them, soaking in the hope that radiated into the air.

"Ah, and look who it is!" Master Tayshin glowed with happiness, and what seemed like pure relief, as he caught her eye. "The one who brought the Guardians of Gold into the light has finally come to join us and lead us to the finish. Albeit a little late, as usual," he teased with a wink. "Welcome back, Miss Belvedor. We've been eagerly awaiting your arrival."

His words rolled smoothly off his tongue, as if it were any normal greeting.

Arianna thought she might lose her stomach for how many pairs of eyes settled on her face then—a collective gasp whisked over Zambienth.

"Is it *really* her?" someone stammered, pointing up.

"I thought that was just a rumor she had come," another said.

Arianna slid all the way back to the other side of the bridge and out of view, dragging Jeom with her.

"What are you hiding for?" he said with a confused chuckle; he was clearly just as stunned by everything, his expression soft with disbelief. "Time to shine! You deserve this, Ara."

He tried to tug her back, but she dug her heels into the ground.

"I'm *not* hiding," she said, chewing on her lip.

Jeom tried to let go of her hand, shaking his head at her; she wouldn't let him go.

He raised an eyebrow. "Huh—"

Arianna returned a sheepish grin. "But you're crazy if you think you're not coming with me. Get ready to jump."

"What do you mean—"

She raced forward, still clutching his hand, her magic pushing them along—suddenly they were flying over the edge of the bridge, the ground rushing toward them.

It was a long way down.

Solza jumped too, transforming into her elegant owl form; she soared down alongside them, using her powers over the wind to help cushion their fall; she perched on a nearby ledge, watching over the gathering.

Arianna and Jeom landed with a thunderous smash in the middle of the crowd, sand and pebbles spewing in every direction; those in the vicinity scurried out of their way, giving them a wide berth. And everyone had astonished looks upon their faces.

Master Tayshin and the others came down from the platform to greet them.

"Master, I—"

"It's been far too long," said Master Tayshin, drawing Arianna into a strong embrace.

She was barely able to wrap her arms around him for how muscular he'd gotten, though he was still quite round in the middle…

She suddenly recognized the version of him that had, undoubtedly, earned the renowned title as a great warrior of the

Olleb.

"I wasn't sure you made it out of Moriamo for a while," she replied, squeezing him back. "Many didn't... I was so glad to hear that you survived."

"I got separated from Cyn and the others in all the commotion," he said in an unsteady voice. "Thankfully, Nico and I were able to bring some of the families here to safety."

She nodded, easily able to pick out the Moriamo people in the surrounding crowd—they were like pockets of wildflowers cropping up in the desert, colorful and bright.

He made room so that Nico could squeeze in.

"Ara, I can't believe it!" he squealed.

"Gods, Nico!" she said, beaming. "Is that really you?"

He flexed a muscled arm, wagging his eyebrows at her; Arianna barely recognized him for how fit he'd gotten.

He looked her up and down with wide, approving eyes.

"How much you've grown," he said with an incredulous smile. "Great to have you back with us, kid."

"Getting a little cocky with your magic now, are we?" said a man with a thick accent. "That was quite some entrance."

"Sergios!" cried Arianna, waving him over. "This is too much."

She laughed as he pushed Nico out of the way to sneak a hug in too, his goatee tickling her face.

"Yeah, couldn't have just taken the stairs?" added Nico, talking with a mouthful of apple.

She shrugged, unabashedly. "I learned it all from you."

"What made you even come back to Zambienth, after everything?" said Jeom, passing out hugs as well.

"We heard rumors that cities were being overrun," said Master Tayshin. "That the districts had fallen, so we circled back to Zambienth once we heard it was safe again." He slapped Jeom on the back. "*Fantastic* what Lessa and Eli did, isn't it?"

"Utterly," agreed Sergios. "I'm still amazed."

"Sure is," mumbled Jeom, looking to his feet.

Arianna caught his eye—it was evident that not everyone was clued in yet about all that had transpired with the Treehouse guardians.

Before they could even figure out where to begin in catching everyone up, Kayode and Tayo made their way forward.

"Kayode…" said Arianna, reaching out to her.

She looked just like she remembered her—vibrant tattoos and proudly won scars filling a pale canvas of skin, long, black braids swinging to her waist, a spear in her grip, and those deep brown eyes… eyes that had seen far too much in their lifetime.

She witnessed her entire village destroyed. Her friends and family… slaughtered.

Arianna felt sadness grip her, for as happy as these reunions were, not everyone who should be there could join them.

They clasped hands, drawing each other into their chests.

She gazed over Kayode's shoulder at Tayo, all smiles despite all he'd lost.

Arianna stepped back, taking them both in. "You made it out." She shook her head. "I wasn't sure—"

"Just barely," replied Tayo, his smile faltering.

"We went back," said Kayode, her expression dark, "but there was nothing left for us."

"So you saw—"

"We buried our fallen brothers and sisters… and Mother Adunni, the way they deserved," said Kayode, tersely, trying to hold back any emotion; Arianna was unsuccessful in this.

Her eyes began to water.

She grasped hands with them both.

"I'm sorry about Mother Adunni," she said. "I've been hoping to tell you that for the longest time. That must've been devastating for you and your people." She swallowed. "I tried…" *I tried and failed.* She shook her head, looking away.

"I'm just so sorry."

"Don't be," said Kayode, squeezing her hand. "Her sacrifice was not for nothing. Moriamo is honored to be fighting by your side in this, Arianna." Her gaze bore into hers, Tayo standing tall by her side in support. "Our people shall hide no longer."

Arianna returned a grateful nod.

"Thank you," she said. "But… who will be Mother of Moriamo now?" She peered around, noticing so many faces of children in the crowd. "Who's your leader? I know that Mother Adunni's role was an important tradition for your village."

Tayo placed his hand on Kayode's shoulder.

"You're looking at her," he said with a wide grin.

A flicker of a shy smile passed over Kayode's lips—it was the first time Arianna had ever seen her not look perfectly composed.

"Is this true?" she gasped, looking her over with new consideration.

Kayode held her head high. "Mother Adunni named me in her place… just before she battled—"

"I'm truly sorry," said Arianna, not wanting to hear his name. *Solomon.* "But she made the right choice by Moriamo. I know you will serve your people well. They deserve nothing less than a protector like you."

"Much agreed," said Tayo, arms across his chest.

"Thank you for your sacrifice as well, Arianna," said Kayode. "For all that you did to help my people escape."

Arianna bowed her head. "I shouldn't have even been there," she said. "Solomon was after—"

Kayode drummed her spear into the earth, now refusing to let her finish her sentence; Arianna shut her lips tight.

"In the name of Mother Adunni," she placed her fist over her heart, staring at her with intensity, "Moriamo stands by you, *always*."

Arianna swept her eyes over the crowd, humbled—the protectors and village people from Moriamo all mirrored Kayode's action.

So many people made it out alive...

She looked back to Kayode, returning the gesture.

"In the name of Mother Adunni," she declared with a slight bow; her thoughts circled around all the ways she planned to avenge her.

Jeom cleared his throat, and Arianna shook out of her darkening daze.

"Oh, sorry about... Kayode, Tayo," she started, "let me introduce you to Jeom. He's one of my closest friends. My family."

Without warning, Tayo closed the distance between them and gave him a huge hug, lifting him off his feet. "Your family is our family," he said.

Jeom grunted, trying to wriggle out of his embrace. "Nice to... meet you... *brother?*"

Kayode and Arianna shared a smirk, trying not to laugh.

Another friendly face suddenly appeared among the crowd, searching Arianna's—she stilled in utter shock.

"Vance..." she stuttered; she had to blink twice to ensure she wasn't seeing things.

Jeom's mouth fell open as Tayo relinquished his hold.

He came toward them.

"But, I thought you were..." She looked between the other guardians, finding troubled expressions on all their faces; she focused back on him, choosing her words carefully. "How did you escape the King?"

Arianna had never expected to see him again, and certainly not after what King Devlindor had done to Iris and Cyn... They had even given him a symbolic burial in the Impenetrable Forest.

Vance shook his head, cupping Arianna's hand between his own, his face shrouded in sadness.

"How did you?" he asked.

A lump formed in her throat, lips quivering.

"I had help," she whispered, her memories bringing her right back to that dungeon with Odessa; she could still recall every detail of her prison, down to the shape of each stone that had been laid to create the impenetrable walls.

He nodded in understanding. "So did I."

In just one glance, she could tell that Vance seemed much changed from the man she remembered. He was not the same elder guardian who had always barked orders at her in potions or spell-casting trainings, nor the person who had challenged her from the onset about all her dreams of freedom from the King.

He'd been broken, and was clearly still on the mend.

"From who?" she asked, gently.

"Iris and Cyn," he replied after a moment.

His words hung in the air, like arrows aiming straight for Arianna's heart.

She choked back a sob, looking to Jeom; he shook his head, his expression full of the crushing sorrow she felt.

"The morning the King came to take us to the city center…" Vance couldn't meet her eyes, "for execution, Iris put up a fight," he explained. "I was able to escape using a potion I had concocted from the scraps of our cage, but the others got caught." He couldn't catch his breath, the words tumbling out. "I kept running. They were so brave, and I—"

He put his hand over his eyes, shuddering.

"It's all right," said Arianna, grasping him by the arms. "There's nothing to be ashamed of. If you had gone back for them, you would have all died together." She shook her head, forcing him to look at her. "And what a *waste* that would've been."

"Thank you." He looked up, eyes rimmed red; he clearly hadn't slept much in weeks. "I'm so glad that you were able to survive as well."

"Me too…" Princess Elisa flashed across her thoughts.

He ran his hand through his hair.

"I just can't believe we have to go back," he said, his voice barely passing his lips.

"We're doing it for them," she replied, meeting his apprehensive gaze. "For everyone we've lost at his hands."

Vance gulped. "I heard there was trouble at the Treehouse," he said—the other elders moved in closer. "Margery?"

"She's perfectly fine," said Arianna with a soft smile; he visibly relaxed.

"She might be, but others aren't," snapped Jeom. He touched eyes with all of them, his voice hitting hard. "Gabriel is dead, and they *have* Lessa. And—"

Arianna grabbed his hand and squeezed; he stopped talking and started taking deep, slow breaths.

They all grew silent.

Master Tayshin pulled at his beard as he thought.

"Rowina has made us aware of the… situation," he finally said; Arianna could tell he had vengeful plans all his own to enact. "She's down at the port as we speak, making sure things are in order." He looked to her. "You're *sure* you want to do this now?"

"I'm sure," she replied without hesitation. "Another month could mean fewer guardians to fight against him. We cannot wait."

She gestured to their dwindling group of elders, leaders.

"He's killed too many of us." She counted on two hands. "Tobias, Iris, Cyn, Gabriel, Kassime, Talis. And Diveena and Mother Adunni… they've all perished by the King's hands before we've *even* marched to his gates. I won't risk adding another name to that list, and we surely won't defeat him if we do.”

She glanced to Vance; he squared his shoulders and returned a supportive nod.

“The guardians have waited long enough to return to Saindora,” she said with authority; Solza swooped down from her ledge at that moment, landing by her side in a burst of magic as a snow leopard. “We have to go, now.”

Arianna knew how much Master Tayshin loved and mourned all of his lost friends, his family—Diveena and his auntie aside, these were men and women he’d taken the time to nurture into the strongest Guardians of Gold that would ever grace the books of history… *if* the rest of them could survive to honor their names.

“Ara, I don’t need convincing,” he replied, holding up his hand. “None of us do. We’re past that. If *you* say the time is now, then let’s not waste another second.” He looked down at her, ever serious. “Lead the way, warrior.”

A sigh of relief whistled from her lips.

“I’m glad you agree,” she said with an apologetic smile. “Because I’ve already sent our ships toward Saindora… and have promised more are on the way.”

Master Tayshin let out a laugh, others joining in.

“Why am I not surprised?” He chuckled again, patting the sword at his hip. “This is your army, child. I was just keeping an eye on it for you.”

Her skin prickled, her magic tingling across it as she looked around at all her warriors.

Thousands, she thought, hope singing in her heart.

Master Tayshin turned his attention back to the crowd too; everyone was waiting anxiously for instruction.

“Ready the ships!” he bellowed out. “We sail tonight.”

With one single order, the entire city dispersed to the beaches and began preparations to take to the seas.

ROWINA WAS IN COMMAND of the complex coordination. She had already accounted for every detail of their trip, down to the tiniest stitch of thread in their uniforms.

She'd ensured that everyone had two sets of their weapons of choice, the essentials in armor, the ingredients for battlefield potions, and a couple months' worth of food and water to share—there was no telling how long this war might last.

She also selected a handful of the finest horses from the Zambienth Stables to join the journey, each finely uniformed just as their riders would be, the head guardians and leaders of the army. Phantom, of course, was among them.

Sergios, on the other hand, had taken the lead in organizing the ship captains and crews; each ship was assigned a crew mixed with capable sorcerers and sorceresses to ensure that the fleet could sail at faster than normal speeds with the aid of magic.

Lastly, Nico and Vance took charge to assemble messengers tasked to ride to the other occupied cities. They spread the word, telling anyone who was willing to fight to meet them at the shores of Saindora as soon as they were able.

It took every single person in the city to get their army situated in just a day's time—two hundred ships on the water—but this was the moment they'd been preparing for.

By nightfall, they were ready to sail into battle.

The elder guardians divided themselves up among a couple of the lead ships, save for Rowina, who stayed behind to oversee the Greenhouse hub. Arianna and Solza boarded a vessel along with Jeom and Master Tayshin.

Nico, Vance, Sergios, and the protectors of Moriamo split up to guide the others.

In what felt like the flicker of a flame, Arianna saw wooden dragons rise all around her, glinting like golden beacons under the moonlight, suspended atop the gentle lull of shimmering black waves—their mighty ships were ready to conquer the vast sea that stretched out before them.

Is this really happening?

"*Indeed, Master, I believe it is,*" Solza said, spying on her thoughts. "*How do you feel?*"

"*Scared, I think,*" said Arianna. "*Yes… definitely a little scared. But, mostly, I feel excited.*"

Solza hummed her gentle laughter.

"*Me too,*" she said. "*We're ready for this.*"

Arianna beamed, savoring the wind on her face. "*I'm glad we found each other, Solza.*"

"*I would not even be me… without you.*"

Arianna brushed her hand through her fur, thinking exactly the same thing.

"Care to do the honors?" asked Master Tayshin, interrupting her racing thoughts.

He looked up, the limp white sail of their ship fluttering gently in the wind; Arianna homed in on the newly formed guardian symbol, the King's snake dead in the jaws of a dragon.

"It'd be my absolute pleasure," she said, unblinking.

Her magic rushed to the surface.

She let a deep breath fill her lungs, then shouted out the two words she'd been itching to say ever since the idea of a guardian army or ships had first entered her imagination…

"Set sail!" she called out across the night, her magic aiding its way so that all would hear.

Sparks flew into the sky, those in charge of navigating calling to their magic to begin their journey.

Sails snapped into place, catching the wind in their grasp. Waves smashed up against the sides of the ships—they were off.

Arianna held tight to the mast to keep steady, and Jeom held tight to her.

Her gaze settled on Zambienth; she wished she had had more time there, to explore freely. *One day, I'll return… I hope.*

The stark white pyramid city shrunk fast in the distance, until soon it disappeared altogether. Everything blended into black, the sea, sand, and night sky melting together as one, darkness cloaking it all.

Arianna shifted her sights to the South Star, to the golden vessels twinkling atop the black waters, following it like a family of firebugs trying to reclaim a friend they had lost. They were putting all their trust in one thing. One golden, bright future…

Just survive.

SEA OF SAINDORA

ARIANNA WAS ROUSED by the incessant rocking of the boat. Her stomach flipflopped, not used to life at sea just yet. Unsteadily, she climbed the stairs up from below deck, clinging to the rail for balance.

"*Finally, you wake,*" said Solza.

The ocean breeze wrapped around her in welcome as she pushed open the door to outside. She looked up, shielding her eyes against the bright rays of sun that peeped in and out from behind thick, gray clouds.

A shadow blotted out the light above her, and suddenly she could see—Solza was again in her dragon form, roaming the skies.

Arianna glowed with happiness at seeing her avatar flying so free; the guardians no longer cared who saw them coming, no longer cared to hide.

"*Enjoying yourself up there, are you?*" she asked, waving.

"*Very much so,*" she replied, sounding particularly relaxed.

She flapped her wings harder, circling the fleet, her silhouette dancing over the azure waters; all Arianna wanted was to join her.

She tore her eyes away from the sky and spotted Master Tayshin lecturing Jeom on something—the conversation seemed somewhat tense.

He paused momentarily to watch Solza fly by, a disbelieving smile stretched across his face, then he resumed his lecture.

Before she had even made her way over to greet them, Jeom had caught her eye; he marched over to her, a frown plastered on his face.

"We need a new plan," he said, a bite to his tone; they met in the center of the ship.

Arianna yawned, still trying to wake herself up.

"Good morning to you, too," she said, pushing past him.

She walked forward to stretch her legs.

Their ship was leading the fleet, so there was nothing but an endless stretch of water as she peered out ahead.

"I'm serious," said Jeom, trailing her, flapping his arms.

It was too early for seriousness; Arianna yawned again.

She would've kept walking to try to shake him, but she came to the bow of the ship. She wrapped her hands around the edge, taking in the view.

Jeom stood next to her, eyes lifted to Solza as she flitted across their line of sight, wings skimming the waters; ocean spray sprinkled Arianna's face, waking her right up.

"All right, I'm listening," she grumbled. She looked at him sidelong. "What's our bad luck now?"

Jeom pointed ahead. "See for yourself."

She followed his gaze and saw only clouds. Dense, dark, fast-moving clouds, the sun sporadically sprinkling down on them only when it could sneak through.

A chill ran across her skin.

She frowned, squeezing the rail tighter. Now she understood why he and Master Tayshin had seemed so anxious this morning. "Tell me."

"The clouds rolled in late last night with no sign of letting up," said Jeom, "according to Master Tayshin. He thinks a storm is brewing… a bad one. If the clouds don't dissipate before nightfall, the navigators will be steering this fleet without the stars or a compass as our guide, and for who knows how long." He threw his arms up in frustration. "What are we going to do?"

Arianna chewed on her lip, thinking. She understood his worry—they didn't have time to waste wandering the seas.

Lessa doesn't have time.

"What about Solza?" she mused. "We could use her eyes. She can follow Sano's scent, like she did before."

Jeom shook his head.

"Master Tayshin doesn't want to risk her flying into a storm to help us navigate. What if she got hurt? And if it gets as bad as he thinks it will, she won't be able to see much anyways." He shrugged. "And we wouldn't be able to see *her*."

She nodded, watching Solza weave in and out of the mammoth clouds.

"*Don't fly too far off*," Arianna warned; Solza turned back.

"Master Tayshin's right," she said to Jeom after a moment of consideration. "If a storm does land, I'll call her back to the ship." She tapped her fingers on the rail, staring at the undulating waves; they thrashed at the sides of the ship, surely foreshadowing the storm to come. "I guess we just have to take our chances with the sea—"

An idea struck her… but it wasn't a great one.

She tossed her head back, howling out to the winds in annoyance; she couldn't ignore it.

It's the only option to ensure our safety.

She glanced back over her shoulder, at the hundreds of ships and thousands of people following her lead—after what happened in Guanamara, she really wouldn't be able to live with herself if these guardians didn't even make it to the battlefield.

"*Master… are you sure?*" asked Solza, shocked at the direction of her thoughts.

The strategy they'd labored over for months seemed to just keep unraveling, step by step.

"*No*," she replied. "*But I don't see another way, do you?*"

Solza was silent a moment, then she said, "*Master Tayshin's right. The storm will be upon us within the hour.*"

Arianna frowned, glaring across the waters.

"*Then we don't have much time.*" She steadied herself toward her choice. "*I guess we can't lean all our hopes on the stars…*"

She searched for it, but the South Star wasn't even visible anymore—the clouds had already consumed its light.

"*Are you going to warn Jeom?*"

Arianna scoffed. "*He'd lock me below deck before he agreed to this.*"

The soft hum of Solza's amusement filled her head. "*Can things ever just be easy for us?*"

Arianna laughed a little too. "*Now, what would be the fun in that?*" she said, dryly.

"What?" barked Jeom, growing agitated at Arianna's silence. He raised an eyebrow at her. "Why do you have that look on your face?"

She hadn't realized she had been smirking, lost in her thoughts with Solza. She quickly composed herself before he got wind of her wild idea.

He faced her fully now, hands on his hips, waiting for her to speak; she scooted away from him and gripped the banister tightly.

"Let's get this over with," she said to Solza.

"When you're ready, I will follow." Solza beat her enormous wings and soared higher; the crew atop every ship cheered and pointed at the skies each time that she neared, their spirits just as high as the dragon. But soon they would comprehend the challenge facing them.

Arianna stripped down to her undergarments.

Jeom looked at her as if she'd lost her mind. *Maybe I have, because this is a terrible idea.*

"Ara… what is it that you think you're doing?" His voice sightly tremored, a glower on his face.

She could tell he already *knew.*

She held up her hand as he took a step nearer. *"Before* you try to talk me out of this, don't."

Jeom slapped his hand to his forehead, howling in frustration.

"No, no, *no,*" he yelled, going purple in the face. "I'm not letting you go." He pointed an accusatory finger at her. "I was hoping my intuition was wrong, but I just knew it would somehow come to this." His voice continued to climb, louder, angrier. "As soon as we stepped foot on this bloody ship, gods be damned, I knew it! Are you *crazy?*"

"He's smarter than he looks," said Solza, impressed. *"Sometimes…"* She chuckled.

Arianna flashed him her toothy 'I'm-sorry-but-doing-this-anyways' grin.

"Wish you had warned me, then. Intuition is never wrong." She spoke matter-of-factly, turning toward the water.

He advanced.

"Ara, wait, you really can't be that senseless," he said, catching her by the wrist. He was pleading now. "Come on. Be sensible here. We'll figure out another way."

"There's no more time for sensibility, Jeom," she said, softening; the clouds whirred in agreement. "There's too many people counting on us."

Her gaze settled on the crew of the ship, and his followed—everyone had stopped to eavesdrop on their conversation.

Jeom visibly deflated, registering their worry.

Arianna smiled at him, nodding. "I don't want to go, but I have to. So, help me up?"

Jeom hesitated.

"Lessa," she mouthed, turning more serious.

He let out an exasperated sigh and lifted her onto the wide rail of the ship; he kept one hand around her waist, steadying her, until she was ready to let go.

Anyone with eyes forward screamed for her to get down. People began to run toward them, waving their hands, frantically.

"What on earth?" she heard Master Tayshin call. "What are you doing? You'll drown!"

"For the record, if you get eaten, I was against this," grumbled Jeom, still holding her steady.

She wobbled as the ship rocked.

"Nothing's going to happen to me," she said, though without much conviction. *Just survive.* "She owes us." She looked to the waves. "I'm ready." He let go of her waist.

Arianna dived, head first, into the sea.

Jeom's voice trailed after her. "Well, if she tries to drain you of your blood, don't come crying to me!"

There were shouts from the ship as Arianna broke through the surface with poise, the waves cupping her in their palms; Solza flattened her wings to her sides and, seemingly, fell from the sky alongside her.

As she did, she shifted from a dragon into the sleek, black and white dolphin that had once graced their easy island days, her avatar transformations effortless now.

The resulting splash soaked everyone on deck of the ship

who had leaned over the rail next to Jeom to watch.

Arianna resurfaced just in time to see him get drenched.

Oh, I wish that Demetrius and Lessa could've seen that!

"That was… *quite…* uncalled for," said Jeom, wiping the water from his face.

She waved back at him to let him know she was fine, giggling all the while.

"*Nice work, Solza,*" she said, still smiling; Solza's chiming laughter rang through her mind.

Arianna felt so much more at ease here than she had on the boat—the waters were warm, rolling her gently across their surface in welcome.

"*Now, let's get going.*"

She and Solza moved as one across the waves, perfectly in sync. She grasped her fin, holding on tight.

"*Where to, Master?*" asked Solza.

"*Deep,*" she replied. She took a big gulp of air. "*As deep as we can get.*"

Solza obeyed and the water engulfed them completely.

Arianna squinted against the rush of water as they submerged. She glanced up to find the golden bottoms of the ships skating over them, like giant fish on the wrong side of the waves.

Her ears popped, and she tugged on Solza's fin to stop.

"*Let's call for her here,*" she said.

"*Are you sure she'll hear?*" Solza appeared anxious; Arianna knew she much preferred the skies or land over water.

This was more Lessa and Sano's terrain.

"*Definitely,*" she replied; she was certain she was already watching, just like when she'd spied on them from these very same waters over the course of their initial journey flying toward the Treehouse. "*She'll make herself known… if she desires.*"

She just hoped that their story would pique the volatile

mermaid's interest even more now.

Solza opened her snout, and the space around them began to ripple violently with the piercing echo that rose up from her throat; Arianna could literally see the soundwaves spreading far and wide, Solza's avatar magic amplifying her voice underwater.

Arianna forced herself to concentrate on one thing, feeling a name lift out from her mind and into Solza's call—*Syrifina Myr.*

When Solza's voice could reach no farther, she instructed her to stop.

"*Did it work?*" asked Solza.

"*Just wait…*" said Arianna—her lungs ached for air, a headache quickly forming.

She let out a gasp of bubbles as something rushed past her, so fast that she'd almost missed it; Solza whipped around to investigate, but Arianna knew what they would find.

Syrifina had answered their call.

The ancient mermaid's hair floated out behind her in bright red ribbons, the flames of a wildfire that not even the water could tame. And her tail was even more dazzling as it swished behind her, scales glinting like a frame of priceless gems had attached themselves to her torso.

It was dark this deep down, but Syrifina shone brightly, eerily; the dazzling rainbow-colored veins of enchanted lifeblood scrawled across her body, vivid and electric.

The sight of her now literally took the last of Arianna's breath away.

She squeezed Solza's fin, urging her to swim back up before it was too late. They broke the surface just in time, the ships gliding around them, stirring the waters as they passed.

Arianna choked on the air, pulling it in greedily.

"*Too close, Master,*" said Solza; Arianna didn't miss the subtle reprimand in her voice.

"*Had to*," she said with a cough, lungs burning.

She blinked, and Syrifina was there—waiting, watching, still as stone among the mounting waves.

Arianna was momentarily stunned to be this close to her again. "I forgot… how fast you were."

Syrifina cocked her head to the side without a word, merely considering her. She sniffed the air, sucking in a deep, full, satisfied breath.

She looked up, and Arianna followed her gaze—many curious young faces peered down at them from the passing ships.

Arianna could almost sense Syrifina's hungry, insatiable heart beating for them.

Her heart thrummed, too, fast and frenzied, as she fully registered the risk she'd taken. *Stay calm. Don't let her see your fear.*

Syrifina looked back in her direction, her gaze sharp, a cynical smile on her lips.

"Have you come for a second chance at life?" she purred; her voice was just as seductive as the last time she'd tried to sway Arianna into the immortal, underwater world. "Or have you just brought me and my sisters dinner?"

She began to circle them like a shark.

"*No*, I brought you here… to talk," said Arianna; her voice came out much shakier than she would've hoped.

She kept one hand on Solza to keep her afloat.

Syrifina swam closer—so close that Arianna could clearly see the veins of silver magic pulsating in her eyes. She reached out a hand to touch her.

Arianna cringed, but did not back away. She kept her gaze steady, strong. *Be a warrior!*

"You're not scared of me… are you now?" Syrifina smirked, her tail twitching behind her, restlessly.

"I'd be a fool if I weren't," said Arianna, feeling every muscle in her body tense; it was like being caressed by pure ice.

Syrifina tossed her head back and laughed, loudly, such a sugary, and yet strangely sour, sound—by the time the laughter had stopped, her fingers were clamped around Arianna's neck, a sneer on her lips.

She squeezed, her grasp like an iron claw.

Arianna didn't struggle, but Solza did.

"*Stay calm, Solza,*" she said, sensing her avatar's defenses flare up.

"*She has five seconds to let you go,*" she snarled, avatar magic streaking across her eyes.

Syrifina didn't miss the threat, her attention settling on Solza.

She released her grip.

"Well, I'd say you're a fool, regardless… considering you have the good sense to be scared and yet have still decided to go for a swim in my waters anyways."

She turned back to Arianna, drawing closer still. Her icy breath sent shivers all the way to her core, her gaze burning into hers.

Arianna stilled as she wrapped her fingers back around her neck, tenderly, though, this time—she caressed the crystal chain that secured the soul of the star.

"You must have *quite* the story to tell," said Syrifina, pinching the brilliant blue stone between her fingers to examine it; her eyes gleamed with interest. "I'm curious to know what else you may have wished for since our last encounter—" She glanced to Solza again. Another dangerous smile. "A dragon, perhaps?"

Arianna felt her bravery soar, thinking…

Who would win between a mermaid and a dragon?

"Would you like to find out?" she said, meeting her challenge; Solza was much stronger now than the first time they'd met.

I won't cower in front of Syrifina! For the gods' sakes, I'm on my way to face the High King.

"*I would love to test her,*" said Solza, not doubting herself in the least.

"*Can't say I don't agree,*" said Arianna. "*But we need her right now.*"

Syrifina snorted, her certainty wavering. She released the stone and swam a little farther back, seemingly studying both her and Solza. It was evident that she was wondering the same thing… who *was* the dominant species in these waters?

"Funny how magic works, isn't it?" she said after a moment.

"I still have *no* idea how it works," said Arianna with sincerity. "It will forever be a mystery to me, no matter how much I learn." She grasped the soul of the star between her fingers, making sure it was safe.

"As are all magical things," said Syrifina, knowingly.

Silence fell between them.

Arianna cleared her throat, attempting to steer Syrifina's erratic focus in the direction she needed it to go. "To answer your earlier question, I have come for a second chance at life… Just *not* the one you refer to."

"Get to your point," she hissed, shifting into a more dangerous animal. "Why have you called me here, into the open like this? Goddess of the Sea as my witness, you had better have a good reason, sorceress, or I'll ensure that your journey for freedom ends here." She spoke with her teeth bared. "I am *not* to be summoned by your kind."

Arianna hoped that her reason was good enough… she stood her watery ground.

"I told you before that I was going to try to take down King Devlindor," she said, evenly, "to try and save Olleb-Yelfra from his devastation. Now, here I am."

Arianna gestured to the seemingly endless fleet around them.

Syrifina lifted her eyes again toward the ships, the mighty dragon heads leading the way to battle.

"So I can see," she whispered, unable to hide the approval in her voice; Arianna grew bolder. "I suppose sparing your life wasn't the worst decision I've ever made… *should* you be successful."

With a fierce glower, she faced them again, her temperament forever unpredictable.

"But I do not like to waste my time." She narrowed her gaze. "What is it that you want from me? Speak freely. Speak now, and do not test my favor, for I would be all too happy to correct my decision."

Arianna lifted her chin high.

"I've called you here to collect on your debt," she said. "It's time to pay up, Syrifina. We… we need your help."

The waves started to roll around them, so vigorously that Arianna had to cling onto Solza just to keep her head above water.

"How *dare* you," she spat, eyes glaring silver. "I owe you nothing!" She bared her sharp teeth, a snarl curling between her lips. "Though, I may yet take something from you before I go."

She inched closer; this time, Solza and Arianna swam back.

"No, you don't owe me," said Arianna, trying to remain calm. "You owe Lessa." She forced herself to meet her frightening gaze. "*She's* the one who needs your favor now."

The waters fell calm.

"Lessa?" Syrifina visibly relaxed, floating a little farther away on her back; she stared to the sky.

Arianna let out a nervous exhale, sticking close to Solza. "Do I have your attention?" she asked.

Syrifina pursed her lips but gave a faint nod.

She flipped her tail back and forth as she floated around, her scales catching the sunlight whenever it was able to stab through the brooding clouds.

"Go on," she said with the wave of her hand.

"Very well," said Arianna, praying every word that came next was persuasive enough for the likes of Syrifina Myr. "Lessa did a great service to you to uncover the cause of your sisters'…" Arianna cleared her throat, not wanting to say it, "deaths—"

"The necromancer," retorted Syrifina, freezing in place; her tail sank beneath the waves, and she turned to face her. "Such a stain on this earth. We swim far clear of the land now, after learning of his dark doings." She brought her hand over the space where her human heart used to be. "His magic cannot harm my family anymore."

"Even Idris? Your *home?*" Arianna was shocked to think that she'd relinquish her beloved island to the King's Shadow.

The waves picked up. "Even Idris."

"I'm sorry to hear that," she replied, finding herself sincere. "You have to do what you can to protect your family." She met her gaze, shaking her head. "I do understand your decision… however, Vladamor's magic can still harm *my* family. He's hunting us, even now."

"What do you mean?" she asked, appearing cautiously concerned.

Arianna leaned in to her angle—somehow, she'd found a way to relate to Syrifina.

"I know you helped Lessa and the other guardians reach the shores of the Impenetrable Forest," she said. "We made camp there, with Diveena Lethander… the last remaining elf of the Nicora Tribe. We had planned to overthrow Guanamara, then bring this fleet to Saindora as a final step."

Syrifina returned a curt nod, growing impatient.

"Yes, and I did that *for* Lessa," she said through her teeth. "You have your fleet. You have your army. Now, your *point?*"

"Sir Vladamor ambushed the guardians in Guanamara

when we attempted to take the city," she explained in a hurry, her voice shaking with the memory. "He killed many of us... including Diveena."

Syrifina's tail whipped through the waters like a sword through flesh.

"*Blasphemy...*" she said, eyes wide. "He truly killed her?" She swam forward, her expression a mixture of grief and fury. "Impossible!"

"It's true. She's gone." Arianna tilted her head as she considered her reaction. "You... you knew her?"

"Of *course* I knew her," said Syrifina, smoldering. She scoffed, as if it were one of the silliest questions ever asked.

Arianna wasn't *that* shocked by hearing this news; however, it was a bit mind-blowing to picture the ancient elf and the ancient mermaid sharing a conversation. Or even the same space in the world for that matter—it just seemed like far too much power and knowledge in close proximity to even wrap her head around.

She shook her head of that baffling image.

"Diveena is... *was* one of the few respected magical beings left to the Olleb, to my knowledge," added Syrifina. "We were both in hiding when the chaos from the King's takeover was still fresh, reinforcing our territories with magic. Her land touches my sea, so it's no miracle that we eventually crossed paths as the years wore on. Though, I cannot remember now the last time I saw her—"

Arianna swore she saw a sparkling tear roll down her cheek.

"Why was she out in the open like that?" she demanded, searching for an explanation. "*Truly...* she's dead?"

"Yes, I'm afraid," said Arianna, bowing her head. "Sir Vladamor poisoned her with dark magic when she tried to save us from him." She grew more forceful, needed her to understand. "Diveena has always supported the Guardians of Gold, and she's the only reason I'm still alive after that attack—"

Her voice cracked; she had the good sense to deliver what came next a little more carefully.

"But Vladamor, he…" she softened her tone, "he captured Lessa during the ambush." She paused a second, letting her words settle in the air. "He's taken her to Saindora as a hostage, in attempt to lure us there. To lure me."

Syrifina stiffened even more. Her eyes grew wide in shock and fear, sorrow and anger—it was as if she'd morphed into a statue of the sea, a woman frozen in the very second she'd learned that she was about to die.

Ice cracked over the waves around her, and Arianna instantly grew cold.

"What did you just say?" Syrifina's lips hadn't even moved, barely a breath of air aiding her voice.

A rumble started deep in her throat, and the next wave shattered the ice that had begun to form; Syrifina swam forward, fast.

"How could you let such a thing happen to your sister? *Our* sister?" she howled. "I delivered her to your friends safely!"

The waves began hurling themselves, as tall as hills, all around them; Solza tapped into her magic over the element to try to keep their area somewhat calm, lest they both drown.

"There was nothing we could have done!" screamed Arianna over the thrashing waters—they mirrored how she felt on the inside, too. "But we're going to get her back. We're going to put a stop to the King and his Shadow Resistance, for once and for all."

"And what do you expect of me, then?" said Syrifina, seething with every word. "Tell it straight."

"As I said, I'm here to collect on a debt… on behalf of Lessa. You owe her, Syrifina." Her voice sounded firm, steady, the complete opposite of how she felt. "On all your honor, on the Olleb's honor, you *know* you do!"

She called to her own elemental magic, alongside Solza's. Together, they were able to bring a stillness to the waves, overpowering Syrifina.

"And more than a debt, I know that you care whether she lives or dies. We need your help to save her." She stared in Syrifina's direction, hoping the magic in her eyes was enough to garner the mermaid's support one last time. "So, what say you?"

"Name your price," she spat, relinquishing her magic. "But after this, my sisters and I owe the guardians nothing more."

"After this, you're *free* to decide what part you wish to play in returning the Olleb to its former glory," agreed Arianna, not bothering to hide her irritation—she wondered if Syrifina would ever come to realize that this war was on her behalf too. "We need to reunite with others in our fleet in the deep sea, off the coast of Saindora, but we can't navigate ourselves with the clouds obstructing the sky as they are."

"A storm's coming," whispered Syrifina, nodding.

"Can I count on the help of you and your sisters to guide us to them quickly and safely? Once we unite all the guardians on the water, we can sail together to the shores as one army. Then this battle can finally begin and we can rescue Lessa."

"Is that *all*?" asked Syrifina with a sardonic grin. "I find that my sisters and I spend a lot of time guiding you and your friends *safely* across our territory. Maybe you should stick to land-walking from now on."

"Maybe." Arianna shrugged. "Just, *please*, bring us to the others," she said. "That's all I ask. Leave the rest to me."

"Very well," said Syrifina, with the slight bow of her head. "We'll guide you to the other guardian ships. My sisters have been keeping an eye on them since they set sail too." Her voice grew sharp. "But after we reunite you, you're on your own."

"We have a deal, then," said Arianna, trying to hide her surprise; she lowered her magical defenses, thankful she wouldn't need to use them. "Although, in case you'd like to say a few words to Vladamor yourself, you're more than welcome to stick around. I have no doubt he'll be waiting to greet us."

At this, Syrifina's sisters began to pop up all around them, encircling Arianna and Solza in the waters. Their eyes glowed fiercely, and she could practically feel the pulse of their anger rolling with the waves.

"We will consider your offer," said Syrifina; the chilling hum of the Myr sisters' song, their hunting hymn, hung in the air; Arianna tried her best to block it out.

Syrifina's enchanted waves had pushed them all the way back toward the front of the fleet; Arianna glanced up and found Jeom waving at her in a panic to return—the blood-sucking mermaids continued to multiply by the tens along the surface.

"It's all right," she called to Jeom. "They won't hurt us."

"*Are you sure, Master?*" Solza grew warier as they quickly became outnumbered, exponentially.

"*Mermaids never break a promise,*" she assured her.

Syrifina followed Arianna's gaze, landing on Jeom.

He gawked down at her in fright; she blew him a kiss and flashed him a wicked smile.

His hand flew to cover the scar at his neck.

"Monster," he growled.

Syrifina laughed, wildly, erratically. "I would say I don't bite, but I'd be lying." She batted her eyelids at him.

"Care for another taste?" he screamed down, his fury overtaking his senses. "Come and get it, you wretched sea witch!"

He summoned the Axe of Crissy without hesitation, pointing the blade toward the water—a strong gust of wind encircled Syrifina and her sisters with the release of his magic, a twister forming atop the surface of the waves.

Everyone had to shield their eyes, magic the only thing keeping them from flying away.

"Jeom, stop!" said Arianna; she and Solza were caught in the cyclone's pull.

Reluctantly, he dispelled it, water splashing down like rain. "Get *out* of the water, Arianna. I'm not asking!"

"My, *my*, how you've both grown into your powers," cooed Syrifina, scrutinizing him.

"Lessa and Demetrius have as well." Arianna spoke with pride. She looked back to her. "We're not the same as you first found us, Syrifina. We're ready for this battle."

"Curious, *very* curious," she mused, considering her. "Beyond my expectations, indeed."

Arianna couldn't help but smile—it was the first, and likely only, compliment humans may have ever received from the likes of Syrifina Myr.

"As I said," added Arianna, "you're more than welcome to fight with us, should you wish to take part in the future."

The sea became riled again, though this time it wasn't Syrifina nor her sisters' doings; the water began to bubble, as if it were boiling hot, bright balloons of colors floating to the surface from beneath them.

The mermaids all looked frightened, Syrifina included. They huddled together away from the disturbance, muttering among themselves in confusion.

Arianna, on the other hand, swam right toward it—in one second, she was consumed by the waters. In the next, she was thrust from the sea into the air, Solza propelling her upward from below.

"Let me know if you change your mind!" Arianna called down as Solza rose high in the sky, a dragon once more; water slid off her wings in sheets, showering the mermaids from above.

There were screeches and hisses of annoyance, but no one attacked; Arianna locked eyes on Syrifina, pleased to witness a genuine smile across her face.

Then, she and her sisters were on the move.

They wove in and out of the ships until they were swimming far ahead of the fleet, to guide them the rest of the way.

Arianna considered her army from this aerial view, thinking the ships looked like magnificent gold and white whales, monsters of the sea, as they climbed across the waves, Syrifina in the lead. It was more than her imagination could have ever conjured up when she had first come to terms with going to war.

She relished the moment—another small success to help them inch toward their final goal. *We're going to make it there, at least.*

With this point of view, observing the battle fleet of the Guardians of Gold, on the back of a dragon, Arianna thought King Devlindor a stupid man…

Thousands had joined the fight against him. District slaves and citizens of the Olleb, from the North to the South alike, had pledged their allegiance to the guardians. And when the Four Corners truly worked together as one, citizen or slave, their strength could not be denied.

Agrarians, who farmed the land for food, supplying their energy source; creators, who built the ships and equipped their fighters with weapons and armor; healers, available to tend to their sick and wounded; and warriors, ready and willing to fight the good fight—they had all come together as one, to stand up to their oppressor.

How had King Devlindor not predicted this future?

Arianna could see the prophecy unfolding with her own eyes.

In creating the Four Corners, King Devlindor had literally molded and shaped the perfect army to fight against him—the young, the able-bodied, and those willing to die for freedom.

The slaves he had condemned to a tortured youth had finally bound together to tap into their magic. And with their newfound strengths, together they could soon bring him to his knees.

"There's no stopping us now," said Arianna as the verses of the Golden Rule ran through her mind. "We're coming."

"You really want to follow Syrifina and her soul-sucking sisters?" yelled Jeom, his voice drawing Arianna's attention as Solza weaved between the sails.

"They'll lead us to our friends," she called back; Solza let out a roar that melted into a clap of thunder. "Then, we march on Saindora!"

Jeom raised his axe into the air, and those aboard his ship repeated the gesture, Master Tayshin included. Soon, every person on the deck of every vessel had lifted their weapons toward Arianna; rallying cries filled the air.

"Hail to the World! Hail to Olleb-Yelfra," they cried.

Solza let out another earsplitting snarl that echoed across the skies and the seas, not to be left out.

Hail to Olleb-Yelfra! *Les, we're almost there.*

AS PROMISED, SYRIFINA AND HER SISTERS swam ahead of the fleet for days on end, guiding them safely through the now treacherous waters; the storm never seemed to end, but at least the rain had let up now.

"This is where we leave you," said Syrifina on the fourteenth night.

She joined Arianna in her human form on the deck of the lead ship, perched on the ledge; Jeom had the good sense to stand back at a safe distance, just as the last of the sunrays were swallowed by the dark.

Arianna thought it strange to be this near to her and not fear for her life, but something had changed between them after two weeks at sea—an unsaid alliance.

Even if Syrifina didn't plan to show up to battle, she finally supported the guardians in their mission and would not stand in their way.

Seeing the ancient mermaid under the spotlight of the moon, suspended above her waters—lifeblood decorating her body in a myriad of iridescent colors, her hair like a river of lava down her back, eyes swirling with unknowable magic—Arianna thought she literally embodied the Goddess of the Sea, keeping watch over her terrain like a majestic queen.

She supposed, in a way, that's exactly what Syrifina Myr was… a queen of the seas. And what a humbling thing it was to stand in the presence of an enchanted queen of Olleb-Yelfra.

"Are you sure this is right?" asked Arianna, nervous to part ways.

She peered out into the darkness and saw no sign of the three guardian ships from the Treehouse.

"I'm sure," she replied; she sucked in a breath through her nose, exhaling deeply. "They're almost here."

Syrifina pointed straight ahead, and Arianna followed her line of sight; she spotted the twinkling firelight in the distance and the ghostly outline of the Saindora palace.

I can't believe I'm back, after all this time…

"The City of Saindora lies not far from this spot," continued Syrifina. "Anchor here. You will not be discovered until you're ready to be."

"How do you mean?" said Arianna. "If we can see them, can't they see us?"

Syrifina shook her head.

"No, they cannot," she said, turning to face her—the ice-silver swirl in her stare was entrancing. "This is my gift to you."

"A gift?" she asked, shifting on her feet.

"Must you question everything?" barked Syrifina.

Arianna chuckled, starting to find her mood changes somewhat comforting. *At least she's consistent.*

Solza giggled.

"How do you think I made it this far?" replied Arianna with a smirk.

Syrifina sighed, looking out over her watery kingdom, toward the one on dry land.

"I simply can't deny that your actions are noble, no matter what ending may befall you," she answered. "My fleeting hope is the only kindness I find fit to offer you now that our deal is done."

"Oh… all right, then," said Arianna—she caught Jeom just as he was sliding his finger across his throat, mocking his own death.

"Not much of a motivational speech, is it?" he muttered under his breath; Syrifina prickled but ignored him.

"Thanks… I suppose," added Arianna. Her smile wavered as she, silently, agreed with Jeom.

"Hmm," said Syrifina, still contemplating her, with far too much intensity to be any kind of reassurance.

In a beat of wind, she was eye level with Arianna, so close that she thought they might morph into one.

Syrifina gripped her, strongly, by the shoulders; Arianna fleetingly considered that she could crush her into a ball, just like that.

"Young sorceress," she whispered, a grave look upon her face, "my truest hope is that you do not fail dearest Lessa." She pressed her forehead into hers, and Arianna felt the importance of the moment; everything seemed to still, the world waiting to see if humans and mermaids had *truly* found peace.

"This hope I have in multitudes."

A collective sigh of relief blew across the deck when she let go, and Jeom's mouth was hanging open.

"Then we share such a hope," said Arianna, firmly.

"We won't fail her," added Jeom, shaking out of his stupor.

Syrifina glared at him, eyes glinting like the edges of his axe.

"I pray not," she snapped. "Alas, it wouldn't be the first time *love* failed a woman."

Jeom puffed out his chest. "If anything does fail, it won't be for lack of love," he retorted.

Syrifina offered him a single nod of approval, which was probably the kindest gesture she'd ever given him. Then she swept her hand in the air, drawing their attention ahead.

Syrifina's sisters began to pop up out of the water in front of the fleet, swimming in sync as if in dance. Glittering tails swished behind them, their seductive song spreading across the night.

Arianna felt the stir of thick magic settle in the air, a blanket of warmth, protection.

A heavy fog began to grow over the waters up ahead, following the mermaids like a trail.

"Beyond the sinking clouds," said Syrifina, pointing to the fog, "you shall meet the sands of Saindora… when you are *ready*. Until then, you'll be—"

"Shielded from sight," finished Arianna, suddenly understanding.

"As I said…" Syrifina smirked. "A gift."

"Look!" shouted Jeom, pointing over the side of the ship; three vessels had suddenly broken through the fog, coming from the left. "There they are. That's them! Oh, *thank* the gods."

Syrifina let out a small hiss in his direction.

"*And* goddesses," he corrected—Diveena and Syrifina clearly had shared similar beliefs.

He grinned, throwing up his hands, whistling and waving in excitement.

"Whoever, whoever, all right, just… *woo!* Thank you!" His voice boomed across the waters, racing to greet their friends.

Master Tayshin laughed, patting Jeom on the back; others began to rejoice and cheer too.

"I believe our thanks is owed to Syrifina," he said, seeming content as the ships neared; then his gaze settled on the shadow of the palace, and a shadow crossed his expression too. "We're off to a good start. Let's pray things keep going our way from here on out."

He signaled to the captain of the ship to make anchor, and the rest of the fleet followed suit as the Treehouse dragons approached them; splashes were heard in the distance for what seemed like miles back.

"Thank you for your help, Syrifina," said Arianna, earnestly. "It will not be forgotten."

She blinked, and Syrifina was perched on the bow of the boat, standing atop the golden dragon head, peering down over them all; everyone craned their necks to get a good look at her, quite the vision.

"Are you sure you won't join us in the fight to come?" asked Master Tayshin, walking forward. "We could certainly use your alliance." He held her gaze. "What's next won't be easy."

"You know what my answer is," she replied, curtly. "Mermaids do not interfere with the battles of mankind. Just look where that got Diveena. I must protect my sisters."

"Indeed," said Master Tayshin with a solemn nod. "But we thank you, nonetheless."

He held out his hand for her to take, and both Arianna

and Jeom gawked at his boldness.

Syrifina hesitated a moment as she considered the offer, then she crouched down to take it.

"No, thank *you*, for defending the magic," she said, steadfastly, knowing well that Master Tayshin was the backbone of the Guardians of Gold; she stood back up, catching Arianna's gaze. "We will be watching… from a safe distance."

Her words irked Arianna. She stepped forward to confront Syrifina Myr one last time.

"This isn't *just* a battle between mankind," she interjected, unable to quiet her opinions any longer. "This is a battle between Olleb-Yelfra and a monster that's trying to squeeze at her life. You know that I'm right, and Diveena knew that too."

"I know a great many things that your mind could never comprehend," she purred, perched on the rail like a cat. "And I know that if you fail, and there's a *good* chance you will, I won't have my sisters anywhere near the massacre that would follow. We've stayed out of the King's eye for centuries and will do so for centuries more, if that's what it takes to survive."

"I know all about survival," said Arianna, looking up at her. "It's the only thing I've ever focused on my entire life. But we've survived long enough, and it's time now to fight back… to take a stand. You're the *original* mermaid of Olleb-Yelfra. Your powers are unparalleled. Is that all you wish to do with your invincibility? Even knowing what the necromancer and the King have done to your family? To Diveena… and Lessa?" She took another step forward, a challenge in her tone. "*Just* survive?"

Syrifina's gaze sharpened, her hair billowing in the wind. Anyone else would have fallen backward into the water as the ship rocked back and forth, but she was perfectly poised as she looked down at her, so many emotions exposed in a single expression.

"I shall never forget the torments that King Devlindor and

his monstrous creation have brought against my family," she replied. "But I will *not* risk the lives of those of us who still live. My sisters are my responsibility, and I'll not endanger them anymore than I already have."

"Very well," said Arianna, unable to hide her disappointment. "Just know that if we do fail, the King will not let another magical being out of his grasp again." She lifted her head high. "The only way to truly ensure their safety is to kill him."

The statement was met with a powerful silence, and a powerful stare.

When Syrifina spoke next, her voice sounded so soft that Arianna thought that it actually held kindness, nothing like her cold, normal self.

"For what it's worth, little witch," she said, "your bravery and courage is hard to challenge. I respect that." She gave a slight bow of her head. "I respect *you*." Her face was swathed in the moonlight, somber and sad. "I pray you do not fail."

With that, Syrifina leaped off the ship, a perfect dive into the sea—the waves reached out to greet her.

Arianna, Jeom, and Master Tayshin ran forward to watch her go; as soon as her body touched the water, a beautiful transformation took place. Her legs and feet morphed back into a fishlike tail, and the sea around her sparkled as the magic fell away.

She disappeared beneath the next wave.

Following her example, the Myr sisters began to sink beneath the water as well, everyone on the ships waving them off. After they were gone and all had quieted, a soft hum reached Arianna's ears, Syrifina's voice somehow lingering.

Near or far, sister, we'll wait for thee…

It was a verse from a spell they'd cast long ago in one last desperate attempt to find Lessa, back when she had turned into a mermaid herself.

Such magic wouldn't be able to save her now.

Arianna tightened her grip on the rail, staring toward the fog. *Lessa isn't lost.*

She hadn't run away, unable to find her way home...

She was trapped, *stolen*, by the right hand of the King, and the only way they were getting her back this time was by bringing an army to the King's doorstep.

Jeom placed his hand atop hers; he had heard Syrifina's song too. "We cannot fail," he said.

"We won't," replied Arianna. "We're ready for this, whether she joins us or not. Syrifina was never part of our plan."

He squeezed her hand—his was shaking—and they both stared ahead at the full moon; a wall of mist enclosed their safe space out in the deep waters.

"I think the storm's letting up," he said.

But Arianna wasn't fooled. "It's just taking a break."

They shared a moment of silence for the unknown fate of Lessa... the unknown fate of all of their futures—when the sun rose the next morning, its fire filling the sky, the Guardians of Gold would finally rise along with it.

Storm or not, the dragons will rise.

PART THREE

18

READY OR NOT

VIBRATIONS SHOT THROUGH ARIANNA'S LEGS as a large plank slammed into the side of her ship—the Treehouse guardians had officially arrived.

"Well, come on over!" called Demetrius, waving at Jeom; he was shaking his head, clearly hesitant as his eyes settled on the dark, crashing waves down below.

Arianna looked too and whistled. One slip and this quest would certainly be over... for him.

"*Glad I got you, Solza!*"

She had morphed back to her snow leopard form.

"*I'd rather not swim at night, though,*" she purred back. "*You're on your own, Master.*"

Arianna scoffed, shooing her forward; Solza pranced across the plank with grace and curled her tail around Demetrius as he fawned over her.

"Why don't you just make your way here?" suggested

Jeom, still warily eyeing the water.

Demetrius snorted, leaning all his weight against his staff.

"Sorry, brother, but I got you beat here." He flashed a coy smile. "I'm sure as heck not walking across that thing on one leg. Hurry it up! We ain't got all night now."

"Damn…" mumbled Jeom, glancing to Arianna.

She shrugged. "He's got you there."

"Well, technically, he's got two since I built—" Arianna pursed her lips. "Right." He tested the plank with the tip of his boot. "Yeah, this is *not* ideal."

"Oh, for the gods' sakes, what are you worried for, really?" said Arianna, tutting at him. "You've been walking planks like this for months in Diveena's world." She gestured to it. "It's the same thing! Seems sturdy enough to me, and I'm *right* behind you."

She placed her hands on her hips, impatiently tapping her foot.

"That's why it's not ideal," he replied, sticking his tongue out at her. He looked forward, readying himself. "And you're one to talk, you know… afraid of heights, yet you lived in the Treehouse for nearly just as long as me *and* ride a dragon around all day in your undergarments for fun." He glanced at her over his shoulder, rolling his eyes. "Give me a break."

She grinned back. "I'll give you a push…"

He feigned calling to his axe, and she took a step forward.

Jeom finally mustered the courage to reunite with his brother. He crossed the plank in just four long strides, and was in Demetrius' arms by the fifth.

"*Whoa*," said Demetrius, hugging him back with a little laugh. "Almost took us off the side of the ship there anyways." They pulled back to look at each other; Demetrius softened. "You all right, then?"

"I'm all right," said Jeom, though his expression said otherwise. "You?"

"Same," said Demetrius, softly.

Sano vied for Jeom's attention—he was curled comfortably across Demetrius' shoulders, looking much better than he had on the morning they'd left the Treehouse.

He bounded into Jeom's arms, snuggling against his chest.

"Ah, Sano, missed you there!" said Jeom, hugging him close. He looked back to Demetrius. "Thanks for taking care of him. I know Lessa would really appreciate—" His voice cracked, his gaze shifting to his feet.

Arianna had yet to hear him speak her name without some kind of emotional outburst; he took a deep breath, trying to calm the storm inside.

"He's part of the family," said Demetrius, softly. He laid a hand on Jeom's shoulder. "Take comfort, brother… as long as he's still alive, so is she."

Jeom gave a faint nod, nuzzling Sano into his chest.

"We're almost there, little buddy," he whispered.

Sano returned the love, then leaped from his arms and onto Solza's back; the two avatars disappeared down the deck, lost in their own happy reunion.

"There she is!" sang Demetrius. He peered around Jeom to find Arianna crossing the plank. "You lot sure did quick work gathering Zambienth and finding us." They embraced. "We've been anchored around the area a few days now, trying to figure out where you might land. I was starting to get worried." He ran his fingers through his long hair. "I know we all agreed to follow the South Star, but it didn't seem like a guarantee that we'd cross paths… especially with that wild storm we had."

"If there's one thing I've learned in all this," said Arianna, "nothing is ever a guarantee."

She smiled, so very glad to see Demetrius again.

"I couldn't agree more," he said, glancing around his ship. "Once again, ole Tobias saved our necks."

He pulled out the gleaming compass from his pocket and gave it a kiss.

"Next time I'm borrowing that," grumbled Jeom, arms crossed at his chest. "And in the new world, everyone gets a bloody compass!"

Arianna laughed, though she didn't disagree.

Demetrius gazed up, squinting at the dark sky—streams of gray slashed through the black, and the stars were starting to shine through, alongside a brilliant moon.

"I think the worst of it's over, though," he said; Arianna's smile pinched. "But the Sea of Saindora is *so* big." He cocked his head to the side. "How did you manage?"

Jeom frowned, rubbing his neck. "You do *not* want to know."

Demetrius raised an eyebrow. "Try me."

Jeom tilted his head, showing off the two silver scars—two painful reminders for their entire group as to just how dangerous Syrifina could be, if she deemed you the enemy. "Care to venture a guess?"

"*No…*" said Demetrius. His gaze flicked to the waters. "The mermaids?" His eyes lit up; he appeared much more excited by the news than frightened. "Syrifina was really with you?"

Arianna chewed on her lip, nodding.

"The Myr sisters guided us all the way from Zambienth to here once we realized we couldn't exactly count on clear weather," she said, pointing up at the cloud-riddled sky. "In any case, Syrifina owed us a favor."

"Damn right, she did!" huffed Jeom with a pout.

Demetrius chuckled, patting him on the arm. "Can't believe you survived her a second time around, brother." Jeom grunted. "She's something, though, that one." He squinted at the sea, as if hoping to catch a glimpse of her. "I'm just glad that idea didn't go sideways."

He shook his head.

"Me too," said Arianna. She peered toward the gray, wispy wall of mist that rolled over the water, a tangible partition separating their past from their future. "The fog was her doing too, actually. Gives us a little time to collect ourselves before…"

They were silent a moment.

"Amazing," said Demetrius. "I can't believe we've made it all the way here. I just hope… well, you know." He gazed toward Saindora, longingly. "I just… *hope*."

"I think we're all hoping the same thing," said Arianna.

Jeom nodded his agreement, and they all set their sights on their final destination.

Others started making their way across the plank.

"Master Tayshin!" said Demetrius, waving as he came to join them.

"Been a long time, son," he said, squeezing him on the shoulder. He beamed, taking him all in—what he'd lost and what he'd clearly gained. "I hear a lot has changed for you, and for the better, it seems."

"Some things certainly have," replied Demetrius, proudly showing off his latest prosthetic—Jeom had crafted him something truly spectacular with the Axe of Crissy this time, something that could withstand a war.

His smile tightened, and Arianna could just tell he was still getting used to his new powers; he looked exactly like how she felt every time she tried to comprehend her animancer magic.

He will master this, in time. Hopefully, we both can…

"So I can see!" said Master Tayshin, an awestruck expression on his face. He looked between the Kane brothers and started laughing, his belly shaking with each breath.

The sound was so uplifting that Arianna's spirit soared. She tried to savor the happy moment, despite the looming threat in the distance.

Down with the King.

Master Tayshin collected himself, gathering everyone around; Sano curled on Arianna's shoulders to say hello, and Solza sat on her haunches by Demetrius, forcing him to pet her.

"It's incredible how far you've all come." He looked between the boys. "Kassime and Talis would be beside themselves to hear you both discovered such strong links to dwarves and elves." He shifted to Arianna, an incredulous expression on his face. "And *animancer* magic? By gods," he shook his head, "truly inconceivable."

Arianna felt herself flutter with nerves—her animancer powers were exactly that, inconceivable. *I still have no idea what I'm doing...*

She feigned confidence.

Master Tayshin turned suddenly serious.

"I was very sorry to hear of Diveena's passing, though." He bowed his head. "Very sorry, indeed… she was a great treasure to the guardians. I can't believe she's no longer on this earth."

"Now *she* was the truly incredible one," stated Demetrius; nobody disagreed.

"Oh, don't worry," said Jeom, breaking the silence. "She's still… on this earth." He nudged his brother, lightheartedly. "Demetrius here turned her into a giant tree."

Demetrius slapped his hand away.

"Is that… so?" said Master Tayshin, scratching his chin as he tried to wrap his head around this statement. "Care to elaborate on that one, boys?"

Demetrius blushed.

"Not really," he muttered. "But I didn't *turn* her into a tree, Jeom." He poked him with his staff so he'd scoot farther away. "I think it was her spirit or something." He shrugged. "I honestly have no idea, but yes… you can definitely still feel her there, in the Impenetrable Forest."

"Well, I think it's an elf thing," said Jeom, smirking. "Wonder what plant you'll transform into at the end."

"Probably something you'll happily chop down for fun," retorted Demetrius.

Jeom winced. "All right, all right—"

"And what's a dwarf thing, then?" he continued. "Goddesses' forbid you turn into a big brown rock."

"*Relax*," said Jeom, tossing his hands up in surrender. "I was only trying to lighten the mood!"

Arianna thought she'd never laughed so hard in her life, the boys still bickering all the while.

She looked up to find Margery running toward them; longer legs than even Jeom boasted carried her quickly across the deck.

"Master!" she said, wiping the sweat from her brow. She towered over them all. "Wonderful to see your face."

"How lovely to see you too," said Master Tayshin, taking her hand in his.

He looked more than relieved to see her again.

They embraced, and he whispered his condolences for Gabriel in her ear; the other guardian elders from Zambienth made their way from their ships to join them in conversation.

"You heard about Diveena, then, too?" asked Margery.

"Yes," he replied. "I was just saying how terrible it was to have lost such a wonderful friend. And to such a monster like that."

Jeom's expression darkened.

"We'll make him suffer for it," he said.

"She was a grand soul," said Nico, greeting Margery and Demetrius with big hugs as well. "And I hear she took *you* in as her apprentice." He put his hands on his hips, smiling. "*What*, I wasn't good enough for you, kid?"

All eyes turned to Demetrius again.

"She did," he said, shyly, his cheeks flushing once more.

"I learned a great deal from her." He focused on the dark sky. "It may take me decades to untangle it all… but she's left me much stronger than whoever I was when she first got to me." He lifted his chin high. "That much I'm sure of."

Arianna nodded, knowingly. She was certain that he would never need a spell to call to his magic—just like her animancer gifts and the girls' avatar powers, just like Jeom's connection to the axe and the air, this was something all his own.

"I'll have to put that to the test," said Sergios, slapping him on the back; Demetrius nearly flew overboard.

"Great to see you too, Sergios," he said with a little cough.

"And Gabriel?" said Vance, keeping his eyes cast down. "Did he at least go… peacefully?"

"I think so," said Arianna, not wanting to remember that; she looked to the battering waters, curling Sano's tail around her finger. "Sir Vladamor didn't waste any time. And in any case, he's in a better place. They all are." She met Vance's eyes. "I watched them go… into the light."

Everyone shifted uncomfortably where they stood, all surely hoping that no one else would have to join them soon.

Vance sniffled. "Any place is better than here, I suppose."

"He was a good lad," said Master Tayshin, his hand fumbling with the hilt of his sword at his belt; Arianna could tell he was struggling to keep his emotions in check. He squeezed Vance's shoulder. "Taken too soon from us."

"They don't all come back," said Margery, softly, rubbing Vance's back. "You're one of the lucky ones."

He frowned, nodding to himself—Arianna knew he felt anything but lucky.

Being a prisoner of the King's was, in fact, worse than death.

Lessa…

She dug her nails into her leg, ripping her mind out of that dark hole before it could annihilate her.

"He was the best," added Jeom, glancing to Demetrius. "If it weren't for Gabriel, we wouldn't even be here right now."

"We'll get him justice," came a new voice from behind. "All of them, we will. No warrior will be forgotten in this fight."

"Well, look who it is," said Master Tayshin, opening his arms wide to welcome him. "I haven't seen that mischievous face in a *long* time. What trouble have you been getting into lately, hmm?"

Arianna turned to find Eli leaning against the side of the ship, a sword at his hip and bare-chested so that all of his tattoos shone under the glare of the bright moon—the clouds curled around the silvery globe like smoke, none able to darken its shine thus far.

Eli's focus was on no one but Arianna.

"Miss me?" he said with his notorious smirk.

She returned it. "Something like that," she replied with a shrug, feeling her skin burn hot. She cocked her head. "Why are you only half-dressed?"

He chuckled and pulled her into his arms, planting a kiss on her lips.

Arianna sunk into it for only a moment, lost in complete bliss—whistles and guffaws ensued from their small audience.

She squirmed with embarrassment, wriggling her way out of his arms. She shook her head up at him, speechless and content.

He leaned forward, eyes locked on hers.

"Well, I certainly missed you," he said in a low voice, so that only she could hear, his sincerity unwavering.

Master Tayshin cleared his throat, and Eli straightened, spinning around on his heels to properly address him.

"My apologies, Master Tayshin! Not sure what, uh…" His eyes flitted to Arianna without shame. "Not sure what came over me there, sir.”

He rubbed the back of his neck, a guilty grin on his face.

“I can take a guess,” said Nico, nudging Arianna in the ribs; she couldn’t meet his eyes but also couldn’t stop smiling.

There were snickers all around, and Margery seemed to be particularly warmed by their display of affection.

Master Tayshin came to Arianna’s side. “The lady asked you a question,” he said, sternly.

“Noah and I were just sparring a bit to get ready,” replied Eli, crossing his arms to try to cover up.

Master Tayshin gave him a reproachful look, then winked. “Best get dressed, boy. Can’t have you distracting our fearless leader all night.” He pinched Arianna’s arm.

She balked—laughter echoed in the air.

“Yes, sir. Right away,” said Eli, offering his hand to him with a shy smile. “It’s good to see you again.” He looked around to the others. “All of you…”

Master Tayshin ignored his hand, instead pulling Eli into his chest for a strong hug.

Arianna found herself more shocked by Master Tayshin’s sudden friendliness this night than anything Eli had ever surprised her with before; they all gave them a little more space.

“You’ve really lived up to your promise, son,” he said to him, an unreadable expression on his face.

Eli reddened, offering a slight bow. “I… thank you, Master,” he said.

“What promise?” interjected Arianna as Eli shook hands with the other elders.

“Why, to take care of you lot!” said Master Tayshin, gesturing to all of them, flippantly. “Always getting yourselves into such tangles.”

He shooed everyone back, forcing Eli to stand in the center as he spoke.

“When Cyn dragged this young man into the Greenhouse,

I thought we were going to have to wipe his memory. But he begged for a chance to prove his loyalty to the guardians, to *you*—" he pointed to Arianna; she looked away "—after the magic you showed him in the desert." Eli let out a loud, nasty cough—but Arianna *swore* he had said 'bombarded me with' through the noise. "Talis and I thought, who better than to keep an eye on four reckless runaways than a strong, willful warrior with something to prove?"

He let out a barking laugh, slapping Eli on the back; Arianna started to wonder if Master Tayshin wasn't a bit tipsy.

"He was prepared to give up everything for our cause," he added, "even with no magic to his name."

"None that we can see," said Margery with a wink.

"Still am…" whispered Eli, green eyes pinned on Arianna, "prepared."

"Well, magic or not, Elijah Neve is a true protector of the Guardians of Gold," declared Master Tayshin, waving his sword at him as if he were being formally appointed to the position. He hugged him again, shaking him a little too violently in his delight.

Yes, he's definitely a bit drunk, Arianna thought.

"You've done good by us, boy!"

"Thank you," said Eli again, shining with pride; the others were also showering him with similar praise. "You're all too kind."

Arianna thought it might have been the first time she'd ever seen Eli *really* blush… and somehow it made him seem even more attractive.

He dipped out from under Master Tayshin's arms, undoubtedly wanting to steer the focus elsewhere; Arianna covered her mouth as she tried not to laugh.

"My, how we've multiplied!" exclaimed Eli, pointing toward the rest of the fleet.

His excitement was exaggerated at first, though when he

stopped to admire the view, it quickly turned real—they had to squint to see it all, lanterns silhouetting their ships in countless rows across the dark waters.

"This is better than we anticipated," he said, glancing to Arianna; she nodded in confirmation—they'd assumed they might not reach the target number in their strategy sessions, just to be on the safe side, yet here they were. *We got so many things wrong.* "How… how many ships is that, then?"

They all peered in the same direction.

"Rowina outdid herself and organized more than two hundred, with about eighty guardians per vessel before she sent us off," said Sergios—he looked so stoic as he gazed to the water, so comfortable; Arianna recalled that he'd spent a good portion of his younger years traveling the seas as a transporter or tradesman. "Suppose that's roughly sixteen thousand men and women to lean on out there."

Eli gave a whistle. "Fantastic."

Sergios patted Nico on the back. "We're expecting a few thousand more to meet us on land in due time," he said.

Nico stepped up.

"Most of them won't have a hold on their magic, though," he added, "but I think against the King's assembled regulators, mostly non-magic folk, we're on pretty even ground."

Vance nodded, his arms wrapped around his chest.

"Plus, his people fear him," he said, "because he's done terrible things to them. We're offering the opportunity now to take revenge against the Crown." He frowned. "Trust me, it's an enticing offer, a motivation that the King's armies won't have."

"I wouldn't be surprised if some defect," said Margery; there were murmurs of agreement from the elders.

"I can vouch that his regulators fear him all the same," said Eli.

"That's the hope," said Master Tayshin. "The bigger our

army, the safer more people will feel to switch sides, especially his warriors."

Arianna felt as if the wind had been knocked out of her, once again considering the impact of what one decision, already years ago, had had on the world…

It had started out as just the two of them, her and Lessa. Then there were four, Jeom and Demetrius added to the ranks—now, there were nearly *twenty* thousand people ready to go to war for the guardians, and maybe even more.

"*You should feel so proud,*" said Solza.

Arianna only felt numb, staggered by their numbers.

"However, the Shadow Resistance is strong," said Sergios, watching Sano as he bounced from person to person. "Many of them are elders with a *long* history in magic." He furrowed his brow. "They outnumber our elder guardians a hundred to one… especially with so many losses on our side."

"We've prepared for this," said Master Tayshin, not letting his remaining leaders sink into doubt. "Don't underestimate the young sorcerers behind us. When their lives depend on it, their magic will not fail them."

"Yes, but let us not forget that Sir Vladamor *still* leads them," said Margery, with a weary expression. "And we haven't even seen a trace of the King yet."

"Arianna, do you feel ready to face Vladamor again?" Vance's words landed like a punch.

She gulped. *No! What a stupid question.*

"Well, I—"

"I hear you've tapped into animancy," he continued, clearly not reading her discomfort, "but Margery and I can cook up the same spells we prepared the last time we tried to go against him and the King… just in case."

Some of the normal Vance was beginning to seep back into his shell of a body, and Arianna supposed that was a good thing. But he was innately skeptical of her, because of her age, and he always announced his doubts at the most frustrating of times.

Arianna averted her gaze to the ground as all attention turned to her.

She had used her animancer powers purposefully only once, and with Diveena's guidance. *And I utterly failed… my only animancer mentor is now dead, because I couldn't do it.*

So how could she look them all in the eyes now, at this pivotal moment in their plan, and say she was ready to face him?

I don't feel ready for any of this…

"You're not alone, Master," said Solza. *"Just tell the truth."*

Before Arianna could even find the courage to respond, Eli had chimed in, one hand on the small of her back.

"It won't hurt to have reinforcement ready when dealing with Sir Vladamor," he agreed. "The necromancer is a trickster, and that's how Diveena died. So let's play it safe and not put all our hopes on one person's shoulders. We have to work together."

Jeom and Demetrius voiced their agreements, and the elders didn't debate it; Arianna relaxed a little, internally thanking her boys for speaking up on her behalf.

Still, she knew that she was the only one… *I'm the only one who can defeat the necromancer for good.*

And if she failed again, more people would die.

She studied Vance as he whispered ideas with Margery—they would be the first to go if they antagonized Sir Vladamor as a distraction on her behalf.

The boat rocked; her stomach churned.

"Our mission has spread farther than the guardians could have ever once hoped," stated Master Tayshin, bringing them all back to attention. "And all thanks to this one here." He squeezed Arianna around the shoulders. "Her persistence has gotten us so very far. May we all celebrate together at the finish!"

"Here, here!" they all agreed, enjoying one last intimate moment between the original Guardians of Gold before they rushed into battle.

The moment was short-lived.

They all had work to do, soldiers to assemble; they dispersed, pairing off to discuss the forthcoming details of the night.

Solza and Sano accompanied the Kane brothers, and Eli pulled Arianna away to speak to her privately.

When they were out of earshot from the others, he took her strongly by the arms and moved to kiss her again. On instinct, she turned so that his lips found her cheek.

He pulled back, a perplexed expression on his face. "Why—"

She returned an apologetic smile, gazing to her feet.

Eli moaned, tossing his head back in frustration, already knowing what she'd say next.

"Not again," he uttered, tugging at his hair.

"When this is *over*," she urged, leaning into him. She wrapped her arms around his waist, compelling him to meet her eyes. "When we win this, then you can kiss me all you want, Eli. Just… not now, all right?" She bowed her head. "Not until we get Lessa back."

He pushed a loose strand of hair away from her face, not saying a word.

"Our blissful Treehouse days are behind us," she said. "We can't afford to be distracted on the cusp of battle." She shook her head, trying to find the right words, trying her best not to ruin this again. "What I'm saying is—" She took a deep breath. "I'm *not* saying I don't want… this. I'm just saying, it has to wait."

She couldn't help but feel slightly uncomfortable making

room for his affection anymore, especially with Jeom in such agony over Lessa and the baby; he hadn't chided Eli for kissing her earlier, but she had seen his face…

He was racked with worry over *his* love, and Arianna didn't want to add to his pain.

What's more, her time away from Eli had offered clarity and space to only focus on the most important thing for their survival—*Down with the King.*

She wished to keep that clarity from here on out.

They held on to each other for another long moment; Arianna could feel Eli's chest rise and fall, his heart pounding.

It felt right. But it just had to wait…

She pulled away.

"I do understand," he said in a steady voice, looking at her with a pained expression. "This time I do. I'll try and back off… for now."

He forced a smile, and Arianna loosed a sigh of relief, wanting a future with him more than ever before.

"Eli, thank you—"

He held up his hand, standing up taller, his voice sounding stronger, his eyes burning into her own.

Was that a flicker of silver I saw?

She melted into his words.

"Even if you won't let me kiss you, which is *all* that I want to do right now, then let me say this…" He cupped his hands around her cheeks, drinking her in. "You are my life, Arianna Belvedor, and I cannot wait until the moment we can throw down our swords and make room for whatever *this* is unraveling to be. No matter what happens out there, I'm fighting for you… for *us*, and I'll wait for you for as long as it takes." She could hardly stand how much she loved him anymore. "Forever, if I must."

"I promise I won't make you wait that long," she said, praying the end of this war proved her sincere.

He smiled, a genuine one. Then he relinquished his loving grip on her.

There were no more words left to say, so they just lingered in each other's space a second longer.

Arianna wished she had the courage to be distracted in the ways that Eli was so persuasively good at, but she was too scared to let her focus drift that way after what had happened in Guanamara. There were just more important things at stake than her love life right now—quite literally, they were floating on the edge of a war to overthrow the High King.

Her mind would never stop reeling.

Eli, the King, magical this, and enchanted that. Rescue Lessa, kill the necromancer, take the throne… she wanted to scream.

It was all so wonderful and so terrible alike.

Reluctantly, she and Eli peeled apart just as Noah came dashing toward them from across the deck; Arianna was thankful for the interruption.

He swept her up in his arms, swinging her around in such excitement.

"Noah," she squealed with laughter. "Put me down! Where have you been hiding?"

"Was below deck, washing up," he said out of breath, letting her go. "Lots to do, lots to do."

She couldn't help but notice how sculpted he'd become since his district days.

"It's good to see you," she said, considering him with pride. She looked between him and Eli. "Who won this time?"

Noah pouted, tossing Eli a shirt. "Who wins every time?"

Eli laid a hand on his shoulder. "You'll be a worthy opponent on the battlefield."

Arianna felt her nerves surge. *It's nearly time.*

"Noah! All is well?" called Jeom as he and Demetrius left their conversation with Sergios to join them; Solza and Sano were trailing them.

"All is well, mate," he replied; they shook hands, firmly. "You know… considering."

"Yes, I know," said Jeom, drawing him into a tight hug. "Trust me, I know."

Noah winced at the touch, pulling away.

"*Ouch*," he said, a hiss escaping his teeth.

"What is it?" asked Jeom, worried. "Are you hurt?"

"No, no," said Noah, waving his hands. "Nothing like that."

He lifted his arm and shirt, and Arianna was shocked to see black ink scrawled across his fair skin—a cursive letter 'K' sat between two crossed swords, a new take on the Warrior's District emblem.

She could've never imagined any of who this new Noah was turning out to be, but she adored him all the same.

"For Kiki?" she asked, her heart warmed.

He nodded with a solemn smile. "For ma lost lady."

He placed his hand over his heart, closing his eyes a moment.

Arianna grieved for Noah inside, knowing her cheery friend had experienced the hardening lessons of love and loss, as many of them had on this dangerous journey; he lifted a leg of his pants to show off the same mark with an 'L' inside.

Arianna softened, contemplating it with full appreciation. *Liam Black, my first, lost love.*

"Beautiful tributes," said Demetrius, examining them.

"Truly," said Arianna; her gaze flicked to Eli, hoping he would never be fated to a mere tribute. "Who did them for you?"

"Well, who do you think, Ara?" She cocked her head. "*Your* love, of course." He gave Eli a little punch.

All the boys chuckled as her face likely turned the brightest of reds.

"I didn't know you were such an artist," she said through her teeth, ignoring them. "Tattoos?"

He shrugged, attempting not to laugh at her expense. "After getting so many of my own, you sort of pick it up."

"What do yours mean?" asked Jeom; he fingered the creator's brand on his arm. "I could never figure it out."

Arianna had not once asked Eli this question, and he had never brought it up. She'd always just assumed that the abstract markings winding across his chest, arms, and back, and all over his body, were meant to be beautiful—for they certainly were.

"I'm surprised not one of you know," he said, a sly smirk stretched across his face. "*Really*, you don't recognize them?"

Silence—he tittered at them.

He traced one of the black, jagged lines across his abdomen; it crisscrossed with many others, leading in various directions.

"I know," said Noah, smugly, wagging his eyebrows.

Eli pointed his finger at him.

"Don't say anything. Let them guess," he demanded.

Moments later, Demetrius clapped his hands in delight.

"I can't believe that I didn't recognize this before, all this time!" he said. "Wow, *yeah*, that's really cool, Eli."

"I don't—" Jeom threw his hand over his mouth. "*Oh*, I just got it!" he said, blinking his eyes over and over as he continued to stare.

"Ara?" asked Eli, tilting his head toward her.

She chewed on her lip, staring at his tattoos intently, trying to find a meaning there. But they just looked like a bunch of lines with no discernable pattern.

She groaned.

"I give up!" she said, throwing her hands into the air. She'd had enough riddles to last her a lifetime, and this one didn't even make the list of things she cared to try to solve. "Just tell me. What do they mean?" She tapped her foot, Solza nuzzling against her legs.

They all sniggered, sharing in the secret; she rolled her eyes, suddenly *really* missing Lessa.

"Fine," he said, "but you should've been the first one to figure it out, and I'm never letting you live this down." He grabbed her hand, letting her trace one of the lines with her finger as he guided it gently along his chest—firebugs began swarming in her stomach again. "It's a map."

"A map?" she repeated as she dropped her hand to her side; she looked him up and down, her eyes widening with under-standing. "*Oh...* it's a map!"

She slapped her hand to her forehead.

"It's my map, to be exact," explained Eli. "A memory of all the places I've been. When I first moved to South Luose, I became obsessed with traveling. Just leaving the Four Corners and journeying from there to my new city was such an amaz-ing experience. After that, all I wanted to do was explore. I never wanted to stop."

"I remember," said Arianna, thinking back to when they had first met—Eli had bragged over ambitious plans to cross the Black Sand Desert alone. "What a future fate had in store for you," she added with a wink.

"Indeed," he said, gazing at her with longing. His eyes shifted to the waters. "I had studied maps for a long time out of interest, so I began to venture to different cities bordering the Nicora Forest. On my travels, I met an artist who asked me if I had anything so special to me that I would be happy to have a permanent reminder." He shook his head, clearly lost in a wonderful memory. "It had to make me smile every time I looked at it, otherwise it wouldn't be worth the trouble. Im-mediately, I said travel!" He clapped his hands. "Plain and sim-ple." He traced the lines on his skin again. "This is my jour-ney... to remember how far I've come."

He turned around, peering over the side of the ship, wind in his hair; Arianna noticed he had shining new designs on his back, black ink surely glinting with a hint of silver as it caught the light.

"And thanks to you all, my journey has continued in the most magical of ways…" he said, still staring off into the distance.

"Who gave you *those*?" asked Arianna, intrigued. "You definitely have some new additions since I saw you last."

She moved closer to inspect his stunning new markings, gliding her hand across his chiseled back; he shivered, then turned to face her with a soft smile.

She wondered if he had firebugs fluttering all over the place, too.

"I did!" said Noah, glowing with pride.

"You?" said Arianna, mouth agape. "But how?"

She found a familiarity with his new markings—they had been a big part of her journey as well.

"Well, I cheated a little," he said, wiggling his fingers as they sparked with magic. "Margery gave me some pointers."

Arianna gave him a stern look. "That could have gone so very wrong," she said.

"Could have," he replied with a smirk.

"Glad it didn't," said Eli, feigning to wipe the sweat from his brow. "But if it had, at least these are on my back. I'd never see them." He pulled on his shirt.

Noah laughed, shaking his head.

"If we make it out of here alive," mused Eli, "I'll have a lot more to add in the future, I'm sure." His voice was much too casual for what his statement really meant.

They all grew quiet, and Arianna knew they were each thinking the same thing—would they have a future?

Will we all make it out… alive?

"Demetrius…" said Arianna, putting her focus on more

serious things. "Are you in control of your powers yet? We're going to need you out there."

"He is," interjected Noah, placing a supportive hand on his back. "It's been a long few weeks, but he's finally starting to get the hang of it."

"It just took some time," said Demetrius, "to cope with all the… information, but Diveena taught me how to meditate like Solomon taught you long ago, Ara." She bristled, wondering how many lessons like that had been a pretense for something else. *Why did he choose me… train me?* "It helps me control my mind, lock away that piece that has tapped into the Nicora Clan's collective knowledge, unless I need it." He looked to his hands. "The trouble is pulling it up now that I've buried it away."

"You'll get the hang of it," Jeom assured him. "That's how I feel wielding the Axe of Crissy, sometimes. We've always had the dwarf and elf in us, suppressed deep inside. The challenge was getting them to come out. Diveena's death allowed you the full breadth of what you're capable of, but it takes time and practice to actually *control* magic that strong." He fingered the tube concealing his axe. "Don't rush it."

"*Maybe* rush it… just a little," said Noah, pinching his fingers together with a nervous laugh. "You know, tyrant king and evil sorcerers coming our way, and whatnot." He shrugged.

That cracked a smile out of all of them.

But Arianna understood Demetrius' fears all too well.

"The same can be said for avatar masters," she added, meeting his worried gaze; Sano scuttled across the back of his shoulders. "But it definitely does get easier."

He nodded. "Thank you," he mouthed.

"Everything happens for a reason, I suppose," said Eli. "Either way, we're here… whether we're ready or not." He knelt down, hugging Solza around the neck.

"I guess we're all in the same boat!" said Jeom with such amusement; his words hung in the air.

Demetrius scoffed, and Arianna and Eli looked between each other disbelievingly.

"Really, Jeom?" said Demetrius after a moment, lifting an eyebrow.

"*Yeah...* that one was no good, mate," said Noah, shaking his head. "I can give you some good tips, though. Later on, maybe? I've got some decent material."

Jeom scowled down at him, and he shrunk back behind Eli.

They all fell into a fit of laughter, Jeom the last to join yet with the largest laugh; when the sounds of cheerfulness died away, all that was left to do was move forward.

Arianna found Sano's bright orange eyes and could sense his uneasiness; he was now atop Jeom's shoulders.

"It's time," she said. "We attack now, while the moon is high in the sky."

They all agreed, leaving the huddle to facilitate their respective duties. Arianna caught Master Tayshin's attention and gave a curt nod—they were ready to go.

He returned it with enthusiasm and released the magical signal to begin; every guardian felt the tingle on their palms telling them that it was time to march to battle.

THEIR FLEET REACHED SAINDORA in the dead of night. They landed on the other side of the port where the coast was clear, the sleeping city completely quiet save for the splash of waves against the shore. And as promised, Syrifina's mystic fog had followed them all the way there, keeping them unnoticed, like ghosts atop the water.

"The time for hiding is done now," Arianna said as their ships met the silent shore. "We're finally here."

"*Reveliantom!*" shouted Jeom—the Axe of Crissy expanded in his palm with a colorful burst. The black of the blades nearly blended in with the night, but the sharp silver edges shone bright.

Arianna closed her eyes for a moment, letting the sparks from his magic warm her to the difficult tasks ahead.

"*Are you ready, Solza?*" she asked.

"*Yes, Master,*" she replied. "*I'm more than ready.*"

"*Then let's not linger, lest we talk ourselves out of this.*"

She opened her eyes and gave Jeom the signal to begin; they pulled their magic to the surface.

With Solza's help, they tapped into their elemental powers over the wind and the water, sweeping the magical mist away like dust. And as the fog dissipated, the City of Saindora came into crystal-clear view.

Arianna felt as if she looked through a window to her past. She cringed as she laid eyes on the palace she'd fled only a few months prior—and just like the King, it seemed to keep watch over everything, steadfast and cold, no matter how much the world crumbled around them.

"Ara… now," said Eli, drawing her out of her daze. "Let's light it up."

Solza ven immito! she thought. She lifted her hands toward the front of the ship.

A large, pink flame grew atop a torch that had been created for solely this purpose—initiating battle—the strong sea winds doing nothing to stop it. And soon, a fire had been lit on every vessel in their fleet so that it looked as if the water had begun to catch fire.

The Guardians of Gold were ready to be seen.

Ladders were cast down the sides of the ships and canoes

were lowered into the sea as the guardian army, sixteen thousand men and women, maneuvered into the shallows of Saindora. They reached the sands quickly and quietly, drawing their weapons and calling to their magic.

It was then that a bell sounded loud in the silent night, ringing across the land like the beating heart of the city; everyone stilled for only a moment, listening to its crying echo.

Arianna felt the hair rise on her skin, more memories from her past ruffled awake as the shriek of the Warrior's District Bell resounded in her heart. She would rip the giant structure down to the ground, set it aflame until it liquified and sounded no longer.

"They know we're coming now," said Master Tayshin, walking up the beach beside Arianna.

"Good," she said, standing watch as their army assembled around her. She narrowed her gaze, searching for a path to the palace. "*Good.*"

The skies were mostly clear now, just darkness and moonlight all around. And with the flickering fires on the waves, Arianna could plainly see just how magnificent the full breadth of the guardians appeared as one …

Everyone donned hooded black cloaks, magicked with a barely noticeable shimmer of red, green, purple, and blue. Interior linings of gold-colored silk fluttered in the soft breeze, and embroidered gilt dragons on the backs of every warrior made it seem as if the army had been plucked straight out of the Golden Age; they glared with gleaming silver eyes.

Each warrior, Arianna included, also wore some form of armor—dark gold metals impressed with patterns that were meant to mimic the sheen of dragon scales, and to protect like them too.

Some, like Jeom, were suited from head to toe. Others—like Arianna, Eli, Noah, Master Tayshin, and nearly everyone who hailed from the Warrior's District—preferred to carry less weight. And many, Demetrius included, opted to carry a shield, the guardian emblem emblazoned on the metal.

The elders, generals, leaders, and Moriamo protectors stood out among the rest in their own unique, stunning ways. However, Arianna, Jeom, Demetrius, and Lessa had been given slightly different attire than the rest…

As the original slaves to steal their freedom, the four had been honored with garbs representing their district beginnings—inspired by the cloak Jillian, Princess Elisa's attendant, had sewn for Arianna the night she escaped Saindora.

Arianna proudly wore that same brilliant red cloak now, and Jeom and Demetrius showed off comparable ones that emphasized their district colors; Lessa's had been stowed away safely on one of the ships, waiting for the moment they could give it to her.

Lastly, each person had been equipped with their choice of weapon from finely crafted metals, thanks to the wealth of Zambienth creators in their fold. Swords, bows and arrows, axes, scythes, daggers, and more were all accounted for this night, all sprinkled throughout the guardians.

Arianna had had her choice weapons with her all along; she drew a single sword from the sheath at her back and noted the foreign inscription on the blade, finally translated for her after so many years by Diveena.

Since her first step outside of the Four Corners, all this time, she'd been carrying around the prophecy—the Golden Rule—before even knowing what it was or all that it would mean to her life in the future. And just like Solomon's swords, it would never be apart from her.

"Why would he give these to me willingly?" she still pondered to herself.

She frowned, thinking of Diveena's words.

These weren't gifted to your master lightly, and I'm sure he did not give them away lightly either. He must really believe in you,' she had said.

Arianna couldn't deny that there'd been a time where Solomon had believed in her for something, chosen her for *something*. But she'd never gotten out of him what it was. And contemplating him now, no matter his change in allegiance, the same thought kept dripping into her mind.

Did he choose me for this?

She dug her boots into the soft sand, finding her balance. She gripped her sword tighter as the army of her dreams organized around her.

The lead guardians gathered on horseback; the rest prepared to march on foot.

"You've got this, Ara," said Jeom, drawing her out of her thoughts and into a firm hug; she could barely breathe for how much metal he wore. "Be safe out there."

"You too," she said as he relinquished his hold. She watched in disbelief as he mounted his horse. "This is so surreal." He nodded, eyes wide. "Don't let go of that axe, you hear?"

He snorted—it was practically glued to his hand at this point, so he didn't have to say what she knew he was thinking. *'They can pry it out of my cold, dead hands if they want it.'*

She turned to Demetrius.

"And you, keep your shield high!"

"Yes, ma'am," he said, straightening.

"I'm *serious*," she warned, pointing her sword at him.

Demetrius softened. "We'll be fine," he said, leaning over to squeeze her hand from atop his horse. "Just stick to the plan, all right? No detours this time. No *sacrifices*, no whims."

She swept her hair back, trying to muster her confidence, on the outside at least.

"Of course," she said with a wink. "Besides, when have I ever not stuck to the plan?"

Demetrius and Jeom smirked at each other.

Noah walked his horse up the beach alongside them; her mouth dropped open.

"*What*, Ara? Never seen a warrior before?" He had a cocky grin on his face.

"Evidently not," she replied, looking him up and down, armor, axe, and all. "You clean up good, Noah. Come here."

They embraced for a short moment, but she was afraid to let him go.

Noah was her oldest friend, and she'd seen him come so far. But never in all her life could she have imagined he was destined to grow into such a wonderful sight, a warrior indeed.

"Liam would be so proud of you," he whispered into her ear.

Arianna hugged him harder. "He'd be proud of you too," she said. "Don't let your guard down out there… *promise* me. Remember everything we practiced. I can't lose you too."

"I promise," he said, the most serious she'd ever seen him.

Her gaze shifted to Eli as he came to join them. "And *no* bets."

Noah cracked a smile. "Now that I can't promise." She scoffed. "I'll be *fine*, Ara," he said as they parted. "If I learned one thing from you, it's how not to die."

"I hope I've learned that lesson well enough, too," she mumbled.

They all stepped back to make room for Eli.

Arianna's heart began to drum faster, all her nervous energy rising to the surface as he neared. She reached out to him, longingly, so many things left to say yet no more time.

There's no more time to tell you that…

"Eli, I—"

Before she could finish her thought, or her sentence (she wasn't even sure if she'd spoken out loud), he had hopped down from Phantom and drawn her into his chest.

He didn't go for the kiss—but she did.

She stood on her tiptoes and pulled him to her lips, hoping that this one kiss might say all the things she hadn't yet been able to.

Vance's words rang in her mind. *'Just in case…'*

It's not the last one, she thought, forcibly, erasing Vance's doubts. *Not the last one.*

She kissed him harder, then, reluctantly, pulled away.

Eli's eyes shimmered as he gazed down at her.

"Just in case?" he asked with a pained expression.

Sometimes Arianna thought that they shared the same link that she had with Solza.

She tried to look away, but he placed both hands on her arms so that she was forced to hear his words; he cleared his throat, surely swallowing the hard truth that they might not kiss again.

"As I said, I'll be waiting for you. So you had *better* come back to me." It wasn't a question, it was a demand; it felt like he was staring straight into the center of her soul, and it glowed for him. "Tell me you hear me, Arianna."

"I hear you," she said. "When this is done."

Noah let out a loud, drawn-out whistle, and Demetrius and Jeom did a little teasing themselves; an embarrassed smile replaced the nerves that were beginning to build up in her chest.

She pointed her sword around the group, playfully.

"Be careful now," said Arianna with a smirk. "I'm in a fighting mood tonight." She turned her sword on Eli, pointing the tip of her blade at his heart and winked.

He put a hand over his chest, as if wounded.

"You got me, Ara. I'm yours," he said, a starry look in his eyes.

The boys howled in even more laughter, and Arianna couldn't help but join in. She felt truly happy in this moment, surrounded by those she loved most, sharing joy with them in the face of such danger—they were just missing one person.

"Sano," she called, suddenly. "Sano, come here."

He'd been perched on the back of Phantom.

He flew to her, twisting around her shoulders and nuzzling into her neck.

"Sano," she said, gently, "we're going to try our best to find Lessa now, and we're going to need you to watch our backs. Can you do that for us, friend? It would be a *great* honor to have you battle by our side."

He hadn't shifted since their separation, his depression evident. But he would be a valuable addition to their fight, if he could find it in him to do so; it had just never occurred to Arianna to actually ask him before…

Thinking of her connection with Solza, she was sure he would understand.

Sano's eyes flooded with silver. He jumped down, transforming into the giant white wolf that would frighten any opponent. And with a mighty howl into the night, he set the tone for their battle.

Don't be brave, little slave. Be a warrior!

Eli, Jeom, Noah, and Demetrius all touched Arianna one last time, on the shoulder, to wish her good luck. Then, with Sano at their heels, they galloped off to the front of the army to assume command with the rest of the original guardians.

"*Time to go, Solza,*" said Arianna. She remained at the rear of the army waiting for Solza to land, now only dragon ships and black waves at her back.

A booming roar ripped through the night before she even saw anything. And she was certain that the city must have heard it too—a dragon, returned to Saindora from across the seas, at long last.

The flap of Solza's mountainous wings sent gusts of wind across the beach, stirring the sand in every direction.

Everyone looked up, shielding their eyes.

It seemed as if Solza had melted out of the darkness, drawing closer with every breath; her sleek, black scales made her appear as one with the night, their silver veins just like sparks of electricity in a thunderous cloud.

Light is light and dark is dark, but never shall they live apart.

Arianna smiled to herself as she watched her dragon dominate the skies, the Golden Rule making an appearance once again.

She landed at the *front* of the army, craning her head toward the clouds, waiting for her master.

"*I wish I didn't have to do this...*" said Arianna. Her heart was racing.

"*Master Tayshin thinks it's an important step to help motivate our people, and so do I,*" Solza replied in a reassuring tone. "*And, Master, you deserve this honor. Get over your fears, and start marching. I shall patiently wait until you arrive.*"

Arianna took a deep breath and began the long walk up the beach to meet her, thinking that she couldn't wait to be in the sky; Solza giggled all the while.

She had to pass through the entire army, countless people, countless faces that she didn't yet know...

They parted for her out of respect, using their magic to light her path with fire all the way to the front, her name circling throughout the crowd like a chant. *I don't know them, but they know me. I have to be brave, for them.*

She held her head high, steadied her sword at her side and kept walking.

Nearing the head of the army atop a small hill, she spotted Kayode and Tayo—they led a large group of people from Moriamo who had pledged to fight alongside the guardians. Their warriors were the only ones gathered who did not wear the guardian uniform. Instead, they stuck to their camouflage comfort zone, their skin and faces streaked with warrior paint.

"Don't let them catch you," said Arianna, speaking to Kayode over the hum of the crowd.

"A coyote never gets caught," she replied, a gleam in her sharp brown eyes.

"So you've proven," said Arianna with a firm nod. "Good luck to you."

"And to you, my friend." She brought her fist to her chest; the Moriamo protectors followed suit.

Arianna returned the gesture, then moved forward.

When she reached the front of the army, she shook hands with all the elder guardians—Nico, Sergios, Vance, and Margery.

Master Tayshin gave her a short hug, his pride for her shining through his gaze, no words left to speak; he patted his armored chest, and she know he meant for her to stay strong.

With another glance around, she found her boys, Sano remaining protectively at their sides—they all stood back, offering her the platform to speak.

Their worry and love were written plain across their faces.

She locked eyes with Eli one last time; he gave her a nod of encouragement, one fist over his heart.

Arianna collected her bravery and finally turned to face the army of the Guardians of Gold in full, finally seeing them for what they truly were—a fierce and beautiful force to be reckoned with.

"*Such a grand view, isn't it?*" said Solza; Arianna couldn't have agreed more. She felt Solza beam. "*Now give them the send-off they deserve, Master. Go on.*"

Her grip sure on her sword, Arianna lifted it into the air, the tip of her blade slashing through the blackness around them.

Her army did the same, raising their weapons to the sky with courage and certainty.

"Hail to the World," she shouted out with such fervor that spit flew from her mouth. "Hail to Olleb-Yelfra!"

The army thundered the phrase back at her, their voices almost knocking her off her feet as they shook their blades; Arianna sheathed her sword and climbed onto Solza's back.

"*Keep your eyes peeled up there,*" she said. "*No telling what King Devlindor has prepared for us.*"

"*No telling what we have prepared for them,*" countered Solza, her passion mirroring the warriors' down below.

She spread her wings, ready to fly.

Arianna looked down to her followers, one final push of inspiration on her tongue. "Remember what it is that you fight for. We are all warriors of the Olleb tonight!"

She thrust her palm into the air, the guardian emblem glimmering there; they cheered more, Sano howling along with them.

"Make it rain," yelled Jeom, cupping his hands around his mouth. He waved his golden axe in camaraderie, the air swishing along with it. "No mercy!"

"Just careful of the trees, Ara!" called Demetrius with a heartening smile; Jeom rolled his eyes.

"You got this," mouthed Eli, Noah at his side.

She beamed, feeling as if they'd already won. *We're all going to be just fine.*

Solza shot into the air, leaving the beach behind; Arianna didn't even have time to glance back, but she heard their cheers and applause follow them the entire way to the city.

They were hovering over the gates of Saindora in minutes.

"*You heard Jeom,*" she said, holding on tight. "*Time to make it rain… we show no mercy to Kyrone.*"

"*Down with the King,*" roared Solza.

She opened her jaw and fire poured into the sky, flames swirling with the clouds. The first phase of their plan had begun—set fire to the kingdom.

INTO THE SHADOWS

ARIANNA AND SOLZA WERE FIRST UP in the scheme to take down the King, the guardian army impatiently waiting for their leader's return back at the beach. Their goal was to draw King Devlindor straight to them so that the guardians could fight on their own terms, send him a message he couldn't refuse—and what better way to do that than by leaving him a fiery trail straight from his palace to the sea?

After the alert of the bell, she was confident that their plan was right on track, their presence in Saindora already well known. Now was the time for action… to create chaos in his stronghold, to weaken their forces before they even got to the fight.

Fire is chaos, Arianna thought—and dragon rider or not, sometimes she still feared its burn.

They flew low to the ground, soaring over the City of Saindora as Solza's earsplitting roars and the sound of the bell shook the night awake; Arianna could tell she was enjoying herself.

She focused on the city, watching as lanterns were lit and people peeked out of windows and doors to investigate the disturbance. She was sure they'd never heard that bell before; everyone who spotted them ran back inside.

With the cover of night, and such a spectacular view from a dragon's back, Arianna had to admit that Saindora proved quite charming, without the sun to highlight its decay…

The city seemed to wind upward toward the palace in stacks of brick and cobblestone, like an inverted tornado. Signs of forest or jungles tapered off here, nothing like that of Guanamara or South Luose. The streets were free of nature, Saindora's borders paving the way for only manmade creations. There were throngs of shops and markets, taverns, homes, and the like for miles between the city gates, the palace, and the sea.

Arianna felt Solza grow warm as she pooled her fire in her belly.

"*Careful of your aim,*" she warned, fighting away her nerves. "*We don't want to hit too many buildings if we can avoid it. There will be enough casualties this night.*"

"*Yes, Master,*" replied Solza. "*I'll try.*"

She recalled the bones of the City of Crissy at the edges of the Black Sand Desert and couldn't help but shudder. "*Try your very best.*"

That wasn't their objective tonight. They didn't want to burn the city to the ground—she just wanted to smoke the snakes out from hiding and lead them into a trap.

She had learned from her time there as a prisoner that the people of Saindora kept mostly to their dwellings in the evenings, no one daring to disturb the King's slumber. Thus, as agreed, Solza would only aim her blazing breath at the main streets which were, thankfully, deserted at this hour.

As if they were of one mind and body, Arianna could feel Solza's fiery magic begin to bubble up in her throat, scorching hot. In the next second, her mighty jaws opened again and fire emptied from them in streams so bright that she had to blink several times before she could see again—this time Solza turned her aim from the sky to the earth.

Her fire consumed the paved paths like a spark to oil, Saindora effectively coming ablaze. And just as discussed, she was somehow able to completely avoid the destruction of *any* buildings.

What in the gods' names… how is she controlling it so well? Arianna wasn't naïve; she'd expected some significant damage.

"*How do I do anything, Master?*" she replied, smugly.

Arianna didn't need to question further. The answer was—so plain, so simple, and so incredibly fantastic—magic.

"*Avatar magic, to be exact,*" she added.

"*What can't you do?*"

It looked as if a flaming river crept throughout the maze-like metropolis, adding its heat to the already warm night. And while fire was known to spread rapidly out of control, not even a flicker traveled out of place.

"*It's just so… contained, like the fire has a mind of its own.*" Arianna was awestruck as the flames continued crawling up a pre-determined path toward the palace, red and orange scorching the white, without Solza needing to add any more to it.

She closed her jaw and continued circling, keeping close watch on this flaming beast she'd conjured.

"*It's my mind,*" explained Solza. "*I'm not just any dragon. And you're not just any sorceress, Master. I can control fire just as well as I can create it… as can you.*"

Arianna let her eyes float closed, inhaling deeply as she sensed the avatar magic course through her. Sure enough, if she concentrated hard, she could feel Solza using their combined powers to tame that trail of fire, leading it to where they wished it to go.

It wasn't long before people began to react—the citizens of Saindora added their screams and panic to the crackling sounds of fire and Solza's terrifying growls.

They pointed to the sky in terror, laying eyes upon a fire-breathing creature they surely didn't even have a name for.

"*They're so scared,*" said Solza; she could sense their discomfort. "*Of me...*"

"*Of us both,*" said Arianna. "*Don't worry, my friend. We knew this would happen. If all goes well, we'll show them soon that we're not the ones they should fear.*"

When they reached the Palace of Saindora, Solza unlocked her fang-riddled jaws once more. She breathed a circle of flames around the outer edges of its base, creating a ring of fire around the King's home.

What a sight, Arianna thought as they hovered there a moment—the palace looked even more frightening and powerful surrounded in flames.

"*Master, look!*" Solza veered her head and her body followed.

Arianna gazed in that direction, and King Devlindor stared back, from the balcony of his chambers.

Solza flew closer, and Arianna fought every urge in her body that told her to turn back.

Even from this distance, the rage was clear in his expression, a rage unlike anything she had yet to see darken that pallid face.

It looked as if he had just been roused from sleep, wearing no shirt nor shoes. Yet, even so, King Damas' crown was fitted firmly atop his head, his fingers wrapped around the ruby-studded staff.

"*Do you think he'll surrender?*" asked Solza.

That had always been their best-case scenario.

"*Not a chance*," said Arianna, unblinking.

Solza flapped her wings harder, and they stayed their ground, kept their gazes locked.

His eyes began to glow a petrifying silver, stark with energy, glaring with power.

"*What's he doing?*"

The ruby of his staff burned a bright red.

"*I've no idea*," said Arianna, pursing her lips. "*But it's not going to be good for us. Go higher, just in case he's targeting us with some kind of spell.*"

Solza flew high into the sky, well out of reach of the King. Still, they circled the palace in anticipation, trying to figure out his next move.

King Devlindor lifted his hand into the air, and the flames around the palace began to dwindle down into nothing.

"*I can't fight him*," shrieked Solza, her connection breaking with the fire—the King had taken over. "*It's avatar magic… my magic! How can this be?*"

"*Don't waste your energy competing with him in this*," said Arianna, remaining calm as they watched their ring of fire die away. "*Remember, he's an avatar master, too. He's strong, but we accomplished what we meant to. Now comes the battle. We'll get our chance at him soon enough.*"

"*Too soon, I think*," warned Solza.

The fear that jolted through her ran straight into Arianna's heart—they connected, and suddenly she could see once more through her avatar's eyes.

Her sight was so crisp that not the night nor the smoke rising could do anything to impair her vision—thousands of people in black cloaks poured out of the palace doors and from around the gardens and grounds as a practiced entity, surrounding his fortress.

Arianna was momentarily taken aback by the sheer

number of followers he'd manage to gather back at Saindora.

The King has been ready for us, too.

She supposed that the moment she'd escaped him, and revealed her greatest weapon, he had finally decided to take her seriously. And in a way, she couldn't help but feel a sense of pride…

At least he respects me enough now to prepare for a fight.

King Devlindor's lips curled up into a disturbing smile. He tipped his crown to her in a gesture that Arianna only took to mean one thing: *challenge accepted.*

He disappeared inside.

Solza sounded the roar of frustration that Arianna felt gathering in her chest; she wanted to burn him where he stood.

We can't let our guard down. Stick to the plan.

She gritted her teeth, squeezing Solza's horn—her promise to Eli gave her all the patience she needed.

"*All right, they're coming now,*" said Arianna—she almost couldn't believe her own statement. *They're coming.* "*Time for phase two. Let's turn around.*"

Solza veered back toward the beach as the King's army, Shadow Resistance and regulators alike, began to march along their fiery path, the golden snake coiled on the backs of their midnight black cloaks. They flew high in the clouds, keeping a bird's-eye view over everything.

The fires receded as the shadows combed through the streets, the King's magic stretching farther than his eyes could possibly see.

Impressive, thought Arianna, trying to suppress her unease. *But not impressive enough.*

King Devlindor's reach was undeniably powerful, but he wouldn't be able to erase the scorch marks left on his streets by dragon fire in mere minutes. And his sorcerers didn't have time to spare to sweep the memories of an entire city whose world had just been burst open wide with new possibilities—

dragons and rebellion against the King's regime.

"*Master, there's many of them,*" said Solza, sniffing at the air. "*There are many more warriors with magic on his side than ours.*"

Arianna urged Solza on faster, leaving the city in their wake—the guardian army finally came back into view.

"*I know, but there's many of us too,*" said Arianna. "*More than them by a good amount… and we have you.*" She patted her on the back. "*And Sano. We're prepared for this.*"

With the King's Shadow Resistance and regulators blanketing the streets of Saindora in a swath of darkness, the guardian army was a glaring contrast.

They gleamed with a brightness that wouldn't easily be overshadowed, their ships so radiant, like golden beacons of light on the waters, and their armor and weapons far outshining their enemies. *Now is our time to prove our worth. Win or die.*

Solza and Arianna landed with a thud at the front of it all, this time facing the city.

She raised her fist high above her head, an enchanted flame twisting in and out of her fingers so that it looked as if she gripped a ball of pink fire.

Her army stood to attention—this was the signal for war.

Arianna savored the delicious sounds that always happened just before a battle… the click of arrows into place, the clink of armor and swords. She couldn't help but glance back to witness the beautiful dragons behind her.

She wanted to memorize all their faces—there wasn't time enough. Yet, seeing them with such a fight and passion in their eyes gave her all the courage she needed for what came next.

And thank the goddesses she *knew* what came next.

No ambush, no surprises.

The Guardians of Gold had summoned their enemies right to them and did not plan to run. With any luck, they'd be able to land some surprises all their own this night...

Archers were positioned stealthily atop the nearest ships lining the shore. And they had the security of rehearsed battle sequences they'd all mastered under the watch of Master Tayshin, Nico, and Sergios—the only remaining survivors of the first failed siege. Anyone without magic was paired up with someone charmed, so no one should feel unprotected against the shadow sorcerers. And with Margery and Vance's supply of powerful defensive potions at the ready, they had come with everything an army could dream of in a fight against the King's.

For once, all was going smoothly for the guardians.

Arianna faced forward, double-checking that her swords and dagger were securely fastened in their sheaths. When she looked up, the Shadow Resistance had emerged from the city gates.

She gripped Solza tighter, straightening her back.

"Here they come." Her heart thrashed in her chest.

Solza crouched low, baring her teeth with a snarl just as the full breadth of the King's army rose into view, at the point where the cobblestone met the sand. They began to quietly fan out on the other side of the vast silver-sanded beach.

Arianna had to blink twice, experiencing a rush of what felt like déjà vu.

But this wasn't complex mind magic at play, as Odessa might've suggested. No, quite the contrary... Arianna had been in this position before.

In fact, her near-death escape from the High City had inspired the beginnings of the takeover strategy the guardians had eventually formed. The only difference was that now she wasn't outnumbered a hundred to one.

Solomon was also, unfortunately, a common factor, leading the shadows just as before. However, he wasn't alone at the front this time—Sir Vladamor, Head of the King's Guard and Shadow Resistance—abductor of Lessa—had assumed full command of the King's force.

The next person she looked for *was* Lessa, but she didn't spot her.

The second was the King.

"Where is Kyrone?" she bellowed out, addressing Sir Vladamor; as their enemies assembled before them, she noticed that the other three members of the King's Guard were not present either.

"*King* Devlindor will receive you…" said Vladamor with the tilt of his head, "when you are dead."

Solza snapped her teeth, itching to let out another burst of fire.

"*Not yet,*" warned Arianna, trying to tame her own temper as well. "*We knew this would likely be the case.*"

They had prayed the King might just lay down his sword at a mere scare tactic, but no one had ever believed that would actually happen. Their core plan had been developed on the very likelihood that the royal monster would not come to face the guardians himself, even once he'd been summoned.

And while the second-best-case scenario had been that this war might end in one fell swoop, right there on that beach with the King buried in the sand, this had also been an unrealistic hope.

King Devlindor only played at one game, and that was his—he wouldn't be giving them the satisfaction of any best-case scenarios.

Arianna was quite certain that, eventually, the guardians would have to breach the palace and fight him in his territory.

"Where's Lessa?" shouted Jeom, guiding his horse forward. The beach became consumed by a heavy gust of wind, Sano close by his side and a low growl rumbling in his throat. "What have you done with her?"

"Why, whatever do you mean?" said Vladamor, turning

his attention to Jeom. "She's right here with me."

He signaled to Solomon, and Arianna stiffened.

"Show her," Solomon commanded to those nearest to them.

Arianna saw Jeom staring at her, petrified—his expression asked only one question.

"Stay calm," she called down to him. "We'll rescue her."

He nodded and faced forward, axe in hand.

The regulators separated to reveal Lessa, wide-eyed, pink-cheeked, and scared—she was trapped in what appeared to be a glass cage.

From just one glance, she could tell she looked sickly, starved for family and likely for food. What's more, her belly had grown much bigger in their weeks of separation; everything about her appearance outraged Arianna even more.

We have to get her and Snow out of there!

Lessa locked eyes with Arianna and stilled, clearly in shock, then she pressed her hand upon the inside of the glass and screamed; her cries were silenced by the cage, but Arianna could feel them, like arrows piercing her chest.

"Let her go, *now*," she said, leaning forward.

Solza took a step too, echoing her wrath; she let out a deadly blast of fire, aiming directly for the shadows guarding Lessa.

They were skilled sorcerers, though. And with Solomon among them, they were able to block the attack.

They can't withstand dragon fire forever, thought Arianna, fury gripping her.

Solza didn't let up.

"Now, now," said Vladamor, wagging his finger at her from atop his horse and from behind a barrier of magic. "Don't waste your energy. You may burn through the guards to get to her, but you'll never break through this glass." He tapped it with a golden-gloved finger. "It's protected by blood magic."

Solza let her fire fade.

Arianna looked down to Jeom for guidance—by her memory, he was the only one with any experience in this realm. She knew little of such things.

"If he's telling the truth, then he's right," he said, growing more agitated by the second; wind lashed around him, his focus locked on Lessa. "It's the same magic that the Axe of Crissy was protected with back in Undor." He slammed the butt of his staff into the ground, magic sizzling, ready to release. "I didn't know about blood magic then, but Diveena helped me to understand…"

He looked up at her, a pained expression.

"*Only* a dwarf of the Undor clan could have obtained the axe." He shook his head. "There's no enchantment stronger, nothing could break such a spell. That's why the King and his armies could never even get close to it, before I came along." He faced forward, glowering at the shadows, jaw set. "He's not of our blood."

She nodded in understanding, already forming a plan to get Lessa out of there.

"I'll gladly cut off a hand if I have to, then," said Arianna, unsheathing a sword.

She looked between Solomon, Vladamor, and Lessa, everyone else all but disappearing before her eyes.

"So…" Her voice rang out, slicing through the fragile quiet, "whose blood will I be taking tonight?"

Sir Vladamor glanced to Solomon and cackled, fingering the ruby stone on the chain at his neck.

"Whose do you think?" he purred, glaring back at her; it was so dark on their side, not a flame in sight, that all she could really make out of him was his chiseled golden mask. "Only the *King's* blood will open it."

Her courage wavered, palms growing sweaty. She couldn't

even look at Jeom to see his reaction.

We knew it would come to this. We knew…

Yet, the more the possibility of having to enter the palace to hunt down the King solidified into a reality, the less she had confidence in their strategy to do it.

"*Stay positive,*" said Solza. "*We can win.*"

Solomon drew his twin swords, the bronze beauties that had carried Arianna so far.

"If you want Lessa back," he said in an even voice, "you will have to get to King Devlindor. And if you want to get to the King, you'll have to first get through us."

With the flick of his blades, the Shadow Resistance army began to light up the night like dark yet colorful lanterns, sinister magic pooling in their hands.

"Better hurry," said Vladamor, one bony hand on Solomon's shoulder from behind. "The air won't last very long in that cage of hers. I made sure of it."

Arianna balked, and she just knew he was smiling underneath his mask.

"How long do you think it will last?" called Demetrius, keeping close to Jeom.

"Not a clue," said Arianna, flashing a terrified glance to Lessa; she looked worse by the second. "Let's not wait to find out."

Master Bell stepped forward, his swords twisting like fans of metal at his sides; he set his gaze on Arianna, beckoning her to him.

She couldn't look away.

Sir Vladamor lifted his fist to the air, and the Shadow Resistance released their magic.

"Solza, fly!" she shouted as their spells raced toward them.

She bolted into the sky at her command, then the Guardians of Gold and the Shadow Resistance rushed forward.

THE SOUND OF SO MANY BODIES colliding with each other fell ill on the ears. With an aerial view, Arianna could already see those who hadn't survived the initial attacks—bodies were scattered across the ground from both sides, dead snakes and dead dragons, one on top of the other.

Solza rolled back and forth in the sky with precision as a group of shadows focused their attacks on bringing her down; Arianna wielded her magic in defense, and an assembly of guardians on board the ships had been specifically trained on covering them when they were in flight.

Still, it was a vulnerable situation for Solza to be in at a time like this—there were reasons dragons no longer existed in the Olleb, and Arianna was willing to bet that war was one of them…

Dragons were not indestructible creatures, *and* they made massive targets in the sky; it was inevitable that some of the attacks would eventually land.

Arianna was unable to concentrate on anything other than holding on and protecting herself and Solza from the thunderous blasts of magic booming around them in the clouds. Meanwhile, Solza was doing as much damage as possible before they forced her from the skies.

The combined guardian efforts just weren't enough; Solza let out a screech of pain and jerked to the side as a spell hit her in the head.

Arianna tried her best to calm her until she could fly steadily again, grasping on to her for dear life. They spun in the air, seemingly out of control, until Solza found her balance again.

"*You all right, girl?*" asked Arianna, panic piercing her.

"*Yes, just a spook…*" said Solza; she let out a deafening roar. "*I'm more than all right.*"

She collected herself, not hesitating one bit to repay the

favor.

She flew straight toward the offenders, showering strings of fire down on them in torrents—and this time, she was aiming to kill.

Between Solza's fire and the magic on both sides, bright bursts all along the shore, it appeared as if the sun were beginning to rise again in the darkness. And yet, the night was still young.

"*Let's get higher, I need to think a moment,*" said Arianna, her thoughts veering back to Lessa; she didn't have time for this.

Who knows how long she'll last in there…

They flew out of reach of attack, orbiting the beach.

When Arianna was able to finally look down and focus on the guardians on the ground, she sucked in a sharp breath, eyes wide.

A zigzag of dragon fire ensnared the beach, a mile long, an ominous light to aid those in battle.

The most talented in magic of her allies had been paired with those best skilled as warriors. Thus, in supporting each other, the Guardians of Gold made worthy opponents to those equally skilled on the King's side.

Arianna gaped in astonishment as archers from their ships sent hundreds of arrows down on their enemies, an incessant rain, all of them lit with pink flames; Nico guided them all the while.

There was also Master Tayshin and Eli, leading the way as they cut through a swarm of shadows with loyal Moriamo protectors at their backs; Kayode and Tayo were a brilliant blur of color among them, proving just how fierce the villagers of the swamp could truly be. They had no mercy.

We're gaining the upper hand, Arianna thought; she felt Solza smile.

She spotted Margery and Vance, too, cooking up the back-up plan to take down Sir Vladamor, their potions crackling and sizzling in sharp blasts all along the shore. And Noah and Sergios had paired up in combat against some very serious sorcerers, weapons churning in the air, spells encircling them like a cyclone.

Jeom was knocking back groups of regulators with little effort, fully channeling the powers of the axe. Blasts of wind followed him wherever he went, and he was clearing a bloody path straight for Lessa; Sano shadowed him closely, aiding the army with his ground-shaking earth powers, tearing apart anyone who dared attack him or his master's other love.

Demetrius, not to be overshadowed by his brother, had successfully honed his elven powers in this time of need; he manipulated the sands as a shield for the guardians or to slow down the opposition, sinking them where they stood. And he called to the nature of the sea, anything that grew from the earth, to defend those around him, no longer caring who got hurt.

"*I think they've got a hold on this now,*" said Arianna, feeling her confidence rise. "*We need to get to Lessa.*"

The blood magic trick had truly not been anticipated, but they'd always known Sir Vladamor would make them work for their win; while getting Lessa back had given them a much-needed nudge to take the final steps toward initiating war, there had been no way to plan for her rescue…

In this, they'd had no idea what to expect.

Now, Arianna was on a tight timeline to figure out how to open that glass box before she suffocated, for she was sure Sir Vladamor wasn't bluffing about her limited air supply and imminent death.

A sudden scream rushed from Arianna's throat as Solza swayed to dodge another attack; she barely had time to hang on, slipping across the smooth scales with a lurch that rose all the way to her stomach.

"I thought we were high enough!" she called, finding a comfortable seat again; her heart was racing, mind spinning. *"That was too close."*

"Not sure anywhere is high enough now, Master," said Solza. *"They want me too badly. And their magic is—"*

"Strong." Stronger than Arianna wanted to admit.

But she knew Solza was right, and they didn't have time to keep playing defense in the skies.

"Watch yourself up there!"

Someone's voice traveled up to them; Arianna peered down to find Eli waving a sword at her. Then, he raced across the battlefield to confront the man who had conjured the spell that had almost thrown Arianna off Solza's back.

She squinted, then recoiled, momentarily taken aback to see who he pursued. *Regulator Roland...*

Looking just as brawny and heartless as she remembered him.

Arianna balled her hand in a fist of magic, ready to return a deadly attack of her own, but Eli had leaped off Phantom to battle him sword-on-sword; oddly, the two appeared evenly matched.

She recognized that Master Tayshin must be suppressing his magic and forced herself to focus elsewhere, swearing on everything that she would slaughter that monster of a man if he hurt either of them.

Her gaze caught Solomon's—he was watching her intently, commanding his armies to attack Solza with all they had.

Arianna gripped on tightly to her horn, leaning forward, a snarl on her lips.

"We have to get on the ground!" she said to Solza—she took a sharp dip toward the beach.

Arianna thrust an attack toward Solomon, but it did little damage with so many concentrated on her.

"There's too many of them. I can't keep them all off your back anymore," she said as the ground rushed toward them; she noticed their guardians aboard the ship had been overwhelmed too. *"Their magic is too strong. Time to change."*

Solza outstretched her claws, the sand nearly upon them— those beneath scattered lest they be crushed.

Arianna jumped off right as they met the ground, Solza swiftly shifting back to her snow leopard form to make for a much smaller target and Arianna landing lithely on her feet.

She unsheathed both her swords, holding them as if an extension of herself; the feeling of being a dragon rider, high in the sky, was unlike anything she'd ever experienced, but nothing could *ever* compare to her first love that was swords— she and Solza flew straight into battle beside their comrades.

She felt so in control now, every decision her own as she battled her way toward Solomon, toward Sir Vladamor.

Toward Lessa.

It wasn't satisfying to see the bodies fall before her blades as she cut through the King's shadows, with an avatar and powerful magic on her side, but it *was* satisfying that she was still alive after successfully defending against such an assault. All her training over the years, all her masters' wisdom, was finally paying off.

And from this vantage point, it still seemed like the Guardians of Gold were winning.

"Heavy losses, though," said Solza—Arianna ignored her, nearing Lessa, feeling invincible with her swords in hand and avatar magic clearing the way before them like a swirling, elemental shield.

She blinked and Sir Vladamor and Solomon were gone.

She and Solza were suddenly blasted off their feet, landing in a heap on the ground.

Disoriented, Arianna peered up to find Solomon and Sir Vladamor hovering over them; they had sent a sudden, calculated attack from behind.

Solomon lifted his electrified sword while she was still trying to gather her thoughts, ears ringing. "You—"

The earth rumbled, rolling her and Solza away from two of the worst monsters she'd ever encountered, out from under their suffocating darkness. A wall of white sand rose to the sky in sheets, separating them from their enemies.

Arianna felt arms wrap around her then, setting her back on her feet.

"Eli," she breathed, sagging in relief.

Jeom, Demetrius, and Sano were right behind him—working as one to control the earth and wind elements together.

When the sands had settled, they were all forced to face the most difficult barrier separating them from Lessa—the Wolf of the East and the King's Shadow.

Jeom dismounted his horse and raised his axe, clearly preparing to run straight into Death's arms if it meant a chance at saving his love.

"Jeom, wait!" said Arianna, holding out her arm. "Something's not right."

"*What?*" he barked, sweat beading on his skin; he dug his armored heels into the ground, but he listened. He swiveled toward her. "What's not right?"

She pointed at them, her face scrunched in confusion. "Why are they not attacking anymore?"

The four stared ahead, and the monsters just stared back.

"She's right," said Demetrius, sliding off his horse too; he repositioned his shield. "Why are they just… just watching us like that?"

She and Eli locked eyes, both seeming equally perplexed and unsettled.

As the battle raged on around them, the four stole a glance away from the commanders of the King's army and toward the other seasoned shadows and regulators across the battle-grounds—they were all waiting for their leaders' next move, too, all seeming to stealthily fall back.

Eli grabbed Arianna's wrist, squeezing so tightly that she could feel the pulse of her own quickened heartbeat rise through her arm. She couldn't even look at him, didn't want to see the panic in his expression.

"*What's going on, Master?*"

Arianna shook her head, though her worries mounted ten-fold—whatever malicious move they were about to make, Solza sensed it too.

The air grew colder, chilling Arianna from the inside out.

Sir Vladamor lifted his mask to reveal his wicked face, his skeletal, sunken features, the mark of the King branded atop his neck and head—just so that Arianna could see him smile; Solomon's expression remained steady, unreadable.

She felt nauseous at the sight of both of them.

"What the…" Demetrius looked to the others, anxious. "Guys, *what* is that? What's he doing?"

The necromancer had plucked a dark-colored velvet pouch from his belt.

"No idea," said Eli, releasing his grip on Arianna so that he could ready his sword. "Though I'm sure it's not going to be pleasant…"

Arianna remained silent, trying to interpret the situation unfolding around them. Trying and failing.

She was missing something, could taste the answer on the tip of her tongue as she stared at Sir Vladamor, at the small bag in his hands. *What am I missing?*

Her instincts were shouting out guidance, but she couldn't focus on them now with all the commotion going on around her, all the arrows and magic flying, swords slashing, screams lashing into the night, warrior cries and final gasps of life alike.

"Argh, *enough* of these games!" growled Jeom, marching

forward, axe in hand; Sano trailed him. "Lessa doesn't have the time."

Solomon shifted his stance slightly away from Sir Vladamor, and Arianna caught another glimpse of Lessa—she was pounding on the glass, crying out as if it were her last breath.

But Arianna could tell that her panic came from something more than just being trapped… her air supply surely thin yet still adequate enough that she remained standing, *wailing*.

She squinted, trying to read her lips, her words muffled by the cage; Jeom was already a few feet ahead, though Sano had retreated, reluctantly seeming to fall back toward the others.

"*Master*—" said Solza in a frightened voice.

"*Wait, Solza, I'm trying to listen*," said Arianna, holding up her hand.

Solza vied for her attention, pawing at her leg.

"*Sano can understand her!*" she implored. "*He hears her. She's saying, 'Run away.'*"

Arianna's eyes widened as her avatar's frantic words filled her mind. *Run away!*

"Jeom…" she stuttered, her voice cracking. "Jeom, *wait*."

He groaned, holding his axe with an iron grip, reluctantly stalling halfway between Solomon and a leering Sir Vladamor.

He looked back to them, and she looked again to the pouch in Sir Vladamor's hand; he opened it and poured its contents onto his palm.

Arianna realized too late what her instincts were trying to say.

A sparkling dust, like a pile of shaved diamonds tinted red, pooled in his palm; he whispered a spell, one that sounded just as malevolent as the shape she realized it would take…

The red dust began to rise into the air, swirling into a fragmented haze that appeared charged with deadly magic.

"What on earth…?" said Demetrius.

Eli was just shaking his head, and Arianna knew he was just as disbelieving as her. *This was not part of the plan.*

Again and again, he repeated this spell.

This curse, thought Arianna; her heart was like a drum with a mind all its own, banging, banging, *banging* in her chest. Screaming out for her to—*Run away!*

Jeom had begun to inch back.

With his magic, Sir Vladamor called forth more diamond-like dust from several other pouches at his belt, each a different color. And each wicked verse he spoke seemed to awaken something within the powdery substance… until it fully came to life before him.

The dust grew into clouds, and the clouds filled with deep, rolling color, bursting with dangerous energy, hissing and buzzing over the battlefield.

Then, the magic solidified into something more…

A terrible, despicable curse.

"Run!" shouted Arianna, feeling her voice quake as she finally understood Lessa's caution. "We have to run, everybody. *Now!*"

Alas, much like everyone else now watching—all the guardians, it seemed—she was frozen in fear.

She just couldn't peel her eyes away, couldn't move an inch.

The clouds lowered to the ground, shifting, morphing, until they were solid and still. When the magic fell away, Syrifina's dead sisters surrounded them.

20

ALLIES

"WE SHOULD HAVE SEEN THIS COMING," said Arianna; she was shaking.

She could see how everything would unfold from here, and this was certainly one moment when she wished to turn back time; the Guanamara massacre teetered in her mind.

"Tell me this isn't happening," said Jeom, instinctively taking a fighting stance.

He called to the powers of his axe, creating a translucent shield of protection around himself, Eli, Demetrius, Arianna, and the avatars.

Arianna stepped up beside him, placing her hand on his arm.

"Breathe," she whispered, maybe more to herself than him; they both inhaled together, and she felt him relax, felt his magic become steadier.

She looked forward, toward the walking dead flanking the

necromancer and Solomon; she couldn't decide which was worse, them or these monstrous versions of the Myr sisters.

The emptiness in their eyes was maybe the most startling—black where Syrifina and her sisters had always boasted silver and brightness.

And still, everything about them was disturbing…

Their lifeblood no longer sparkled on their skin like a rainbow of living color. Instead, strings of oily, dark hues slowly moved across their bodies, as if it had been caked over in mud, congealed and hardened in true death.

And though *dead* they certainly were, these mermaid manifestations had not come back as ghosts but as fully formed, blood-thirsty beasts.

"What are they?" said Eli, a shaky grip on his sword. "Are they…" He cleared his throat. "I thought Syrifina was on our side. They helped us. Are those really her sisters?"

"They used to be," replied Arianna, her voice low, trembling.

Now that she'd said it aloud, there was no denying this atrocity was real.

To think that a singular moment in the past, forgotten and shifted from the mind, could hold such important clues for what the future might bring was more than bewildering. Yet, here they were, witnessing Syrifina Myr's mystery finally resolve itself with an unimaginable and horrifying conclusion.

She sheathed her blades, turning to him.

"Don't you remember Lessa's story from back in the Greenhouse, that night we snuck out?" she asked, keeping one eye on the mermaids—they had yet to move a muscle.

He furrowed his brow. "I'm not sure I do…"

She sighed, hurrying to catch him up.

"The whole reason she agreed to turn into a mermaid—" Jeom scoffed "—was so that we could get off that island with Syrifina's aid. In return, Les was supposed to help her figure out why her sisters were leaving the water during the daylight, even though it meant their sure demise." He was nodding. "Well, she *did* find out." Demetrius pointed to Sir Vladamor, making a strange face that surely meant death. "And these are those ill-fated mermaids… resurrected in darkness."

After the necromancy was said and done, five mermaids had emerged from the pouches at his belt. They stood stone still as Sir Vladamor put the finishing touches on his spell.

"Gods, *that's* why he was luring them out into the sun," said Demetrius, piecing the puzzle together for himself. "He captured their souls as they died." He pointed ahead with his staff. "He somehow bottled up their essence."

"But how could they be in a solid form like this?" said Jeom, visibly frightened as he focused on holding the barrier magic. "If they died, shouldn't they only reappear as… as ghosts?" His words flew out in a panic. "How could the necromancer even get his hands on such powerful creatures? I don't understand!"

"Breathe," she mouthed; he inhaled.

"These are no ghosts," mumbled Demetrius, commanding nature to reinforce Jeom's shield.

Syrifina had never not scared them, but these creatures solicited an entirely new sensation of fear. There would be no reasoning with these mermaids, no negotiations nor discussions this time for a chance at sparing their lives—this was the King's favorite game in its truest form, and right now he held some very dangerous cards.

Arianna gulped, questioning her fate again. *Win or die?*

"I suppose, they were never *really* alive to begin with…" she said. "A mermaid is not fully human. She forfeits that piece of herself when she turns, so what's left, I think, must be something different, a magical vessel of sorts, maybe?"

She squinted, trying to see any flicker of life in their eyes.

"While remnants of the human soul may live on in a

mermaid," she continued, "it's just that, a remnant." She shook her head, saddened. "Sir Vladamor let the sun turn those vessels to dust so that he could use the strong, magical properties for himself." She gazed past the mermaids—Lessa had scooted all the way to the back of her glass prison, mouth hanging open in disbelief. "If they were never truly alive, no wonder the necromancer could so easily manipulate them to their true deaths in the first place." She touched the soul of the star at her neck, knowing it wouldn't be helping her out of this. "It's his domain. He controls Death, masterfully."

"He just had to lure them to the land," finished Eli as the pieces of the story clicked together for him too.

She nodded, solemnly, thinking that Syrifina was smart to leave the Island of Idris far behind after all.

"It isn't right," muttered Demetrius. "This isn't how they're meant to be…" Vines shot up from the earth as he readied his defenses. He moved to Arianna's side; they locked eyes. "This goes against nature. The essence of a mermaid is *supposed* to go hand in hand with a human. Without the human side of them to help channel the magic, they'll be left… completely unchecked."

"Not unchecked," said Eli, gesturing to the necromancer. "They're being controlled."

"So what do we do?" said Jeom.

They fell silent—if they couldn't even stand against Syrifina and her 'somewhat' sane sisters, how in the gods' names would they be able to defeat these darker ones?

Arianna's focus shifted to the ruby Sir Vladamor forever wore around his neck—it had begun to glow a vicious red.

The eyes of the mermaids risen from the dead started to shine the same color, as if freshly drawn blood filled their pupils to the brim.

Then, they attacked.

Arianna's breath caught in her throat in the same

second—she'd barely even noticed when the mermaids scattered.

Their speed was unparalleled by anything, so they ripped across the beach in a mere moment.

One of the mermaids paused in front of their protective bubble, so Arianna helped to reinforce it with her magic too. Between her, Demetrius, and Jeom, it was the strongest protection they'd ever conjured… and yet a thick layer of magic between this monster and them just didn't feel like enough.

"*Stay behind me, Solza,*" she commanded, thinking of the time Syrifina had attempted to drown her and Sano.

"*I've got your back,*" she said, though Arianna didn't miss the shake in her voice.

The mermaid tiptoed around their barrier, not even trying to test the magic. She studied them, like an animal contemplating its prey, intrigued by the challenge.

Her skin was strikingly pale under the moonlight, and waves of dark black hair rolled down her back; in a way, she reminded Arianna so much of her mother, and yet she knew there was not a shred of her there.

Sir Vladamor erased her… killed them.

He killed Diveena.

He murdered my friends!

Arianna felt Solza's calming effects press into her mind; she could not lose herself right now. She knew she had to grasp onto her elusive animancer powers… but she would *not* risk disconnecting with her avatar again, not with so many of the enemy surrounding them. *No, it's too dangerous. How else can I tap in? Think!*

The mermaid glanced over her shoulder, looking back to Sir Vladamor, waiting for his command… just a single nod and she was obedient to his every unspoken desire.

She turned again to face Arianna and her friends, blood-red eyes touching each of theirs as she sized them up.

She smiled and launched herself *over* the barrier and into the thick of the battle—she tore through the guardian army like paper.

"Fall back!" they heard Master Tayshin cry only moments later; Arianna hadn't even laid eyes on him in hours.

She prayed she would see him again, but doubts swarmed her mind. *I won't if my powers don't come! We'll all die.*

She screamed out with wasted effort as she searched inside herself.

"Take your time," whispered Eli, trying to be supportive.

"There isn't time!" bellowed Jeom, watching horrors unfold.

Arianna and Demetrius met eyes; he gave her an encouraging nod—she clung to his stare, searching, *searching.*

"It's only locked away, Ara," he said, knowingly. "You just need the key."

She kept trying, whereas her friends kept dying…

Hesitant at what they'd find, they each peeled their focus away from Sir Vladamor to take in the rest of the battlefield—only a minute had passed.

The war had transformed into a slaughter spree; Guanamara didn't even compare to this nightmare.

Cries of anguish from those who fought valiantly for the Olleb replaced their former cheers of courage as the mermaids ripped through them mercilessly; the black-haired one was already covered in gore, dark red stains covering her face and hands.

Arianna spotted another with skin like black velvet, almost purple in the moonlight. Tight curls framed her face, and a mouth of perfect white teeth was bared like a lioness'—her attention was glued to Kayode's back.

"Kayode, watch out!" yelled Arianna over the mayhem.

She tried to lunge forward, out of the protective space, but Eli wouldn't allow it.

"Focus, Arianna!" he said, losing his composure; he tried to collect it in the face of her horrified expression, but it was too late.

"I know… I'm trying," she growled, gritting her teeth. *But everyone's dying. Everyone's dying!*

"*Focus, Master,*" urged Solza. "*Focus. It's the only way.*"

"*How can I focus when everyone is dying?*" she retorted.

At Arianna's warning, Kayode had whipped around to face-off with the mermaid, magic whirling in her hands and lacing the tip of her spear as she waited for the attack; Arianna held her breath, knowing it wouldn't matter.

The mermaid pounced, and Kayode tried to thrust her spear forward; however, Tayo, her most devoted comrade, threw his body in front of her like a shield.

"*No!*" Kayode pitched to the side, watching her friend's ending in utter horror.

The mermaid had already sunk her teeth into Tayo's throat before either of them had even the chance to understand what they were dealing with. In the next second, she had tossed his lifeless body aside—there was nothing she could've done… magic, spear, or otherwise.

Arianna screamed out again, her throat scratchy and dry as tears welled in her eyes. *Focus,* she thought in desperation. *Why can I tap into my other powers so easily yet not this?*

"*It wasn't always easy…*" said Solza.

Kayode threw a blast of distracting magic toward the mermaid, then ran in the opposite direction, surely knowing it wouldn't be enough to delay her for long.

Arianna wasn't confident that *any* magic could actually harm them, and there were five, blood-thirsty monsters using the beach as their hunting grounds.

She and the boys observed with tortured expressions as Sir Vladamor's creatures wreaked havoc across the shores, relishing the carnage they left behind with their every step—she had never seen so much death in her life.

"This is worse than all of my years in the Four Corners combined," said Eli, running a hand through his hair.

What Arianna would give to go back to those simple times in this moment. "*Solza, have I fated all our freed friends to this?*"

"*You have the power to stop this, Master,*" she said. "*It's not your guilt to bear, but you must focus! Find it. I know you can.*"

"*Diveena had faith in me too…*"
And now she's dead.

She pressed her hands to her temples, closing her eyes, anything to try to conjure that power that didn't mean sacrificing her connection to Solza right now; she just knew Sir Vladamor would sense it and hit them when they were vulnerable.

Her gaze again drifted to the battlefield turned overflowing graveyard.

Those with magic attempted to hold the mermaids back and to protect the others, but they could hardly withstand the monsters' relentless fight. The situation became more dire still as the Shadow Resistance and regulators took this moment of weakness to strike their own deadly blows to the guardians as well.

"They're tearing them apart out there!" said Jeom, arms shaking as he held most of the weight of the barrier.

A tear rolled down Demetrius' cheek. "We were winning."

"Ara, is there anything else we can do?" asked Eli. "How do we stop these things?"

"Let me think," she said, crouching down with her head bowed low. "I can't think!"

She turned away from the havoc, her eyes resting again upon Solomon and Sir Vladamor.

They stood their ground, watching with a victorious confidence to see the guardians scatter like spooked birds. It made her sick to see them now, with nothing but fear flooding her mind.

She looked to Lessa, wishing to hear her words of wisdom again. If anyone would know what to do in this time of peril, it was her—after all, she'd been one of them before.

Lessa caught her eye and stood, pressing her hand upon the glass again; Arianna could tell she was breathing quite heavily, the way her chest rose so slowly up and down. She appeared to be concentrating hard on something, her stare fierce.

She blinked, and her eyes suddenly filled with magic.

Arianna gasped. *She's fighting their suppressive spells!*

No one was paying Lessa any attention now, but Arianna wondered if carrying Snow might be giving her an enchanted boost.

She felt compelled to mirror her, pressing her palm against the magical barrier—her avatar magic ignited as she linked with Solza.

She glanced down and Solza *and* Sano were both staring toward Lessa, too, their eyes bright bulbs of silver.

"Ara… what's going on?" she heard Demetrius say. *Focus.* She ignored him and everything else. "What are you about to—"

His voice was drowned out as Lessa's filled her head, and Arianna echoed every verse:

> *Near or far, sister, hear our call,*
> *Across land or sea, we beckon thee,*
> *May our voices erase the space between,*
> *Near or far, sister, we'll wait for thee!*

Jeom's protective shield snapped back like a whip, his magic drained. And without him, the rest of their barriers proved weak against a mermaid's strength.

Arianna's connection with Lessa and their avatars was severed by the disturbance. And now they were just as vulnerable as everyone else.

"Excellent," she saw Sir Vladamor mouth, sneering back at them.

Jeom leaned all his weight on his axe, trying to regain control.

"You need time to rest," said Demetrius, worried.

Jeom glowered at him, and Arianna turned in circles to see the chaos around them.

There is no time.

The necromancer pulled his mask back down and lifted his fist into the air. At his unspoken command, Arianna and her friends were suddenly surrounded by all five of the mermaids.

"Win or die," said Arianna, withdrawing her swords.

Animancer magic or not, she wasn't going down without a fight.

"Win or die!" the boys repeated, taking their fighting stances.

The mermaids were crouched, revolving around them like a pack of hungry wolves who had rounded up their kill.

Arianna and her friends moved back to back, weapons held out at their fronts in an attempt to keep the creatures at a distance; Solza and Sano snapped their teeth, threateningly; the mermaids snapped back.

No one dared to even blink as each woman clearly selected their choice victim.

As they slowly revolved, waiting for them to strike, Arianna found herself facing the water—she couldn't help but notice it, even with hungry red eyes assessing her.

It had become strangely riled, the guardian ships thrashing back and forth as the waves grew abnormally high; she gazed up, wondering if the earlier storm had returned to finish them off—all was cloudy but clear.

Soon, everyone was mesmerized as the sea seemingly came to life; Sir Vladamor turned his attention to the water too, and his mermaids did as well.

"Do you have any ideas how to get out of this?" said Eli, seizing the distraction.

"Lessa did," she said with a small smile of relief, pointing ahead.

They all turned to face the water.

As if a gift delivered from the Goddess of the Sea herself, Syrifina Myr walked onto their battlefield, spotlighted under the moon just like the first day Arianna had laid eyes on her. Although, this time, she wasn't hunting Jeom.

"Déjà vu," he muttered under his breath—yet he looked more than relieved to see her this time around.

A fierce and threatening energy radiated around her as she moved toward the guardians and shadows, each step purposeful and poised. And the closer she got, the angrier she became—she was accompanied by her sisters, and they all looked just the same.

The vibrant colors of their collective lifeblood were a stark contrast to that of the ones Sir Vladamor controlled, and they moved with a fluidness and freedom which could only be achieved in life.

All eyes laid on Syrifina now, the original mermaid of Olleb-Yelfra, and her furious family; the battle had come to a halt.

"Sisters!" cried Syrifina, raising her arms, calling to those that surrounded Arianna and her friends. "What has become of you, my truest loves?"

The mermaids snapped their eyes in her direction but did not speak. They just looked on at her, swaying back and forth like dolls on strings.

Syrifina hissed, locking a savage stare on Sir Vladamor.

"You!" she roared, suddenly looking like the most menacing creature on this beach; her expression darkened so visibly that Arianna almost thought she was turning into one of his puppets. "What have you *done* to my beloved family?"

She was so still, a statue frozen in time, though her hair whipped around her like ribbons of fire in wind.

Arianna was afraid to move even a muscle.

She had *never* seen Syrifina express such ire before, and it was not a comforting sight.

"He controls them now, Syrifina," she said in barely a whisper. "They're not your sisters any longer." She offered a single nod. "Be careful."

She knew she had heard her warning. She waited, on edge, as the ancient mermaid shifted through confusion, sadness, and fury all at once, unable to land on one emotion, searching the faces of those she had once loved dearly. Then she seemed to notice the dead, scattered at her feet and across the sand by the hundreds.

In this moment, Arianna thought she actually witnessed something of remorse in Syrifina's expression…

But when she finally saw Lessa, it shifted right back to fury. She closed her eyes, as if to try to center herself.

"We're here for you… our sisters," she uttered. She snapped her eyes open and looked to Arianna. "Tonight, we fight by your side, young sorceress of the Olleb."

Arianna opened her mouth to respond, but by the time she had, Syrifina and her sisters were already at her side—a giant wave smashed onto the beach right behind them as they collided with the ghostly versions of themselves.

She and her friends jumped out of the way, scrambling to get to safety as they threw each other around the beach, like boulders slamming into one another, watery magic surrounding them.

"Things are getting out of control," shouted Demetrius;

he whipped at a regulator with his staff, a wave of earth magic striking with it.

"We have to get to Lessa and regroup!" said Jeom—with the mermaids now occupied, the battle instantly started up again.

"Syrifina bought us some time," huffed Eli, running alongside him. "Let's try and free her now, then we fall back."

Arianna was already racing in that direction, Solza and Sano at her heels; they climbed up the sandy bank toward Sir Vladamor and Solomon.

"Even if we get to her, the blood magic may not give," said Jeom as they inched up a small hill—he knocked shadows aside with his axe like an enraged bull.

"What do you suppose we do?" asked Eli, sprinting behind him, thrashing through opponents with his sword as he went.

"We'll figure something out," said Arianna, clearing their path with her magic. "We have to."

Jeom let out a roar—the next opponent they passed didn't even see his axe coming.

"What about Vladamor and Solomon?" said Demetrius, manipulating the earth to guide him up the hill, too, burying anyone with sand who got in his way. "They'll never let us near her. Does *anyone* have even an inkling of a plan here?"

Arianna couldn't help but smirk back at Eli.

"Do we ever?" she said.

It seemed like they ran forever in place as the war raged on around them, hindering their way to Lessa.

Eli's voice suddenly shook her eardrums from behind. "Ara, look out!"

She tore her focus from Lessa too late; her body collided with something rock hard, and she was thrust through the air.

She landed on her back with a thud, coughing up sand. It took her a moment to orient herself, but when she did, any pain she felt was replaced with adrenaline and fear—the dark-skinned mermaid who had killed Tayo targeted her now.

She was splintered off from her friends, swords scattered at her feet; she picked herself up from the sand, wincing with the movement as she went to collect them.

Her blood stained the handles, dripping from a large gash at her arm. And she'd caught her leg in the fall, earning a limp.

She needed a healer, and quickly, if she had any hope of making it through the night...

When she looked up, she found the mermaid licking her lips, devoid of anything other than thirst; she had homed in on her arm.

And past her, she found Sir Vladamor waiting eagerly for her death. *Not yet. We're so close.*

Her friends tried to go to her aid, but the Shadow Resistance cut them off. Following Solomon's command, they bombarded them with attack after attack. Not even Solza nor Sano could save her now as they fought for their own lives—Arianna was on her own against this mermaid-monster of the night.

"You're at the end now," Vladamor called down to her. "There's no one left to save you."

"I never said I needed saving," she said, keeping her focus on the mermaid. She aimed her weapons in her direction.

She had stood against a mermaid before and survived. And she'd since learned a thing or two—most importantly that mermaids were *not* invincible creatures, not fully immortal...

"Thanks to you, Vladamor," she said under her breath.

As everything, they were born into this world and could just as soon leave it. Even still, she wouldn't be talking her way out of this battle, as she'd done with Syrifina long ago.

So, how to defeat a mermaid for good?

She remembered how her swords hadn't fazed Syrifina that terrifying night in Idris, yet her dagger *had* kept her at a distance; she longed to unsheathe Aurora now but didn't think she had the time enough to switch weapons before this *thing* attacked.

Diveena pressed into her mind then as she considered her elven-made blades, the only weapons standing between her and this monster. She'd taught Arianna a very crucial lesson of balance that rang clear in her thoughts now...

Without nature, there'd be no air. Without water, there'd be no earth. And just as easily as the wind could snuff out a fire, a fire could melt ice into a puddle until it was nothing.

The entire world was created equal, nothing without its weakness or strength. *Vladamor, too.*

A strange sensation hummed inside her, but it was faint yet; she kept on her train of thought, thinking of Syrifina's weakness.

Mermaids fear the sun for a reason.

They were creatures of the night... for a *reason.*

Luckily, with her avatar by her side, Arianna had started to become very good at taming the sun. *Solza ven immito!*

The magic resonated in her heart, and her swords came ablaze.

She drew a circle of fire around herself, and the mermaid reacted just as she had hoped...

With a frightful screech, she leaped back to shield herself from the heat of the flames.

"Follow Arianna!" she heard Noah yell from somewhere down the beach. "Follow your leader."

She thanked the gods that her friend was still alive somehow, and that he had such quick thinking as to spread the word—her idea was replicated by many other sorcerers until, soon, the entire battlefield was lit up in a magical blaze.

"Those fires won't help you for long," said Vladamor. "Even if they did, I could easily finish the job myself. Did you already forget those you lost in Guanamara... *Diveena?*" He cackled. "Not you nor the Guardians of Gold combined are match enough for me and my king.”

He tilted his gaze past her, and Arianna turned to find his sights set on Noah now; Sir Vladamor clenched his fist, and Noah dropped to his knees, pulling at the cloth over his heart.

“I can’t… breathe,” he choked out.

Arianna tightened her grip on her swords, unable to do anything. “Let him go!”

As she observed her young friend traveling toward death, the mermaid continued to circle her.

Frantically, she searched for Vance and Margery, but they were in disarray, still fending off attacks of their own. Whatever spells they’d been planning to cast on Sir Vladamor to buy her more time had been thwarted by his mermaid monsters.

“Release your fire,” commanded Vladamor, squeezing harder at Noah’s life. “Release it, or he dies.”

She knew that Sir Vladamor clutched at Noah’s soul. He meant to yank it straight from his chest, and it rattled her beyond belief that he probably would do it, no matter what.

Eli ran to Noah on her behalf, dropping to his knees beside him as he tried to help—it was a fruitless effort.

Noah didn’t have power enough to fight off a necromancer, and Eli didn’t have power at all. And not even Diveena, a formidable opponent, had been able to survive him.

The fifty bodies of the fallen guardians in Guanamara flashed across her mind… she was witnessing firsthand just how they’d died; Sir Vladamor had collected their souls, one by one, his to control, just like his mermaids—and all it had taken was the snap of his fingers.

Arianna gritted her teeth as she comprehended the truth of his threat. *He’s toying with us…*

He always had been and always would be, until they put a stop to the necromancer, permanently.

Eli looked back to her, shaking his head.

"Ara, I don't know what to do," he called, eyes watering; his sword was discarded in the sand.

He held Noah in his arms as he began to lose consciousness.

Arianna started shaking with anger, feeling her magic swell.

"I'll kill you!" she screamed at Sir Vladamor, seeing nothing but fire—she swiftly snuffed them out to try to save Noah.

Sir Vladamor laughed again, the sound slapping her right in the face as he unclenched his fist…

It was the first time she'd ever seen him keep a promise

Noah breathed in deeply; Eli let out a shout of joy, then swiftly got to his feet, just in time to send his sword straight into an enemy trying to attack them while their guard was down.

The fires elsewhere across the beach had, at least, been enough to hinder the ghostly mermaids from attacking any other guardians; Syrifina and her sisters were slowly winning the battle over their fallen kind.

Arianna remained in peril. She was *still* face-to-face with a mermaid, now nothing separating them from each other and no one near enough to intervene.

Before she could even think of her next move, the mermaid had a stone-cold grip around her neck.

Her swords fell from her hands as she scratched at her fingers, trying to peel them back so she could breathe; it was like scraping at steel. Tiny, white stars began to sprinkle her vision as the air left her body.

Arianna gazed into the mermaid's empty eyes and presumed that this would be it—with one click of her fingers, she could snap her neck.

Or, in another thirty seconds, she would simply run out of air.

"*This is not it*," came a steady voice.

It seemed distant, her mind already drifting away.

Then, a burst of brilliant light filled the space behind the mermaid, encouraging her to hold on a little longer. *Solza!*

She had shifted back into a dragon, a soul-shaking roar completing the transformation.

The monster didn't even have time to turn her head; Solza whipped her massive tail across her body.

Both the mermaid and Arianna went flying, but at least she could breathe again—she gasped for air.

Solza had knocked them so far up the beach that they landed with a crash atop the large cage where Lessa was trapped, their blood smearing the glass; she and Lessa looked at each other, then a resounding '*crack*' split the night.

The mermaid leaped to the ground, and Arianna followed her lead; she rolled off the top of the cage, just as the glass disintegrated into a glittering rainfall.

Lessa was free, left out in the open and crouching with her hands over her head as any trace of the glass prison magically vanished around her; she inhaled, deeply, some of her normal color already beginning to return.

"Are you all right?" called Lessa, crawling toward her when all seemed safe. "I can't believe we both almost suffocated together. What a way to go."

Arianna couldn't move for a moment, completely in shock, but she felt Lessa's hands on her skin, starting to work over her wounds with precision.

"How did that happen?" she stuttered after a moment, feeling instant relief. "I thought... Vladamor said the cage was spelled with blood magic?"

Lessa shrugged, her focus set on hasty healing.

"Sir Vladamor didn't lie about my dwindling air supply," she replied, "but he's not known for honesty, is he? My guess is that no glass, no matter *how* enchanted, can withstand the weight of a mermaid."

Arianna shook her head, trying to snap out of her daze. "Are you all right? You look—"

They grasped hands. "Can you stand?" Lessa asked. She put one hand on her stomach as she got to her feet, then she helped Arianna up.

"I… I think so," she replied with a wince, wobbling on her injured leg; it felt better with Lessa's quick fix but not great. "Is the baby—"

"Later," mouthed Lessa, gaze pinned on the black-haired mermaid; they squeezed hands and let go.

The monster paid them no mind now, for Solza had her full attention.

Arianna could sense how inconsolable Solza was at the moment, and it scared her. *The Three-Headed Dragon of Crissy had probably been scared too…*

Her avatar had been so provoked by all the dangers around them this night, all the threats to her family, that she didn't think Solza would even hear her words right now if she'd commanded her to stand down. In fact, she didn't think she could hear anything but the voice of her own fear and rage.

"Move back!" She whipped around to find Eli coming up behind her; she lurched toward him, yanking him out of the way.

Jeom was by his side, Lessa in his arms in the same second, and Sano at their heels.

They all ran out of the line of fire just as Solza opened her mighty jaws to release a magnificent flame.

Her fire engulfed the mermaid, making her appear like a black granite statue consumed by a tunnel of blazing water; she tried to walk forward, attempting to fight it, but each step grew more sluggish than the next.

Everyone paused to watch, to *witness* what would prove more powerful—a dragon or an 'undying' creature of the sea.

The scene was so shocking that even Syrifina was humbled by it, the thrashing waves abruptly quieting.

It didn't happen quickly nor without pain, but eventually the mermaid *did* die. Under the relentless force of dragon fire, she had crumpled back into a pile of smoldering dust.

Sir Vladamor tried to revive her with his magic—but it was to no avail. Solza's flame had reduced the mermaid's body to ashes for the earth to claim again, as was Nature's way.

There was nothing for him to salvage this time.

"Solza, that's enough," ordered Arianna, standing safely to the side with the others. "Stop, now!" Everyone shielded themselves from the heat as she continued to release her lethal fire.

"*Solza, you're out of control!*" she said, forcing herself into her mind.

Solza eventually clamped her jaws shut and lowered her head to the sand.

"*I'm sorry, Master,*" she said, ashamed. "*That thing was hurting you. I had to do something.*"

"*I know…*" said Arianna, limping over to her with Eli still at her side. "*I'm fine now, though. You did the right thing.*" She sighed in relief. "*Thank you, Solza.*"

She sniffled in reply, and Arianna just hoped this would all be over soon.

"Ara, behind you!" said Lessa—both she and Jeom looked ready to run to their aid.

With quick reflexes, Arianna and Eli jumped out of the way just as a regulator tried to attack from behind. However, before she could even reach for her sword, the man was blown off his feet; he slammed back to the ground from such a height that there was no chance he would ever get back up again.

She looked up to find Lessa had joined once more with Sano—their eyes glowed like jewels as they manipulated the air element, more in tune than ever.

"Glad to have you back," said Arianna, having hardly the time to process the moment yet.

Lessa flashed her a smile, then turned her attention to the enemies closing in.

"*Solza, fly!*" said Arianna as more shadows surrounded them, their weapons raised, their magic rolling. "*Don't come down until I call for you.*"

She launched into the sky, trying to smother her longing to set the battlefield aflame and end this one way or another.

"I *said*, no more fire!" snarled Vladamor at the top of his lungs as he watched her soar across the beach. "This ends now."

He clenched his fist and suddenly moans of pain were heard from all across the battlefield. Those in mid-fight fell to their knees.

"No!" cried Arianna, scanning the area as many of her friends and fellow warriors were killed, solely because of Sir Vladamor's interference.

She saw Master Tayshin, not far down the beach, take a hit to the side from a sword, clutching at his chest in agony; she hoped his armor had proved effective. He had managed to unarm his opponent before falling to the ground; still, it mattered not, if Sir Vladamor was set on killing him.

"We have to do something," said Lessa in a panic, one hand on Jeom as he crumpled to the sand—the necromancer's magic had targeted him too.

Lessa stared at him in disbelief, tears swimming in her eyes; he had one hand on her cheek, and one hand on her belly.

"Jeom…" said Demetrius, gazing on helplessly as his brother writhed on the ground at their feet.

"Ara—" Eli uttered from behind.

She felt his support give way before he also collapsed; he slid to the ground, thrashing violently.

"*No,* wait," she said, turning in circles to find everyone she ever cared about… dying. And, just like the last time, she couldn't do anything to stop it.

She couldn't keep the tips of blades from entering the bodies of her defenseless friends, or help the archers who toppled forward into the sea as Sir Vladamor tugged on their souls.

There was no way to help them.

Unless I kill the necromancer. She felt that strange flicker of magic come stronger, brighter. *What is the key? What is the key?*

She thought of Demetrius, of how he'd finally discovered his true self, his purpose as a descendant of the elves.

She lifted her eyes—Sir Vladamor was observing the chaos with a smug satisfaction, Solomon still loyally by his side.

As long as Sir Vladamor existed, the upper hand would always remain with the Shadow Resistance. He was King Devlindor's greatest weapon, and he didn't need an army to inflict catastrophic damage on their opponents—he *was* the catastrophe.

Diveena's teachings enveloped Arianna. *'His weakness is the same as his strength.'*

Yes, yes… but what is the key to my powers to defeat him? Think, Arianna, think!

She understood now that life and death were equally matched when stripped down bare, each born from one another, the cycle continuous. And necromancy and animancy—these were no longer mysteries to her.

If one can manipulate life, one can manipulate death.

By now, she had proven to herself that she could access the animancer gifts, magic that essentially countered necromancy, if she willed it hard enough. She no longer doubted it was there.

I'm willing! I'm willing, she thought, more frustrated than ever.

She considered Solza, remembering how resistant she'd

been to her at first, to her avatar side. She hadn't wanted to accept her out of… *fear*. She hadn't wanted to let the unknown in.

That's when it clicked—she saw the lock materialize within her mind. Just beyond it her animancer powers were ready and waiting.

I'm terrified, she thought. *What if I can't control it? What if I fail? What if it consumes me, like Sir Vladamor's has?*

"*Nobody knows the future, Master*," whispered Solza from somewhere in the clouds. "*If you don't try, you will never know.*"

She thought of her avatar's light-filled gaze, utterly grateful that she'd found the strength to accept her, despite all her fears.

She dug her heels into the ground. *This is the end. But whatever happens now, I won't be afraid.*

With nothing left to lose, it was then that Arianna felt that wonderful warmth overcome her once more, filling her—she gripped it tight, not letting it slip away this time.

TT WAS A FAMILIAR SENSATION, the energy of her animancer powers originating from somewhere deep inside of her. But unlike the other times when this magic had surfaced, what she felt now was undeniably stronger, more resilient, whole.

Just like her avatar magic and that which she was born with, her animancer gifts were now hers to control.

She realized she hadn't needed to give any of herself up to make *room* for it. It was part of her. She had just needed the key to that lock, to accept her full self.

Onasyuda.

She willed the power of life into her command and felt her magic call out to every soul who had ever suffered from the curse that was the King and his necromancer.

The souls responded to her cry.

The night began to pop into life, bright flickers high in the sky, drawing closer to the earth. It appeared as if thousands of stars fell from their places in the heavens.

They settled atop the waters, far out at sea—lustrous and bright, like ships searching for the shore.

In a wave of glaring white, they neared the beach. And, soon, the shimmers, the stars, began to take shape.

"Ara, are… are *you* doing this?" asked Lessa.

Arianna couldn't speak, concentrating with every bone in her body to harness this magic inside.

Demetrius nearly toppled over, setting aside his shield.

"*Gods*, do you see that?" He looked to Jeom, ecstatic. "I can see them! Oh, *my* goddesses of the Olleb," he exclaimed, waving his hand. "I can see ghosts!"

Arianna felt all the hair rise on her body, the air cooling around them, dramatically, as if a winter storm had just blown in across the sea all the way from the Jar.

"I can too," stuttered Eli. He was clutching his heart, sucking in rasped breaths; Sir Vladamor's powers were waning.

Eli is alive, she thought with pure relief.

He slowly got to his feet, and Arianna felt her powers flourish.

Jeom and Master Tayshin followed suit, shaking off the soul-clenching spell. And with each person she freed, she grew only stronger still; soon, every guardian who Sir Vladamor had tried to send to the grave had been released from his magic.

The ghosts atop the water continued to approach, an avalanche of light bowling toward the shoreline.

Her plea had reached through to another world, the same one where her animancy had been born. And with it, she had released these scarred souls from Sir Vladamor's hold, giving them back their freewill; she had also called to anyone who had ever felt the sting of his magic, whether he kept their souls or not.

She had built a bridge through astral planes that connected whatever afterlife they wandered to her place of the living.

Thus, the otherworldly beings began to cross over into their realm for *all* to see—ghosts from the past flocked to the battlefield, an army made of starlight marching on the water.

They finally reached the shore, and the armies of the living were swept over by this one of the dead; the bloody battlefield was doused in a much-needed light.

Generations of life were all accounted for, coming to stand together as a united entity alongside the Guardians of Gold.

There were those decorated in the garments, weapons, and armor of a buried history, souls that had perished in the Golden Age; giants hovered tall over the rest, fairies dotted the sky like firebugs, sorcerers and sorceresses appeared from all walks of life, and even dwarves stood to attention, their armor and gems shining bright.

Among Jeom's fallen kin, Arianna recognized one of the first ghosts she'd ever laid eyes upon—General Indra of the City of Undor.

This noble dwarf had been the first of her Golden Age allies in this war for freedom, before she had even known what the war was. He had introduced her to the Golden Rule before her journey had barely even begun.

He bowed his head to her now in respect, and she bowed back.

His presence was suddenly overshadowed by another of his kind.

"Is that—" Jeom stepped forward, then dropped to his knees in reverence, clinging to the staff of his axe, eyes brimming with tears.

Dwarf King Undoriamus had appeared at General Indra's side, gripping a ghostly version of the Axe of Crissy.

The fallen dwarf king smiled, gesturing for Jeom to rise.

"You've made us proud, halfling," he spoke, his voice a deep echo across the wind. "You shall always remain welcome in the dwarf kingdom."

Jeom, along with the rest of the thousands of people who had surely never seen a ghost before, fell speechless.

By now, countless faces from the ethereal plane, both familiar and not, had emerged. And no one, guardian nor shadow, was determined enough to continue battling.

Even the mermaids under Sir Vladamor's control had ceased their attacks on their kin—they stared to Syrifina and their sisters in utter bewilderment.

As if the light had been slammed back into their bodies, their eyes rimmed with silver, the blood-red and the black fading away in its wake.

"We're sorry, Mother!" they suddenly wailed out in unison—they ran into Syrifina's open arms.

Syrifina appeared just as shocked as everyone else, but she held them close, coddling each one of them as they showered her in apologies and explanations.

"There, *there*, my sisters," she said in a gentle voice. "It was not of your doing, and so you shall not keep the blame." Their living sisters circled them in support. "I just hope the journey of death is as adventurous as the life you lived with me under the sea. Go in peace now."

Syrifina kissed them each goodbye and stood back.

"Thank you, sister," they called to Arianna before they turned into a glistening dust—only their ethereal souls remained. "You've freed us."

They melted in alongside the army of ghosts.

The spirits hailing from the Nicora Elven Clan were the next to take shape, marching up the beach behind their leader,

Master Lethander; Diveena was at his side.

They stopped before Demetrius, surrounding him with support.

"See, Father?" said Diveena, the proudest expression on her face. "I told you he was worthy."

"Aye," said Master Lethander with a firm nod, his gaze probing and deep as he looked at him. "So he has proven. The Nicora Clan may yet live on."

Demetrius gawked back, gripping his staff tightly.

"Thank you, sir," he stuttered after a moment, a blush rising to his cheeks.

"You do not thank us," said another elf whom Arianna did not know—she was an exquisite creature, standing regally at the other side of Master Lethander; she appeared to be nearly an exact replica of Diveena. "We thank *you*."

"You must be..." Demetrius looked to Diveena, uncertain; she grinned. "Are you... Delira?"

"My sister," said Diveena with a nod—she looked so at peace, glistening with her own essence and joy.

Delira offered him a soft smile.

"I've heard a lot about you," she replied.

"And I you," said Demetrius, unable to blink.

Diveena beamed at him as he tried to suck back his tears.

"Come, sister," she said, signaling for Delira to follow. "Vladamor is waiting for us." Her voice came sharp, intent; she tossed one last glance to Demetrius. "Good luck to you, brother. I know you'll do us a great honor. And come back to my forest, won't you? You shall always be welcome."

He placed his hand over his heart, unable to respond as they glided on.

Diveena and Master Lethander lingered as they passed by Arianna—they placed their palms atop her shoulder.

Arianna jumped slightly, surprised to find that she could actually *feel* their touch; it fed her energy.

Her powers grew stronger.

She could see the reflection of herself in their lustrous forms—her eyes were glowing like two solid silver coins.

"I see you have found your army," said Master Lethander, hand still upon her.

Arianna noticed with great astonishment that he held a ghostly white staff... it was the very same that was in the King's possession at present; after so many sessions with him, she'd all but memorized its every detail.

"She's found a great many things," added Diveena with a knowing look. "She just needed to believe."

They removed their hands, and moved on, ever so slowly, toward Sir Vladamor—he had not moved from his spot, frozen in what could be terror, although Arianna felt as if her magic might be tethering him there.

As more ethereal creatures of the Golden Age made their way up the beach, flowing from the sea to the shore, following in the footsteps of the others, Arianna began to recognize more faces.

Fallen Guardians of Gold, both long-lost and recently taken, drifted by her with nods of approval—they each placed supportive hands upon her shoulders as well.

Master Tayshin and the other living elder guardians brought their fists to their hearts in salute to those who had been lost in the first battle of Saindora; and Arianna finally got to look upon the faces of those she thought she'd never have the fortune to meet.

The ghosts of Gabriel and Iris earned a wave of cheers from the living guardians as they materialized next. They led the fallen dragons of Guanamara *and* those who'd perished on this fateful night, true leaders even in death; they each stopped before Arianna, whispering their gratitude and wishes for luck to her and her friends.

"You kept your promise well," said Gabriel, grinning wide;

she felt the touch of his palm and glowed brighter.

"Kiki!" Noah nearly buckled over with tears of joy; the young warrior followed Gabriel's lead.

She turned to him, a smirk on her face as she twisted her iridescent flail in the air.

Noah cupped his hands around his mouth and cried out, "I love you, Kiki. I love you!" He flexed his bicep at her, showing off her tribute.

She blew him a kiss, and he caught it in his palm.

Mother Adunni and the ones who had perished in the ambush of Moriamo emerged too, pausing a moment to formally address Arianna.

"You did well, child," said Mother Adunni with a chuckle as she glided by, a cane in hand and Tayo as her escort; he waved eagerly at Kayode, and it was the first time Arianna had ever seen her cry.

"Wasn't sure you were going to make it..." continued Mother Adunni, as blunt as ever, "if I'm to be honest." She found Kayode in the crowd and smiled. "Proved us all wrong, *thank* the gods." She turned serious, looking her up and down. "What a gem you truly are."

Arianna couldn't find the strength to speak back, the animancer magic nearly overpowering her as more and more ghosts appeared to grant the guardians their blessing.

"And a dragon rider is born again," came the powerful voice of a woman—Arianna recognized it immediately.

Kayode, and all her people, bowed low as Queen Moriamo herself floated to the front of the procession. She wore a crown atop her head, and a look of genuine pride on her face.

Evios, her avatar lion, followed loyally at her heels; he paused before Sano, studying him with great interest. Then, his gaze flicked to the sky, searching for Solza.

Queen Moriamo glanced up too.

"The chosen one, indeed," she breathed with approval.

Arianna sucked in a deep, satisfying breath as Mother Adunni and Queen Moriamo placed their hands upon her, her powers building exponentially with each gesture of support.

Odessa was the next to pay her respects, swaying awkwardly among the gathering, as if she'd been born to be a ghost.

Her eyes swirled with secrets, even in death, and an all-knowing smile twisted on her lips as she contemplated Arianna—what future did she see for her now?

She felt the warmth of tears brush her cheeks. She had so much she wanted to say to these beings, her lost friends, but her voice would not come.

Odessa didn't linger, did not speak. However, as in life, she gifted Arianna the energy to keep going once more, her hand atop her shoulder.

The full breadth of her animancer magic consumed her, like a searing fire within her mind, though welcome and exhilarating. She could feel herself shaking, breathing heavy, needing a release.

It was then that she found the faces of those she had once loved and respected the most, taken too soon from her by this cruel world...

Liam Black and Keeper Kassime. Tobias, Talis Churry, and Cyn... *Oh, dearest Cyn.* Innocent Pippa, and even her kind-hearted Luose palace attendant, Lily, encircled them now.

"Oh, Talis," stammered Lessa, reaching toward him; Jeom wrapped his arms around her as she buckled.

"Lessa," he replied, eyes twinkling. "You're absolutely glowing, aren't you?"

"So are you, Master," she choked, laughing through her tears.

"Liam..." said Noah; his mouth fell open. "Is that really you, mate?"

"*Me?*" said Liam as he glided around him in circles. "Look at you! In all my years." He shook his head, an astonished expression on his face. "A warrior you've become." He patted his ethereal sword. "Stay strong, my friend."

Noah puffed up his chest, giving him a brave nod.

Arianna could barely concentrate now, so overwhelmed by this new sensation. If her fallen friends spoke to her, she couldn't hear. Faintly, though, she considered that this feeling must be pure *love*—from every single one of the spirits who surrounded her.

They touched her gently, lovingly, on the shoulder; her heart sang, and her magic soared.

A panicked shout stole her attention.

"Where are you going?" said Sir Vladamor. "Get back here!"

All eyes were drawn to him as he watched what remained of his Shadow Resistance army begin to fall back—they leaped on their horses and fled away from the beach.

Even Solomon had the good sense to follow.

"Bell, you *traitor!*" he roared, shaking his fist after him; it appeared that the necromancer was not, in fact, frozen in terror but literally could not move from the place where he stood—Arianna realized now for certain that her magic was pinning him to the sand, weighing on him like a thousand tons. "Your soul will never be free, if it's the last thing I do."

Solomon turned to face him. For a moment it appeared as if he might stand his ground.

His eyes found his former guardian family—Cyn, Talis, and Keeper Kassime all stared after him with sorrowful expressions.

"You can try," he said to Sir Vladamor, flatly. "Though, I don't think you have any last moves left."

He hopped on a horse and disappeared over a sandbank and into the night.

All was quiet now as Arianna finally turned to face Sir Vladamor, her army of ghosts joining her like wings of light.

"So be it," said Vladamor with a shaky voice, finding her eyes. "I will not run away from a *slave*."

Arianna smirked, for he couldn't run… even if he tried.

She stretched her magic further, weighing on him even more.

Sir Vladamor screamed with the effort it took to gather his darkest magic in his palms. He began to attack, throwing blast after blast at Arianna, just like he'd done in Guanamara.

This time, though, she barely needed to lift a finger to block his cursed shadows. Her entire being was like a shield of impenetrable light.

She went to meet him at the top of the hill, his darkness rolling off her like water on skin. She stopped just a few feet in front of him, her army of light locking them both in a ring.

She felt more ghostly hands on her shoulders and back. And those behind them held each other, creating an unbreakable link that all led back to her—thousands shared their lifeforce with Arianna, and Sir Vladamor grew weaker by the second.

The necromancer, the darkest most monstrous thing that had maybe ever walked the Olleb, was absolutely and justifiably scared.

She felt her power building, Sir Vladamor waiting for her to attack, incensed by his position; his energy dwindled with each blast he threw, dark magic singed into nothing every time it landed against her.

Her hands began to glow with a silvery-white essence, power pooling in her palms; Sir Vladamor cowered where he stood.

"You can do this," said Liam, his voice like a calming song. "Now's the time to take your freedom, Arianna."

She glanced back to find her fallen masters and friends,

their encouragement, love, and support plain on their faces.

"I won't see you all again?" she whispered, finally finding the strength to speak as Sir Vladamor all but disappeared from her thoughts.

He was of such insignificance to her now that she couldn't even remember what it was about him that had once chilled her to her core in the first place—she was light, and he was dark, and now the balance had shifted.

"We'll always be with you, dear," said Cyn in her gentlest tone; Arianna felt her heartbeat quicken, wanting so badly to hug her, to remain in the safety of her arms forever. "You know that by now." She smiled. "And you were so very brave."

She looked so at peace in her soft yellow cloak, the healer's crest showing proudly in the stitching—just like how Arianna remembered her, glowing with kindness and joy.

"Yes, magic has a mind all its own, someone wise once said," added Talis, finding her gaze; he shrugged. "You just *never* know what might happen next."

She felt her voice croak out in a little laugh. "Master Churry..." was all she could bring herself to say.

Keeper Kassime beamed, hand upon Talis' shoulder.

"Wiser words have never been spoken," he said. He cocked his head to the side, his slender, luminous crown tilting with it. "With your tenacity, Miss Belvedor, somehow I'm sure we'll meet again."

Tobias tipped his hat in agreement, and Pippa and Lily joined hands—it was such a bittersweet moment.

Arianna smiled to honor it, though her silent tears kept falling.

Lessa, Demetrius, Eli, and Jeom had all come to join her at the very top of the hill. They placed their hands upon her shoulders as well, each bearing witness to the necromancer's last moments of life while surrounded by those that had ushered them so far on this journey.

"We bid you farewell," called Master Lethander from the other side of the swelling circle; King Undoriamus' hand was upon his shoulder.

"The Olleb needs you to stay strong," added Mother Adunni, with a serious look. "This war is not yet won."

"Fight well, children," said Diveena, Delira standing tall by her side. "We'll be watching."

"You know what to do now," urged Talis. "You've known all along. And don't forget what I told you the last time we spoke." He winked, then mouthed, "Trust."

Arianna felt her magic surge, her mind holding it in like a cage ready to burst.

She understood for the first time, *truly*, what Sir Vladamor's weakness was…

She had been carrying the answer with her, in her heart, ever since the first time she'd tasted life after death.

"Go on now!" urged Pippa, her freckled friend seeming just as spirited as she remembered her.

"*Yeah*, what are you waiting for, miss?" Lily beamed bright, standing by Pippa's side.

She heard Tobias exclaim, "I just can't wait to see what happens next. Good riddance, Vladamor."

"I'm ready," she said, closing her eyes.

A familiar magical word sat on her tongue, and only in this moment did she grasp what it *truly* meant—a word that could just as easily translate to mean 'life'… as equally as it could mean 'death.' An enchantment that had given her a second and *third* chance at the world, strengthening her against the lure of darkness twice over.

Arianna breathed this word out of herself now, tapping into the deepest realm of her animancy, unchaining the innocent souls from the necromancer's grip and letting them move on in peace—and when they did, she knew they would take the darkness with them, for once and for all.

Unlike her, Sir Vladamor wasn't strong enough to fight such magic again, and this time he wouldn't survive.

She opened her eyes, and spoke the word aloud. "*Onasyuda!*"

She released the power from her mind, her hands, her body, and felt the rush of energy from the souls so linked—her animancer magic emanated around her, its force so strong that she was lifted off her feet above it all.

A bright, white cloudlike burst bloomed within the circle, then the army of ghosts rushed in.

Sir Vladamor tried to fight back, but his dark powers were no match for all the light that enveloped him now.

He had made enemies of several generations' worth of souls—those he'd murdered, those he'd taken control of to use in his dark deeds even after death, and those who had never even left the Olleb, by *choice*, as they waited for someone to help fix what he and the King had helped destroy…

They all devoured him now.

A pulsating blackness grew around Sir Vladamor as he tried to combat this storm of revenge, but it was quickly diminished—and now, the ghosts poured into *him*, possessing him with their light.

All Arianna could see of Sir Vladamor was his black, beady eyes, swirling among a tornado of silvery-white.

Lessa and the others had to shield their faces; it was too bright for them to look at. But Arianna kept her eyes wide open as the magic she emptied from her soul joined her ghostly allies in one last powerful push.

With a deafening scream, Sir Vladamor was consumed fully by their light; his body was obliterated in an explosive blaze that bathed the area in white.

The ghosts disappeared along with it, rising back toward the stars, Solza weaving in and out between their glittering trails; she showered them with her own form of love, a fantastic fiery flight.

However, unlike their otherworldly allies, Arianna didn't see the necromancer's soul soar to the heavens… only a dark, simmering bubble of black remained, hovering before them in the air.

Arianna let her hold on her animancy go, floating back down to the earth. As she did, the seething shadow faded away into the darkness of the night, into *nothing*.

All was quiet.

And all that remained of Sir Vladamor—Head of the King's Guard, the King's Shadow, and known necromancer of Olleb-Yelfra—was his golden mask and the long chain with the ruby pendant.

Arianna just hoped that the afterlife awaiting him would not be pleasant.

When the ghostly army had fully vanished, the light dissipating along with it, the night settled back around the guardians left standing.

Arianna collapsed to her knees.

Eli was the first to run to her. "How do you feel?" he asked, hesitantly; he seemed afraid to get too close. "Are you…?"

Arianna nodded, not even sure what he'd meant to say.

What words would be appropriate for a time like this? she thought in a daze. *What would one say?*

"*The necromancer's dead!*" cheered Solza, still dancing in the stars; Sano howled in happiness, then shifted back into his monkey form.

Arianna beamed, feeling as if she'd just sipped on a shadowleaf potion that left her not with a headache but a high; she tried to shake off the magical haze that had enveloped her—it felt as if she'd been in a deep sleep the entire time, a beautiful dream.

Sir Vladamor's necklace glinted up at her from the ground.

Warily, she plucked it from the sand, studying the ruby.

Something told her that it held the secrets to some of his power, though she wasn't sure how…

The stone had sharp, jagged edges, almost as if a piece of it had been carved away or broken off at some point in time.

Feeling the burn of eyes on her, Arianna looked up; Lessa, Jeom, and Demetrius were all gathered around, gawking, grinning.

She stood, holding the necklace in her hand, disbelieving. Then each of her friends took a turn to touch Sir Vladamor's most prized possession, the reality sinking in.

"I can't believe he's really… dead," said Demetrius after a moment, eyes watering; his gaze averted to his prosthetic leg.

Jeom laid a hand on his back, letting out a sigh of relief.

"May he never rest in peace," he said, giving the ruby a flick—it spiraled out of control, gleaming in the night.

Solza roared her agreements from the skies, and Eli hugged Arianna around the waist.

Lessa bundled Sano up in her arms. "He deserved every bit of that torture," she said, snuggling him close. "Now on to the next."

Arianna peered off into the distance, toward the City of Saindora, just as the last of the Shadow Resistance army disappeared through the gates.

Solomon Bell is their leader now, she thought.

She clutched the ruby, feeling the stone dig into her palm—there was just one more obstacle left before they could finally face the King.

21

MARCH TO FREEDOM

"THEY'VE FALLEN BACK!" shouted someone from below. "I think we're winning."

Cheers suddenly swept across the battlefield, the Guardians of Gold relishing this major victory; Arianna and the others returned to join the stupefied crowd on the beach.

"We haven't won yet," said Master Tayshin in a raspy voice.

He was hunched over on his side, his face pale.

Margery and some of the other guardians ran to help him. They gently rolled him over to inspect his injuries.

"You've been wounded," said Arianna, hovering over them as they worked—a magicked sword had broken through his armor, blood smearing the metal.

"I'll be fine," he said through clenched teeth. "I've always made for such a big target." He tried to laugh it off, but the gesture was stifled by a gasp of pain.

Margery glanced up to Arianna and shook her head, slightly—the same way she'd done when Diveena was on her last breath.

They peeled off his armor to find a deep, infected gash at his middle.

"Lessa, we need Sano!" called Arianna.

Lessa and Sano pushed through the worried crowd.

"Can you fix him?" asked Sergios, limping over to them; Vance had one arm around his waist. "There's still a long way to go until this battle can be called a true victory. We need him with us."

They were both bloodied and bruised, having fought heroically this night, as had all the survivors.

"I think so," said Lessa.

She hugged Sano tightly to her chest, reluctant to put him down.

"I've missed you so much," she whispered. "You were so brave through all this, but there will be time for our reunion later. Please, you must help Master Tayshin."

Sano gazed deep into Lessa's eyes, then halfheartedly leaped from the safety of her hold. He went over to Master Tayshin and placed his small silver paw across the open wound at his hip.

Those watching remained silent as his unique healing powers soon wiped away any remnant of blood—Master Tayshin boasted a shining scar across his stomach not moments later.

"Thank you, my friend," he stuttered, inspecting his new scar in admiration; he looked to Lessa, reaching out to her. "I'm so glad to see you alive and well again, child. It's been a long time."

"You too, Master," said Lessa with a solemn smile. "I'm just sorry that it's under such… similar circumstances as the last."

"The last time we all fought together was on the beaches of Zambienth," said Jeom, drawing Lessa into his arms. "This is different. This time, no one is running, and no one will be left behind." He kissed her square on the lips.

"Right you are," said Demetrius; he gazed around, such a joy-filled expression. "Whatever happens next, at least we're together again."

"Here, here," said Master Tayshin, shooing everyone back. He beckoned to Arianna, holding out his hand. "Ara, help me up, would you?"

She knelt down beside him.

"Maybe you should just lie here for a moment and rest." She gently tried to push him back down. "You took a nasty hit."

He nodded, then grasped her hand and tugged her close.

"Enemies cannot be left to live," he said so that only she could hear. "Take no prisoners until the war is won. Do you understand me? If they don't fight with you, they're against you. There's just one more stretch, and then this is over. We cannot take *any* chances now."

Arianna hesitated as his words registered—kill those who had fought against them yet did not succeed, to prevent even the slightest chance that they might heal and steer the outcome of this war back into the King's favor.

With many of the Shadow Resistance dead or wounded, and Sir Vladamor removed from command, the Guardians of Gold had the advantage now.

We cannot take any chances.

Arianna closed her eyes, contemplating her cold district days. The bottom of the Pit flashed through her mind, the bones of the slaves who would never make it to the other side of the mountains, lives unjustly stolen from the Olleb far too soon...

If the tide should turn against them again, if the King did

win at the end of this, then the bones in the Pit, in the Tunnel of Tombs—all across the lands of Olleb-Yelfra—they'd only stack higher until the world overflowed with death. That's what his Shadow Resistance slaves fought for.

"Yes, I understand," she said, gravely, helping him to his feet.

The sun began to peek awake on the horizon, casting a soft glow over the beach. Arianna couldn't even begin to count the number of dead, friend and foe, scattered across the battlefield.

Every guardian left standing came to gather around, and Arianna could see the weight of their exhaustion plain on their faces; their breath came heavy and hard, sweat drenched their skin, and their armor and blades were painted in blood.

Not a single person was free of injury—wounds, bruises, and broken bones were suffered by all.

"We fought well," said Arianna as a silence hovered in the air, each person considering the losses shown by the wearily rising sun. "The enemy has retreated, and we are still standing. *You* are still standing!"

She felt her heart pounding in her chest with adrenaline, still coming down from all that had just occurred.

"You've seen the magic on their side, but ours has proven greater." Her voice shook with courage. "Our passion is stronger. We have defeated the King's Shadow, a necromancer! Now, there's nothing standing in our way to take down the King. He cannot hide behind his slaves any longer. We will remove him from the throne!"

The gathering listened intently, impassioned by their leader's words, clearly still mesmerized by her earlier demonstration of power; they howled in support, finding enough energy left to shout praises.

"There's still a long battle ahead," she said, raising her hand for quiet. "We cannot let down our guard now." She unsheathed her sword, glancing to Lessa; she nodded her encouragement. "We cannot celebrate, cannot mourn, cannot *stop*… not until we remove King Devlindor's crown—"

She lifted her blade into the air, turning in circles as she met the eyes of all; Solza let out another roar across the skies in response.

"Another day is nearly upon us, and when night falls once more, we must be ready to *finish* this fight." Her eyes swept the beach. "Tend to your wounds, bury our fallen friends, rest and replenish. For, with the moon, we will rise again."

"Hail to the World. Hail to Olleb-Yelfra!" they all cheered in unison, pushing their weapons into the air to join hers.

At that moment, a man crawling through the sand on the edge of their gathering caught Arianna's attention.

Noah was behind him in seconds.

"Where should we put him?" he asked, twisting his axe in his hand; Arianna hesitated.

"I'll handle it," said Eli, walking forward.

She held out her arm to stop him.

"No, I've got this one," she said with determination.

She relieved Noah of the task.

The man was tangled in a bloodstained, black cloak, a golden snake glaring up at her from the cloth; Arianna had seen him use magic skillfully on the battlefield, to kill who knows how many younger, inexperienced guardians—her friends.

He is the enemy.

"Please…" he spluttered, trying to crawl away as he held a hand against his wounded thigh. "I surrender."

Arianna looked back to Master Tayshin with a heavy heart; he gave a single, unforgiving nod.

She turned back around to face him, hardening herself to her duty as a guardian.

"You cannot surrender if you've already lost," she declared so that all might hear, her sword catching the first rays of light;

she knelt down, whispering in his ear. "You fought for the wrong side in this war. Kyrone Devlindor is not our rightful ruler, and you know it."

The man stopped struggling and stared Arianna straight in the eyes, clearly comprehending the finality of her statement.

"Yes, I do know," he replied. "I made my choice long ago…"

She was a bit taken aback by his candor.

"I understand all about choices," she said, studying him. "They're never easy to make… but each come with their own consequences that must be faced."

"Do not lecture me about consequences!" he snapped, glowering up at her. "Do what you must, young warrior. But know this, all that blood on your sword is consequence for *your* choices, to wage a war you cannot win—"

Arianna drove her sword straight through his heart before he could say another word. "Go in peace."

When she withdrew it, his blood covering her blade, he gasped and the light left his eyes.

She marched back to her people, resolute in her decision.

"We take no prisoners until this war is done," she commanded, repeating Master Tayshin's words. "And make no mistake, this war is *not* yet over." She wiped the blood from her blade. "Dismissed."

Everyone began rushing to prepare for what would come with the night, no one questioning the hard choice she'd made.

Arianna heard the finality of arrows landing in flesh and swords taking more lives as her most seasoned guardian-warriors set out to finish off any enemies still alive in their midst.

Alas, they knew a good number of the surviving Shadow Resistance and faithful regulators to the King *had* found their way safely back to the palace. They'd be waiting for them in the maze of dark halls and rooms where anyone could hide…

The guardians had no choice now but to fight in the King's territory, no telling what traps he may have laid for them.

Before the gathering had a chance to fully disperse, Lessa stepped up to make an announcement of her own; Jeom was glued to her side.

"Anyone who has the skill of a healer, tend to the wounded," she ordered. "Sano will do what he can to help, but it's all hands on deck." She left him to wander the battlefield in search of the most severely wounded.

"You've come a long way," said Nico, drawing her into a big hug once Sano and the healers set off to care for their injured friends. "From a healer-slave to a Guardian of Gold, and a *baby* on the way." He pointed to her stomach in disbelief. "Yet still fighting. I'm so proud of you!" He laughed, shaking his head. "I can barely wrap my arms around you now."

"Oh, Nico," she said, squeezing him back. "It's good to see you too. I know… I can't believe any of this."

"Well, believe it," he said. "You did good, kid."

"Thanks," she said with a slight blush.

He left to help guide the others.

Lessa looked to Arianna next; they had hardly spoken to each other since her rescue, too busy trying not to die.

"That means you too," she said, hands on her hips. "You're bleeding, you know? Or do you not feel pain now with all your new powers." She smirked.

Arianna shook her head, smiling. "Trust me, getting tossed around like a ragdoll *still* hurts."

Lessa began to examine the large gash on her arm from when the mermaid had attacked her.

"I'll be *all right*," she said, squirming away. "Others need you more. It's just a scratch. Besides, I think you already cleaned it up well enough earlier."

Lessa rolled her eyes.

"Oh right… you mean in between dodging attacks from mermaids and Sir Vladamor's near massacre of our people?" She poked Arianna's wound; Arianna let out a loud hiss, slapping away her hand. "Drink up," Lessa demanded, plopping a small vial in her hand. "We can't have our leader spilling blood everywhere she goes, now can we?"

"Do you go anywhere without a supply of prillyberry juice?" Arianna laughed. "By gods, Les, I mean, you were kidnapped…"

"It would be just poor planning if I didn't, seeing as someone's always getting hurt," she replied. "I guess I'm lucky I didn't need it myself…"

Arianna swallowed, looking her over—she didn't seem to have suffered any harsh physical beatings, but she didn't look her healthiest either.

Lessa could sense the concerned assessment.

"I'm fine," she said, averting her gaze. "Honestly, the worst part was how long they just left me alone…" Arianna touched her arm, knowingly; Lessa shrugged, trying to act strong. "I think the King was so busy making preparations for *this* that I was all but forgotten about during captivity."

"I'm sorry," said Arianna. "I couldn't stop—"

"We don't have time for this," said Lessa, firmly. "You did everything perfectly. You *rescued* me, so now let me help you." She focused her stare. "*Helthra saludis emencia.*"

Arianna felt her skin stitch back together in a sizzling sensation, almost instantly. When she wiped the blood off her arm, there was not even a scar.

"You're getting *too* good at this," she said with a whistle.

"Yes, quite the natural," purred a voice from behind.

They turned to find that Syrifina Myr had joined them, red hair billowing in the light wind of the lifting night.

"I'm so happy you came!" Lessa threw her arms around her without hesitation. "Thank you, Syrifina. We would've all surely perished had you not."

Arianna heard Jeom gasp as he looked up from what he was doing. In fact, everyone in the vicinity stared on in astonishment, to see one of their nearly ill-fated leaders hug the most blood-sucking, unpredictable mermaid of Olleb-Yelfra.

Syrifina remained rigid, then, quite extraordinarily, she returned the gesture.

Her sea-faring sisters observed from a distance, seeming unsure of the exchange. They murmured among themselves as they backed away toward the receding waters.

"Thank you," said Lessa again, letting her go after a long moment. "I will never forget this, Syrifina. Not ever."

"Neither shall we," she replied, considering her with something like wonder; her eyes flicked to her stomach. "Try not to get into any more trouble, will you? I'd hate for you to die now that we've rescued you so many times."

"I could *never* promise such a thing," said Lessa with a smirk. "It's not in my nature."

"No... no, I suppose it is not," said Syrifina with a chuckle; she straightened, reverting back to her indifferent self. "But who am I to judge?"

"Why did you decide to come in the end?" asked Arianna.

Syrifina laughed her delicate sound, turning toward her. She appeared to drink in every detail of her face with those penetrating, silver-lined eyes.

"In the end, my reasons were many," she finally said. "But for your *simple* minds..." She sighed. "You called, so we came."

"Would you care to share those reasons with us?" asked Demetrius, in his most polite voice; he walked closer to them. "We couldn't be more grateful for your help out there, Syrifina, *really.*"

Syrifina narrowed her eyes at him, then obliged—she'd always carried a soft spot for Demetrius, it seemed.

Jeom grimaced, and Demetrius drew closer to listen.

"Lessa was in trouble, for one," she started. "Without her, we would have never known what was driving our sisters to the surface." She looked to the girls. "When we heard their song, we came to the shallows and witnessed what the necromancer was doing with our departed's beloved souls. We had no choice then but to interfere. He besmirched their memories, and we could not just stand by and watch after seeing it with our own eyes." She pursed her lips, glancing to Demetrius' leg. Then she considered the guardians as a whole. "As the old saying goes, the enemy of my enemy is my friend."

"Does that make us friends now, then?" said Arianna, unable to hide her skeptical expression.

Jeom made a sound quite like he was dying; he folded his arms at his chest.

Syrifina grinned, her perfect, pink lips curling over sharp, pearly white teeth.

"After tonight, it *just* may," she said. "We owe you a great many thanks, Arianna Belvedor, and not just for helping us to rid this world of the necromancer."

"What do you mean?" She cocked her head to the side. "Why else would I be deserving of your gratitude?"

Syrifina stepped closer to her, eyes boring into hers; she placed her hand upon her shoulder; it was a different, harder sensation than when the ghosts had done it... and yet, she still somehow felt energized just the same.

"For giving us real faith," she replied with more sincerity than Arianna had thought possible for her. "I daresay, there's another Golden Age on the horizon."

Demetrius coughed.

"Speaking of horizon..." he said, tugging at Arianna's cloak. He pointed across the sea with his staff.

They all turned to find the slivers of sun growing at the edges of the horizon, the sky lightening more and more with every passing second.

"You'd better go now," said Lessa, squeezing Syrifina's hand one last time. "The sun will fully rise soon."

Her sisters had already retreated to the safety of the water.

Syrifina gazed at her with an unreadable expression.

"I hope with the next rise of the moon, we will again be welcomed on these shores," she uttered after a moment, "and that victory will be yours."

She turned to leave, nearing the water in seconds.

Arianna and Lessa followed all the way to the edge of the shore; their ships glinted in the climbing sun, Syrifina's sisters sprinkled throughout the bobbing dragons.

Everyone watched and waved their goodbyes to the mystic saviors from the sea.

"Lessa… there's something else you should know," said Syrifina before stepping into the water; her sisters had since shifted from their human forms, tails shimmering amid the waves. "There's another reason I came for you." She shifted from side to side, appearing somewhat nervous. "I told you I would always protect my family—"

"I completely understand," said Lessa, dismissing her with the wave of her hand. "I spent a month as your sister… and I know you still see me as such." She smiled. "I cherish that time with you, too, more than you know."

Syrifina tilted her head with a little chuckle. Then, she gently pressed her hand against Lessa's stomach.

"When I shared my life story with you, I told you that I've always watched over those who share my blood." She moved her hand to wrap around Lessa's. "No matter how far inland my descendants may travel, nor how much my surname may shift over time, I know who remains *my* blood. And you, Lessa Thur, are in fact, my descendant." She stood tall, dropping her hands back by her sides. "You, and all that may be born of your blood, are *Myrs* through and through. I have *no* doubt of this."

Arianna's mouth fell open, eyes wide; she looked back and forth between Lessa and Syrifina in utter bewilderment.

"What are you *talking* about?" said Lessa, astounded. She shook her head back and forth, as though she might burst into laughter at any moment. "I... I don't understand. How could you think—"

Syrifina bristled.

"My Maddison, my baby girl, *is* your ancestor," she snapped; Lessa turned serious, understanding this was no joke. "You don't only carry the sea in your eyes but also in your soul, Lessa Thur." She poked at her heart. "That is why you're so very drawn to us. They always are, in the end."

Lessa looked to her feet, rubbing her belly as she tried to find her words.

"You're saying that my mother... could be your descendant?" She twisted a strand of hair around her finger; it nearly broke off. "But... I don't even know who she is." She chewed on her lip. "It feels impossible."

Syrifina threw her head back in laughter.

"That phrase always seemed so preposterous to me," she said. "If so many things are so very possible, then what truly do we know of the impossible? I'm not sure the word carries any meaning at all, if you really think about it." She moved backward so that the water began to rise above her ankles. "For example, once you were a mermaid, and now you are not. What's the possibility of that?"

"Wait, I don't understand!" said Lessa, running after her.

She went as far as she could go without getting wet.

Syrifina was in up to her waist now, her gem-like tail already swishing back and forth in the waves.

"I think that you understand more than you know," said Syrifina. "I will always be watching over you, Lessa Thur. *Or...* should I say 'Myr'?" She smirked, glancing to Arianna.

"I will always be watching over you both, wherever my waters touch. You're our sisters now, no matter what life you choose to live."

Syrifina glanced over her shoulder to the other mermaids.

"Girls!" she sang out. "Let's show them what it means to truly be a Myr."

A beautiful hum rose into the air as they all joined their voices together in song.

"Cover your ears," warned Jeom to Demetrius, still not trusting them in the slightest; Demetrius moved closer to listen.

The waters began to glow a silvery-blue, as if magic had leaked out of the mermaids while they swam, their song enchanting the waves. Then, one by one, each of Syrifina's sisters blew a kiss toward Lessa and Arianna, carrying their watery magic with it on the gentle breeze.

Syrifina sent her kiss last, and the girls were suddenly engulfed in a cocoon of icy magic.

Arianna recalled the time she had shifted into a mermaid before and thought, for a panicked moment, that it was happening again. However, the enchantment swiftly and painlessly concluded, the shell of magic glittering away like grains of sand. And when all was said and done, nothing had seemed to have changed.

"What *was* that?" she breathed, inspecting herself.

"No idea…" said Lessa, pushing the hair out of her eyes; Jeom and Demetrius came toward them.

"Are you hurt?" said Jeom, catching Lessa's hand with a wild look in his eye; he looked her up and down, expectantly.

"I don't think so," she stuttered, glancing to Arianna with a bewildered expression; Arianna just shrugged, feeling exactly the same. "Jeom… so did you happen to hear what Syrifina said about—"

"What's this?" he shrieked, eyes wide as he turned Lessa's

palm over in his hand.

A shimmering blue vein had appeared on her skin; it pulsed with life, traveling from her wrist and swirling up her arm like some kind of highlife jewelry.

"Ara?" said Demetrius, raising an eyebrow at her.

She cautiously examined her own hand to find a similar streak—only hers was a sizzling red.

"It's… by gods, it's our lifeblood, Les," she stammered.

Lessa gently covered it with her hand. "But, I—"

"What did you do to them?" yelled Jeom, shaking his fists toward the water.

Syrifina waved back at them from the safety of the sea, observing their reactions with plain amusement.

"You'll see," she said, her words carried to them on the breeze; she looked directly at Lessa and Arianna. "Whenever the urge arises, you're always welcome to join us now. All you need do is sink beneath the waves and call to the Myr magic within." She smiled. "I *know* you know how." She winked, flipping her hair back. "Hope to see you again soon someday, little witches, in a different type of world."

"Hey, and what about us?" called Jeom, gesturing to himself and Demetrius. "You still plan to dine on innocent *men* in this new world, or what?"

He tossed his hands up, clearly presuming that the answer was yes.

"Don't you worry yourself anymore, *half-blood*," hissed Syrifina, baring her teeth. "You get to keep your head. My sisters and I will never touch anyone with the guardian mark again." Jeom gawked; she blew him a kiss that he was extra careful to dodge. "Besides, we don't have much of a palate for *dwarf* anyways."

Jeom cared nothing for her insult. He pumped his fist in the air, kicking up the sand in celebration.

"Good riddance!" he shouted, actually drawing a genuine

laugh out of Syrifina and her sisters.

Demetrius waved them off in good spirits, along with Arianna and Lessa, speechless as they were.

"Fare thee well, young guardians," she said with the slight bow of her head. "Until we meet again."

Syrifina Myr and her sisters sank beneath the sea, just as the sun began to fully shine.

ARIANNA AND LESSA WALKED BACK toward Jeom and Demetrius after the mermaids had vanished from view.

"At least you don't have to worry about Syrifina coming after you anymore," said Lessa, poking Jeom in the side. "You really know how to pick your enemies, huh?"

"Yeah, now I just have to worry about *you*," he said, pretending to be frightened of her. "Just don't ever bite me, all right?"

Lessa gave a toothy smile. "Again, I make no promises."

Jeom rounded on her then, drawing her into a deep, passionate kiss; the others looked away.

"I thought that I'd lost you," he whispered, stroking her cheek. "Lost you both."

He gently laid a hand on her stomach; his eyes lit up as the little baby inside of her nudged his hand.

"I think she may have missed you," said Lessa.

Jeom smiled. "You still think it's going to be a girl?" he asked. "I don't know… that felt like a man's kick!"

Arianna scoffed. "Have you ever seen Lessa in hand-on-hand combat? If a strong kick is what you're basing your guess on, then trust me, *it's* a girl."

"Shall we make this interesting?" asked Demetrius,

pinching a coin between his fingers.

Jeom let out a loud laugh, plucking the coin out of his brother's hand; he held it up to the sunshine for a better look.

"How on *earth* have you managed to keep this after so much time?"

It was the silver coinage they'd discovered in the City of Undor, the Axe of Crissy engraved on one side, the dwarf word for 'prosperity' on the other.

"I thought it might be lucky," he replied with a shrug. "It's special to me. My first taste of magic was stumbling through that hidden door and you lot coming to my rescue."

"Well, then I wouldn't wager it," said Lessa.

She took it out of Jeom's hands, studying it fondly before tucking it safely back in Demetrius' pocket.

Demetrius pulled her into a tight hug. "Glad to have you back, sis!" he said. "That was brutal without you there."

"You too," she said with a happy sigh.

She let go, addressing them all with a pained expression.

"I was afraid I… that I wouldn't see any of you again," she said, choking up a little. "Thank you for coming to *my* rescue this time."

"I don't know about everyone else, but I sure owed you one," said Demetrius with a wink, trying to lighten the mood.

"I suppose that you've saved my neck on an occasion or two," said Arianna with a grin. She turned serious. "But after how the King treated me, there was no *way* I was going to let them keep you there for long."

"I'm certainly glad of that," said Lessa, bowing her head; a tear fell to the sand.

"Besides, you're already *quite* pale," added Jeom, tilting her chin up and gently wiping away the tears. "Imagine if we had let you turn into a ghost, of all things!"

He winked down at her.

"They really are *quite* pale, though, hmm?" he added,

brow furrowing as he thought. "I'm not sure what I had envisioned all this time…"

There was a moment of silence, then they all burst out laughing, the sound a much-needed light to dent some of the darkness.

"Jeom, you idiot," mumbled Lessa, hugging him around the waist. "That's a horrid joke. But speaking of ghosts… I'm glad we got to say goodbye to everyone." Her smile twisted into something sadder. "I was shocked to see Diveena among them."

Arianna bowed her head, the others too.

"You did good, Ara," said Demetrius, squeezing her hand. "Now what do you want us to do?"

"Rest," said Master Tayshin, walking over to them, still looking very weak; Eli and Noah flanked him, making sure he was all right. "You've certainly earned it. The Shadow Resistance have fled back to the palace, back to the King. We haven't even felt his dark magic yet, so the best thing for us to do now is bury our dead, replenish our energy, and plan for the next battle."

"We've already organized everything so that each guardian who is able has a task," said Eli.

"Yeah, no need for you all to worry too much over coordinating the next phase," added Noah, seeming much more the leader now than ever. "Go see a healer and rest up for tonight, you hear?"

"Just one last thing," said Master Tayshin; he gestured to Eli, and he pulled a sparkling blue cloak from his pack, presenting it to Lessa. "This was collecting dust, but I'd wager that you probably want to look the part for when you take your revenge." She beamed. "Rowina sends her regards."

Lessa graciously accepted it, admiring the golden silk accents and emblem on the back.

"Thank you," she said. "I'm more than ready to go back

to the palace." Her eyes streaked with silver, and Arianna knew that she was thirsting for blood.

They all dispersed to help out around the beach.

What remained of their army soon retreated back to the ships for food, water, and rest while they sharpened their weapons and reinforced their armor.

Several hours later, when the sun was high in the sky and the air was warmer, Arianna and the other head guardians led their army from the safety of the ships back to the beach.

In the harsh light, they found the white sands bathed in the blood of both enemy and ally.

The tide will wash this memory away, thought Arianna. *We can start afresh when this is over.*

"Prepare the horses!" commanded Sergios.

It was time to move on.

With Arianna and her friends in the lead, the Guardians of Gold marched through the City of Saindora, no longer hiding and no longer afraid. The King knew they were coming, so they would enter through the front gates of the palace and confront the enemy straight on.

They walked confidently through the city streets, their army spreading out to fill the narrow cobblestone paths as they climbed upward toward the palace.

Arianna had seen Saindora before on a normal day—citizens working through their routines and highlifes leisurely wandering the grounds. But it was eerily quiet now.

It seemed as if all life had deserted the area on this bright, sunny afternoon, though Arianna knew it still stirred behind the shadows. People peered out at them from windows and whispers reached her ears as they marched, the High City residents spying on them from the shelter of their homes.

The citizens of Saindora probably remembered Arianna's face more strongly than most she'd encountered on this tireless journey. They would recall how King Devlindor had publicly tormented and humiliated her, and how they'd supported him through it all.

Now, here she was, leading an army through their streets.

But like she'd promised herself she would during that ill-fated time, she had already forgiven them… and today, she planned on upholding her vow to do everything in her power to expose to them the truth of who their King really was.

She held her head high as they marched, sitting proudly atop her horse at the front of the procession. The wind rolled off the sea, ushering them along.

And with the taste of sweet salt on her tongue and the help of the warm, southern sun, she felt a bitter coldness in her heart finally begin to melt away… she became lost in thoughts of years gone by, the palace rising into view.

There, in that monstrous beauty overlooking this robust seaside metropolis, her journey would finally end.

And as the palace grew taller, growing closer with every footfall, all the life-altering moments that had brought her such a wondrous view suddenly flooded her mind.

IN THE JAR, I WAS A WARRIOR-SLAVE in training with worries concerning only myself, my freedom, my future—my name.

I was thick-headed and unrounded.

I thought I was strong, when I was very weak. I thought I knew everything, when I had known nothing at all. I thought pain was something familiar… until I truly felt its agony. But, mostly, I was confident that I could take my freedom by simply winning a game…

What a fool I had been after all.

Now, here I stand, in the High City of Saindora, a chance to make sure there will be no more Four Corners or Free Falls Festivals.

I could help bring about the day when the Gathering Balls must yield to an unmasking. All would shed their slave colors to become one united Olleb, assembling for a new Golden Age and celebrating freedom.

There would be no more Transition Weeks, and the Opalls would be disbanded. There would be no more daily verses or bent knees to the King—there would be no more of this bitter cold.

Once I was a child, but that was then…

Now, I know what it takes to truly win my freedom, and what's at stake if I don't.

"ALL RIGHT THERE?" SAID ELI, catching up to her atop Phantom; Arianna focused back on the present.

"Just thinking," she murmured, still staring ahead.

"I'm sure we're all thinking along the same lines…" he said, trying to be reassuring.

They entered the thick of the city, and Arianna couldn't help but notice the number of people beginning to show their faces—such fearful eyes yet such curiosity.

"I think you're on now," she said, gesturing to them. "You've got this?"

"Always do," he replied with a wink.

He pulled back on the reins of his horse, letting her continue on ahead.

Arianna had no doubt that Eli's blood ran thick with magic—maybe not the kind that was visible to the eyes or useful in a battle, but it was definitely perceptible to the ears. In her gut, she had known this when she'd first heard him sing.

Eli's *voice* was his magic. His words were his power, and what a powerful tool they had already proven to be.

He separated himself from the procession, calling out to those who remained in hiding.

"Citizens of Saindora!" His voice rang out over the march of their footsteps. "We too are *citizens*, of Olleb-Yelfra. From the North to the South, we are Guardians of Gold, freed slaves from the Four Corners and beyond. And thanks to Arianna Belvedor and her friends, we no longer bow to your king."

"Here, here!" came the impressive echo of the army.

People began to slink out of the shadows, lured by his words.

"No one has ever openly questioned His Majesty, until now," he continued, galloping on the outskirts of the marching guardians. "Have you ever stopped to wonder how King Devlindor grew to have so much power? Or why our history mentions *nothing* of any other kings or queens?" He raised his voice. "What you think you know, what King Devlindor has fed us for centuries, is false! Our existence did not begin with him, and it will not end with him either. He is a tyrant who has unlawfully taken the throne and unlawfully taken your freedom, stripped you of your enchanted essence." He pointed his sword at those watching, listening. "We fight him now, for *you* and for our Olleb."

"Hail to the World. Hail to Olleb-Yelfra!" shouted the guardians, throwing bouts of magic to the air.

"Join us as we take back what is ours," he called to them. "See what powers we hone together. We are stronger *to-gether*." He lifted his head high. "And as we have all certainly bled under Devlindor's sword, by the end of this, together, we will ensure Olleb-Yelfra shall no longer bleed for the monster named King."

At this, some people slammed their doors and windows shut, retreating back into their hiding spaces. However, others began to inch out of their homes and from the alleyways, weapons in hand, merging with their group to fill out what had been lost.

Arianna saw the passion in their eyes, the opportunity as they seized it. It made her even more hopeful for the future the guardians were carving…

And no matter what another cycle of the sun might reveal, everyone, guardian or not, would remember it for centuries to come.

"Your song is a powerful one," said Arianna as Eli caught up with her again.

"I only sing for you, my lady," he said with a mock bow.

Arianna sighed. "Will you always be so flattering?" she asked, sarcastically.

"Until I die," he replied, matter-of-factly.

He leaned across Phantom and stole a kiss.

She felt herself blush a little, taken aback; there were snickers from behind.

"This is definitely *not* the time," she said through her teeth.

He shrugged, clearly unworried.

"Just in case," he said with a coy smile.

Lessa giggled at them as she held tight to Jeom, and Demetrius clapped his approval.

Arianna tried not to smile, trotting ahead in front of them all to try to focus. But it was hard not to show her hopefulness in this moment, too; with Sir Vladamor finally out of the way, their original planning could really fall into place.

That's when Eli graced them with one final song, his voice resounding through the streets as he sang to the steady beat of the guardians marching into battle:

When the sky is clear,
And the moon is bright,
Be brave, little slave.
Fear not tonight.

And if the light falls down,
Darkness all around,
Be brave, little slave,
There are monsters about.

Though some shadows are kind,
And fear's controlling your mind,
Still be brave, little slave.
Don't let your guard down.

But, when the last of the moon disappears,
Death whispers much too near.
Don't be brave, little slave.
Be a warrior.

Arianna could recite each word of the Warrior's District anthem from memory. But tonight, she felt the words resonate with her more truly than ever before, booming in her heart.

Soon, all those who followed were singing along with him, their voices chasing away any fear that had been there before and replacing it with courage. It was only when they reached the city center did their voices die away…

King Devlindor's gargantuan, golden statue reminded them that they still needed to remain vigilant.

The procession crossed through the city center, thousands of guardians swarming the area where the King normally held his morning commendations.

Arianna brought her horse to a halt in front of the marble white fountain where the statue had been erected, flames filling its bed instead of water, snakes encircling its perimeters. As she considered the tribute, from the black granite jaguar at his feet to the stolen crown atop his head, all she felt was a blazing anger—she recalled the first time she'd looked upon that statue.

An image of Cyn replaced her vision, her final words of encouragement ringing in her ears.

'This is where it counts, dear,' she had said. *'When you're more frightened than you're even able to admit. You must be brave.'*

"I will," she said, a single tear rolling down her cheek, re-membering the beautiful, ghostly version of her instead of the beaten and broken memory King Devlindor had tried to leave her with.

She wiped the tear away and clutched the reins of her horse, feeling her magic come.

Solza swooped down over the city at her beckon, so low to the ground that she riled the horses, a great gust of wind en-circling their procession. She set her sights on the King's statue, and a river of fire flowed from her jaws, leveling it into nothing but a pool of molten metal in the bed of the flaming fountain.

The liquified gold overflowed, dripping onto the tiled area.

Everyone watched their step as it gathered in the cracks and crevices of the colored stone, eventually pooling in the center of the mosaic pattern that created the emblem of the Four Corners across the grounds.

"*Come now, Solza,*" said Arianna, calling her avatar back to her side. "*Take a break from terrorizing the kingdom.*"

Obediently, she shrunk from her dragon form into an owl, soaring just overhead alongside their march; no one even both-ered to look back as they left the city center behind.

They came upon the palace not long after and stopped,

the army gathered at the King's locked gates, thousands of people deep. A long, clean, white path led from there all the way to the main courtyard, and the front doors.

The sunlight caused the sharp, peak-like towers to cast ominous shadows across the lands; Arianna faintly pondered if the Saindora palace hadn't been partly inspired by the Blancoren Mountains… before *the King's time or after?*

Soon, the sun would reach above its claws, set beyond the horizon, and the shadows would melt once again into the night.

She surveyed the path, surveyed the palace. *We're so close.*

Her gaze settled on the high marble balcony that overlooked the main entrance—it was the very same where she'd first laid eyes on Princess Elisa, *and* which had, subsequently, been her path to escape.

This time, though, instead of the beautiful Princess, she found King Devlindor glaring down at her with a dark, brooding stare.

Arianna couldn't help but note that he had at least paid them respect enough now to properly prepare for the battle to come…

Swathed in black from head to toe, he was fully cloaked and armored, a decorated sword at his belt. And with the golden snake imprinted on his chest plate, the jeweled crown placed firmly on his head, and his staff in hand, his costume looked complete.

But that's all it was—a king's *costume.*

Never forget.

The most disturbing part of his appearance, though, was not him at all… it was the black snake that joined him, curled around the railing of the balcony; Arianna tried to stifle her shock, but it was certainly the most enormous and petrifying species of serpent she'd ever seen, silver tongue licking at the air.

It seemed to see her, too, bright yellow eyes attempting to peer straight into her soul. She couldn't look away.

"*Whoa,*" said Noah in a small voice as all the head guardians led their horses to the front, "so that's where the snake emblem comes from. I always wondered…"

She would've been fine with never knowing.

"It's his avatar, Raja," she said, spellbound as it twisted across the banister; sleek, black, lustrous skin and a silver underbelly made her appear as if she were a vein of lifeblood, just as dark and corrupted as that which had sullied Syrifina's departed sisters. "Her earth form is the jaguar, and I've seen the air form as a hawk—"

"Then a snake must be the avatar's water shape," interjected Lessa in a shaky voice, glancing to Sano; he had shifted back to his warrior wolf form for the march. "He's mastered three elements."

"Maybe… maybe four," said Arianna, looking to her; Lessa's expression reflected her concern. "We don't yet know."

They looked back to the King, wondering what other surprises he might have in store.

He stood there with such poise, peering down on them, seemingly untroubled by the army at his gates. Long, white draperies fluttered in the wind at his back; her attention was drawn to them.

She saw the ghosts of King Damas and his son, Prince Neas, floating behind him, almost imperceptible to the eye— they blended so finely into the sheer material of the curtains.

Arianna knew that Sir Vladamor had had nothing to do with their ability to move on… these royal spirits would not rest until King Devlindor was dead alongside them. More encouraging still, she knew that he could not see them, for he had yet to die.

I have surprises of my own, she thought, feeling her animancer light rise. *Tonight, I will ensure he meets the afterlife.*

They raised their palms in encouragement, then vanished.

The King waved his hand, silencing the agitated crowd; Arianna tightened the grip on her reins, bothered that he still had that much control over them.

"It seems that you miss your place here in the palace, Arianna Belvedor," he called down to her as a hush swept over the city; she could tell that his voice was carried by magic, its evil echo surging loud through the air—Arianna shuddered, feeling as if he was again in her mind. "You know, you're *always* most welcome here. Likewise, we can surely make room for more guardian guests."

King Devlindor opened up his arms as if to usher them right through the closed gates. As he did, the long pathway to the palace was suddenly lit up on both sides, hundreds of torches igniting with magical flame—all the way from the gates to the looming, black doors.

He lifted his gaze past Arianna, to everyone else.

"Citizens of Saindora and those of you who have traveled far across the Olleb, blindly following children to my doorstep, I speak to you now. Ask yourself, what is it that you seek?"

He rolled his shoulders back, stroking a finger along Raja.

"Think carefully over what you do next," he said, his tone sharp, pointed. "I am not known to be merciful, but I'm known to be fair. If you feel you've been tricked, coerced, or misguided by these slaves who would do anything to *steal* the freedom you've so rightfully earned, now is the time to come forward."

His voice boomed across the land, the iron gates rattling from the vibrations of his enchantment.

"Drop your weapons where you stand, and go back to where you came from! And if you do, you shall not be held accountable for these acts of *treason*." The word rolled off his tongue, a hiss from Raja along with it. "By the gods, this I swear, you *will* be pardoned for your offenses." He homed in on Arianna, pursing his lips. "For this is quite an… unusual circumstance in our history."

Arianna squeezed her eyes shut, a chill scratching up her spine; the repulsive ring of metal on stone suddenly reverberated in her ears, replacing his voice—the sound of deserters.

Hurried whispers began to sneak up toward the frontline, the steadfast guardians urging the newest recruits not to go.

Arianna took several deep breaths.

Jeom whipped around on them, his thunderous voice nearly outdoing the King's. "If they cower at just the mere words of a man, they would die here today with certainty. Let them go!" He turned back around, fists clenched. "We don't have time for cowards."

"Jeom is right," said Demetrius, more calmly. "We must show those who are not yet ready to fight the reason why we're here today… to fight *for* them." The earth rose to his defense upon command.

"Fine," snapped Eli; he pulled the sword from its sheath. "They can thank us later, then."

"*Reveliantom!*" shouted Jeom.

The Axe of Crissy grew alive again in his palm; Arianna saw the King's eyes dance with greed.

It gave her courage to know that their army had powers he coveted, despite him slightly denting their numbers by just a little speech.

"Your necromancer tried to take this from my friend," called Arianna, gesturing to Jeom's axe, "but he did not succeed." She cocked her head to the side, a mock pout on her lips. "Now, he is dead. What promises did you make to him?"

Her voice danced with arrogance, but she didn't care.

"I promised him a swift death should he fail me again!" said King Devlindor, no sign of remorse; he appeared to grow agitated, impatient, then his calm settled right back over him.

"And so, I prove I am a man of my word."

He gave a slight bow, a smile twisting on his lips.

"A man with no integrity is not a man at all," growled Master Tayshin, his horse pawing at the ground. "Surrender while you still have the chance!"

"*Ah*, Master Tayshin," said the King. "What a surprise to see you still alive." He softened. "At least, there's someone here with worthy experience." His sights settled on Vance. "And I see you've brought other familiar faces from your original *lizard* clan, or what's left of you."

He gave a nasty chuckle and a sickening sneer.

Vance squared his shoulders, chin lifted, trembling with rage; Margery whispered words of calm in his ear, then Nico and Sergios stepped up to show their support.

The King gave a derisive snort, jaw set.

"Very well," he said, almost bored. "I'm sure you all remember Master Solomon Bell, then?"

He gestured toward the front of the palace where his Shadow Resistance was already positioned; their numbers were not comparable, but their magic was—it hovered in an expansive dark cloud above their heads, ready to discharge, and Solomon waited obediently at the head.

"You'll pay for what you've done!" screamed Vance, shocking even Arianna as magic flooded his eyes.

King Devlindor hardly acknowledged the outburst, turning his attention back to her.

"Command your army to stand down, or you will all die here today," he said in the most menacing voice he could muster; it shook through to her bones. "Admit who you really are, Twenty-Two. Throw down your weapons, and I'll consider sparing the lives of your friends."

Arianna felt her fury boiling over as he reminded her exactly how far she'd come from being *just* number Twenty-Two.

She knew that King Devlindor believed every word he spoke to be infallibly true, knew that he believed himself something greater than *just* a man—a god, with the power to control the future, life and death, *everything*, everyone.

But he was fooling himself…

Witnessing the true death of mermaids and a necromancer had been all the proof she'd needed to know, without a doubt, that nothing and no one—no matter how strong—was truly immortal in this world. King Devlindor was *just* a man, and she was now a woman with the power and army big enough to challenge him and his iron grip over the Olleb.

In her eyes, they were equally matched, and she would die if she had to to prove it.

"You spoke of the gods earlier, Kyrone, but what do you really know of them?" she asked as the gathering grew quiet once more. "Do you think they're listening to you now? Backing your empty promises when you've broken yours so surely?"

At this moment Solza swooped down from the air to the ground in a transformation that would dazzle even a Devlindor; she was a snow leopard once more, positioned at the front of the army alongside her master.

The King's knuckles whitened as he clung to his staff, forehead wrinkling with impatience.

Arianna let out a scornful laugh, incredulous. "Or do you actually think yourself *one* of them…"

His expression remained unreadable, though she swore she saw the corner of his lip twitch up into a faint smile.

Her voice turned cold as she glared in disgust.

"You're a disgrace to Olleb-Yelfra!" she shouted up at him. "And by the *gods*, I shall do them the favor of ridding her of you."

She signaled to Jeom, and he swiftly swung his axe into the ground—a razor-sharp gust of air blasted across the path and toward the balcony.

The King flicked his hand, and a barrier grew around himself and Raja; Jeom's magic ricocheted off it and into the trees next to the palace. It landed with such a force that some of them toppled to the ground with a booming crash that shook the land.

Demetrius winced as the earth settled.

Jeom seethed, gripping his axe even tighter.

"Very impressive, boy," said the King, almost genuinely. "You've tapped into the axe's powers." He shrugged, making gentle circles with his staff; the wind seemed to circle with it. "Alas, it'll take more than a little puff of air to move me from this place."

"We're just getting started!" he bellowed back, eager to fight.

"He's baiting us," said Lessa. "We have to be careful. Let's not do anything rash."

"So be it," said the King, his words like acid. "The disease you guardians have spread across my lands ends here and now. And if you're so lucky as to even make it through my palace doors, I will be here waiting for you with open arms to deliver your punishment." His eyes flooded with silver, Raja's too.

The wind picked up all across Saindora, howling, *screeching*, far stronger than that which Jeom had conjured.

King Devlindor opened his arms wide, lifting his staff and hands to the air, his cloak billowing out behind him in waves of the deepest black… as if he were, in fact, a god.

Arianna had to look away, hair whipping her face violently, and everyone was forced to shield their eyes.

The iron gates blew open, welcoming their army inside.

22

BEAUTIFUL CHAOS

THE SHADOW RESISTANCE COLLIDED with the Guardians of Gold. Black armor versus gold, thick smoke blotting out the sun. Deafening cries and the crack of metal rang out across the land all at once. The ground shook beneath their feet as explosive magical attacks were conjured up from both sides.

In the moment, it was impossible to tell who might win…

And as the opposing armies tangled with one another, the Palace of Saindora towered over them, like a foreboding god hungrily hoping for yet more bloodshed.

It was a race to the doors, every guardian with the same goal—enter the palace and kill the King. They aimed to drive the Shadow Resistance back, until they were forced to retreat inside where they couldn't attack so openly.

That's when the most skillful guardians would spread out to try to get a steady foothold on the palace; the rest would hold their ground from the outside, giving the King and his snakes no choice but to slither out into the open.

Nobody really knew what it would take to accomplish the final task. No amount of planning could have equipped them for it, nor how to manage the chaos that was unfolding without sizable losses. However, any of the seasoned guardians would have been all too happy to have the honor to take the King's life.

Thus, whichever group could corner him first would be the lucky—or unlucky—ones to take him on… if they could ever breach the doors.

With every step the guardians took forward, they were slammed backward with incomprehensible force, the Shadow Resistance equally as organized in their methods.

"Take no prisoners!" Master Tayshin yelled from somewhere far ahead, thrusting his broadsword forward without mercy.

Arianna leaped off her horse, slashing her swords against her enemies faster than her mind could keep up with. It seemed as if the Shadow Resistance moved upon her in a ceaseless wave of black. She had not a moment to think about anything else other than blocking attacks and hitting back.

She could hardly even catch her breath as she poured all her energy into surviving the initial collision.

Solza managed to remain by her side as she was pushed and pulled in different directions, trying to defend against strikes from all angles; each time she eliminated one enemy, two more would take their comrade's place, pursuing her with both magic and weapon. She screamed with the effort to try to push back the endless onslaught, spinning about her enemies with carefully-practiced skill and dodging their attempts to steal her life.

"*Just breathe, Master,*" said Solza, whispering words of encouragement to Arianna as they fought side by side.

Her avatar snapped her teeth at anyone who dared try to

attack them up close, and she wielded her power over the elements to defend her master at all costs. Anything went, except for transforming into a dragon again.

Not until the time was right.

Arianna didn't want to risk putting another large target on her back so close to the King's domain. Nor could she risk burning down the ancient, Golden Age palace in the heat of battle… if they could avoid it.

The elder guardians had warned Arianna from the beginning that she and Solza would be a primary target, and they had been wholly right. But all the preparation in the world couldn't have readied her for the reality of the situation.

For years, she had been ruthlessly hunted by some of the most powerful and dangerous people in the world—now, they were all laying their eyes on her at once.

The Shadow Resistance followers who had survived after her defeat of Sir Vladamor seemed even more motivated than before, methodical and merciless in their approach. And even worse, the guardians were fighting on pure rival territory this time, just magic and skill to rely on.

No mermaids would be coming to their rescue again; they were too far inland. And the ghost army she had summoned previously for help would have no effect on enemies with beating hearts. The only ones they could count on to finish this were themselves.

Arianna whipped around to face an attacker, driving her sword through his middle. Then she took in the most motivational view—the guardians nearest to her were fanned out behind her like an unstoppable human shield, marching upon the Palace of Saindora with nothing but bravery in their eyes.

Just as the Shadow Resistance had showed up in a dark flood to defend the King's position, the Guardians of Gold, *even* after all the lives they'd lost the night before, had showed up in full force to defend the integrity of the Olleb. Alongside the protectors of Moriamo, their magic sparked in bright bouts of light as they did anything but bend or bow to their opponents.

Better still, true to their word, the citizens from the most inland regions had finally showed up as a surprise addition, and just in time to join the fight.

Arianna was astounded when she also found the familiar faces of many of the drifters she'd offered a second chance to after escaping Solomon; they battled fearlessly by her side.

Some she called family, others she called friends, and most she had never even known, but seeing so many groups come together to fight against one common enemy gave her all the confidence she needed in this moment. Finally, her dream had come to fruition, and she wasn't going to let anyone down by dying at the King's doorstep.

Arianna emptied her mind and kept her focus; all her nerves fell away to be replaced with pure energy. If anyone did wound her, she probably wouldn't notice until later. She couldn't see but what was in front of her, inching her way closer to the palace as bodies fell to her feet by her blade and ruthless battle magic.

She stayed in close proximity to her friends as she and the most experienced guardians led by example, watching each other's backs and working together to carve out the shadows. They moved as one unit, always in sync as they cut their way through the horde.

It was hard not to notice Jeom leveling Shadow Resistance sorcerers by the tens, aided by the impressive powers of the Axe of Crissy. Its double-sided blade was already dripping red with blood, his air magic skills and his creator-born, hammer-like swing clearing any obstacles before him.

Demetrius was also difficult to ignore—it didn't matter that one of his legs was made of metal, for he made a worthy opponent to anyone. He manipulated the nearby gardens and trees to defend himself and those around him.

Roots and limbs crawled across the battlefield without forgiveness, condemning any enemy in their path to sink beneath the earth; no one could get close to Demetrius with his heightened command over nature and Jeom at his back…

Together, the Kane brothers were an unstoppable force to be reckoned with.

Eli danced back and forth across Arianna's line of sight as well, expertly wielding his sword and always staying within a few feet of her. Even throughout all the mayhem, she knew he kept a close eye on her every move.

In turn, she protected him against any magical attacks that his sword and armor might not be able to withstand.

Luzcora, she thought—a potent electric blast struck down a sorceress who had cornered him.

"Owe you one!" Eli called back before he delivered a final blow with his sword.

Arianna ran toward him, ducking behind Vance and Nico who had teamed up against some of the more experienced Shadow Resistance supporters. As she watched them in the thick of a duel, she couldn't help but be impressed.

Vance, who touted his brilliance yet proved useless in a traditional battle, made up for his lack of skill in weaponry with defensive magic in a big way. And Nico, who had always struck Arianna as not much of a warrior, could dodge nearly any attack, so nimble and practiced in his movements. Together, they made quite the pair as they played off each other's strengths.

Arianna made a mental note to ask them for more pointers later, should this have a happy ending. Only now did she realize just how short her time had been under the care of the elder guardians—no matter her status in this war, there was still a lot she could do well to learn.

"*Master, now's not the time to ponder over what skills*

you're lacking," snapped Solza—then she sank her fangs into a regulator who'd inched too close.

Arianna lunged at another attacker. "*Right you are, my friend.*"

Both her sword and powers were such an extension of her now that her mind almost felt free to wander, to let the metal and magic do all the work. *Almost.*

She focused on the palace doors ahead; they were getting closer.

Then, she felt Eli at her back.

They were both facing off with different opponents, sorcerers.

"Eli, you should stay close to Solza," said Arianna as they twisted their weapons in hand, mirroring their opponents' steps and mirroring each other. "She can protect you against magic while I deal with this snake."

"*Ha!* Why don't you both stay close to me?" he yelled as he thrust his blade forward, dodging a sharp bout of magic and striking his opponent dead.

He swept up a discarded shield just as the other sorcerer aimed his attack his way in revenge; it ricocheted off the magicked armor and back at him, killing him instantly.

"Hey!" said Arianna, whirling around to face him. "He was mine." She narrowed her eyes in his direction. "You had better not have made another bet with Noah…"

Eli flashed his teeth.

"I *think* what you meant to say was thank you," he countered with a boastful grin; he looked her up and down. "Not even a scratch on you yet, hmm?" He cocked his head to the side with a mocking expression. "I must say, I am a *little* surprised, Belvedor."

Arianna scoffed.

"The same could be said for you." An attacker rounded on him from behind, and she let her get a little too close before she did anything. *Levantis bora!* The sorceress was knocked backward off her feet. "Maybe I should stop saving you so much and see how well you fare?"

She gently shoved him aside, and he feigned to be wounded.

As the battle ensued around them, Arianna could tell that Eli was starting to have some fun with it; in a way, she was too.

In fact, with one look at the guardians, anyone who hailed from the Warrior's District could be easily spotted—they appeared to be in their element, calm and collected with their weapons in hand.

Arianna would never make light of such a situation, but she and Eli had both been bred in the Warrior's District, taught to be fearless and take pain in their stride. So *this*, battling in the greatest war they'd probably ever see in their lifetime, and on the frontlines no less, was more than enough reason for two former warrior-slaves to grow a little excited.

"Shall we race to the finish?" he asked with a slight bow, before stepping around her to spar with a non-magical opponent; with the twirl of his sword it ended quickly and in his favor.

"You would lose—"

As Arianna turned again to face him, she saw several metal spikes flying straight toward the back of his head.

She gasped, "*Ni passe!*"

A magical barrier expanded behind him, the spikes slamming into it in the next second before falling to the ground.

He jumped, looking down to the ground with wide eyes, the spikes smoking with magic.

"Let's not get too overconfident yet," she said, shaken back to seriousness by such a close call. "There's still a long way to go."

Eli returned a nod of agreement, nervously running his hand through his hair.

"Thanks," he mumbled.

"Don't mention it," she said, letting out a long breath.

The battle had cleared up a little in their area, the more concentrated places appearing both ahead and behind.

Arianna turned her sights on the one who had nearly killed Eli, preparing to cut him down. In another blink of the eye, an enchanted arrow had soared over their heads, piercing the man through the heart.

Eli and Arianna both looked back to find Lessa waving down at them, enthusiastically.

"Watch your backs!" she called from high up; she was pointing toward the palace. "There's more coming your way."

As part of their strategy, Demetrius had used his powers to help Lessa—along with Margery and many other guardians skilled in both archery and magic—to settle safely in the trees surrounding the palace. They were able to defend their peers from a higher position and remain clear of any direct danger; only when the guardians breached the palace would they leave their positions to join them on the ground.

"Thank you!" said Arianna, waving a sword back at her.

Lessa was already focused elsewhere, lacing magicked arrow after arrow to rain down on their enemies.

She looked like a watchful spirit hiding among the trees, her blond hair glowing in the falling sun. Her eyes shone bright blue and silver as she connected with Sano down below—he, evidently, had a vengeance all his own to satisfy.

He ripped into anyone who stepped across his path and stayed close to those less skilled.

"Now's not the time to be stubborn," said Arianna, raising her voice over the noise as she and Eli flew back into battle. "You need magical protection if you're going to stay so close to the frontline. We've been over this." She lunged at an opponent, taking her out with a swing from each blade. "We're supposed to fight in pairs. It was your idea!"

Eli and Arianna played off each other's movements like a beautiful, flawless dance—attack and defend—so that there was never a moment for the enemy to rest.

"Fine, all right," he grunted as Arianna blocked another deadly blast of magic. "I was just having a little fun. But I'm right behind you!"

Arianna huffed, marching forward with Eli at her heels.

"*Solza, please don't let this fool die,*" she said.

"*Very well, Master, but he's not making it easy.*"

They both shared in a laugh, then linked minds and obliterated the shadows before them with an eruption of avatar fire; Solza didn't need to be in her dragon form for them to wield the flame.

With the path to the doors now scorched and somewhat cleared, soon most of the elder guardians had cut and blasted their way to the front of the palace alongside them.

Master Tayshin showed no mercy with his spells nor his blade as he marched behind Arianna and her friends—Sergios, Noah, and Kayode flanked him.

"Still a long way to go, but I think the plan is working," said Arianna as she and Eli both ducked to avoid a spell; it had been sent directly from the palace. "They seem to be slowly retreating inside."

Shadow Resistance sorcerers sent deadly magic down from the tall towers, and enemy archers had a clear view of their heads, positioned much higher than the trees could ever reach—the passage to the palace entry was still heavily blocked.

Nevertheless, the guardians were making good progress.

Eli glanced at her sidelong, a happy and hopeful glow on his face; Arianna knew what he was thinking as they neared the doors…

This could really end in our favor.

She couldn't help but feel a bit giddy at the thought that

things might work out for them after all, just as they'd hoped. For, as it stood, the Shadow Resistance was beginning to withdraw into the palace as the Guardians of Gold forced their way closer.

We just need to get inside and locate the King.

THE HOURS TICKED ON, both sides growing tired. Early night blanketed the battlefield, the last embers of sun sinking beneath the earth. A full moon and army of stars began to awaken in its place, a steady brightness in the mounting dark.

Arrow after arrow flew overhead, their tips burning bright with pink flames, streaking through a dark navy sky; Arianna didn't have to turn to know that Lessa still had her back as the battle drew on, just like she always did. She continued forward with confidence, never letting up.

And thanks to Solza, her energy never waned.

No matter the hopefulness she had for their futures, it was hard to remain *fully* optimistic once she saw the dead starting to pile up, guardians and shadows alike—the closer they got to their goal, the bigger the pile grew.

It was too soon to celebrate their victory.

"Ara, look out!" Demetrius was waving frantically at her with his staff and shield some distance away across the path.

Arianna whipped around just in time to block a near-fatal attack from Solomon; he had run up behind her, two swords raised, screaming with the effort it took as he brought them down against her with all his strength.

If not for Demetrius, she'd have been added to the pile of her fallen friends and foes.

She shoved off him with her blades, her magic exploding

around her so that they both blew backward—neither lost their grip on their swords.

Arianna landed on her feet; she ran forward to return the assault… master versus apprentice with the King's palace grounds as the unlikely arena.

"You've come a long way," said Solomon, sweat dripping from his forehead as he elegantly manipulated his blades. "And you've brought your friends. I must say, I'm actually quite impressed by how long you've managed to survive after such desperate beginnings…"

"Indeed, I've traveled far," replied Arianna, her jaw set as she concentrated; she matched his movements almost perfectly, as if they were mirror images of each other. "I'm not the same person I used to be."

She lunged at him, and he sidestepped her.

He furrowed his brow, twisting his swords at his front as he considered her.

"Aren't you, though?" he said, his eyes like slits. "It seems to me that you haven't changed one bit, not at your core." He gave the slight shake of his head. "You're still hungry for freedom." He paused in his attack, taking her aback. "Tell me, Arianna, who else has to die for you to get what you want? Have you not sacrificed enough? Do you not have *enough?*"

He gestured to the doors, not far behind him.

"All this just to die at the King's feet?" He looked at her incredulously. "You *are* persistent, though, I will say that… there's something about you that just yearns for death."

Arianna felt a roar of rage grow inside her; her swords ignited in flames. She couldn't even speak for fear she might actually breathe fire herself.

"Lovely magic," he said, somewhat genuinely. "Alas, I'm afraid it won't help you against me. I know everything you know… and more."

In the next instant, Solomon's swords grew ablaze with a

magic Arianna didn't even have a name for, glowing with what looked to be a lavender flame. He dived toward her.

Their blades met, scraping and sparking off one another, adding a sweltering heat to the already stifling night.

"Age may have given you more experience, but my path has led me to understand a great many things," snapped Arianna, her avatar magic flooding to the surface. "You'd be lucky to know everything that I know now. You are *not* my only master."

She ducked, and Solza leaped over her with Solomon in her sights; he dodged her by a hair.

Solza landed on the nearest enemy, ripping into a sorcerer's throat.

"That may be so," replied Solomon, cautiously getting to his feet; he kept one eye on Solza, but she was occupied with her new prey. "However, you still have much to learn as a warrior."

He lifted his sword and began to circle her, almost as if they were warming up for training; he lectured her just the same.

"When your emotions run hot, you tend to rush, Arianna. That's when you're the most vulnerable to be struck down. Patience and perseverance are key to any long-term achievement, and that includes battle. You must stay focused, even when there's only chaos. You have to let go of your feelings and *focus* on what's happening, at all points around you." He dropped his sword to his side. "Never let your guard down… or you will die."

It was then that two of his regulators snuck up behind her, surrounding her from either side. She was forced to confront them with her weapons, leaving her defenseless against Solomon.

His boot met her chest, sending her flying backward.

She skidded across the ground, feeling the wind knocked

out of her. She rolled onto her side, coughing up blood.

The ones who had ambushed her took this moment to pin her down using magic. They kicked her swords out of reach.

"Get away from her!" yelled Eli, racing to her aid.

Before Eli could reach her, Solomon had tackled him to the ground with an enchantment. He restrained him by the throat.

Arianna craned her neck to see, trying to resist her captors; it looked as if Eli could barely breathe.

"Get *off* of me," growled Arianna.

Her magic surged, and a barrier burst around her before the suppressive spells could sink too deep—the sorcerers pinning her down, along with their stifling magic, were blasted away.

She rolled onto her hands and knees.

"Stop it, Solomon, you'll kill him!" she cried, seeing as Eli struggled for air.

"My, my, does this feels familiar," he said, his eyes emanating a dangerous silver glow. "Tell your armies to surrender! If not, I'll crush his throat before you can even think of a spell to stop me."

"No... Ara," Eli choked out, his hands gripped around Solomon's as he tried to pull them away—they stayed steady as stone. "*Don't.*"

Arianna didn't move an inch, not wanting to test Solomon's threat, but she could see Eli was running out of time. His face grew paler by the second as he desperately tried to pull air into his lungs.

Before she could even think of what to do to buy time for his life, she heard a *whoosh* as a flaming arrow sliced through the air right past her head—it was aimed straight for Solomon's heart.

With a master warrior's instinct, Solomon released his hold on Eli and crossed his swords at his chest; the arrow reversed its direction. As if it were one of his blades, it sliced a path back toward the place where it had originated so fast that Arianna barely had time to duck out of harm's way.

Eli seized his opportunity to crawl away from Solomon and to the safety of nearby guardians with magic; he signaled he was all right.

That was too close...

She smiled back at him, signaling her next move; Eli's expression fell, eyes wide and terrified.

His gaze lifted toward the trees.

"What is it?" she called, panic seizing her.

Her mind was slow to catch up to what had happened.

Jeom let out a heart-wrenching cry. He rushed past her, and suddenly she couldn't breathe.

Arianna felt as if she'd somehow frozen in place as the war raged on around her. All the sounds of battle had turned into a medley that she just couldn't comprehend, everything blending together in a haze as time seemed to skid to a stop. All she could do was observe, mind racing, eyes unblinking.

Eli was suddenly at her side.

She heard his voice but couldn't truly grasp what he was saying. He'd dropped down to his knees beside her, shaking her, speaking words she just couldn't hear...

It wasn't until she saw Solomon turn to walk away, retreating back to the palace, that Arianna seemed to regain awareness.

She shoved Eli away and turned around to face the horror she couldn't bear to be true—the very arrow meant for Solomon was sticking out of Lessa's chest, the smoke from her magical flame rising into the air to join the clouds.

Then, she fell from the treetops.

Magic appeared to cushion her body as she tumbled down, and Jeom was there to catch her before she hit the ground.

He rocked her in his arms, crying out her name.

Arianna seized, as if someone had squeezed her heart in their hand. She spun around to search for Solomon, rage filling her mind. All her hope crumbled away in the same second, as if it had never even existed.

"I'll kill you!" she shouted.

She swept up her swords and got to her feet, ready to run after him.

Solomon turned to face her as her threat met his ears; he stood in the entryway of the palace.

We were so close…

With the slight bow of his head, he vanished inside.

"Ara, *please*, do something!" she heard Jeom call, just as she made to go after Solomon. "She's barely breathing."

Arianna let out a scream of anger so loud that her throat ached. She gripped her swords, thinking that the hilts might snap right off—it took everything for her not to go after Solomon, but Lessa needed her more.

She sheathed her weapons and ran in the opposite direction, Eli and Solza following directly behind.

Demetrius was already there, the vines he controlled gently unraveling from around Lessa's body.

"I caught her…" he stammered, tears swimming in his eyes as Arianna and Eli met him and Jeom at the horrific scene.

"Good, that's good," said Arianna, her voice shaky.

Jeom cradled Lessa's head, and Arianna gently reached for her hand.

"She barely has a pulse…" She looked around, trying to remain calm. "Guardians, we need a healer!"

Nobody came. Everyone was too occupied with the battle.

Margery called down to them from the trees. "Is she still alive?"

"Barely hanging on," said Eli, giving them room. "Can you help?"

Margery was sending ceaseless cascades of enchanted

arrows down onto their enemies, leading the archers now with Lessa wounded.

She shook her head with a somber expression.

"I can't leave them," she said, using her magic to shield those who fought around her.

"It doesn't matter," said Arianna, suddenly. "Her magic won't work. We *need* Sano."

She knew no healer's spell was strong enough to reverse this kind of damage, not without the proper remedies. And with everyone working to stay alive, Sano was their only hope.

She connected with Solza. "*Find him!*" she commanded.

Lessa had ordered him to fight with those on the ground, thinking herself safe in the cover of the trees.

How wrong she had been…

Solza threw herself back into battle without hesitation, searching for Sano.

"I'll go with her!" said Eli, already racing after her avatar.

Arianna prayed that Sano could sense her master's dire state in this moment. *He'll come to her rescue in time. He has to.*

Lessa's eyes fluttered open, finding Arianna's. She squeezed her hand.

"*Les…*" said Arianna, gripping her tight. "Are you—"

"The baby," she gasped, blood spluttering from her lips; she reached for Jeom's face. "Save… her."

Jeom couldn't reply, overwhelmed with tears as he held her.

"No," said Arianna, forcing a smile. "No, Les, it won't come to that. We've got you. Sano…" She looked up, searching the frenzied battle. "He's coming." She nodded to herself. "He's going to arrive any second now."

She squeezed her hand harder; Lessa's grip was getting weaker.

"Yeah," stuttered Jeom, trying to be strong for her. "It's

going to be all right. Just hang in there, you hear? Sano would never let you down."

Lessa faintly nodded, her cheek resting on his palm.

"Is there anything we can do?" whispered Demetrius as they all huddled around her; he smoothed back her hair, then laid a hand on Jeom's shoulder.

"I... I don't think so," said Arianna, bowing her head. "We just need Sano."

Jeom glowered at her. "Just try *something*, anything, Ara!"

She'd never seen him look so scared... not the weeks Lessa had disappeared as a mermaid. And not even throughout all the days she was being held captive by Sir Vladamor.

Arianna met his red-rimmed gaze.

"Breathe," she mouthed.

He nodded, over and over, trying to steady his emotions.

Arianna slipped the half-empty prillyberry potion from Lessa's robes and forced her to drink. "Maybe this will steady her while we wait for Sano to show..."

Demetrius conjured his magic to buy them a little extra time, creating an impenetrable barrier of nature between them and the battle.

"*Helthra saludis emencia*," said Arianna, repeating the phrase Lessa had taught her long ago.

They waited for a moment, but it didn't seem to have any effect.

"Why isn't it doing anything?" said Jeom, all his muscles clenched. "Try again!"

"I... I think we have to remove the arrow first," said Arianna, beginning to panic; Lessa's hand had started to grow cold. "But I'm not a true healer, and she could bleed out even quicker if we do. I don't have any other remedies with me, and this wound—"

She gazed at her hands, Lessa's blood covering them.

"Ara, what else can we do?" said Demetrius, stroking her

forehead; her face was so pale. "We can't... let her die. Not like this."

Arianna just stared down at her, helpless. This time, she just didn't have the answer.

"It's all right," breathed Lessa, her words barely audible—they all grew quiet to hear her.

She squeezed Arianna's hand again, as if in reassurance, then she touched eyes with Demetrius, her expression softening. Her gaze set on Jeom last, and she parted her lips. "I love you all..."

Her voice trailed off; Arianna felt her grip release, her hand falling down to her side.

They all stared in disbelief as Lessa's eyes, always so blue and so bright, lost their shine.

"No, no, *no...* Les!" said Arianna, gently slapping her cheeks to try to wake her up; she didn't move. "We just got you back. Don't do this now. Stay with us!" She looked around again, desperate. "*Sano!* Where are you?"

Jeom collapsed across her body, looking up at his brother with a pleading expression.

"Wake her up, Demetrius," he whimpered, so helpless in this moment. "*Please*, brother, you have to help her. She can't be—"

He scrunched his eyes closed, burying his face in her robes.

Demetrius leaned over to check her pulse.

He put his arms around his brother.

"I'm so sorry, Jeom," he said, tears in his eyes. "I'm sorry... she's gone."

Jeom shrugged him off, howling to the sky in agony. "Bring her *back!*"

Arianna wobbled to her feet, Lessa's blood still staining her hands. She gazed around, feeling as if she were in a dream, unable to comprehend the loss of her closest friend. It had all happened so suddenly, and now her mind was filled with thoughts of only her.

She recalled one so vividly now, could taste the snow on her tongue from a night so far gone—they'd played under the moonlight in the Warrior's District, witnessing a star plummet from its place in the sky.

Arianna felt herself grow just as cold now as if she were standing outside in that very snowfall.

Her hand flew to her neck, feeling the soul of the star there—she prayed, more than *anything*, that she hadn't used her last wish on her own life when she'd jumped off that bridge.

Bring her back!

In an instant, her kind and loving friend had been snuffed out of this world like the flicker of a candle turned to smoke on the wind. There was no more magic in her eyes, and her skin was like ice, the silvery-blue feather of her very own arrow sticking out from her chest.

Eli's voice boomed over the madness. "We found Sano!"

Demetrius let the barrier of nature fall away as he and Solza made their way back to the group; the Shadow Resistance still surrounded them on all sides.

Eli skidded to a halt, his mouth falling open. "Is she—"

One look at Arianna was all the answer he needed; he stiffened, placing his fist over his heart. Then he spun around to defend against another assault. He channeled all their sorrow and anger on anyone who dared to try to get near them.

A howl ripped through the night—Sano was rushing toward them, the ground rolling beneath his feet.

"Is it too late?" muttered Jeom, a little bit of hope returning to his voice; they cleared the way for her avatar.

Nobody could say for certain, but even Arianna was unable to stifle the little bit of faith that had seeped through her devastation with Sano's arrival.

Collectively, they held their breath as he summoned his

unique healer magic.

When he laid his paws across Lessa's chest, his magic appeared to work as usual, a silver glow originating from him and flowing into her—yet nothing seemed to be happening as a result.

After too much time had passed with no change, Sano's magic died away. He sat back on his haunches and began to howl at the glaring moon; the sound sent stabbing aches straight into Arianna's heart.

That's when she felt herself truly go numb, shaking her head in disbelief as she gazed down at Lessa's lifeless body.

"I can't..." Demetrius looked to Arianna, quivering. "She's really gone?"

Jeom was utterly inconsolable, now crying into his brother's arms. He couldn't even look at her anymore.

Arianna reached out to Sano as the poor thing continued to howl and howl into the night, his voice full of pain, his orange eyes glowing abnormally bright.

She thought he would collapse at any moment.

"I think..." Arianna gulped, looking to the boys in yet more fear. "Sano's going to die too."

"This is too much to bear," said Jeom with a moan, his entire body shuddering.

They all gazed to Sano and locked hands, waiting for his inevitable ending to come too, as was recorded of the avatar race...

"What's happening to him?" whimpered Demetrius.

They all jumped back, eyes wide as an extraordinary, magical vortex suddenly ensnared Sano—even as his howls of sadness still echoed out into the world.

"It looks like he's... transforming," said Arianna, moving to a safe distance with the others; she'd seen enough to know. She wiped her eyes, gaping all the while.

"But I thought an avatar would die without its master?"

said Jeom, shielding his eyes from the brightness. "Is this death?"

"That's what I understood, too," said Demetrius, nodding.

Arianna shook her head, just as confused. "Yes, but this… this looks *nothing* like death."

Something new was growing among them, lighting up the darkness that had begun to suffocate them all.

"What's going on with Sano?" gasped Eli, finding his way over when it was safe for him to turn his back on the battle.

Nobody replied, all struck speechless as they waited and watched.

"*Solza, stay close,*" said Arianna, feeling her avatar nudge up against her, equally full of sorrow.

"By gods," breathed Demetrius—all their sadness seemed to shift to wonderment. "It can't be."

Sano's shocking transformation was complete, a rain of magic spilling down around him.

They all stared in quiet astonishment as a white dragon with glittering, almost translucent scales had wholly replaced the wolf they'd come to know. His body was so large that he spanned from one edge of the pathway to the other, spilling over into the gardens and cutting off access for anyone else to cross to the other side. And he was curled, protectively, around Lessa's body, hiding her from view.

"Sano? Is that you?" whispered Arianna, cautiously stepping toward him.

The dragon lifted its mammoth head, lowering it to eye level so that Arianna could look straight into the bright orange bulbs that could only signify Lessa's loyal avatar.

"I don't understand…" said Jeom, reaching out to touch him.

Sano gently nudged a scaly cheek against his palm.

Jeom perked up. "Sano, is Lessa *alive?*"

Jeom clutched at Arianna so hard now that she thought she could feel the pulse of his heart through his armor, one that wished with all its being that Lessa had somehow been revived.

She desperately wanted to believe this too—that maybe Lessa had survived or had been given a new chance at life because of some twist of fate, some unheard-of avatar blessing.

Sano was a healer, too, after all.

And as she witnessed another mythical dragon materialize before her, she recalled the scroll regarding the avatar species...

It was suggested that the avatar would follow their master to the grave shortly after death. *Or* they could lay down their life in exchange for their master's, if they so chose.

Arianna clung to that scripture now, praying with everything in her power that there had been a loophole they had missed, one which had consequently allowed Lessa to return to life. For, as it stood, not only was her avatar alive and well but Sano had *transformed* into a dragon, the final stage of the avatar cycle.

"Sano..." said Arianna, pleading. "Let us see. Is Lessa—"

He slowly uncurled his body.

Arianna's hands flew over her mouth as she cried into them; Jeom dropped to his knees, head in his palms. His tears came like a flood.

"How can this be?" said Demetrius, his voice trembling with a watery gaze.

No one could even begin to comprehend what was before them. Arianna found the strength to address Sano, reading the fear in his eyes.

"It's all right, Sano," she said, walking forward. "We're all going to be... all right."

Her voice cracked on the last word as she stepped into the protective circle Sano had made around Lessa's body. Arianna couldn't do anything but stare for a moment—in shock, in sadness, in wonder.

Lessa's body was nowhere to be found.

Instead, in her place, tangled within her bright blue guardian cloak, there remained a beautiful baby with dark, gray-blue eyes and light brown skin. She was tucked safely near Sano's belly, one nearly transparent to the fire within.

"It's all right," she said again, the tears falling in streams now; Sano seemed a little defensive toward her, a rumble growing in his throat. "I'm *not* going to hurt her, Sano. It's me."

He calmed, and Arianna gently climbed over him to lift the baby into her arms, wrapping her in Lessa's cloak. As she did, she noticed a swirl of silver marking the space above her heart—a birthmark, mirroring the scar Lessa had earned on her neck from the day she and Sano had first joined as avatar and avatar master.

Arianna looked the child over, its big eyes flicking around in curiosity. Did she notice a spark of silver there, too? Its little arms and legs wiggled about as she tried to hold it steady.

"What in the gods' names," said Eli, running his hand through his hair, staring at the baby with his mouth agape.

Arianna let out a deep sigh, rocking the child in her arms. "Sano is a healer," she said with acceptance.

His mouth just formed an 'O' as he stood back.

It was incomprehensible in some ways, and in others it made the perfect sense.

Lessa's avatar was a healer by trade, gifted powers beyond belief to help continue *life*. And with the miraculous birth of Lessa's baby, here his powers had truly shown...

Sano had done the impossible.

At this moment, rocking Lessa's baby in her arms, Arianna understood exactly what Syrifina had meant about that word—it just didn't mean a thing.

"*Anything* is possible," she whispered as she sank deep into the child's gaze.

It was one of the saddest moments of her life, knowing certainly that her best friend had been snatched from this world too soon. And yet, in a way, it was also one of the happiest outcomes they could have asked for in such a situation.

Someone they had all cherished greatly had left something so beautiful behind in her memory for them to hold on to, a gift to be rejoiced in and protected.

This bright, innocent life, born amid such darkness by the hand of magic, gave Arianna more hope than even the soul of the star had ever been able to conjure—a wish granted she didn't even know she had had in her heart all along.

"Is it… hurt?" asked Jeom, slowly getting to his feet.

"I don't think so," she said, examining her. "And *it's* a girl." Arianna looked up, smiling through the tears. "Jeom, you have a baby girl."

She walked over to him, urging him to take her.

At first, he refused, too distraught to even consider this possibility. But when Arianna placed the baby carefully in his arms, Jeom's demeanor immediately changed.

"Of course, it's a girl," he said, awestruck as he gazed down at her. "Lessa is always right."

"What can we call her?" asked Demetrius, slipping a finger into her tight grip as she squeezed.

Jeom met Arianna's eyes, and she nodded in reassurance.

"Her name is Snow," he replied without reluctance.

Arianna returned a solemn smile. "How nice to finally meet you, Snow," she said.

"Your timing is… unexpected," said Demetrius with a sad chuckle. "But we'll make sure you stay safe, little one."

Sano got to his feet, startling them all back to the present—there was still a war to be won.

He reared his head to the black sky and anyone near scurried away, dropping their weapons in a panic lest they be crushed. He opened his jaw, releasing a gut-wrenching sound to the air.

The battle seemed to still, everyone gawking as Sano rose into the sky, a beautifully terrifying sight, uncontrollable in his sadness.

"What's happened here?" shouted Master Tayshin, rushing to the scene now that the area was somewhat clear; Nico trailed him.

They gazed from the baby to Sano in confusion.

"Lessa's dead," said Demetrius, head bowed. "But Sano transformed into a dragon and… somehow saved her…" he scratched his head at the riddle, "unborn child?"

Master Tayshin appeared stunned for a moment, the statement sounding so utterly ridiculous. Yet, when he looked again to Snow in Jeom's arms, he nodded in understanding.

"He's a healer," he said, his expression dark. "An avatar's magic knows no bounds."

"Yes, but aren't avatars supposed to follow their masters into death?" said Jeom, sounding frustrated, his focus never leaving Snow. "This is what we learned."

He clearly needed an answer he could grasp, in order to accept that Lessa was really gone.

"I think, I finally get it now," said Arianna, watching Sano flood the sky with his pain, setting the night on fire. "Avatars *must* be the embodiment of blood magic." A shiver rolled up her spine, and everyone quieted as they looked at her—she touched the silver scar on her arm, noting the one on Snow's chest. "It's painful when you bond with an avatar, unlike anything you've ever felt."

"Except for maybe this…" said Jeom through his teeth.

"Except for maybe this," agreed Arianna, gently. "But just think, if such pain and suffering comes from an avatar union, then maybe it's because of some type of blood bond forming through magic, right? Why else would we need to survive their attack before completing the transition?"

There were so many mysteries floating around the link to avatars and their masters, yet Arianna felt steadfast in her deduction the more she pieced everything together.

"Blood magic is the strongest of them all," said Master Tayshin, musing over this idea.

"Exactly," said Arianna. "And if I'm correct, Sano was able to keep Snow alive not just because he's a healer but because they are, by nature, bound by blood, *too.*"

Demetrius tapped his chin. "Lessa's dying wish was also to save the baby…"

Arianna glanced to Solza, recalling how she had stayed atop the hill in the desert when she'd sacrificed herself to Sir Vladamor, knowing very well that they would both die together.

"*Don't remind me of this,*" said Solza, pinning herself to her side.

"*You did that because I commanded it.*"

"*Yes,*" said Solza. "*You are my master.*"

Arianna nodded to herself, then looked to the others.

"An avatar would never defy their master's wishes," she explained, "even if death is what they faced. However, in this case, because of Sano's unique healing powers to be able to keep Snow alive somehow, it seems he was granted a second chance at life." She looked down to little Snow, pale against Jeom's arms. "Lessa's blood flows through her child's veins. Thus, the avatar blood magic goes on unaffected." All eyes settled on Snow as Arianna drew to her conclusion. "I think Sano lives to serve a *new* master now."

Jeom gave a weak smile. "Like a magical inheritance," he said, nuzzling her to his face. "It's like Snow *inherited* Sano." He sighed. "How lucky that we didn't lose them both."

"If what you're saying is true," said Demetrius, "that would mean avatars *could*, presumably, live on forever…

serving generations of avatar masters to come."

Arianna knelt down to Solza, stroking her fur. "*May you never die.*"

"*I wouldn't want to live without you,*" replied Solza, just as shaken by the death of Lessa as everyone else.

Arianna averted her eyes to the sky as Sano continued to grieve for the loss of his first love, his first leader.

"*Nor I you,*" she said. "*I think you should go be with him… Sano needs your support.*"

"*Yes, Master,*" agreed Solza. "*Although, I doubt he will hear me now.*"

"*We all have to keep going,*" said Arianna, mustering up her own strength. "*For Lessa. She can't have died for nothing. Make him hear you.*"

With her command, Solza shifted into her fiery form.

With the flap of her wings, she floated into the sky, joining Sano in a devastating yet stunning dance among the clouds. Fire streamed from their mighty jaws, as if they screamed out loud to honor their fallen friend. Now, not one but *two* dragons conquered the skies of Olleb-Yelfra, their black and white scales melting together into one as they swirled across the stars, leaving a silver trail behind them.

It was then that Lessa's death truly hit Arianna, standing side by side with her broken family, eyes all lifted to the sky.

An uncontrollable anger gripped her in that moment; her magic flooded her mind, uninvited, just as it used to when she was first learning to master her avatar powers.

She closed her eyes, finding herself suddenly connected with Solza, their minds linking as one. And in doing so, she realized that she could actually *speak* to Sano in Solza's tongue.

"*We have to end this,*" she called to them both, fury feeding her words. "*In Lessa's name, we have to kill the King.*" She couldn't stop the command. "*Do whatever it takes. Get us into that gods-forsaken palace!*"

The avatars' eyes lit up like the stars in the sky around them; Arianna could practically feel the force of their combined powers radiating in the air.

Then came Sano's voice. "*For Master Lessa!*"

It reverberated loud throughout Arianna's mind, deep and strong, and full of fire.

When she opened her eyes, the avatar state had fully consumed her; she used her powers to shield all the guardians still standing.

Sano and Solza released a rain of fire down on their enemies. It fell in a terrifying wave, creating a bloody and charred path straight into the Palace of Saindora.

THE CHOSEN ONE

ARIANNA FELT EVERY LICK OF FIRE leave Solza's jaws, unbidden tears streaming down her cheeks as she held steadfast to her avatar connection. The Shadow Resistance had fully retreated inside the palace, Solomon included.

The ones who did not make it in time were burned alive.

The avatar dragons had taken matters into their own hands—Solza and Sano gleamed under the moonlight, their large shadows consuming the land.

"Ara, snap out of it." Someone was shaking her. "It's too much. This wasn't part of the plan!"

She felt the sting of a hand strike across her face, her magic rolling back with a *snap*.

She looked up to find Master Tayshin standing over her, his palm just as red as her cheek probably was; Eli released his grip on her shoulders, standing by his side.

Nico, Demetrius, and Jeom had moved a safe distance

away with the baby.

As she fully relinquished her connection with Solza, she fell forward, collapsing into Eli's arms.

"You slapped me," she mumbled, weak from the exertion as she glanced up at Master Tayshin.

"I had to do something to bring you back," he said, his breath heavy. "Just look around us. We don't have time for this, Arianna! We're so close."

"He's right," said Nico, more gently, his expression grave. "This is not what Lessa would want."

Arianna noticed that Jeom had conjured a protective shield over all of them—the fires had grown out of the avatars' control, eating through Demetrius' nature-made barriers.

"You all right?" Jeom called to her, rocking Snow in one arm and holding the Axe of Crissy with the other.

She shook her head, comprehending the frenzy she'd caused.

It was apparent now how quickly fire could spread without being checked, burning away at anything in its path with nothing to stop it. It had only been minutes since Solza and Sano had taken on their fiery forms, and already Arianna saw the extensive damage they'd done to the area of the city bordering the palace. Even her own people looked frightened of them; Sano burned anything and *anyone* in his path, Solza not far off behind him.

If not for Arianna's protective enchantment, they would probably all be dead.

She was depleted of energy now, and her magic had since worn off. Thus, those in the vicinity ran for cover, using defensive magic to hide. It was every man and woman for themselves.

No longer were the armies focused on fighting for their respective causes—instead, both enemy and ally fought merely to survive.

"You have to do something," shouted Demetrius, horrified as the surrounding woodlands went up in flames. "They'll destroy everything, Ara."

"Sano… he's heartbroken," said Arianna, pressing her hand to her head.

"We all are," said Eli, turning to face her, desperate for her to hear him, "but we can't let them burn the city to the ground. If we destroy it so completely, how can we say that we're any better than the King? *Why* would the people follow? This city is part of Olleb-Yelfra too. It's our home."

Home…

The word resonated with Arianna to her core. What would such a place look like without Lessa?

She couldn't really picture it, but she knew that Eli was right.

The people of the Olleb would never trust the guardians if they burned the High City of Saindora to ashes, and Arianna knew very well that it was a real possibility…

The remains of the City of Crissy were the historical, Golden Age reminder—and that had been just *one* dragon's doing.

Fire didn't discriminate between good nor evil, guardian nor shadow.

Likewise, avatars were only as good as their masters.

Arianna had been granted extraordinary gifts that could help shift the overwhelming darkness consuming the world to make room for the light, bringing balance back to the land.

The Golden Rule.

Or she could follow in the King's footsteps and destroy it.

I am nothing like that monster, she thought, gazing to Sano. *And neither was Lessa.*

She peered toward the palace; flames licked at the structure, scorching away its surroundings, its foundation.

There was nobody guarding the doors anymore—they

stood open and waiting.

Although not according to plan, the Guardians of Gold *had* made it to the final stage in their strategy. But Eli was right...

Burning Saindora to the ground is not part of it.

"Jeom, let me out from this barrier," demanded Arianna, pushing off Eli and standing up straight.

"Are you sure?" he asked.

"Yes, I've got my magic under control now," she said, concentrating hard—she was drained, but she knew Solza would remedy that.

With the flick of his axe, their shield of protection rolled back to safeguard only Jeom, Demetrius, and the baby, leaving everyone else out in the open.

A smoldering wall of heat smacked her so hard that she nearly lost her balance.

Everyone was coughing, choking on the air around them. She had to act fast.

I can do this! She'd already mastered all the elements, so now all she needed to do was accept them, just like her animancer gifts. *Just like Lessa's death... I must accept it.*

She craned her neck to the smoke-riddled sky and connected again with Solza. She channeled the pain she felt over the loss of Lessa into something more powerful than destruction.

This time, she was so in control and aware of herself that she could practically feel Solza's belly full of fire, the warmth tingling within her own body in a wonderful sensation; Arianna homed in on that fire, knowing it was hers to tame.

"*Sano, I'm sorry... I'm so sorry, but this has to stop now,*" she said through Solza. He didn't let up, but Solza stopped immediately. "*I said, enough! Lessa wouldn't want this of you. Enough now. The palace is open. Your work is done.*"

Sano still did not respond. Though, observing him

through Solza's eyes, Arianna could tell he had begun to relax.

"*Come back to us,*" she said, more gently now. "*We need you...*"

"*Lessa needed me,*" he growled.

"*She still does,*" said Arianna, her voice steady. "*But not like this.*"

The dragons began to circle back toward the palace; they landed right in front of her, the ground shaking beneath her feet.

Arianna ran to Sano; he lowered his head to her height.

"I know you're heartbroken, my friend," she whispered, peering into his saddened gaze. "I am too, but you will do your master the most justice by ensuring no harm comes to Snow."

"*I will protect her with my life,*" he declared, setting his attention on Jeom and the baby; Jeom rocked uneasily on his feet, staring into the dragon's fire-filled eyes.

"Ara, the flames," cried Demetrius, going over to them. He laid a consoling hand on Sano's scaly cheek, looking at her in concern. "They'll destroy everything. What can we do?"

"I can handle this," she said.

She lifted her hands to the air, easily able to manipulate the fires without help. She smothered them into nothing but smoke and scorch marks. And when all seemed under control, she relinquished her avatar state, as well as her connection to Sano.

Nico let out a loud whistle. "Close call," he stuttered, taking in all the damage; everything in the vicinity had been charred to a crisp, but the palace still stood.

Demetrius loosed a long exhale, already using his magic to help regrow some of the nature that had been lost.

"That was... *utterly* terrifying," said Eli, gawking at Arianna. "And yet, brilliant."

With the fires stifled and the Shadow Resistance holed up indoors, a calm had settled in the air; after all was said and done, Arianna noted that a good number of the guardians who had made it past the mermaid massacre were still standing strong.

Not all… but many. *We aren't defeated yet.*

"You should be grateful that you were able to take control back before they turned their sights on the rest of the city," snapped Master Tayshin, visibly relieved. "The damage seems pretty well contained to the palace grounds." He grew quiet, his voice sharp. "Don't let something like that *ever* happen again."

"Never," she replied, feeling guilty. "I promise. And thank you for helping me to focus. I just… lost myself a bit." *Lost Lessa.*

He returned a curt nod.

She put her attention on Sano and Solza; their allies were still cowering in their presence.

"We could use you both back on the ground," she pleaded. "I think we've all seen enough fire for now."

There were murmurs of strong agreement from all around, and the avatars obliged.

Transformative magic encircled both Solza and Sano, shrinking them exponentially, until soon they were back to their original forms—Solza a snow leopard and Sano a miniature monkey.

Neither inspired fear compared to that of their dragon personas; there was a collective sigh of relief from the surrounding crowd.

Sano flew to perch on Jeom's shoulders as soon as the transformation was done; his gaze was pinned to Snow.

"How's she doing?" asked Arianna, walking over to them.

"Fine, I think," he replied with a shrug. His expression twisted with uncertainty. "Ara… I don't know what to do with her. I *have* to fight. I have to finish this… for Lessa."

"Let me protect her," came the voice of a woman.

They all turned around to find Kayode marching toward them. She was covered in soot and blood, a spear in hand and a curved sword slung across her back.

Jeom eyed her, warily.

"Those from Moriamo are familiar with children," said Nico. "I'm sure it's all right."

"Are *you?*" said Jeom, looking to Arianna as he rocked Snow back and forth in his arms—out of some miracle, she had fallen asleep during all the chaos.

"Yes, don't worry, Jeom," said Arianna, gesturing to Kayode. "We can trust her. She's just as strong a fighter as we are. There's nobody better to keep watch over Snow than her… Mother of Moriamo."

Kayode reddened, but she kept her chin high.

"I can vouch for that too," said Master Tayshin, firmly.

Arianna smiled. "Snow will be just fine."

"I suppose… there's really no other option," said Jeom with a heaviness; he pointed to Sano. "You stay close to her now, too, you here? Do *not* take your eyes off this one."

Sano pressed into Jeom's neck, affectionately, then jumped to the ground, shifting into a gallant white wolf. He went to sit protectively by Kayode's side.

Kayode held out her arms. "I *won't* let any harm come to her," she said, unwavering.

Reluctantly, Jeom passed Snow to her, planting a kiss atop her head before he fully let her go; Kayode bowed to him, his child secure in her arms, swaddled in his lost love's guardian robes.

"She will be returned to you at the end. This I swear on my life," she said. "It's the least I can do to honor your sacrifices, guardians of the Olleb."

"Thank you," replied Jeom, entirely defeated. "Please… just, keep her safe. No matter what happens."

"I won't take her near the palace until the King is dead,"

said Kayode, firmly.

She locked eyes with Arianna, offering her a small smile. Then she slipped away from the gathering crowd, taking Snow, hopefully, somewhere safe; Jeom's gaze lingered on them until they were fully out of sight.

"All right, guardians and allies," said Master Tayshin as more people began to join them. He hugged Arianna around the shoulders. "Gather 'round. We've come a *long* way, but not without great loss to acknowledge—"

With the setting of the sun, the second great battle in the war to capture the High City of Saindora had already come and gone. Arianna didn't know how much time had flown by nor who had even survived. Everything had passed by in a blur.

Now, as the dust began to settle, she could see the truth of it…

Those who still remained stood to attention, waiting for the next command of action; the far too many absent faces were a harsh reality to bear.

Arianna could see that many of their friends and allies had already been taken in this bloody battle, just like the last. And like Lessa, all that was left of them now were bodies to bury or the memory of their sacrifice—it was a cold reminder that, just as fire, Death did not discriminate.

There will only be more souls to deliver into his waiting arms by the end of this…

"Do not linger on that loss now," continued Master Tayshin. "Linger on the faces that survived, the ones who remain by your side. There's still a hard battle to be fought, and those who stand with you now are the ones who will make sure you see it through to the end. If we're to avenge the lives of our fallen guardians, our friends, our allies, we must endure on their behalf." He gestured to the palace. "The worst of the Shadow Resistance is waiting for us in there, and this isn't the first time we've faced them. I'll be damned if we lose twice to these monsters, so remember your trainings and fight well… for each other."

He held up his palm to the sky so that the golden dragon shone clearly, then he made a fist and brought it across his bloodstained, armored chest. Everyone mimicked the gesture, Arianna included, the drum of her own heartbeat reminding her not to give up yet.

Just survive!

With Lessa still drowning out her thoughts, she touched eyes with those she considered family, those who still lived—Jeom, Eli, Demetrius, Noah, and Master Tayshin.

She knew that the next hours could potentially bring forth more unwelcome goodbyes; every guardian knew it as they mentally prepared for the final phase in their plan…

Down with the King!

"See you on the other side," she said to those closest to her, unsheathing her weapons—she raised a sword, her voice rising with it. "Let's go and take back our freedom!"

The crowd roared their agreement.

"You heard her. Fan out!" commanded Eli. "Just like we practiced." Everyone rushed to assemble as his voice rang out. "Those of you assigned to the palace, don't even *dare* turn a corner alone, but leave *no* corner unexplored. By the end of this, the Palace of Saindora will be ours."

"And whoever locates the King first, *no* mercy!" screamed Jeom, pushing his axe into the air; Arianna had never seen him look more like a warrior, ready to kill.

Now that King Devlindor was trapped inside, their plan was to neutralize what remained of the Shadow Resistance, to slowly draw him out and into the open, just as they'd rehearsed; small units of highly skilled warriors and sorcerers started to infiltrate the palace, each led by an experienced guardian or Moriamo protector.

Master Tayshin and Margery were the only elders to remain *outside* of the palace, overseeing a large defense of the less experienced fighters. They would focus on fortifying the palace grounds with heavy enchantments, in preparation to contain the King should he try to flee. And they were also tasked to impede any of his followers who might try to escape.

As the small units disappeared inside—Noah, Nico, Vance, and Sergios among them—Arianna, Jeom, Demetrius, and Eli were the last to follow.

"Ready?" asked Eli, marching in step with Arianna to the palace doors, Solza not far behind.

"Not at all," she said, Lessa still swirling in her mind.

She gazed up at the palace, a monster with its mouth wide open, teeth bared—she knew inside she'd find a whole new, dark and dangerous world, another plane of existence to survive.

She took a deep breath and stepped through the threshold; as she did, she was hit with the realization that she would either exit that same way victorious or would never leave the Palace of Saindora again.

AS SOON AS THEY WERE INSIDE, it was chaos. They immediately had to duck from a blast of magic that shook the old walls with a force so strong a brilliant, jeweled chandelier ripped from its chains, smashing to the floor in a million pieces.

Arianna saw Noah at the top of the winding stairwell in the main gallery, using defensive magic she'd taught him not so long ago, protecting her and her friends from the backlash.

"Thanks for the cover, mate," said Jeom, brushing the rubble from his hair.

"Hurry! Get out of the foyer," he yelled back before disappearing down a hall on the second floor—others in his group raced behind him.

The four stood frozen in the main entrance, trying to unravel the scene unfolding around them; Arianna could think of no way to describe it other than 'pandemonium.'

"*Stay close, Solza,*" she said, looking around in horror.

The quiet, pristine palace she'd first entered as Solomon's captive had exploded into a mess of loud, crackling noises and screams, the war for freedom swelling inside its gold-trimmed walls and rolling down the marble-plated halls.

"Let's go!" shouted Eli, waving everyone forward.

They all followed his lead, each using their magic to protect him and each other from the battle spells flying haphazardly about.

They kept getting caught in the crossfire of everyone else—Guardians of Gold versus Shadow Resistance, battling to the death more ferociously than ever before.

People were being pushed from balconies, landing on their feet or in piles. And opponents were slammed against walls so forcibly that the stone crumbled at their backs.

Both the wounded and the dead sprawled across lush carpets and tiled floors, hanging out of broken windows and over marble banisters; the residues of both dark and light magic smoked off their bodies—they were ripping each other apart.

"Which way do we go from here?" called Demetrius over all the commotion as he moved ahead of the group—he manipulated the limbs of a tree that had smashed into the palace to save a fellow guardian from her opponent's deadly strike. "Think anyone has made it near the King yet?"

A regulator tried to attack Arianna from behind; Jeom caught him by the neck, slamming him against the wall, ready to end him.

"How could anybody even get close to him when scum

like *this* keep getting in our way?" He squeezed tighter.

Demetrius quickly pulled out a pinch of sleeping powder and sprinkled it in the man's face.

Jeom rounded on his brother, anger flooding his eyes.

"Why'd you go on and do that now?" he barked, letting the regulator slide to the floor in a crumpled ball; he snoozed in the most unfortunate of places.

"We all have enough blood on our hands," he said, evenly. "You'll thank me later."

"Come on. More are coming!" said Eli, pointing to a gang of shadows who had set their sights on them from across the foyer. "Ara, can you tell which way we should go?"

They had gone over maps countless times before, but the palace had been flipped upside down. Nothing was as it seemed, so all they could really rely on was her actual experience, *that* and a little luck.

She knew where King Devlindor was waiting, but she wasn't ready to face him just yet. With the necromancer out of the picture, they needed to stick to the original plan and secure the entire palace first—leave no door unopened or corner unturned, and defeat the last of his royal guard.

Solomon must die.

She readied both her swords, unsure of what they'd find.

"Follow me!" she said, using the memory of her ethereal walk through the palace to guide her.

And from where they stood now, with all the damage to the main hall, the only safe direction to go was up…

They reached the velvet-lined staircase where they had spotted Noah earlier and carefully climbed.

When they came to the top, Arianna raced down a long, familiar hallway, summoned by a memory; the others blasted open all the doors along the way behind her, making sure the area was clear.

At the end of the hall, she paused in front of a circular

door. Serpents were engraved on it—once again, she found herself standing before the entrance to King Devlindor's sleeping quarters, though this time in the flesh.

She couldn't help but look inside. *Operium undrio!*

The door flew open with a bang. She cautiously walked forward, assessing the chamber from the doorway.

Across the firelit room, she saw that the terrace overlooking the garden was open. Gossamer curtains billowed ominously in the wind, like trapped ghosts, and everything about the room looked harshly unchanged… except for that the royal serpent's bed was empty.

She groaned in frustration, staring at the sheets where she'd seen him so restlessly sleep.

"If only I could've killed him sooner…" she muttered to herself. "Then Lessa would still be alive."

"Don't worry," said Eli, glancing toward her from the hall. "It's almost over—" There was a sharp intake of breath. "Ara, get down!"

He shoved her farther into the room, protecting her from a surprise attack of magic; the others were forced back down the hall, dodging the blasts.

Arianna looked up from the floor, spotting Jeom racing in an entirely different direction than the others, his axe raised, shouting at the top of his lungs; Demetrius followed at his heels, nature trailing behind him.

"Eli, you all right?" she called; he was left battling the sorceress who'd just attacked them, Solza focused on defending him with her elemental magic.

Arianna got to her feet and collected her weapons.

As she started toward Eli, someone moved into her peripheral vision, out of the shadows near the door.

"It's just you and me now, child," said a familiar voice.

Solomon Bell stepped into the light of the fire, twin swords in hand.

"Ara!" she heard Eli yell as he and Solza ran back toward the room.

Solomon was quicker.

He slammed the door shut, locking her friends out and reinforcing it with powerful magic so that not even an avatar could smash it open.

Arianna could hear Eli's muffled voice calling to her from the other side; he banged his fists against the door, but it wouldn't budge—she was trapped alone with the wolf.

"How did you know to find me here?" she said with a sneer, never letting her eyes off him.

"I know how you think," he replied, tutting at her. "Of course, your curiosity would lead you astray, even as the palace falls down around you. But you've wasted your time. You won't find the King here. This is *not* his true domain."

She gritted her teeth, barely able to see past her own rage. "I said I would kill you, and I truly meant it."

"Well, you're certainly going to have to in order to have any chance at the King," he replied. He gave a slight bow. "Shall we?"

Solomon twisted his swords in his palms, the blades glinting in the light of lanterns strung about the room.

"As you wish, *Master*," she said, barely able to pass the word between her lips.

She let out a scream and lunged forward with all her strength, all her fire. The wrath she felt over the loss of Lessa burned sharp in her chest, and she channeled every ounce of that pain into demanding the same fate for Solomon—a life for a life.

He blocked her first attack swiftly, then they began a deadly dance about the room… the last she hoped to ever do with him.

Neither of them used magic to begin; Arianna couldn't bring herself to throw the first blast, and Solomon's eyes never even twitched toward silver.

This was a sword-on-sword battle, and they both knew it, both fighting to determine the better warrior at long last.

Solomon had once told Arianna that she had bested him… for how else could she have obtained his swords? And Diveena had later confirmed that the priceless elven-made weapons were, in fact, rightfully hers.

Still, such affirmations had never been enough to satisfy her.

Arianna had always known that she had not fairly *won* the blades she wielded now—they had been a gift.

But tonight, she intended to earn them.

"You killed Lessa!" she said, finding her voice between attacks. "And Liam—their blood is on *your* hands."

Solomon expertly defended, but Arianna forced him back.

She threw all her strength, all her sorrow and rage, into each blow. "You killed Kassime, you killed Mother Adunni, *and* you're responsible for Cyn and Talis' deaths!"

She slashed one sword after the other as they battled around the chambers, forcing Solomon back, back, *back*— suddenly, they fell through the thick curtains, as if passing through an ethereal barrier to the outside.

"Now, it's your turn," hissed Arianna, never missing a step.

The fight continued in a whirl, back and forth, across the King's expansive balcony, metal twisting and slicing through the air, shrieking into the night each time their blades kissed.

She landed a jab at Solomon's side, and one of his swords clanked to the ground as he gasped—it was the first time Arianna had *ever* rid him of a weapon, had ever even drawn his blood.

She faltered, so shocked to see Solomon's blood on his blade. *My blade.*

"I do not control death," he said, using her lapse in

attention to return her attack; he sliced at her arm, the bronze sword biting into her skin. "I control *nothing*."

Arianna felt a searing pain as her skin ripped open, but it only enraged her more, *empowered* her more.

I'm doing this for all the lost guardians!

She swallowed back her tears and spun around, throwing her full weight at him as she sent a kick to his stomach; she was surprised he hadn't seen it coming.

Her boot met his middle and he buckled, stumbling backward into the banister—it split open.

Solomon yelled out as he teetered dangerously on the edge of the high balcony; he was forced to drop his other sword as he tried to regain balance.

And as the sound of his blade, her very first sword, clanged to the ground with that familiar ring of surrender, Arianna hesitated. She stared down at it in disbelief.

I finally did it. I finally won.

She realized he was about to plummet to his death—her first master, her former friend…

Her heartbeat quickened, beads of sweat rolling down her back. *I won't be like him.*

Against all that she ever thought she'd known about herself, she threw her swords to the ground and ran forward to try to help. She placed one hand onto the broken banister and used the other to grasp for the neck of his cloak—Solomon lurched backward, arms flailing, feet slipping.

Now, the only thing keeping him from falling was *her*, and she didn't think she could hold him up for much longer.

"Why, *why* did you choose me?" she cried as she clutched at his robes; she realized she was sobbing. "Tell me, Master! *Why?* How could you do all of this to me, to your friends?"

The cloth tore between her fingers, a chain ripping off his neck—it clanked to the floor at her feet.

Solomon let out a moan of relief, startling Arianna so

much that she let go; he grabbed her wrist, staring into her eyes. Suddenly, his eyes seemed so different, so full of life, just like before.

"Because… I love you, Arianna." Her heart nearly stopped as they both wavered on the edge of the terrace; a glowing smile, one just as genuine as those she had come to miss the most from her district days, was stretched across Solomon's face. "And *love* is a powerful thing," he said.

Her gaze flicked to the broken chain—its pendant a dark red ruby, with a sharp, jagged edge.

The banister snapped under their weight, and Solomon let go.

Arianna understood everything far too late as he slipped through her fingers. There was nothing she could do now but watch as her first master fell toward the ground, a bird without wings.

She squeezed her eyes shut just as Solomon landed with a sickening thud on the cobblestone path below, though not before the image of his regal robes, fanned out around him in a tangle of black and gold, was imprinted in her memories—the Wolf of the East was gone for good.

Her breath came ragged, her heartbeat the same; with shaky hands, she pulled Sir Vladamor's chain from her robe pocket.

She knelt down to examine its stone against Solomon's.

Please, don't be true…

The cracks in the rubies lined up seamlessly, a perfect match.

Silent tears rolled down her cheeks.

Solomon Bell was never against us at all.

Just like Sir Vladamor, he had been the King's puppet all along, though surely not of his free will.

Arianna gripped both rubies in her palm until she felt her skin break. She closed her eyes and let her fire come hot and unforgiving, forging the two halves back together as she screamed in grief.

When her throat ran dry, she peeled herself from the balcony floor and peered down—people had gathered around Solomon's body in disbelief, *fear*, Shadow Resistance and guardians alike.

He was a former friend and commander to both sides, a man with two faces, two lives, and his death had sent those below into an uproar; a new battle had ensued between the shadows fleeing the palace and the guardians fortifying the grounds, and it grew even wilder with the foreboding presence of the wolf's body.

Master Tayshin looked up, catching her eye. He stopped battling, reading the gravity of her expression.

Arianna raised her sword to the sky—*Solomon's* sword.

"He's one of us!" she cried down, tears swimming in her eyes. "He was one of us, all along. To the very end." She glowered down at the shadows. "He was a *slave* to the King all this time!"

A myriad of emotions seemed to cross Master Tayshin's face as her words floated down to them. Then, he and the other guardians threw all their energy into battling for Solomon's honor.

Arianna had to look away from the horrid scene, neither side knowing so truly what she'd only just learned…

Dark magic had evidently bound Solomon to the King's service. However, she guessed that Solomon had never had a *choice* in his actions, unlike the necromancer. The double life that he had lived—Guardian of Gold versus Wolf of the East and King's Guard—had at some point wholly consumed him.

Arianna backed away from the ledge.

She bowed her head, trying to steady her spinning thoughts. Her eyes were glued to a single spot on the balcony floor—a faint golden shimmer, a *smear*. She thought it could've been a worn splatter of paint, but there was no way to know.

She remained fixated on the dull spot of gold, thinking of her goal at hand, thinking of anything other than the searing aches of loss that threatened to tear her apart from the inside out.

Kill the King. Kill the King. Kill the King!

Arianna felt like she had been standing in the same position for hours, though only minutes could have passed.

Droplets of water started to draw her attention as they fell around the golden stain. She couldn't find the strength to even cry, so she knew it had to be rain.

Then, the thunder added its deafening drum to the battle.

She lifted her eyes to the sky just as it flickered with a sliver of lightning. She placed her hand on the dagger Solomon had gifted her long ago. She slipped it from her sheath… it boasted its own lightning streak at the center.

She gazed down at it just as more electricity burned across the night—it was then that she saw her destiny, strikingly clear.

The rain began to pour, soaking her to the skin.

She closed her eyes, savoring this moment of peace.

"*Helthra saludis emencia,*" she whispered, summoning the water's special healing properties as she let it cool her face and wash away some of the pain.

Lessa was gone. Solomon was gone. So many others… *gone.*

But their spirits still remained.

They all urged Arianna to finish this, for the sake of their memories and the futures of those who still lived.

The battle was nearing an end now, the thunder drowning out the final clashes of metal and magic throughout the night.

The dull pitter-patter of the rain cleansed the land's wounds, a fresh start just waiting to be exposed after the worst of this storm was over. And as Arianna took in the City of Saindora—all the way from the palace grounds to the sea— she found it calmer and quieter, the world ready for something new to arise with the morning sun.

24

CURSES AND VOWS

AN EXPLOSION FROM BEHIND drew Arianna's focus. She sheathed her dagger, collected her swords, and burst back into the room, ready to cut out the throat of anyone else who might try to stand in her way. But just as she lunged, her weapons already raised, she realized there was no threat at all.

"Eli," she stuttered as he, thankfully, sidestepped her attack. She sheathed her swords. "Sorry, I thought—"

He ran to her, hugging her into his chest.

"I thought *you* were dead," he said, seeming shaken. "Solza was finally able to break down the door…" Arianna knew it was because Solomon was gone, along with his magic. *His light.* "You all right? What happened?"

Eli squeezed her so tightly that she thought she might lose her breath; she didn't want him to let go.

She wrapped her arms around his neck, resting her head on his shoulder for only a moment.

"Nothing is all right." Her eyes flicked back to the balcony; the curtains still fluttered in the wind, between worlds. "Solomon is dead."

Eli pulled back, trying to read her expression—he didn't yet understand that this was no victory to be recorded.

He noted the new gash on her arm.

"You're hurt," he said, assessing the injury. "We should find you a healer." He looked toward the window. "I think it's starting to die down out there. We can get you some help outside."

Arianna shook her head, covering the wound with her hand just as Solza brushed up against her legs, purring; she knew she'd heard everything that had happened between her and her former master. *Friend...*

"I have to end this now. Solomon—" She couldn't push the truth from her lips. She pressed her forehead to his. "I have to end this, for all those who have lost their lives to the King."

"*You didn't know, Master,*" said Solza, gently. "*Nobody did. It was out of your control.*" Still, Arianna couldn't help but hate herself for not seeing through such a wicked trick.

"*I can't believe that Solomon was a prisoner all this time...*" she said, her heart constricting even more.

"I don't get it," said Eli, pushing a strand of hair from her eyes. "He killed Lessa." His brow furrowed. "Isn't this what you wanted? You *won*, Ara. And you're lucky to be alive." He tilted his head, staring at her intently. "What am I missing here?"

She looked away, recalling the advice from the ghost of Liam Black, long ago on her journey, the second time she'd died; he had urged her to stay dedicated to the goal at hand, to push aside any other distractions that might shift her focus from the King.

Arianna hadn't understood him then, but she did now.

"Solomon was not the enemy," she said, finally able to

voice the harsh reality. "He never was." Eli shook his head, disbelieving. "There's only *one* person to blame for Lessa... for any of this." *Never forget!* She peered up at him, wiping her eyes. "We have to kill Kyrone."

She pulled away from his hold, marching out of the King's bedroom with one final mission in her mind.

Eli and Solza followed her out into the hall.

"There you are!" called Jeom from much farther down. He was waving his axe in the air to get their attention. "What took you all so long? You have to come, *quick.*"

There was an urgency in his voice, and Arianna wasn't eager to find out what else had gone wrong. They rushed to meet him, passing by the grand staircase on the way.

She glanced down to the ravaged first floor just as a mismatched group of Moriamo protectors, drifters, and guardians ran back outside to join the final battles—there were no Shadow Resistance followers in sight, not in this part of the palace.

The main foyer had been all but destroyed, the doors to the outside world standing wide open, creaking in the wind. Fires burned here and there from magic gone awry, and bodies were strewn among the rubble; the only notable thing still intact was the two-story tall, stained-glass window that looked as if a portion of the sea had found its way onto the land.

Arianna had admired this on her first visit to the palace, pondering whether or not it might be enchanted. Now she knew with certainty, for the fact that it still stood, that it *must've* been touched by magic. *Old magic...*

The beautiful Hall of Maps came to mind, pushing aside some of her pain.

Magic will always find a way.

And things did seem a bit calmer now, the sounds of battle only seeping in from the courtyard or from distant places within the palace.

"I think we could really win this!" said Eli, his voice pitching in excitement as he took in the foyer alongside her. "Seems like we cleared most of the palace much faster than we calculated."

"We can't win until the King is dead," replied Arianna, drawn back to the task at hand. "That's the *only* way." Her mind drifted to the necromancer, to Solomon, knowing that there was still one more battle left. "And I'm sure no one has succeeded yet, or we'd know."

Eli laid his hand atop hers on the banister. "What really happened back there, Ara? You can tell me."

She was about to respond—about to confess that she'd killed her master in a duel when what he'd really needed was rescuing all long—when Jeom ran to meet them, huffing and puffing.

"Come *on*," he urged, grabbing Arianna by the wrist. "You need to hurry!"

He dragged her forward, but when she peered ahead, she didn't see Demetrius with him anymore. Her stomach twisted in knots as she considered that another member of her family may have been snatched from this world too soon.

"Where's your brother?" she asked, fearful for the answer; she forced him to stop. "He's not..."

"Gods, no!" said Jeom, letting go of her, walking briskly ahead. "You think I'd still be standing?"

Arianna felt her entire body sag in relief.

"Then what's the matter?" said Eli.

They had to jog to keep up with him.

"You just need to see this for yourself," he said, glancing at them from over his shoulder. "We found Princess Elisa..."

Just her name made Arianna recoil.

Princess Elisa Devlindor may have rescued her in the end, but she still supported the King in so many other horrendous deeds. And each time she'd fed and bathed her after her brother's countless torturous sessions, she had felt more humiliated than the last.

"What do you mean you *found* the Princess?" said Eli, balking. "Dead or alive?"

They all picked up the pace.

"Alive, in her chambers and surrounded by regulators. Another group of guardians flagged her to us. You'd think she was waiting for her supper or something..." Jeom frowned, using his axe like a walking staff. "Would you *believe* she was even drinking wine? Meanwhile, the sky is falling down around her!"

"*So...* you killed her, then?" asked Eli; he and Arianna shared an anxious glance.

Jeom shook his head. "We captured her." He rolled his eyes. "You know Demetrius," he said with a whine. "He won't let me use my axe for anything!"

Arianna gaped at him. "Are you saying that you left your brother *alone* with a Devlindor?"

"Yeah... but don't worry," he said, raising an eyebrow. "He's so powerful now, and he's not alone. He's with Noah."

Arianna was sure she'd lost all the color in her face—she'd been around Princess Elisa enough times to know that she was just as practiced as the King in both magic and weapon.

There was no way the two of them could hold her, even with all the powers Demetrius had attained from Diveena... he just wasn't that experienced yet.

"We have to help them!" said Arianna, switching back to her warrior mindset. "Where is she?"

"Down that way," said Jeom, gesturing up the hall. "There's another stairwell a bit farther back. We found her in her chambers on the first floor, near some gardens, but—"

Before he could finish his sentence, Arianna had dashed off, allowing her memory to guide her to Princess Elisa's wing of the palace.

She skidded to a halt at the stone archway; the embroidered silver door, one engraved with flowers and vines—like the entryway to a secret garden—had been flung wide open.

Arianna peered from the doorway, a bit staggered to be back in this lavish hallway again; it had always felt like leaving the palace altogether, nothing like anywhere else within these walls. She remembered it like the back of her hand, decorated from the top to the bottom with the finest flourishes one could dream up and charmed with so much Golden Age splendor.

What she looked upon now was barely a remnant of that.

The essence of Princess Elisa was still there, but the statues of lovers and sorcerers Arianna had before admired were nothing but piles of rubble at her feet, and the long, pastel draperies had fallen to the floor in tangles. The portraits of mysterious lands hung at odd angles on the walls, mostly ripped to shreds, and her Golden Age collection of knickknacks and ornaments was scattered like trash among the debris.

What's more, regulators lined the carpeted floors from the entrance of the hall all the way to the Princess's bedroom—all looked very dead.

She hesitated to step a foot inside, lest she end up like them…

The adjacent gardens appeared to have broken into the palace to join the fight, the windows of this gallery completely shattered as vines and tree limbs forced their way inside; the nature still pulsated with life, twisting ominously along the floor, smothering the ill-fated regulators who had tried to protect the King's sister.

Solza, Jeom, and Eli caught up to her quickly.

"Watch where you step," said Jeom, eying the plants with caution. "But we should be fine. Follow me."

He guided them inside.

"Looks like we sure missed a party," mumbled Eli, kicking at the head of a broken sculpture.

"You're saying… Demetrius did all this?" asked Arianna. "He killed all these people?"

"They're not dead, just sleeping," said Jeom, shaking his head. "He pinned them down, then I used air magic to suck the oxygen out of the room until they fell unconscious."

She exhaled in relief, counting the soldiers—there were at least a hundred in this hall alone. She was glad that they hadn't been added to the mounting death toll, even if they fought for the wrong side.

Limp swords still poked out from under the thick, unmovable vines.

Jeom twisted his axe in hand, a pout on his face.

"I'm telling you, he won't let me do a *thing*," he huffed under his breath. "I sent the other guardians who were here away to help out elsewhere, since, as you can see, they weren't really needed…"

He grunted in annoyance, and she wondered how long he would last without breaking down about Lessa again.

How long will I last?

Her eyes found a face among the rubble that she surely recognized—Regulator Roland stared up at her with deadened eyes, magic smoking off his body and a deep gash at his side.

"*You'll last until the King looks just like that,*" said Solza.

Arianna nodded, not letting herself get sucked back into memories of her horrid dungeon days.

"This one put up a nasty fight," said Jeom, following her gaze. "He's the only one that tasted steel." He used his cloak to wipe the blood from his blade, not a hint of remorse in his voice.

Arianna continued on, not wishing to consider him a second longer. "Pity I wasn't part of it."

"What happened to you lot back there anyhow? We lost you," said Jeom, falling in step with her. "Why didn't you follow?" His expression was twisted with emotion, anxious. "We need to try to stick together. We're nearing the end."

"Solomon attacked me," she said, gravely, averting her gaze.

Jeom blanched.

"He *what?*" She could feel the air magic beginning to swirl around him, his grief resurfacing again. "I'll kill him! I'll *slaughter* him for what he did to Lessa." He slammed the butt of his axe down, the tile shrieking in response. "Where is he?"

Arianna grabbed his hand to try to calm him; he was shaking, his expression violent.

"Nothing is as it seems, Jeom," she said, softly, her eyes watering. "But you needn't worry. Solomon is dead."

He relaxed, the air fizzling away.

"Oh," was all he said.

Before he could inquire further, they had reached the entrance to Princess Elisa's bedroom.

Arianna used her magic to blow open the door, preparing for battle; Solza let out a roar to announce them.

But there was none to be fought…

Noah greeted them from across the room, a haughty smile on his face as he registered Arianna's shock. "Surprised I'm still alive, are you?"

He looked tired and beaten, but he was still standing and forever cheerful—even as he held his axe to the Princess's throat.

She was seated on her canopy bed, arms and legs bound to the poles on either side by long vines, head bowed and silvery-white hair hanging long over her face. Her tiara was still fixed on her properly, but Arianna's friends had had the good sense to at least remove her favored weapon; her leather lash was strewn across the pale pink carpets in the middle of the room.

Jillian, her attendant, was there too, hunched over on a sofa and seemingly fast asleep.

Arianna chewed on her lip as she took in the scene.

"Well… this is not what I was expecting."

"See, I *knew* it!" said Noah, waving his free hand in the air. "Always with the doubt. Yet, I have one Devlindor, and you have *no* Devlindors. I think that means I'm winning."

He puffed out his chest.

"It's not a contest," muttered Jeom. "Keep steady on that axe."

Noah straightened, concentrating on the Princess.

"I'm a little *confused*," said Eli, scratching his head.

"You and me both," said Arianna, not sure what to do.

They moved farther inside the dome-shaped chamber.

She thought this was probably the only part of the palace that didn't look overrun by death and destruction—it was just as bright and cheery as the first day she'd laid eyes on it.

The tall, lace-lined windows were shut and locked, so they couldn't hear the battle. And the gentle hues of every piece of décor, including the dazzling gem-studded chandelier, made it seem as if it were sunny outside.

Arianna glanced to the wall-length canvas of Saindora. *We're going to bring you back.*

"Noah didn't do anything either," mumbled Jeom, leaning into Arianna. "It was all Demetrius—"

"I *heard* that," he snapped, though he didn't dispute it.

They all looked to Demetrius then.

He was seated in a chair, facing the Princess in front of the bed. He didn't speak a word to acknowledge that they were there, and when Arianna leaned over to greet him, she could tell he was concentrating very hard, his eyes clasped shut.

He appeared to be fully immersed in his elven mind, the vines from the hall continuing to wriggle with life as they slithered through the room, binding their hostage tightly to the bed.

It appeared that Princess Elisa couldn't move at all—*that* or she wasn't even trying.

"What should we do with her?" asked Demetrius, surely feeling her gaze; he opened his eyes, and they shone like silver balls of light. "Do you want me to kill her?"

Arianna was struck speechless to hear this out of his mouth.

He had always been so against killing when it could be avoided, yet it was clear he would make an exception for a Devlindor…

She didn't readily respond; Demetrius let the vines squeeze tighter at the Princess's life.

Princess Elisa couldn't speak, her mouth and neck completely covered, but she lifted her head and looked straight at Arianna—a startling emerald gaze bore into hers.

"No, not yet," said Arianna, holding up her hand. "She… saved me, remember? Let's at least see what she has to say first."

Demetrius gave a small sigh of relief, letting some of the vines fall away. As the pressure was released, the Princess leaned forward, gasping for air.

Arianna unsheathed one of her swords and walked closer.

"I was wondering when we'd meet again," said the Princess, glaring toward her; her voice was raspy, and stripes of bright red skin lined her throat from where Demetrius had left his mark. "You wasted no time in returning for your revenge."

"It's not revenge that I seek," she replied. "Not anymore."

"What is it that you're searching for, then?" she asked, tilting her head so that Arianna saw her own reflection gleaming back at her in the silver tiara.

"I seek your brother," she snapped, twisting her sword in her palm. She stepped closer. "For a fair fight at freedom."

Princess Elisa's eyes flicked to her weapon and back. "Where is Solomon?" Her words flew out like a reflex. "Have you seen him out there?" She looked toward the door, lowering her voice. "He was supposed to be here by now."

Arianna pursed her lips, tired of repeating herself. Tired of thinking of him, of how she had *finally* earned these blades in her hands.

It was all for nothing. Just another wasted life.

"Solomon… is dead," she said, flatly. "He won't be coming to save you."

Demetrius' eyes widened in shock, quite like the Princess's.

Her cool façade seemed to crack, her expression incredulous, eyes narrow. "You lie—" Her voice splintered.

Arianna shook her head, then she realized who she was talking to…

How many truths had Princess Elisa helped to bury so that she could keep that crown on her head? And had she even played a part in shackling dear Solomon to the dark?

An inkling told her 'yes,' for they had always been not far apart from one another during her captivity. And she was aware of their history as clandestine lovers.

Had that been of his own free will?

"*The Devlindors don't believe in free will,*" spoke Solza.

Arianna stepped closer. "I would never *lie* to you," she said—her blade itched for blood.

Princess Elisa seemed to grow disconcerted, forgetting her situation. "How?" she demanded, the emotion rising in her voice.

Arianna felt herself obliged to respond, the Princess so authoritative even now.

"He fell," she said, "from the King's bedroom terrace after a duel… with me."

She slipped out the warped ruby and set it on the nearest table so she could see. *See that I know the truth.*

A gasp caught in her throat. Her eyes lingered on the stone, a single tear rolling down her cheek.

"I loved him, you know?" she finally said, head bowed.

"I've loved him since the day he came into our lives." She peered up at Arianna, a serious expression on her face. Her voice was firm, almost resentful. "And he *always* loved you, even with the King controlling his soul all this time."

"I knew it," said Arianna. Her rage ripped through her again. She slashed her sword through the air at her side and the boys gave her a wide berth. "So, it's true then!"

Hearing of Solomon's appalling fate as fact from the mouth of a Devlindor made it all the more horribly real.

"What does she mean, Ara?" asked Demetrius, looking between them, bewildered. "What's true?"

Eli caught his attention, shaking his head in warning; Jeom appeared indifferent, still not understanding her grief; Noah just shrugged, still holding the axe, no clue of what had transpired.

Princess Elisa composed herself, fixated on Arianna, her jaw set. "Solomon had been so near death the day he helped you escape the Four Corners, but—"

"But *what?*" she demanded, lunging forward.

She swiped her sword at her shoulder, the Princess's garments ripping, red blood streaking her porcelain skin.

The Princess let out a small cry, but quickly reined it back in—the Devlindors were practiced in many realms of pain, it would seem.

Arianna slid the tip of her sword under her chin so that she was forced to look at her, her breath hitched in her throat; Noah stood back.

"But, what?" she asked again, her patience slipping.

Princess Elisa's lips turned downward. "He lived."

She felt her palms grow sweaty, her sword hand trembling. She didn't understand, and wasn't sure that she wanted to.

She didn't *want* to know the horrible details about what Solomon had been forced to endure in the King's captivity…

Because of me. It's all because of me! And I still don't

understand, why…

"*Because he loved you,*" said Solza, coming to her aid. "*He clearly did. He told you so.*"

"*But why?*" her thoughts screamed back.

For this, her wise young avatar did not have an answer.

The Princess continued. "Alas, the King recognized his treachery right away. He's no fool, and the trace of one's magic is potent. He knew that Solomon had betrayed him in helping someone escape… you." *Me.*

She lowered her sword, utterly defeated with this knowledge.

"Why didn't the King just let him die?" she asked, her curiosity to know more overcoming her hatred for the Princess. "Why not just kill Solomon, then, if he was so sure of his treason?"

Princess Elisa let out a little laugh, still so poised even in restraints.

"Child, King Devlindor has never been known to be forgiving," she said, shooting Arianna a glance as if to say 'you should know better'; she did. "Killing Solomon would have been a *kindness* after all he'd discovered about him."

Arianna rocked back and forth on her feet, trying to quiet her rampant heart. "What do you—"

"His entire disguise unraveled into nothing after he saved you, years of work, *gone.*" Arianna flinched. "He found out what he was," said the Princess, coolly, holding her gaze. "To let him die with honor in the eyes of the Guardians of Gold?" She scoffed, shaking her head, silver hair glinting in the chandelier light. "That was never an option."

Noah's mouth fell open, clearly catching on. "You mean Solomon was never…" Eli nodded; the axe fell limp in his hand.

Jeom's mouth formed an 'O', and Demetrius just bowed his head, some more of the vines loosening.

Arianna didn't have the heart to respond, but Princess Elisa did.

"Solomon was the King's most prized slave," she answered, glancing to Noah; her eyes flicked to his blade. "He was much too valuable to kill. Maybe even more so than you, Arianna." She glowered in her direction; Arianna averted her eyes. "The greatest punishment the King could devise was to force him to be a loyal servant to the Crown, to the Shadow Resistance. Forever, or until death, compelled to abide by his wishes, and *always* against his will."

"So all this time—" said Jeom, piecing the story together.

"He was under a spell," finished Demetrius.

Arianna took slow, deep breaths, her hand pressed upon her temple as she listened to Princess Elisa's version of the story that painted Solomon as a martyr, a hero. She loathed herself for ever thinking that he had turned his back on them when, in fact, it had been the other way around—the Guardians of Gold had shut him out at a time when he'd needed them most.

"Sir Vladamor held tightly to Solomon's soul with his dark magic so that it would not cross over into the safety of Death's arms," added the Princess. "And once he was well enough again, the King split the curse which bound the necromancer to his servitude *with* Solomon." A shadow fell across her expression, and Arianna thought she appeared truly regretful. "He never had a choice in any of his doings. No one could fight such magic alone."

They locked stares.

"Even with the necromancer gone, the King still had his grip on him." She looked away. "But even still, I believe his love for you remained… somewhere deep down, throughout all of it."

Every moment with Solomon since they first parted at the Vanishing Tunnels pushed into Arianna's mind—it all looked so different now as the Princess's words settled with her.

A man so near death would have been absolutely vulnerable to the necromancer's curse. And Arianna had seen what Sir Vladamor could do once he had a soul in his clutches…

She'd witnessed ghosts and even just the memories of flesh and bone turn to slaves at his bidding. Mermaids risen from nothing but dust, sculpted into monsters who served only him—Solomon Bell, fatally wounded and trying to hold off a swarm of district regulators all on his own, would've been an easy target to capture.

"But he hadn't been easy to hold…" said Arianna, suddenly grasping something the Princess had said. "He *struggled* against the necromancy, didn't he?"

She thought back to their first reunion in South Luose, trying to find some redemption for him there; Solomon had murdered Liam in cold blood and ended Keeper Kassime's life, but when Arianna had fled from his attacks in the Luose palace attic, he had not followed. What's more, Lessa had previously mentioned that she'd found their enchanted attic still intact when they had retaken the city.

Yes, he could have easily destroyed it, she thought.

They had crossed paths again in the Four Corners, yet he had not slain her when he'd had the opportunity. He could have taken her to the King as a corpse but… *Instead, he took me as a prisoner.*

Finally, on the long journey to Saindora, *somehow* Arianna had ended up with a fighting chance, slipping out of his grasp once again before meeting the King.

"Nothing was by chance," she whispered, contemplating the warped ruby.

The Princess followed her gaze.

"That stone is one of the most dangerous black magic conduits that exist, to my knowledge, now that it's been so tampered with," said the Princess, something of fear in her expression. "Solomon may not have had chains on his ankles, but the chain around his neck enslaved him just the same. He resisted always, but the darkness ate away at him day by day." She nodded to herself. "For the guardians, though, he did *try* to fight it."

"I'll destroy it," growled Arianna, staring at it, intently—she wondered how such a beautiful thing could breed such wickedness.

Princess Elisa shook her head.

"You cannot," she replied. "Elf magic and darkness is deep-rooted in that stone now. Its poisonous magic would only be released into the world, and there's no telling what it would do. You know this… magic has a mind all its own." Arianna bristled, thinking of all the lost masters who had taught her this crucial lesson. "This is a combination of King Devlindor's power and a *necromancer's* curse, trapped in an elven-made bottle." She snorted, practically rolling her eyes. "I suggest you hold on to it for safekeeping."

"Better listen to her on that one," said Demetrius, eyeing the stone, warily.

Arianna returned a curt nod, signaling to Jeom who slipped it safely into his pocket; she would heed the warning.

"You should hide it," added the Princess. "Bury that magic deep where it can never be found again." She chewed on her lip as she thought. "Regrettably, though, there's still one more left… one which never leaves the King's hand."

Arianna cocked her head to the side, considering her with more focus now that Solomon's story had wound to an end—she was growing tired of this conversation. *Games… a distraction.*

"Just like you, Princess, for the last three centuries," she said, walking back over to her. She knelt down so she could look her in the eye. "Your bloodline should not even be allowed to *exist* anymore for all the evil you've created," her voice came softly, like the gentle kiss of death she hoped to deliver soon with her sword, "so give me one good reason not to kill you right now."

She leaned forward.

"And I don't *care* if you rescued me before… but because you did, I'll allow you one," she held up a finger, "chance to plead for your life."

Princess Elisa was unblinking, her confidence steadfast.

"I don't know if there's any reason good enough to offer salvation for my crimes, or the crimes of my brother," she replied, evenly, "but the King is not my only blood. Would you go so far as to eradicate *every* Devlindor in this world, even if they were innocent of our crimes?"

Arianna hesitated, glancing to the boys; they appeared just as puzzled by her words.

"What do you mean?" she asked, turning back to her. "Be straight with it, or I swear this will be the last riddle you will ever speak."

"So be it," she retorted, her eyes shining fiercely. "Didn't you ever wonder why Solomon, the greatest swordsman of the present day, would choose you, a slave of nothing… no skill, no merit, *nothing*, to be his apprentice not only in battle but in *magic?*"

Arianna froze, eyes wide. *Yes, but how could she know that?*

She faintly considered Odessa, wondering…

The Princess smirked, her voice as steady as a pointed sword. "Like I said, Arianna, he always loved you, from the moment he laid eyes on you." She leaned forward, pulling against her restraints. "That moment was *not* in the Four Corners."

Arianna stood, glowering down at her, sword ready at her side. "What in the gods' names do you *mean?*" she said through her teeth, forcibly rejecting the only explanation that fell into her mind.

The Princess merely smiled, as if waiting for her to draw the conclusion herself.

Arianna lunged, not willing to listen to another word of this. "All you Devlindors ever do is lie!"

Princess Elisa's eyes shot to silver, and Arianna stumbled backward, only having time enough to create a barrier in front of her and Noah; a powerful electrified force bloomed around the bed, colliding with her magic.

She and Noah flew backward, smashing against the far wall, and the vines strapping the Princess down fell to the ground in ashes.

Demetrius jumped up from his chair, startled out of his trance. "What happened?"

He looked to his hands in bewilderment, trying to regain control.

Arianna got to her feet, pulling her magic with her.

"*Master, do you need me?*" said Solza, a growl building in her throat.

"*No, she's mine!*"

She ran to meet her in the middle of the room just as she stood from the bed; the Princess looked as regal as ever, re-laxed, *even* with Arianna's elven-made steel pointed again at her throat.

Eli ran to help Noah, and Jeom pulled Demetrius a safe distance away; Solza remained at the ready.

The Princess took a small step forward, meeting her challenge without arms, letting her magical defenses fall; Arianna hesitated.

"Solomon met you the first day you were born," she said, resolutely.

Arianna felt her entire world tremble, then she realized her magic was making the earth shake beneath their feet; the boys clung to pillars or furniture to steady themselves.

"And I placed you in his arms, right in this very room," she added, as if it were the most natural thing to say; the words fell heavy to Arianna's ears, like a stone in her stomach.

The Princess opened up her palms, exposing her chest, her heart. *My sword. Solomon's sword…* She directed it there.

"You are his, *and* you are mine."

"*Lies!*" screamed Arianna, spit flying from her mouth; her magic pulsated all the way down to the edge of her sword, tears of anger streaking her face.

I could end her. I could end these lies!

"*Master, wait…*" She pushed Solza away, but she felt her calm the tremors.

"My brother *tore* you from my arms," said the Princess, stepping forward. "Just like every other baby in this world—" Arianna shook her head; her voice grew stronger, more un-yielding "—he fated you to the Opalls to be raised into slav-ery… *Twenty-Two.*"

"No…" she said, barely audible.

Princess Elisa pointed an accusatory finger at her; Arianna took a step back, not lowering her weapon.

"It's only by *luck* that he didn't kill you before your first breath, girl." She sighed. "Even monsters have their limits."

Arianna felt as if she would never breathe again.

"But he spared you…" The Princess averted her gaze.

I could strike her dead now, so that she can never look at me again. But her blade wouldn't listen, her body numbed by this poison the Princess spilled from her mouth. *Lies… just like the King!*

"*Not lies, Master, listen.*"

"I couldn't bear for my only child to face this cruel world alone, so I begged Solomon to follow you," she continued. "The King thought him loyal for a long time, even though I had learned of his secret…" She frowned, shaking her head. "A spy for the guardians—"

Arianna heard Jeom mutter, "*How?*"

Princess Elisa had become impassioned by her confession, hardly seeming to notice Arianna, nor any of the others, anymore.

"But I loved him anyways." Her shoulders sagged. "And mostly, I have always *hated* Kyrone," she added.

She took a deep breath, as if the memory exhausted her.

"Eventually, the King granted Solomon's wish to retire to the Four Corners as a master trainer, and there he found you. The rest is... *well...*" They gazed at each other, Arianna and the Princess; she lowered her weapon. "Now you understand why I rescued you that night from the dungeons, despite the punishment awaiting me—"

She unbuttoned her shirt and turned around so that Arianna could see the deep scars on her flesh.

Demetrius gasped from behind. "By gods..."

Arianna couldn't help but weakly wonder if they were all so new, or if some hadn't been earned long before her time.

"I'm surprised he let you live," she found herself saying.

The Princess frowned, covering herself back up. "He always does." She sounded almost disappointed.

She looked deep into Arianna's eyes now, uncomfortably deep; she squirmed.

"I *just...*" She cleared her throat, lowering her gaze. "I just couldn't tolerate the thought of *my* blood being tortured for eternity by my ghastly brother."

The Princess shrugged with the finality of her story, and Arianna felt as if she'd been stabbed in the heart.

"*Breathe,*" Solza whispered.

She couldn't think straight. *My blood? Her brother? Solomon? The King? Her... the Princess?*

"*I can't—*"

She stumbled backward, feeling faint, but Eli was there to catch her.

"Does he know who she is?" he asked, his panicked voice drawing Arianna out of her daze; she steadied herself by his side, sheathing her sword—he unsheathed his. "Does the King know Arianna is of his blood?"

The hair on her skin rose. *Of the King's blood?*

"No, he does not," she said, crisply. "I think he's forgotten that it happened. And even if he does remember that ill-fated birth, he still has yet to uncover my, well, former relationship with Solomon." She looked away. "My brother can be brutal, but not always the brightest. I often take lovers." Arianna heard Jeom gag. "Besides, if he *had* ever put together the puzzle of my and Solomon's loyalty to this little slave girl from the Warrior's District," she gestured to Arianna, "it would only be more of a reason for him to kill you."

She let out a cynical laugh, covering her mouth with her hand. "But I suppose it matters not. You've given him reason enough."

Arianna opened her mouth to respond, but no words came out; Solza had also gone utterly quiet.

She looked to Eli for any reassurance but didn't find it there. In fact, all of her friends were gazing at her with the same stunned expression that was surely plastered across her own face.

She swallowed, her throat bone dry.

"It can't be true," she finally said.

Princess Elisa merely blinked back at her, not even bothering to acknowledge such a statement.

"My brother could never bring himself to kill me," she said, walking up to her. "I'm all that he has. Still, I can assure you, I am *no* exception to the King's law." She pushed the hair from her face. "You will have to decide for yourself if this is reason enough to spare me, for I do not deny all the horrors I've partaken in—"

She came closer, so close now that Arianna could look

nowhere but straight into her bright green eyes.

"Devlindor *is* my name, but you must understand… it is also, rightfully, yours."

Each word felt like a chisel to her gravestone. Arianna wanted to look away but couldn't. "I—"

"To help keep you safe, Solomon and I combined our surnames to give to you… Miss *Belvedor.*" She grinned, as if still satisfied with the choice. "Arianna was the name of my mother. Though, I doubt Kyrone even remembers her now." She scoffed.

Eli jumped back from Arianna as if she were on fire. "I don't believe this…"

Noah looked dizzied, mouth agape, looking between everyone.

"Solomon Bell," stuttered Jeom, hand to his head, "and Elisa Devlindor? Bell… *and* Devlindor?" His mouth fell open too.

"Ara," said Demetrius, "by the King's law, that would make you…" he ran his hand through his hair, "a *royal* by birth."

At this, Arianna seemed to snap out of her stupor.

"Real power is earned," she retorted, squeezing Solomon's sword. "Not granted as a birthright." She pushed Princess Elisa away. "Besides, we no longer recognize the King's law."

"I couldn't agree more," said the Princess, carefully. She stood back. "Neither I nor my brother deserve our titles. We've dishonored our family name."

"The world," mumbled Noah, crossing his arms at his chest.

Princess Elisa suddenly removed the tiara from her head and set it aside.

There was an intake of breath from the boys; Arianna just stared, feeling her anger rise.

"I saved you," she said, quietly. "I helped you escape. I'm

hardly looking to fight you, Arianna. I surrender." The Princess held out her hands, the silver magic fully fleeing from her eyes. "I've done enough fighting to last me a lifetime. If that lifetime must end now, then end it shall." She inhaled, deeply. "The decision is yours."

Arianna reached for the hilt of her sword; Eli and the others scooted closer to each other, everyone afraid to move or speak.

"*Remember, Master,*" Solza said, "*blood or not, you're no Devlindor.*"

Arianna held the Princess's fate in her hands, and if she was even going to consider sparing her life, she wanted some kind of proof of this outlandish story; it struck her then that she carried the evidence in her own memories…

Her balance nearly escaped her as she traveled to the past—one where Apprentice Aridyn had had all the control.

Keeper Kassime had once explained that in order to create the illusion for Arianna and her friends to have different appearances to the public, the potion they consumed would manifest a new identity *based* on each of their unique dormant traits; as she recalled the face of Aridyn now, she saw an undeniable likeness to that of Princess Elisa—fair features and all.

"Arianna?" asked Eli, gently, drawing her out of a spiral into her past. "What do you want to do? We have to decide now. We can't stay here."

She gritted her teeth, then she released the grip on her sword.

"Let's not follow in the footsteps of the King," she said, trying to steady her mind. "After all, she is my… mother."

The boys were utterly speechless.

"You believe her, then?" asked Demetrius after a moment; he glared at the Princess. "It could be a trick."

"It's not a trick," said Arianna, weary, unable to even look at them.

"How can you be certain?" said Jeom. He squared his shoulders, leveling his axe toward the Princess. "If you have an issue killing her, I'm happy to—"

"Apprentice Aridyn Lareigh." She sighed, meeting their eyes; she adored them so much, protective of her till the end. "Don't you remember her?"

"Aridyn, but—" Jeom's eyes widened as his own memories caught up; Demetrius pressed his lips together in understanding.

"She has to be my mother," she said again, the word sounding so strange.

She looked to the ceiling, trying to think of what to do next.

"We'll take her… as prisoner," she said, nodding.

"And what about that one?" asked Noah, pointing his axe at Jillian; she still slept soundly on the sofa.

"Her too," said Arianna, without hesitation. "She was kind to me before, but *don't* let her age fool you. They will both need strong magical restraints."

Arianna noticed the Princess relax a little, knowing she wasn't going to die today.

"If you're sure," said Demetrius.

"I'm sure," she said, decisively. "Let's find Master Tayshin. He'll know how to handle this."

"Gladly, Ara," said Eli, stepping up to do the honors.

He grabbed a handful of sleeping powder from his belt and blew it in the Princess's face.

Princess Elisa grinned, purposefully sucking in a big gulp of the smoky air; Demetrius then spelled the vines to restrain her again, tying her hands behind her back; Noah used his magic to levitate Jillian above them.

They were ready to escort the royal and her attendant outside.

"Now all that remains is to coax the King out from

hiding," said Arianna, determination in her heart.

Princess Elisa chuckled, the sleeping powder already taking effect. "King Devlindor never hides," she replied. "You know this. He's waiting for you, surely… to kneel."

Arianna felt her lips curl into a sneer. "Then he shall wait forever," she said, standing up straighter.

Eli looked down at her, his expression somber. "It's time…" he said.

She returned a curt nod.

The Princess began to wobble, her eyes drooping heavily.

"Be careful," she said. "Don't you understand now? If you fight him, you'll die… it's destined." She swayed, dangerously.

"*What?*" said Arianna, taken aback.

Princess Elisa tried, unsuccessfully, to focus.

"It's the Golden Rule," she slurred. "Blood relatives, fighting… such opposite sides. You and Kyrone are probably more linked to the prophecy than any other beings alive today."

The Princess collapsed, and Jeom caught her in his arms.

"Take her to Master Tayshin and the others," Arianna ordered to Jeom. "Get her somewhere where she cannot escape again."

"But what was that?" said Noah, looking worried. "What does she mean that you'll die?"

Arianna waved him off. "I'm not going anywhere."

She tried to offer a reassuring smile, but inside she knew.

It's the Golden Rule.

"But are you coming with us?" he asked.

She was silent; Noah recoiled.

"Ara…" said Demetrius, eyeing her warily. "We should discuss this—"

"Don't," she said, trying to laugh it off; the boys weren't buying it. "Everything will be fine. I think… I think I know what needs to be done now."

"I don't understand what's going on," said Jeom, hoisting the Princess over his shoulder.

Demetrius rushed over to him in a panic. "We've been staring at the Golden Rule for years now. Recite it!"

"Light is light and dark is dark, but never shall they live apart," said Jeom in a bored voice. He pouted. "I don't—"

"That's not all of it," said Arianna with a knowing sigh.

She recalled the first moment she had read the full scripture—the day they had escaped the Four Corners. And since that day, she'd always carried the words in her heart:

Light is light and dark is dark,
but never shall they live apart.
One shall seek what the other denies.
If it is found, thus follows the demise.
When one eclipses over the other,
life shall end for he and his brother.

"I still don't understand," Jeom said, huffing

Noah scratched his head. "Yeah—"

"She's a *blood* relative of the King," said Eli, abruptly.

Arianna could tell he'd grown agitated. "*Eli…*"

"That's how she was able to break Lessa's glass cage," he added, his voice rising, "because she's a damn Devlindor!" His cheeks burned red with understanding; he bowed his head. "The Golden Rule, the prophecy, is one of balance. If they can't both *exist* together, then—" His voice cracked.

Demetrius, Jeom, and Noah all looked to her.

"If I kill the King… knowing what we know now, I suppose it's possible that I may also die," said Arianna, stating the words so factually that she almost accepted them.

"Well, that's just not part of the plan!" said Noah, looking at her incredulously. "We said we'd fight him together, so… so you don't even have to be there, Ara." He looked to the others. "We'll go. You stay." Even as he said the words, she could tell he knew they were empty.

Eli pressed his hand to his forehead, breathing hard, and Demetrius and Jeom were speechless.

Noah was rambling. "Or maybe, we can find Master Tayshin and—" He threw his hands up. "Someone could've already killed him for all we know!"

Arianna shook her head, somehow certain *she* would know.

"It's all so clear now," she said, placing a hand on his shoulder. "Fate has led me right where I'm supposed to be, given me every possible tool in order to help me stand an even chance against… my blood."

Arianna felt the weight of her dagger, firm against her thigh; her swords, sure at her back; her powerful magic, finally within reach; and Solza…

"*Ready to fight,*" she purred.

She cleared her throat, garnering the attention of the boys.

"When the time comes, it seems that Destiny may yet demand one last sacrifice for us to triumph," she stated, holding her head high. "And I think I have to do this alone."

"Why would he even try to kill you in the first place though?" asked Jeom, growing desperate for answers. "He's known the prophecy all along!"

"Because he doesn't understand it," said Arianna, piecing her own thoughts together. "He's never really understood its meaning, and he *definitely* doesn't realize that I'm his sister's child that he spared long ago." Eli was shaking a fist at Princess Elisa. "If he did, I would already be dead, regardless of this prophecy."

She glanced to the sleeping beauty.

"Solomon, he knew all along," she said with a heavy heart. "This is what he trained me for… why he *chose* me."

"Just in case?" muttered Eli, arms crossed at his chest.

She nodded. "Just in case…"

And Master Bell was never wrong.

She felt herself grow cold.

"In setting me free, he sacrificed his soul to the darkness," added Arianna. "I must honor his memory." She contemplated the dragon mark on her palm. "We made a vow to protect the Olleb and its magic. *This* is the Golden Rule we pledge to. This is why we fight." She balled her hand into a fist, looking up. "If I must die so that you all can live, then so be it. I made that decision long ago, and I'm not going to change it now."

Jeom walked up to her, towering above her, taller than he'd ever been, a princess across his shoulder.

"Are you sure we can't change your mind? Are you sure you want to do this al—"

"*Positive*," she said. She was afraid if he asked one more time, she might very well not go through with it.

"You're strong," he said, averting his gaze; she could still see his eyes swimming with tears. "You're a warrior. You'll survive. This isn't goodbye." He shook his head. "I know it's not. I won't lose another—" His voice splintered. "I *know* it's not goodbye."

"I hope not," she whispered, hugging him around the waist.

He sniffled, turning away so that she couldn't see him cry.

"Will you be all right?" said Demetrius, resigned to her decision; Arianna just shrugged.

He grasped her hand and squeezed.

"I will see you again," he said, offering her the most encouraging smile he could muster. "And remember, *no* sacrifices." He managed a heartwarming wink.

She tried to memorize his face like this, knowing she would need Demetrius-like reinforcement soon enough.

For his sake and hers, she held her tongue when she

thought, *But this isn't a whim...*

Noah ran to her, throwing his arms around her with a sob.

"*Please*, Ara, don't leave us," he moaned. "We can find another way."

"There is no other way," she said, sternly, peeling his arms back, then she wiped his teary eyes with the back of her sleeve.

He tried to smile, but he just couldn't.

"It's all going to be fine," she said, smiling for him. "Go now... all of you. Get to safety outside of these walls."

Noah bowed his head, joining the Kane brothers.

Reluctantly, Jeom led the way out of the room with Princess Elisa in his arms. Demetrius and Noah followed, Jillian floating eerily behind their procession; Solza nudged them all in the legs as they passed through the doorway.

Each one of her boys looked back before they disappeared from sight... each one surely silently praying to see her again just as strongly as she prayed the same.

Eli hadn't budged.

"You should go with them," she said to Eli when they were alone; he had been quiet for some time, standing near the bed. "The others may need your help in these last throes of battle."

"I'm not going anywhere," he said, firmly.

Arianna opened her mouth to protest, but Eli padded across the room so quickly that she didn't even have time to think before his lips were pressed against hers, his hands cradling her head.

The world disappeared then, all her worries and fears falling away. She would have stayed there, forever in his arms, if she could...

The King was waiting for her, and so she pulled away.

"Eli..." she breathed, her forehead pressed against his; she tasted the salt of her tears mixed with his own. "You should *go.*"

He shook his head, hand upon her cheek, staring into her

eyes. "I won't."

"Very well then," she said after a moment—in truth, she didn't want to go alone.

She took his hand in hers, and they walked back down the long corridor in silence, Solza marching protectively behind.

ARIANNA DIDN'T RUSH THIS TIME, no longer racing to get to the next phase in the plan.

This was it, the final push toward freedom.

And now that it was here, so close to her grasp, she realized all that she'd have to give up—all she'd *already* given up—just to get it. She told herself it was worth it, that her sacrifice could be what was right for the Olleb, but with Eli's hand in hers, she was terrified to let go.

It would be selfish not to, she thought.

They crossed the now empty foyer; sounds of battle had fallen silent.

Instead of going outside where they saw the Guardians of Gold had gathered, rounding up what remained of the Shadow Resistance as prisoners in the first hints of morning light, they climbed over fallen stones and pillars toward the throne room.

Bodies littered their path, both enemy and ally. And the closer they got to the gilded-glass entrance of the King's true domain, only more death they found.

"It seems like the guardians gave up trying to get to him," said Eli—it was just death all around. "They're probably re-grouping to figure out how to—"

They had arrived at the doors.

She peered up at him, and just knew he could somehow

hear the words in her mind… *I'm not letting anyone else near here. He wants me alone.*

She let go of his hand, growing instantly cold.

She placed her hands upon the handles, Solza at her side, knowing without a doubt what she would find on the other side.

"This is as far as you go," she said to Eli, staring ahead.

He touched her arm, and she looked up.

"I know," he said, his voice cracking; he brushed the hair back behind her ears.

She averted her eyes. This was the final chapter in her quest for freedom, yet, if Princess Elisa's words were true, she would not be seeing that freedom in this lifetime…

But my friends will. Eli will.

"Find the others," she said, trying to sound strong. "Make sure they're safe. Make this… worth it." She faltered.

He tilted her chin up, and Arianna couldn't help but get lost a little in his shining stare.

"*Nothing* is worth this," he said. "I pray, to every higher being I know the name of, that the Princess is wrong. Stay strong, and come back to me, Ara." He swallowed. "Promise me that you'll come back if I let you go."

She placed her hand on his cheek, studying him, thinking of the wonderful future they might have had together in a different, better world—it was torture to even consider that it had all been just a dream.

"I can only hope," she whispered, drawing him into one last kiss; it was shorter than the last, more final. "But you'll have to let me go either way…" She turned to face the doors. "Goodbye, Elijah Neve."

"Dammit, Ara, this is *not* goodbye!" he said, more tears swelling in his eyes. "I'll be waiting."

He lifted his fist to his heart and stepped back to let her face the destiny they had both known she'd always meet one day.

With no strength to look back, Arianna pulled the doors open and stepped inside, Solza at her heels—and with a rush of magic, not of her own making, the doors slammed closed.

25

THE FINAL FREE FALLS

THE WAR OUTSIDE was instantly wiped away as Arianna leaned against the doors, taking a moment to find her bearings—she felt as if she'd stepped into another, even darker world.

She had been in this chamber before, not long ago, forced to kneel before King Devlindor as Solomon's prized captive.

This time, though, she would not bow without a fight.

The chamber was shrouded in shadows, as his throne room always was, but they felt more permanent than before. Candles flickered from a vast crystal chandelier that took on a new, inverted, fiery life, an endless reflection in the mirrored ceiling. And slender flames shot up from the floor along the outer walls, illuminating a collection of statues with most frightening expressions—whatever happened in here, they would be the only witnesses.

Tilting her head up, Arianna found her reflection

multiplied across the ceiling along with the candles, statues, and flames. The silky, black granite tile, firm beneath her feet, made it seem as if she were floating, lost somewhere in space.

She recoiled a little as her eyes steadied on her own reflection in the glass, floating there like a lost, broken spirit. She hardly even recognized herself. She looked beaten and bruised, clothes ripped and hair matted with blood. Armor dented, wounds deep…

I can't believe I'm still standing.

And yet, somehow, she still felt stronger than ever before; Solza's energy radiated around her, replenishing her strength for the truest battle to come.

With much reluctance, she looked across the expansive room, fearful of what she would find. For in this chamber echoed another's slow-drawn breath.

She saw him first in the mirrors, his jeweled crown glaring against the firelight. His black hair curling down around his neck, a striking contrast against his pale skin. And when she lowered her gaze from the ceiling to face the monster in waiting, she found his eyes—dark and smiling.

King Devlindor sat there upon his gilded, fire-like throne, contemplating her in all his glory. He looked ever the false king in his glistening armor and fitted robes, his ruby-studded staff firmly in hand; his avatar was now back to her original form, a stunning jaguar, sprawled out lazily across the velvet stairs.

Arianna glanced down to Solza, alert and focused at her side; she looked equally, if not more, impressive.

A low growl was building in her throat, and, dimly, Arianna thought she heard the same coming from the other side of the room.

She couldn't help but think that Fate had a twisted sense of humor…

"*By the looks of it, we don't seem much different,*" she

said to Solza.

"*It matters not how one looks,*" she replied. "*It's our choices that make us who we are.*" She was resolute with her words, pulling knowledge from somewhere Arianna could not name. "*Us and them… we are not the same.*"

"*No, we are not,*" she agreed. "*But are we ready to face them? To find out who is the stronger pair?*"

Solza was silent a moment.

"*Master,*" she said, resigned, "*at this point, does it really matter? We fight either way.*"

Arianna frowned. "*I suppose you're right,*" she said. "*Good luck to you, my friend.*"

"*And to you, Master,*" said Solza. "*With you until the very end.*"

Arianna laid a hand on her avatar's head, then she took a step forward. Her boots made a loud clacking sound against the tiled floors that seemed to echo on forever.

"Arianna Belvedor," said King Devlindor, reacting to her movement; he sounded both shocked and impressed. "You've come very far, indeed."

His voice ricocheted sharply across the great expanse of the chamber, and she could hear the confidence there, even as his palace burned down around him.

She took another step, this time drawing her swords.

"I'm not often surprised by anyone these days, but you…" He looked her dead in the eyes, his dark stare streaking with silver as he clicked his tongue against his teeth. "You certainly have surprised me."

His mouth twitched up into a smile, as if he enjoyed some sense of pride that she'd made it this far in his game.

"You've brought an army to my doorstep and resurrected the Guardians of Gold," he said. "You *killed* my necromancer!" He looked to Raja, shaking his head in bemusement. "This I still cannot believe." He looked back in her direction.

"And you've torn open centuries of secrets I've shielded from the world."

He rested his chin in his hands.

"*My*, the mess you've made. What will I do with you now?"

"Shielded?" she retorted, a gut reaction. "You mean to say stolen. Magic was never yours to take!"

Even as the words flew out of her mouth, she couldn't really believe it—it was finally her moment to confront him, to stand up to the High King, on behalf of Olleb-Yelfra.

"I was protecting the people… this world," he said, cocking his head to the side with an incredulous stare, as if confused by her response. "Not everyone is deserving of magic. But you and I—"

He pointed his staff toward her, the red ruby glowing bright.

Arianna stilled, its radiance reflected all around her in the mirrors. She knew now that he'd used this very staff and stone to manipulate Solomon to his death…

"We are stronger than the rest," he continued. "I'm nothing if not true to my foundation, and I *always* keep a place open for strength in my world." He held out his hand. "Join me, and I shall let you live." The sudden force of his voice nearly pushed her back against the doors; he leaned forward. "*Kneel!*"

He pressed the butt of the staff to the ground, softening into something more snakelike.

"Or take another step, and I will rip out your heart and keep it forever as a trophy. A reminder to anyone else who dares to think they could do anything but live under my reign." He tapped his fingers against the arm of his throne, narrowing his gaze. "I'll allow you a moment to consider your options."

Raja suddenly got to her feet, a snarl tearing from her jaws;

its sound was harsh and unyielding, mirroring the King's threat.

Then, all grew quiet, nothing but the sound of crackling fires.

Arianna lifted her gaze to the colossal portrait of the King and Princess Elisa above his throne; she felt as if the Princess were staring straight through her, with those steely green eyes. She could almost hear her voice again, sure and sweet… *'You'll die.'*

"*Not if we rip out his heart first, Master,*" snapped Solza. "*And his avatar's throat!*" She responded to the King's offer with a roar of her own—it shook the chamber, the chandelier rattling.

"*You read my mind,*" said Arianna, bolstering her bravery to match Solza's.

"Is that your answer, then?" he said; his voice made a chill curl down her spine.

She could tell that he was readying his magic, his fearless façade crumbling away as he recognized their threat.

In fact, he wouldn't even be offering them a deal at all if he didn't somewhat fear her and her avatar—and the more she comprehended this, the more confident she became.

Down with the King!

For the first time in Kyrone's life, someone stood to *truly* challenge his claim to the throne. *Just survive.*

She took another step forward.

Her swords an extension of her, Arianna called to her magic to feed them. It glided from her hands all the way down to the tips of each blade, adding a warm, glowing light to the cold chamber.

The King stiffened, considering her a moment from his perch. He smoothed back his hair and stood, his robes layering the stairs.

"Very well then," he said; he leaned the staff against his

throne. "Let's see what you've learned, avatar master."

His power seemed to ripple around him like a thunderous wave, and when he clapped his hands together, his magic exploded across the chamber, dark and dazzling all at once.

Arianna's reflexes were quick as she blocked, but the impact was so forceful that it pushed her several feet backward. She was momentarily stunned, recognizing the magic—it was an avatar master's manipulation of the air element, just on a greater scale than she'd ever summoned without losing herself fully to her and Solza's combined strength.

She peered back at him, her bravery lessening.

He's so in control…

"Come on," he said with a derisive laugh, drawing the decorated sword at his belt. "Isn't this what you've been waiting for?" He flashed a toothy grin, opening up his arms. "Or would you like to reconsider those options?"

Arianna hesitated for only a moment, then she ran forward, her loudest warrior cry yet tearing from her throat, shaking through to her bones; Solza outpaced her.

With her swords twisting at her sides, and Solza's spells surrounding her, she closed the distance between them.

King Devlindor and his avatar met them in the middle, along with all his magic and might; Arianna matched him in a deafening collision, the palace shuddering around them.

Arianna felt like their battleground had instantly become engulfed by a tornado of energy, their combined powers threatening to rip their limbs apart as she dodged the King's attacks and sent her own toward him. Solza and Raja were in a deathly tangle all their own, claws and teeth bared, their snarls adding to the chilling sounds of war.

In a blink, she was blasted off her feet, skidding across the sleek floor on her back; thanks to Solza, she had avoided a near-fatal strike from the King's electrified sword.

Before she had time to get back to her feet, Raja sent a

bone-crushing blast of wind toward her; she rolled to the side to dodge it, but the glowering statue at her back was shattered into pieces, showering them with stone.

"Is that what Jon Tayshin taught you?" he called after her. "To run and cower?" He scoffed. "I know these aren't Solomon's teachings. He would have never turned his back to me."

"Do not speak his name," said Arianna, standing, *seething*; she conjured an attack of her own, fire balls spitting toward him from the chandelier, scorching everything beneath in pink flame.

He pointed his glittering sword straight up, and an umbrella-like shield of magic expanded over him. Somehow he looked even more indestructible then, standing beneath a rain of fire without so much as breaking a sweat.

He undid his cloak, letting it fall to the floor to reveal the full breadth of his elegant, black armor.

"Then *fight* me!" he yelled, his voice crashing into her like a wall, filling every crevice of her mind.

Get out, get out, get out!

He ran forward, a sneer on his face.

With swift precision, the King began to manipulate the water from the air, pulling the particles together until they morphed into a huge swirling sphere.

How is he doing that? Arianna hadn't even considered attempting something like this before in all her training…

He cupped his lips and blew, his air magic lacing his breath as he sent it howling toward her.

She didn't have time to maneuver herself out of its hungry path—she took a deep breath, and the water absorbed her.

The sphere lifted her off her feet, high above the ground, toward the lofty glass ceilings.

The fiery magic lacing her swords was instantly snuffed out; they floated alongside her, useless in this watery world.

It would seem as if she were swimming, except there was

no surface to escape to this time. And through the rippling waters, she saw King Devlindor relishing her demise…

She struggled to breathe.

She looked anywhere but down at him, not giving him the satisfaction. *There's got to be a way out.*

With this unfortunate aerial view, she saw that Solza was beginning to wane against Raja's expertise, too. It confirmed one of her biggest fears at one of the worst possible times— King Devlindor and his avatar were more experienced, more capable, in both magic and might.

Thus, she and Solza, alone, would likely not be enough to defeat them. *How can we win?*

She just couldn't believe that all her triumphs and failures would've led her here without a fair chance to overcome him.

There must be a way…

As the sphere of water rose higher, the King never letting up, Arianna thought it might smack into the ceiling and pop, sending her hurling toward the floor. She was so close now that she could see every detail of her reflection in the mirrors when she looked up, trying to swim out of this watery trap.

Frankly, she wasn't even sure if she could survive either outcome—another minute in here or the fall back down.

Her mind began to grow hazy from lack of air, though she tried to stay lucid, tried to *think*.

Think…

She sank into a memory—or possibly a dream—from long ago… a mysterious figure dragging her into an ice-cold river, holding her under until the air had gone from her lungs, until she froze.

The figure had floated there before her, taunting her to give in as she tried to drown her in darkness.

But Arianna hadn't drowned at all.

She'd swum up and out.

The darkness cannot hold me down!

After so many tests of courage and strength, all that was left in her heart was the certainty of light, no matter how dark and cold the world around her grew.

Now, as she peered through the water to see her own face staring back, that figure in the mirrors, her truest reflection, had wholly changed. It reached out its hand for her to take, a beautiful, warm spirit, guiding her back out of the dark. *Just survive!*

She grasped it, feeling her avatar magic take hold again.

She found the strength to tap into her own control over the water element, snatching it from the King's. The sphere began to solidify around her in ice, then she shattered it with an explosion so strong that he had to pull his defenses back to shield himself, frozen spikes slashing toward him and Raja.

Arianna plummeted to the floor, her magic cushioning her landing. Her swords dropped down to the ground with a bang.

She scooped them up, along with a big gulp of air, feeling awakened by the frigid cold, feeling her magic burn hot in her veins, and surely like silver flames in her eyes.

The King's anger betrayed his confidence then. He screamed out in frustration, throwing his sword to the side and reclaiming his staff instead.

He lunged at her again, relying on magic over weapon; Arianna conjured dangerous attacks of her own, never relinquishing her blades.

She was quick, but he was faster....

While she called to her greatest avatar powers and traditional magic to try to wound him, the King *always* managed to thwart her attempts; and using his staff, he blocked every strike of her swords with maddening expertise.

Beyond infuriated, Arianna couldn't help but wonder if the King hadn't trained Solomon Bell himself at one point in time, given his long history and their close relationship.

I wouldn't be surprised...

"*But you beat him, Master.*"

The grip on the hilts of her swords tightened. "*Anything is possible, I suppose.*"

She took another swing.

"Do you really think you can defeat me, Twenty-Two?" he said as they darted around the chamber. "I am a master of sword, of magic, of avatar… and with centuries more experience than you. I am your king!" He snorted, smugly, seeming so invigorated by her challenge. "You cannot win."

Rage filled her. She put more energy behind her attacks.

He lunged, she lunged. He parried, she parried. He conjured a spell, she blasted back. And Solza and Sano toiled beside them…

He hadn't taken one decent hit yet, and she was already covered in bruises and blood.

As much as she wanted to deem him a liar, she knew in this moment that she and King Devlindor had never *really* been evenly matched… she had been naïve to think she could duel him that way.

The King evaded another one of her spells and crouched down. He pressed his fingertips to the ground, and the floor rolled beneath him, bowling toward her; Arianna wobbled but did not fall as the granite groaned and cracked underneath her feet.

She called for her fire. *Solza ven immito!*

Her blades burst back to life, and she ran forward, catching him off guard before he could fully stand. She put all her strength behind the swing of each sword, the slender blades slicing into his magic with a hiss every time; she savored when the tip of one sliced through his palm; he had held up his hand to block, but she was faster this time.

He sucked a breath in through his teeth, but like his sister, he did not scream.

"Win or die, isn't it?" she said with a satisfied smirk. "I'll happily take my chances." She twisted her swords at her sides. "I never got to finish my Free Falls Festival, you know?"

The King's gaze traveled to his pale hand, bright blood smeared across it. He steadied his focus back on her. They both took a moment to breathe.

Arianna thought that he actually seemed *frightened*, to see his own blood drawn in battle. She mused that, like Sir Vladamor, he probably hadn't felt pain in a very long time...

Sir Vladamor is dead. Arianna felt Solza smile.

Alas, anything she took for fright in his expression quickly turned to fury.

"I haven't even begun to show you my strength," uttered the King, standing up tall. "You're already on your last life, when all you've managed to do is nick me."

He wagged his finger at her, blood dripping down his hand, then he showcased his palm with an arrogant shrug; Arianna watched in horror as the wound stitched back together, his healing magic working over it with such speed as she'd only ever seen Sano conjure.

"As I said, Twenty-Two, you cannot win." He shook his head, almost in pity. "Nobody can win against me."

Arianna glimpsed Solza on the other side of the room; she looked to *really* be struggling against Raja now.

"*How are you holding up, girl?*"

"*I'll be fine, Master,*" she replied. "*Stay focused.*"

Arianna could sense Solza's panicked mind as Raja snapped her teeth at her; they were using their earth-shaking powers against one another in a desperate desire to gain the upper hand.

The King followed her gaze, then suddenly threw his staff to the ground—he marched toward Arianna, weaponless.

She pointed her weapons forward, taken aback.

"See! Your avatar is just as weak as you are," he said, nearing fast; her heartbeat raced, sweat beading her skin, but she stayed her ground, trying to determine his next move. "I grow tired of your games now." His voice came dry, bored; she readied her magic. "This ends now."

Arianna felt her body go rigid.

Her swords fell to the ground with a clang that ricocheted sharply across the room. She hadn't needed to hear the spell spoken, she knew it well, remembered it in her bones—Keeper Kassime had introduced her to it long ago. *'Cementas cuerpal.'*

It was one she always found difficult to block, especially when caught off guard. And once the enchantment sank in, she had yet to learn a way to shake out of it.

The King was in her face now, so close that she could feel his warm breath on her skin. She couldn't move a muscle to even cringe away—the only thing that did seem to move was her heart, vibrating the inside of her chest like an internal earthquake.

"Have I lived up to your expectations?" he whispered, moving the hair from her face.

In the next moment, his palm met her cheek. He'd slapped her so hard that she heard her cheekbone fracture.

Unbidden tears welled in her eyes; she tried to scream, to release the pain with her voice, but he held it in his grasp, her lips locked just like her limbs. Her stomach twisted, her tormented cry swirling there with no way out. She thought she would burst open from the pain.

"I'm sorry..." said the King with mock concern. "Did you have something you wanted to say before you die?"

With the snap of his fingers, her lips parted.

"I asked you a question. So speak!" he bellowed, spit flying. He got closer to her face. "I *said*, have I now lived up to your expectations as High King of the Olleb?"

Arianna gazed at him, fear spreading up her spine.

"*Master, I can't hold her off much longer,*" cried Solza. "*I cannot help you. She's too strong. Her magic is... too strong.*"

"*I know, dear friend,*" said Arianna, trying to remain calm. "*It's all going to be all right. Keep fighting… until you can't anymore. It's all right.*"

Arianna put her attention back on the King.

"You're exactly what I've always imagined," she replied. "A coward through and through. At least *I'm* not afraid to meet Death." Pain seared across her face as she tried to smile. "But you should be."

"What did you just say to me?" he said, straightening up, seeming apprehensive.

"I said that *you* should be afraid of Death," said Arianna.

She found the strength to smirk, her gaze steady and sharp, her voice just the same.

"I mean, it's clear you already are… *you*, who created the Four Corners, a city of slaves, just to avoid it." She snorted. "Like I said, a coward." Her voice strengthened, her courage mounting. "Now that I stand here, I see that you're just a man. A lonely man at that, with no one by his side. And when someone is truly alone, *that's* when they're most vulnerable." She swallowed, wishing for the encouragement of her friends, yet knowing this was one sacrifice she'd finally gotten right; she found Demetrius' warm smile in her mind's eye. "I learned that long ago… but it seems you never did."

"Lonely, you say," hissed the King as he paced around her, crouched like a jaguar himself, itching to pounce, to dig his claws into her chest and rip her heart out. "And how do you gather this?"

"You were granted the greatest power and position in the world, and an opportunity to use it to make the Olleb a better place," said Arianna, evenly, "yet you're so afraid of losing power that instead of lifting people up, you order them to fall at your feet, give their lives for you just so that you feel safe from those that might one day rise against you." She licked her lips; they were cracked with blood. "In doing this, in leading with fear and terror, you have gained no followers, no *friends.* Only slaves."

Her eyes flicked to Solza.

"A friend would lay down their life for you willingly, fight for your honor." She paused, eyes flitting around. "Where are your friends now, Your *Majesty?* Even if you kill me right here in the throne room you stole, is there anyone out there who will fight for you and help you win this war to keep it? Are you certain that if you walk out of this chamber to command your people that you will find anybody left to command?"

The King visibly shook with her words, balling his hands into fists by his sides; white-hot, sweltering magic wove in and out of swollen knuckles; Arianna could feel its heat sifting toward her, seeking her out.

I won't be afraid.

Her bravery grew—yet all she had was her words, her magical mind suppressed by his sheer will.

Her avatar, waylaid by another of greater strength.

Her swords, surrendered to the black.

"I may meet Death by your hand sooner than I'd hoped, but I've accomplished what I set out to do," she said, voice shaking. "I *did* bring an army to your doorstep, and they're still out there, waiting for me. If it's you they meet instead, do you think that your power can defeat them all? The thousands of men and women who *chose* to follow me and the Guardians of Gold?"

"They will follow me or die," he replied, flatly, his stare filling with more magic.

"That may be so," she said, swallowing back that hard truth. "But just so you know… they are all *willing* to die. And if you kill every last one of the slaves in your kingdom, who will be left for you to rule?"

The King shook his head now, unaccepting. "They will bow to me again," he said, trembling with anger.

"Those who might've followed you out of fear are either dead, captured, or converted to our side," replied Arianna, curtly. "Hear me now, Kyrone." His eyes widened, face growing paler by the second. "The Shadow Resistance has fallen against the Guardians of Gold, and all of Olleb-Yelfra has witnessed this turning of the tide. The world sees another way now."

She took a deep breath.

"So tell me, Your Highness, do you really think they will choose *you* without a fight?" She smirked again, her lips quivering from the pain. "I don't think so. I think your reign is over... whether I die here or not."

He let out an enraged howl, his concentration shattering; the spell rolled away, and Arianna collapsed to the ground.

"Your tongue is quick, little witch, but power is pure and measurable," he said, kneeling down in front of her to look her in the eye. "The fact remains that power and strength is life, and *weakness* is death." He pushed a loose strand of hair from his face, seeming to collect himself, his kingly mask placed right back on. "The Guardians of Gold are weak and always have been—"

He tilted her chin up so that she had to look straight into the depths of his darkness.

"Neither you nor your foolish army are powerful enough to beat me. History has proven time and time again that nobody is." King Devlindor raised his magic-laced palm. "In *my* favor is the only way that any war ends, and now that magic is out for everyone to see, all you've done is make me stronger."

He laughed, the sound like needles on her skin.

"And once the people see your limp body and the display of my *true* powers," he said, "they will surely bow even lower." He narrowed his shadow-sunken gaze, a joyless smile on his lips. "Like I said before, I need only to show them your heart."

He plunged his fist into her chest, his magic searing

straight through her chainmail and armor.

Arianna didn't even have the time to scream, her voice merely a murmur of shock.

She grabbed him by the wrist with both hands, trying to push him back, their gaze still locked.

His face was tight with arrogance, glowing with pleasure.

Hers was surely twisted in anguish, darkening from pain.

When the shock wore off a moment later, the King's strength surpassing hers, she felt the truth of his magic all at once—a cry escaped her lips that echoed between the walls, resounded against the mirrors, shattered her pride.

He reached for her heart without mercy, his deadly enchantment burning a hole through everything she was… metal, flesh, magic, and bone. It was an agony even worse than when she and Solza had first connected, the King's hand digging around in her chest, searching for her most prized possession; she thought she would pass out at any moment.

A *whoosh* of air distracted her from above.

Arianna and the King looked up.

Solza had transformed into her owl form to escape Raja, her fury now aimed at the King. The wind magic she conjured was so forceful that he was blown backward, rolling away like a log. He released his death grip on Arianna before it was too late.

Solza… is it… too late?

Hot tears streaked her face, and she toppled to her side, blood sputtering from her mouth. She kept one hand over the place where the King's had entered.

His magic slammed into her again like a boulder, before she could even gather her next thought. She sailed through the air, smashing into the portrait above the throne—it ripped off the wall, falling to the floor with a crash, along with Arianna.

She rolled down the velvet steps, stilling at the bottom.

Her vision was spotted with black, with white, with Solza.

Raja had attacked her again, and they were struggling not far from where she'd fallen.

With the last of her strength, she crawled toward her.

"I'll kill you!" The King's voice chased after her.

He marched toward his throne, toward the fire he'd instilled upon his kingdom, to her pile of a body at the bottom.

He picked up the staff from the ground, his hands still covered in her blood as they were, smearing the white wood.

He surely planned to drive it straight through her for the final blow, to utterly destroy her before revealing her mangled body to her people. She could see his desire for that plainly.

She only had one move left, no energy left to conjure magic.

"*Solza… you have to transform.*" Her head spun, but she focused enough to communicate with her avatar.

"*I don't know if I can,*" she whispered back; Raja had cornered her in her hawk form, ready to rip into her again, talons flexed.

Arianna could sense she was badly hurt too.

"*Yes, you can,*" she said, calmer now, being brave for them both. "*You're stronger than her. We're both stronger in ways we don't even realize…*" She tasted the blood on her teeth, coppery and warm, wrong. "*They're afraid of Death, but we are not.*"

"*Yes, Master,*" she said with more confidence. "*Let Death come! As long as they meet him too.*"

"*We'll make sure of it,*" she replied. "*One way or another, girl. Let's give the Olleb our very best.*"

Arianna had to squint as the darkness was enveloped in a spectacular kaleidoscopic light, the mirrors refracting it into every shadowed corner of the chamber, the fire-forged throne of gold gleaming.

You did it, girl! She focused on Solza, on her beauty, on her embodiment of the Golden Age. *The Guardians of Gold.*

Solza had tapped back into her fire, a magnificent dragon to behold—even the King took pause to see her up close, and inside his palace.

Raja hurried to her master lest she be crushed as the top of Solza's head hit the high ceiling; the chandelier fell to the floor with a splintering crash, diamonds dancing across the floor.

Solza positioned herself protectively over her master; King Devlindor could no longer stand between them.

Then, Arianna felt a little of her fire returning too.

Solza reared her mighty head, fire flooding from her jaws, engulfing the throne room in streams of red-orange light. The portrait was singed into ash, the statues melted into nothing—all that remained was the throne, blending with the fire.

The King roared with the effort to protect himself and Raja from the force of her unforgiving flame, hiding behind a shield of magic. The fire ricocheted off his spell and shot up through the mirrored ceiling.

More glass rained down, revealing a crystal-clear sky—the night was beginning to lift.

Levantis bora. Arianna used the remnants of her energy to retrieve her swords, then she climbed onto Solza's back, preparing to flee.

"Not so fast!" called the King, a menacing sneer on his lips as he glared up at her.

Raja had begun to undergo a transformation too…

Arianna and Solza stared on in horror, in disbelief, as what they had only guessed at before was made a reality right before their eyes—King Devlindor's avatar had morphed into a dragon with liquid black scales.

"You thought you were the only one who had mastered all the elements?" He laughed, as if he'd been *hoping*, somewhere deep down, to reveal this card all along—he was conceited to the very end. "How do you think dragons went extinct in the first place?"

He clicked his tongue at her, shaking his head in mock disappointment when she didn't respond.

"An avatar dragon is the master of *all* dragons," he said. "And just like people, dragons bow to kings of their own kind. In this case… a queen." King Devlindor laid a hand on Raja's scaly side. "Say hello, Raja."

She let out a roar that seemed to shake the earth, even stronger than Solza's. Then she stooped down low, allowing her master to climb onto her back in a practiced method.

He patted her, something like adoration in his expression, though Arianna thought it was an unrecognizable trait for him.

"You don't even know the power you possess," he said to her—they glowered at each other from atop their dragons.

Arianna was grateful for the bed of Solza's horns, otherwise she thought she might slide right off, her strength dangerously dwindling.

"You ordered the *queen* of dragons… to murder… all her subjects?" she said after a moment.

Even as she said the words, she couldn't comprehend them; she was dizzy, her clothes and skin sticky with blood.

He let out a loud cackle that drifted off into the night.

"Quite the contrary," he replied. "Her subjects are just sleeping, waiting to be woken by us at any time." She recoiled, unable to fathom such a thing as King Devlindor with an army of dragons in his arsenal; Raja's molten-yellow eyes glinted. "If you do not surrender, I will make sure the Guardians of Gold die by the fire they so love, to mark the beginning of a new era under my reign. And thanks to you, magic, under my control, will surely be part of it."

Arianna's headache was worsening, her mind reeling, her body deteriorating.

"*Solza… could dragons still exist somewhere in the Ol-leb?*" she asked. "*Is he telling the truth?*"

"Anything is possible, Master." Her normally strong and steady voice sounded soft, weak.

"Even if you are telling the truth," said Arianna, pulling the fragments of her courage and strength to the surface, "there's a new avatar dragon to challenge Raja's place as queen." She pressed her body against Solza. *You can do this, girl.* "Just as I challenge you now."

"His avatar is strong," said Solza, scared. *"She's mastered all the elements too. I don't know how I can beat her..."*

"The King is strong as well," said Arianna, *"but he's just reminded me of something... something important, I think."* She latched onto a memory that formed into an idea, praying that both she and Solza had the strength left to allow her to test it. *"I might know a way to defeat him. I didn't realize it before..."* She shook her head. *"Solza, I need to get close to him again."*

"We'll see about that," said the King, drawing their attention.

"Let's go, Solza," she urged, holding on as tightly as she could—her thought gave her a slight boost of energy, for Solza could no longer do so. *"This will all be over soon, one way or another."*

"Yes, one way or another, Master. My heart is with you."

Solza unfurled her wings, filling the chamber. She launched upward, breaking through what remained of the glass ceiling and into the sky.

"After them," she heard the King yell from below. "Fly!"

ARIANNA AND SOLZA BROKE FREE of the palace, flying high into the lightening sky and ripping through the clouds. Their friends and followers were down below, watching their every move.

She had been right in her statement to the King—the Guardians of Gold had won this war, and now it was up to her to return to them with the crown, and the King's head.

Her bravery boosted a little more, her grip on her life a little tighter. *I can do this, for them.*

The wind tore through her long hair and invigorated her deepest, fullest breaths.

She forced herself to turn away from the future and glance back to the present that refused to let go, to drift away into the past, into nothing—King Devlindor and Raja were on their tail, slicing through the clouds right behind them.

With the King in pursuit, they soared toward the rising sun, its rays burning like the breath of a dragon on the horizon, just over the sea; Arianna lingered on the water, thinking of the peaceful days she'd spent with Solza flying over its endless reach, wondering if they'd ever get to do so again. And as she did, she swore she saw Syrifina and her sisters wading at the shores by the ships, waiting to see what might come of the Olleb with the new day.

Raja let out a blast of fire, and Arianna felt the heat near her back, heavy and unwanted; Solza returned it, and thus a fiery war in the skies had begun.

It was hard to tell up from down as the enemy dragons rolled among the clouds, attacking each other from all angles. Claws outstretched, slashing into scales. Fangs were bared, sinking into flesh. Fire blasted and burned, and the King's deadly magic kept a clean target on Arianna.

Everything was a blur—blue sky, white clouds, red flames, and black magic.

Solza could do nothing but fight and fly for her life, and Arianna struggled to defend them both, growing only weaker from the wound she'd suffered over her heart. She was surprised, in this tumble through the clouds, that it hadn't slipped right out of her chest to plummet to the ground.

She was getting tired, too tired to keep hanging on.

Just survive… until the end.

This battle was coming to a close.

"You will not survive this!" she heard the King scream over the thrashing, dragon-made winds… over the screams of their dragons.

His voice and threats were just an annoying whisper in her ears now. Her thoughts drowned him out, her focus so occupied on her idea—with every second, it grew clearer, surer in her heart.

King Devlindor didn't realize what Arianna was beginning to feel so certain of… *Neither one of us will survive this.*

A giant, white cloud seemed to suddenly spew fire.

Arianna blinked away from her thoughts to find that Sano had joined the fight, his scales shimmering like a snowfall in the skies of Saindora, fire pouring from his mouth like an exploding volcano; he and Solza fought together in unison, so in sync with one another it appeared as if they'd flown a thousand years by each other's side.

Now, it was two against one.

Arianna didn't miss the King's terrified expression—he'd been so sheltered during this war that he clearly hadn't even noticed another avatar dragon existed.

Raja tumbled to the side, surprised just the same; Sano took the lead now, allowing Arianna and Solza time to find their bearings.

"*Thank you, Sano,*" said Arianna, speaking to him through Solza. "*Lessa would be proud.*"

Sano's voice boomed back, as he attacked with everything he had. "*She would be the most proud of you, Master Arianna… don't forget that.*"

She averted her thoughts to Solza, knowing what Sano

surely did too.

"*It's time*," she said. "*Do you understand what has to happen now? This can only end in fire.*"

"*I understand, Master,*" she replied, reading every thought in her mind. "*I wish it didn't have to be this way...*" Arianna relished the powerful soothing tones of Solza's voice. It vibrated through her with warmth, just as it had done on the first day it had formed—though she trembled with tears. "*I would have liked to live a thousand lives with you.*"

"*Every minute has been more than a blessing,*" said Arianna, stroking her, gently. "*Let's make the final ones count.*"

She felt Solza harden to the task ahead. "*Hang on!*"

She rounded on Raja, locking her claws deep into her belly; Arianna squeezed her eyes shut.

Sano had been the perfect distraction to allow them the upper hand. There would be no escaping Solza's iron grip now—Arianna, King Devlindor, and their avatars fell from the sky as one.

They landed with a crash behind the palace, in a courtyard that backed up against a thriving forest. And both the King and Arianna did what they could to cushion the blow with magic, otherwise they all would've certainly died.

Arianna cried out, crumpled on her side. She struggled to roll onto her hands and feet, sharp shooting pains traveling through her body.

Raja was still in her dragon form but badly wounded from the fall and the fight, curled into a ball not far from her—Sano had done his duty well; he remained in flight.

Arianna didn't need to see Solza to know that she was on her last breath, not much better off than Raja. She glimpsed her on the other side of the courtyard, a weak transformation shifting her back to her more comfortable snow leopard form.

She wanted so badly to tend to her, but she didn't have time; the King was already on his feet, throwing more deadly magic her way.

Arianna barely blocked it, its scorching residue tearing at her skin. She crawled in the opposite direction, her throat too dry to even cry out from the pain.

"You have come to your end," he said through staggered breaths—he had to use his staff to walk, limping toward her.

Arianna turned to face him, still inching across grass.

The crown had fallen from his head during the crash; she glimpsed it a few feet away, gold and glinting.

And without it, Kyrone looked so different... nothing like a king at all.

He picked it up and placed it back on his head, as if afraid to be seen without it.

She didn't have her swords anymore, but they had aided her enough on this journey. It was time to let them go.

Slowly, the King approached.

She called to her magic.

It was faint, but it was there, so she stopped trying to crawl farther away and just held on to that warmth.

King Devlindor was straddling her in the next moment. He pressed the bar of his staff against her throat so hard that she could barely breathe, struggling under his weight.

She kicked her legs, but it was fruitless. She stilled.

Just hold on to the magic.

"Any last words?" he growled, drool dripping onto her face; his expression was livid, splotched with blood.

He could see nothing but her and she saw nothing but him... all of him, Kyrone Devlindor.

The end of the staff began to glow a bright red, matching his anger—there was no telling what type of magic he might use to end her life.

"I hope you burn forever in death!" she choked out, her tears now dry.

She gritted her teeth, and he made to smile. *Win or die.*

Arianna felt her hand clutch the hilt of her dagger, firm and cool in her palm. She ripped it from the sheath at her thigh and drove it into the King's chest, just over his heart.

Aurora's blade cut smoothly through his armor to enter his flesh, its special properties unparalleled—only the hilt with the electric jeweled pommel remained sticking out from his chest.

His smile faltered, softening with shock. And with her hand still upon the dagger, she could feel his entire body tremble in fear.

For a moment, as he lay on top of her, the King appeared frozen in time, unable to utter a word. Then she felt his grip on the staff release as it fell from his hands.

His body sank into her, vulnerable and weak.

The King tried to speak. "What did you—"

Arianna found the strength to push him off her; she sat up, her grip on the dagger tighter.

She placed both hands around the hilt, and he put both his hands over hers.

He tried to pull, but she pushed.

She straddled him now, forcing Aurora in deeper, imagining its sparkling black blade slicing his wretched heart in two. There was no force in the world that could pull her grip from that blade.

The warmth of her magic grew, and Arianna saw the reflection of it in his dark eyes, silver and bright—she summoned her flame and it came without hesitation, without fright. *Solza ven immito!*

Pink fire pooled in the palm of her hand, glowing atop her skin. And just as it had done that curious night at the Treehouse, Eli protectively at her side, it poured into the pommel of the dagger, blazing bright.

The world seemed to stop turning in this moment. Enemy, friend, magic… all of it ceased to exist around her.

She only saw Kyrone.

And his dark eyes were now void of any trace of magic.

A strange sensation began to creep under her skin as she kept calling to her flame, like an itch growing into something much worse. Still, she held the dagger steady against his heart, knowing nothing could pull her hand away, unless she made the choice.

She could feel her fire manipulating the aura and ora stones, sparking its magical properties into life. The blade danced with energy as it sank deeper into the King's chest, its magic deeper into his body.

"What's happening to me?" he stuttered, suddenly finding his voice.

He tried to make her stop. *Nothing will make me stop.*

Tears beaded in his eyes, making him look suddenly and unnaturally fragile. Fear had consumed him, gripped his heart, just as tightly as she gripped the dagger.

Only now did Arianna truly comprehend the extraordinary magic her guardian relic was capable of, what those spellbinding ribbons in the sky had really been made of—it had been magic, in its purest form.

She sensed her powers amplify. *The dagger's a magical conduit!* Just like the ruby on the King's staff.

In the back of her mind, she wondered if Diveena had known all along. Had the last Nicora elf granted her dagger the very gift meant to destroy the King?

Had Solomon known, too?

Her lips twitched up into a smile, the past and the future baffling her evermore.

It was similar to the feeling when Solza gave her a boost of her own energy, yet she knew that whatever Aurora was giving her now could not be taken away, would not fade over time or with distance.

As her power seemed increased, her warmth became

overwhelming, unstable—she didn't have the room for it. Didn't want it. *I have to hold on, for the Guardians of Gold.*

She screamed against the effort, against this mounting new kind of pain as this foreign, curious energy tried to find its place in her body.

The King screamed out too, demanding an answer. "What's happening?"

"Don't you get it?" she choked out, barely able to speak as she concentrated. She closed her eyes and recited the familiar verse. "When one eclipses over the other, life shall end for he and his brother—"

"The prophecy…" stammered the King—another scream. Her flame grew brighter, her power grew. "I don't understand."

"It's the Golden Rule, you monster," retorted Arianna, yelling in frustration. "And if you *did* understand it, we wouldn't be in this situation at all!"

"What do you mean?" he said in a rasped whisper, his lips turned down. He looked at her with something of desperation in his expression, his voice. "What's… what's *happening* to me?"

Arianna felt as if her fingers might break for how tightly she held on.

"I'm stripping you of your magic," she said, knowing surely that she spoke a truth; she kept her gaze steady on his. "You don't deserve an ounce of it."

He opened his mouth to speak, but with merely a thought she silenced him, never wanting to hear his poisonous words again; he choked on his tongue, still clutching desperately at her hands.

"And when *you* meet Death, you'll be completely powerless against him." She felt another surge of power as the King's magic flowed into hers. "May the gods and goddesses of the Olleb offer you as much mercy in his hands as you bestowed upon your kingdom."

His eyes bulged in terror, in pain. He convulsed beneath her.

A rainbow of dark hues, just like the ones she'd seen light up the night sky at the Treehouse, just as were forged into her dagger, began to engulf the King in an electrified and smoky cocoon of magic, eating away at his lifeforce, Arianna's fire twisting along with it. Aurora's powerful magic seeped out of every crevice in his body, consuming him from the inside out, just as he'd tried to consume the world.

But while the King was overcome with this profound, ruthless magic, so was Arianna.

Everything that poured out of him, flowed into her, a powerful energy spreading through the dagger and transferring into her body. She knew if she looked, the light in Aurora's pommel would be writhing and bright, *too* bright.

I can't let go. I have to hold on… until the King is destroyed.

She screamed out again in agony as she consumed everything that he was, though the Princess pushed back into her mind.

'You'll die.'

King Devlindor's eyes suddenly grew wide with true understanding, his expression panicked as he felt his magic disappearing, himself vanishing. He grasped Arianna's hand even tighter, pleading for his life.

"Let go, and we both live," he implored. "There are *far* worse monsters than I which lurk on this plane, and they will rise again if you release all the magic in the Olleb." His expression grew wild, eyes disturbingly dark, shadows forming under his pallid skin, revealing the truth of his decrepit self, brittle and broken. Frail and imperfect… fallible. Vincible. *Not a king at all.* "You don't know what you're doing. Let go of your flame!"

Arianna felt her lips curl into a sneer, refusing to listen to more of his lies.

"It's our destiny to die," she said, without reservation, her magic overflowing so much that she felt her hair and her clothes raise all around her. Then they too began to float in the air, a king impaled beneath a dagger, a dragon consuming its power. "And there's nobody but yourself to blame." They rose higher. "The Olleb deserves her freedom now, and you… *you* deserve whatever despicable afterlife has been waiting for you all this time. No one is immortal."

He shook his head, his expression pleading, angered, scared.

The verses of the Golden Rule repeated in Arianna's mind, and she was certain that her connection with the King now let him hear it too—this time to comprehend their true meaning:

> *Light is light and dark is dark,*
> *But never shall they live apart.*
> *One shall seek what the other denies.*
> *If it is found, thus follows the demise.*
> *When one eclipses over the other,*
> *Life shall end for he and his brother.*

"Arianna, let go!" She heard Eli's voice seep into their bubble, but magic and power and pain had overtaken her almost completely. "Don't do this, *please!*"

Although she could not oblige, she took comfort in that she would go surrounded by those left in the world who she cared for the most. Finally, she knew her family would be safe.

Her guardian allies crowded around them now, but they didn't dare interfere.

"Sister…" spluttered the King, spotting Princess Elisa among them; Master Tayshin had her in restraints, clearly suppressing her magic—King Devlindor released one hand from

Arianna's and reached out to her in desperation. "Save me, Elisa."

"Brother," she replied, coolly, her jaw set, "you *are* being saved." She lifted her gaze from him to look at Arianna. "Finally, we can say goodbye."

Arianna caught her eye, and the Princess gave her a firm nod.

"You traitor!" he cried, his tears shining for all to see. "You always were a traitor to our name. I should have killed you. I should have killed you, Elisa, when I had the chance!"

"That's good," said Arianna, evenly, the pain beginning to numb her from the inside out. "Now you understand that you have no more chances left."

As the King begged for his life, she found the faces of Demetrius and Jeom—Demetrius was holding Solza's head in his lap, and Jeom was restraining Eli by the arms so that he couldn't intervene.

There were tears in all of their eyes, but what she saw in their expressions gave her the courage to keep holding on to that dagger.

Down with the King!

She felt Solza's warmth enter her mind, lessening some of the pain. "*Down with the King, Master. Down with the King!*"

She tore her eyes from her friends and set them back on Kyrone. He was shriveling into an old man before her eyes, the bones in his cheeks protruding, the magic eating him alive as it vacated his body.

"We love you, Ara!" she heard Noah call to her from below.

"*You can do this, Arianna. For the Olleb!*" Every soul she had touched with her animancy spoke to her from somewhere beyond it all, echoing within her heart.

Win or die, she thought, ironically.

She knew she could not live.

The crushing heaviness of the King's power inside of her began to be too much to withstand. She thought she might explode at any moment.

And with nowhere to go but out, the magic began to take shape atop her skin, golden veins spreading up her arms and all across her body as if alive, a new lifeblood settling in.

With the rest of her strength, she called her flame brighter, letting King Devlindor's power consume her completely— every last ounce of his magic and lifeforce was suddenly drained from his body.

"Please…" he said. "Let go. I… I don't want to die."

Arianna hesitated, noting the first truth she'd ever heard him speak.

It's far too late for mercy. The balance must be restored.

"Neither do I," she whispered, "but our time has now come."

Arianna let go of her fire, and King Devlindor let out a painful gasp.

All fell quiet as she and Kyrone locked eyes, sharing this final moment of life together. There was nothing left to say.

Arianna yanked Aurora from his chest and the cocoon of life-sucking magic fell away.

For a moment, they remained there, the sky as their arena, the guardian allies their witnesses—it was as if the world held its breath to see if the King might actually die.

Still, somehow, it seemed impossible, though Arianna knew better than to think that by now.

In the same moment, a dark shadow grew over the sun that now sat high in the sky; with their last grain of energy, Arianna and the King shifted their gaze toward the clouds.

The day fell eerily to night as the moon forced its way back into focus, like a blanket suddenly drawn over the bright sun. It was a phenomenon Arianna had only ever heard rumors of—an eclipse.

The sun's fiery, vibrant crown was now the only thing visible in what was now unequivocally night; everyone had to shield their eyes, but the King and Arianna just stared in wonder.

At that moment, Sano soared across the sky, his silvery-white body illuminated against the backdrop of the eclipse, his roar solidifying the balance now righted in the world.

Arianna smiled.

"I suppose… you win," choked the King.

He no longer struggled now, his arms hanging in the air, limp alongside him; Arianna was still teeming with lethal power.

"*Free* for the slaves who earn their citizenship," she snapped back. "*Falls* for the ones who die."

They both crashed back to the earth in an explosive blast.

Arianna rolled away to the side as he began to writhe violently.

"Hail to Olleb-Yelfra," she breathed, unblinking.

The King wailed in agony during his last moments of life, his body slowly and brutally ripped apart from the inside out, ultimately destroyed by the nothingness that Arianna had left him with. He *was* nothing.

His body, his screams, his horrors… just dust on the wind, to be left somewhere in the past.

Arianna hoped that the suffering he'd felt as he'd vanished would remain with his soul forevermore. It had been, after all, the consequence for his choices.

In the split second that Kyrone Devlindor's life was finally over, a sureness washed over Arianna. She glanced to the crown he'd left behind, still gleaming bright, despite the darkest times it had suffered.

All will be all right now. The guardians… we survived.

She fell onto her back atop the grass, Aurora still in her

grasp. She gazed upon the eclipse, both darkness and lightness, creating the most enchanting sky she had ever dreamed to look upon.

There were cheers from the surrounding crowd, but they seemed so far away.

Les, we did it, she thought.

Arianna's heart suddenly constricted in pain, her body fighting to withstand the addition of King Devlindor's powers, the golden veins of magic her own lifeblood, consuming her entirely.

She glimpsed her friends, rushing toward her to help, but she wished they'd stop.

It's too late... she thought, tormented enough by such knowledge. She couldn't bear to hear their cries.

She knew she would not survive.

This was my truest fate all along. My destiny was to die.

And she'd finally accepted it.

The last thing she heard was the voice of Solza in her mind, erasing all else. She sang to her a comforting melody from her past, to help ease the pain... to say goodbye:

Now I only see ahead,
As I'm sailing with the clouds.
Drifting with the wind,
Happiness I've found.
Free and alive,
Goodbye, I've left my past behind.
It is my dream,
Finally, I am free.

26

THE ECLIPSE

THE GATHERING WAS SILENT as they all stared upon the ashes of the long-reigning High King of Olleb-Yelfra… and the lifeless body of Arianna Belvedor.

Soft golden streaks of light still pulsated across her skin.

She looked as if she could be sleeping, resting atop the grass, her gold and crimson cloak swaddling her, long curls spread out beneath her like a fan…

She would look as if she were sleeping, if not for her eyes.

They remained open. And there was no more magic there.

The Aurora dagger rested in her dirtied palm, the glittering black blade dripping with blood—the crown and staff had fallen beside her, her swords not far away.

Her armor still shimmered, beneath the scuffs, scorch marks, and scratches. And her skin still held the warmth of life, though what was visible was badly beaten.

Yes, she would look as if she were sleeping, if not for her

bottomless brown eyes... and the space above her heart—metal, skin, and bone, torn open to reveal the strength inside.

Arianna's soul had drifted on.

"NO!" SCREAMED ELI. He fell to his knees at her side, pulling her into his arms.

She was still warm to the touch.

"Wake up," he pleaded, gently rocking her, his tears splattering her face. "*Please*, Ara. Oh, please, you must wake up!"

He felt a strong hand grip his shoulder.

"She's gone, son," said Master Tayshin; Eli peered up at him, finding a hopeless expression on his face, looking just as lost as he felt. "We have to let her go."

He whimpered, shaking his head, unable to process this cruel reality where the love of his life lay dead in his arms.

He glanced to the jeweled crown glinting up at him from the ground, mocking him.

How can Kyrone Devlindor truly be dead, yet you're not here to rejoice with us?

His tears continued to fall, ceaselessly.

"We were so close..." he muttered into her hair, caressing her bruised cheek. "You promised me, Ara. This can't be goodbye." His voice cracked, anger and sadness both trying to take front and center. "You promised!"

Deep down, though, he knew that she hadn't.

Her last words rang in his head, sharp as her swords...

'I can only hope...'

He covered his mouth with his hand, trying to stifle his sobs. Then, reluctantly, he slid away from her to make room for Master Tayshin; he wanted to make his peace with his apprentice.

Princess Elisa was still in restraints by his side. She stared upon Arianna with dry eyes, her expression unreadable.

Master Tayshin gave his own farewells to Arianna, gently moving her free hand to cover her heart; the Princess took his lapse in attention as an opportunity to kneel down too.

She whispered something in Arianna's ear. Her expression remained stoic, emotionless, unmoved.

Eli shoved her away with a warrior's wrath. She fell onto her back on the grass.

"Get her out of here!" he snarled, seconds away from ending her life—his sword was pointed at her so fast that he hadn't even noticed he'd drawn it again.

Master Tayshin yanked the Princess back to her feet by the crook of her arm.

"Is there anything we can do to help?" said Nico—he and Sergios had broken apart from the surrounding circle, everyone recognizing that all was now safe.

"Isolate her from the others," ordered Master Tayshin, sounding ever the confident leader—Eli didn't see how he managed. He felt as if his entire body, his mind, had withered from the inside out. "Make sure she has no means of escape."

"Yes, sir," said Sergios.

Nico nodded, and they both made to carry her off.

But not before they paid their respects to Arianna—they lifted their fists to their chests in salute, then walked away.

"Sano!" Demetrius' fear-stricken voice struck like another sharp stab to Eli's heart. "Come down here, hurry!"

He sheathed his blade and glanced over.

Demetrius was sitting on the ground next to where Solza had landed; she remained in her snow leopard form, her tattered body curled into itself.

Eli couldn't bear to go any farther from Arianna, so he called out to him, concerned. "What is it? What's wrong?"

Demetrius shook his head, clearly distressed. "It's Solza... she's dying."

Sano was still soaring high in the sky, nearly camouflaged against the puffy, white clouds. He swept down toward the courtyard. As soon as his feet touched the ground, he transformed from the stunning white dragon into his infinitely smaller monkey self.

He bounded over to Solza, laying his silver paws across her.

"You know that won't work..." said Jeom, solemnly, standing over them.

Sano's healing magic had no effect, and eventually, he gave up. He scuttled onto Jeom's shoulders.

"I know..." said Demetrius. He looked to Jeom with agony in his eyes. "But we had to try."

Jeom scrunched his lips, nodding in understanding—he looked just as devastated as everyone else.

Demetrius gazed back down to Solza, stroking her fur with a shaking hand.

"It's all right, girl," he said. "You can go to her now."

"We'll never forget you," said Jeom, kneeling down beside them, one hand on his axe. He glanced toward Arianna, eyes rimmed red. "None of our girls."

Eli swallowed the lump bulging in his throat, growing even sadder to know that another truly felt his pain—Jeom's love had also vanished before his eyes.

With one last purr of affection, Solza collapsed on Demetrius' lap, her electric blue eyes closing for good. Her body was engulfed in smoky wisps of white magic, as if she might transform at any moment.

Alas, when the magic fell away, there was nothing left of Arianna's avatar to suggest that she had ever even existed at all—except for an extraordinary patch of wildflowers that had sprouted up from the ground in her place.

They boasted all the vibrant hues Solza's soul had surely been made of… green, blue, purple, and a blazing red. Their stems were made of gold.

They all stared at the wildflowers in awe, disbelieving.

"Rest in peace, Solza," murmured Eli, bowing his head.

Everyone turned their attention to Raja then, waiting for the inevitable. She was still in her dragon form, a mountainous black presence in the courtyard—she gave one last exhausted roar before she too vanished in a magical wisp.

All that remained in her place was broken earth where her body had smashed the grass.

"Arianna's really… gone?" whimpered Noah, running up to them, his face splotched with tears.

He looked back and forth between Eli, Demetrius, and Jeom; no one responded.

He sniffled. "What… *what* are we going to do now? She was my best—"

"She was mine, too," said Demetrius, grasping his hand—Noah helped him to his feet. "She was my family, and you were hers." He pulled him into a tight hug. "That makes you one of us, and families stick together."

"He's right, Noah," said Jeom, holding his head high—he couldn't even look in Arianna's direction without seeming to tremble. "We'll get through this… together."

Noah started weeping; Jeom hugged him around the shoulders, trying to stay strong, even as silent tears betrayed him, streaking his dirtied cheeks.

They all walked over to join Eli and Master Tayshin, surrounding Arianna's mangled body in support. They just stood over her and stared, side by side, no words feeling right enough to speak, just soundless tears to cry.

Kayode was the first to break the silence. She emerged from the crowd, baby Snow safe in her arms and fast asleep; it appeared as if she'd been hiding among the trees all this time, protecting Lessa's child from all the horrors of war, just as promised.

"I'm truly sorry for this ending, guardians," she said, her voice full of regret—she passed baby Snow back to Jeom, and he took her with open arms.

Her gaze drifted downward.

"Arianna Belvedor and all those who gave their lives to this battle will forever be honored by the people of Moriamo." She straightened, slamming the butt of her spear into the ground. "You have my word. Your sacrifices will not be forgotten."

She placed her fist across her chest, bowing low to them, then to Arianna.

"You let them catch you," she whispered, her lips pressed into a firm line, "but you died a dragon."

"Thank you for protecting Snow," said Jeom, cradling her close. "And for fighting with us." They all glanced behind her to take in their survivors—there was drastically less color, less of Moriamo, present. "I'm sorry for all of the family you lost, too."

She returned a grateful nod and gently, lovingly, caressed Snow's cheek. She gave another bow and left to join what remained of the guardian allies.

The other leaders in this war stepped forward from the crowd to pay their respects.

"If only our fallen dragons were here to see this," said Sergios, one hand over his heart—the remaining elders all looked down upon Arianna with such pride, such sorrow, such gratitude.

"They would be so honored," said Margery, wiping her eyes.

She leaned all her weight on Vance, badly wounded.

"I can't believe… it's over," added Nico, a mixture of pity and disbelief on his face. "Just like that."

"Who knew," said Vance, wiping a tear from his eye;

Margery patted him on the arm. "She really was the one the prophecy spoke of… all this time."

Master Tayshin put his hands on his hips, nodding. "Never doubted her for a second."

Eli looked down too, standing among the other survivors who had helped forge this journey alongside Arianna, forced to face the truth.

"You were strong," he said, sucking back his tears; his entire body ached for her. "Until the very end, you were strong, Ara. And we will not let you die in vain."

He kneeled down beside her again and placed one last kiss upon her lips—it was colder than all the rest had been, nothing of her warmth left.

Nico offered him a hand as he got to his feet.

Then, what remained of the original Guardians of Gold and Arianna's family all turned to face the gathering, a new day, a new era, upon them.

"The prophecy has come to pass," said Master Tayshin, calling for everyone's attention—the courtyard fell quiet. "King Devlindor is dead!"

There were scattered claps.

He looked down upon his apprentice in both sword and magic. His voice softened.

"Arianna Belvedor is dead… but with their deaths comes new opportunity, new beginnings." He held up his dragon-painted palm. "Arianna died for this, for us!"

The applause exploded, cries of support drowning out all else, people thrusting their palms and weapons into the air.

Master Tayshin let it go on until their breath ran out.

"The Golden Rule is one of balance," he said, after the crowd had calmed again, "an equilibrium resting in the beating heart of our world. Now, Olleb-Yelfra has finally spoken, *awoken*—"

He pointed to where the dead king's crown lay discarded.

"History cannot be changed," he continued, his passion strong, his voice booming. "Our pain and losses cannot be erased, but there's no room for all light or all dark in the future we carve. They *must* come together as one in order for our land to thrive. Let us not make the same mistakes as we have done before. Let us preserve the balance."

He ended to a round of applause, then a heavy, uncertain silence lingered in its place—as if to say, *'What next?'*

Everyone was clearly shaken by the loss of their true leader, and by the horrific death of the King.

Master Tayshin turned to Eli, stepping aside to offer him a chance to address those he had helped lead.

"Son, is there anything you'd like to say?" he asked. "Before we move on?" He offered him an encouraging smile. "I think they need to hear from you."

Eli considered Arianna with a heavy heart, wanting only to honor her memory. He lifted his eyes away from her, to her people in waiting. *I won't let you down.*

He stepped forward, facing all those who had fought valiantly by his side, and by hers.

"I know this conclusion may be difficult to grasp," he said, finding his courage, his voice again, "but Arianna understood the prophecy better than anyone in her final hours, even more so than Kyrone." He paced before them, hand on the hilt of his sword to steady his nerves. "And still, *knowing* her fate, she sacrificed herself so that we could begin anew, the Four Corners finally united once again... all of us, together."

He looked to the enemy regulators and shadows who had since laid down their weapons.

"That was the King's greatest mistake," he growled, "hoarding magic and trying to keep us from it by separating us in the districts—" he found Kayode in the crowd, the Moriamo people, the drifters "—or forcing us into hiding."

He looked to the eclipse, watching in wonderment as the

sun and moon slowly moved apart.

"I've seen now an enchanted world, and no matter the dangers it can possess or the new enemies it might release, it's *so* much better than no magic at all." He wiped his tears, lifting his chest high, vowing to himself that he would never forget the magic Arianna had shown him. "There's no stopping dragons from rising again," he said, finding that he was smiling—the flames of daylight gradually grew brighter, the night dwindling away.

Magical, golden bursts exploded in the sky to join the reigning sun, his allies voicing their agreement.

Master Tayshin waved his sword in the air.

"Those of you who fought against us, hear me now," he yelled, his fury breaking through. "We are Guardians of Gold, protectors of Olleb-Yelfra and all her natural glory."

He tightened his grip on his weapon, pointing it toward the enemy.

"If you too are a guardian of the Olleb and not a *slave* to a dead tyrant, pledge your fealty now to the gods she serves…"

"Or die," finished Eli, withdrawing his blade once more, this time with the intent to use it. "Make your choice."

Master Tayshin, Eli, Jeom, Demetrius, Noah, and what remained of the elder guardians all stood together to face what was left of the King's Shadow Resistance, now prisoners of war. Each looked just as broken as the palace they had once resided in.

One by one, they dropped to their knees, swords to the ground as they pledged their oaths to the Olleb—*Hail to the World!*

Those that refused were shown no mercy.

ONASYUDA.

The sound, the word, is faint but familiar. It keeps ringing in my head, like a whisper from someone's last attempt to save me, or memories from attempts in the past. But it's empty here, this place without magic. Just a meaningless, powerless word.

Onasyuda… *Life.*

I know it in my heart, or the memory of my heart, that I'm already quite dead—too dead for such a spell to work, anyhow.

I stare on into that memory, where my heart remains.

I can see them all so clearly now, maybe more clearly than I had ever seen them before, my family… or what's left of them.

"Eli!" *I call.* "Jeom, Noah, Demetrius. I'm here! I'm still with you."

I desperately want to run to them, to feel safe again with them near, now that all the fighting has stopped.

They cannot hear my voice…

In a daze, I look around. Smoke rises to the sky in stacks above the war-torn city, merging with the clouds. There are no more sounds of battle, an enduring quiet in its place. The eclipse is still draped above my final arena, dark and burning.

The Golden Rule in its most tangible form, *I think.*

I gaze upon it with new eyes, but I can't bear to look for long. It just reminds me of the ending… of my horrible ending. And all that I'll never get back.

I tear my eyes away as the moon and sun slowly begin to separate, the daylight again taking over to continue on, as if the dark had never even existed. As if I never existed.

The sun still shines on.

I focus on my friends, the familiar sound of their voices.

Eli and Master Tayshin seem in control of the situation. Good, *I think.*

They'll make sure none of this falls apart. I trust them to do what's right by the Olleb and to help the land heal.

Jeom and Demetrius are still there, too, holding Noah and baby Snow between them. I want to cry out that I'm right here, that there's no need to mourn me.

That I've gone nowhere. I'm still here!

Yet, I know… I know what I am.

I think of all the souls that I encountered on my journey in life, lost and wandering on the wrong plane, waiting for the ending that has already passed.

They're gone. I set them free, and now I am one of them, tethered still to this spot where I died.

For what reason, I can't possibly know. What else could my soul desire with the High King dead by my own hands? What else is left for me to yearn for now that my quest is complete?

Who will set me free, if I'm the animancer?

I have no answer. All I have is the horrible certainty that I might be stuck here a while, in this limbo between what was and what comes next.

Time is different here, I muse.

It feels as if hours have passed, though I can see, plainly, that those still living are moving at a much slower speed than me, still processing that I've died.

It's torture to see life, the beautiful future I helped create, go on without me. I look upon my friends, my family, my allies… I want to be happy in this moment for all those who survived, but there's an emptiness forming inside my soul, carving out the space where joy used to live.

I am mourning, too.

I'm mourning those who did not survive the King and his rampage. And I'm mourning those who will have to live a life without the ones they loved and lost. However, most of all, most selfishly, I can't help but mourn myself…

I am dead.

Confronting that truth, knowing that there's a barrier between life and death—knowing that I'm now stuck on the other side, with no hope of being pulled back by some bout of luck or magic—is most difficult to digest.

I try to wipe away the tears that must be falling; there are none. My eyes linger on my hand.

Only when I see what I am does it become irrevocably real.
I am a ghost.

My skin sparkles like diamonds, translucent almost, and all the blood and bruises from before have been wiped away, as if with a healer's glittering brush—there's no more hole above my heart, nothing to suggest the High King of Olleb-Yelfra had ever tried to kill me.

Long, luscious brown curls lay perfectly across my shoulders, glowing with a magical essence that had never once belonged to me in life. And I can feel no more pain, none except for the sadness surrounding my soul.

I'm still in my guardian uniform, armor and all, except the cloth of my cloak, the metal on my skin, is in pristine condition. I even don ghostly versions of my swords, my dagger, though I consider how useless they must be in such a state. They're weightless, like me, nothing compared to the real thing.

"Can anyone hear me?" I cry out again. I am a ghost. *"I'm here. I'm still here! I don't want to go."*

Nobody turns, everyone doing their best not to even glance my way anymore. Why don't they look?

Out of curiosity, I peek down, scared of what I might find.

A gasp escapes me, and I can't help but cringe as I stare into my own dead eyes.

I reach toward her, wanting to weep for the girl who struggled for so many years, experienced so much loss, just to end up dead. It's painful to even look at such a reflection, this lifeless version of myself... Even though she isn't me.

"I'm still here!" I scream again.

Nobody listens. Nobody turns. The guardians are already making plans for the future, plans that don't include me.

I kneel beside my former self, wanting to push the hair from her eyes. Instead, my ghostly fingers meet nothing. They move straight through her body—a cold emptiness swathes me, pulls me… down, down, down.

I yank my hand back to safety.

She is not me!

There's another sensation gnawing at my mind in this ghostly state. I can't ignore it any longer, though I want to.

"Solza…" I whimper.

My gaze drifts toward the bed of glorious wildflowers swaying in the gentle breeze, golden stems glinting in the budding sun.

I know it in my soul that my loyal avatar is gone for good—she has not followed me here.

The emptiness grows deeper.

I focus on my body and see Aurora, the real version, a fusion of colorful stones, just as peculiar as they are priceless. I try to grasp the hilt of the mysterious blade that had ended it all, to feel its familiar, steady warmth in my palm.

Alas, it doesn't belong to me anymore, and its magic cannot guide me home. I can't touch anything in this ethereal shape! The former version of myself, this person I hardly recognize, has claimed it forevermore. And all I feel is cold.

I shout to the sky, shaking my fists toward the sun and the moon as they move on, leaving me behind.

I feel as if I need to wake up from a dream, drowning in this strange dimension where I am nothing but a spectator, unable to feel anything except for my own distraught emotions, my tangled thoughts.

Yet, I know this is not a dream from which I wake.

My scream dies in my throat with no one to hear. I sigh, a

long exhale, and tear my eyes away from my broken body, anger flooding me. I notice the King's crown, still shining in the muck, a rainbow of jewels still twinkling atop the gold, tainted not by the sinful soul who had worn it for centuries.

King Devlindor is dead… and my body lies in his ashes.

It's the oddest thing, though, not to feel anger toward him anymore. All I feel is sad, lonely, a longing to go home. Furious at my situation, more questions of the future forming again, a future I wasn't ready for.

I wished for this moment for so long, that the King might finally meet his maker—yet now that it's here, I'm not sure what I'm meant to do, not sure of how to feel.

I always imagined I'd be celebrating, rejoicing in his death. But I'm dead, too. I didn't wish for it to end like this…

I look to Eli. I want to go home.

Faintly, I realize, that's probably why I haven't moved on. It all happened too suddenly, no chance for proper goodbyes. I'm not ready to leave my family behind.

I didn't want to say goodbye! I still don't.

Death has yet to claim me in his arms, so I use the time I have left to memorize this image. My friends, my family, the victorious dragons, my army of dreams…

I wonder when he'll come.

IT FEELS LIKE DAYS PASS ON, though I can still see the guardian army gathered in the courtyard. I can still see the sun high in the sky, the moon slipping away to sleep again until night.

I hear a rumble, a groan across the land—the earth moves beneath me. I can see the ground shake, the trees sway.

And though I cannot feel it, the living can.

The survivors begin to panic as the small earthquake grows to something more—they can feel it, I can hear it.

I look up and all eyes are suddenly on me, on my body at least.

"Can you see me?" I call in desperation.

I turn to face them, an unfounded hope filling the void growing inside.

They just stare, silent and scared, at the spot where my body lies. What has them so frightened?

Their eyes lift to the sky, and so do mine.

I watch in wonder and terror as a swirl of colorful energy—wind, light?—descends from the clouds, vibrant hues turning together in a hungry vortex that's aimed right at me.

There's no time to even move out of harm's way. I shield my eyes from the glaring brightness as the vortex lands, surrounding me, trapping me, in its epicenter.

It transforms, solidifies, into four radiant walls—they seem to reach all the way from the sky to the earth, locking me, my body, and the King's remains between them.

I reach out to touch the luminous barrier. I think I will just step through to the outside.

My fingers caress the wall and, with a screech, I yank my hand back—I felt that pain, like a shock all the way to the space where my heart used to be.

I'm trapped.

I squint to try to see through the walls of electric energy; my friends are still somewhat visible, the barriers somewhat transparent, like a tinted veil separates me from them.

They seem frantic, pointing toward me, huddling together, eyes wide.

It's difficult to see what exactly is happening out there, but I am certain that they can see this too… whatever this is.

I might recognize it, vaguely, if it were magic. But I can't place it with words.

No, but there's no magic here, *I think.*

Something about this barrier is different, much stronger than anything that could possibly be described by such a worldly element. I can feel it in my soul... whatever power created this partition far exceeded anything I've ever encountered in the Olleb.

Each of the four walls are tinted with a different striking color—Green. Blue. Purple. Red.

"What's going on?" I say, reaching out again, cautiously this time, to test the crimson side.

I can feel the warmth radiating from the wall as my palm hovers near; I'm too wary to touch it.

"What is this... magic?" *I have no other word in my language to describe it, though I'm certain that's not the right one.*

The entire barrier seems to undulate, like water disturbed by a pebble.

I leap back to the center as the most unbelievable beings, unlike anything I have ever laid eyes upon before, materialize from out of each wall, towering over me from every angle. They must be from another time and space, another earth, though I can hardly comprehend the thought.

I gawk up at them in sheer astonishment, utter fear, to think what they might be... I look away. I can't even fathom that I'm dead, let alone what new dangers death might bring.

Nevertheless, I sense the intensity of the power these mysterious beings must hold, so much so that I'm afraid to even lift my eyes to see them properly.

In the ghostly plane, I have no magic and no tangible weapons—I have nothing but my soul and my memories.

Unable to protect myself, I drop to my knees, floating amid the King's ashes, cowering before this new presence, wondering what new beings might demand the allegiance of my soul. Wondering what it means to be a warrior here. How can I fight?

"Rise, child of light." A brilliant voice surrounds me, filling every bit of space between the walls, like the sound of light itself. "You need not kneel here. This is your land now. The gods of Olleb-Yelfra have spoken."

27

ALL THAT REMAINS

ARIANNA FELT AS IF A BOLT of electricity ran through her soul. The voice enveloped her, awakened her—allowed her to *feel* again as if she were still one with her body.

Still, she was terrified to raise her eyes.

"Look at me, child," the voice commanded again.

It belonged to a woman, she thought. Or something with a sound much like a woman.

The being laughed when Arianna still did not move, a delicate, chiming ring that sounded as if music filled the atmosphere around them.

"Do not be afraid," she said. "We greet you as friends."

Obedient, Arianna slowly glanced toward the voice, only to sink into even more disbelief.

A tall woman with dark skin and striking sapphire eyes stared down at her. A crown of pearls sat atop her head and decorated her neck, like the froth of waves. She was adorned in thin wrappings of silvery-blue that clung to her body; every time she moved even the tiniest bit, the essence of magic followed her, like a sparkling trail of watery dust in the air.

She seemed to be forged straight from the Sea of Saindora, more majestic than even the mother of mermaids herself.

Arianna couldn't find her voice as she contemplated the remarkable being. However, in her soul, she knew what she was… *A god? Can it be?*

She recalled the detailed depictions of the gods and goddesses of Olleb-Yelfra, those that she'd witnessed both in Moriamo and in the Hall of Maps—it was as if those portrayals had come to glittering life before her, the proof of their existence solidified only in death.

"Are you…" Her words struggled to follow her racing thoughts. "I mean, you are…" stuttered Arianna. She cleared her throat. "Are *you* the God of the Sea?"

The being offered a slight nod.

"I go by many names," she replied with a small smile. "Though, I do quite prefer *Goddess.* It bears more authority where I come from."

Arianna loosed a long exhale ; she hadn't realized she had been holding her breath (or the memory of a breath, at least).

"And… where is that?" she mustered the courage to ask.

The Goddess of the Sea laughed again, like the tinkling splash of waves against a shore.

"I see the fire in you that got you so very far, young one," she said. "Where I come from matters little." She cocked her head, hair glistening, eyes twinkling. "What concerns me is where you'll go next. We've been watching you, Arianna. You constantly teeter between this world and that, and we're curious to see which way you'll land."

The Goddess of the Sea glanced toward the wall of red— it seemed to flicker in and out, like the glow of a magical flame.

Before the wall stood another being, also in the figure of a woman, and just as enthralling to behold as the first. She wore a fierce scowl, and a warmth tinted her light skin, as if she'd spent too many days under the hot sun. She boasted waves of dark orange hair, which made her look as if her head had caught fire, and she flaunted a brilliant, gilded crown; much like King Devlindor's throne, it had been forged in the figure of flames.

What's more, her flowing gown seemed to spark and sizzle with magic, red, orange, yellow, and gold sliding across her skin in spellbinding strands.

"The fire is there in her heart, indeed," she spoke, her voice just as alluring as fire itself.

"The Goddess of the Sun…" said Arianna, shifting her attention to her.

She was still on her knees. She couldn't keep from shaking.

"It's good you're frightened," she replied, her lips pressed into a firm line. "That means you're smarter than you look."

Arianna blinked, a bit taken aback. "Do I look unwise?"

The goddess smirked, toying with a bulb of fire she held in her palm.

"You look as if you are dead," she said, matter-of-factly. "And yes, the dead, especially those who perish young, are typically deemed 'unwise,' if only per the fact of their predicament." Her eyes burned into hers. "Staying alive tends to take some skill in the world of Olleb-Yelfra. Wouldn't you agree?"

Arianna considered her words for a moment. She couldn't help but chuckle a little.

"I suppose I can't really argue with that," she murmured, eyes cast down.

"Rise," commanded the Goddess of the Sun.

Without thought, Arianna stood, feeling so light in her ethereal body, as if she might float away at any second; her feet skimmed the ground, drifting just above the earth she'd almost left behind.

She gathered her bravery to address the goddesses before her.

"I may be dead," she said, empowered by hearing her own voice speak that hard truth, "a ghost… but, even now, Death can't seem to grasp me. Why am I tethered here still if I've served my purpose?" She looked to her hands, truly wanting the answers. "What does it make me if Death cannot hold me down? Am I… not worthy?"

"I say, it makes you *worthy* of the great honor of Life," came the smooth voice of a man, like the kiss of a gentle breeze.

Arianna whipped around to find an elegant creature leaning against a smoky, violet wall. He was quite tan, hair tumbling down to his chest.

Silks of maroon and lavender swathed his skin, the cloth resting on him like the gusts of wind. And with every flick of his hand, the air seemed to visibly churn around him; like the others, he also wore a crown, one embedded with a vibrant assortment of jewels reminiscent of the many hues of a sky somewhere between a sunrise and sunset.

"Here, here!" came the deep voice of another man; the earth seemed to vibrate with it. "And there's still so much more of the world for your young eyes to see… should you wish to, Arianna."

She turned to her right to face the last of the beings who joined them—she found the mischievous eyes and sly grin of a man with fair skin.

His hair was of the blackest black, and atop it sat a crown of vivid silver crafted in the form of leaves. He flaunted magnificent robes of glittering green, the cloth coiling about him quite in the same manner as the vines that forever twisted around Demetrius.

"The God of the Earth," stated Arianna, gaping up at him.

He returned a single nod, standing confidently before an

emerald wall that seemed to sprout to life with otherworldly nature.

"And… the God of the Air?" she said to the other, noting the purplish-white, puffy wall at his back—she considered it might literally be made of the clouds just before a storm.

"Very good," he replied, a sound like the whoosh of wind. She gulped.

"What… what do you all want of me?" she asked, trying to understand. "Are you here to… take me away?"

She glanced toward her friends, trying to make out their faces—they were all so blurry now.

Worry gripped her tighter.

I don't want to go! I'm not ready to say goodbye.

She felt as if her mind would tear apart with the effort to try to contemplate her future, one where gods and goddesses were real and her friends were not.

"We are the creators of the earth, air, sea, and sun," said the Goddess of the Sea, her gentle demeanor shifting to one of unquestionable authority. Her voice crashing down on her, like an unruly wave. "We are *your* creators, and we've come to bear you witness, Arianna Belvedor, child of light."

"The youthful aren't meant to meet Death, you know?" said the God of the Air, his casualness disconcerting. "It's always such a tragic loss when human life gets cut short."

He snapped his fingers, and the air seemed to crack, like the breaking of bones.

"That is not what we wish for your futures," added the God of the Earth, the deep tremor in his voice somewhat soothing. "We want our creations to flourish… to discover all the magic and good this world has to offer." He smiled, and Arianna felt overwhelmingly reassured. "It's truly plentiful. One of our best yet."

She shook her head, as if to shake away a trance—their words and voices combined were like a spell. She looked back to the Goddess of the Sea, trying to remain focused.

"Bear witness to what?" she said with a quiver. "I don't understand. The King is already dead." She pointed to her body. "*I'm* dead." She looked between them. "What more could there be?"

"Kyrone Devlindor was no rightful king!" said the Goddess of the Sun, her words lashing like a flaming whip. "A crown atop one's head does not make you a ruler." She snatched the crown of golden flames from her hair and held it before their eyes. "And power does not make you strong. That is why he is dead, and you are still here..." She softened, a smug expression on her face. "Somewhat."

She placed her crown back on.

The Goddess of the Sea drew Arianna's attention.

"Your life was chosen, tangled up in a conclusion that had been a long time in the making," she explained. "It was not an easy journey, but step by step, you crossed the Olleb to bring her justice, taking her burden under your wing. For that, we thank you," she leaned forward, pearls jangling, "and have come to bear *witness* to your triumphs."

Arianna straightened, throat dry, mind throbbing.

"It was tragic to see what that terrible soul did to our Olleb," said the God of the Earth, vines weaving in and out of his fingers. "His actions will not go unpunished."

His statement seemed to echo deep into the earth.

"I should hope not," whispered Arianna—just the thought of Kyrone's soul still existing somewhere made her feel ill.

"You were born with the flame at the center of your heart, Arianna, a warrior of light," said the Goddess of the Sun. "You did not close it to the rest of the world. Instead, you used your flame to *spread* that light. That's why the world has stayed by your side all this time."

She tilted her head. "Stayed by my side?"

"You humans may refer to this as 'luck,'" replied the God

of the Earth with a chuckle; he and the God of the Air shared a furtive glance. "Such a silly notion."

"Your avatar is one of those very *lucky* gifts," clarified the Goddess of the Sun. "Avatars are the mouthpieces… for those like us." She gestured between her kin.

Arianna perked up with this new understanding, then she grew sadder still.

"She's gone now, though," she said, wishing so badly to share this moment with Solza.

"Yes, she's gone," replied the goddess with a solemn expression; Arianna felt the heat of her gaze. "Because you're gone."

"Nevertheless, avatars are one in a million," said the God of the Air. "A rarity since the creation of Olleb-Yelfra." He wagged his finger, and the air waved with it. "We do not grant them lightly."

"It's a shame that avatar Raja couldn't help change Kyrone's direction, tainted just the same," said the God of the Earth, pursing his lips; he looked to the others. "Alas, we couldn't have known."

There were murmurs of agreement.

"Quite right," said the Goddess of the Sun, firmly. She turned her attention back to Arianna. "But your Solza *believed* in you, and so we believe in you too. Especially for all the good you've both done with your gift."

The Goddess of the Sea nodded.

"You've done us an incredible honor by taking the burden upon yourself to rid our land and waters of that filth," she said, kicking at the King's ashes. "Kyrone's darkness grew like a sickness. And until you, there was nothing to stop it from spreading."

Arianna chewed on her lip.

"But why couldn't you just end him yourselves?" she asked, feeling as if she were drowning in knowledge. "You're…

all-powerful beings." She cocked her head, considering them. "Aren't you?"

She realized she knew very little of gods and goddesses—up until now, they had only been a belief, a possibility. A faith in the unknown.

"We do not interfere in the doings of the souls we create," stated the God of the Air. "If anything, we just try to nudge you all on the right path." He opened his arms out wide, strings of wind curling gently between them. "But not even gods can predict the true future when humans are presented with *so* many different choices. Nothing can." He raised an eyebrow. "Didn't your seer teach you that?"

Odessa floated into her mind. Arianna wondered if she'd seen the faces of these beings before in one of her many visions; she smiled, knowing she most surely had.

"But we're always watching," added the Goddess of the Sea, turning serious. "And you, Arianna Belvedor, set the magic free again."

"Now," spoke the Goddess of the Sun. Arianna jumped a little. "You have *one* last wish." She gazed into the flame she still held in her palm. "How do you intend to use it?"

Arianna blinked several times, unsure she'd heard her correctly. "I…" She swallowed. "What do you mean a wish?"

The Goddess of the Sun sighed, her flame flickering. She twisted her hand in the air, magic spinning with it.

Arianna watched in bewilderment as her necklace was enchanted away from her cold body—the soul of the star sparkled before their eyes.

"A beauty this one," said the Goddess of the Sun, nodding to herself; she manipulated the stone so that it turned in slow circles, as if suspended from a string that connected all the way to the sky from which it was born.

"Yes, quite incredible," agreed the God of the Air, leaning forward for a closer look. "A strong star, indeed."

"You're fortunate it chose you to share its magic with," added the Goddess of the Sun. "How you made it this far without using all your wishes, I'll never understand." She looked to Arianna and laughed. "*Hmm*, maybe you are smarter than you look." She held up her finger, voice firm. "You have one more wish left."

"No..." stammered Arianna, shaking her head as she looked to the twinkling stone, still mesmerized by its depth; she glanced up. "I used my last wish when I was escaping from Solomon... at the bridge." She furrowed her brow, thinking back to that moment, trying to find the memory in her mind's eye. "My wish saved me from a deadly fall when I jumped into the river."

The goddesses and gods whispered between themselves in a language unknown to her; it sounded like the hum of the universe, unintelligible yet familiar all the same.

"Are you *quite* sure of that, child?" asked the Goddess of the Sea, a grin on her face. She cupped her hand around her ear. "The river has told me otherwise."

Arianna hesitated. "But I thought—"

"Don't think," she replied with the clap of her hands. "*See!*"

The goddess somehow created water from nothing, shifting it into a flat, glassy surface in front of her eyes.

Arianna's hand flew over her mouth. As she peered into the enchanted surface, she realized she was somehow observing the bridge battle of her past from an aerial position.

In disbelief, she watched as she made the daring climb over the railing of the bridge, then she took the treacherous leap; as her past self fell away from view, toward the roaring river, Arianna's eyes turned to Solomon—he was bent over the side of the bridge.

From this angle, contrary to her memory, he didn't appear angry at all as she jumped. In fact, he looked outright terrified.

"*Levantis bora!*" she heard him scream, reaching for her—his magic raced her toward the water.

She covered her face with her hands, not wanting to see.

"Oh, Solomon…" she whimpered. "He wasn't trying to kill me at all."

She looked up to find the beings observing her, intently; each of their somber expressions told her that her guess was right.

She tried to stifle a sob, a mixture of shock, sadness, and guilt.

Solomon, I'm sorry I didn't see!

She had always believed that her final wish had been used on saving her life that day.

I survived that fall because of him.

Even magically bound to the King and the necromancer, he had still found the strength to fight them, just as Princess Elisa had said—and instead of using it to save himself, he'd expended his energy on her, to save her.

The Goddess of the Sea recalled her magic, and Arianna closed her eyes, remembering that moment differently now; when the mighty arms of water had reached up to catch her, cushioning her fall, they had been Solomon's all along… catching her one last time.

"So what'll it be, then?" asked the God of the Air, a tenderness about him. "We're here to honor that it is done, even in death."

"Will you choose life?" asked the God of the Earth, clearly ecstatic at the thought, as if she were the grandest of entertainment to him—she considered that maybe she was. "Or, *perhaps*, there's something else you desire even more?" He pressed the tips of his fingers together as he waited.

Arianna looked again to the enchanted star stone, its existence in her life still such a mystery. "I have one last wish?"

She spoke more to herself, trying to comprehend the truth

of her past—Solomon had saved her, and she had only used *two* wishes before her death.

The beings nodded, the air charged with their anticipation.

She looked down to her body. *Do I wish to live?*

She peered through the hazy walls of magic back to her friends, her family, and longed to be with them again.

If I have another chance at life, why shouldn't I take it?

She opened her mouth to utter her final wish, what seemed like such an obvious decision; the words caught on her tongue as her eyes found baby Snow, cradled in Jeom's arms.

For a moment, she lingered on Lessa's memory, whose child now had no mother—and from there, her thoughts spiraled, wandering over everyone who had died for this cause.

Diveena, Gabriel, Cyn, Odessa, and Mother Adunni. Talis, Tobias, Iris, Lily, Tayo, and Keeper Kassime. Liam Black and Solomon Bell. Of the newest guardians and the people of Moriamo, many of them snatched from the world too soon. Of the mermaids, elves, dwarves, and giants who had been slain by the Shadow Resistance, entire families and races wiped off the face of the Olleb.

There was even young Pippa, who had never made it past the mountains. *Solza!*

All the innocent lives stolen by the King… they stacked so high. And they were all equal. If one wish could truly grant a life back, she could no more choose between Lessa and Solomon than she could between that of an innocent child of Moriamo or Pippa.

Who am I to decide who deserves to live, out of the countless people and enchanted beings who were slaughtered in this war, all fighting and dying for the same freedom?

And most certainly, she would not even consider that her life might outweigh any one of them.

So many had sacrificed their futures for this very moment,

the King's ashes littering the ground. It was a priceless thing to witness. Yet, for many, their futures had ended long ago, before Arianna had even plunged the dagger into his chest.

She thought of the thousands of ghosts who had joined her in finishing Sir Vladamor, supported her and the guardians despite their unjust endings.

Death is the journey after, not to be feared...

That was the greatest lesson Arianna had ever learned from her first master, Solomon Bell, in the bitter cold of the Jar. And now, with this momentous decision weighing on her, it was all that she could think of—she wouldn't shun his wisdom now, not after all he'd sacrificed for her.

"WHAT HAPPENS IF I LOSE?" asked a young Arianna, during a practice duel. "What happens if, out there, someone beats me... and I—"

"Die?" Solomon slowly circled her, hand behind his back and sword down by his side; it had a decorated handle of gems unlike anything she'd ever seen wielded in the Warrior's District. "We all die someday, even kings," he said, matching every step she made. "The most valuable aspect of the life we live is all that remains of us after it's gone."

"What do you mean?" she said, trying to mirror him without tripping.

"Death is inescapable in our world, an inevitable fate for all," he replied, his voice so steady and so sure of the end that Arianna wondered if he'd experienced it before. "What matters most is the impact that a life makes on the world and those we leave behind before the moment of death."

He twisted his blade in his hand, striking at her like a

snake—she parried, then struck him right back.

His lips twitched up, a faint smirk of approval.

"How long one manages to survive matters little," said Solomon after a moment. "And warriors… we do not fear Death." He lifted his sword again, eyes as sharp as his blade. "The wisest of us are not so arrogant to think that we can evade him forever."

He opened up his arms wide.

"In fact, we welcome Death as an old friend, one we've been in search of for a long while… if we're so lucky as to search for long—"

He beckoned her forward; Arianna tightened her grip on her twin swords, bronze blades gleaming.

"Death is to be respected, Ara," he added, a seriousness in his expression, "for we will all meet him one day. And when you do, do not be afraid." He pointed his slender sword toward her, narrowing his gaze. "Just make sure you're ready. Make sure that the life you leave behind you is one you can be proud to claim at the end." He placed his hand over his heart, as if he might close his eyes and drift away. "That's a warrior's greatest honor."

Arianna squared her shoulders, readying for his attack.

"I'm not afraid to die," she said with unfounded confidence; she averted her gaze, not wanting to reveal the doubt that was surely in her eyes. "I just… wondered what came next."

Solomon beamed, his smile shining through all her worries.

"Your curiosity will take you far," he said with a little laugh. Then he spoke under his breath, though she didn't miss what followed. "I hope so, anyways."

She hesitated.

He took a small step forward, his sword targeting her with a certainty that made her heartbeat quicken.

"However, I urge you not to walk into Death's arms will-ingly," he added, a warning in his tone, *"for he shall not let you go once you do."*

Arianna crouched down, widening her stance, her focus set; Solomon returned a slight bow, his respect for her plain.

She hoped that this time she might beat him…

"Just put up a damn good fight, Ara," he said, *"then no matter what happens, you'll be ready to take his hand, when the time comes for you."* He winked.

With that, he advanced, and they began yet another duel—an enthralling dance between a wise wolf and a budding dragon.

"TIME TO MAKE YOUR CHOICE," urged the Goddess of the Sun.

The soul of the star still hovered in the air, taunting Ari-anna with its infinite power.

She tore her eyes away from her friends, away from her past.

"My last wish is what's true in my heart," she said with conviction, "what's been truest all along." She looked straight into the goddess's fiery gaze, like staring at the sun itself. "I have never once *asked* to return to life." She lifted her chin high. "I am not afraid of Death."

She gazed again to her broken body, thinking of just how good of a fight she did put up in the end.

Solomon would be proud.

"If it's my time now, then I'm ready to meet him." She gave a firm nod, bracing herself for the difficult choice she was making. "All I have ever sought was freedom for myself and for the innocent souls who have been victims of King Devlindor's oppression. Every life that he has ruined deserves to find peace, either in that world—" she glanced to the guardians, then she shifted her gaze again to her body "—or this one."

The goddess's stare deepened, brightened; the others leaned in.

Arianna didn't look away. She kept her voice steady. "This includes those that may linger in this… in-between."

She gestured to the barrier, to her ghostly self.

There was a hum of disapproval and surprise. The beings conversed again in their strange language, surely already knowing the wish that had settled in her heart.

"What is it that you ask?" said the Goddess of the Sea, her voice low, like the drone of the deepest waters she and Solza used to swim. "You must speak it aloud." She tilted her head. "But think *carefully* of what you say next. There is only one wish left."

Arianna stood her ground, touching eyes with each of them.

"For my last granted wish, I beg only for your forgiveness on behalf of two souls misguided during these dark times," she stated; her focus was fixed again on the soul of the star. She considered how much it had given her throughout her life's journey. "Please guide them through the dark, like this star has guided me."

Her mind flitted to the first ghosts she had ever met on her quest—Jacob and Damon, two friends from the Creator's District who had tried to escape the Four Corners together, in the beginning of the King's terrible reign.

They had not succeeded.

In the end, they had taken their own lives rather than fade away in the darkness, in the bowels of the Olleb. And in doing so, they'd forfeited their souls' futures, never permitted to move on in the journey of death.

Thus, their sad stories were forever bound to the darkest parts of the Vanishing Tunnels.

Arianna remembered that first ghostly conversation with Jacob like it was yesterday…

"When you die, your soul is supposed to move on from this world and into the next life," he had said. *"But by taking our own lives, we naively made a declaration to the gods that our souls were not worthy of… of whatever comes next. Of course, had we known that at the time—"*

She had nothing but fond and grateful thoughts of both him and Damon, her earliest saviors on the daring pursuit to freedom. They were worthy of so much more than an afterlife of darkness—they had helped her through her very first steps toward this ending, steered her safely through the Vanishing Tunnels and protected her from General Ivo, her first true adversary.

What's more, she'd learned from her friends that they had also helped guide thousands of other slaves to the same freedom, when the Four Corners had fallen.

The gods and goddesses stayed silent, but Arianna remained steadfast, wishing with everything she had that her request would be accepted.

"I learned long ago from a *friend* that if one takes their own life, they might never be allowed to move on," she continued, "held back from the comfort of death and forever tethered to the physical world to watch life go on without them. I know you see sacrificing one's life as a rejection of your gift, but I believe those souls have atoned enough for their choices." She found her own vacant stare once more. "And life can be unbearable at times…" She bowed her head, hands clasped at her front. "I leave it to you to decide."

The beings looked between each other, seemingly stunned.

"Are you *sure* this is your wish?" asked the Goddess of the

Sun, her voice pitching. "To pardon those already deemed dishonorable, rather than save yourself… or even a loved one?"

"I am," said Arianna.

The goddess merely blinked at her in bewilderment

"Very well," said the God of the Earth; he looked to the others, and, grudgingly, they nodded back. "We know of whom you speak."

The God of the Air rubbed his fingers together, magic sparking between them, growing into a cloudlike substance that filled the barrier in the space above their heads.

Within seconds, the ghosts of Jacob and Damon lowered out of the smoky haze, settling next to Arianna in the center.

"Arianna?" gasped Jacob, Damon close by his side. "What's going on—"

He gaped as he recognized those who joined them, his voice catching in his throat.

"Jacob Marcissus and Damon Lorel," stated the Goddess of the Sun, her tone firm, "you are hereby pardoned of your offenses. You are free to move on now." She had a resigned yet reproachful expression. She leaned forward, studying them each in a way that they might never forget her sun-kissed face. "May you respect your souls more in death than you did in life, *hmm?*"

"Yes, Your Excellency," implored Jacob—he and Damon both bowed low, glowing with utter joy. They trembled with fear, with astonishment. "We are forever grateful for your mercy!"

"It isn't I who deserves your eternal gratitude," the goddess replied, gesturing to Arianna.

She stepped back, allowing them room to speak.

"Why… if it isn't Miss Belvedor," said Jacob, nearly struck speechless as he turned to her. He shook his head, an awestruck expression on his gentle face. "Your story continues to surprise me." He chuckled, slapping Damon on the back.

"I daresay the world will be telling tales of her for a *long* time to come, right?"

"I can't wait to hear them all," said Damon, grinning wide.

"Maybe," said Arianna with a shrug, content with her choice either way. "Guess I'll never know."

"Somehow, I doubt that," added Jacob with a warm laugh, eyes glittering in excitement at the future he now had.

She returned a soft smile.

Then, they all watched in respectful silence as the Goddess of the Sun gently settled the soul of the star back onto Arianna's body, its last wish finally spent.

"I see you found your stone," mused Jacob—his gaze was pinned to the necklace, then the crown. "Quite a journey that was etched there for you, wasn't it?" He cocked his head to the side, eyes reading her now. "It seems you had a grand destiny after all, Arianna."

He stared at her with so much wonder that it made her blush (though, she was sure her cheeks had not actually reddened).

She considered the stone in such a light. *My destiny?*

She couldn't help but laugh, thinking of how much had transpired since he'd offered her that first lesson on such a complex concept.

"You have *no* idea, Jacob," she replied after a moment.

She reached out, finding that she could actually touch them; they were, after all, ghosts... just like her.

They embraced in a long, comforting hug.

"Thank you... to you both, for all that you've done for me and my family," she said. "*And* for the Olleb. I hope you'll find peace now. You deserve every bit of it."

They pushed her to arm's length, gazing at her with the warmest of expressions.

"I wish for you the very same," said Jacob, sincerely.

"See you on the other side?" asked Damon.

"I suppose I will," said Arianna, swallowing back her fears as that reality started to sink in.

Jacob gave her one last deep, contemplative stare.

"One day, maybe," he said after a moment, a smirk on his lips.

He grasped Damon's hand and they both bowed low once again, this time to her. Then they disappeared in a glittering burst, onward to their next journey.

Arianna let out a sigh of relief, feeling that she'd made the right decision in freeing them from an eternity of unfair punishment.

Now she had to face her own uncertain future.

"What will happen to me now?" she asked, her nerves plain as she gave her attention back to the beings.

"Well," snapped the Goddess of the Sun, hands on her hips as she studied her. "Truly, I'm staggered. I wasn't expecting such self-sacrifice from you, Arianna. Not in this final moment. *You*, who have spent years trying to obtain the freedom to live your life outside the King's law." She waved her hand in the air. "When you finally have the choice to grasp it, you give it away!"

"It was the right thing to do," she retorted, unable to stop her brazen side from shining through, even now. "And maybe you should consider reevaluating such punishments."

The goddess bristled, though her lips twitched up, and Arianna thought she might've appreciated the challenge.

"*Oh, I must agree...*" said a familiar voice, ringing in her ears—it didn't belong to anyone in sight.

Arianna jumped. "Did you hear something?"

The beings were quiet, their expressions unreadable.

She looked all around in a panic, thinking she'd finally lost her mind.

"*You used your one last wish on a selfless act of kindness,*" came another. "*That kind of deed does not go unnoticed, especially when you're dead."*

Arianna felt a wave of shock and joy wash over her as the unmistakable voices of her fallen masters and friends, Solomon Bell and Talis Churry, sounded in the air.

"I told you the trouble would be worth it, old man!" she heard Solomon say.

"I suppose, this time, you were right," Talis said with a chuckle. *"She was definitely worth starting an uprising for."*

"What's going on?" cried Arianna, looking around everywhere for their faces—they were just voices in her head, yet clear as day.

"You sacrificed yourself… *again*, and this time for two lives," said the God of the Air, a sly grin on his face. "So, two more lives shall you gain."

The God of the Earth held up two fingers.

She looked between them, growing more anxious by the second. "I don't under—"

The Goddess of the Sea held up her hand, stepping forward. "But this time, *we* will decide who is deserving," she said, her voice pleasant. "Do you have anything that could represent the departed Lessa Thur?"

Arianna felt as if she'd just been slapped awake. *Lessa? They're not saying…*

"We don't have all day." The goddess held out her hand, expectantly. "I can't make something from nothing." Arianna pondered just how exactly the Olleb was created, though she figured it was far above her comprehension to even bother asking. "I need a starting point."

Her reeling mind drifted from Solomon and Talis to Snow; without overthinking it, she pointed toward the ground.

"In the lining of my dagger's sheath…" she said, not fully comprehending the moment as she gestured to her body. "There's a small snowflower, preserved in glass."

Arianna had sewn it there for safekeeping sometime after fleeing South Luose. She'd been carrying it with her for so long, a token from the beginning of her quest, that she'd almost forgotten it was even there; it had been a gift from her old attendant, Lily, who died in the siege of the palace.

The Goddess of the Sea used her magic to pull it from Arianna's sheath and into her hand. She brought the glass ball to her lips, then she tossed it into the wall of waves behind her; the water turned into a shimmering sapphire vortex, a portal to another world.

Lessa emerged, from somewhere beyond, materializing in a physical form inside their barrier.

When she stepped out of the watery partition, she looked like a goddess herself. Magic literally dripped off her in glittery beads, pooling at her feet as if she walked on water.

Arianna was stunned into silence, blinking over and over to make sure it was true.

When the magic fell away, Lessa remained in dazzling sapphire robes, pink-cheeked and smiling. It was as if she'd never died at all, her battle-earned scars still shining bright on her skin. She had gained a new one too—a brilliant blue swirl—where the arrow had pierced her heart.

Better still, the ghosts of Solomon Bell and Talis Churry were floating by her side, her chivalrous escorts from the beyond.

"Ara…" stuttered Lessa, looking dazed and disoriented.

Arianna wanted desperately to run into her arms, but she couldn't in this ethereal state. They just stared at each other.

When Lessa finally found her bearings, she whimpered, hand flying over her mouth—she'd noticed Arianna's body on the ground.

"We won?" she stammered, looking back up, tears in her eyes.

"We won," Arianna choked out, hardly able to believe

Lessa was alive and well before her.

Solomon and Talis smiled, approvingly.

"As for you, Arianna Belvedor," said the Goddess of the Sun, closing the distance between them; Lessa's mouth fell open as she registered their company.

Arianna gulped, staggering backward.

"Yes?" she said in a small voice, feeling the sweltering heat that radiated off her.

"This will now be your *fourth* chance at life." She clicked her tongue. "Where I come from, four is all you get." The other beings emphatically confirmed her statement. "Do not waste it."

Arianna shook her head. "I—"

The Goddess of the Sun laid her hand over where her heart was supposed to be and pushed.

In a painful jolt, suddenly, Arianna could feel again—the heat pulsating from the goddess's touch felt like the breath of dragon fire scorching her from the inside out. She looked down, unable to move nor speak as a glowing light began to grow over her chest.

Then, it consumed her.

The earth gave way, the world disappeared. She was falling, no time to even let out a cry for help.

It was as if she had been dropped through an endless white space, memories from her past flashing by her in a blur. There was so much noise around her, too, that everything seemed to blend together… the sound of laughter and screams, of singing and whispers, of spells and script.

She hit the ground—and all of the sound, all of the memories came crashing down.

Everything stilled into darkness, quiet; she could hear her heart beating in her ears, her breath rising and falling in her chest, filling her with life.

She clung to Eli's voice. *Just breathe.*

With a gasp, her eyes flew open. She slowly sat up, feeling as heavy as stone.

She considered that it had all been a dream… the war, her death, the ghosts, the gods, Lessa, *all* of it. But when she again found focus, the gods and goddesses remained there within the walls of magic, along with the ghosts of Solomon and Talis. And, sure enough, Lessa was still there, too, in the flesh.

"I'm back in my body?"

Lessa bit down on her lip in her excitement, nodding.

Arianna lifted her hand to her head. It was throbbing.

"Ouch," she said with a little laugh, so grateful to be able to feel again.

With a quick assessment, she noticed that her chest was still covered in blood.

"I'm bleeding…" She started giggling, hysterical with pure wonder, savoring the way her tears warmed her cheeks, the blood sticky on her skin. "I… I'm alive?" she exclaimed.

"We're alive!" said Lessa as the realization also hit her.

Arianna recognized the weight of Aurora, still resting in her palm—she wrapped her fingers around the winged hilt and wiped the blade clean on her robes, ridding the precious dagger of the King's corrupted blood.

She sheathed it right back where it belonged.

"Here," said Lessa, reaching out to help her stand—they grasped hands.

Another wave of exhilaration came over her, the firmness of Lessa's grip confirming that they were both truly of flesh and bone; she got to her feet, standing by her side.

As she found herself upright, her ailments began to settle back in, the high of new life wearing off just as suddenly. The aches from the battle made themselves known all over her body again—her tears of happiness shifted to tears of agony.

"Keep still," said the Goddess of the Sea, gesturing for Lessa to move aside.

Arianna sucked back her tears and obeyed.

The otherworldly beings each rested a hand on her arms, squeezing tightly. Their eyes burned with unfathomable magic, the colors of the elements shining bright.

Their power began to course through her, licking her wounds clean, from the deepest cuts to the faintest scrapes. And when they finally pulled away, Arianna felt as if she'd drunk an entire carafe of prillyberry juice. She was still in her ripped clothes and bloody armor but had been completely healed, just like Lessa.

With a shaky hand, she touched the place where the King had ripped open her armor, to try to get to her heart. She sighed in relief, the pain drifting away into memory.

You did not succeed.

She glanced down, noting the thick new veins of a scar, a fiery red, spreading over the right side of her chest.

"Ara, I'm so proud of you," said Solomon, seizing this moment to address her.

She looked to him, feeling all her strength returned, her body and warrior spirit restored. Her magic was there, too, stirring beneath the surface with a fierce, new energy, as if it knew it had finally been liberated.

It felt different than before…

In his ghostly form, Solomon truly shone. He looked just as healthy and strong as on the day she'd first laid eyes on him in the Warrior's District, swords sheathed at his hips and a regal robe gliding behind him, even in death.

"Thank you, Master," murmured Arianna. She bowed her head. "For everything. I don't know where to even begin." She felt a lump catch in her throat, her lips quivering. "I'm sorry we didn't know you needed saving too…" She averted her gaze. "You were always there when I needed you, and I let you down."

He contemplated her, a solemn smile on his lips, his

expression soft; she wondered if he knew that Princess Elisa had confessed to her just exactly why he had always cared for her so much.

Master Bell is my… father.

"Absolutely not," he replied before she could bring herself to ask. "Do not *ever* think you let me down, child. Quite the opposite, in fact!" His booming laughter of her fondest memories filled her ears; she looked up to find his expression full of joy. "You surprised me in the best ways possible." He gestured to those around them. "With the goddesses and gods of Olleb-Yelfra as sure witnesses, you saved our world."

They nodded their support.

Arianna felt her face run hot—this time, she was certain her cheeks had turned a bright red, her face splotched from crying.

"But… I couldn't save *you*," she said, the tears coming harder.

"I never need saving," he said, smugly, hands on his hips. "Just like you." He looked down at her, turning serious. "Arianna, my choices were mine, and mine alone. And if I hadn't made them, I wouldn't have had you… my daughter—" she froze, eyes wide, mouth dry "—my greatest apprentice, *and* the Olleb's liberator."

She wiped her eyes, wanting so much to wrap her arms around him, to tell him every single battle she'd overcome since they'd separated in the districts, to erase all the terrible things she'd ever thought about him these past years. "Master Bell—"

"Child, everything happens for a reason," he said with a firmness she'd missed. "But you've slain the monsters, just like I taught you. For that, I will forever be proud."

She sucked back her tears.

"Are you going to be all right?" she asked, glancing back toward the vortex still swirling behind him. "I mean… in the afterlife?"

"What do we say about Death now?" he demanded in a voice much like the Master Bell who had always forced her to be strong. He pointed his ethereal sword in her direction, smirking from ear to ear.

"We do not fear him," she said, loudly, standing up straighter.

"*Warriors* do not fear him," he said with an approving nod; he sheathed his blade. "I've been ready for a long time. Plus, I have a good friend to lean on in this next journey." He patted Talis on the shoulder. "That makes all the difference. I'm sure you know that by now."

He winked at Lessa, then offered Talis a moment to say goodbye as well.

"Master Churry," said Lessa, stepping toward him; he looked as content and wise as ever. "I'm going to miss you…" She sniffled. "I have been missing you for a while."

He chuckled.

"Well, I hope you miss me a while more," he replied, wagging his finger at her. "I don't want to see you again now for a *long* time, you hear? Take care of Snow." He glanced through the barrier, toward Jeom. "If she's anything like you, you'll have your hands full before you know it, girl!" He twisted his beard around his finger, eyes twinkling with admiration as he considered his apprentice. "May she be just as mischievous as her mother."

"Oh, Talis," she said, tears streaming down her cheeks; Arianna reached again for her hand, holding it tight. "What will we do without you both to guide us?"

"You got this far, didn't you?" said Solomon, bemused. "Two slaves from the Warrior's and Healer's Districts." He cocked his head. "In the end, you freed magic, took the Four Corners, killed the long-reigning King, and were granted another chance at life by the literal hands of your creators."

The beings tittered, observing their exchange.

"We didn't even accomplish that much in our time," said Talis. "And we're *much* older than you."

"Yes, I think you'll be all right this time around," said Solomon. "Just try not to trip and break your neck or something, since there's no one left to battle." He snorted, looking to Talis. "I won't be surprised if she dies in a practice duel, though."

"And Lessa from drinking a bad prillyberry batch," said Talis, glaring her way. "They're just that *lucky.*"

Solomon and Talis howled in laughter, so contagious that even the goddesses and gods couldn't help but join in; Arianna and Lessa barely refrained from rolling their eyes one last time at their first and greatest masters.

The girls grinned, both shaking their heads.

"Goodbye, children," said Talis, collecting himself. "Take care of each other now." He narrowed a probing gaze in both their directions. "We'll be keeping a *close* eye on you."

"May there be no more monsters to slay in your futures," added Solomon. "But if the day should come where you must battle again, I daresay the monsters won't last very long against either of you." He flashed them a smile so bright and reassuring that Arianna felt anything but sad at this final farewell.

"Master, I—"

He lifted a finger into the air, a sly grin on his face, surely about to leave her with one last tidbit of wisdom.

"You must learn from Kyrone's mistakes. The secret to *true* happiness has nothing to do with longevity, nor strength nor magic. It's laughter and love." He gave her a serious, knowing, Master Bell look. "Make room for it, Arianna… if you want to make the most of this new life."

"Yes, Ara," said Talis. "Give that boy a chance!"

She blushed, chewing on her lip, thinking that she most certainly would.

The ghosts of Talis Churry and Solomon Bell stepped back into the vortex, vanishing in a burst of glittering light, their laughter lingering behind them.

Arianna and Lessa wiped their eyes of their tears as the silence settled over them again. They put their attention back to the gods and goddesses.

"Thank you," said Lessa in an awed voice, still holding Arianna's hand, "for giving us our lives back."

Arianna placed her other hand over her heart, her scar.

"We are forever in your debt," she said. "But… what would you have us do now?"

The thought of leaving this barrier, entering back into the real world suddenly seemed so daunting.

"That is entirely up to you," said the Goddess of the Sun, softening toward her. "You shall start off this new era strong and whole. But remember… if one pillar falls, the rest crumble. Make sure you reinforce what you know now to be true for generations more to come. The future of the Olleb depends on it."

"We're counting on you both to maintain this new peace," added the Goddess of the Sea, her gaze fixed on Lessa.

The God of the Air suddenly used his magic to lift King Devlindor's discarded crown into the air, cushioning it on a puffy cloud.

"Take it," he urged Arianna. "It's yours now."

She balked, letting go of Lessa's hand as she stumbled backward.

"Absolutely not," she said, eyes bulging. "I couldn't possibly take on such a responsibility…"

Her heart drummed in her chest.

"*Yes*, you can," said the God of the Earth—the ground rolled beneath her feet, carrying her back toward it. "You just have to keep your faith." He smiled, a very Demetrius-like one.

"Like I said before, Arianna, a crown does not make a ruler," added the Goddess of the Sun. "A ruler *earns* their crown." She tapped the golden fire atop her head.

"No, I can't—"

Before Arianna could protest further, Lessa had plucked the brilliant crown from the cloud of magic and shoved it into her hands.

"You deserve this," she said, with a determined expression. "There's no one I'd rather see take the throne, Ara, and I didn't come all the way back to life to let it fall into the wrong hands again." She poked her in the chest, right above her broken armor. "Neither did you." She smirked, hands on her hips, looking her up and down. "Besides, rumors in the afterlife tell me that you have royal blood in your veins."

Arianna opened her mouth, but Lessa held up her hand; her fierce stare sparked with silver.

"This is *meant* for you," she said, leaving no room for discussion. "You literally gave your life for the Olleb, more than once. Royal blood or not, you earned this power. Do not take it lightly. But *take* it, all the same."

"I... I..."

Lessa glared at her, daring her to refuse.

Arianna averted her eyes, her attention back on the crown, considering it—the metal felt dense, heavy in her hands.

I'm stronger than the last man who carried it, she thought.

She looked up.

"I won't take it lightly," she murmured.

Lessa visibly relaxed.

Arianna glanced between the gods and goddesses, holding her head higher now, acknowledging the duty to pick up the pieces King Devlindor had left behind.

She bowed to each of them.

"I accept your gracious honor."

Abruptly, the walls of magic began to melt away, sucking

back up into the sky.

"Fare thee well, children," said the Goddess of the Sun, beaming back at them.

The Goddess of the Sea blew a kiss. "May you both live a long and magical life."

"Hail to the Queen!" sang the Gods of Earth and Air. "Hail to Olleb-Yelfra."

The otherworldly barrier fully dissipated, exposing Arianna and Lessa to the outside.

AS FATE WOULD HAVE IT

THERE WAS AN INTAKE OF BREATH from all around the courtyard, thousands of people staring their way with mouths agape, expressions awed and fearful—the goddesses and gods of the Olleb still remained among them, visible for all to see.

Then, the divine beings departed, faster than Arianna could even comprehend. But not before all of Saindora had witnessed their existence; she was certain that they had purposefully stayed long enough to make true believers out of anyone watching, and their resounding voices lingered in the air behind them, declaring her as the next ruler of Olleb-Yelfra.

Before she could even think of what to do or say next, a voice filled her ears—one that only she could hear.

It was the Goddess of the Sun, speaking to her from somewhere beyond…

"*I just couldn't help myself,*" she said, a smile in her voice. "*Solza… very aptly named.*" She chuckled. "*I hope your flame never goes out, Arianna. It is more special than you know.*"

The goddess's voice died away, and Lessa tugged at Arianna's arm, excitedly pointing to the sky.

The sun was shining so bright now, its fiery arms stretching out all across the land—in a burst of flames, Solza appeared in her dragon form, born again straight from the sun's belly of fire.

The gathering cried out their astonishment as her confident roar filled the skies, her blazing breath joining the sun in an incredible display of life.

"*We did it, Master!*" sang Solza.

Arianna let out a cry of laughter to hear her avatar's voice once more. Tears of joy streamed down her cheeks, and she instantly felt whole again.

"*That we did, girl!*" she said, beaming as Solza soared in circles above their heads. "*So glad to have you back, dear friend.*" She wiped her eyes, twisting the soul of the star between her fingers. "*The future would've been so dull without you. Are you ready for it?*"

"*Only if you are,*" she replied.

Another roar weaved through the clouds.

"*Come join me then,*" said Arianna, reaching toward her.

Solza landed gracefully before her and Lessa. And when she did, her extraordinary gifts rippled across the courtyard— the flowers and trees destroyed from the earlier battles were suddenly reborn, dusting the air with nature's magic.

Arianna looked all around the vicinity, stunned as plants shot up from the earth, as if Diveena were there to coax them back to existence with only the snap of her fingers; Solza had returned to the world of the living more powerful than she'd left it.

"Thank you," she whispered to the Goddess of the Sun, knowing somehow that she would hear.

She could barely contain herself as she found her avatar's

fiery gaze. "*I thought that I'd lost you for good,*" she mumbled, voice quivering. "*But seems you and I refuse to die.*"

"*I'm happy to live a little longer with you,*" said Solza, gently nudging her.

She transformed, shrinking back into the beloved snow leopard from their beginnings, as beautiful and energetic as she'd ever been.

"Ara, look!" Lessa said. She held out her forearm. "Look, you have one too…"

Sure enough, glowing on her skin was a new magical mark of some kind—between this, the scar from Solza and the King, her guardian symbol, and Syrifina's enchanted gift of mermaid lifeblood, she considered that she was beginning to resemble Eli more and more.

Lessa poked at it, examining herself closely.

"It's the emblem of the Four Corners," she said with a frown. "Why would they mark us like this?"

The four district colors shone in what looked like bright ink on their skins—red, blue, purple, and green. Black and white strokes spun in the middle to connect them all, just like the flag in the Warrior's District Arianna had spent so many years loathing.

But seeing it now, imprinted on her body forevermore, gave her an epiphany.

"It's not," she said, tracing the mark with her finger. "It's not the emblem of the Four Corners at all, Les." She shook her head, mind spinning with wonder. "It's… the symbol of the goddesses and gods."

Lessa's mouth formed an 'O'.

Arianna understood the mark now for what it truly meant—the King had tried to remake the ancient symbol for himself, had believed himself a god of sorts. But no matter how hard Kyrone had tried to persuade the world that his power was the greatest in the history of the Olleb, in the end, he had failed…

Centuries later, many people still had faith in something more, some greater presence out there that could be held responsible for both the good and bad of their world. Whispers of the existence of a number of gods and goddesses had even crept into the Jar, and they spread wider still across his kingdom.

And now, with the thousands of witnesses gathered around them, that belief would surely grow stronger—who was any one man to suggest that a higher being wasn't real, if he was not at the beginning of creation to see what came before? Who was any one man to claim that he was greater than all the rest, when he'd been born the exact same way as everyone else?

We were all created equal, and we all, equally, deserve a chance at a free life, no matter what we choose to believe.

The symbol embedded in Arianna's and Lessa's skin was not one derived and owned by the High King, and it was not a reminder of the slavery they had once endured. It was a gift from the *creators* of Olleb-Yelfra, an acknowledgment of the magical and all-powerful beings who truly governed this kingdom, forever enforcing the Golden Rule… should the girls choose to recognize the emblem with new hearts.

Arianna closed her eyes a moment; she could still feel their power, coursing through her veins from when they had laid their hands upon her, blessing her with another chance.

She looked again at King Devlindor's crown in her grasp—just like the emblem of the Four Corners, it had never really belonged to him.

Though the tyrant had ruled with it atop his head for nearly three centuries, its rightful owner was the last monarch of the Golden Age, King Damas.

"*And its future owner is holding it in her hands,*" mused Solza.

Every second her avatar was by her side, Arianna felt herself fill up with even more power. And unlike when she'd consumed the magic of the King, this power had room to spread inside her, room to grow. She was *so* glad that her return to life included nothing of him. So glad that the gods and goddesses had revived her without that poisoned piece of his soul.

I don't need one bit of that monster's magic to lead.

A shimmer of silver suddenly engulfed the jeweled relic—an enchantment sweeping away King Devlindor's tainted memory and transforming it into something new, something better.

"God-touched," breathed Lessa, peering over her shoulder to see the charmed crown. "Just like us…"

The crown pulsed with a magical energy unlike any material item they'd ever seen, the colors of the four true elements shifting in and out of translucence across the gold.

"We thought you both were dead!" Jeom's voice boomed across the courtyard, drawing their attention.

The girls glanced up to see the Kane brothers closing in; Demetrius nearly tripped and fell to the ground in his excitement, and Jeom was barely able to skid to a stop before colliding into them. He leaned on his axe and his air magic to slow him down.

"Oh, Jeom," said Lessa, crying and laughing at the same time. "Demetrius!"

"I'm never taking my eyes off you girls again," said Jeom, a mystified grin on his face and tears wetting his cheeks; he kissed Lessa with such intensity that Arianna thought he would never pull away.

"I can't believe it," squealed Demetrius, steadying himself as he looked between the two. He reached for Arianna's hand. "You're both really here… am I dreaming?"

She shook her head.

"You're definitely not dreaming," she said, giving him a

big hug. "We're here."

In a blur of white and a gust of wind, Sano appeared in his monkey form, falling into Lessa's open arms as she and Jeom finally parted. He peered up at her with watery orange eyes, clearly overjoyed to have his first master back.

"Sano, my love, it's so good to see you!" He scuttled across her shoulders, planting himself there firmly; she gasped, a look of astonishment on her face. "Oh my, and… *hear* you?"

Arianna offered a reassuring smile. "You're not crazy," she whispered.

Lessa ran her fingers through her hair, contemplating Sano. "I was so scared when I—" She choked on her words, face blanching. She pressed her hand to her stomach, gazing to Jeom with such worry. "Snow…"

"She's perfectly fine," said Jeom, pulling her closer to him. "I don't know how he did it, but looks like Sano has *two* masters now."

"He's a healer," said Demetrius, nodding.

"Thank the gods," stated Jeom.

Lessa and Arianna shared a glance, eyes wide.

"I couldn't agree more," added Lessa, standing on her tiptoes as she peered toward the crowd. "Where is she?" She was shaking with eagerness.

"Don't worry," said Demetrius, pointing with his staff. "She's safe with Eli."

Arianna swiveled in that direction—Eli stood at the very front of the gathering—Phantom, the luckiest horse in the world, was somehow still by his side.

He was flanked by Noah, who jumped up and down in his happiness, and Master Tayshin, who couldn't have looked more at peace while he watched the unbelievable reunion unfold. The other elder guardians were there, too, Kayode among them.

Arianna felt her whole heart glow at the sight of them all,

but her focus remained on Eli; he rocked baby Snow in one arm and lifted his hand over his heart with the other, eyes only for Arianna.

"Never again," he mouthed with the shake of his head, a beautiful smirk growing across his lips.

Arianna's entire body sagged with relief, a slight blush warming her cheeks. She knew exactly what he meant—she would never say goodbye to him again either.

"I love you," she mouthed back.

Eli let out a moan of relief, gazing to the sky.

"Finally," he said.

Lessa whimpered as she laid eyes on Snow, leaning into Jeom.

"Thank you for saving her," she whispered to Sano, stroking him. "I love you both so much."

"Come," said Jeom, taking her hand. "It's time you met—"

His words ended in a scream as a powerful gust of sparkling wind swooped down from the clouds and engulfed him in a buzzing cyclone; the others barely had time to move out of the way.

When it faded, he too had the symbol of the Four Corners emblazoned upon his forearm. What's more, a bright purple jewel had been implanted into the other. *And* he looked just as majestic as Lessa, vibrant violet robes settling around him in a sprinkle of magic.

"What on earth was that!" he screeched, completely frazzled as he tugged at his clothes and examined his new, permanent additions.

"That had nothing to do with the earth," said Lessa, grinning to the sky. "That was the God of the Air. Seems we have some friends in high places."

The girl's showed off their own similar markings.

Jeom's mouth dropped open.

"Pardon me?" he squeaked in a voice quite unlike his own, eyes flicking toward the clouds.

Demetrius squinted at the sparkling gem; it glowed bright against Jeom's dark skin.

"Looks like you're officially a dwarf now, brother," he said, slapping him on the back.

Jeom was about to retort when the ground started trembling, directly underneath Demetrius.

"What's going on?" he yelled as he wavered back and forth; the grass rolled beneath him. "What's happening?"

Arianna signaled to the others to stand back, knowing that he was about to also experience something special—roots and vines climbed up his body with a mind of their own, engulfing him in an orb of nature's magic.

Moments later, the earth again settled and the magic dissipated, leaving behind so much more—he had been cloaked in glittering green robes that made him appear as if he and Jeom were truly two halves of one whole.

"*Goddesses*, I… I can't believe this," said Demetrius, staring down at himself in disbelief. "I thought it would take me days to wash up."

"Now *that* was the God of the Earth," said Lessa, sending praises toward the ground.

Arianna looked Demetrius up and down in admiration.

"It's not just your clothes," she said, softly, pointing to his arms. "See…"

On one, he bore the same colorful marking as the others; and on the backs of both hands, he'd earned new tattoos of shining silver that wrapped around his wrists.

He traced one in reverence. "Those are from Diveena, I think," he muttered, mystified and smiling.

Arianna gave a slight chuckle. "No doubt she's colluding with the gods."

They all held out their forearms with the district symbols

to compare—each was a perfect match to the other.

Arianna felt the tingle of a new sort of magic pooling there, bonding them together forever; she considered her guardian mark and wondered what special enchantments a god-touched one might bring.

"What do they mean?" asked Jeom, shifting his arm back and forth so that the variety of colors caught the sun.

Arianna let out a little laugh. "It means… we have a lot more work to do."

She knelt down to pick up the King's staff and used her magic to dislodge the ruby, tucking it safely away in her pocket.

Then, she passed the staff to Demetrius.

"Why me?" he stuttered, taken aback.

"It was Master Lethander's," she said, matter-of-factly. "It's only right that you have it now." She gestured to the Axe of Crissy forever glued to Jeom's palm. "You have a legacy to uphold, just like your brother."

Lessa and Jeom agreed wholeheartedly, and he accepted it with a gracious bow.

Arianna considered each one of them now… her family whole again, their avatars safe.

She squeezed the crown between her fingers, accepting what must be done.

"We *all* have a legacy to uphold," she declared. "The Golden Rule has finally been restored, so let's use the gifts the Olleb has given us to ensure that it can never be broken again."

In that moment, with her family again by her side, and her friends and followers in waiting, Arianna knew that it was their duty and destiny to take Olleb-Yelfra into the next chapter— a glorious and golden one.

And with the King's ashes at their feet and the gods and the goddesses of their world watching from the heavens above, nothing and no one could stand in their way.

The air around them seemed to grow silent and still as Arianna raised her arms, slowly, feeling the weight of the power she was about to accept heavy in her hands.

I am strong enough for this, to be the leader we deserve.

She let go of any last doubt, let go of her past where a High King had reigned through terror. *Never forget…*

She placed the god-touched crown firmly atop her head and stepped forward to face all those who had gathered around.

Otherworldly magic washed over her, originating from the crown—her robes, her armor, and even the air around her exploded in a dazzling display fit for a royal of the Golden Age.

Colors she didn't even have names for sparkled and surged across the courtyard. And Arianna remained at the center of it all, enveloped in warmth.

It was almost like the time she had transformed into a mermaid… *Almost,* but not quite.

This transformation felt much more permanent; and when it was complete, she truly looked the part of the queen the gods had deemed her to be, shrouded in brilliant red and gold, as if the crown had been made for her all along.

"*Whoa…*" she heard Demetrius breathe. "Now that's one for the books."

One last thing, she thought, before lifting her eyes to the anxious crowd.

Arianna located her swords in the grass and scooped them up, relishing the familiar weight in her hands, cherishing how she'd gotten them, earned them. *Thank you, Solomon.*

Solza was at her side, and her friends stood loyally behind her, all facing the future, together; she glanced back to them, and they gave her encouraging nods, prepared to follow her forward in this final step of their quest for freedom.

All right, I'm ready for what comes next…

She caught Master Tayshin's eye. With a deep breath and

a booming heart, she gave a single nod.

He beamed with pride, then dropped to one knee, sword to the ground as he pledged his allegiance to a new ruler. "Hail to Arianna Belvedor, High Queen of Olleb-Yelfra!" he roared.

Without hesitation, Eli and the other guardians, and all their allies, followed his lead, heads bowed low, weapons merging with the earth in unity with her. Lessa, Jeom, and Demetrius bowed, too… even Solza and Sano.

In an overwhelming wave, every single person in Saindora who had come to witness the end of the war fell to their knees before her.

"Hail to the Queen!" they exclaimed, bursts of bright magic exploding in the air. "Hail to Olleb-Yelfra."

Arianna listened to their voices joined together, ringing out across the High City of Saindora to pronounce her queen—she no longer had a doubt in her soul about who she was meant to be, not her purpose nor her destiny.

She gazed around at everyone, glowing with joy.

We survived.

BY THE FALL OF NIGHT, word had spread of Arianna's defeat of Kyrone Devlindor. Thus, a time that would've been marked as the 290th Free Falls Festivals under his rule was instead recorded in history as the High King's death day—it was also her twenty-first year of life.

And just like the marker of the end of each annual Free Falls, paper lanterns, with flames burning bright at their centers, were released all over the Olleb, this time in celebration of freedom and in honor of all those who had been lost on the way.

It was finally the start of a new era.

There was only one thing left to do before it could begin…

Arianna entered the war-torn Palace of Saindora with Solza at her heels. She followed the familiar halls, locating the great black cellar door of her ethereal memories.

It towered over her now, daring her to try to enter again.

A soft fluttering hum sounded in her ears as she contemplated the mysterious threshold; she turned, spotting the culprit—a striking, black-winged dragonfly, its body a shimmering turquoise, had somehow found its way into the depths of the palace, hidden away safely throughout the chaos.

Such a beautiful creature, she thought, following its unpredictable path with her eyes.

She blinked, and it was gone—the ghosts of Prince Neas and King Damas smiled back at her.

She gasped, then bowed low. "Your Majesties," she said.

"I suppose we could say the same to you… my queen," replied King Damas, a bright grin upon his face.

He returned the gesture, and Prince Neas bowed too.

Arianna straightened, still getting used to the crown.

"You know what to do now?" asked Prince Neas, looking her up and down with an incredulous smirk.

"I do," she said with confidence, gaze flicking toward the door. "The world is ready to see it now, all of the magic that belongs to them."

"Good," he replied with a smug nod of approval. "Seems that you're not such a novice after all… for a Devlindor." He crossed his arms at his chest.

Arianna pursed her lips, and he laughed.

"Well, I had a little help along the way," she replied after a moment, "to overcome my shortcomings."

The Prince snorted, and she couldn't help but crack a smile.

"*A lot of help…*" added Solza; Arianna scoffed.

"There's nothing wrong with asking for help sometimes," said King Damas, as if he'd heard her avatar's snide comment. "You'll do well to remember that when you're seated on the throne and all the world's problems are brought to your feet."

She swallowed back her nerves, then faintly wondered if the King's version of the throne was even still standing.

"Another word of advice," said Prince Neas, more serious now. "Don't *ever* forget that magic has a mind of its own." He gazed toward her pocket—did he sense the ruby's dark magic? "There's still a lot left for you to uncover, and just because you have a happy ending today doesn't mean that everything that follows will be as pleasant." He gestured to her crown. "Especially not with that retched thing making you such a pretty target."

The crown suddenly felt much heavier.

"Wise words, son," said King Damas. "But do take the time… to celebrate today. You certainly have earned it." He offered her a reassuring nod.

Arianna lifted her chin high, touching eyes with them both. "Trust me… I won't forget anything I've learned," she said with conviction, "nor what I've earned."

King Damas seemed to sigh out all of his burdens.

"Then we can bid you farewell," he said, a weightiness clearly lifting off his shoulders, so much so that he was seconds from floating away. "The Olleb is *finally* in good hands."

His expression was so soft and pleasant while he regarded her, as if all the decades he'd watched Kyrone wreak havoc on his land had been wiped away.

"No doubt about that," he whispered. "That crown fits you just right."

"I couldn't agree more, Father," said Prince Neas, flashing her a genuine smile. He gave a little wave. "Fare thee well… Your Majesty."

"I'll see you on the other side," she said with the slight bow of her head, heart hammering in her chest. *Just not yet.*

They turned to go.

"Oh, and Arianna," called King Damas, glancing back, "best give it a little taste of who you truly are now… *just* to be on the safe side." He glanced to the door.

"Wait, what—"

He winked, and they both vanished in a glittering '*pop.*'

She was again alone, Solza her only company in this airless part of the palace.

Arianna went up to the cellar door, King Damas' final words still ringing in her thoughts. As she considered how to enter, she suddenly understood just what he'd meant…

This door was one protected by strong blood magic, so strong that it had repelled her even during astral projection.

This time, though, she was here in the flesh and had just what she needed to coax it open—the blood of Kyrone Devlindor.

"*Be careful, Master,*" warned Solza.

"*Don't worry,*" said Arianna, sizing up her next opponent, the lingering magic of the King. "*I know what to do.*"

She withdrew the very dagger that had taken his life; she ran Aurora's blade across her palm, slicing it open. Her skin pooled with crimson, and she sucked a breath in through her teeth.

Then, she pressed her bloody hand upon the door.

"*Who goes there?*" demanded a deep voice that seemed to resound within her thoughts. "*Answer at your own risk.*"

Arianna cleared her throat, squaring her shoulders.

"It is I," she replied, her words steady.

"*And who might that be?*" pried the voice, this powerful magic not yet satisfied.

Arianna felt her confidence swell, thankful that she no longer had uncertainties about this answer. She placed a fist over her heart and swore to never forget her humble beginnings as number Twenty-Two. However, the scar the King had given her made her so much more.

I survived.

She was proud now to declare just exactly who she was.

"I am a warrior, a witch, and a Guardian of Gold," she stated. "I am an avatar master, an animancer, and a child of light." Her voice grew louder, more assertive with every word spoken. "I am Arianna Belvedor, High Queen of Olleb-Yelfra… and I demand to claim what is mine!"

Silence—Arianna twisted the star stone between her fingers, closing her eyes. *I am the daughter of Solomon Bell and Princess Elisa… I am a Devlindor.*

The magic spoke. "*You may proceed, my queen.*"

She felt the blood magic protection fall away, felt the future of the Olleb rush toward her. *I'm ready.* She opened her eyes, wrapped her hand around the golden serpent handle and pushed.

A cool breeze engulfed her as the door creaked open—she vowed that it would never be locked again.

At long last, all the magic buried during the King's exacting reign, hidden away in the confines of his palace, would be released for all to see… and after everything that had happened, anyone would be a fool not to believe it.

Solza ven immito!

Arianna stepped across the dark threshold with her avatar by her side, letting all the light pour in behind her.

EMBERS RISE

THE WORLD CHANGED AFTER THAT, healed slowly by the hands of those pronounced 'god-touched,' under the rule of Arianna Belvedor, High Queen of Olleb-Yelfra.

The little that was left of Kyrone Devlindor and his laws were buried without ceremony in the Tunnel of Tombs, and all the bodies of those who had never made it out of the Jar were exhumed from the Vanishing Tunnels, reburied in the light.

The King's sister, Princess Elisa, was spared a death sentence thanks to her final acts of kindness. She was banished to the Island of Idris to live out her days in solitude, under the rigorous watch of the Sea and without the taste of magic.

Heeding the Princess's warning, they buried the tainted rubies deep beneath the Saindora palace in the dungeons, in the very chamber the Devlindors had built for Arianna at the end of their reign. They secured them with the strongest barrier spells they could conjure, in the hope that the dark magic injected into them by the King and his necromancer would never be unbound.

However, most significantly, with the support of the Guardians of Gold, Arianna, Jeom, Demetrius, and Lessa used their extraordinary gifts to release the suppressed magic across the kingdom. And Solza and Sano literally helped to breathe life back into the Olleb with their unique, restorative powers.

Together, they rebuilt the cities destroyed by the wars and returned children to their parents, abolishing the Opalls forever.

The people of Moriamo finally came out of hiding, and guardian sanctuaries everywhere were revealed to the public. Libraries and schools once meant for studying and revering magic were uncovered and restored all across the land, for anyone to learn. And the enchanted beings forced into near extinction began to emerge from the Olleb's darkest places—fairies returned to their forests, giants made themselves known, and clans of dwarves and elves repopulated the land, Demetrius and Jeom spearheading their reemergence.

Even mermaids were welcomed back to city shores across Saindora, under Lessa's strict supervision.

Gradually, the stains of death on the land were removed as new and enchanting opportunities were gifted to every citizen who wished to grasp them and discover their magic within. Better still, the use of imagination became *highly* encouraged in order to make any of it possible—from the ashes of King Devlindor's kingdom birthed new and beautiful life.

However, the greatest achievement of all under Arianna's just reign became known as the *Rebirth of Dragons!*

Just as the King had divulged in his final moments of life, the guardians came to learn that the dragons of Golden Age legend still existed in the world of the living; not long after Arianna took the throne, she ordered that his statement be validated…

The bewitching beasts were discovered to be sleeping soundly beneath the Black Sand Desert, where the King and avatar Raja had laid them to rest. But with Solza and Sano, the new avatar dragons ruling the skies, Arianna and Lessa were able to resurrect the Olleb's ancient, fiery protectors, drawing them out of their enchanted slumber.

Thus, on the back of dragons in a blazing storm, Arianna and her friends returned to the Four Corners one last time.

They burned the slave city to the ground and magicked the dragons' flames so that they might never be put out, capsuled forever in the claws of the mountains. The fires transformed the Jar, where so many young souls had been tortured and slain, into a glowing lantern… so bright that the Blancoren Mountains could never be known as a dark place again, a memorial to last the ages.

In that spectacular moment, as Arianna Belvedor soared away on the back of Solza, her friends surrounding her in the skies of the Olleb, the City of the Four Corners burning down behind them, she had only one thought—*Finally, we are free!*

Dear Ruler of Olleb-Yelfra

Well that was sure unexpected! I'm so thankful you survived and that King Devlindor is no more. I'm sure you're very busy figuring out what to do next, with all your freedom, power, and whatnot...

Might I suggest a motivational speech to your new, loyal subjects? I'm certain the world is more than eager to follow your lead now that you hold the crown.

What's the main thing you would want them to know about your ultimate triumph? Own the platform you've created.

Hold your head high and speak your truth on

amazon goodreads BookBub

Thank you for your commitment to this trying quest, warrior. I'm compelled to say 'The End,' but I'm no seer. How could I possibly know the future?

Sincerely,
Ashleigh B.

ACKNOWLEDGMENTS

That's a wrap, bookworms! I can't even begin to tell you how amazing this writing journey has been. This very moment—writing the acknowledgments to the final draft of my final story in the *Belvedor Saga*—marks nearly a decade since the first draft of *Belvedor and the Four Corners* was written.

I submitted a horribly rough version to a novel contest back in October 2012 before even publishing, and that was the first and cherished step Arianna and I took on this extraordinary adventure.

Of course, I didn't win, but it fueled a fire in me to figure out how to become a better writer and to tell the story of the girl in search for freedom. And every failure or setback since has only fanned that flame. Finally, we made it to the finish line!

The completion of this book and series is truly a dream come true, encompassing many large and small milestones, just as many letdowns as wins, and so many beautiful life lessons. It's been a long road—with over 730,000 words penned—before getting to '*The End*,' and I couldn't have done it without a guardian-ship-load of encouragement.

To my Four Corners of support

Mom, the Cyn I'll always need—thank you for telling me to keep going on the hardest days, for reading every first draft, and for being just as excited for me with the small wins as the big. I'll never forget how quickly you binge-read the finale, then didn't actually know how it ended because you were so tired from staying up too late (lol!).

Dad, the Solomon of advisors—thanks for being the sounding board for all my goals for the future, and for keeping me grounded with every step. I would've been lost without you, though I humbly ask that you waive the counseling fee you've been threatening me with for years. I've racked up quite the bill.

Christina, the Demetrius to my Jeom—thank you for caring for me through every phase, even when we're far apart. I've learned so much from you in life, including the very important lesson of how to make a decent pot of coffee (that got me through countless revisions!). I'm lucky to have a big sister like you.

Lisa, the Lessa to my Arianna—fate clearly knew what she was doing when she brought us together. I could *not* have finished these stories without your unending support and advice. It's been quite the surprising adventure! Thank you for sticking by my side through each and every battle, and for cheering me on to the end.

To the Masters of editing and design

Hannah McCall, master healer of words—you deserve a round of applause from every Belvedor Bookworm out there. Thank you immensely for the time and effort you poured into my books, for being an advocate for my characters, and for asking the questions that challenged me to bring this story to the next level. I never thought I could trust someone else so fully with my words, but I have found that in you as an editor.

Mirella Santana, master creator of covers—never in my wildest dreams could I have imagined such enchanting covers as the ones you designed. Now all my readers will be immersed into a true epic fantasy adventure before even page one.

Jessica Khoury, master creator of worlds—it was such a special moment to see my imagination mapped out through your gorgeous illustrations. No one could have created Olleb-Yelfra better! Thank you for your attention to detail and touch of magic to my fantasy world.

To the family and friends who aided me on my quest

Niki and Rachel, my Aura and Ora stones—you're both two of my earliest adventure buddies; our childhood curiosity and imagination knew no bounds! No matter how long we're apart, I know I can always count on you to still light the way home. Thanks for rooting me on from Missouri.

Danielle, the Aridyn by my side—life's too fun procrastinating with you. You've always been in step with me (in heels!) through the ups and downs of this maddening city version of 'adulthood.' I'd hate to know a Brooklyn that didn't include you. Thanks for lifting me up, and for dressing me for success.

Megan, the Odessa in my life—oh, how we've bonded through despair. The 2020 apocalypse would've been so lonely without you, among other eras. Thanks for celebrating the little and big book milestones with me during the pandemic, and for getting me through those darker days! … *"Is this now?"*

Grandpa, the Master Churry in my family—thank you for loving me as I am, no matter how I chose to write my story… and for the years of free medical advice.

My peers in search of adventure—the friends I made when I lived out of a suitcase (Mexico, Spain, South Korea, Belgium, Kuwait, Zambia, Uganda), you know who you are! Whether or not we kept in touch, thank you for being my interim family throughout those wilder years; we had the adventures of a lifetime, and many of them helped Arianna's world flourish.

My City of Saindora—New York City can be such a transient and lonely place at times; I'm grateful for the community and friends, both in my past and present, who traveled part of this journey with me. Thank you for making me feel at home, and for all the fun we've had while we chased our dreams.

To the allies who helped me strategize for battle

Lisa and Allison, my Greenhouse guardians—being able to lean on our women-only masterminds group for help and collaboration about the business side of Belvedor was a huge relief. I wish you both much success with your own endeavors and can't wait to see what time makes of all our goals. *Check out your fellow Belvedor Bookworms at:*

- ◊ **HolaLittleOne.com**—download easy, fun crafts and activities for busy little ones.

◊　**VivaLaTravelista.com**—the ultimate guide for anyone considering a trip to Playa del Carmen, Mexico.

The Alliance of Independent Authors (ALLi)—as a self-published, independent author, I have been faced with too many options, endless questions, and so many uncertainties about publishing over the years. ALLi has been like a guardian sanctuary through it all, a trustworthy hub of like-minded authors steering each other in the right direction. Thank you!

To the OG Belvedor Bookworms

Whether you have you been cheering me on from Missouri, gave feedback on the earliest editions (hi, Kristie!), or took a chance on my stories before they were likely even edited, I'm so grateful for the time you gave to supporting my work and growth as a writer. Old friends and family alike, thank you for your kindness!

The first Belvedor Bookworm—Grace, I love how much you adored Arianna's beginnings. Thanks for uplifting me as a new author; oh, and Francis Howell North High, represent!

The Cannonball crew—your family has probably purchased and promoted more of my books than anyone else combined. You're all so amazing! I cherish the support.

To all the Belvedor Bookworms of the present day, honorary Guardians of Gold—to YOU.

It's been the absolute pleasure of my life to create the world of Olleb-Yelfra and to welcome you into it. I wouldn't have been able to fulfill my dream of being a storyteller without dedicated readers like you. And I hope Arianna's journey has left you with the courage to follow your own dreams, too.

From the bottom of my heart, thank you for reading the *Belvedor Saga*. And keep chasing the magic! I swear on the South Star that I'll do the same.

ARE YOU DYING TO READ MORE ABOUT
THE MERMAIDS IN OLLEB-YELFRA?

CHECK OUT ASHLEIGH BELLO'S
LATEST RELEASE - A DARK & SPICY
MERMAID-VAMPIRE ROMANTASY.

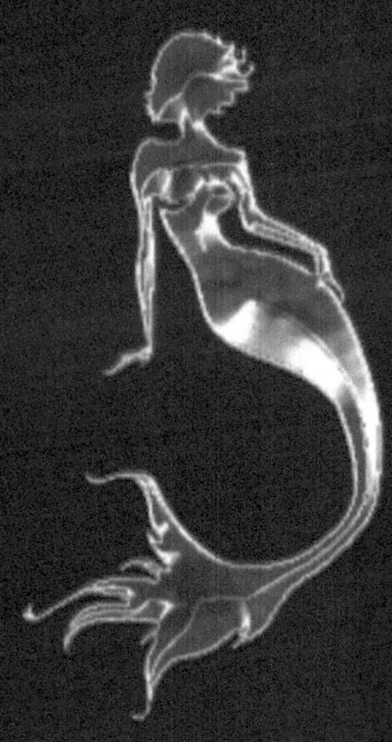

A MYRMAID'S KISS

Are you a
BELVEDOR BOOKWORM YET?

If you answered "YES!", then add your name to the
Belvedor Bookworms newsletter for even more
bonus materials. Get to know the person behind the
books and be the first to receive exclusive news,
author updates, giveaways, and more.

I can't wait to connect with you!

Scan me!

www.ashleighbello.com/belvedor-bookworms

Turn the page for

BELVEDOR
BONUS MATERIALS

Behind the Scenes with the Author

Real World Magic

A Letter to My Readers

BEHIND THE SCENES

Ashleigh Bello answers questions from the Belvedor Bookworms!

What books and authors inspired the writer in you?

Although the *Belvedor Saga* is epic fantasy, I didn't read that much in this genre growing up. I'm only now discovering some great authors in my lane like Sarah J. Mass. Instead, I was a bit hooked on commercial urban fantasy (hello, *Hunger Games* and *Twilight)*. I just couldn't resist those fast, fun reads… and still can't!

I also remember *Charlie Bone* and *Eragon* fondly, and I tore through the *Harry Potter* books every time they were released—*Harry Potter and the Goblet of Fire* is one of my favorite books; it inspired me to build a colorful fantasy world that came alive through the details.

Last but not least, my teenage obsession with V.C. Andrews novels remains unmatched; I was definitely too young to be reading those stories, but I regret nothing. *Flowers in the Attic* is so twisted. Love.

I've also always appreciated a good murder mystery, psychological thriller, or straight up Stephen King scaries. Classics like the *Great Gatsby* and *Pride and Prejudice* have a permanent place on my bookshelf, and the occasional 'follow your dreams' reminders, like the *Alchemist,* are a must when I need a pick-me-up.

Follow me on Goodreads if you're curious about what's on my bookshelf.
@ashleighbello

If you didn't read much epic fantasy, what do you think motivated you to write in this genre?

I have been devouring fantasy stories and fiction since I was a child, and that includes through movies and television. I'll watch anything that has to do with fantasy! While books pave the way for my interest, my fascination with all things magic likewise began with the *Neverending Story*, became solidified by *Aladdin*, settled in as part of my identity with *Charmed* (and the occasional backyard séance with my bestie), then spiraled out of control with *Harry Potter*.

I may have missed the boat on reading some great epic fantasy books in my youth, but I'll get to them. And I already watched *all* the movies—a movie mindset even motivated me to be as visual as possible with some of my more colorful scenes.

What was your favorite scene to write in the finale?

I'm tossing between two with Solza in her dragon form: the one with all the guardian ships gathered at sea, Solza flying overhead, and the one on the battlefield where Sir Vladamor's resurrected mermaid faces off with her. I *think* I'll go with the latter… the mermaid fighting dragon fire in slow motion is very visual in my mind, almost like a scene playing out in a movie, like I mention above.

What's it like coordinating a battle sequence?

Daunting and thrilling all at once. I had to keep reminding myself that there were no rules in war. Anything goes, so I tried to set aside my character biases to make things feel more realistic—both sides had terrible causalities in the end.

I also learned a lot about medieval weapons and battles throughout the years of research; when I first started working with my editor, Hannah McCall, she would always school me on Lessa's poor archery form and lingo! I've already forgotten what's correct, so it's a good thing I've written it all down ☺

Okay, tell us. What's with the number 22?

Fine, just don't make fun of me… I was born on October 22 and somehow ended up being one of those die hard lucky number people (whose with me!? Cue the crickets). I also love celebrating birthdays, so that probably gave the number a bit of a lift in my mind. But whether or not #22 adds any magic to my life, I have fun believing that it does.

On that note, the first edition of *Belvedor and the Golden Rule* was published on 2-22-20. And I re-released the second edition of *Belvedor and the Golden Rule* on 2-22-22 along with the first publication of *Trail of Fire*—I wanted to give myself the best shot at seeing Belvedor books on the big screen one day, *just* in case my inkling is right. Fingers crossed!

What's one thing that your readers would be surprised to learn about you?

I've got a big dose of extrovert in me. The amount of hours I spent alone in my imagination to write a fantasy series that totals at 2000+ pages baffles me sometimes. No one asked me to start or finish Arianna's story, so it's safe to say I truly enjoyed the process of being alone with my words. That said, it's kind of shocking how much I love socializing and pushing myself out of my comfort zone to experience new things. It's seems like an odd combination, but that's me in a nutshell. Odd as can be ☺

What's next for you now that Arianna's story is done? Will we see more from Olleb-Yelfra?

I can't make any promises because I can only write if there's a story to be told. However, there *just* might be room for more books in the Belvedor universe, if the inspiration comes.

For now, I just want to have fun and see what happens. I've been wrapped up in developing this series for almost ten years, so I'm looking forward to having the space for new creativity. Who knows where the magic will lead me next. I just follow its lead—Stay tuned!

2024 NEW BOOK RELEASE UPDATE!
A Myrmaid's Kiss by Ashleigh Bello is now available on Amazon and other retailers.

REAL WORLD MAGIC

The adventure of your dreams could be just outside your door.
Take the leap and go explore!

The finale of the *Belvedor Saga* was packed with nods to real places. Take Starr Caverns for example—the idea for this location struck me on a solo trip to Bermuda. I toured a famous cavern that took my breath away and knew it had to be a setting in my storyline. I can't even describe how enthralled I was with a magnificent banyan tree sitting right outside the cavern entrance; it had our dear Diveena written all over it!

I tried to capture its essence when she underwent her transformation from elf to the heart of the Impenetrable Forest, but it's better to see it with your own eyes.

Photo of the magical Banyan tree. (Bermuda, 2019).

Photo of the enchanting Crystal Caves. (Bermuda, 2019).

I was also lucky enough to have witnessed the rare total solar eclipse that occurred on November 3, 2013. It was only viewable in its entirety from a handful of remote places, including a small town called Pakwach, Uganda. And by lucky, I mean it was a wholly unplanned experience!

I just so happened to have arrived in Uganda for work days before it took place and was invited to the special viewing event hosted by local officials; the sky was such a spectacular sight to behold, unlike anything I've ever seen, so it was fitting that Arianna should also get to witness this beautiful, otherworldly phenomenon at the end of her quest.

Photo of Total Solar Eclipse. (Pakwach, Uganda, 2013).
Photo credit and fellow travel buddy:
Joey De Smet, Instagram @photo_by_joey

A Letter to My Readers

WHEN I FIRST BEGAN WRITING THIS STORY, it was the summer of 2012. I was twenty-three, living in a small studio in South Korea and working as an English teacher. It was the kind of summer that should have been filled with magic, but at the time I was feeling very lonely. Traveling is one of the most wonderful experiences I can wish for anyone, and I've been blessed to have explored many parts of the world, but it can come with a cost—as any fellow traveler will probably understand, eventually you are forced to part ways with the friends you meet abroad… your adventure buddies, your interim family, your home away from home.

So, there I was, in between semesters and alone in South Korea as most of my friends had moved on. I took to writing to pass the time and to work through my emotions (before eventually meeting locals in my town, now lifelong friends!). I never thought once that Arianna Belvedor would take on such life as I jotted down the first words, but her story and world gripped me so fiercely that I couldn't stop writing once I had started. Suddenly, I didn't feel so alone anymore, and looking back, this period in my past where things felt so uncomfortable turned out to be one of the best things that had ever happened to me—I just hadn't realized it yet.

The first draft of the first edition of *Belvedor and the Four Corners* was completed in two short months and published two years later (on December 17, 2014).

I never thought of myself as a true 'writer' back then; I wrote most of the series while focusing on nine-to-five jobs, wishing that I *could* be a full-time author.

But as I'm writing this now, knowing what the ending turned out to be, knowing that I was even able to finish the series while navigating the wonderful madness that comes with making a home in New York City, I can tell you that crafting the *Belvedor Saga* has been the highlight of my life so far. No matter what it took to get this book done and to write all the rest, and no matter where my career goes as an author, it's been an honor to share a piece of my soul in this way with you. I'm certainly better for it.

I hope that Arianna's journey has encouraged you in some small way too. As with any book, what it means to me probably looks entirely different to what it means to some-one else, but if it's added even a touch of magic to your life, then I've achieved my goal.

Ultimately, I want to thank you for choosing to read my story. I know there's a wealth of beautiful fantasy books out there all waiting to be devoured, so however my book found its way into your hands, whatever made you pick it out of the many, know it genuinely means the world to me that you did.

The only thing I have loved more than writing these books is hearing what my readers have to say about the fantasy world I built. It's been an incredible opportunity to engage with readers from all walks of life throughout the years, and it's the biggest reward I could ask for as an independent, self-published author.

I really want to know what you think! The best way to share your thoughts and show your support for my work is by leaving a review or sharing a Belvedor book on your favorite social or reader platform—it would mean so much to me.

Again, I thank you for choosing to read the *Belvedor Saga*, and I sincerely hope you close this book satisfied. Arianna's journey for freedom may be over now, but who knows what might come next.

Until next time,

Ashleigh B.

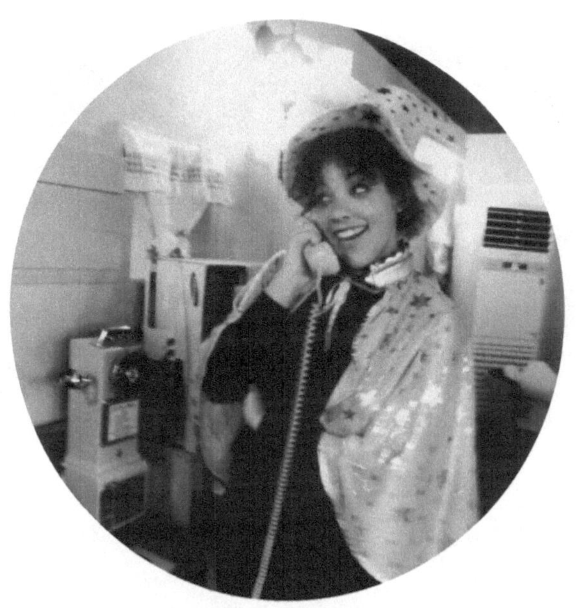

Photo Caption: Somewhere in South Korea,
letting my imagination run wild
(no, it's not Halloween). ☺

THE BELVEDOR SAGA

By Ashleigh Bello

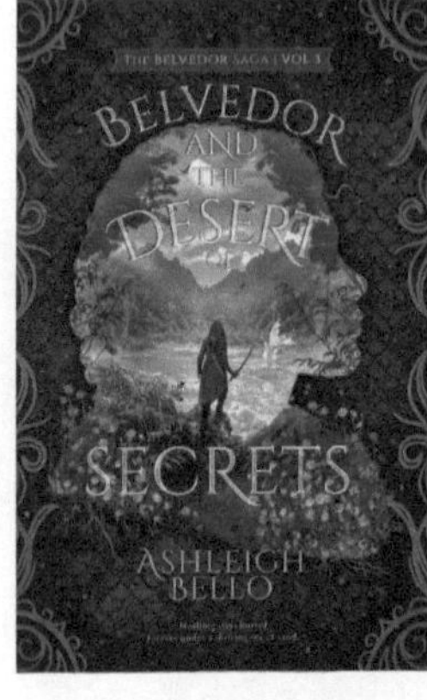

Follow the author on Amazon or Goodreads
for updates on future book releases.

amazon

A S H L E I G H   B E L L O is the author of *A Myrmaid's Kiss* and the *Belvedor Saga*. She graduated from the University of Missouri-Columbia and currently lives in Brooklyn, New York. She also teaches and practices vinyasa yoga in her community and is the co-founder of Yoga Block Party, a female-owned yoga events and retreats business. She enjoys spending time with friends and family every chance she gets and is always daydreaming about her next novel. Her endless passion for travel and spontaneous adventure continues to be her inspiration for future works in the enchanting world of Olleb-Yelfra and beyond.

Connect with the Author
www.ashleighbello.com
@ashleighbello

Follow Ashleigh Bello on TikTok!
Scan the QR code to visit her bookish social account

Returning hate for hate multiplies hate,
adding deeper darkness to a night
already devoid of stars.

Darkness cannot drive out darkness;
only light can do that. Hate cannot
drive out hate; only love can do that."

-Dr. Martin Luther King, Jr.